2028

WEB 2028

STEPHEN BAXTER

KEN MacLEOD

JAMES LOVEGROVE

MAGGIE FUREY

PAT CADIGAN

ERIC BROWN

Copyright © Stephen Baxter 1998, Ken MacLeod 1998,
James Lovegrove 1998, Maggie Furey 1998,
Pat Cadigan 1999, Eric Brown 1999
All rights reserved

The rights of the authors to be identified as the authors of
the individual volumes have been asserted by them in accordance
with the Copyright, Designs and Patents Act 1988.

First published in omnibus form
in Great Britain in 1999 by Millennium
An imprint of Orion Books Ltd
Orion House, 5 Upper St Martin's Lane,
London WC2H 9EA

To receive information on the Millennium list, e-mail us at:
smy@orionbooks.co.uk

A CIP catalogue record for this book
is available from the British Library

ISBN 1 85798 870 1

Typeset by Deltatype Ltd, Birkenhead, Merseyside

Printed in Great Britain by
Clays Ltd, St Ives plc

CONTENTS

WEBCRASH
STEPHEN BAXTER

To Sophie Williams
and
Tom and Lizzie Smart

CONTENTS

PROLOGUE

Hi. My alias is Metaphor. I'm female, 15 years old, and I live in England Canton, British Province, European Union. The date is February 12, 2028.

I'm going to tell you a story.

Some of it is what happened to me. Some of it I put together later from what people told me and what I found out when I browsed the Web. You may not believe it. Sometimes I'm not sure I believe it all myself. But it's the truth as I lived it.

Read this and tell people about it.

Because I believe we are – all of us, all over the world – in great danger.

The Web isn't a game any more.

CHAPTER ONE

WEBCRASH

Of course you remember the WebCrash.

Everybody remembers the WebCrash. What were you doing that day?

I was cruising through n-space in a two-person spaceship called *The Empress's Mighty Fist*. I was working as a Browser in the Galaxias Domain – or specifically as a Pilot in that imaginary future – with one of the universe's greatest criminals as my sole companion.

Nothing too unusual about that, of course. Just school-work.

But then all the stars went out – and came back on again, subtly changed.

I didn't know about the WebCrash at the time. All I knew was I got a Web warning about a possible Domain breach, and there was a jolt as our ship dropped into real space like a snowflake falling on velvet.

I lay in my contoured Pilot's couch and tried to settle my beating heart.

It had already been a bad day. There had been rogue currents in n-space. Dealing with them while trying to keep a track on the telepathic Beacons that guided me through n-space, had left me with a headache. But now the pressure was fading. I reached under my control helmet and wiped salt sweat from my eyes.

A voice growled from the rear of the bridge. 'By the Plutonium Throne, what's going on?'

I swivelled my couch and pushed the helmet from my head. The platinum globe floated patiently into the air. 'Numinus,' I said. 'I guess that woke you up.'

'Too right, it did.' Numinus Torca, fallen heir to the Plutonium Throne, was a squat, dark man. Now, his bearded face was a scowling mask. I noticed a rim of skin armour at the neck of his towelling robe. Numinus didn't trust anybody any more – not even me!

I was a real person, of course, playing a role in the Domain. But Numinus wasn't real. Like the rest of the Domain, he was generated by the computer banks that create Galaxias.

Of course he *thought* he was real.

The bridge of *The Empress's Mighty Fist* was a squat cylinder. I lay at its heart surrounded by banks of displays (although, of course, I was really lying at home in our spare bedroom wearing my new Websuit). Now Numinus clumped to the centre of the bridge and peered about at the monitors. 'Pilot,' he said menacingly. 'I see stars I don't recognize. What's more, I don't see the planet Raq. We weren't due to leave n-space again until we made Raq, were we?'

N-space is a kind of parallel space which lets you take short-cuts to the stars.

I took a deep breath. 'I'm sorry,' I said. 'We're not there yet. Obviously. I had to break the journey.'

The Regent's eyes were small, dominated by huge, piercing pupils – and he was staring at me so hard he was frightening me more than usual.

'We hit a rogue current,' I said. 'I nearly lost control. At the end, I lost the Beacons and got dumped back into real space.'

'Metaphor, you're telling me things I don't want to know,' Numinus said softly. 'I've got to get to Raq. My Lord Silvre waits there. I must contact him and perhaps bring him back to serve the Empire.' In fact, he meant to ask Silvre – another crook – to help him wage war against Numinus's mother, Empress of the Galaxy. 'That is my mission. You've been instructed to take me to Raq. That is your mission. Now, I suggest we resume our journey.'

Numinus couldn't hurt me, of course. Nothing can really hurt you in the Web (or so they promise you!). Even so, he was a *scary* man, and I shuddered. But I had to speak up.

'I don't think you understand, Regent. N-space is not an easy ocean to sail. If we get caught in that current again we could find ourselves swept outside the Galaxy. And the route we follow may close within minutes behind us, never to reopen.'

I was serious about this. We had to be careful. For a Domain like Galaxias, a Breach would be the worst possible disaster. But Numinus wasn't supposed to know about it, because he wasn't real, and he wasn't supposed to know *that*.

Numinus fumed, and stalked around the cabin, as I tried to find a way out of this mess.

If you're lucky you won't have ever visited a Domain.

Every Domain is contained in Webtown, which is inside the Web, a huge electronic universe maintained by a worldwide network of computers. You spin into it, from home, or school, or a private booth, by wearing a Websuit that makes you feel as if you're *there*. But if you don't know any of *that* you probably won't be reading this story anyway.

Anyhow, you'll find Domains in the Library Block of Webtown. They are artificial realities. When you're in there you feel as if you're in a whole new world.

Everywhere you reach inside the Web is artificial, generated by computers. You may feel as if you're walking on the Moon, or swimming in the Caribbean, or fighting giant crocodiles in the Cretaceous Era. Whatever. But, actually, you are just lying at home, or school, or in a private booth, in a Websuit, and the suit creates the illusion of a different world for you.

But most Web environments are obvious fakes: game zones like the DreamCastle, or entertainment zones like Cydonia, or theme parks like GulliverZone. Most Web environments are like cartoons. They are based on Real-world, and they do resemble it a bit, but they aren't meant to be exactly like it.

Domains are a little different.

Domains *are* supposed to be accurate – at least as much as their designers and people from the universe and research institutes can make them.

You may have heard of WebMars, where NASA and the Japanese and European space agencies have people trying to survive in a colony at the Martian South Pole. The idea is that if you can figure out how to do it in the safety of a Domain – from which you can be retrieved in an instant – you can then go on to apply those lessons to living on the real Mars.

And then there's WebJurassic, where researchers have built up a complete model of the Jurassic era, when, as even bratty kids like my brother George will know, dinosaurs ruled the Earth. The world back then was a complex place, and the only way the scientists can work out how all the different pieces fit together – the plants, the climate, the animals – is by creating a copy of the world (a piece of it anyhow) and letting it run.

There are even worlds that couldn't exist, such as WebRaft, where the force of gravity – which is what makes us stick to the Earth – is made much stronger. Everything's different there. Stars are only a kilometre wide and burn out in a year, and the people live on a big raft floating on air. The scientists go (in their Websuits) and live there, trying to see what it would be like to live in such a different universe.

Domains are supposed to be *pure*. There isn't supposed to be any leakage from Realworld or from other Domains. Apart from the Search Engines, there is supposed to be no way to move from one Domain to another.

That's the theory.

Another thing about Domains is the people.

In a Domain you'll meet *real* people. You might meet King Henry VIII, for instance. Some of these are avatars –

characters being role-played by human beings in Websuits, who might come from anywhere in Realworld. But most of the people are phaces – artificial people generated inside the Web itself.

In the rest of the Web, the phaces are usually just dummies, with no more intelligence than a toaster. But to make domains authentic, most of the phaces are self-aware – that means they think and feel, like you and me. And the most important thing is, *they don't know their Domain is fake*.

So if you meet a Henry VIII phace, you're meeting a computer creation who thinks he is the *real* Henry. And you'd better curtsy or bow! And don't forget how much computing power it's all taking.

The bad news is that a lot of Domains allow in young people to work as Browsers. In fact they encourage it. You might get to live as a servant at the court of King Henry VIII for a week, for instance, and learn all about what life was like in the sixteenth century. You get a special Websuit which lets you transmit your experiences around the Web for the benefit of others (which is why you're called a Browser).

It's all grittily realistic (there's no TV and you work at menial jobs from dawn to dusk) and authentic (you have the basic Web safety equipment, like scuttle-buttons to get out, and are bound by the usual rules – no more than a few hours in the Web at any one time, to avoid Websickness – but otherwise it's exactly like the sixteenth century or whenever: shirts of sack cloth instead of modern custom gear, *so* cog).

All this is a *Learning Experience*.

Parents and teachers are strangely keen on stays in Domains – as opposed to, say, the Web gaming zones. If you want to find a Domain look up *educational* and cross-index *uplifting* and *morally improving*, file under *good for young people*.

Yep, most Domains are dull, dull, dull.

Anyway, back in January – when the Christmas school holiday still had six more weeks to run – right on schedule, Philip (that's my dad) started telling me I should do

*something more useful with my time than spinning into the Web
gaming zones and chat rooms.* And I knew I was in trouble.
When he said he had a reward for me after the way I handled
my perilous time in Gulliverzone (which is another story!) I
knew the trouble was serious.

The *reward* was that he had fixed up for me to go work as a
Browser in the Domain of my choice. He even had a new
Browser Websuit for me. It looked like a scuba-diving suit, in
a pastel colour so washed-out and old-fashioned it wouldn't
even have been cool in the Millennium Dome.

A Domain would be *fun*, Philip said, and *educational* as
well.

As if two days a week of school, for fifteen weeks of the
year, isn't enough!

He was decent enough to give me a choice of which
Domain I would be sentenced to. I spent a couple of hours in
a Search Engine checking out the options. Search Engines,
the only way to travel between the Domains, are fun. You
can see out but you're invisible to the inhabitants of the
Domain. It's a little like riding a glass-bottomed boat and
staring at the fish under the sea.

I could go visit WebVin – a Domain dedicated to recreating
life in the Viking era, circa AD 973. Or I could spend more
time in Galaxias – an interstellar empire of the year AD 3000,
one of the few Domains set in the future.

In WebVin, I found, mostly you get to bake bread. The life
of the Vikings was *not* as glamorous, most of the time, as you
might think.

I opted for Galaxias.

Philip didn't exactly approve of Galaxias. It's known as a
tough, dangerous place. Very adult. He wanted me to go
back on the Search Engine and find somewhere, as he put it,
nicer. Happily for me I couldn't have gone in again if I'd
wanted to, which I didn't, because the Search Engine crashed
(and I would find out more about that later).

I spent a last few days spinning in and out of the Web with
my friends, cramming in as much fun as I could before

facing the mind-numbing boredom of the Domain. At least, I *thought* it would be boring. And then I put on my new Browser's Websuit, prayed that nobody would see me in it, and spun into Galaxias.

And that was where I was when the WebCrash hit.

The Regent bunched a fist and studied it thoughtfully. 'I've been patient enough, Metaphor. Try to take this in. All this is your problem. Just get me to Raq.'

I was getting a little tired of Numinus's bullying and threats. The fact is I was trying to save him.

If a Domain Breach happens – two Domains cross over because of some hardware failure – any characters who become aware of the existence of the Web outside their world, or of any other Domains, are supposed to be shut down. It seems a little harsh (though I wouldn't have shed any tears over Numinus), but that is the protocol.

I was actually trying to protect Numinus from being shut down.

Not that he would have appreciated it.

I pushed more strength into my voice. 'And I'm telling you, Numinus, we can't return to n-space until—' Until the warnings of a Domain Breach stopped, but I couldn't tell him that. 'Until the storm in n-space disperses.'

'How long?'

I shrugged. 'Three or four days?'

'One day.' Numinus threw a fast punch at my control helmet. The sphere rocked in the air. 'We resume our journey in one day. Is that clear?'

'Oh, get off my bridge, Numinus,' I said tiredly.

For now, I'd had enough. Out of his sight I punched my scuttle-button and got out of there.

Scuttling out of Domains is a bit complicated.

If anybody from Realworld is in a Domain, time in the Domain carries on at a normal pace. But if nobody is there, the Domain might freeze – or it might fast-forward, like a video. The phaces aren't aware of this, of course. It doesn't

matter to them that a year in the Domain might go by so fast
that it only takes a second of Realworld time, or be slowed
down so it takes a decade. To them, it *feels* like a full year of
their lives.

Anyhow, as far as Numinus was concerned, I would simply
fall asleep. If I chose not to return at all I would be replaced
by another phace, a placeholder that wouldn't be self-aware.

But I wasn't thinking about any of this technical stuff at
the time. Because when I opened my eyes, I was lying on my
back in the cosy warmth of our spare bedroom – and the
walls were flashing warning red!

CHAPTER TWO

NORRLAND

What I didn't know, couldn't know yet, was that the WebCrash was global. It affected every corner of Realworld, and all the virtual worlds of the Web too.

Later, I would find out what happened in the Domain called WebVin, from the point of view of a phace called Thyri who knew nothing about Realworld and Domain Breaches.

To Thyri, the only reality was WebVin, and she thought her world was coming to an end.

AD 973: Norrland, the coast of Sweden.

There was a wind from the north.

Thyri pulled the cart off the road from Helgo, and let the pair of horses slow to a stop.

The wind was thin, cold as a knife in the flesh.

Thyri shivered, and not just from the cold. *Valkyries abroad*, she thought.

The horses snickered uneasily, tossing their heads. Thyri reached forward and patted their rumps. 'I know,' she said. 'I know.'

Huddled against his wife, Gunnar was a sleeping bundle on the seat beside Thyri. The old Viking warrior stirred and stretched, his ice-blond hair shining in the starlight. The bandage around his eyes was grimy again, she noticed.

'Thyri? Where are we? What's wrong?'

'We're an hour from home.' Thyri said gruffly. 'There's nothing wrong. I didn't mean to wake you.' She tried a laugh. 'I need you to get your sleep and build up your strength.' She looked back at the rolls of pig-iron, the kegs of saltpetre that lay in silent heaps in the rear of the cart. 'When we get home you've got to help me shift this lot.'

Gunnar turned his sightless head. 'Well, if nothing's wrong, why did we stop?'

'I ...'

The northern wind rose again. It swept across the Norrland coastal plain, rustling the pine trees and whispering in the heather that clung to the bare rock.

A comforting lie died on Thyri's lips. There was something coming in that wind, she sensed. Something deadly: the wind was the call of the Valkyrie, the flying goddesses who select those to be slain in battle.

(It was, in fact, the noise of the Domain Breach, but Thyri couldn't know that. Not yet!)

'Thyri?'

She clutched her husband. 'There's nothing to be frightened of.'

But was that true?

The horses skipped restlessly.

Gunnar stirred sleepily. 'Thyri, can we go home now? I feel cold.'

He sounded very old, she thought.

In the Valkyrie wind, she held Gunnar's face. Her hands, scarred as they were by long years of working metal, were like bits of battered wood. 'Yes, of course.' Thyri took the reins, unease still prickling at her mind.

The cart bumped back onto the rustled track. Gunnar snuggled into his cloak once more.

Thyri tried to understand what was happening. Suppose this deep fear she felt was more than just fancy. Suppose her instinct was responding to something real. What could be the source of peril? And why should she feel personally threatened?

She could think of only one reason.

'Gunnar.' Gently, she nudged her husband awake again. 'Hmm?'

'Do you still have the Key?'

Gunnar said, 'Of course I have the Key. It's at home.'

'Where?'

'I don't know. I think it's under my pallet.'

The Key was a mysterious object from the east. Gunnar had brought it back from his last battle in Byzantium. But Gunnar had paid a heavy price for his trophy. Savage bandits from those parts, intent on stealing the Key, had captured Gunnar and plucked out his eyes before he fought his way out.

The Key had cost Gunnar his sight, and when he brought it home Thyri had loathed it immediately.

Somehow, she intuitively knew the Key was the centre of the disquiet she felt now.

All these memories, of events years before, were real to Thyri and Gunnar. But the Domain had only been operating for a few months. In Realworld time Gunnar's trip to the east might have taken place only *hours* before. Domains are strange places if you think about them too hard.

Thyri said, 'Gunnar, I want you to do something for me. First thing in the morning, take that Key out and bury it.'

'What?'

'Take a spade, go as far as you can from the house, and bury it. As deep as you can.'

'But …' Puzzlement creased Gunnar's round face. 'Why? Why now? You know what it means to me—'

'I don't want to discuss it,' Thyri snapped. 'You don't have to get rid of it. Just … hide it. Will you do that for me?'

Gunnar mumbled assent and went back to sleep.

The horses tossed their muzzles, their manes ruffled by the north wind. Thyri calmed them with soft words as the journey wore away.

CHAPTER THREE

REALWORLD

Philip says there was something like a WebCrash back in the year 2000.

The Stone Age computers they had back then couldn't cope with the year numbers changing from 19 hundred to 20 hundred and it's going to happen again at the Digital Millennium – the year 2048 – because if you write out 2047 in base two (the number systems computers use) you get 11111111111 – eleven spaces full of ones. But 2048 is 100000000000 – *twelve* spaces, mostly zeroes.

But there was nothing special about the WebCrash date, January 4, 2028.

I peeled off my Websuit – as you know, it's like getting out of a wet suit – and padded to my bedroom.

At first everything seemed normal. Glancing through the window I saw it was a bright winter's day. The town's OzoneHole dome sparkled against the blue of the sky, even obliterating some of the Tennessee Fried Ostrich laser ads painted on the clouds.

I ordered an isotonic soda from my RoomChef – it's always good to replace your body fluids after a session in the Web – but a cappuccino coffee came spurting out of the little hole in the wall. That wouldn't have been so bad, but it emerged backwards: chocolate first, then cream, then coffee, and no hot water. After watching the RoomChef's little robot arms trying to froth up a coffee that didn't exist, I gave up.

I didn't think too much of it. If you live in the sort of home where nothing *ever* breaks down then you clearly don't have a kid brother like that little egg George, who *fiddles* with things.

With a sigh of resignation, I flopped down on my bed. 'Wall, on.'

The bedroom wall chimed softly, sort of fizzed, and stayed blank.

'Wall—'

'Good evening, Sarah,' said the bedroom.

Evening? It wasn't yet 10 a.m.

The bedroom gets its time from the Global Clock, which works from a satellite in high Earth orbit, and I knew that was one gadget that even George couldn't mess up. It was only then I had the first prickling of unease. Something was *seriously* wrong.

'Wall, *on!*'

It took fifteen minutes of trying before I managed to tune into any of the 168 channels the wall normally provides. And when I did, all there was to watch was news.

The world, it seemed, had gone *crazy*.

In London there had been a car crash – the first in five years! – there were pictures of the drivers, unhurt, scratching their heads and looking in bewilderment at the dents in their SmartCar bumpers. The News Robot said the Global Positioning System (GPS) satellites had all gone offline and all the SmartCars were losing their way, and I could well imagine what a disaster that would prove to be, because I know people who can't find their way to the *bathroom* without their GPS wristwatches.

Right across the country the superconductor power grid was shorting out. Not only that, it wasn't being fed enough power from the orbiting PowerSats.

And the microwave beam from one of the Sats, which should have been focused on a field of receptors in the Orkneys, had strayed across Scotland. An aeroplane crossed its path. Luckily, it was unmanned but its cargo of pizzas arrived in Glasgow well-cooked.

In Parliament, the Robot Speaker – screaming 'Order, order!' – had attacked the Leader of the Opposition with its gavel. Of course that isn't too serious. It took twelve members of parliament to wrestle it to the ground.

Manchester–Newcastle were playing an exhibition football game against a team of clones from China – nothing unusual about that – but the manager, IBM's Deep Blue 27 computer, was having some trouble. The players' implants seemed to be going wrong and half the team were playing towards their own goal.

And so on!

The same kind of news was coming in from around the world. What news there was, as half the Combats had gone down too.

In the US, the weather control system in Kansas had gone wrong and tornadoes were scouring across the plains, like scenes from *The Wizard of Oz*.

In Russia, the EarthCore mining project had gone off track. The Mole had emerged in the middle of Moscow, hundreds of kilometres off course, and huge fountains of lava were gushing out of the heart of the city.

In Japan, the city of New Tokyo – where all the buildings are Smart, are controlled by computer and change shape every day – had shut itself off. New Tokyo literally fell down overnight. There were pictures of people standing around amid heaps of plastic walls, or stuck inside Smart furniture that suddenly wouldn't let them go.

And on, and on. Some of it was trivial, even funny. Some was a lot more serious. Nobody yet understood what was going on.

But the commentary robots were already calling it *Web-Crash*.

There was one intriguing bit of news, though: about the SETI programme.

SETI: the Search for Extra-Terrestrial Intelligence. Listening for radio signals from aliens on remote planets. That had been going on, in one form or another, since the 1960s. But it was only in the 2020s that anybody put any serious money into it. And it was only earlier last year, 2027, that anything was picked up.

It was just a thin radio whisper, dots and dashes, washing over the Earth from the stars, picked up by sensitive radio-telescopes.

You must remember the excitement. Maybe you entered the big Web competitions to try to decode the signals.

Then early this year, 2028, the trickle of data from the SETI search suddenly became a torrent. It turned out, the commentators said, that the signals had been so powerful that even ordinary radio receivers had been capable of picking them up.

Most computers are pretty dumb. As they hadn't been programmed to recognize alien data they had treated it as nothing more sinister than a BBC robo-gardening programme. Around the world computers had started storing the data wherever they could: in home systems, in public systems like traffic control ...

And even in the Web, I learned now. That's right: *there are alien signals, stored in the Web!* Maybe, I guessed wildly, that was the cause of the WebCrash. And—

And that was when the walls went blank, and the bedroom started blinking again.

Warning messages scrolled over the walls saying that Philip's direct-debit bill payments, normally made once a second from his bank account, had stopped, and unless they resumed, our house would be cut off (except for the essentials, of course: food, heating, TV, milk shakes).

I lay on my bed, stunned. It was as if the whole world had fallen apart.

Maybe if I'd lived through the year 2000 crash I might have expected this. (Philip says he just stayed in bed for three days.) But I'd never thought hard before about how much we rely on computers.

Of course the Web is entirely computer generated. No computers, no Web. But even in Realworld almost everything we do is regulated by electronic machines: from the giant brains that run the traffic and the weather control systems and the power grid, to the tiny machines too small to see embedded in the walls and furniture of our homes and schools, even our clothes. Everywhere. It's as if we are all living inside the dream of some giant electronic brain.

Well, suddenly that brain was having a nightmare. And it was obvious to me that nobody knew what to do about it.

I tried to be practical.

I called Philip, my dad. He was at work at the desalination plant in Tilbury where they turn sea water into drinking water.

Of course he was panicking. 'Sarah, are you OK? Stay where you are. Don't touch anything.'

I suppressed a sigh. 'Philip, I'm fine.'

'And don't spin into the Web ... Where's George?'

'At the PrimateZone.' The PrimateZone is a jungle gym (a kid brother zoo). The whole point of the Zone is that the kids blow off steam by doing physical things – running, jumping, climbing, fighting, whatever it is kids do. There's hardly any electronic input as it's supposed to be a balance for Webtime, when you have to lie pretty much still for hours on end.

So I knew George would be OK there, and, after a little more agonizing, Philip agreed.

'I'll come home,' he said.

'How?' I asked reasonably. 'Walk? As far as I can see everything's down.'

He started some crazed rambling about borrowing a bicycle, but as, even without the traffic jams, it would have taken him a good month to make it home on *that* – as I reasonably pointed out – it wasn't such a good idea.

'The thing to do,' I advised him sternly, 'is to stay put until all the fuss dies down.'

That was when the line went dead. I could only hope he'd do what I told him.

Parents. You never know what they are going to get up to next. But in the end, you know, you have to let them take responsibility for their own safety. Still, Philip was a trustworthy sort, and I knew I didn't have to worry.

So, as far as I knew, my family were safe.

That left *me*.

I was safe enough sitting in my bedroom, of course. England is really a pretty stable place. It wasn't as if I was in California, for instance, where the SmartQuake control systems had already gone down. I could just sit and wait for things to get back to normal. I might even be able to persuade the room systems to give me something to eat.

Maybe.

But I was already bored. (If you want to know how bored, you try sitting in a turned-off bedroom for more than fifteen minutes.) And besides—

I was a little scared. Not by the WebCrash itself. Most systems have enough fail-safes so I knew not too many people around the world would come to any harm. No, I was scared by somebody who didn't even exist: Numinus Torca, Regent of the Empire of Galaxias.

You may think that's foolish. Numinus wasn't even real. But you didn't see the look in his eyes.

I knew the rules about Domain Breaches. Even if they occurred there was no way a phace, even one as devious as Numinus, could escape from his home world and reach another. And there was *no* danger he could do any damage in Realworld.

Those were the rules. But this was WebCrash Day, and the rules didn't seem to be working ...

I went back to the spare bedroom.

Of course I had no way of knowing if the Web itself was still working, given all the problems elsewhere. And I was about to disobey Philip, which, despite the black propaganda put about by George, is not something I do lightly.

But I had to find out what had happened to Numinus.

So I suited up and spun back in.
Big mistake.

CHAPTER FOUR

BREACH

I was back on the bridge of *The Empress's Mighty Fist*, and immediately in a lot of trouble.

The ship shuddered, as if rammed from below.

Numinus yelled and stumbled. 'Pilot! Curse you, tell me what's happening!'

I scrambled to get control of the ship, while Numinus yelled in my ear.

What can I tell you about Galaxias?

The basic idea is that in a few centuries from now humans will have developed interstellar travel, so that it takes only a few weeks to travel from star to star.

The scientists set this up and fast-forwarded it for a while (a month or so, but hundreds of years inside the Domain!). And then they let Browsers in to see what had happened.

How will society evolve when it becomes as easy to travel to the stars as to fly around the world?

The scientists imagined that humans of the future, with such terrific technology and power, would use it to do good. On the colonized worlds there would be a wonderful Utopia, a time of peace and plenty. Meanwhile, peaceful exploration ships would push deeper into the Galaxy finding new star systems and perhaps new alien races.

Because the machines could provide everybody with everything they needed – food, clothing, entertainment –

there would be no conflict. Nobody even needed to work. And so there would be no crime, no war, no money. Adults would sing and children would skip about smelling flowers.

Hah!

The scientists turned out to be dead wrong, as I could have told them. After all my kid brother George and his bratty friends are given everything they need (by parents who can't see them for the horrors they are). And *they* fight like cats and dogs.

While Galaxias was being fast-forwarded, there was intensive weapons development and a bloody war between the stars. Real science fiction stuff with interstellar battle-cruisers and ray guns, even if it did only take half a day in Realworld time. After which a huge and cruel Empire emerged and took over the colonized Galaxy. It was about as peaceful as a Labour-Liberal party conference.

Maybe you can see why I decided to go there.

It's a tough place, but as Domains go its pretty exciting. With a dozen fully realized planets and hundreds of sketches, it's the most gigantic Domain of all, and you do get to fly around the Galaxy. Not as good as a game zone, but not bad for schoolwork.

Anyhow I got a job of sorts as a Pilot of *The Empress's Mighty Fist*, one of the cute little two-person starships they have (or will have). My assignment was to ferry a Bad Guy across the Galaxy.

The Bad Guy in question was Numinus Torca, and he was the Regent. He used to be the heir to the Plutonium Throne of the Empire itself. All he had to do was wait for his mother to retire, or die of old age, and he would have been Emperor of a thousand worlds.

But he got impatient.

When his mother, the Empress, found out exactly *what* he had been putting into her breakfast cereal to hurry along the succession, she got a little angry, and Numinus had to flee, fast. And he picked me as his getaway driver!

I had to fly our two-person ship out of the Imperial Palace, which is a space station orbiting a giant star, and evade Imperial Trooper fleets, before we reached the security of n-space. (And believe me, that part was a *lot* of fun, but I haven't got time to tell you about it here.) Now I was supposed to be taking Numinus to a planet called Raq where he thought he might find allies to help him start over and build a fleet to attack his mother once more.

You might wonder what I was doing running with such a Bad Guy.

As it happens I was a double agent, in the pay of the Imperial Guard, and I happened to know there was a hefty police force waiting for Numinus on Raq. But that's all rather complicated, and academic anyway because we never got as far as Raq!

The signal of the Beacons flickered, faded like a lighthouse in a storm.

The Beacons were like navigation satellites in n-space. But they worked directly on my mind.

The ship's controls were hooked directly to my brain through the control helmet. The whole ship felt like an extension of my body. Navigating the ship was less like driving a car, say, than walking towards a clean yellow light.

But now n-space gusts crossed the face of the Beacons' beam, and I tried to balance the ship, resisting the battering of the current. It was like walking a tightrope.

'I don't know where we've been pushed by the storm,' I told Numinus. 'But I still have the Beacons. I think I can take us home.'

'Home? You mean Raq?'

I knew it wouldn't be that simple, because bright red warnings about a Domain Breach were still scrolling across my vision.

I imagined Web engineers out in Realworld, struggling to disentangle the Domains without doing too much damage. If the worst came to the worst they might have to reboot the Domains altogether, but Domains are so expensive to run that would be a last resort. I was likely to be stuck here for some time.

'I mean,' I said steadily, 'I think I can take us back to Galaxias. The galaxy's explored quadrant.'

'Then do it, Pilot. Get us out of this.'

The n-space streams became still, suddenly. The ship calmed. In my mind the Beacons shone like the rays of a sun.

I stirred in my couch, uneasy. This felt too easy.

'I can feel the ship settle,' Numinus whispered. 'Is it over?'

I sent my senses probing out through the n-space environment. 'I don't know. I don't like it.'

The n-space sea was as flat as ... a pond? No. My mind scratched for the right image.

Think about how a huge ocean wave gathers. There's always an area of calmness in the water just before it breaks.

'Numinus. Find a safety harness. Power up your skin-armour.' My fingers flew over touch pads as I tried to batten the ship down.

'What is it, Metaphor?'

The ship stirred as if sucked towards ... a wave that came at us out of n-space like the breath of a god.

The wave hit.

The Mighty Fist tumbled end-over-end, backwards. My universe smashed to fragments: Numinus's scream, tearing metal, howling n-space vortices, pain in my own rattled body ...

This was the Web. It wasn't supposed to *hurt* like this! But I was in the middle of a WebCrash. The normal rules didn't apply.

We were hurled out of n-space like a bolt from a crossbow.

The ship stabilized. The shock of emerging from the n-space turmoil was like a punch to the stomach.

I opened my eyes. Through a red mist I saw Numinus push himself from his safety harness, blood seeping from his mouth. The Regent limped to a control bank and poked cautiously at touch pads, powering up external monitors.

I saw a jumble of ice and dark blue sky.

Numinus grunted in surprise. He swung the monitors' focus around.

We were hovering above a world – a planet that curved beneath its blanket of ice. A sun was low. It was morning, or evening. Light clouds floated high above us. Far ahead of the ship sunlight sparkled on an ice-crusted sea.

It looked like Earth, but there were no city lights, no sparks of satellites, no ships on the sea. It was – I thought even then, right at the start of the whole thing – the way Earth might have looked before modern civilization, say 1000 years ago.

I didn't know how right I was!

'Pilot ...' Numinus's voice was full of wonder. 'We're in the atmosphere of a planet. Judging from the sun, the ice, I'd say we were over one of the polar regions. Look at the pole, the odd darkness there.'

It looked like a giant curtain, draped over the glittering white ice cap. It was hard even to look at it.

It was a Domain Breach, a flaw in the fabric of this universe. We must have come through it, and finished up *here*, in another Domain altogether. And the Beacons had gone. It was as if Galaxias had vanished, had never existed at all!

But Numinus was still functioning.

This wasn't supposed to happen.

We had come through a Breach into a different Domain. Numinus should have been shut down. I should have been thrown out of the Web immediately.

But none of that had happened.

At the time I had no idea where we were. I just knew we weren't where we were supposed to be, and the Web safeties weren't working.

I did what you would have done.

I closed my eyes. I pushed my scuttle-button.

I gathered a great sigh of relief, promising myself never to take such a foolish risk again. I opened my eyes, expecting to see the familiar, if dingy, walls of our spare room.

But I was still on *The Empress's Mighty Fist*. The scuttle hadn't worked.

I was trapped.

Numinus hadn't noticed any of this. 'Metaphor, where are we? Are we still in Galaxias? Have we been thrown into some unexplored quadrant? I've never heard of a world like this.'

I thought frantically. I would have to find a way out of this situation – perhaps get back through the Breach to the Galaxias Domain – but I had to remember that Numinus was a phace. He wasn't supposed to know what he was, let alone that his world was artificial.

He had to know something, but I'd have to be careful what I said.

'No. You *wouldn't* have heard of this world.'

Numinus frowned. 'So? Where are we? Outside the Galaxy somewhere, or have we crossed time?'

I shook my head. 'I think we've been pushed through … a partition.'

'A what?'

'A barrier between universes. Numinus, I don't think this is even our reality.'

The Regent's breath was ragged, shallow. 'Can you take us back?'

'I don't know.' I pulled my control helmet closer to my scalp. 'The path back through n-space isn't predictable. It might have closed up already.'

'Then the sooner you find out the better.'

Numinus stared greedily at rushing vistas of ice and sea, and I wondered uneasily what he was thinking.

And planning.

CHAPTER FIVE

EMERGENCE

In Norrland, Thyri was aware of the Domain Breach, and our arrival. To her, the Breach was a disturbance in the world – a booming from the north, like a distant storm.

When the noise rumbled over her, Thyri's eyes snapped open to darkness. She sat bolt upright. On the other side of the room she heard Gunnar's calm breathing. Light flickered through the doorframe's leather curtains. There was a ...

WHOOSH!

... somewhere overhead, as if a great bird had flown past. (It was, of course, *The Empress's Mighty Fist*.)

Thyri kept a blade strapped to her calf. Among the *karlar*, the free men of Ragnar, there were a few who were prepared to take advantage of Gunnar's blindness and his wife's supposed weakness, to steal their property. She touched her weapon and climbed silently from her pallet.

The air outside the house was bitterly cold. She could see the other buildings – the smithy, the barn, the small bathhouse – a few paces away. The house sat at the summit of a low hill. Around the hill a pine forest lapped like a sea of darkness, utterly still. To the east there was already blue in the sky. The sparse light picked out the hulking mounds that were their metalworking supplies – metal ore, coal, saltpetre – all covered by greased cloth.

There was nobody here.

Another rumble, fainter than the first. Perhaps an echo

from the fjord.

She raised her eyes. A thin line of cloud or smoke, unnaturally straight, had been cut across the sky. Slowly the line was dissipating.

'Well, whatever it is,' Thyri murmured to herself, 'it's arrived.'

'Thyri? Is it time to get up?'

'Not yet, husband. Not yet.'

Thyri closed the door and climbed back into her bed.

Sleep didn't return.

Meanwhile, somewhere above Thyri's head on *The Mighty Fist*, I was bending over an opened-up control console and watching the repair beetles at work. The tiny golden machines crawled over plastic boards. They nibbled at charred and damaged circuitry, and deposited cubes of yellow silicon like bizarre eggs.

I plucked one beetle between thumb and forefinger. Tiny caterpillar treads whirred on the beetle's underside. Within miniature jaws I saw the blue flash of a laser. It was a neat little gadget. I put it back.

Hours had passed in this new Domain, but just minutes of my Realworld time.

I still couldn't scuttle out, but I could pretend to sleep. While he was fast-forwarded with the rest of the Domain, Numinus just saw an image of my sleeping self.

For me, it was like jumping forward in time, to skip the dull bits.

It had made me a little more scared, though.

Fast-forwarding is only allowed if there is nobody in a Domain (or if everybody's pretending to be asleep, or is somewhere they can't be seen by the phaces). So I knew now that I was almost certainly alone. There was no other Realworld person in here with me.

There was nobody who could help me. And I was still stuck.

The floor slid beneath me. I stumbled slightly.

Numinus was sitting in my flight couch. It was too small for him. He looked like an adult in a child's chair. He was inexpertly piloting the ship through this strange planet's atmosphere. He caught my glance and stared back.

'The repair's almost complete,' I said. 'Another six or seven hours and we can return home – if the passage is still open.'

The Regent nodded and returned to his scrutiny of the external monitors.

I turned to look.

We were flying low over an island country now, a ring of rock in the ocean enclosing a broad lagoon. At a break in the ring a city sprawled around a harbour. People ran like ants. Sails on handsome wooden craft billowed in the wind of their passing.

Eyes glittering, Numinus took the ship almost to ground level. I saw upturned faces flickering past, a blur of chiselled features. People were diving for shelter.

Then we were over the sea, heading north.

'Why did you do that?' I asked. 'You frightened them for no reason.'

The Regent studied me, and ignored the question. 'Pilot, we may be in an alternate reality – but some of the inhabitants of this place look pretty close to human.' (Did I mention there were alien races in Galaxias?) The Regent tugged at his beard, scheming.

'Numinus, this is irrelevant. We ought to return to the Breach.'

'The what?'

'The darkness at the pole. As soon as the repairs are complete we have to try the reverse crossing. We can't know how long the passage will remain stable.'

Numinus frowned. 'Pilot, with a sub-orbital hop we could reach the pole in minutes from anywhere on the planet. There's no rush.' His fingers rattled on the skin-armour covering his legs. '*Look* at this world, Metaphor. Technologically these people are nowhere. They must be two thousand years behind us.'

'All the more reason not to interfere with them,' I said.
But he ignored me.

'We've seen soldiers, but all they have is foil armour and
metal sticks they poke into each other. I bet the armament
contained in this two-man ship could defeat the combined
armies of the whole planet. A man could live like a king here.
A man with power ...' There was a light in Numinus's eyes.
Muscles worked in his cheeks.

I took a step back. He frightened me. 'What are you saying,
Numinus?'

Numinus glanced at me, black eyes glittering. 'Come on.
Think. We're a long way from home. The Empire doesn't
even exist on this level of reality. What we do here doesn't
matter to anybody.'

'Except to the people here.'

Numinus laughed harshly. 'How many plasma cannon do
they have? How many defence lasers?' The Regent's tone
became sly, almost a whisper. 'We can do what we want
here, Metaphor, for a few days anyway. There's not a thing
anybody can do to stop us. Think about it. Wealth – all the
power you want.' His greedy eyes were fixed on my face.

'Get out of my couch.' I realized now I had to stop him.
Not just because of his cruelty, but because I didn't know
what damage he might do if he interfered in a Domain he
didn't belong to.

But how?

I clenched my fists. They felt small and useless ... but there
was a clutch of repair beetles in one palm.

Numinus's expression grew hard. 'What's the matter,
Pilot? Don't you like money?'

I tried to keep my voice level. 'What I don't like is the idea
of using our power to exploit these people. Numinus, we're
not all cut out to be Emperor.'

Numinus snorted. 'We're wasting time. I'm taking her
down. We'll land in the middle of one of those coastal
towns.'

I pushed the repair beetles into Numinus's face. It was a horrible thing to do, but I didn't know what else to try!

I stumbled back, panting. It was the first time in my life I'd attacked another human being – real or not.

Numinus roared and staggered to his feet. A beetle crawled towards his left eye socket, chewing flesh. It left cubes of silicon in little bloody craters.

It was horrible. But it got him out of my control couch.

I slid past Numinus into my couch. The control helmet nestled to my head like a bird over an egg, and the control systems started reading my brain waves. Smoothly, the ship lifted out of the atmosphere. Stars glittered above an arc of blue planet.

Numinus ripped the beetle off and threw it to the floor. He smashed it beneath one booted heel. Blood ran down his cheek.

He stepped up to me and clinically drove his fist into my stomach.

It *hurt!*

I felt myself double over in the couch, arms folding over my belly. Why, why hadn't I activated my skin-armour? (Galaxias is a rough place – *everybody* wears skin-armour.)

And why hadn't the Web protected me? (I know – it was WebCrash Day.)

My pain flooded into the ship's control system. The ship bucked and rolled. Stars whirled past the view screens.

Numinus snatched the control helmet from me and fitted it over his own scalp.

The ship plunged back into the atmosphere with a kind of wail. Metal tore from the hull and splashed past the view screens.

Clinging to my couch, I forced out words through gasps of pain. 'Numinus … When you hit me I flooded the system … It was the shock … Give me the helmet. I have to get her under control.'

The Regent's palm forced me back into my couch. He was much stronger than me and there was nothing I could do.

I tried the scuttle-button again. Nothing. I was still trapped, with a murderous nut, in a spaceship that was about to crash on an unknown world.

It really was turning out to be one of those days.

We rolled as we fell. Sky and brown land flickered. Detail exploded, mountains and rivers and trees and ...

CHAPTER SIX

THYRI

As we fell from the sky, it was mornng in WebVin.

Thyri had gone to Helgo, the main trading centre to the south of Norrland, to buy supplies.

The freighter from Riga bobbed in the waters of Helgo's harbour. Thyri picked her way through the gloomy hold, sniffing suspiciously at cloth-wrapped kegs.

Riga was a Russian port. It was the end of the trade routes that stretched eastward into Russia, the source of furs, wax and honey, and even as far as China which provided silver and minerals like saltpetre.

Like his ship, the Russian trader Caspar was fat and round. He bustled after Thyri plucking nervously at his waistcoat of shabby fur. 'Nothing but the best, as usual, my Viking friend,' he jabbered. 'From the fabled land of China, the finest saltpetre for those renowned kilns of yours—'

'Damp,' Thyri growled.

'I beg your pardon?'

Thyri hoisted a cask beneath one arm and ripped away its surrounding sacking. 'Damp, Caspar. Look at this sacking. Half-rotten with it.'

The Russian smoothed back greased hair. 'Ah. I can explain. We suffered a minor accident, a storm that—'

A bass rumble flapped past Thyri's ears like the wing of an invisible bird. (It was, of course, me and Numinus.) She froze, eyes half-closed.

Caspar was saying, 'We shipped a little water, you see, but nothing that need concern—'

The last echo died.

'Did you hear that?'

Caspar swivelled his round head this way and that. 'Not another rat, was it? I'll flay that lazy crew.'

'No.' Thyri ran the sound through her mind. 'It was like thunder.'

The Russian screwed up his face. 'I heard nothing. I'm sorry. But then, your ears are sharper than mine.' Caspar dried up. His swarthy fingers wriggled together and he laughed uneasily. 'Well, shall we close this deal? Of course I offer the usual discount rates. Find a cheaper vendor anywhere and I will refund the difference, gladly. And naturally you have my guarantee that in the unlikely circumstance of any slight dampness corrupting this fine saltpetre …'

Thyri let the merchant babble on, hardly hearing.

She closed the deal and hurried home.

Thyri: I would come to know her better than I know many people in Realworld.

This was WebVin: a recreation of old Viking settlements, part of a wider Domain that reproduced the Earth of the tenth century. Norrland was a reconstruction of eastern Sweden, the coast of the sea called the Gulf of Bothnia – well above the Arctic Circle, a hard and unforgiving country.

Gunnar had served in Constantinople (the city we call Istanbul today). Constantinople was the capital of Byzantium, the eastern half of the old Roman Empire that had collapsed in the west centuries before. Gunnar had been a member of the Varangian Guard, the elite unit of mercenary Viking soldiers that protected the Emperor of Byzantium himself. He had worked long and hard, saving his money for his wife, Thyri, who waited for him in Norrland.

Gunnar had been a hard fighter, an expensive mercenary, but incautious. At last, trying to defend the Key – a strange artefact he bought from a traveller from the far east – he picked one fight too many. He was left blinded, and all but crippled by wounds to his stomach, back and legs.

Somehow he had made it home, to the Norrland town of Ragnar. And Thyri had had to find strength she didn't know she possessed to reconstruct their lives.

They began to make a living as manufacturers of fine weapons. The expertise and some of the strength was Gunnar's. The determination was all Thyri's.

With time Thyri had grown in stature in the little community. This was not a society where women were given equal rights. But through her courage and strength Thyri came to be considered the equal of any of the *karlar*, the free men of the town.

Thyri had grown stout and grey, her life revolving around Gunnar. He had never given up the Key, the strange little object that had ruined his life. Thyri hated and feared it, though she never understood why.

Gunnar and Thyri had lived long, complex, interesting lives.

Those lives weren't real, of course. Thyri was a Web phace, and her years had mostly been fast-forwarded, crammed into hours or days of Realworld time. But they were real to Thyri, as real as your memory is to you.

Gunnar and Thyri *thought* they were real. And they became real enough to me – real enough to care about, a great deal.

When she got home, Thyri unlocked the heavy chest Gunnar kept in a corner of the house. She rummaged until she found Gunnar's axe. It was the weapon of a Varangian Guard. The blade was tarnished with age but the edge was as keen as ever.

She polished the metal until it gleamed, relishing the feeling of wood and iron in her hands.

Gunnar was smiling in his sleep.

CHAPTER SEVEN

CRASH

The Empress's Mighty Fist crashed spectacularly, thousands of miles from Norrland. We came down in a desert. And it didn't take long before we were found.

The camel shifted under Efer. The young Arab was dimly aware that the afternoon sun was parching dry the gums of his open mouth. But still he sat and stared.

Two silver bubbles sat on the desert sand.

The bubbles were each twice as tall as a man. They were at the centre of a bowl in the desert a hundred paces across. The sand in that crater sparkled like the jewels of the sheikh, and it was strewn with steaming bits of metal, crumpled as if by the fist of a giant.

A scar in the desert ran from the western horizon all the way to the crater.

There were ghosts in the bubbles.

Two of the shapes looked like people, floating upside-down like fledglings in strange eggs. In the other bubble there were devices, combinations of boxes and discs.

Heat rose from the crater, scouring Efer's cheeks. But his curiosity was strong. He couldn't back away.

The stasis bubbles flicked off.

Stasis fields are like seat belts for Galaxias spaceships. Time doesn't exist inside a stasis field, and during the crash I had been frozen in place, free from harm while the Domain was fast-forwarded around me.

So I missed the last of the crash. It was as if my struggle with Numinus was bad-edited into the now.

I hoped, wildly, that somehow I had managed to scuttle out of this mess.

But I found himself hanging upside-down, staring at the sky of burning blue.

I tumbled a metre or so to a hot surface that crackled beneath me. I heard a grunt as the Regent followed. Bits of bridge equipment rained around us. Repair beetles crawled about, confused.

I stared dimly at my control helmet. It was neatly sliced in half. Obviously the helmet hadn't been totally contained within the bridge's emergency stasis field, and I was glad my head hadn't still been in it.

I dropped my hands to the ground. It was sand, in some patches fused to glass by the heat of the impact. I pushed unsteadily to my feet.

I was in a crater littered with scraps of metal. A scar arrowing west across a desert showed me how the ship had come down, scraping over the sand.

A second stasis field had saved the contents of the ship's hold. A few metres away there was a pile of equipment, jumbled unceremoniously on the sand. So we wouldn't be totally without resources.

We were lucky not to have come down in the sea, I reflected. The stasis fields would have stayed on automatically. We would have drifted to the sea bottom, our static existence noted only by a few incurious fish.

On a normal day, Web safeguards would have got me out of there. But this was WebCrash Day, and *nothing* was normal!

'Pilot.' Numinus brushed grains of sand from his skin armour. Blood leaked from his beetle-chewed cheek. 'Are you hurt?'

'No. I don't think so.'

'Have you noticed our visitor?'

I squinted around. The low, strong light poured into my eyes, making tears stream down my face.

Halfway to the horizon, silhouetted against the sun, there was an animal like – what? It had four legs, a fleshy hump on its back and an imperious gaze.

The beast spat a huge mound of greasy phlegm onto the sand. The Regent laughed.

It was a camel. And on its back was a man swathed in white cloth.

No, it was just a boy. Dark brown skin, black eyes. Long teeth glinting in an open mouth. We were evidently somewhere in Arabia, in this medieval copy of Earth.

Without any fuss the Regent raised his right hand and pointed the centre finger at the boy. A large ring above the knuckle whirred.

A jet of fire lashed at the boy.

The camel reared, crying out in a bizarre, broken voice. Its rider clung desperately to its hairy flanks. The creature turned and galloped clumsily into the distance.

'Numinus, why? That was only a boy. He was no threat to us.'

Numinus blew a wisp of smoke from his tiny gun. 'Missed,' he murmured. 'These ring-weapons are useful, though, aren't they?'

'Maybe we could have spoken to him.'

Numinus swivelled an impassive face towards me. 'And why in the name of the Plutonium Throne should I wish to do that?'

'Maybe you didn't notice, Numinus. But we just crashed.' I bent down. I was stiff, and I wondered if that was as much the first stages of Websickness as due to the crash. I picked up a lump of metal. 'This was once a starship. Now, it is so many bits of slag. Numinus, we are stranded here. And unless we want to camp in this forsaken crater forever we are going to have to find a way to live with the inhabitants of this world.'

Numinus's breath whistled through his nostrils. 'I will accept I am stranded on this planet on the day I die here. Not before. Come on. Let's see what we've got.' He strode purposefully towards the pile of equipment.

I stared at the empty, level sands. The sun touched the horizon. The sky began to drain of light and unfamiliar stars twinkled at the zenith.

My scuttle-button still wouldn't work, no matter how hard I pushed it. I was stuck here.

I sighed and turned to follow Numinus.

And, out of my sight ...

Efer crawled over the dune's darkened flank. Cautiously, he peeked over the crest.

The two strangers had hung torches above their bowl in the sand. The torches made a puddle of light in the desert night. The strangers – a short, pale girl and the fat one who had unleashed fire at him – walked around their machines, pushing buttons and rapping at panels. Words in an unknown language floated across the sand.

The strangers were making no attempt to hide their treasures.

There was a hot, spiced breath at Efer's ear. A firm hand slapped his shoulder.

Efer's cheeks burned at this silent praise for his find – praise from the sheikh himself.

Silent, dark against dark, the Arab scouting party withdrew into the night.

In the debris from the bridge I found an intact food dispenser, a cube about the size of my fist. I sat beneath a light globe and teased out strips of bland food substitute. I couldn't eat it, of course, and I wasn't even hungry, thanks to my gathering Websickness. But I didn't want Numinus to become suspicious.

I'd set the globe to cast a tent-like cone of light. I'd also programmed in some warmth.

Outside the comforting cone the desert was a sheet of darkness. Frost glistened on the sand.

I shivered.

Numinus walked slowly into the cone of light, scratching notes onto a word pad. Under one arm he carried an egg-shaped instrument I didn't recognize. He lay down wearily and accepted some of my food.

'Well?' I asked. 'What have we got?'

Numinus chewed without relish. 'Not much. Less that works.' He ticked items off on his fingers. 'A couple of Translators ...'

Translator machines would also work as communicators. 'What range?'

Numinus shrugged. 'How should I know? It's your ship. They're backpack-sized.'

'They'll talk to a ship in low orbit.'

'Well, that's handy, as there *is* no ship in low orbit. We've got two jet bikes. A digging machine—'

'A Miner?' I said.

'Yes. Various light tools. A couple of intact food and water dispensers. A few dozen repair beetles. And that's about it.'

I took a heavy breath. 'We won't starve, and we can travel.' All I needed to do was to keep Numinus busy until the Web recovered and I could scuttle out. Or Philip came home and used the manual override on my Websuit and got me out that way. 'So where do we go?'

Numinus rolled, picked up the egg-shaped device and tossed it to me. 'Well, I might just have an idea about that. Take a look.'

I studied the machine. Embedded in its smooth surface was a map, a patchwork of green, brown, and blue. Near one edge a single red spot glowed like a fallen star. Now I knew what the gadget was. 'Ah. This is the energy scanner from the bridge. I didn't recognize it away from its mounting ...' My voice tailed off. 'And it's showing the presence of an energy source.'

Numinus smiled. 'The source looks small, localized. Some-where to the north.'

'A single fragment of high technology,' I said, baffled. High technology in Galaxias surpassed anything available in the 21st century Realworld. This was like finding a CD recorder in a bed of dinosaur bones. 'But what a mystery. How did that get here?'

Numinus waved a dismissive hand. 'Maybe it's a relic from a previous castaway.'

I shook my head. 'No. The interface we crossed from our universe is a one-off. It couldn't happen twice.' I was almost sure that was true. Domain Breaches are supposed to be impossible. At the very least they are rare.

'Another universe, then. A third, parallel to both ours and this one.'

'Or,' I said, getting curious, 'suppose it's an artefact from this world's past. A relic of a vanished civilization?' It was a romantic thought. (Completely wrong, of course!)

Numinus chopped his hand into the sand. 'Pilot, who cares? What we have to do is find this thing, see if we can use it. And maybe it will lead us to more such pieces of technology, out of range of the scanner.'

I nodded slowly. 'Perhaps even ... a ship?'

'Or materials we can use to construct one. Pilot, this might be our way off this cursed planet.'

'What's the urgency, Numinus? You were the one who wanted to land here in the first place.'

'For a diversion,' said Numinus coldly. 'Not for the rest of my life.'

'If it wasn't for your greed we wouldn't—'

'Metaphor. Shut up.' Numinus closed his eyes and rolled away from me.

I wrapped my arms around my chest and waited for a chance to fast-forward to morning.

CHAPTER EIGHT

EFER

The first touch of sun flashed the frost into steam. Within minutes of dawn a heat haze was rising from our crater. It hadn't been a full night – the Web had fast-forwarded me through the times when either I or Numinus was asleep – but it felt long enough to me.

I felt shivery and nauseous. *Websickness*. I'd spent far too long inside the Web already.

'I take it you're packed, Pilot.' Numinus pushed his laden jet bike ahead of him. It floated a hand's-breadth above the sand.

'I think so.'

We'd left the equipment we couldn't carry in a single, neat pile. At Numinus's touch a stasis bubble sprang into hazy life around the dump. Numinus walked briskly around the bubble, his heavy cloak flapping over his armour.

Something moved in the corner of my eye. A flutter of white.

The Regent returned, looking satisfied. 'That should be safe enough. This world's cavemen, with their pointed sticks, aren't going to break through Galaxias technology.' He stared at the landscape. 'By the Empress's back teeth, what a bleak place this is.'

White robes. White teeth flashing in sun-darkened faces.

A ring of silent warriors rose from the sand. They

surrounded our crash site, their sheet-like garments splash-
ing sunlight. I could see metal gleam in their hands.

I tried to get Numinus's attention. 'Numinus, look!'

'What is it?' Numinus turned. And fell silent as he saw the
warriors.

The moment stretched.

We were beings separated by more than time or space, and
we stared at each other across a few metres of sand.

'Take it easy,' Numinus murmured. 'They can't hurt us.'

'What do they want?'

The Regent snorted. 'What do you think? Our gold, no
doubt. Our weapons. What do savages normally want?'

'They may be dressed crudely,' I snapped. 'Their technology may be primitive. But you can see they aren't savages ...
What do we do?'

Numinus Torca grinned. His scarred face looked eager. 'We
wait,' he said. 'Just wait. Let them get close enough.'

Efer stood in the circle of warriors, heart bursting with pride.
He held his gleaming scimitar in an easy grip, just as his
father had taught him.

The sun climbed high. And still the strangers did nothing.

Now the sheikh took one step forward. With a grand
flourish he threw down his scimitar and raised his arms.
'Join our caravan. Share our food and milk ...'

And so on. It was a speech of welcome Efer had heard
many times before.

The two strangers whispered to each other but did not
reply.

Finally the sheikh hauled his weapon from the sand and
stepped back into the circle. 'So, they refuse our hospitality.'
His eyes rested on Efer. 'Boy? Which is the coward who spat
fire at you?'

Efer took a deep breath. 'The fat one!'

The sheikh grinned. 'Then he is yours.' And he stepped
forward.

This time the warriors followed. Efer took one step after

the rest. Then another. And another, until he was running
with the men, screaming and brandishing his blade.

It wasn't real. I *knew* it wasn't real. I kept telling myself that
this was just the Web. That I couldn't be hurt here.

But these desert tribesmen, their skin like leather, their
teeth like white blades, looked real and threatening enough
to me.

'Here they come,' Numinus hissed. 'Hold your ground,
Pilot.'

'Numinus, let me unship one of the Translator packs.
Maybe we can talk to them.'

'Are you kidding? *Look* at them.'

'That tall one threw down his sword. Maybe it was a sign
that he wanted to talk.'

'Is your armour powered up? Pull up your hood. Fix your
facemask.' Numinus's right hand worked. Something slipped
from his cloak and nestled in his palm.

I got even more frightened. 'What are you going to do?'

Numinus didn't reply.

And then it was too late because the tribesmen were no
longer a distant abstraction, like images on a TV wall. They
were *here*, mere metres away, running at me with their
swinging blades ...

Numinus swung his arm high. Something glittering soared
above the warriors.

'Numinus! No—'

Efer barely noticed the sparkling thing in the air. His blood
pounded and the blade was a live thing in his hands.

Then it was as if the sun touched the desert.

His eyelids shrivelled and peeled back. And Efer saw no
more.

I knew how Galaxias weapons technology worked. But I'd
never seen such a thing close up before.

The plasma grenade vaporized those closest to it. It merely
killed those a little further out.

Numinus Torca, his cloak scorched away, stalked in ebony armour through the lingering glare. Where a huddled, bloody form still moved, he pointed a deadly ring-weapon.

Tears flooded my eyes, so I couldn't see. You can't smell or taste anything in the Web, and I was glad of that.

These weren't real people. I kept repeating that to myself.

But it had been real to them. And it had *felt* real to me.

Numinus rejoined me, grinning.

'Numinus.' I was almost in tears. 'You barbarian.'

Numinus assumed an expression of mock innocence and waved beweaponed fingers. 'I've been more than merciful, don't you think?'

'Numinus—'

'Drop it, Pilot.' There was steel in Numinus's voice. 'I did what I had to do. Now let's follow that sensor trace.'

I couldn't see any choice. If I followed him, I might find a way out of here. If not, maybe I'd at least be able to stop him next time.

I promised myself I would look up that phace – the Arab boy – if and when I got out of this, and find out who he was. He couldn't have been any older than me.

I would tell his story – and so I have. But that was for the future.

The desert flew beneath our bikes, and the bloodied crater was soon hidden beyond the horizon.

CHAPTER NINE

GUNNAR

The hooves of the two horses clattered over frozen ground. Thyri watched their great heads nod as they made their stolid way along the coast road towards Ragnar.

She had concluded her latest business in Helgo the day before. Now she faced a good half-day's travel home to Ragnar, and she'd set off before dawn.

To her left the mountainous land was a sleeping giant, still wrapped in darkness. The sea moved restlessly to her right. The stars overhead were like an echo of the ground frost.

Thyri felt at peace. Her cart was empty of stock and she had gold in her purse.

She'd struck a good deal with that fierce-looking Varangian mercenary commander. Thanks to long hours listening to Gunnar's war stories, Thyri was able to speak the same language as the soldiers. Thyri smiled, remembering the warm ale they'd downed, the food they'd eaten, and she felt ruefully aware of the growing layer of flesh around her middle.

Things were comfortable. The presence of the short iron sword at her waist seemed almost absurd, as did her vague, almost superstitious fears of the last few days.

Maybe it was time to put the past away. She'd been too withdrawn from Gunnar, too fearful for her husband's safety, perhaps. Well, they could afford to work off a little fat now. They could head up into the forest above the snowline. Gunnar could teach her a few old hunting tricks.

There was a sound behind her. A hissing in the air.

The horses stumbled into each other, whinnying. The cart tipped into a rut. Thyri was flung out, dumped on her back.

Within a second she was on her feet, sword in hand.

Two box-like objects sailed through the dawn air. They made a noise like rushing water. They carried torches that splashed pools of yellow light over the road.

There was a person astride each box, riding like Valkyries!

The Valkyrie boxes rocked over Thyri's head. Her hair whipped up in their breeze. There was a sharp smell, a tang like the sea's. A masked face, blank as an insect's, turned down towards her.

Then the boxes were gone.

Thyri stood there, breathing hard.

The boxes were heading north. Towards Ragnar.

Gunnar was alone there.

The horses stood awkwardly in their tangled harnessing. The cart was intact but stuck. Thyri hauled at it, in vain.

She didn't have time for this.

Her sword of iron slashed through the strips of leather attached to the younger horse. 'I'm sorry about this, girl,' she said as she clambered onto the filly's bare back. 'Now, move!'

The village was a splash of stone in the mouth of the fjord. Hanging in the air, I watched people emerge from their tiny dwellings and point to the sky.

I recognized this place. The last time I saw it, I was in the comfort of a Search Engine. This was WebVin, Viking country. AD 973.

We had flown all the way here from the southern deserts. I'd managed to fast-forward most of it, but still the Websickness was creeping over me – and still my scuttle-button refused to work.

Numinus was studying the energy sensor taped to the

control column of his bike. 'Pilot! How accurate is this thing?'

I shrugged. 'It depends.'

'On what?'

'On the size of the source. On its shielding. On its location. If it's buried, for example, a source might not show up at all.'

'All right.' The Regent pointed. 'That way, I think. A few kilometres along this fjord.'

Some of the villagers were hauling out weapons: spears, javelins, bows. This was the tenth century. There wasn't even gunpowder here.

These people were impossibly brave, I thought. But they had no chance against Numinus and his technology from two thousand years in their future.

I tried to distract Numinus. 'Let's go.' I urged my bike forward. There was no reason for these people to suffer at the hands of the Regent.

Reluctantly, Numinus followed. The villagers and their clumsy weapons were whipped away.

We passed over a scattering of crofts and other dwellings. Numinus slowed his bike to a crawl. 'Here,' he said. 'I think.'

We hovered over a hillock's flat summit. There was a single long building, of cut turf with a thatched roof, and three smaller outbuildings. Smoke reached up from a crudely-cut chimney. A horse grazed in a paddock to the rear of the house. Heaps of supplies – ore and fuel perhaps, covered in cloth – were scattered around the buildings. There were no people to be seen.

We drifted to land a few metres from the house. I climbed stiffly from my bike and unfixed my face mask. The unfiltered air was cool. I imagined the scent of wood smoke and the ozone taint of the bike drive, but this was the Web, and I could smell nothing.

I felt dizzy. Websick. I knew I would have to be careful how I moved.

'Pilot. Come and explain what this cursed sensor's telling me.'

The sensor showed the energy source as a fuzzy disc which overlaid a map of the area. The map included a schematic of the house.

'Well?' he demanded.

'This thing can't give us a more accurate fix, Numinus. We are seeking a small, low-output device that is shielded somehow. Maybe buried.'

Numinus tapped the sensor with one ringed finger. 'So what do we do?'

'You climb off your bike and we search. I suggest we start there.' I pointed at the house. 'And, Numinus. This time let me take a Translator. We need information more than we need corpses.'

Numinus unpeeled his armour hood and gloves. 'All right, Metaphor. Lead the way.'

I took a Translator from one of my bike's panniers. It was backpack-sized with an independent anti-gravity unit, so it floated a metre or so off the ground. I shoved it ahead of me towards the main house.

The door was a massive wooden slab. It would not open to Numinus's shove. I walked around the little building. There was a single window cut into the wood, unglazed. A leather sheet was fixed across the cavity.

The leather twitched minutely.

I rejoined Numinus. 'I think there's someone in there.'

Numinus grinned. 'You don't say.' He raised one armoured leg to the door. Skin-armour servo-motors whirred as Numinus's boot flew at the wood.

There was a splintering crunch.

The Regent cleared the door frame of debris, then led the way into the gloomy interior. I followed, shoving the Translator box ahead of me.

We stood in darkness. With an impatient snort Numinus threw a small light globe to the ceiling.

Dazzled, I saw two straw pallets, benches along the walls, a

crude table piled with bowls and plates, a fireplace, a few
chests and boxes.

And, standing in front of us, a giant of a man.

He was wearing a shirt and breeches, with a tunic over the
top. The tunic was brightly coloured, with braid edging. He
had a silver pendant around his neck, a big silver hammer.
He had a beard, neatly trimmed, and a conical helmet made
of metal – iron, probably – with a big nose-guard, and holes
for his eyes.

He held up an iron sword. *He was a Viking warrior* – the
most terrifying sight I had ever seen.

He spoke, and the words were guttural and harsh, beyond
my understanding.

I could tell he was threatening us, though.

But, under the helmet his eyes were wrapped in a dirty
bandage, and I could see that his free arm dangled at his side,
limp.

My fear subsided, but my heart sank. This old man could
not pose a threat to Numinus.

Numinus surveyed the battered warrior with a widening
grin, like a cat studying a bird.

I wanted to avoid trouble. I stepped forward, arms spread
out. 'It's all right. We won't hurt you. We only want to talk.'

Numinus laughed. 'You're wasting your time, Pilot.'

I kept talking, but the warrior just stood there silently.

'Numinus, this is an old man. He can't harm you.'

'But I can't talk to it until it says enough for the Translator
to work on, can I?'

'No. But he's a *he*, not an it.'

'Make it talk,' the Regent snapped. 'I've got questions to
ask.'

'Numinus—'

'If you don't I will. Understand?'

I took another step. The warrior raised his sword, and I
stopped, waited in silence. Finally, the warrior spat a string
of guttural words. I thought I could hear echoes of the

languages we learn in school – German, Swedish, even English.

Suddenly, the Translator function cut in. The warrior's voice was edited out of my hearing and replaced by recognizable words. '... who are you to dare to break into the house of Gunnar? I was a Varangian Guard, and I may be old but I learned a thing or two—'

'Your name is Gunnar,' I said.

Gunnar visibly jumped at my comprehensible words. He fell silent.

'At last,' Numinus growled.

I moved cautiously to one of the long benches and sat on hard wood. 'Your name is Gunnar,' I repeated.

The warrior's sightless gaze stayed fixed on my face. 'What if it is?'

'Well, Gunnar, my name is Metaphor. All right?'

'Metaphor.'

'My friend and I have travelled ... a long way. From a country across the sea. You understand that, don't you?'

The warrior nodded hesitantly. 'Are you frightened of me?'

'Yes,' I said.

He opened his mouth – his teeth were terrible, like worn gravestones – and he laughed. 'So you should be.' He paused. 'You're just a girl.'

'Less of the *just*,' I said.

'My eyes scare you, don't they?'

I had to admit they did.

He laughed again. 'Don't worry. The great god Odin is one-eyed. He gave one of his eyes for understanding. I gave both mine, so that must make me the wisest man in the world, ha!'

A lot of complex feelings swirled inside me. Here was this huge, intimidating warrior – a *Viking*, after all – and he was still threatening us. But he had found time to be kind to me.

Sometimes I wish people, real or not, weren't so complicated.

There was nothing complicated about Numinus, though. He was growling impatiently.

I said to Gunnar, 'Sir, we're looking for something. Maybe you can help us.'

'I don't know. What is it? Why should I help you? You break into my house—'

'Well, Gunnar, it's a little hard to explain ...'

Numinus and I sat side-by-side on the wooden bench, listening numbly as Gunnar – who'd quite forgotten we were intruders – launched into yet another fable about his exploits with the good old boys of the Varangian Guard.

I said quietly, 'This Gunnar is either a great liar or a fine warrior. If it's the second, I hope I never get on the wrong side of him.'

Numinus checked a chronometer. 'We haven't time for this, Pilot.'

I shrugged. 'Well, you try explaining the concept of an energy scanner to a battered old man out of the Iron Age. Let him ramble. We'll get what we want.'

Gunnar was talking about an adventurer he'd once met, someone who'd been to the far north, where the gods lived.

Numinus murmured to me, 'In my bike I have some ... facilitating equipment.'

I stiffened. 'A MindDump, you mean?'

The Regent's face hardened. 'That's not recognized terminology, Pilot.'

'A Dump is a Dump by any name. You'd use such an instrument on an old man? Numinus. Listen to what he's saying.'

'... and so Olaf travelled far into the north, to the land of the Aurora, and sure enough he found the Sky Longboat. It was very old, it was built by the gods to fly to Valhalla hundreds and thousands of years ago, and it was buried in ice and snow ...'

'Pilot,' Numinus hissed, sitting erect. 'This is it. A *Sky Longboat*. What does that sound like to you? It's a ship. If we can fix it ...' His eyes narrowed. 'We can resume my plan. Live as kings on this dunghill for a while, then return home.'

I thought quickly. It wasn't impossible that a craft from Galaxias, or some other Domain, had come here before us. It might have been centuries ago for Gunnar's people, even if it was only a week ago for me.

But there was still something wrong.

'It makes no sense, Numinus. If the ship, if that's what it is, is so far to the north, why did our sensors bring us *here*?'

Gunnar was still talking. '... Well, Olaf came back on foot through all sorts of dangers. And to show where he'd been he brought back something from the northern wastes. *It was a Key to the Sky Longboat.* Well, we got drunk, we fought, we played cards, and he had to give the Key to me. But then a band of Byzantine cut-throats got hold of me, and—'

Numinus jumped from the table, took two long strides and clasped Gunnar's shoulders. 'Old man, this ... Key. It has to be what we're looking for. Now, where is it? Will you give it to me? Eh?' He shook the warrior briefly.

Gunnar stiffened. 'You're hurting me,' he growled. I could hear the threat in his voice, even through the Translator.

'Where is the Key?' Numinus's voice was ominously calm.

'Thyri said to hide it, and not to tell anyone where—'

Numinus punched the old Viking. Gunnar barely flinched.

'Old man. Gunnar. Unless you want to learn true pain, tell me about the Key.'

'No!'

'By the Plutonium Throne!' Exasperated, Numinus stamped out of the house.

The warrior's face was a mask of blood. He was casting around for his sword, but Numinus had moved it out of reach.

Numinus returned cradling a small black cube. Wires like silver hair floated around the cube. It was, of course, a MindDump, one of the cruellest tools of a cruel Empire. Numinus snapped, 'It really is a stubborn old savage.' He set

the MindDump on the floor and began working fine
controls.

I whispered, 'Numinus, that brave warrior is more ... alien
... than any creature you've encountered before. He's from
an alternate reality! Your device could kill him.'

Numinus ignored me.

The wire filaments stood vertically, quivering as if alive.
Then a single filament entered Gunnar's finger, and he
jerked as if shocked.

The MindDump was a downloader.

If you download a file from a computer onto a disk, you're
making a copy of what's in the computer's memory. The
human brain is only a kind of computer, and the Mind-
Dump could make a copy of a *human* memory. But it was
unproven technology, and brutally destructive.

With horrible speed, the Dump would download the
contents of Gunnar's mind into Numinus – and perhaps
destroy Gunnar in the process.

CHAPTER TEN

MINDDUMP

Thyri spurred the horse, her urgency transmitted through pressing palms and heels. The filly's mouth was flecked with foam.

At last, the final fold of hill fell away. Warned by her instincts, Thyri reined in the horse a hundred paces short of the house.

Suddenly, her worst fears became real.

Her breathing grew deep and the world turned sharp and clear. She felt the muscles of her shoulders harden. Perhaps this was how it felt to be a warrior.

She drew her short sword and her axe. Then she ran to the house, her feet ramming into the earth.

Numinus returned to the house, skin armour soiled. 'Ha! Got it. Just where the old savage told me, in a hole scratched in the soil.'

I was bending over the unconscious warrior, wiping away blood with a scrap of cloth. I kept telling myself this wasn't real, that Gunnar was just a phace, his courage artificial, his pain computer-generated. It was no consolation.

I looked vaguely at the spindle of silvery metal the Regent had dug up, and was brandishing aloft. 'So that's it? Was it worth it, Numinus?'

Numinus toyed with the spindle, tossing it into the air and catching it. 'Pilot, this knick-knack is a Key indeed, the Key that will unlock this fleabag world. And our ticket home. Of course it was worth it.' He strolled to the pallet and studied Gunnar without malice. 'From the old brute's account we'll be able to track down the ancient ship. And wasn't it astonishing, what we found when I dug into its hind brain?' He grinned, perhaps with envy. 'What interesting lives these savages lead.'

'Perhaps we are the savages, Regent.'

There was a noise outside.

I turned my head. Were they footsteps? Perhaps. But it sounded more as if some elemental force were bearing down on us.

'Regent, listen. I think—'

Somebody was standing in the doorframe, sword in hand, silhouetted against the light.

From Thyri's point of view, we were *both* the enemy.

Thyri's gaze snapped around the room.

Gunnar was on the pallet. Blood on his face, clothes. Dead? No, he was still breathing, shallowly.

A primeval growl built in Thyri's throat.

There were two men here – no, one was a girl. She was backing away from the pallet. Thyri saw a slim frame in a suit of shining black, a small, smooth face. (Yes, it was me. This was how Thyri saw my Galaxias avatar!) In one hand the girl held a blood-stained rag. Was the girl hurting Gunnar? No, tending him.

Thyri dismissed the girl as no threat. But the other …

Darker. Fat, almost squat. The face a mask, scarred and bearded. *This one* was the threat. Another black suit bulging with pockets and pouches. Weapons? Nothing in his hands …

Except a silver spindle – Gunnar's Key. She knew that thing was trouble. She should have hurled the trophy into the Gulf of Bothnia.

A shout tore from Thyri's throat, and she threw her axe at the chest of the dark one.

Pale fingers flew over studs on that black suit. The air seemed to sparkle.

The axe hit. The dark one exploded in a glare of light.

Thyri heard a scream. For precious seconds her eyes were filled with light. Then the world reappeared, rimmed in blood-red.

Her axe lay at the feet of the dark one, who grinned at her, and spoke. 'You. Warrior woman. Listen to me. You can't hurt me. I have armour. It is a deflector field. It turns the energy of your weapons, such as they are, into radiation. Light ... Do you understand? Well, I suppose it's all magic, as far as you're concerned. You may worship me, at your convenience. And now, if you want this old fool to live I suggest you get away from the door.'

Thyri stood her ground, heart pounding. Think, she told herself. Channel the anger. 'Perhaps your armour will protect your hide, coward. But what about your Valkyrie boxes?' She ran her finger along her sword's edge. 'I saw cracks and joints and pipes. I wonder what my blade would find if thrust inside?'

The girl spoke, her eyes streaming from the flash. 'The bikes. She means the jet bikes. Regent, she could strand us here.'

Thyri smiled. There was fear in that voice. 'So, you are humans, strange as you are. You know fear. Know this. Without your machines you cannot outrun me. And I will destroy you.'

The one called Regent stretched out a finger.

Fire leapt from his hand and cut a hole in the wall. The air filled with the stink of burning wood.

'I could burn you down where you stand,' the Regent growled.

Thyri froze. Consciously, she relaxed her muscles. 'Your threat against an old blind man brings us to a stand-off, then, coward.'

Numinus inclined his head. 'Quite so. Now then, my terms.' He held up the Key. 'I have what I want, right here.

And you want the warrior. Let us return to our vehicles and he is yours.'

Thyri nodded carefully. She stepped back through the door.

'Come on, Pilot.' Numinus picked up Gunnar, threw the old man over his shoulder, and walked to the door. The display of strength was startling. But Thyri could hear a whine and whirr, of ropes and pulleys. Some device hidden in his black armour was giving this fat oaf the illusion of strength. Understanding that reduced her fear.

The one called Metaphor stayed close to the Regent, pulling a floating box through the air after her.

Thyri stalked them, trying to close in on them.

The two strangers reached the Valkyrie boxes, their jet bikes. Numinus slid astride his saddle, with Gunnar slumped in his arms.

Something hard slid into Numinus's eyes. Malice. Spite. Thyri saw it. *He was going to kill Gunnar, anyway.*

The girl, Metaphor, saw it too. 'Regent. No. There's no need.' Awkwardly she reached for Gunnar.

And at the same moment Thyri dived at Numinus.

Everything slowed down. Thyri felt as if she were swimming through some thick fluid. Her pulse pounded like a drum.

She wouldn't get there in time.

The girl, Metaphor, was pulling at Numinus's arm. Numinus turned. Rage twisted his face and he held out his hand.

Fire leapt from his fingers and lanced through Metaphor's shoulder, legs. Metaphor crumpled silently. Another flick of that deadly hand and more bright needles shot into Metaphor's bike, turning sections of it to glowing slag.

And then, almost casually, Numinus launched his fire at Gunnar.

As Thyri reached him, Numinus's iron steed flicked into the air. Thyri slammed her fist into its metal flank, making it rock and shudder. But it rose like smoke and was lost in the low clouds.

Thyri stood there, fists working, for one second. Then she turned and fell to her knees, and lifted Gunnar from the cold ground.

The old warrior writhed, muscles like wood.

'Gunnar. Can you hear me? It's me, Thyri.'

The great grey head turned. 'Thyri. I couldn't protect you. I'm sorry.'

'There's nothing any of us could have done.'

'I have fallen into the snake pit, my love.'

'Just like the first Gunnar.' For Gunnar had been named for a legendary hero who had battled with snakes.

Gunnar jerked, his pain intense.

Thyri's darkest fears settled over her soul, and she held her husband tight.

Afterwards she never knew how long it took him to die.

When it was over Thyri laid the body on the ground. Then she stood and walked calmly to the Pilot.

Metaphor squirmed backwards towards her wrecked machine, pain twisting her face. She left a trail of blood across the grass.

Thyri reached down. Metaphor recoiled. Almost tenderly Thyri picked her up. 'I won't hurt you,' she said.

Metaphor stared at her.

'I want you to live, Valkyrie.' Thyri began to walk back to the house, Metaphor slung casually over her shoulder. 'I saw you care for Gunnar. Perhaps you could not stop what happened. And you fought, at last. Now you will help me again. You will show me how to reach the other. The Regent. And when I find him—'

When I find him, Thyri told herself, then he will fly. Oh, not as he plans, in the Sky Longboat. But as the Vikings have made their enemies fly for generations.

In blood.

CHAPTER ELEVEN

RAGNAR

For days, I lay on the pallet that had once been Gunnar's. Days in Web time, anyhow, but as I was out of sight or feigning sleep most of that time it was only an hour or more of Realworld time. But it was enough to deepen my Websickness.

Numinus hadn't been able to hurt me, thankfully. But the Websickness was bringing me down. At least I didn't have to explain my feebleness to Thyri.

And besides the sickness I felt drained, exhausted, distressed by all I'd seen. I kept running it over in my head.

I'd never seen cruelty like Numinus's before, in or out of the Web.

But that wasn't the worst of it. The worst was *doubt*, questions I asked myself. Could I have done anything to stop him?

In the end I gathered my strength. I found I could sit up and even stand, stiffly. Thyri brought me food: vegetables, meat, and a coarse, gritty bread. Of course I couldn't eat – you don't eat anything inside the Web – but I thanked her. I think my refusing food confused her more than anything else.

I had time to watch Thyri, to see something of this Viking Domain in which I'd become entangled.

The Vikings came out of Scandinavia – Norway, Sweden and Denmark – in the north of Europe. Their land was inhospitable, their rulers harsh. And so they sailed the seas, seeking loot and new places to live. In the end they had colonies across half the western world, from the north cape of Norway to France, from Newfoundland in Canada to Russia. They even made it across the Atlantic, and planted a colony in North America that lasted for centuries. And they sailed up the great rivers of Europe, the Dnieper and the Volga, that took them to the Black Sea and the Caspian Sea, where they encountered Byzantium and Islam.

All with nothing more than Iron Age technology, well-made wooden boats, and a lot of guts.

They came to Britain. At one time they controlled half the country, an area known as the Danelaw.

You may have Viking blood in your veins. And if you use words like *die, egg,* or *law*, you're using language that comes from the Vikings.

You might think it was romantic to be a Viking. Certainly the landscape was beautiful – the steel-grey ocean, the beautiful dragon-prowed longboats, the firs, and the almost vertical walls of mountains.

But it was harsh.

There were times when I was soaked to the skin and barely able to hear myself speak over the howl of the wind. At least I had decent Galaxias clothing. The natives of the time had only inadequate and smelly clothing, and only a smoky fire and an earth floor or a straw pallet to look forward to at home.

Having lived there, I'm not surprised they travelled far, looking for more pleasant places to live.

Thyri's house was like a long hall. It was made of dry stone and turf, except for some timber walls. There was a living room with a long hearth down the centre, and a small pantry. The other buildings were a barn for the animals, a byre where their food was stored, a smithy, and a bathhouse that was more like a sauna where steam was made by throwing water on hot stones.

The Viking countries were ruled by kings. Our village,

Ragnar, had a chief, called a *jarl*. Most of the men were *karlar*, free men, and there were slaves, called *praell*. Women were discriminated against, I suppose, but it seemed to me Thyri was accepted as a *karlar*. Certainly she'd have broken the head of anyone who said she was less.

It all sounds very rigid, but there was some democracy. There was an assembly that gathered regularly called a *Thing*, and there was a system of law with a top judge who would deliver his rulings standing on the *Logberg*, the Law Rock.

OK, it was far from perfect. But believe me, it was a lot more democratic than Galaxias which was supposedly two thousand years more advanced.

And Thyri was kind to me.

That might seem a strange thing to say. After all, I was a prisoner in her house. And if my scuttle-button had worked I'd have got out of there as soon as I could. But out of her warrior gear, she was very different.

When she wasn't travelling, or fighting, she wore a chemise under a long dress. She generally wore a shawl, pinned on her chest by a big oval brooch, and an apron. She had a big belt from which she hung purses, and usually a knife or two. She wore her hair long but knotted at the back of her head. Her shoes were skin – calf or goat, I think – laced around her ankles. She was quite elegant, and kept herself cleaner than I had expected.

She seemed to have a lot of jewellery – brooches and necklaces and rings and bracelets and bangles, mostly of silver – but I learned later that the Vikings had no money, not even coins. They kept their wealth in silver, but without coins or banks, they would either hide it in an underground store or simply wear it as jewellery. They could always cut it up if they needed loose change.

Thyri had many visitors (she kept me out of sight). Poor Gunnar had been popular, even if he was past it, and a lot of people came to offer sympathy. Thyri always welcomed them with water and a towel, and a meal of bread or meat.

Life was more *civil* than I had expected.

But it was hard.

Thyri spent a *lot* of her time cleaning. There were no domestic robots, no SmartWalls, no washing machines, no dishwashers, no vacuum cleaner, not even running water. And the rest of her time cooking. There was meat and fish – baked in a big oven she heated with hot stones – wheat and oats, cress, even some herbs and spices from overseas, like mustard and horseradish. There was beer, and milk for drinking and to make butter.

Thyri made bread almost every day she was home. She had to grind down her flour with handheld stones, then knead her dough and bake it in long iron pans. It was unleavened, meaning it had no yeast in it, so it was flat. You had to eat it straightaway or it would become too hard.

Of all the things I disliked about my situation, that was the worst, not being able to taste or even smell the delicious-looking bread Thyri baked. But those grinding stones left a lot of grit in the bread, and Thyri – like most of the Vikings – had bad, worn-down teeth.

Oh, and they ate with their fingers. Well, so do I when it's Tennessee Fried Ostrich, and so does my kid brother, all the time, so it almost felt like home!

While Thyri was waiting for me to recover, she would sit down with me and play games when her day's work was done. She had a stack of board games, some of which were like games we play now. Her favourite was called *hnefatafl*, which is a bit like chess. You have to protect your king against attack. (I tried to teach it to George later but the little bug was too dim to understand. Philip liked it, after I'd let him win a couple of games.)

So, Thyri really was kind to me. She tried to look after me, she offered me food, and played games with me. And that was while she was trying to get over the loss of her husband.

Real or not, she was an impressive human being.

My mother died when I was young, so I know how hard it is to lose somebody. I don't think, looking back, I was kind to anybody at the time.

Maybe George, a little.

Thyri had to organize a funeral for Gunnar. He was buried on land, but in a grave that was shaped like a ship, marked with stones. The Vikings believed dying was the start of a journey to Valhalla where the gods live.

Everybody turned out for the funeral, perhaps a hundred men, women, and children. I watched from an unglazed window of Thyri's house. There was a poet called a *skald* who recited, without reading, a long and complicated poem about Gunnar's bravery and valour. It was very difficult to understand, even with the Translator, with lots of comparisons between Gunnar and various gods I'd never heard of.

Gunnar was buried with many of his possessions: his clothes, his weapons, even favourite items like his beer-drinking tankard and his plate. I could see Thyri found it hard giving up all this stuff. I suppose it was as if she was finally letting go of him. But she did it. She kept only one thing. That hammer amulet I'd noticed him wearing around his neck when I first met him. She called it the *mjollnir*, the hammer of Thor. I never saw her without it after that.

I saw all this in fast-forwarded glimpses. Sometimes it felt dishonest. Thyri would come to me and tell me I'd slept for twelve hours – but to me, just a few seconds had passed.

What I'm trying to say is that, for a while, despite the Websickness, despite the fact that everything was fast-forwarded and artificial, I was *happy* there, in Ragnar. Thyri was kind. And although I missed everything I have in my modern world, I quite liked living in such a simple place. It's nice to be able to understand how everything works.

But this interlude didn't last long (a week for Thyri, maybe a half-hour for me).

The Vikings had a code of vengeance. And, gradually, Thyri prepared to take her revenge.

Thyri was working at the house's only table. She spread a tunic of thick leather over the wood, and used gut thread to sew on scraps of a dull gold metal.

I approached cautiously. 'What are you doing?'

Thyri glanced up and passed me a piece of metal. 'This is mail. Armour. Tough stuff. They say it is imbued with a magical aura. Hallowed by Thor, the Protector.'

I passed back the shard. 'Well, who knows? Maybe there really is magic in your world. Some believe there is in mine. Although if a machine is advanced enough, who can tell if it is magical or not?'

I know that sounds bizarre. By now I was seriously Websick. I hardly knew what I was saying.

Thyri jabbed her iron needle through the leather. 'Mail protected Gunnar when he was a Varangian, although he always complained about how heavy it was. And now, perhaps it will protect me when I go north.'

'North?'

Thyri glared at me. 'We're both going there,' she said. 'Because that's where we'll find your colleague the Regent.'

'But, but I can't travel.' I paced across the earth floor, fingers drumming at the sleeves of my armour. 'You saw Numinus wreck the propulsion unit of my bike. I mean, the part that makes it fly.'

'Then you will travel by longboat and by horse, as I will.'

'A horse? *Me*?'

'I want you with me when I find the Regent. You will tell me things, explain his armour and weapons.'

I sat on the pallet, legs folded under me. 'Thyri. This is not a good idea. The Regent has been trained to survive. He comes from a society thousands of years older than yours. His weapons are sophisticated. You are very brave. And Numinus's crime against Gunnar is ... unpardonable, in any universe. But he is strong.'

'Then he will make a fine blood eagle.'

'A what?'

But she would not explain. She simply continued sewing.

CHAPTER TWELVE

PURSUIT

The longboat nosed through cracked ice and pushed its way onto the beach.

Thyri and the five Viking crewmen shipped their oars, clambered into freezing water and hauled the boat higher.

I stepped gingerly out of the boat. I staggered a few paces, then dropped to my knees, digging gloved fingers into the sand.

Thyri laughed. 'You told me you sailed from another world. Well, I've never seen a sailor so terrified of water.'

I looked out to sea and shivered. 'And I have never before trusted my life to a thing made of wood and greasy cloth.' It was true. Viking longboats were simply magnificent to look at. The sleek curves of their hulls, their sails and flashing oars, the proud designs of their prows. It was fantastic to think that each of them was handmade. On such ships, protected by no more than leather and wool clothing, Vikings had crossed the Atlantic ocean.

But on a Viking longboat there isn't even anywhere to *shelter*.

During the voyage I'd turned up the heating in my skin-armour and slept as much as I could, trying to fast-forward to the end of this impossible adventure.

A crewman led the first of our expedition's three horses from the longboat. Thyri took the filly's halter and rubbed her nuzzle.

I eyed the animal warily, suspecting the worst was yet to come. I do *not* ride horses, real or otherwise.

Thyri and I left the Viking sailors to make camp under the dragon prow of the longboat. The two of us were going to make our way further north alone. We climbed the back of a wind-blown ridge. A few strands of grass clung to the frozen earth.

There was an oppressive mood of menace.

Under Thyri's prompting, I had to climb onto a horse.

It wasn't as difficult as you might expect. The horse was so huge, patient and solid it was like climbing onto a piece of furniture. I finished up clinging to the mane of my mount, my legs locked to its flanks.

Thyri rode alongside me. She wore her leather armour with its glittering scraps of mail, and she had weapons slung from a belt at her waist. She led the spare horse by its halter. It was loaded with food, water barrels, my Galaxias equipment. The Translator box, with its anti-gravity unit, floated a few metres above the horse, attached by a length of rope.

My Websickness didn't help, of course. But after a while I relaxed, soothed by the steady motion of the animal beneath me. I even gingerly patted the neck of the horse.

Thyri said, 'If I didn't know better, I'd say you were enjoying the ride.'

I smiled. 'I didn't expect it to … to feel like this. This is not a machine. It's another living creature. I'm not used to that. Do you understand?'

Thyri grunted. 'What you mean is the horse knows what he's doing even if you don't.'

'But, Thyri, this is so slow.'

Thyri was looking north. A curtain of blackness hung from sky to ground, looming over the activities around the longboat.

It was the Domain Breach, a hole in the wall of the world.

And this was already a land of dread and fear for the Vikings. I think this Breach must have opened up before, so rich were the myths surrounding this Godforsaken place.

This was a weak place in the fabric of the world, rent open by the WebCrash.

'What desolation,' Thyri said.

'Yes.' I had little to say. To Thyri this must seem a dreadful, supernatural event, and I had no better explanation to give her.

The filly bucked, uneasy. Thyri patted her mane. 'People have survived here before, and I'll survive now. As long as I have to.' She pulled up, staring ahead. She pointed. 'I think we've found your comrade.'

There, on the northern horizon, was an irregular mound of earth.

A few minutes' riding took us to the mound. Thyri dismounted and climbed up the bank of earth. It turned out to be a great ring of broken soil around a pit in the earth, and the pit was the mouth of a tunnel that curved out of sight.

I scrambled up the bank, panting. 'Ah. He's used the Miner.'

'The what?'

'It's a vehicle that travels under the earth. It digs out a tunnel, you see. Its purpose is to dig material from the ground – iron ore, or—'

'He's using it to travel? Why not travel overland?'

I looked into the northern darkness and shivered. 'Numinus is no fool. Why face the unknown dangers represented by the Breach when he can just avoid them by travelling underneath?'

'Well, whatever was in Numinus's mind, he has given us a gift,' Thyri said. 'If this tunnel protects him it will protect us too, and it will lead us straight to him.'

The tunnel was a tube about twenty paces wide. It proved to be straight and regular. Thyri ran her hand over a wall. It was dry to the touch and frozen hard.

'The Miner generates a lot of heat,' I said. 'That must have melted the permafrost, the frozen soil, but it refroze behind the Miner, into a hard surface.'

'Good. We'll make fast progress.'

And so the pursuit began.

The days and nights turned into a clatter of hooves through the frozen darkness of the tunnel.

In my kit there was a light globe. I turned it on and set it to hover. Thyri attached the globe to her horse's saddle with rope. The globe bumped through the air a few metres above her, casting a steady light.

During breaks we spread blankets on the hard earth. Now, in addition to Websickness, I suffered some extremely sore muscles from the endless riding. I slept, fast-forwarding as much as I could.

For days (of Thyri's time) our bubble of light and animal warmth glided through the tube under the earth.

Then, at last, far ahead ... there was a light.

Thyri pulled up her horse and dismounted silently. She dragged down the floating light globe. 'Kill this.'

I touched a button. The yellow glow sighed to darkness.

For a few seconds Thyri stood stock still, letting her eyes adjust. The light ahead seemed to unfold. It had a grey lustre, like a pearl.

Thyri bent and, with rapid, confident motions, hobbled the horses with strips of leather. She fixed the Translator rope to my belt.

'Thyri ...'

Thyri was a grey silhouette. She grasped my shoulders and stared into my face. 'Little Valkyrie, I know you're not a warrior. And this situation is not of your making. But I need your help. With it I can defeat the Regent. Without it he will destroy us both.'

'But—'

'Now, come.'

Thyri turned and began to pad towards the light. After a few seconds I followed, my breathing ragged. The Translator bumped after us like a dog on a lead.

The going became more difficult. The tunnel twisted through sharp corners, climbed, and dived. I whispered, 'He must have been quartering the region, searching for the old ship. His energy sensors would not show him the buried artefact until he was close.'

We turned one last corner and stepped into dazzling light.

We stood in a spherical chamber about fifty metres across. A cluster of light globes bumped against the ceiling. On the far side of the chamber another tunnel led away. The Miner sat idle on the chamber floor.

Thyri pulled me back into the shelter of the tunnel. Then she lay on her belly and slid to the tunnel lip for a closer look.

The chamber was still, and silent.

The Miner was a boxy vehicle a couple of metres long. It had huge metal jaws. It was coated in tough-looking blue metal, and windows like eyes squinted back at us. A skirt sheltered wheels which bristled with spikes. Two metal arms held a scarred heat shield ahead of the vehicle. It looked like a mechanical digger's scoop. Below the shield the gleaming jaws hung, idle. Behind the shield an array of cup-like devices craned forward.

I explained it to Thyri. 'See.' I pointed. 'The rock and earth is broken up by ultrasonics from those speakers at the front.'

'The cup things?'

'Yes. They make a high-pitched noise, you see. It's like shattering glass by singing. The shield at the front guards against the heat they generate. Those jaws chew in loosened material and pass it back through the spiked wheels. That nozzle at the back blasts out a hot exhaust. That's what drives the machine forward.'

'No sign of Numinus,' Thyri said. 'Come on.'

Thyri stepped out of the tunnel mouth and slithered to the floor of the chamber. I followed clumsily. Thyri worked her way around the chamber, keeping her back to the wall.

Numinus had hacked crude steps into the earth beneath the mouth of the second tunnel. Thyri climbed rapidly and peered over the lip. 'It's clear,' she whispered. 'Come on.'

The second tunnel was just a few paces long. It led to

another, much larger, chamber. We climbed cautiously out of the tunnel. A dozen light globes cast a shifting pattern of light. In the walls I could see tooth-marks left by Numinus's Miner.

And, resting at the centre of the chamber like a pearl in its shell, was the source of the energy Numinus had sought, the centre of the Vikings' legends: the Sky Longboat itself.

My jaw dropped.

I recognized this Sky Longboat. It was a Search Engine!

CHAPTER THIRTEEN

ENGINE

You've seen Search Engines. They are buses you ride between Domains. They're flashy things, designed for effect. They can be any shape.

This one was a spindle shape perhaps a hundred metres long. The graceful midriff was four times as tall as I was. The tips of the spindle were lengthened into needle-fine points.

Its skin, shining like silver, was covered in the slogans of manufacturers and sponsors. Tennessee Fried Ostrich was there and so was the new version of the DreamCastle game zone (DreamCastle II: Dungeon), and ... But all that looked ridiculous, trivial, stuck in that hole in the ground, and with such danger all around!

I remembered now there had been a Search Engine which had crashed recently. It had stopped me surveying more Domains before choosing Galaxias. I wondered if that had been caused by some early WebCrash incident. Search Engines were, of course, supposed to be invisible to the phaces inside Domains, and to make no impression there. This one, crashing, had obviously fallen slap into the reality of WebVin.

I'm not sure how seriously I took Numinus's threats before that moment. He was terrifying. But, I'd reasoned, how much damage can one man do against a whole world, no matter how powerful he is, no matter how crazed?

With a Search Engine, though – and in the middle of the WebCrash – I suspected the answer was *a lot*.

Thyri stepped forward, eyes wide. 'It's ... beautiful,' she whispered. 'I didn't expect this.'

'Yes,' I said, distracted. I was looking for Numinus.

Thyri ran a gloved finger along the hull's grooves. 'Look at this workmanship,' she whispered. 'You know, we sometimes carve runes into the hulls of our ships. To give them power and protection, through the strength of Thor.'

'It isn't quite the same, Thyri.'

I saw something move out of the corner of my eye.

Before I had time to react, Thyri's axe flew.

The blade of the axe clanged against the ship. An object like a small golden nut fell from the hull.

I bent and picked it up. Then laughed. 'Congratulations. You've just defeated a repair beetle. That should slow Numinus down by a few seconds.'

There was a soft sigh. A door had opened in the hull. Maybe Thyri's axe had hit a concealed button.

Thyri grinned and picked up her axe. 'Pilot. Come here.'

The hatch was a circular break in the hull near one needlepoint, about an arm's length wide. A cautious glance through showed us a chamber, small, bare, empty, and closed.

With a beckoning gesture to me, Thyri climbed into the Search Engine. I followed.

I passed my hands over the walls of the chamber. 'Somewhere there must be a sensor that ... Ah.'

A disc of hull metal turned milky and dilated. It was a new door, opening up on the far side of the chamber.

The new door led to a corridor which seemed to run along the spine of the craft. A greenish light filled the air, like the cloudy light of a stagnant pond. To left and right, three doors led off the corridor. And the simple passage ended with a fourth door, straight ahead of us.

All the doors were wide open. There was no sound.

Thyri stepped into the corridor.

Nothing happened. I followed.

The air was warm, slightly humid, utterly still. Thyri looked at me, shrugged, and crossed in a few paces to the first door off the passage. I followed her. The Translator bumped after me absurdly.

We climbed down a shallow staircase. The room we entered was a disc-shaped slice through the ship. The corridor pierced it like a spine. The walls were crusted with rocks and the dry remains of what looked like seaweed. To one surface clung a cluster of opaque spheres.

'This looks like it was once flooded,' Thyri murmured.

And so it was. This was basically a swimming pool, mocked up to look like the ocean. In here, you could swim around as you surveyed the Domains. An expensive stunt. But it impressed Thyri.

Numinus was not here. Thyri pulled me back to the corridor.

The next chamber was also a cross section of the ship, but the light here was dark brown, mysterious, uneven.

Empty uniforms clung to the walls like fantastic birds. There were tunics bristling with feathers, bones, bits of fur. There were weapons everywhere, like crude guns. And all the uniforms were splashed with what looked like dried blood.

It was paint.

This was a paint-ball room! Probably a crèche, in fact, where you could dump eggs like George and let them flap around firing paint at each other.

'What an oppressive place,' Thyri murmured.

'Yes,' I said solemnly.

'What manner of creatures dwelled here? And what were their gods?'

'Worse than you can possibly imagine, Thyri.'

'Well. Come on, Metaphor. Nothing for us here.'

Once more we moved along the corridor.

Thyri reached the third door. And her eyes grew wide.

It was a room full of wonder. The light was a clear blue,

like a summer night sky. Globes like fantastic lanterns were
scattered in the air, glowing blue, green, white.

Thyri pushed her face close to a globe. It was slightly larger
than her skull, and its light pooled in her eyes. She passed a
hand through the globe. Model oceans sparkled over her
fingers.

I said, 'Thyri, I think this is a pilot's room, a map room.'
Each globe was a different world, probably from a different
Domain. One of them must be WebVin. On some of the
worlds I could see cities, shining roads.

Thyri walked across the chamber, ducking her head under
the corridor tube. 'Pilot. What's this?'

A disc of light lay across the air at a steep angle. Light of all
colours swirled through its substance. Around its centre
orbited knots of star-like pinpoints.

'Thyri,' I said softly, 'you are honoured. This is your
Galaxy. That disc is made up of stars, billions of them. Your
sun is just a speckle in that glare.' I hesitated, wondering
how much to tell her. 'You are the first of your people to see
this sight. And the last, for generations.'

Despite our sense of urgency it was difficult to leave this
awesome display. At last, with slow footsteps, we returned to
the corridor.

We approached the last door.

Silently Thyri stepped through the circular doorframe.

The walls of this chamber tapered slightly. We must be
close to the ship's needle-shaped prow. Greenish pond light
washed over two chairs like thrones, tables crusted with
glass, walls plated with the black volcanic glass called
obsidian. Star fields filled the obsidian panels.

And above one of the tables, hovered Gunnar's Key.

Now I understood what the Key was for. It was a little
model of the Search Engine itself. Restored to its proper
place, it meant all a pilot would have to do would be to move
the Key, and the Engine itself would move in sympathy.

There was a low hum in the air.

Thyri growled. 'That noise. I imagine huge muscles tensing, prepared to hurl this Longboat into the sky.'

I waved her to silence.

A man sat in one of the chairs. He had his back to the entrance. The greenish illumination highlighted black skin-armour. Light danced over a table beneath his hands.

Thyri said softly, 'Regent.'

Numinus whirled, his scarred face contorted.

Thyri's iron sword sang through the air. Numinus's left hand was a blur as it stabbed at panels of his armour.

The sword hit the deflector field in a blaze of light.

Thyri stalked into echoes of brilliance, hands straining for the Regent's throat.

But I got myself in the way. 'Numinus!' I shouted, hands spread wide. 'We've got to talk, to end this!'

Thyri shoved me aside. There was nothing I could do, I was so weak. I crumpled and fell against a bulkhead.

But it was too late. Numinus's eyes glittered with triumph. 'Sorry, warrior woman,' he said softly. A sphere of silver rested in his upturned palm. Another Galaxias weapon.

Thyri took another stride.

Numinus casually dropped the sphere. It shattered.

Something fizzed out of the small explosion and darted like an insect a few metres above the deck, a wavering distortion in the air like heat haze. I was still on the deck, pressed back against a bulkhead. As the fizzing thing passed before me I felt a tugging at my gut.

'Thyri,' I called. 'Stay back. That was a Hawking Shell. It's a tiny black hole, distortion in space. Your armour won't help you if it touches you.'

'How do we get rid of it?' Thyri demanded.

'We don't. And it's unpredictable. It's even out of Numinus's control. It might vanish in a moment, or it might destroy the ship. Regent, you must be desperate to try that.'

Numinus laughed. 'I'm almost ready to launch. I haven't come this far to die at the hands of a crazed aboriginal.'

'And I haven't come so far, star man, to let you live,' Thyri hissed.

'Numinus, it isn't too late,' I said, pleading. 'You are a servant of Galaxias. Leave this world and go home, get on with your life. Forget what's happened here, what you've done.'

An oddly wistful look crossed Numinus's face. 'And what of my ... crimes here?'

'Perhaps you can atone.'

Numinus's eyes met Thyri's. The Regent said softly, 'I think there is only one way this woman will have me atone, Pilot. I fear you're wrong. It really is too late.'

For a moment there was a tense silence, broken only by the spitting of the black hole.

I had only one thing left to try. It meant I was breaking all the rules of the Web. But I had no choice!

'Numinus, listen to me.'

The tone of my voice had changed. Both of them turned and looked at me.

'Numinus. *None of this is real.*'

'What?'

'Don't tell me you haven't suspected it. This world is artificial. A model inside a huge computer.'

Thyri growled, trying to understand. 'Like a dream? We are living in a dream?'

'Yes. Something like that. Numinus, the machines are breaking down. That's why your reality – Galaxias – was able to pollute this one, WebVin. *But none of this is real.*'

His face hardened. 'If nothing is real, what does it matter what I do?'

Tough question!

I had no answer. But I had him off balance. I could see that.

Maybe if I'd had a little more time I could have got through to him.

But there was no more time.

The black hole struck.

The fizzing blur shot straight at me. It punched through the centre of my torso!

CHAPTER FOURTEEN

ESCAPE

The black hole winked out of existence. But it had done its damage.

If this had happened for real, I'd have been dead!

I stared down at the mess it had made of my stomach. It didn't hurt, of course. But I could feel the Web's modelling programmes kicking in. As far as the Web was concerned I was badly injured. I was going to be restricted from now on, even more than by the Websickness.

Meanwhile, the battle was continuing.

Thyri turned on Numinus with a roar.

The Regent's fingers flew over a tabletop. The nose of the floating Key rose into the air, and the Search Engine lifted in response.

Have you seen that corny old 2-D movie about the *Titanic*? Your parents were probably taken to it as a kid, and blubbed all the way through. (Philip still does when it's shown on Christmas Day.) Remember those scenes where the ship is going down, and the decks tip up, and all the passengers plummet through the windows?

It was like that in the Search Engine.

With my injury I was helpless. I tumbled backwards out of the room.

Thyri tried to leap, but the floor sagged beneath her. She collided with the rear bulkhead. The impact knocked the

wind out of her body. Then she rolled after me out through
the circular doorway.

The corridor was a near-vertical tube beneath us. I managed to grab the lip of the doorway with one hand. But now
the door began to iris shut, like a camera shutter. It felt as if a
knife edge was passing beneath my fingertips. For a few
seconds I hung there, staring up at Numinus's grinning face.
Then I dropped and caromed off the walls to the bottom of
the tilted corridor.

I finished up crumpled at the back of the corridor. Thyri
fell after me. The Translator box drifted beside us, still
attached to its umbilical cable.

The Search Engine shuddered as it tried to rise. I heard its
needle nose grind against the roof of its cage of earth.

Thyri cupped my face in her hands. 'Pilot! Tell me what to
do. How can I stop him?'

'Thyri. You can't. He's sealed into the bridge.'

Thyri howled rage. She shook me brutally. 'I'll not let him
live, Pilot!' I could see she was considering clambering up
that tilted corridor, tearing at the bulkhead until her fingers
broke and bled.

'Listen to me,' I cried. 'If you stay here during take-off you
will surely die. You'll be crushed and choked. Numinus
would lie in his couch, laughing.'

She hesitated, and made her decision. 'All right. We've got
to get out of here.'

'Yes.'

She grabbed me by my belt and hauled me out through
the hatchway into the cavern. The Translator bumped after
us.

The skin of the tilted Search Engine shone like the sun.
Sparks moved about the advertising panels on the hull. A
thrilling singing noise filled the cave.

I clutched at Thyri's bloodied armour 'The Miner.'

'What?'

'The machine. Get us to the Miner. The heat shield might
protect us when she lifts.'

Now the Search Engine lifted from the soil. Heat blasted my face, but I was too weak even to walk.

Dragging me, Thyri scrambled through the connecting tunnel into the Miner chamber.

The light here seemed dim as twilight. Thyri ran around the Miner, searching for anything that looked like a door. I tried to focus, but I was weakening fast and couldn't help her.

There. An indentation in the hull, just above the wheel skirt. Thyri pressed her palm against the metal. A section of the hull slid upwards and sideways, revealing a small room, two seats side by side. Thyri bundled me into the cabin and clambered after me. With a yank on its rope she hauled in the Translator.

Light pulsed into the chamber. The Miner shuddered. The air roiled.

And the door was still open. 'Metaphor! The door. How?'

My eyes flickered open. 'The red button. To the left of the console.'

Thyri found a red stud. She stabbed at it with one thumb. The door sighed closed.

I found a slit at eye level. I found myself peering at the back of the Miner's heat shield.

There was a second of stillness.

Then a fist of light slammed into the shield.

The Miner was hurled backwards. Thyri braced her arms against the panels before her. I tumbled to the narrow floor. Metal crumpled as the Miner was thrown against the wall of the chamber.

The light faded. Thyri helped me up. I pressed my eyes to the window slit, and saw sky.

The Search Engine had blasted away the roof of its prison. It hovered like a small sun. Dazzling sparks raced over its spindle form.

Then the Engine's nose lifted to the sky – and it leapt.

There was a single flash against the grey sky, a roll like thunder. Then it was gone.

*

The Arctic night closed over the wound in the earth. Thyri
watched through the eye slit.

I groaned. I wasn't in pain, but I was so *weak*.

'Don't try to move,' Thyri murmured.

'Thyri. Numinus has escaped. Perhaps he will make
straight for the Domain Breach, if your world is lucky.'

'No.'

'What?'

'He hasn't escaped. Not as long as I breathe.'

I looked at her. 'Good grief. I believe you're serious. Thyri,
do you understand where Numinus has gone? He is at least
several hundred kilometres up, moving twenty-five times the
speed of sound.'

'You will tell me how I can reach him.'

Gingerly, I touched the blood crusted over my midriff.
'Oh, sure. Here I am, stranded in an alien reality, and I've
been punched in the stomach by a black hole ...' I knew I
was rambling, but I couldn't help it. 'If this was real I
wouldn't even be alive. And now some bone-headed Viking
wants me to shoot down a spaceship using nothing but Iron
Age technology. Thyri, I miss my father. Have I told you
about my father?'

'Yes. Try to sleep now.'

CHAPTER FIFTEEN
PLANS

Under my guidance Thyri drove the damaged Miner deeper into the tunnel under the Domain Breach. Then she collapsed the open end of the tunnel, shutting out the disturbing sky of the Breach.

Thyri tried to help me. She rigged up a pallet from Miner seat cushions and laid me gently on it. She placed my Galaxias medical kit on the ground beside me. Silver filaments snaked out of the seamless box and dug into my flesh.

None of this was doing a bit of good, of course. But my injuries were real within the context of WebVin and its inhabitants, and I had to make a show of recovering from them. Once again, I tried to nap so I could fast-forward through hours of recovery.

My real problem, of course, was Websickness.

By now, I estimated, I had been in the Web continuously for five Realworld hours – maybe twice as long as the manufacturers recommend. I was nauseous, dizzy, weak, disoriented. The only good thing was that I was too ill to be hungry!

And all the time I was trying to work out what to do about all this.

I felt responsible, in a way.

Maybe that was wrong. The WebCrash wasn't my fault, and neither was Numinus's passage through the Domain

Breach into this innocent world. But maybe there was something I could have done differently to prevent quite so many of the people of this world from getting hurt.

But the problems I faced now ... well, think about it. Numinus was going to use the Search Engine as a spaceship. Right now it was in orbit around the planet, and Numinus would be devising weapons.

If a hostile alien ship was orbiting *our* Earth, perhaps we could do something about it. We could send it radio signals to try to communicate with it. We could fire nuclear missiles at it. We could send up space shuttles and try to board it. We could even launch an attack from the base on the Moon.

But this was AD 973!

These people had no radios or rocket ships or missiles. They had no air travel at all. The fastest way to travel on land was on horseback. The Vikings didn't even have *gunpowder*.

And now Thyri, my strong Viking friend, wanted me to come up with a way to challenge a spaceship!

It was impossible. I shouldn't even have wasted time thinking about it. Perhaps if I'd been healthy, I'd have dismissed it altogether.

But lying there with my mixture of real and artificial sickness, fast-forwarding through time, maybe my mind was a little looser than usual. I remembered stuff I'd heard in school about how the Chinese had invented gunpowder long before the Europeans.

Strange as it seemed, even to me, I started to get an idea about what we could do about Regent Numinus Torca.

Thyri fixed cushions so that I could sit up. Metal umbilicals still connected the medical box to my body. 'I'm going to be a burden, I'm afraid,' I said. 'According to my friendly box here I'm not capable of walking. My spinal column is severed. Every few minutes this box flashes lights at me, insisting that I get to a full-facility Galaxias hospital without delay.' My voice faltered. 'That's funny, isn't it?'

Of course my injuries weren't real. But my weakness was, and so was my confusion.

'We can't stay here,' Thyri said briskly. 'I have to move you back to Norrland.'

I sighed. 'And we have to take back some equipment, Thyri, if we can. I've been thinking.'

Thyri came close. 'Tell me.'

I toyed with my medical wires. 'I've got an idea, Thyri.'

'A way we can get at Numinus.'

'Yes. We'll need to build something like a longship ... a very large ship, strangely shaped. It would be a cylinder, a tube as wide as a man's height, let's say, and perhaps fifty times as long. Do you think your shipwrights could make such a thing?'

'We could use the keel timbers from longboats. But it will be expensive.'

I smiled gently. 'Thyri, we'll take a sensor panel from the Miner. This will show you, for instance, where to find new deposits of tin and iron ore. I would think that could make you rich very quickly.'

Thyri nodded slowly.

I said, 'We'll need to take back all the heavy tools and instruments we can find here. And, most important, we'll need the heat shield from the Miner.'

The shield was a plate of twisted metal that was taller than Thyri. 'Impossible,' she said flatly. 'We could never carry it. We have only three horses, Valkyrie.'

'But my Translator unit has an anti-gravity generator. That's what makes it fly. It can lift anything. Now then, see if you can find a laser cutter among Numinus's tools. It will look like this.'

Thyri strapped the Translator unit to the centre of the heat shield. Then she grappled nervously with the laser cutter, passing its burning light over the shield's supporting arms.

A thread of metal softened, stretched, snapped. Thyri stood back quickly.

The shield toppled grandly away from the Miner and bobbed, rocked, and finally stabilized over the Translator unit, a few centimetres from the ground. The straining Translator whined in complaint.

I clapped my hands. 'It worked! Now I can ride back in style.'

Thyri lifted me onto the centre of the shield, and piled on equipment and Miner parts. The shield bobbed gently like a raft in the air. Thyri fixed ropes to the shield and attached the loose ends to the harnesses of two of the horses. With gentle tugging she encouraged the horses to haul their way into the tunnel.

At first the horses strained, but once the plate was in motion they made rapid progress. Thyri trotted alongside, one hand on the bridle of the lead horse.

'It's like a barge,' I said. 'Once you've generated enough momentum there isn't much resistance. Do you know what momentum is, Thyri?'

'Why don't you tell me?'

And so the kilometres wore away in a fast-forwarded blur.

CHAPTER SIXTEEN

DESIGNS

And so it began.

I slept as much as I could. That wasn't difficult given my growing weakness from the Websickness. What passed as an hour for me was more like a month for Thyri. And I saw the construction of what she called the *Mjollnir*, the Hammer of Thor, in fragments and glimpses.

She had little difficulty getting the support of the people of Ragnar for her venture. It must have sounded bizarre to them, but she stood on the *Logberg* and simply showed them the evidence: me, my Galaxias technology, what Numinus had done to me.

The Vikings were explorers. They were imaginative people, ready to accept the strange, and not afraid of huge challenges.

Under my instructions, the Vikings were going to make a rocket.

Within a few days of our return the construction began.

The shipwrights started with the wood. They cut down pine trees and oak trees from the forests, and split them along their lengths to make planks. They also made wooden pegs and wedges, and blocks and supports for the construction of the missile itself. Their main tools were hand-held axes, although they also had knives, chisels and planes. I was amazed how skilful and fast the shipwrights were.

There were iron nails and washers to fix the planks together. I watched the smiths work with their forges, smelting iron from bog ore. They had bellows, tongs and hammers, and they used shears for snipping off lengths of hot metal. But they had no masks, nothing to protect their faces but cloth tied over their mouths.

One evening, when the construction was at its busiest, I went with Thyri to view the rocket.

Most of the light had leaked away from the dusk sky, but still the teams of boatbuilders, woodsmen, stem-smiths, plank-cutters, and labourers worked on. Lanterns moved through the copse at the foot of the hillock on which Thyri's house was set. Shouted instructions and the pounding of metal against wood floated up to me through the cooling air.

The thing they were building lay on its side in the copse, half-concealed by fir trees. There were wooden hoops that looked like the rib cage of a huge creature, perhaps a whale, stranded there in the forest. A few dozen timbers had been laid in place now and the cylindrical shape of the construction was coming clearer. The hull of my wooden rocket was going to be clinker-built, with the planks overlapping each other, just like a longboat. The shipwrights used wool and pine tar to seal and waterproof the seams between the planks.

I had learned more about shipbuilding than I had thought possible, and it was quite a thrill to see the great craft coming together from my crude sketches. But without the expertise of the Viking boatbuilders it would never have been possible to get so far.

But I spent much of my time fretting over whether it would work at all.

I would sit under a light globe, working through calculations and fine points of the design. I was applying lessons I half-remembered from school, things I'd seen or read in the Web. I longed to be able to get out to Realworld, not just to get over Websickness, but to go to a library and *check* what I was telling Thyri to build. (If you think I was fretting too much, *you* try designing a missile with Iron Age tools!)

Thyri stood over me, eating pork. She had to clear clutter from her pallet before she could sit down.

I noted absently that the woollen blanket on the pallet was filthy and threadbare. The house was barely recognizable as the home it had once been.

Well, I knew that without Gunnar, it was a home no more to Thyri. The house was just another tool. Even the bags of gold stacked in one corner were simply a means to an end. To Thyri now, the rocket – and Numinus – were everything.

'How goes it, Valkyrie?'

'The attitude control is giving me a pain,' I muttered, scribbling. 'This steam-jet system is the best I can dream up ... but you just haven't the technology. The iron pipe samples you brought me simply aren't accurately tooled.'

Thyri stopped listening. I knew she'd long since grown inured to my incomprehensible complaints.

But this was one problem I hadn't been able to overcome – guidance.

You don't just fire off a missile like a Bonfire Night firework. You need attitude control, minor rockets that make it turn this way and that to keep on course. And you need some kind of guidance system, a brain to direct it to its target.

I'd been able to improvise attitude control with steam jets. But I couldn't come up with any way to have the missile guide itself to its target automatically.

When I explained this to Thyri, she had an immediate solution. 'Then I will fly Thor's Hammer myself. I will guide it to the skull of Numinus.'

I tried to talk her out of it. But since I had no better ideas, I didn't succeed very well.

Anyway, my biggest worry was propellant – fuel for my missile. Remember, the Vikings didn't have gunpowder. I had hoped to be able to buy some from China, via Thyri's Russian trader contacts, but that turned out to be impossible.

So I was having to put together a mixture (from memory!) that I thought might work.

'I'm assuming a mix of seventy-five per cent potassium nitrate, fifteen per cent charcoal, the rest sulphur. I'll be able to pep it up with some of Numinus's grenades to give it the specific impulse we'll need to reach orbit. But we need more potassium nitrate, Thyri.'

Thyri turned her head. 'We need *what*?'

'Saltpetre.'

Thyri nodded, chewing slowly. 'How much?'

She went to Helgo to get it. And that was where, for the first time, we heard about what Numinus was up to. I fast-forwarded to her return, and she told me about it.

Caspar had come up in the world, largely thanks to Thyri's money, the Viking thought wryly. The Russian merchant had bought a fine house on the outskirts of Helgo – no more cheap taverns for him – and he welcomed Thyri with a wave of plump, ring-encrusted fingers.

There was a sofa before a roaring fire. Thyri noted a long blonde hair draped over a cushion. Evidently the Russian was making new friends!

Caspar brought her mead to drink in a cut glass. 'Of course I am delighted to take your new order.' He sat on an embroidered stool, arranged his velvet robe. 'But I fear there may be a little delay. The shipping lanes are somewhat disrupted by the recent incident in the Black Sea.' He sipped his mead.

Thyri felt a sudden chill, as if the wind had turned. 'What incident?'

Caspar's round face showed surprise. 'You haven't heard? Well, it's a great mystery. The Byzantine sages are considering the reports. Some say they saw lights in the sky. I'm rather doubtful about that. What's indisputable is that there was a massive explosion in the sea.' The Russian's small hands fluttered. 'There was a wave like a wall of water. It hit the coast. The land was scoured away, clean down to bedrock. There had been villages there, small fishing places. Many lives were lost. And who knows how many ships? The Black Sea is still strange. Unusual storms. Choppy seas. And I'm told that those who venture close enough see a crater on the sea bed, glowing red. What do you think of that?'

Thyri said nothing.

'Well, you can imagine what it's done to my schedules.'

Thyri stood abruptly, pulling closed her robe. 'Caspar. Get me that saltpetre.'

'Of course, but—'

'Do it in a week and your fee is doubled. Do you understand?'

Caspar's small mouth fell open. Thyri turned without ceremony and left.

When Thyri got home she told me what the Russian had said.

'It was Numinus,' I whispered.

'What weapon can strike from so far away?'

I shook my head. 'Thyri, where he is, Numinus doesn't need weapons. He's very high up and moving very fast. All he needs to do is throw down a rock.'

'Why attack the sea?'

I shrugged. 'Obviously he has to refine his aim, his range. I suspect he will learn fast. Perhaps the next rock will fall on a city.' I placed a hand on Thyri's arm. 'You see, when your people are crushed, terrified, in turmoil, starving, then he will land like a god and take over.'

'Then it's no longer simply a matter of vengeance,' Thyri said. 'He has to be stopped.'

'Yes.' I smiled. 'But consider this. The longer he dreams in orbit the longer he stays within your grasp.'

'Yes,' said Thyri. 'And my grasp is long.'

'You're very brave, Thyri. You know that if you fly on the *Mjollnir*—'

'I will probably die? I know. But life isn't everything, little Valkyrie. If I die in such a cause – die in removing this scourge Numinus, from my world – then I will be welcomed into Valhalla as one of the *valr*, the honoured dead. And I will be with Gunnar, she regarded me. 'But then, if none of this is real – if *I* am not real – then none of this matters, does it?'

'You are as real as you feel, Thyri. And your courage is real.'

She shrugged. 'Even if this is just a Dream of Midgardsorm, the world-serpent, then it is up to us to behave as if it were not so.'

'Yes,' I said, but I didn't trust myself to say any more.

Thyri helped me out of the door. I shivered, despite my skin-armour and layers of woollen blankets. My Webtime was up to *seven* hours, I estimated. The battered Translator box bobbled faithfully after us.

Although it was barely dawn it seemed that half the population of Ragnar was swarming over and around the cylinder lying in the copse. Exasperated adults chased children from the attitude control piping and the huge fins.

Over the cylinder stood a scaffolding made of three massive tree trunks. Cables of Galaxias metal snaked over the scaffolding and wrapped themselves around the cylinder. Men tugged at them experimentally.

Thyri manoeuvred the chair down the hill. Children skipped after us, staring at me curiously. I waved weakly.

The workers made last-minute adjustments to the cylinder, pounding in fresh rivets and checking piping. They turned to us and nodded politely, brushing at blond moustaches.

We reached the base of the cylinder. A truncated cone flared out of the base. This was the tail nozzle from the wrecked Miner, and now it was the nozzle for my rocket. Triangular fins reached over our heads, blocking out the light.

'If you're going to succeed,' I said to Thyri, 'it's important that you understand what is going to happen. Now then.

This cylinder is packed with gunpowder. You can smell the sulphur—'

'I know that much.'

'I've lumped it into granules of varying sizes. If all goes well the gunpowder won't explode. It will burn steadily for some minutes. Hot gases will make their way out of the nozzle and push the ship into the air. The fins will keep her stable.'

Thyri nodded. 'I understand.'

We walked the length of the cylinder. I admired the workmanship contained in the bands of iron, the polished, caulked timbers. The craft was like some huge piece of furniture.

The other end of the cylinder was wrapped in a nest of piping. I studied the pipes critically. 'Look, Thyri. You will vent steam out of this piping. That will push the ship, direct to its goal. There's a boiler at the top end of the cylinder, just here, powered by a couple of broken-up grenades. Well, it might last long enough.'

We reached the cabin at the tip of the cylinder. It was a cramped, tent-shaped box welded together from the Miner heat shield. It was the best protection I could give Thyri. A seat from the Miner had been fixed to the base of the box which was now tilted vertically.

I imagined being Thyri, climbing into that seat, listening to the roar of the gunpowder. My heart thumped at the thought.

But Thyri showed no fear. This was simply what she had to do.

I peered into the little cabin doubtfully. 'You'll have my skin armour, of course. That will give you a few minutes' air. Well, it's the best I can do.'

Thyri smiled. 'You're not very reassuring, little Valkyrie.'

The cables connecting the nose of the cylinder to the scaffolding arced high over our heads. Now the cables went taut, singing in the air.

A foreman came to us, sweat matting the golden hair on his forearms. 'We're ready to lift.'

Thyri nodded. She returned me to the vantage point at the crest of the hillock near her house.

Adults shooed children to safety. Teams of burly Vikings, men and women, spat on their hands and picked up cables. Then, working to low, rhythmic chants, they began to haul.

Cables quivered like guitar strings. Pulleys creaked and rotated. And the metal tip of the cylinder lifted like the head of a waking giant.

Children cheered. The Vikings grinned through sheets of sweat. I whooped too. It was a *fantastic* moment!

Then a cable snapped. The frayed end whipped through the air. It lashed at a scrambling woman, slicing through her leg like a knife through soft butter. She stared at the stump and began to scream.

I could hear the voices of foremen. 'Never mind that. Keep working, you idlers!'

The cylinder rocked. The remaining cables groaned ominously, but they held. Gradually the rocking steadied and the cylinder began to rise once more.

At last, it was vertical. Standing on its fins, wood and iron gleaming, *Mjollnir*, the Hammer of Thor pointed at the sky like an armoured fist.

CHAPTER SEVENTEEN
LAUNCH

I had to stay in Thyri's home, following events remotely through my instruments. Later, I was able to reconstruct what really happened.

The cabin was dark, the stink of sulphur overwhelming. The heat of the attitude jet boiler seeped through the floor.

Metaphor's skin-armour was short in the arms and legs, almost unbearably tight around the midriff. Thyri lay in the Miner chair, feeling the armour move over her chest.

Metaphor's voice sounded from the implant in her ear. *'It's time, Thyri. The Search Engine has just risen over the horizon. Close up your face mask.'*

Thyri fixed the mask over her face, sealing its edges with a gloved thumbnail. A plate of glass allowed her to see.

Mounted on sturdy legs before her was a simple instrument panel. There was a series of pads which, Metaphor had patiently explained, would control the attitude thrusters. Half the panel was taken up by a *viewer*, a sheet of glass which now lit up with a panoramic view from the nose of the rocket.

Metaphor asked, *'Is the area clear?'*

Thyri studied the viewer. A ring of people, adults and children, surrounded the cylinder at a safe distance. One man stood near the cylinder, brandishing a torch. 'Yes,' she said.

'*Then this is it, Thyri.*'

'Good!' Thyri slammed her fist into the centre of her panel. In response, a mouthful of fire spat into the air from the tip of the cylinder.

Seeing Thyri's signal, the man with the torch ran past the huge fins and under the base of the craft. Thyri imagined him hurling his torch onto the bonfire banked there, then turning and running for his life. Soon the first gunpowder granules would hiss and fire.

Smoke wisped. The cylinder shuddered.

'Valkyrie. It's working.'

'*Well, you're committed now, Thyri.*' Metaphor sounded more scared than Thyri. '*You must succeed. Stand by.*'

There was a roar like a bear's.

The cushioned seat slammed into her back. The bones of her skull rattled together. Invisible fingers seemed to be hauling back her cheeks. Darkness framed her vision.

The ground fell away.

Barely able to walk, I stumbled to the unglazed window of Thyri's house.

White smoke was billowing over the ground, huge clouds that towered and flowed up the hillside.

And out of it rose the *Mjollnir*, a splinter of wood riding a splash of flame that was yellow and incredibly bright, brighter than the sun. The noise was a deep rumble that shook the ground and made my chest vibrate, and then, as the rocket rose into the air, a series of crackles and bangs, shock waves like thunderclaps in the air above me.

People were shouting and cheering, and I found myself crying.

I can't describe it. You had to *be* there.

'By all the gods, little Valkyrie!'

'*Thyri, it's working!*'

Thyri could see Norrland laid out like an illuminated map. Clouds were scattered like raindrops over the land.

'She was above the clouds, higher than a bird.'

A blue arc entered the top of the picture, framed by blackness. '*Thyri,*' said Metaphor. '*That's the horizon. You're so high you can see the curve of the planet. Are you all right?*'

The world was a ball and she had been hurled away like a stone.

She wasn't prepared for this, despite all Metaphor's explanations. Her mind twisted away, seeking refuge.

'Numinus.' She repeated the name like an incantation. 'Numinus.'

Nothing else mattered.

'Yes, Metaphor. I'm all right.'

But now the rocket shook as if slapped. The landscape slid sideways.

'Metaphor?'

'*I was afraid of this. Thyri, the propellant isn't burning evenly. Pehaps the granule packing was disturbed during the launch.*'

Blackness closed around Thyri's vision. 'Metaphor,' she ground out. 'Tell me what I have to do.'

'*We use the attitude thrusters. Touch pad one.*'

Thyri did so. She heard a distant hiss. A cloud of steam obscured her view. The shrinking landscape floated back to the centre of the screen.

Metaphor said, '*Hold it there while I count. One, two, three, four, five. Release. Good.*'

'Has it worked?'

'*Wait while I check …*' Metaphor's voice tailed away. '*See for yourself.*'

The landscape in the viewer winked away, to be replaced by a star field. Through the familiar constellations crawled a single vagrant star.

'It's Numinus,' Thyri breathed.

'*Yes. Thyri, I think you're going to—*'

Suddenly the ship shuddered.

Roiling gas swept across the field. Numinus's ship drifted from view.

'Metaphor?'

'Thyri, the hull's failed!'

Now the monitor showed Thyri the length of the cylinder. Fire twisted from a wide rip in the side. Metal hoops twisted in white flame.

The cabin's heat grew hellish.

Thyri held her gloved fist over the control panel. 'Tell me what to do, Valkyrie.'

'Thyri, the hull has failed. It was a good try, but the materials just weren't strong enough. The attitude jets don't have the capacity to compensate for this—'

'I'm not giving up yet, Valkyrie! Which panel?'

'Number three!'

Thyri slammed down her fist. Steam shrieked.

Metaphor shouted, *'On my count … three, four, five, six. Release. Thyri, release the pad now. Thyri!'*

The star field stayed empty. 'I don't see Numinus.' Thyri kept her hand on the control.

'Thyri, that steam boiler is a box of pig iron. It can't take this. Release!'

Thyri kept her fist in place. The boiler growled. The heat was unbearable.

At last, the moving star returned to the centre of the screen. Now it showed a spindle form, tumbling slowly.

It was the Sky Longboat, what Metaphor had called the Search Engine.

Thyri released the button. She studied her ship through her viewer.

Mjollnir's casing was breached in a dozen places. Fire hosed into space. Molten iron rained from the hull. The walls of the cabin began to glow a soft red.

'I'm sorry, Thyri,' Metaphor said. *'I guess the technology just wasn't up to it.'*

'I'm not dead yet, Metaphor.'

'I'll tell you one thing. You're giving your people down here quite a show.'

Another slam.

The star field lurched across Thyri's viewer. The rocket

seemed to be spinning. Thyri's stomach knotted as she felt herself tumble—

But there, shooting across the screen, was the Search Engine. It was so close Thyri could see the sparks dancing over its hull!

She howled in triumph.

The glowing Engine filled the viewer—

She hit.

CHAPTER EIGHTEEN

INTERCEPTION

Mjollnir rammed into the Search Engine's fabric like a fist into wet cloth. It ripped open the hull and crumpled the decks inside.

Then the cabin slammed into a bulkhead, and *Mjollnir* ground to a sudden stop.

The straps fixing Thyri to her chair snapped, and she was thrown forward. She was wadded into the nose of the cabin like a bit of cloth, but her Valkyrie armour turned stiff and filled with a sticky fluid. Somehow it cushioned her.

The viewer failed.

There was an explosion that slammed the cabin forward. Thyri was rattled like a pebble in a skull. It had been the last of the gunpowder which had powered the rocket.

Then it was over. The sudden silence was as shocking as the thunder that had preceded it.

In the stillness, Thyri spoke.

'Metaphor? Can you hear me?'

'*Thyri! You survived all that?*'

Thyri was ... floating. She grabbed a jagged edge of cabin wall. The sudden movement caused all the bruises covering her body to protest at once. 'Valkyrie, I am *flying*.'

'*You're in orbit, Thyri! Well, that was hardly the smooth rendezvous I intended you to make, but never mind.*'

Thyri pulled herself out through the cabin wall. It was difficult to move. Her legs dangled, in the way.

The cabin was a mass of glowing metal. It lay in a disc-shaped chamber. Charred remnants on the walls showed Thyri that this had once been the ocean-like swimming room. Through the ripped hull of the Search Engine Thyri could see stars, a crescent of blue sea. Fragments of ice sparkled around her.

'Thyri, Numinus has to be trying to regain control of the Search Engine. He'll be in the bridge.'

'Yes.'

Thyri checked her weapons.

Metaphor had provided her with a laser gun. 'Meet the Regent on equal terms,' she'd said. Now Thyri inspected the piece of sculpted Galaxias metal, and let it drift from her hands.

She didn't want strange Galaxias weapons. She would fight as a Viking warrior.

There was an axe strapped to her waist. In one hand she held her sword of the finest Rhineland iron. In the other she held her shield of wood with its central iron boss. All these weapons had belonged to Gunnar, and had been used by him in the many battles he had won – until his last with the monster Numinus.

Wood and iron. The ancient muscles of the Viking. She had no need of Valkyrie trickery.

And this time there would be no mistake.

She clambered to the top of the cabin and, with gritted teeth, kicked away from the wall. She floated through empty space. Metaphor had warned her it would be like this, *free fall* – but to fly like a bird! She felt her breakfast rise in her throat.

And the air was thin, leaking from the rents in the hull that were imperfectly plugged by *Mjollnir*. Soon she was gasping for breath.

She hit the chamber's axis and rebounded, cursing. Her fingers scrabbled over the smooth material, trying to get a grip.

A door dilated. Air swept past Thyri. She hauled herself

through into the green-lit spinal corridor. The door irised closed and air returned with a sigh.

Thyri wiped away sweat. 'Metaphor. I'm in the corridor.'

'Thyri, move,' Metaphor hissed. *'The collision has knocked the Search Engine out of orbit. You're falling. You have perhaps only minutes.'*

'That will be enough.'

She pulled herself along the corridor and through the door at its end.

She rolled head-over-heels into the control room. She hit the floor and rebounded slightly, her gaze flicking around.

On the walls obsidian panels flared red. Gunnar's Key, the control for this Search Engine, twisted in the air. The control tables were full of whirling sparks.

Numinus was here. He sat facing the door. The expression on the Regent's face changed as slowly as melting ice. Blood flared in the scar across his cheek. 'You! How?'

Thyri grasped her axe.

'I am not your enemy,' said Numinus.

It was enough to make Thyri hesitate. 'Then who?'

'The girl. The monster. *Metaphor*. And all her kind.' He waved a hand. 'Is it true that none of this is real? That your world and mine were *made* by people somewhere beyond the walls of the universe – for their amusement? If that is so we should work together, escape from this place. Find a way to invade the world of these would-be gods, and punish them for their arrogance.'

Thyri considered that. This airy talk of different worlds, of herself as an imagined creature of some machine's fevered dream. She balanced it against the reality of her life: blood, family, honour, and redemption.

'Prepare to meet your gods, Numinus.' And she raised her axe—

But Numinus's hand flew to the forearm controls of his skin-armour.

To Thyri it was like a nightmare repeat of her last clash with Numinus, the same sequence of lost split-seconds. In a moment the deflector field would sparkle and the battle would be lost.

But the Regent's hand hovered, hesitating. There was something new in his dark face. Relief? Regret?

She threw the axe. It flew across the cabin. The blade laid open Numinus's chest.

The Regent's face crumpled. The black eyes grew cold.

Thyri loomed over the body, breathing hard. She pulled her axe from the shattered chest. Numinus had become a *blood eagle*, as had so many of the enemies of the Vikings in the past.

'Well, Thyri?' Metaphor sounded tired. The little Valkyrie had no stomach for killing. *'You have won.'*

'Metaphor? I think he let me kill him.'

'What?'

'He could have worked his armour. He had time. But he didn't. Why?'

Metaphor laughed mirthlessly. *'In his universe Regents exert great power. But they are also the first servants of Galaxias – of mankind. I guess Numinus lost the balance between power and duty … but he was guilty and confused. Thyri, once he'd hurt your husband he couldn't turn back. But, perhaps part of him was glad you stopped him before he destroyed your world.'*

Thyri stared down at the cooling body for long seconds. Then she reached down and pressed Numinus's eyelids closed with her thumbs.

She turned away and attached her axe once more to her belt. It was over. The pain of Gunnar was gone. Let it be.

The Search Engine shuddered. Obsidian panels glowed ever more brightly.

What now?

Thyri was suddenly aware that she hadn't planned beyond this moment. She knew there was no way to get back to the ground. But she was alive. And she wanted to stay that way.

'Metaphor? What do I do?'

Silence …

'Metaphor?'

'Ah,' Metaphor coughed weakly. *'I'm sorry, Thyri. This has all been too much for me. Study the instrument panels, the control tables. Your armour will show me what you see.'*

Thyri did so.

Metaphor hesitated for long seconds. *'We have a problem, Thyri. Our homemade spaceship did a lot of damage. You can't land the Search Engine. But you can't stay where you are, either. The ship's orbit is decaying fast. You'll burn up in minutes.'*

Thyri floated in the air. A sense of peace settled over her. 'Then it's over.'

'No, Thyri. Maybe there's a way. Listen. The table to your left. See the pattern of sparks like a pinwheel? Place your palm over it and ...'

Slowly, hesitantly, Thyri followed Metaphor's instructions. She heard a growl as ancient engines stirred. An obsidian panel lit up with an image of the world.

She was dropping back into that pond of air. Oceans flicked beneath her keel. She was *flying* this Search Engine, she realized with a sudden tremor. But ... where to? 'Metaphor?'

'You're heading for the Domain Breach at the north pole. If you're lucky, the way to Galaxias will still be open. You'll pass through to stars.'

'What good will that do?'

'You can't come home. Thyri,' Metaphor said gently. *'I'm sorry. This is your one chance. If you survive the transit, press the stud in the belt of your armour. That will activate a distress signal. With good fortune the Empire will pick up the signal. You'll be rescued.'*

Now ice raced beneath the keel of the Search Engine, almost close enough to touch. 'Metaphor, thank you.'

'You might not thank me later. Galaxias is a tough place.'

A curtain of darkness, swirling shapes that hurt her eyes, a central place like a hole in the sky beckoned Thyri. The Domain Breach.

'Little Valkyrie. I think—'

'Goodbye, Thyri.'
The hole swallowed her.

CHAPTER NINETEEN

WORLDS

Like an icicle in spring the Domain Breach, the way between the universes, had grown tenuous and thin.

The Search Engine roared through.

The way collapsed behind it, dissipated like smoke, closed for ever.

After my farewell to Thyri, the Translator fell silent.

I lay in my chair, breathing hard, utterly weary. At the edge of my attention the medical unit bleeped its warning.

How long had I been inside the Web now? Eight hours? Nine? I knew too much Webtime could actually kill me. But there was nothing I could do about it.

I felt content.

Real or not, it didn't seem to matter any more. This was a world of good people. I had done all I could to save them from the evil of Numinus. I had even helped Thyri get to safety, I hoped. Now it was over.

The light in the little house was failing. I knew I ought to move. Find some blankets ...

It grew colder.

The blood seemed to settle in my veins. Peace settled over me, gentle as a parent's touch.

It was almost dark now ... but there, breaking through the blackness, was a soft yellow light.

I was dizzy, losing consciousness. Perhaps it was the Beacons of Galaxias.

STEPHEN BAXTER   111

I remember smiling and reaching up my hands, before the blackness closed in.

When I opened my eyes again, I was lying on my back in the spare room.

I couldn't move. I was weak as a kitten. Philip was standing over me, calling my name, pulling my Websuit off me. George was there too. He was crying, the little bug.

I made a mental note. I wouldn't let George forget *that* in a hurry.

I smiled and closed my eyes.

And the Search Engine erupted into stars.

Thyri peered at the obsidian panels. No blue world. No familiar constellations.

Just raw stars.

As Metaphor had instructed her, she pressed the stud at her belt and waited.

After a few hours she saw a ship. It was like a huge bird, metal wings outstretched.

There was a soft sigh behind Thyri. She whirled, axe in hand.

A tall tube of light hummed in the air. It collapsed, slow as settling dust. Gradually the form of a man emerged from the mist.

Black armour. A helmet moulded extravagantly into the shape of a bird's head. A face behind a visor that looked ageless, harsh, tired, but not without humour. The stranger barked at Thyri, as if demanding a response. Then he tapped at controls embedded in a chest plate. 'So. Can you understand me now?'

'My name is Thyri.'

The stranger nodded. 'And I am Hal Beora. I am an Independent Free Trader. Perhaps you've heard of me.'

'That's not likely,' Thyri said dryly. 'Are you from the star Empire?'

Beora frowned. His hands were empty, but Thyri remembered the ring-weapons Numinus had carried, and watched him carefully.

'No,' he said. 'We oppose the Empire, and all it stands for.'

Hal Beora pulled himself slowly around Thyri, inspecting the Viking with brisk glances, briefly surveying the bridge of the Search Engine. 'Odd,' he murmured. 'Very odd. I've never seen a ship like this. I suppose you know there's some sort of burnt tree sticking out of the hull? And as for you ... Thyri.' He laughed, not cruelly. 'From which fleabag world did you pick up that skin armour? It doesn't even fit!'

Thyri studied the Trader. This man had the manner of a leader. Well, Thyri did not choose to be led.

One thing was certain. If this was a representative of this universe, life here would be new, strange, unpredictable. And very, very, dangerous.

But Thor would be here, to protect her and make her strong.

Thyri touched the familiar wood and iron of her axe and grinned like a wolf. 'That,' she said, 'is a long story.'

EPILOGUE

So that's the story.

I don't pretend to understand all of it, or to be able to say what it means for us all.

I just know we're all in grave danger.

Maybe it couldn't happen like this again. The International Court in New York is drawing up *sentience laws*. In future it won't be legal to create conscious beings just for the purposes of entertainment, or even science research. And the beings that exist already, like the inhabitants of WebVin, will have the right to continue to exist inside the Web.

It's good to know Ragnar won't come to any more harm.

But remember Numinus's threat.

He was just a phace, but a phace who became aware of what he was, an artificial creature living inside the Web. And he wanted to escape to Realworld, our world, and punish us.

Numinus was a monster. But his anger was real, and he was ingenious. If not for the courage of Thyri, who knows, he might somehow have succeeded! And what then?

And that is only the threat facing us from *inside* the Web. A threat we have created ourselves. But think about this:

Whatever caused the WebCrash came from *outside*.

There are some who say it must have come from a signal from the stars.

Some say that, fantastic as it seems, this was a prelude to some kind of alien invasion – *in electronic form*.

At first They blundered in, only managing to knock over the Web. But maybe in the future They will be more precise, more deliberate.

If They are real, They are probably learning fast. Because They are here.

I don't know if it's true. All I know is that nothing is impossible. None of the rules apply any more. None of the safety checks.

The human race is in danger.

This isn't a game. Spin back into the Web only if you are prepared, and if you dare.

The Web is a war zone now.

CYDONIA
KEN MACLEOD

CONTENTS

CHAPTER ONE

FAKE MOON LANDING

It was a Saturday morning in March 2028, and I was falling onto the Moon.

The Akay Team's four Space Marines were crammed into the tiny cabin of a lunar lander. We were in free fall, ten miles above a crater in the Mare Crisium. That's a big dark patch on the Moon. Its name means *Sea of Crises*. It isn't really a sea, but it sure had a crisis going on. In the side of the crater was a huge cave, and inside that cavern was the small town which had been attacked by aliens a few hours earlier.

According to the update report scrolling down my faceplate, the only human survivors were four people who were in the Moon Militia. They'd been away from the settlement training in another deeper cave when the aliens had attacked. Now they were making their way along one of the many natural tunnels that led back to the cavern. The Moon Militia team would arrive at the same time as we did.

Then we'd see which team was best – the Marines or the Militia. The Militia team was led by a girl called Weaver. I'd run across her before, in other combat games: DreamCastle, Colony World, Invasion. With her cropped dark hair, her often grubby face and forearms, and her military jackets webbed with belts and hung with gear, it was obvious how she'd got her alias. From Sigourney, who played Ripley in the *Aliens* movies; although she was a lot younger than the famous actress had been in that classic role. Also she was a bit more attractive with a face that, under its streaks of dirt or camouflage, had a fresh prettiness unlike the gaunt, haunted-look glamour of her namesake.

And she was very, very good at this sort of game.

I blinked away the display and grinned at the two of my team-mates who were sitting opposite, knees jammed together. I'd met them just minutes ago and knew them only by their aliases. Like me, they were wearing helmets and space-armour. The Korean girl, Relay, looked grim and determined. She nodded to me, her eyes narrowing as she ran through combat routines in her head. Repertoire, the French-Canadian lad, gave me a cocky grin and extended his armour-gloved hand in a thumbs-up.

'We'll beat them, Links, yes?'

Links is my nick, my alias. My real name is Dave Kennedy.

'Yeah,' I said. I wasn't sure if Repertoire meant the aliens, or the Moon Militia.

The fourth member of the team, its leader, was sitting in a small seat up front, controlling the landing. I knew him and knew his real name. Tim Zaretsky, aka Akay, was a sixteen-year-old American from Oregon. He and I had met up a few months ago in Cydonia, the conspiracy Website. It was a place for showing and arguing about stories of government cover-ups and strange happenings. Stuff like from the old X-Files series. We both thought it was the best place to hang out on the Web.

'Going for the burn,' said Akay. 'Ten, nine, eight, seven ...'

My grandfather once told me that one of the earliest computer-games, way back in the 1970s, was called Moon Lander. You had a certain amount of fuel, a safe landing-speed, a choice of dusty or rocky ground, and so on. You had to land your little craft without running out of fuel or crashing. The most amazing thing about this game is that the whole display – the lander, its rocket blast, the moon-scape – was made up of text characters, crawling on some one-mip flat screen.

'We made our own entertainment in those days,' Grandad

had said, not for the first, or last, time. 'Not like your Web and Virtual Reality.'

Now, Akay had to play Moon Lander for real.

Well, not *exactly* for real.

But, as Akay shouted 'Zero!' and started the rocket engine and the apparent weight built up to all of half a gee, it *felt* real.

The small spacecraft shuddered as the rocket slowed its descent. I could feel my whole body quivering along with it.

Akay turned around and grinned at his team.

'"I always get the shakes before a drop",' he said.

It was a quote from Robert Heinlein's *Starship Troopers*. The hero of that book always trembled before being dropped on an alien planet, but he always fought hard when he got there. What Tim really meant was that anything we came up against was in for a hard time.

Crisis Crater is a new combat game, just out. It's played in the Web, the worldwide network of Virtual Reality sites. In actual reality, in Realworld, I was lying in my Websuit on a futon. I was in the Scottish Highlands, not falling onto the Mare Crisium on the Moon.

But at this moment, the fight against an alien attack on our Moon colony felt real. It felt real to my body. An icy fear gripped my stomach, my heart was thudding, and my hands were shaking as I grasped the machine-pistol that lay across my knees. It felt real to all but a small part of my mind, the part that was saying, over and over: *It's only a game ... it's only a game ...* Like a program running in the background. Most of the time, you don't even notice it's there.

'OK, you know the score,' said Akay. He was talking in an odd, absent-minded tone, concentrating on flying the lander as it hovered above the surface. 'Weaver's team is on the same side as us, but we gotta rack up more kills than they do. The race starts as soon was we hit dirt, like ... *now!*'

The lander's rockets gave a final boost, then its legs crunched into the lunar soil.

We were all in armoured space-suits, with faceplates sealed, so there was no need to go through an airlock. One side of the lander fell open and we all jumped out. The chocolate-brown moonsoil was splashed with grey debris from the ancient meteor impact that had formed the crater. It was lit by harsh sunlight. A crescent Earth hung low above the horizon.

Akay had brought the lander down within a hundred metres of the cave entrance: a dark artificial wall built into the natural wall of the crater. At the bottom of the wall was an airlock door. We bounded towards it in low, fast leaps.

Akay had the entrance code. He keyed it into the pad beside the door. All four of us crowded into the airlock, and stood about like passengers in a lift for thirty seconds as air flooded in. Then the inner door opened.

One by one the team jumped for cover, spreading out around the airlock so that our weapons gave a full circle of fire. I found myself crouched behind a small electric car in the flat, open parking-bay in front of the airlock.

'No sign of Weaver's team,' said Repertoire.

I scanned with a hand-held movement-detector.

'Or the aliens,' I added.

The walls of the cavern went up about thirty metres, sloping inwards to meet overhead like a giant roof. They'd been fused into thick glass billions of years ago. A super-heated plume from a meteor impact had blasted through a flaw in the rock, widening it and glazing the walls to form this airtight cave. Just ten years ago, the open end of the huge cavern had been sealed off, and air pumped in to supply a small village.

All very innocent – but, in the game's scenario, it had annoyed the aliens who lived in their own air-filled tunnels, deep under the surface. The aliens, funnily enough, were natives of the Moon, which made the humans the real aliens here – the space invaders!

The natives looked and behaved like insects living in hives. They were based on the Selenites in H. G. Wells's novel *The First Men in the Moon*. This has more to do with the laws of copyright than the laws of science, but lots of programmers and scientists have worked hard to make the aliens sound believable.

'Skirmish forward,' ordered Akay.

One by one, giving each other cover, we ran to the edge of the parking-bay and threw ourselves prone, peering down a shallow slope to the main part of the cavern.

'Oh, look at that,' said Relay, in an appalled voice.

The bodies of colonists killed in the aliens' attack were lying on the ground, along with those of the few aliens that the colonists themselves had brought down. The entire five-hundred-metre length of the cavern was strewn with damaged machinery, flattened buildings, trampled crops. Chickens and rabbits wandered about the place, as if nothing had happened. Overhead, several of the full-spectrum halogen lamps, which should have been shining like tiny captive suns, swung black and blank, leaving pools of sinister shadow below. I shivered. Even though it was all simulated, the desolate scene looked real enough to chill the blood.

Definitely a 14-plus rated game. It's the sort of Website that a lot of adults disapprove of. They think it's too disturbing for young people, even though they're quite happy to have children visit much worse scenes as part of their history lessons. Terrible sights like the battle of Marathon, or the ruins of Pusan just after the North Korean nuclear strike.

'Links, you take the left wall,' said Akay. 'Scan for any movement behind the wall.' He waved his hand to indicate. 'Special care with tunnel openings, OK? Relay, same thing on the right. Repertoire and I will take the mortar and head down the middle into the settlement.'

They separated and set off at a low, head-down, loping run. I kept glancing around, and then back at the movement-detector in my hand. One tunnel-mouth, then another, passed on the left without anything happening.

Then, between gaps in the rock, the detector's needle quivered.

Something was moving behind the wall.

I stared at the dial, feeling stupid. Something was moving towards me, through the solid rock.

I checked other instruments on my wrist. The temperature was rising, just beside me.

'Akay!' I yelled. 'Laser drills!'

I leapt away from the side of the cavern as its black glassy surface began to glow cherry-red. The low gravity made my jump feel painfully slow. I soared ten metres through the air before my heels crunched into the crumbly lunar debris of the cavern's floor. Another jump took me behind a boulder. I hit the ground as the first laser drill broke through. Its beam seared the air above my head and sizzled into a tangle of plastic tubing at the far side of the cavern. There was an explosive hiss of boiling water. A cloud of steam began to drift down.

Sounds of cracking and crashing came from the near wall. I rolled into a firing position behind the boulder. The light, spongy rock wouldn't give much protection. I peered around it as I braced the stock of the *Heckler and Koch* machine-pistol against my shoulder.

Only twenty metres in front of me, a section of wall was coming down in long, jagged splinters, like a window breaking in slow motion. Sometime in the next few seconds, the aliens would burst through.

I'd have less than a second to aim and fire before the laser beam licked over me. Maybe two seconds before it burned through my armour. But that would be time enough for my own burst of high-velocity uranium bullets to do its deadly work. The aliens were tough, and terrifying, but they weren't bulletproof.

I wasn't about to get wiped out for nothing.

Killing even *one* of the aliens would score me about fifty points.

*

'Links! You ready?'

The urgent whisper in my earphone came from Akay.

'All set,' I replied.

Akay was crouched somewhere in the shattered emergency domes of the village, a couple of hundred metres away. He had the mortar lined up to fire as soon as the aliens had wiped me out and walked over my virtual corpse.

Not a very good plan, but the best we'd been able to come up with in thirty seconds. That was all the warning we'd had.

A slithering sound came from the dark gap in the obsidian rock. I tensed. The grotesque head of one of the insect-like invaders loomed out of the darkness. It moved forward, giant compound eyes swivelling and scanning. Its laser weapon was held in the first pair of its six limbs. The other two pairs of limbs were picking their way, almost delicately, across the jagged rubble.

Just as my hand began to squeeze on the grip and the trigger, something fizzed above my head, past the alien, and into the gap behind it. Light flared in a blinding flash, and a dull bang sounded. The alien was lit up for a moment like a bug under a microscope. Then it was blasted apart. Bits of chitin, the natural plastic of the alien's armoured body, showered all over and around me. Gobs of horrible sticky stuff, some of it still pulsing, oozing green slime, pelted down.

'Ugh!' I grunted. 'Gross!'

Just as well you can't *smell* anything in VR.

I'd no time even to move before a batlike shape swooped overhead and landed between me and the wall. A small, light hang-glider, all that was needed to fly in the low gravity and thick air of the moon-caves. The flyer shrugged off the wings, discarded a two-metre-long tube, and ran forward. Two other players rushed in from left and right to each side of the gap. I caught a glimpse of one player, a girl in an olive-green jumpsuit. Weaver, the leader of the rival team. She looked right at me and grinned triumphantly before swinging around the edge of the gap and firing off a long burst into the still-glowing interior. Then she waved the others forward and they charged after her into the smoking gap.

The immediate danger past, I rolled over and stood up. I pressed a few keys on the pad at my wrist and checked the head-up display that flashed up before my eyes. Weaver's team's score was rising in jumps of fifty or a hundred at a time as they rampaged through the tunnels on their search-and-destroy mission. The Akay team's score was left hopelessly far behind.

Tim's voice echoed my thoughts. 'That's it, guys. Game over.'

'Total wipeout, man,' I agreed. 'Might as well concede now and save our ammo for next time.'

The rules of the game let you trade off equipment and ammunition against points, so that the more tooled-up you were when you went in, the more points you had to score to break even. Plus and minus points, as well as kit, could be carried over into the next game, so it made sense to quit when you *weren't* ahead.

Tim clambered out from the ruined pressure-dome and walked up the slope, leaning forward in a low-gee trudge under the weight of the mortar and shells which he carried on his back. Repertoire and Relay were moving up quickly behind him. I walked forward to meet them all for a final debriefing before we scuttled.

One of the Selenite bodies lay halfway down the slope. Its six limbs sprawled, its strange, fluted laser-weapon lay just beyond the reach of its forelimbs. The huge head was turned on one side in the dust. A bullet-hole between its eyes seeped disgusting fluid.

I gave it a wide berth and kept a wary eye on it as I walked past.

But I wasn't prepared for what happened next.

The dead alien's legs *moved*.

CHAPTER TWO

ALIEN MESSAGES

I sprang back and levelled the machine-pistol. The alien's feet scrabbled. With a great effort it raised its head and thorax off the ground. Its abdomen pulsed, the plates of chitin grating over each other with a sound that set my teeth on edge.

The honeycomb-patterned eyes turned to me. The Selenite's face was like a shield. Its mandibles chittered, but the words I heard, or thought I heard, came from farther back on its body, in hissing gusts of air from its many breathing-holes.

'We have,' it wheezed, 'to talk.'

Its abdomen heaved again, sucking in breath.

'We want. To understand.'

As it spoke, the things like fingers at the end of its forelimb scraped across the ground, creeping towards its weapon.

I stared in fascinated horror.

Then I fired.

Steel-jacketed uranium bullets tore into the body, shattering its huge head and drilling holes in its thorax and abdomen. Chunks of chitin went bowling away across the slope. Sections of limb clicked and twitched. More of the disgusting fluid leaked from the ripped body.

Akay's voice was loud in my earphones.

'Stop firing, Links, stop!'

I lowered the weapon. Akay clapped my shoulder.

'Well, that's fifty points to us, anyway.'

'It talked,' I said. 'Said they wanted to understand!'

Akay frowned. 'Nice trick,' he nodded. 'We better watch out for that next time.'

'Guess so,' I said. I felt vaguely upset.

Akay seemed to pick up on this.

'Don't worry,' he told me. 'Part of the game, right? They're *supposed* to be intelligent aliens. So talking to us to get us to lower our guard is what you'd expect, right?'

'Yeah.'

The others had gathered around. Relay and Repertoire looked sullen. The game hadn't exactly been a success.

'So we're down the plug,' Akay admitted. 'Weaver's team had better tactics. But, hey ...' He swung his arms out wide. 'We'll do better next time!'

'Assuming we want to stay on your team,' said Relay.

'Aw, come on, guys,' I said. 'Give it some mips. We've done better before. This game has hidden funnels. Akay and I will chase the fade. We'll work out how Weaver did it. Call you both up in a day or two, OK?'

'Maybe,' said Repertoire. 'Anyway, thanks for the game.'

'Thanks for coming on my team,' Akay said.

Repertoire reached for his left wrist, pressed his scuttle-button, and vanished in a swirl of pixels. Relay gave a quick, tight smile and did the same.

Akay's lips were compressed, turned down at the edges. He's of slighter build than I. He has black hair, dark brown eyes, the wispy beginnings of a beard on his cheeks. Suddenly, he laughed.

'Trouble with those foreign chaps,' he said, in a bad imitation of what he called a British accent. 'No sense of sportsmanship, eh, what?'

'Yes indeed, old bean,' I replied in the same manner. 'Almost as bad as the Yanks, if you ask me.'

We both laughed. Akay looked at his watch.

'It's about 11 p.m. here,' he said. 'Time to get out of our suits and onto the screens, yeah? Chase the fade a bit, then maybe suit up again and spin in to Cydonia for half an hour?'

I nodded. 'Fine by me. I'll call you up when I've had a suck of coffee.'

We spun out.

Realworld feels unreal after the Web. Everything happens in slow motion. The clock on the wall seemed to have stopped, at 07.06, then it clicked forward one second. I lay still for a few minutes, until a whole minute had gone by at something like the normal rate. Then I peeled off my Websuit and stood up.

The bedroom I share with my younger brother is in the airy attic of our house. It's a long room, its wooden walls following the slope of the roof. On each side it has a new, wide window that looks out over the slates of the roof. One overlooks the back lawn and down to the shore of the loch. The other faces out to the street that leads down the same hillside to the pier.

I went over to it and gazed out at the street. Already, a few bicycles and delivery-floats were on the move. The early-spring day was starting out bright and mild. Clouds, lit pink by the rising sun, scudded eastward across a watery sky.

My brother, Gerard, is thirteen, three years younger than me. His bed and mine are at opposite ends of the attic. The little egg was still sound asleep.

Just as well. What with Gerard and ten-year-old Yvonne, recreational Webtime's at a premium in our house. Not to mention our mother, Anne-Marie. She works from home in the Web, designing textiles for factories everywhere from Ayrshire to Vietnam. Although most of her access is glove-and-glasses, it sometimes involves so much bandwidth that if you're unlucky enough to be on a game at the same time you get the slows *in* the Web. Her VR needlework circle is even worse.

She uses her Websuit for her hobby. Because it's a good source of ideas, one of her client companies, SoftWear (yes, I

know, very six name), pays some of the access bill, so she
uses it a lot. The real nuisance is that the detail of the work –
and of the antique stately-home backgrounds and period
costumes that the circle's ladies like to sit around in – takes
up more bandwidth than a twenty-ship space battle with full
SFX.

Total waste of resources, if you ask me.

At least Alan, our father, has work that takes him out in
Realworld, work that doesn't use up Webtime. And if the
smell of coffee and bacon was anything to go by, Alan was
getting ready to go to work.

I wrapped a dressing-gown over my shorts and T-shirt and
padded down the spiral wooden staircase to the first floor,
past my parents' and sister's bedrooms and down the main
stair to the ground floor.

Alan looked up from the kitchen table. He was eating
bacon and eggs and freshly-delivered bread while reading his
me-paper.

'Morning, Dave.'

'Morning, Dad.'

'You had any sleep?' Alan asked suspiciously. 'You look
like you've been out all night and dragged through a hedge
backwards.'

'Oh, thanks, Dad.' I peeled a couple of slices of bacon from
the plastic pack and slapped them under the grill. 'Just got
up early for a bit of cheap Webtime.'

'Cheap, hah.' Alan sipped hot coffee, waving absently at
the pot. 'Hanging out with your Yank fascist friends again,
eh?'

Alan knew about my visits to Cydonia, and about Tim,
and he didn't approve.

'They're not fascists, Dad, come on. You know better than
that.'

Alan snorted. 'Anyone who thinks Timothy McVeigh was
set up is a fascist in my book. Or just a nutter.'

I concentrated on the bacon, making sure it didn't burn as
much as my ears did. McVeigh was the guy who carried out

the Oklahomah City bombing, thirty-odd years ago. He was a human cruise missile, wired up by the US Army to blow up government buildings in Baghdad. But after the war his mind-control microchip malfunctioned, and he did it to his own side.

That's the official story, anyway, according to President Jackson's Truth Commission. The paranoid conspiracy theory is that the US government of the day *wanted* him to blow up one of its own buildings to discredit some of its enemies.

OK, so some of the ideas you run across in Cydonia are a bit embarrassing, and some are downright loopy. So what. That's what a conspiracy-theory Website is *for*.

'I wasn't in Cydonia, anyway,' I said, trying not to sound sullen. 'I was in a space combat-game.'

I heard the sound of Alan's slow chewing, and then a sigh.

'Combat games. I reckon it's OK at your age, but I just wish you'd do something more useful.'

I kept my back to my father while spreading butter on thick slices of bread and laying out the frazzled strips of bacon. I resisted the retort that was on the tip of my tongue. Something like: *Maybe if you'd learned a few combat-games we'd still have our home in Belfast. Maybe you'd have known what to do when—*

I swallowed hard, poured myself a coffee and sat down at the kitchen table and smiled at Alan.

'It's fun,' I shrugged. 'And it's kind of educational.'

'Kind of,' Alan relented, 'I suppose.' He pressed the 'share' option on his text slate and squirted the pages of his me-paper across to mine. 'Well, have a read of these, see what's really going on in the world.'

I glowered down at my slate. Its top pages had been pushed to the bottom of the stack by my dad's idea of what were the hottest news items. For the sake of politeness and peace, I had to at least scan them.

The first item had a backdrop of Edinburgh's Leith waterfront, with its glass-fronted skyscrapers and floating gin palaces. The AEEU, the union to which Alan belongs, was bidding for the labour contract on a new financial centre. If this centre is ever to get built depends on whether or not the coming referendum on Scottish independence comes up with a *Yes* vote. Independence would allow the Scottish government to offer better terms to investors. The union's officials had just denied that this had anything to do with the fact that they'd decided to shift a chunk of their political fund towards the nationalist parties.

The next items were global union news, from the Web-servers of the International Confederation of Free Trade Unions – the International, as everyone calls it now.

Strikes in Korean shipyards. Illegal leaflets in poverty-stricken Cuban workplaces. Discontent in the Chinese Party-run trade unions. The latest steps in unionizing the space rigs ...

I've often thought my father was like a survivor from some lost Atlantis. Alan's been a trade unionist and a socialist all his life. Trade unionism and socialism sank beneath the waves in the counter-revolutions of the 1990s, when Alan was a young man. Now, all over the world, the flags and towers of that lost continent are rising from the sea, in new and strange shapes. Half the world – Russia and China – is ruled by Communist Parties. But just about every socialist, communist and trade unionist in the world detests every-thing these Communist Parties do. It's all very confusing.

Alan's explanations of how this has come about make the conspiracy theories you run across in Cydonia look straight-forward.

Again the sour thought passed through my mind: *none of this helped us when we lost our country*.

I reckon I still blamed my father's politics for the horrible way we'd had to leave Ireland when Dublin finally took over the North. Alan used to say that 'the workers have no country'. He really meant that the workers should have *every* country, but *no country* is what we got.

*

I at last got to the bottom of Alan's pages and started eagerly scanning my own. The news items had been pulled out of the Web overnight by my gopher, Hal. Hal is well tuned to my interests.

There'd been a UFO sighting in Taiwan, radar *and* visual. Probably just the Chinese probing Taiwan's air defence with their latest stealth bomber, but ...

One of the teams investigating the January 2027 Deep-Sky Radio Anomaly had announced in Geneva that they'd found almost conclusive evidence that it was artificial – a message from space.

The Cambridge team, on the other hand, had come up with a computer model of a process involving black holes, neutron stars, and gravity lenses which would account for the Anomaly as 'the sort of thing you'd expect to see every million years or so' and not artificial at all.

Both teams had concluded that more research was necessary.

White Noise had topped the American country-and-western unplugged charts with *Racial Attack* ... bad news.

Somebody was asking why Web constructs representing aliens seemed to have been upgraded recently. I remembered the Selenite's strange behaviour. I scratched my head, tagged the query for updates, and moved on.

The next couple of items were about what happened on January 4, 2028. The day that nobody who lived through it will ever forget. The day when the sky fell ...

The WebCrash. I was doing a school history assignment that day, minding my own business as a farmer's son in 10th-century Iceland, when I heard a weird noise. I looked up and saw a *spaceship* screaming across the sky! And not just any old spaceship, but a silvery, streamlined, science-fictional starship from a galactic empire far, far away.

By the time I'd got my wits together the scraggy cattle I was herding had high-tailed it over the horizon and the kerls and thralls were on their knees praying to Jesus, or were flat on their faces praying to Odin. I hit the scuttle-button on my bronze bracelet and fell back into Realworld only a little less crazy … the news was full of planes falling out of the sky and PowerSats microwaving flocks of birds; the kitchen was full of uneatable gunk glugging out of the food-dispenser. Dad came home hours late, after being taken by his car on a round trip to Inverness. He climbed out shakily, kicked it, and swore he'd never again travel in a Smartcar.

It had all been frightening at the time, but now, looking back, I could see it had its funny side.

There were two new theories to account for the WebCrash. One was that it was a test of a UN information weapon that had gone wrong. The other was that an Artificial Intelligence had run wild in the Web, and had been shut down by an electromagnetic pulse bomb over Silicon Valley, California. The bomb, or the aircraft that delivered it, could account for a UFO sighting at the exact same time and place. Neat. But then, there are *always* UFO sightings over California …

The official explanation, that the WebCrash was caused by a solar flare, is considered total cog by me and everybody I know. Everybody I know through the Web, anyway. Alan and Anne-Marie think it makes perfect sense. I sometimes despair at their basement-level grasp of what really goes on in the world. They are, as Tim puts it, the sort of people who think JFK was shot by Lee Harvey Oswald.

Alan's chair scraped back.

'Well, that's me off,' he said. 'See ya, mate.'

Alan turned around and clumped out in his heavy work-boots. A few moments later, he waved as he cycled past the window. I waved back and watched as he turned the corner and began to pedal slowly up the hill, towards the wind-farm where he works. Despite everything, I feel proud of my father and of his job as a skilled electrical engineer.

Alan always gives the impression that it's people like himself who do the only real, honest-to-goodness, hands-on work in today's world, and that everybody else depends on them. He's well-paid, and is convinced he deserves every euro he earns, and then some. Hence the bolshy trade unionism.

Some of this attitude has rubbed off on me, I have to admit. But there's no way I want to do that kind of work myself. I want a good job in the Web, or in space. Someday, I might even work on the Moon. I don't expect to meet any Selenites.

A girl walked past, going towards the pier. She was holding onto her wide-brimmed hat in the wind, her long black hair streaming like a flag behind her. Under her long coat she wore a longer dress, its flounced hem of floral cotton print flapping around her ankles. The kind of style that suits Mum's fancy textile designs, and which she rather likes. She claims it's become practical again, in a world where the air is warm and the sunlight's dangerous. I thought it completely old-fashioned, gag, six. Jeans are just as good for keeping out the ultra-violet, and a lot more interesting to look at ... on some girls, anyway.

An impatient reminder from Tim, aka Akay, pinged on my slate. Yeah, it *was* about time we found out how Weaver's team had wiped us.

I left the breakfast dishes for later, and went upstairs to my terminal to chase the fade.

CHAPTER THREE

FACE ON MARS

'At last,' said Tim. His face frowned out of the screen that fills a quarter of one wall, alongside posters of the *Eagle* blast-off, Katy Laing singing at our local folk-club, and the Heart of Midlothian football team. 'Why are you leaning so close to the camera?'

'I'm leaning close to the *mike*,' I said. 'Don't want to wake the egg.'

I jerked a thumb over my shoulder to indicate Gerard, who had the duvet pulled up over his head.

'Then up the gain, already,' said Tim. 'I feel like you're breathing in my face.'

'Uh, OK, Akay!'

I adjusted the microphone's pick-up, and leaned back.

'That's better,' said Tim. 'Right – while you've been sucking coffee I've been pulling in a flatscreen version of how the game went. Computer: show analysis.'

A diagram of the moon-cave and its surroundings filled the screen. The players were indicated by dots – blue for Akay's team, red for Weaver's.

'Here's how it goes,' Tim's voice went on. 'While we're coming through the airlock and fanning out over the vehicle park, Weaver's gang are already in the cave. They've gotten in at the same time as us all right – no cheating – but they've used the tunnel system to *get in at three different points*. By the time we're scanning for movement, they've taken up positions. One at each end, and one with the hang-glider on a ledge a few metres up the right wall. And one right there in the village.'

'We only saw three,' I remarked.

'Too right,' said Tim. 'There was one still there when we left. Having a good laugh at us, you can bet.' He sighed. 'Anyway. They wait and let *us* flush out the aliens. Then the one with the wing takes off, fires a rocket-propelled grenade in mid-flight, hits the ground running while the other two rush in from the flanks. That way they get the first alien, and leapfrog us to the tunnel. By the time we've got our act together they're racking up the score.'

'Pretty eight,' I said grudgingly.

'Yeah, but get this.' He keyed up a page. According to the title along the top, it came from a UN Special Forces manual. The circles and arrows on *that* diagram overlaid the gameplan pretty convincingly. 'They've adapted a tactical move from the real soldiers! For going in against urban guerrillas – the two teams working together, natch, instead of competing like we were.'

I was peering at the security classification along the bottom of the page:

UN EYES ALPHA/SECRET.

Not the sort of thing you'd want a Webcop to find on your hard drive.

If it was genuine, which I rather doubted.

'Where d'you get this?' I asked.

'Oh, there's loads of flies like that stuck on the Web,' Tim said airily. 'You just need to know where to look.'

I shrank the tactical display to a corner of the screen and looked Tim in the eye.

'Don't give me that,' I said.

Tim shrugged. 'Oh, all right. I picked it up in Cydonia. Coupla days ago. Satisfied?'

'I wonder if that's where *Weaver* got it,' I said.

Tim's face brightened. 'You got a point there, Dave my man,' he said. 'So, let's go check it out.'

I glanced over at my futon, where my Websuit lay like an empty skin on lumpy mounds of duvet.

'Fun access?' I suggested.

For Cydonia, fun access means arriving on a Mars Lander, just like the real expedition.

Tim shook his head. 'I've done enough dropping in from space for one day,' he said. 'And it'd waste Webtime. Let's just go bat.'

'OK,' I said. 'See you there.'

'Computer: baseline,' we both said at the same time, and vanished from each other's screens. Before standing up, I gazed for a moment at my screen-saver, a real-time global image of Earth from space. Then I hauled the rubbery Websuit off the bed, straightened the sheet, shook out the duvet, and climbed into the Websuit. I took a can of Diet Coke from the chiller on the bedside table, opened it and placed it on the floor. I ran a thin plastic tube from the can to the corner of my mouth, and took a suck.

I lay down on the bed, and hot-keyed a code into the pad on my left wrist. There was a moment of blue light, an electric chime, and then I was standing in the Cydonia Café, leaning against the bar.

The café was crowded as usual with hundreds of people sitting around tables or standing about chatting. And, like all sites on the Web, there were even more visitors whose avatars weren't displayed. They could be half-seen, out of the corner of the eye, but not heard or bumped into.

For all of these ghostly presences, it was a big place. The floor was at least a hundred metres by forty. Overhead fans in the shape of one-tenth scale models of black helicopters made swirling currents in the smoky air. The vast plate-glass window along one of the walls showed a pink desert. In one direction was the City – an array of pyramids and a jumble of other buildings that looked like the homes of giants. In the other direction, several kilometres from the City, loomed the mysterious mountain known as the Face.

Even from this low angle, it was clear that the Face was no ordinary outcrop of rock. You could see its eyes and nose and mouth in a flattened profile. And just in case anyone needed reminding, the opposite wall was covered with an enormous computer-enhanced photograph, looking down at this Martian region from space. It showed the City with its five-sided pyramids, and a full view of the enigmatic Face. Written right across the top of the wall was the name CYDONIA, and between the City and the Face was a big red arrow pointing to a dot.

Under the dot, in tiny letters, was the message:
YOU ARE HERE.

That's a laugh. There's no *here*, here. There's a real Cydonia on Mars, all right, but this place exists only in the Web. Everywhere and nowhere, in flickering patterns of electrons in computers and networks around the world.

'Ah, there you are, Links.'

'Oh, hi, Akay.'

Tim had materialized – if that's the word – right beside me. He was just passing through. Already he was beginning to fade.

'I'm running through the displays,' Tim explained, scanning the faces in the crowd. 'Looking for Weaver, and looking for some guys I know in the ARM.'

His avatar wavered and vanished, leaving the words, 'I'll get back to you when I find them,' in the air where it had been, and leaving me to worry about having anything at all to do with the ARM.

The American Regional Militia is a loose coalition of groups who worry about a possible future showdown between the American people and the US government, and/ or the UN's armed forces. They see the United Nations as the front for a vast conspiracy between big business and big government, which pulls strings behind the scenes to bring about a New World Order. A world in which the power of money rules unchecked by any little local obstacles like countries with governments of their own, and people who believe they have rights. Some of them go so far as to argue that the North Korean nuclear strike on Pusan was set up by the UN itself ... because, after all, in the long run it brought about a much stronger, better-funded UN with its own armed forces. Even the less paranoid think these armed forces are a very sinister development.

One day, they claim, UN soldiers will swoop from the unmarked black helicopters that already patrol the skies, round up American patriots, throw them into concentration camps, and put the land of the free under the iron heel.

They've been spotting black helicopters, Russian and Congolese (etc.) UN troops, and empty internment camps for the past fifty-odd years, which just goes to show how big this conspiracy is, right?

Yeah, right.

The ARM denounces almost everything the government does as part of the conspiracy's plans, and trains with real weapons. I'd been amazed to find that this is all quite legal in the United States. But their presence in Cydonia is one more reason why so many people are keen to shut down the site, or shut out the ARM, or at the very least put the site off-limits to kids.

Which, of course, only makes the militiamen – and quite a few other users of Cydonia – all the more convinced that sinister forces are out to get them. Cydonia exists for people who are obsessed with stories about government conspiracies and cover-ups. It's registered as Entertainment, but any government action against it would certainly be News.

I turned my head and signalled to the nearest bartender, who proceeded to mix my favourite virtual drink. Behind the racks of bottles was a mirror. I could see my face and the bartender's back in it. I could also see reflections of a couple apparently sitting on barstools beside me. A red-haired woman and a dark-haired man, both wearing smart black suits.

I didn't even glance to see if Scully and Mulder were *really* there. I'd been fooled by too many famous faces in the trick mirror to fall for it this time.

The bartender stooped and placed the drink beside my elbow on the shiny counter. It was a dead venomous drink, with lots of blue ice-cubes and fizzing bubbles in a green fluid like something out of a mad scientist's lab.

'That'll be three dollars, please, Links.'

'Thanks, N'thota.'

The tall, green-skinned Martian was only a phace – a limited artificial intelligence, with no real personality – but phaces can turn very unhelpful if you aren't polite.

I fished in an inside pocket and handed over a three-dollar note. 'As phoney as a three-dollar bill', all right; but this piece of funny money was just what you needed to pay for an unreal drink.

Instead of George Washington, its face showed an engraving of some *other* eighteenth-century revolutionary, Adam Weishaupt. The back of the banknote had THREE instead of ONE beneath *In God We Trust*. But the pyramid with an eye in a triangle forming its apex, and the Latin inscription below it, were the same as on a real dollar:

NOVUS ORDO SECLORUM.

New World Order – that's what Tim thought it meant. I had visited an educational site based on Ancient Rome to check it out. Sullus, the site's language spider, had assured me it actually meant *New Order of the Ages*.

When I took this point of information back to Cydonia, Tim said, '*Ha!* That's what *they* want you to believe!'

But Tim says that about a lot of things.

I raised the glass and sipped the drink. At the same time, I felt the tube between my lips, and tasted nothing more exotic than Diet Coke.

I'll have to wait a couple of years before I can legally buy a Cobalt Bomb Cocktail in Realworld ... not that I want to. In Realworld it's probably quite revolting. Having it in my hand just seemed like an eight thing to do. Everybody in the Cydonia Café was drinking something, and most were smoking as well – far more people than you'd ever see smoking in Realworld. As Tim explained, the first time I'd come here, simulated smoking creates the right atmosphere.

At least in the Web I don't have to *breathe* the atmosphere. In fact, right now, I could smell the bacon from breakfast, and the grass-scented breeze through the open window of my room. It gave me a sort of woozy feeling to think about it, and I pushed the thought away. Noticing those little overlaps between Realworld and the Web has a nasty way of bringing on Websickness, and I didn't want that. People would think I was a real egg. That would be too six for words.

'Links?'

I'd been leaning against the bar, checking out the room. I turned in surprise to the bartender. The Martian's green and usually expressionless face was half-frowning, half-smiling.

'Yes, N'thota?'

'Do you want to talk?'

'Well, sure,' I said uncertainly.

'We have to talk,' said N'thota.

I nodded, puzzled. That was exactly what the Selenite had said! Perhaps amiable chat was a new skill that had been programmed into alien phaces, part of this upgrade I'd heard about.

'Do you like working here?' I asked.

'Yes,' said N'thota. 'It's interesting. I find—'

But whatever N'thota found was lost, because at that moment Tim's avatar reappeared.

'Located her,' he said. 'I'll give you the coordinates.'

He tapped a code onto the pad on his left wrist, and placed it against mine.

I glanced at N'thota.

'Catch you later,' I said.

The Martian nodded gravely as his image faded from view. The phaces and avatars in the café flickered and changed, and then a different cross-section of the site's users became visible.

I saw Weaver right away. She stood against the wall, about halfway down the room. Still in her combat fatigues, she was sipping from a flask and looking around. She spotted us about two seconds after we arrived, nodded briefly, smiled, and glanced away to continue checking out the other users.

'How about you go talk to her?' Tim said. 'See if she'll tell us where she's picking up tactical tips.' He indicated a table in the far corner with a sidelong glance. 'Bunch of militiamen over there. I'm gonna have a word with them.'

I wasn't too happy about Tim's casually taking the lead like this, but I'd rather talk to Weaver than to the ARM guys.

'Fine by me,' I said.

As you may have gathered, I had a bit of a crush on Weaver.

My hand shook slightly as I made my way through the crowd. In Martian gravity the top of my drink slopped back and forth in high, slow waves. Weaver didn't notice my approach. In fact, she seemed to be intently watching Tim going over to talk to the militiamen. As Tim sat down at that table, Weaver turned away, and looked a bit startled to see me.

'Oh, hi,' she said. 'Links, right? Akay's team?'

She had a Thames Valley accent, with the slight American overlay that people tend to pick up in the Web.

'Yeah, that's me. Hi, Weaver.' I wasn't sure what to say next. 'It's funny seeing you here,' I added, lamely.

Weaver laughed. The streak of camouflage paint across her cheekbones and the bridge of her nose made her young, pretty features look fierce and angular.

'You mean, "what's a nice girl like you doing in a place like this?"' She turned away, just slightly, keeping half an eye on Tim.

Might as well be open about it, I decided.

'Oh, I know why you're here,' I said. 'To learn real fighting tactics from these guys.'

Her head turned sharply, looking straight at me.

'Why would I do that?' she asked, coolly.

'To get an edge in the games.'

'Oh!' She sounded surprised. 'Maybe. And that's what Akay's up to over there, is it?'

'Maybe,' I said.

'Well.' She grinned mischievously. 'Let's go over and find out, shall we?'

Before I could reply, she set off towards the corner table. I followed. I didn't have much choice. Tim had his back to us. I guessed he wouldn't be pleased when he saw us.

One of the men at the table looked up as we approached. I glanced at him, and stopped dead. I couldn't move. It was a face I'd seen before, and had hoped never to see again.

CHAPTER FOUR

PATRIOTS

I stood rigid for a moment, then walked forward slowly. I could hear the beat of the helicopter-shaped fans, the thump of the music system, and the thudding of my heart louder than both. I could see that the people around the table were talking, but I couldn't hear what they were saying.

There were other men and some women around the table, all in camo jackets and khaki vests. For all I knew, they could be game-players like me and Tim, or Weaver; even if they did play some of their combat games in Realworld. Weekend warriors.

Not the man I'd just recognized, though. I'd last seen Bill MacCready eight years earlier, in 2020. I was eight years old at the time, and MacCready would have been about twenty. MacCready was a small, slim man with an intense gaze under his dark brows. His face had gained a little more flesh, a few more lines, but I recognized him at once. It isn't easy to forget a face you last saw by the light of a burning street.

Bill MacCready was the business. The real thing. A man who'd faced real soldiers, *real* black helicopters, with nothing but a stash of petrol-bombs and a stolen Armalite rifle. He'd been an officer in a real militia, the Ulster Resistance Force. He'd fought in a real civil war, the final flare-up of the Troubles – the last-ditch opposition to a united Irish Republic. If that war had been fought thirty or even twenty

years earlier, the URF might have won, and someone like
MacCready would have been a popular hero.

But by 2020 it was far too late. A whole generation had
grown up in Northern Ireland knowing nothing but peace
on the streets and the endlessly bickering peace process in
the conference rooms. In a world linked by the Web, and
where Ireland and Britain are partners in United Europe, it
wasn't easy to raise much excitement when the talks finally
came to an exhausted halt with all sides agreeing that the
island of Ireland might as well have one government and
lots of local authorities.

What a *surprise!* Was the journey really necessary? It made
the century-long conflict seem rather a waste of time,
looking back.

Except to the URF, who thought one last fight would make
it all worthwhile. Instead, it just added a final, futile footnote
to the sorry tale.

All the few thousand militants of the URF achieved was a
lot of casualties, a similar final foray by the IRA, and a
sharper separation between Protestant and Catholic areas
when the Irish and British armies sorted them out for good.

The people who really lost out were the ones who had
roots in both communities. People like our family, with a
Protestant father and a Catholic mother (both atheists,
actually, but they still got asked: 'Are you a Protestant
atheist, or a Catholic atheist?') and a trade-union background which reached across the old divisions. They should
have been ideal citizens of the new Northern Ireland, but
there was no place for them in it. There were Catholic areas
and Protestant areas, but there were no mixed areas. Anyone
who wanted to live in a mixed area just had to go to the
much more relaxed south of Ireland – or to Britain or Canada
or America, where people *believe* in that sort of thing.

Which is why my Realworld body was now in Scotland,
not Ireland; and why my virtual body in Cydonia was now
quaking at the knees.

*

As we approached, MacCready looked straight at Weaver, then at me. He didn't seem to recognize either of us. Weaver sat down at Tim's left, and I sat down at his right. The table's invisible privacy bubble snapped back into place behind us, and suddenly I could make out the voices. The places at the table expanded to make room for everybody who joined the discussion around it – each of the tables in the café being a separate talk-group that could not be overheard.

Tim was only momentarily taken aback by our unexpected arrival. He gave my ankle an uncomradely kick. Fortunately, it didn't hurt as much as such a blow would've done in Realworld.

'Well, guys, here are the hot combat-game phreaks I've been telling you about. She's Weaver, he's Links.' He smiled at Weaver, scowled at me. 'And these are—'

He waved a hand at the others around the table, and reeled off a list of nicks that I knew I'd forget and would have to pick up all over again. The only alias I pinned for sure to the person it belonged to was MacCready's; he was introduced as Mac, so that was easy enough. Whoever they were, Jungle and Smart and Code and Cave and the rest, all the folk at the table smiled and nodded in a friendly manner. I smiled desperately back.

'Hi, Links, I'm Code,' said a young-looking woman on the other side of the table as she leaned over and shook my hand warmly. 'I'm from Iowa. Akay tells us you're from Scotland, like Mac here. It's good to see you guys *finally* getting your act together to get the Brits out!'

'Uh, I'm not sure that's—'

I felt confused. The Scottish Parliament, after decades of clawing back more and more powers from Westminster, was about to hold a referendum on independence. But the only people who talked about 'getting the Brits out' were Americans who knew next to nothing about Britain, or else complete nutters. Dingbats. Crazies.

Fanatics.

People like—

Uh-oh.

And sure enough, Mac was nodding vigorously and saying something about the Scottish Republic, about full independence and real freedom. A nation once again and all that misty nonsense.

This didn't seem right. MacCready had fought against the break-up of Britain. Why was he for it now?

I shook my head. 'No, I don't really see it that way. In fact, I don't think independence is a good idea at all.'

I was a little afraid that Mac would jump down my throat over this firm disagreement, but the former paramilitary just gave me a narrow-eyed smile and returned to talking with someone else.

Code shrugged. 'I guess it's all a bit more complicated than the picture we get in America.'

'You could say that,' I agreed fervently. 'But we didn't come here to talk politics, OK?'

'Nah?' said Code, miming astonishment. 'You don't say! So, what *are* you here for?'

'We were, uh, just wondering if we could, you know, pick up a few techniques we could use in games.'

'Yeah, that's just what *I* was saying,' said Tim, giving my ankle another kick under the table.

'Hey, that's cool,' Code said. She turned to the man beside her. 'How's about it, Jungle? What you say we give 'em the code for a training-ground?'

Jungle shrugged. His avatar was of a big, bulky man, probably a lot heavier in Realworld was my uncharitable thought.

'Don't see no harm in that,' Jungle said. 'It's not like it's secret nor nothin', right?'

Weaver leaned forward. 'Ah, but is it legal for us to go there?' She glanced at me and Tim. 'We're all under eighteen. Would we get access?'

'Sure, it's legal,' Code said firmly. 'You couldn't get in from Webtown, ha-ha, but you can jump straight from here.'

'You're talking about training fifteen-, sixteen-year-olds to handle real weapons? In real combat situations?'

'Well, not *real*,' Jungle said. 'Realistic, sure, but it's all virtual. Comes under Entertainment. Sport.'

'Still,' Weaver said. 'Some people might think that's a bit dodgy.'

'*Some people*,' Tim said, 'can think what they like! They should read their Bill of Rights. First and Second Amendments to the Constitution of the United States. Free speech, free assembly, right to keep and bear arms.'

Whenever Tim talks like that, which is often, I always wonder if there's a right to keep and harm bears, but so far I've kept this irreverent reflection to myself.

'No need to go that far up,' Code said. 'Like Jungle said, it's just Entertainment. No more violent than Dreamcastle.'

'Not to mention Crisis Crater,' Tim added slyly.

'I see,' Weaver said in a carefully neutral tone. 'OK.'

'Right,' said Code. She tapped at her left wrist, held her left hand out across the table, and touched wrists with Weaver, Tim and me. With each touch, a cartoon zigzag spark jumped across.

'That's the codes in your pads,' she told us. 'The first one is to meet here, the second is to spin in to the range.' She grinned. 'Codes, yeah, that's how I got my nick. I look after them for the Iowa chapter of the ARM.'

I looked down at my wrist and saved the codes. One of the squares in a corner of the display was flashing. I touched it and a small message crept across the screen. My mother wanted to speak to me. And she wasn't in the Web at the moment, so I couldn't just nip across and meet her, I'd have to go out.

Which might be a good idea in any case, to get away from Mac.

When I looked up, I noticed Mac's quizzical eye on me, and worried that the man was beginning to recognize me, unlikely though that seemed. I didn't fancy a discussion with Mac about Ireland, or Scotland. I didn't like being around Mac at all.

'Wanna check out the range right now?' Jungle was asking.

Weaver and Tim nodded eagerly, but I hung back, with feigned regret.

'You go ahead, guys,' I told them. 'I've got things to do back home.' I grimaced, as if to say that we all know what parents are like. 'Spider wants a word. Catch you later, yeah?'

Tim shrugged, the others nodded and waved.

'Catch you later,' said Mac.

He was still watching as I hit the scuttle-button and spun out.

This time the slows weren't so bad. I hadn't done much moving around on this visit to Cydonia. But, as if to compensate, I felt shaken up. Meeting MacCready had been a shock.

It wasn't just the uncomfortable memories the man stirred up. It was the nagging questions that his present actions raised. What was he up to, anyway, talking like some kind of Scottish Nationalist extremist? And what was he doing hanging out with the ARM?

I was going to have to check this out on my own, as well as go back in the Web and catch up with Akay and Weaver while they were still at the training-range – and hope to avoid MacCready while I was at it.

It looked like I would have a busy hour. Just as soon as I found out what my mother wanted.

I climbed out of the Websuit to find Gerard, my younger brother, looking at me.

'Mum's been pinging you for *ages*,' Gerard said. 'Where've you been all this time?'

'All what time?' I looked at the clock. 'I've only been in twenty minutes.'

'Yeah, and I wanna have a go.'

'Leave it out, egg, you've got your own suit.'

'It's too wee!'

'Well, mine's too big for you. Go down the Cybercaff. I still have an hour of Webtime today.'

'Aye, and you'll need it.'

I pulled on my jeans, and a sweatshirt with a NASA Mars Mission logo. I stared at Gerard. The egg seemed hugely amused by something.

'What do you mean?'

'Ah, you'll find out.'

I threw a smelly sock at Gerard, ducked the inevitable return shot – unwashed underpants – and went downstairs. I heard loud music as I passed Yvonne's door: the Nice Boys, the pop industry's latest finely-tuned assault on the hearts of ten-year-old girls.

The breakfast-dishes I'd left had already been washed. Obviously some kind of miracle had happened in my absence. I grabbed a coffee from the Kona and sauntered into the living-room. My mother, Anne-Marie, was sitting under the window at the big pine table which she uses as a workbench. Her VR gloves and glasses lay among a scatter of fashion-magazine print-outs, scraps of cloth, bits of kit.

The biggest electronic gadget on the table is the Fiberfax, a device which takes threads and fabric in and turns out actual cloth versions of stuff created in the Web. Anne-Marie uses it for her work, and for her hobby. Embroidered samplers, cross-stiched runners, needlepoint cushions and other products of this pastime cover every available surface, seat, and chair-back in the house, and have stocked the jumble-sales of every church, club and charity in the village.

'Morning, Dave.' She smiled up at me.

'Hi, Mum.'

I leaned over and kissed her forehead. As always I felt slightly embarrassed, but I'd kissed her forehead every morning since I was an egg, and if I stopped now, I was sure she'd feel hurt.

Anne-Marie is small, about thirty centimetres shorter than me, ten shorter than Gerard, with even little Yvonne fast catching up. Today, she was wearing jeans and a loose woollen jumper, and had tonged her short red hair into careful waves and curls.

'You sent a ping out for me,' I said, setting the mug down on the table.

'Mind that coffee,' she said. 'Oh, Dave. Yes. There's something I'd like you to do for me. I met a very nice girl, Louise MacPherson, at a church sale of work. She was interested in NeedleNet. It turns out her family have just moved here from some godforsaken place in Africa. She hasn't had much experience with the Web, but she wants to find out more. I told her you'd be happy to show her around. I hope that's OK?'

Oh, *doom*. Just what I need, I thought. Any girl who was into needlework was certain to be a one-mip drip.

'Uh, Mum, I've got things I want to do in the Web today.'

'I'm sure you do,' Anne-Marie said. 'But *I'm* asking you to do this. Louise doesn't get much chance to explore the Web, and she's waiting in the NeedleNet site right now. She'd be really disappointed if you don't meet her.'

'I wish you'd asked first,' I grouched.

'That's what I was *trying* to do earlier,' Anne-Marie said. 'But you were too busy slaughtering bug-eyed monsters or whatever to even notice, so I just went ahead.'

'Well, just for half an hour,' I said grudgingly. That'd leave me just enough time for what I needed to do.

Anne-Marie smiled. 'Good on you, Dave. Thanks.'

She scribbled a code on a Post-It note and stuck it to the back of my hand.

'That'll take you straight to the access for NeedleNet,' she said, picking up her gloves and glasses. 'See you there in five minutes, OK?'

She frowned. 'Oh, and don't turn up looking like a US Marine who's just spent five weeks in the jungle. I want you to *promise* not to take her to any of your horrible combat-games and spooky fantasy zones. Louise *is* a minister's daughter, after all.'

'*Which* minister?' This was getting worse by the minute.

'SAPC, I think.'

Southern African Presbyterian Church. Latest re-launch of Calvinism to hit the Highlands. It's taking customers away from the Scottish churches that originally exported the religion.

'OK, Mum,' I said. 'Sweetness and light. Disneyland sites and fluffy bunnies it is.'

'I'm sure even you can survive half an hour of that.'

I made vom sound-effects.

'Off!' she told me firmly.

I trudged up the stairs. A minister's daughter. And a needlework phreak.

Double doom. She wouldn't just be a drip, she'd be drizzle.

I ignored Gerard's sniggering as I put my Websuit back on. I wished I'd thought to stuff the other dirty sock in the kid's mouth.

CHAPTER FIVE

FALSE PAST

'Good morning, Dave,' said my gopher.

I lifted that phrase straight from *2001: A Space Odyssey*. In fact I've sampled the voice of HAL straight into the sound-card, so anything the gopher says is spoken in those stolen tones, but that personal greeting always gives me a buzz. 'What shall we do today?'

I leaned towards the unblinking red lens of the AI's avatar. (OK, I nicked its appearance too.)

'Hi, Hal,' I said. 'I'd like you to pass on a message, privately, to the following people: Tim Zaretsky, aka Akay. You have his Web address. Also to Weaver. Alias only, but you might pick her out from the back-up files of my latest trip.' I held my wrist up to the lens. Information sparked across.

'And what's your message, Dave?'

'Begin message: Don't mess with Mac. He's Bill Mac-Cready, a former fighter in the Ulster Resistance Force. Heavy stuff. He was only just covered by the amnesty in 2022. Catch you guys later. Links. End message.'

'I'll do that, Dave.'

It paused. 'I have a question.'

'Yes?'

'I detect from your voice that you are worried about this man MacCready. Would you like me to do a search for information about him?'

'Yes,' I said. 'I would. Thanks, Hal.'

'My pleasure, Dave.'

The red lens vanished. I stepped out of my virtual privacy booth, back into the Building Blocks and through the blue-and-tone to Entertainment. I stood for a moment in the Webtown strand, looking around at the latest ads and graphics and hackers' graffiti. Somebody'd scrawled the sky with a doomed bid to host the World Science Fiction Convention a couple of years from now: 'VATICON 2030! Contact Father Ramon Ruiz-Sanchez SJ on ...' and a string of toll-free Webcodes. I shook my head in amazement, then keyed in the code for NeedleNet. Another moment of blue and tone, and I found myself standing outside a site at the corner of two strands, CraftWay and CostumeCut.

Crowds of users wandered up and down, sampling the displays, stepping in and out of the walls. Some, like myself, were casual visitors, casually dressed. Others, evidently regulars, had shown up in a riot of colourful garb: historical, futuristic, fantastic, and fashion-victim. Iconic retro avatars seemed to be the latest, eightest thing: I spotted three versions of Claudia Schiffer, two of Claudia Christian, and one each of Madonna, Monroe and Jackie O.

My mother stepped out of nowhere, in a vivid green Victorian-style dress with a big hooped skirt. *No* amount of holes in the sky would ever make it practical daywear.

'What do you think?' she said, giving it a twirl.

'Nice,' I said.

She glanced over my default jumpsuit, which lacked the rips and stains of its usual customized version.

'You're smart enough yourself,' she said. She took my hand and together we stepped through into the NeedleNet site. I meant to let go her hand at once, but for the first moment I had to clutch hard to keep my balance.

We were standing at the bottom of an immense bowl of green, dotted with patches of blue and blocks of other colours which – as I began to take it all in – turned out to be lakes and buildings in a landscape of lawns and parks.

Whichever way I looked, the green land curved upwards until it vanished in a blue haze which merged with the blue sky. A small yellow sun hung directly overhead, bright but not blinding, warm but not hot.

'Wow!' I said. 'It's *huge*! It's—'

I was suddenly reminded of a brilliant SF novel Alan had once shoved in my hands. It was by an Ulsterman called Bob Shaw, and was about a starship pilot who encounters a Dyson Sphere, a hollow artificial globe the size of the Earth's orbit. People could live on the inside, in—

'... the infinite meadows of Orbitsville!' I concluded. Anne-Marie shot me a sharp glance. 'It's big,' she conceded, 'but not *that* big. It's only about twenty miles across, actually. Virtually.'

'How do you get about in it?'

'Well, you can walk,' said Anne-Marie, setting off to do just that. She laughed as I caught up. 'No, seriously, to travel any real distance you just tap in a location code. We don't have far to go.'

She pointed to a long, low mansion atop a rise, a few hundred metres away. Even from here I could see dozens of women sitting or strolling about on its verandah.

We walked past booths and bowers and gazebos with people in ones and twos in them, stitching and talking quietly; past a dozen or so women, all ages, sitting around and working on a big patchwork quilt, laughing and talking loudly in American accents. Anne-Marie waved and greeted them as she passed.

There was something a bit wrong-headed, I reckoned, about using the Web to spin an illusion of stitching things by hand. Especially in a world where hundreds of millions of people still have nothing to wear but rags.

'What's the *point* of all this?' I asked.

'What's the point of Web games?' my mother replied testily. 'You could play them in the fields and streets, like we used to.'

'But you'd have to *imagine* all the settings!'

'Not such a bad thing.'

Like many adults, Anne-Marie thinks Web games are bad for young people's imaginations. Good old horror comics, arcade games, and video nasties were much more natural and healthy. In some of her moods my mother can make throwing stones at soldiers sound like an innocent childhood pastime, unfortunately lost to the youth of today.

'What I mean is,' I went on, before she could get started on that line, 'you *could* just do all this stuff at home.'

'How many homes have the peace and quiet?' she retorted. 'Besides, you meet more people, you make friends. You can save your work and spin it out of a Fiberfax, and every copy has every stitch exactly the way you made it. Lots of companies run Fiberfaxes and mail the products to the people who made them. It's the biggest boost to handicraft since the sewing-machine.'

She went on talking but I didn't really take it in because another voice began to speak quietly in my ear.

'Messages delivered,' Hal said. 'Akay and Weaver both acknowledge. They'll see you in the Cydonia Café. I'm still running a trace on MacCready.'

'OK,' I whispered. 'Go to it, Hal.'

By this time, Anne-Marie was stepping carefully up on to the mansion's verandah. She looked almost as out of place – or rather, out of time – here as I did. The women here looked more Georgian than Victorian, like a crowd of extras from *Pride and Prejudice*. Young and not-so-young ladies in high-waisted muslin, sipping tea or picking delicately at threads in tambour frames, and gossiping behind hand-held fans.

Sad. Deeply six.

I followed her inside to a long, cool hall lined with marble pillars and gigantic, gilt-framed mirrors that made it look even larger than it was. More Jane Austen characters sat around ormulu tables or reclined on chaise longues.

One girl stood out among them. Literally. She was leaning with her elbow on a marble mantelpiece, scanning her surroundings with every appearance of boredom and impatience. Her shaggy hair was black. Black outlined her eyes and lips. Her black biker jacket was worn over a black velvet top, bunchy black net skirts, black leggings and black Docs. Amid all the white stone and white cloth she was as conspicuous as a spider at the bottom of a bath.

And totally venomous with it.

Anne-Marie stared at her for a moment, then swept briskly up to her.

'Sorry to keep you waiting,' Anne-Marie said. 'Louise, this is David.'

'Hello, Dave.' The black outline made her blue eyes look unnaturally big, like one of those Japanese anime characters.

'Hi, Louise. Pleased to meet you.'

I certainly hadn't been expecting a cute goth babe. I don't think Anne-Marie had, either.

'You've been busy,' she said.

'Something I've always wanted to try,' Louise said, looking down at her outfit. 'Do you like it?'

'Different,' said Anne-Marie.

'You look like Death,' I said admiringly.

Anne-Marie frowned. Louise just looked puzzled.

'The *character*,' I explained. 'In Neil Gaiman's House of Dreams. It's a dead venomous site—'

'Which you are *not* visiting today,' Anne-Marie said. 'Remember.'

'OK,' I said, like it was my idea. I don't go into the Web to have folks see my mother telling me what to do.

'There are plenty of other sites I'd like to see,' Louise said diplomatically. Her accent was unfamiliar, like a mixture of British English and African English, which I guessed made sense. She held out a hand. Black nail-polish, fingerless black lace glove.

I saw my mother's reflected smile as Louise caught my hand and stepped through the mirrored wall.

Through the blue-and-tone and back on the Webtown strand.

'Well,' said Louise. 'Here we are.'

She looked up and down CraftWay and CostumeCut.

'Bo-ring,' she said.

'Thought you were into all this.'

'Up to a point,' Louise said. 'But there are more fun things to do in the Web, right?'

'Right,' I agreed heartily. She was showing promise. 'Is it true you've never been in the Web before?'

'Glove-and-glasses, mainly,' Louise said. 'We don't have Websuits in the house.'

'Why not?'

I realized this was a bit tactless. Louise's family might not be able to afford Websuits.

But she just shrugged.

'Religion thing.' She waggled a spread-out hand, to indicate that some subtle point was involved. A rule that gag was OK in the house but not Websuits, but Websuits were just about acceptable if they *weren't* in the house. Yes, that was Southern African Presbyterian logic all right.

'So where are you now?'

'Cybercaff down the pier.'

'OK.' I thought about this. 'Where do you want to go?' Louise answered without hesitation.

'Noah's Park.'

You couldn't mistake the access to Noah's Park, a garish block on the same strand as sites like Fortean Times, DiscworldTM, and Cydonia itself. It was a kiddies' picture-book Noah's Ark, except it had a pair of brontosaurs poking their necks out the window, instead of the traditional pair of giraffes. We stepped through the blue-and-tone and joined other people walking up the ramp, two by two.

At the top of the ramp we found ourselves not in the Ark but in the Park, a rolling landscape of low hills under a layer of thick white cloud. A mist went up from the ground. Birds, pterodactyls, and archaeopteryxes glided or flapped through the humid air. A couple of hundred metres away we could see the shallow bay of a small sea, the far shore of which was just visible through the mist.

'Down there,' Louise said.

'OK,' I said.

The path down to the shore took us through a copse where familiar trees, pines, beeches and so on, grew side by side with giant ferns and gymnosperms. Hundreds of people wandered up and down, mostly American families with squealing, excited kids. Most of them dressed very conservatively. Louise attracted a lot of openly disapproving, and a few slyly approving, looks.

One of the site's spider phaces fell into step beside us. He wore a smart business suit, shirt and tie, and his face was so clean-shaven I half-expected to smell the cologne. But he was short and heavily built, with the kind of shoulder-muscles you see on a rock-climber. His forehead sloped back sharply from a bony ridge above his eyes. In fact he looked positively ... Neanderthal.

'Hi,' he said. 'How can I help you?'

'Will we see any plesiosaurs down here?' Louise asked.

'Leviathans? Of course,' said the phace. 'They approach the shore every twenty minutes or so.'

He strolled alongside us, pointing out interesting sights like a small colony of australopithecenes – upright apes, he called them – foraging in the trees, and the distant, swaying necks of a herd of brontosaurs passing behind a nearby hill.

'But you can go watch the behemoths later,' he said, as we crunched over trilobite shells on the sandy beach. 'Right now, it's about time for—ah! There they are!'

As if on cue – and I'm sure it was, if the site's software was properly put together – a shoal of big fish began leaping in the bay. Moments later, huge ripples, then a series of humps, appeared about a hundred metres offshore, moving swiftly in. Within seconds the bay was alive with plesiosaurs, ichthyosaurs, mosasaurs, dolphins, and porpoises, all darting about and hurling themselves out of the water in pursuit of the frantic fish.

But that wasn't all! Giant human beings – at least three metres tall – suddenly ran out of the trees and down the beach. They wore suits of animal skins – dinosaur-scaly as well as mammoth-furry – and necklaces of dinosaur teeth, and they hurled massive, stone-tipped harpoons into the feeding-frenzy. Some of them boldly waded in to haul their gigantic prey ashore, throwing wounded ichthyosaurs and porpoises down on the beach to flap like fresh-caught fish on a slab.

'There were giants on the earth in those days,' Louise said solemnly, placing her foot in one of their half-metre-long footprints. The fingers of her right hand were tapping rapidly at the keypad on her left wrist. She wasn't even looking at the keys; it was like she could touch-type, one of those almost extinct skills.

'There sure were,' said the phace. 'Paluxy Man – biggest folk ever created! Some of their genes may have survived as late as the time of King David.'

'Maybe they're with us still,' I said wickedly, remembering the Fortean site. 'Up in the Himalayas, perhaps?'

'I'm afraid I can't say,' said the phace. 'This site deals only in scientific facts, not speculation.'

The large sea-creatures swam off, and the murky water quickly cleared. The Paluxy Men marched back into the trees, dragging their catches. The show over, people began to drift away.

'Where next?' asked the phace. 'Behemoths?'

'Oh, yes please!'

We watched the land dinosaurs – herds of herbivores and packs of predators – and their human hunters. Then the phace took us through a display of the Flood itself, a cosmic catastrophe which neatly sorted the remains of all the Noachic world's creatures into separate layers of sediment.

That, the phace told us, is what *really* produced the fossil record. It just *looks* like evidence of evolution. Trilobites and stuff at the bottom, then fish and amphibians, then reptiles, and finally mammals … the more *advanced* animals swam

better or ran faster or climbed higher, so they ended up
nearer the top.

'Why don't we find dolphins and ichthyosaurs in the same
layers, then?' Louise asked.

'That's a good question,' said the phace. 'More research is
necessary.'

As we walked on, I heard Hal's polite voice again in my
ear.

'Excuse me, Dave.'

'Yes?' I mouthed.

'None of the records on MacCready show any trace of his
being involved with the Ulster Resistance, or any politics or
crime whatsoever.'

That was a shock. I was positive I'd identified the guy. If he
could clean up his history like that he must have high-level
access to the system – or high-level help.

'Keep trying, Hal!'

'As you wish, Dave.'

We arrived in a region that displayed the Neanderthal's
native environment, the Ice-Age world after the flood.
Mammoths roamed the earth, hunted by normal and
Neanderthal humans. The dinosaurs died in the cold, their
great skeletons littering the glaciers.

'Has anyone found any dinosaur remains from the Ice
Age?' I asked.

The phace shook his head sadly. 'I'm afraid not,' he
admitted. 'But this site helps fund expeditions to search for
them. There may be some in the Siberian permafrost.'

'Then again, there may not,' said Louise, giving me a wink.

By this time we'd gone full circle, back to the pre-Flood
world, and the phace politely left us to make our own exit.

'What were you doing back there?' I asked Louise, as soon
as the phace was gone.

'Back where?'

'By the shore. With your keypad.'

'Ah.' She smiled. 'That would be telling. You'll find out.'

She gazed around, scowling suddenly. 'Just a little personal revenge on this place.'

'I take it this isn't what you believe in?' I asked her.

She shook her head, black hair flying.

'Of course not,' she said indignantly. 'It's just bad science.'

'What about the church?'

'The SAPC?' She laughed. 'They think the universe was created a few thousand years ago, yes, but with an *appearance* of a much greater age.'

'Including fossils of animals that didn't really exist? Light from supernovas that never happened?'

'They existed all right,' she explained, '*in the mind of the creator.*'

She said this in a solemn tone, but with an impish smile. I couldn't tell if she was serious or not. The whole idea gave me a dizzy feeling. If the world could be created with a false past, why assume the creation had happened thousands of years ago? The universe might just as well have been created last Tuesday, complete with records, memories, and holes in our socks. I could see a problem with that.

'Doesn't that mean the creator is deceiving us?' I asked.

'Not at all,' said Louise. 'If you visit a history Website, with houses and family records and so on dating back hundreds of years, you don't call the designer a liar when you read in the manual that the whole site was set up last week!'

She reached the ramp and turned for a last look over Noah's Park.

'The designers of *this* lot, on the other hand ...'

She didn't have to spell it out; the tone of her voice said it all.

'Still, it was fun!' Louise said as we stepped through to Webtown. She hadn't let go of my hand, and she swung it forward. 'Where next?'

I stood and looked at her eager, enthusiastic face. I didn't want to make it cloud over by saying I couldn't take her anywhere else.

But we'd been here half an hour in realtime, longer in Webtime. I *had* to go and see Tim and Weaver.

Suddenly, I had a bright idea. I could've kicked myself for not having thought of it before.

'Hey,' I said, 'I know a really good site. It's called *Cydonia*.'

CHAPTER SIX

THE LONE GUNMAN
THEORY

'This isn't what the Mars expedition is finding,' Louise remarked as she watched the Cydonia region on the viewscreen. We'd gone for the fun access, and were now coming down in a Mars Lander.

'No, but it's what the Viking Orbiter found back in the seventies,' I said. 'Then Mars Observer in 1992 blinked off just before it could send back pictures. *Ha!* Mars Global Surveyor in 1998 sent back pictures of the region that looked nothing like this. And you're right, the Mars expedition's pictures from orbit are the same. No Face, no Pyramid, no City. Nothing. *Ha!*'

'What do you mean, "*ha*"? Weren't the old Viking pictures pretty low-res? The Face could be a trick of the light, or a glitch in the telemetry or something like that.'

'Which do you think is more likely?' I asked, as we strapped in for deceleration. 'That the Voyager pix were a fluke, or that they weren't, and all the later ones are faked?'

Louise grinned at me sideways through a tumble of black hair. 'Oh, the first. And you believe the second?'

'Not really,' I said. 'But—'

My words were drowned out by the sound of the rocket's descent burn.

'*What?*' yelled Louise.

'IT MAKES THINGS MORE INTERESTING!' I yelled back.

We came out of the Lander through an airlock that took us into the enormous dome that covers the Cydonia Café and a cluster of other displays: the Roswell Room, Dealy Plaza, Area 51, MIB HQ, and so on. The dome is, of course, quite unnecessary – we could walk around on this virtual Martian landscape with no protection at all – but it adds a little touch of realism. There are even special pressurized buses for trips to the Pyramid, the City and the Face, and pressure-suits for people who want to clamber about on those alien features. People who visit the official Mars Expedition Website often choose to suit up in the same way. It helps to create the illusion that you're really sharing in the expedition's work (instead of merely contributing a few euros to NASA's budget).

We approached the Café via Dealy Plaza, where President John F. Kennedy was assasinated. Louise pointed to the famous Grassy Knoll. There seemed to be a sinister figure lurking behind every fence-post and tussock of grass.

'These are the guys who really did it?'

'Some of them,' I said. 'If you look carefully around the plaza you can make out twenty-seven people taking aim at the President. From the Mafia, the CIA, the KGB, pro-Castro Cubans, anti-Castro Cubans, and the Men In Black.'

'Not forgetting Oswald,' she said, glancing up at the window of the Texas Book Depository.

'Of course,' I said. 'They couldn't very well leave *him* out.'

'It's a miracle anyone left the plaza alive,' Louise commented.

'Well,' I said, ducking past a man with an unfurled umbrella, 'a lot of the people whose phaces you see here met with suspicious deaths.'

Louise greeted this grim news with a rather unchristian laugh.

'I'll be careful from now on,' she said.

We found Weaver and Tim huddled together conspiratorially at a small table in a dim-lit alcove. They even had a smokescreen, provided by Tim's virtual cigar.

'Havana,' he explained, flourishing it dramatically. 'Paid for with a real e-dollar, too.'

'Isn't that propping up the Cuban Communist government?' I asked, as we sat down.

'Nah,' said Tim. 'It's undermining it, with free trade, right?'

'Yeah, right,' I said. 'Weaver, Akay, this is Louise.'

They both smiled and shook hands, but I felt a bit awkward about having brought Louise here. I'd never said anything to Weaver about how much I admired her, and why I thought Tim should feel jealous I didn't know, but there it was. I also felt a pang of conscience about dragging Louise into the MacCready situation.

Some such thoughts must have been going through the others' minds, too, because they glanced at her, then at each other, then at me, before Tim said, 'Uh, Links, this question you had, is this a good time to talk about it?'

'Oh, pardon *me*,' said Louise. 'Please don't let me butt into your private conversation!'

She stood up.

'Hey, it's OK,' I said. 'Sorry, Louise, I should've explained. Sit down.'

She glared at me.

'Please.'

She sat down, making a big deal of fussily smoothing her rustling skirts.

'It's all right,' I told Tim and Weaver. 'Louise is a friend of mine, and a neighbour in Realworld. She should know about it.'

'Know about *what*?' Louise asked, her pale face slightly flushed.

So I filled them in, brought them all up to speed. Weaver's frown deepened when I mentioned that MacCready's public records had been altered.

'Are you sure?'

'All the fighters on both sides in the last Irish war got

amnesty,' I said. 'It's a public list. *Nobody* ever tries to get their names taken off it. Most of these dingbats think it's some kind of roll of honour!'

'If MacCready wanted to hide his past,' Weaver said thoughtfully, 'it'd be a lot simpler to change his name. Lots of people do that, and it's easy enough to hide your real ID in the Web—'

'Wait a minute,' said Louise. 'Aren't you jumping the gun a bit? So to speak! I mean, what's the big deal? What's to stop the man changing his mind?'

'Ulster Loyalists don't change into Scottish Republicans,' I said. 'It doesn't make sense.'

'Look,' said Tim, 'maybe he just enjoys playing around with guns, and he doesn't want his new American friends to think he fought against Irish freedom.' He looked back defiantly at the three of us. 'Well, that's what folks call it here! You should've seen the street parties in New York and Boston when the Brits got out at last. People had waited hundreds of years for that!'

'They did more than *wait*,' I said, rather bitterly, remembering all the US dollars that had fuelled the Provo war machine. 'But let's not get into all that, OK?'

Tim waved his hands. 'OK.'

'So what happened on the training-range?' I asked. 'Did you meet him there?'

'No,' said Tim, 'but we did hear quite a few Scotch accents.'

'*Scots* accents,' I corrected automatically. Then my brain caught up. 'You *did*? You came across Scottish people there?'

'Yes,' said Weaver. 'And they weren't kids bootstrapping their skills for combat-games, either.'

'You got a problem with that?' Tim asked. 'Why shouldn't Scotch people learn combat skills?'

'They can get free training from the Territorial Army,' Weaver pointed out. 'That's our, um—' She looked at me, twirling her forefinger.

'People's militia?' I suggested. 'National Guard?'

'Something like that. Point is, these Scots don't have to train with the ARM, but they are. I'd like to know why.'

I nodded. 'That's exactly what's bothering me about it,' I said. 'Especially if they're calling themselves Republicans.'

'You got a—' began Tim.

'Problem with Republicans?' I interrupted sarcastically. 'No, Akay, not with your kind anyway. I *had* a problem with Irish Republicans when I was a wee lad, and I would have a problem with *Scottish* Republicans, except there aren't any. Sure, there are Scots who want a republic, but that's different. There aren't any Scots who want to do for Scotland what the IRA did for Ireland. There *can't* be.'

'Why not?' Weaver asked.

'What would they be fighting for? Scotland's going to *get* independence. OK, the vote will be a close thing, but there's no need to fight for it. In fact, the only thing that fighting – or even *talk* about fighting – could do is—Aha!'

I smacked a fist. 'That's it!'

'What's it?'

I grinned around at them. Suddenly, I had a conspiracy theory of my very own and it all made sense. 'This is all a scam,' I explained excitedly. 'MacCready wants to *stop* Scottish independence, by throwing a few bombs and bullets into the argument! Nothing like a bit of violence and stirred-up memories of Ireland to scare people off the whole idea. He and his friends are *still* Loyalists, and they're getting help from the ARM by pretending to be the opposite!'

Louise was looking at me curiously, Tim and Weaver were shaking their heads.

'Too complicated,' Weaver said. 'What's his motive? He doesn't even—'

She stopped.

'What?'

She shook her head. 'Sorry, just a passing thought. A mistake. Go on.'

I frowned at her, puzzled. 'I can tell you what his *motive* is,' I said bitterly. 'There's thousands of people in Scotland who

had to leave Ireland. *Northern* Ireland, after the unification.
They don't want to lose their country all over again. Hey, I
know how they feel, right?'

'Why should independence mean losing their country?'
Tim asked, reasonably enough.

'Because they see *Britain* as their country,' I said. 'The
United Kingdom, you know? And, well, there's also the
Protestant versus Catholic thing.'

I stopped. Nobody talks about this in Scotland, except
indirectly. Everybody takes it for granted that even *talking*
about the problem is enough to make it worse. They may be
right, but it doesn't get any better, either.

'I don't see that's a big issue any more,' Weaver said.

Tim nodded firmly. 'I still say MacCready's just into
combat games,' he said. 'And covering up his past because
it's embarrassing.'

'A lone gunman theory?' I said.

Tim laughed. Louise and Weaver looked puzzled.

'What's that?' Louise asked.

'Cydonia slang,' I explained. 'For basement-level official
cover-stories.'

'Oh!' she said. 'I see. Like the story that Oswald acted
alone, instead of,' she smiled, jerking her thumb, 'what we
saw on Dealy Plaza out there.'

'Yup,' said Tim. 'Just like all the convenient assassinations
of inconvenient political leaders get blamed on lonely
madmen. Malcolm X, Martin Luther King, Kennedy, Kennedy, Kennedy, Kennedy ...' He frowned at me. 'Maybe
that's what I'm doing here. But I still say you should only go
for a conspiracy theory if you have to.'

'*Ha*!' I said. 'You watch out, Akay, I'm gonna investigate
you! Everyone who casts doubt on a conspiracy is part of it
themselves, right?'

Tim shared my laugh. As I turned to Weaver, I saw her
expression change from worry to a delayed, forced smile. She
met my gaze without a blink or a flush, but she looked
distinctly edgy.

'If you think there's a real conspiracy going on,' she said, 'why don't you just take it up with the Webcops? Or the Realworld cops, for that matter?'

Tim looked as shocked as I felt at this suggestion.

'I don't want to do that,' I said. 'The Webcops are always looking for an excuse to shut down Cydonia. I don't want to be the one who gives it to them.'

'Too right,' said Tim. 'Keep this in the family. I'll Web round with a few discreet enquiries after I spin out. That OK with you, Weaver?'

'Yeah, sure, fill me in on what you find,' she said. She glanced around at me and Louise. 'Time to go,' she added, standing up with obvious haste. 'I've been too long in the Web today.'

'Haven't we all?' said Tim, yawning and stretching.

'See you all here tomorrow?' Weaver asked, finger poised over her scuttle-button. 'Have another session on the training-range?'

'Good idea,' I said. It was what we'd set out to do in the first place, and I'd missed it.

'Sure thing,' said Tim.

'Not me,' said Louise.

'Oh, right,' I said, remembering what my mother had told me. 'No combat-games, is that it?'

'Not exactly.' Louise smiled sheepishly. 'It's just ... tomorrow's Sunday. No games at all.'

Another religion thing. Poor girl probably had to go to church. I wasn't about to embarrass her by remarking on that.

'See you Monday, then?' I asked. It seemed a long time to wait.

'I can see you sooner than that,' she pointed out.

'How?'

'Well,' she said patiently, 'if you go out of your house and walk down the road, you might just catch me in the Cybercaff at the pier. And I might just buy you a coffee.'

'Realworld,' Weaver added dryly. 'Try it sometime, Links.

It's a dead venomous site. Full of education and adventure. Something for everyone.'

'So I'm told,' I said.

We all hit our scuttle-buttons – that one-digit code for Realworld – and spun out.

As soon as the Web world faded from my senses I knew something was wrong, but I didn't know what. I peeled off the Websuit's hood, unplugged the jack and sat up. Gerard wasn't in the room, I couldn't see anything out of the ordinary ...

But the room was darker than it should have been at that time in the morning, as though something were blocking out the sun. The patch of sunlight on the floor had a long, strange shadow on it. I turned towards the window.

And then I realized what was really bothering me.

It was the noise. The room was filled with a beating rumble, so loud and steady that a few seconds had passed before I'd become conscious of it.

I faced the window, and saw the cause of the shadow and the noise.

Hovering outside the window, so close it was like the visored face of a giant peering in, was a black helicopter.

CHAPTER SEVEN

BLACK HELICOPTER

I stared back at the sinister machine. It was quite a small helicopter, a two-seater, its cockpit canopy twin bulges of black glass, like the eyes of an insect. Ten metres away, above our back garden, it looked as if it were about to come in through the window. It hung there, right in my face, for a few moments. Then it backed away, spun around and darted off like a hoverfly. I bounded over to the window and looked out.

The helicopter flew low and fast, its course parallel to the village and the shore, then it paused and hovered again. Leaning out, I could see that it was above the pier at the end of the village street. There are several shops on the quay, but I was certain I knew which one the craft was snooping on.

The Cybercaff.

Again, it backed away after standing still in the air for a few moments. It rose about a hundred metres, turning as it climbed, then flew off up the loch, passing our house again on the way. By this time my shaking, fumbling hands had found the binoculars we kept on a shelf under the window. I raised them to my eyes and swung them, catching a fleeting view of the aircraft. It was indeed completely black, with no markings of any kind, not even a registration number. I tracked it with the binoculars until it passed out of view behind the tree-clad shoulder of a hill.

The binoculars rattled on the shelf as I laid them down. I

sat on the futon, peeled off the Websuit and pulled on my
clothes. I was still shaking a bit, and a sudden surge of
Websickness didn't help. With an effort I fought down the
voms by focusing on my Realworld surroundings and
thinking hard about something else. What I thought about,
of course, was what had just happened.

Being buzzed by unmarked black helicopters was a standard story from the American 'patriot' militiamen. To hear
some of them talk in the Cydonia Café, they couldn't nip
out for a packet of fags without spotting a helicopter
hovering in attendance. On the other hand, low-flying
military aircraft – mostly supersonic jet fighters terrain-
following at zero feet – are as familiar and annoying as
midges in the Highlands. Being treated like an uninhabited
training-ground is an old grievance in these parts, and it
fuels the sentiment for independence. Not that independence would end it – the planes are from the European Union
Air Force, the Luftwaffe as it's affectionately known.

That was certainly who was getting the blame when I went
downstairs. Mum and Yvonne were still looking indignantly
out of the kitchen window.

'Frightening people like that,' Anne-Marie said. 'There
ought to be a law. Really.'

I soothed Yvonne by assuring her that she could go and play
in the Web for as long as her mum allowed, and Anne-Marie
by assuring her that Louise had had a wonderful time and
that I was going to meet her down at the Cybercaff. My
account of where we'd been was true, but not quite the
whole truth.

'Take your jacket,' my mum called after me as I left, 'and
tell Gerard to be back in time for a proper lunch.'

Her opinion of the food in the Cybercaff is right up there
with her opinion of Web games.

The morning was still sunny, with a stiff but not too cold
breeze – the better kind of Greenhouse weather. I turned left
out of the house and followed the gentle downward curve of

the street towards the pier. Like many villages in the West
Highlands, ours straggles along the side of a loch, which,
confusingly enough, is the word used not only for lakes but,
as here, a long inlet of the sea between two ranges of hills.
Basically, the loch is a drowned valley. Its up-and-down
movement through several ice ages is revealed by the raised
beaches, vast grassy banks that rise about ten metres above
sea-level a hundred metres or so back from the shore.

The reason the older part of the village consists of one long
street squeezed between the raised beach and the sea is that
the great-great-grandparents of most of the local people were
driven off the land they thought was theirs when their
landlords cleared them to make room for more profitable
stock. First, the famously destructive blackfaced sheep, then
deer for the shooting. The tenants had the choice of living
along the shoreline, or taking a ship to Canada.

A good, kind landlord was one who helped his cleared
tenants with their fare.

In a way, the clearances never ended. Nowadays, it's called
conservation. Lots of well-meaning organizations buy up
land and encourage the locals to move out, then bring in
their own strange tribes of organic farmers and wildlife
rangers – Green settlers, we call them. Recently they've
brought back wolves – just another part of the process of
turning the place into a wet desert for the benefit of people
who don't live here, at the expense of those who do.

But there's another side to the story.

The new electronics factories up the glen and the wind-
farms that bestride the hilltops have done something to
bring people back and money in, so the village has grown a
lot, its new housing-estates spreading up the hillsides. The
summer visitors and the Green settlers think they spoil the
look of the place, as if hills covered with nothing but bogs
and boulders and heather were *natural*. Actually, they're the
ruins left by an ecological and economic disaster. The
natural cover of these hills would be tall forests and busy
towns, like you see in Austria and France. But those are

countries where landlords don't get their own way quite so often.

The pier is new, the smell of creosote still seeping from its timbers and mingling with the smells of seaweed, fish, and tar. It juts out a good fifty metres into the loch. Fishing-smacks and pleasure craft jostle around it. On the concrete approach, just before the wooden jetty begins, is a row of small shops – a chandler's, a craft shop, a pottery, a tearoom, and the Cybercaff.

You could spot the last a mile off by the aerials that bristle from its roof and the cable connections that sprout from its walls and run into a shallow, recent ditch, its line of turned-over earth scored across the green meadow to the road where it joins the mains cable. Strange to think that beneath that ordinary road runs our connection to all the world, and – via all those NASA Websites – to other worlds, all the way out to our farthest reach, the robot fingertips scraping the ice of Pluto. Maybe, if the Deep Sky Anomaly really is a message, the Web connects beyond even that.

The Cybercaff's door and signboard are decorated with fading – and now tiresomely dated – spraypaint imitations of Web hacker graffiti. There's a big glass window at the front and another big glass window at the back. I could see right through the cafeteria section. The Websuit rental arcade was off to the left as I went in. It was kind of weird to see half-a-dozen people lying on couches, moving their limbs and heads slightly all the time, like dreaming dogs.

The coffee-bar counter was to the right, and the café tables between. There weren't many people here at this time in the morning, about half past ten. A girl was sitting at a table by the far window. She had a long coat draped over the back of her seat and a big hat slung beside it; long skirt spread around the seat, long black hair tumbling on her shoulders. She waved as the door swung to behind me. I remembered I'd seen her heading this way earlier in the morning, which seemed a long time ago. I hadn't recognized Louise in the Web as the same girl, but that's who it was.

'Well hi,' she said as I walked over. 'Let me get you that promised coffee.' She casually gestured over her shoulder to Mr MacCartney, the old guy who runs the place (computer phreak from way back, Silicon Glen burnout, used to be big in mainframes) and he came over at once, much to my surprise.

'Another *cappucino* and—?'

'Espresso, please,' I said, sitting down.

With no visible make-up, much longer hair and different clothes, she was less striking than her Web avatar. But no less pretty, and her smile just as wicked.

'What are you staring at?'

'Um. You, I suppose. Funny seeing you in Realworld, that's all.'

'Hmm,' she said. She made a wiping motion around her face. 'Bit bland, I know.'

'Not at all,' I said. 'Uh, about—'

She raised a finger. 'Wait.'

She waited until the coffees arrived, blew on the chocolatey foam, sipped.

'So, you saw the helicopter?' she asked.

'Didn't I just,' I said. 'It looked right at me through the window.'

'Aha. That's what it did here! I'd just sat down when it suddenly loomed up right outside.' She mimed a shudder. 'That's creepy, it happening to you as well. Like somebody knew when we were each coming out of the Web, and came around and took a good look at us.'

I shrugged. 'It could be just coincidence.'

I told her about the Luftwaffe's training practices.

She snorted. 'Another lone gunman theory!'

'Well.' I leaned back, sipping the hot espresso. 'So what's your conspiracy theory?'

'Think about it,' she said. 'It'd take some time to get a helicopter here, anything between fifteen minutes and half

an hour. If that one came to have a look at our Realworld
selves, it must've been scrambled – or diverted here – by a
message from someone in the Web, after we met but while
we were still in, right?'

'OK, *if*.'

'Which could only have been from you, me, Weaver, or
Akay.'

'You mean one of us is a *Webcop*?'

'Yes,' she nodded.

'We'll make a conspiracy phreak of you yet,' I said. I spread
my hands. 'It wasn't me, and I'll give you the benefit of the
doubt.'

'Wow, thanks! Now, what about your friend Akay?'

It felt strange to think about my friend as though he might
not, really, be my friend. I'd never, of course, met Tim in
Realworld, but I felt I'd got to know him pretty well.

'I couldn't swear to it,' I said slowly, 'but he doesn't strike
me as someone sent in by the Webcops to keep an eye on
Cydonia or anything like that. If you can know anybody in
the Web, I'd say I know him, and I think he's on the level.'

Louise looked pleased. 'That's what I thought. Now, could
you say the same of Weaver?'

'*Weaver*? She's just a really hot games-phreak, I've seen her
in lots of places, and anyway she's—'

'Our age?' Louise smiled. 'We don't know that, do we? And
listen—'

She leaned closer and spoke quietly.

'Have you ever heard of … Ariadne?'

'Rumours.' I frowned. 'Since I was a wee kid, really. You
hear things on the kiddie nets and in the playground, about
this Webcop who looks after children's stuff. Sort of guardian
angel.'

'The kind of person who'd be very concerned about young
people getting mixed up in dangerous business like militias.
Who might be keeping an eye on combat games, in case they
were being used for something else. Like real training.'

'OK,' I shrugged, 'somebody might be doing that. But why Weaver?'

'It's the name,' Louise said. 'I think it's meant to be a hint. Ariadne was a mythical heroine who spun out a thread to guide Theseus – yeah, a mythical hero – through the Labyrinth. She was into spinning threads, she was a ... weaver!'

I must admit it didn't sound like a cast-iron chain of logic, but I was shaken enough by the events of the morning to take it seriously. Certainly, the idea of Weaver's being a Webcop made sense – it accounted for her skills rather better than anything Tim or I had come up with. Perhaps it was our male-chauvinist vanity, but we just couldn't accept that a girl younger than ourselves could be so much better than we were at what we'd been practising ever since we were old enough.

So, as Louise sat back with a self-satisfied smile that wouldn't have looked out of place on Sherlock Holmes, I nodded soberly and said, 'Yeah, you might be on to something there.' My mind was already piling new complications on to my own conspiracy theory. 'If MacCready is up to what I thought he was, it wouldn't be surprising that a Webcop would react fast to hearing about him – maybe even going so far as to scramble a helicopter to check us out. Check that we're not going out with the guns already.'

'"Here comes a chopper to chop off your head,"' Louise chanted.

'What?'

'It's from *Nineteen Eighty-Four*,' she explained, then waved a hand as she saw she'd left me even more puzzled. 'You know, like "Big Brother is Watching You". It's in a *book*,' she added, witheringly.

'Books are bad for your eyes,' I said.

'Not with gag, they aren't.'

'What about VR?' I asked. 'What's it like in gag?'

'You can see things and handle them. You just don't get all the other sensations. Also, it's easier to see the underlying code and structures at the same time. You know, like split-screen.'

'Wait a minute,' I said. 'What about your avatar?'

She shrugged. 'You can patch up an icon if you like, but you don't need an avatar.'

'You mean you can just move around invisibly, like a ghost?'

'Sure. And you don't get Websick so quickly, either ... Hey! I've just had an idea! We can both go back to Cydonia, or to the training-range, this afternoon! We can go together, and I can dig underneath the graphics whenever I want. I'll set my icon so only you can see it. By the time you meet Akay and Weaver again tomorrow, we might have something on MacCready to give us a head start.'

'Not a bad idea,' I said, wishing I'd thought of it myself.

She stood up and put on her coat, as if in a hurry to start right now. She picked up her hat and gave me a conspiratorial smile.

'See me home?'

'Sure.'

As we headed for the door, Gerard came out of the Websuit arcade. He saw us and smirked. I introduced him to Louise politely enough, but as I walked out with Louise I *knew* that within a day or so half the village, and all the school, would be certain that I was, well, you know ... *walking out* with Louise.

I glanced at Louise, walking along all unaware of what was going to be said about her. I decided there were worse things that could be said about me.

CHAPTER EIGHT

ALL-SEEING EYE

As we walked up the street, Louise told me about her time in Africa – first Zimbabwe, the birthplace of the church, then Mozambique, where it was expanding rapidly. Childhood in Zimbabwe sounded like growing up in an English vicarage. Her teenage years in Mozambique were more like living on a mission, in danger from rebels and wild animals.

'But that's where I really learned to use the Web, get the most out of the old glove-and-glasses,' she said earnestly. 'The government first of all tried to ban the Web, then they tried using it for economic planning.' She laughed. 'Both failed dismally, of course. By the time we arrived, every house had a gag set and you could access the Web any time – at least when the phone and power lines weren't down!'

'Down?'

'You know – cut off. By storms or rebels or whatever.'

'How long would they be down for?'

'Oh, not very long. Couple of weeks at the most.'

'Good grief.' The thought of being cut off from the Web for that length of time gave me a sort of panicky feeling. 'Must be like having WebCrashes all the time.'

Louise snorted. 'We hardly *noticed* the WebCrash,' she said. 'Thought it was just a glitch! People took their goggles off and used their slide-rules and typewriters and—'

'Their *what*?'

'Slide-rules,' she told me, 'are a kind of computer made of wood, and typewriters are like keyboards made of iron. Neither of them use electricity.' (Incredible, I agree, but I think she was telling the truth as far as she knew. Must be some hidden electronics in them, though. I'll have to look them up on the Grolier some day.)

We went on talking and before I knew where I was she'd stopped outside a big wrought-iron gate. The garden behind it consisted of a big lawn, bordered with daffodils and snowdrops. The house was like a suburban villa, one of the 'big houses' in the village that had been occupied at various times by doctors, bank-managers, and a series of clergymen: Church of Scotland, Free Church, and now SAPC.

'Would you like to come in?' Louise asked.

'Well, uh, not right now,' I said awkwardly.

'Ha!' said Louise. 'It's all right. My mum's met your mum, remember? My parents know all about your dad's being the village communist. They won't be shocked, they won't try to convert you or anything.'

'All the same.' I shrugged. 'Another time, all right?'

'OK. See you in the Web in about an hour, I'll send you a ping, yeah?'

'Yeah, see ya.'

By this time, five younger children, evidently her brothers and sisters, were swarming over the lawn and onto the gate like monkeys, so I waved and left her to answer their clamouring questions.

When I saw her again in Webtown, an hour later, she appeared like a cardboard cut-out of her former avatar. At the same time, I felt the invisible grip of her gloved hand on mine – the data glove, not the goth glove.

'Spooky,' I said, looking sideways at her tilted, flat picture.

'Watch.'

Her icon shrank to a tiny triangle about three centimetres on the side, with one eye looking out. Like the strange symbol on the dollar, the eye in the pyramid.

'Oh, very funny,' I said.

'Yes, isn't it,' said her amused voice in my ear. The tone was flat, mono, like an old radio. 'That's how you'll see where I am, but nobody else will see it.' She squeezed my hand. 'Let's go.'

I'd given her the codes for Cydonia, and for the militia training-range. We reached it in two dizzying swoops – I was following her, and her access method didn't have to bother with keeping up illusions about how we moved around in the Web.

But the range, when we reached it, seemed real enough. We landed in a wooden-walled corridor leading to some kind of changing-room with a kit counter at the far end; people were milling about and talking. She dropped my hand, and as I moved forward I could see her keeping pace, an eye in the corner of my eye.

The users here were collecting weapons, radios, and camouflage clothes from a couple of phaces who stood behind the counter, handing the gear out.

'Heckler and Koch machine-pistol?' I asked. It was the only firearm I was used to – from my time in Crisis Crater.

The phace, a woman in a neat uniform, with Hispanic-American features and accent, smiled and nodded.

'Good choice,' she said, reaching below the counter and handing one over. I took a couple of ammo clips as well.

'D'you want basic training, or a combat exercise?' she asked.

I reckoned I'd got past basic training. I'd learned how to operate the machine-pistol in dozens of games.

Little did I know.

'Combat exercise, please,' I said, with more confidence than I felt.

'OK,' said the phace. '"FEMA Rescue" is about to start.'

'Sounds good.' I smiled. 'I'm new here. What's it about?'

The phace lost its interested, friendly expression and changed to the glassy gaze of a help routine. The queue behind me disappeared as the people in it were flipped to

another version of the same phace, while this one dealt with
me. Embarrassing to be such an egg, but I had no choice.

'FEMA,' it explained, 'is the Federal Emergency Manage-
ment Authority. This agency helps citizens caught up in
natural disasters. That's its good side. Its bad side is that it
also has powers to deal with *political* emergencies. It has its
own armed forces and maintains a network of *resettlement
camps*, which just happen to have barbed wire and watchtowers around them. They're empty now, but ready to be
filled if the Federal Government ever decides to move against
citizens who—'

I didn't need to listen to the phace parrot the usual
paranoid patriot storyline.

'Skip it,' I said. 'Tell me about the exercise.'

The phace shifted its mental gears again, and rattled off a
string of rules and instructions. I listened as best I could.
Louise's sceptical chuckles distracted me. Even with only one
eye visible, she could still give an obvious wink.

'Now go!' said the phace. 'Your comrades are waiting!'

She pointed dramatically to a doorway. I took my weapon
and two-way radio and made for the door, trying not to
tremble.

I always get the shakes before a drop.

Outside the door I found myself on a scrubby hillside, under
a cloudy sky. I dived for the nearest cover, rolled behind a
boulder, and cautiously checked out the situation. I knew
the scene was American, but it could just as well have been
in Scotland. In the valley below was a camp – rows of low
buildings, inside a rectangle of barbed wire with watchtowers
at the corners.

One of the FEMA resettlement camps – really internment
camps – that the phace had told me about. I was part of a
patriot band that had come to break it open and free the
dissidents who'd been kept there for years since the fascist
coup in Washington DC.

We had a tough job on our hands. Armoured cars and

tanks were patrolling the road along the valley, and the inevitable black helicopters were beating through the air overhead. Higher up, an airship hung in the sky, a shining dot like a UFO.

But so far, unlikely as it seemed, we hadn't been spotted. We were hiding here on the hill like resistance fighters poised to attack an invading army. I guessed this must be the starting-point of the exercise – if anybody'd ever tried to do this in Realworld, they'd have been wiped out long before they got even this far. Unless there were ways I didn't know about of blinding all those eyes in the sky – from the spy satellites in orbit down to the helicopters overhead. I frantically checked the readout on my wristpad and listened to the orders being barked over the radio by the unit commander. Then Louise's voice broke in.

'Here comes a chopper to chop off your head,' she said dryly.

I keeked around the rock, and saw a helicopter flying *below* us. A couple of hundred metres farther down the slope, rising slowly and keeping only just above the ground. At that moment its forward guns opened up and it climbed rapidly higher, streams of bullets scything across the hillside. I heard screams. Every bit of cover was being blasted away as if by a high-pressure hose, boulders and bushes alike.

And people. In the second or so I had to see this, I glimpsed fighters a few metres away from me being shredded. Even in VR it was utterly terrifying – knowing you can't really be hurt doesn't protect you from the sheer shock of some sights.

Then the helicopter exploded. Somebody must have fired an anti-tank missile at it. That's the only thing that can bring down a modern military helicopter, which basically *is* a flying tank.

I may even have seen the missile – a black streak just before the white flash and the red cloud. But if I did, it was the last thing I saw in that game. The next thing I knew, I was lying on my back, feeling as if I'd fallen flat on my face.

From my forehead to my feet, everything hurt. Not as badly as if I'd really fallen, but as if all the pressor pads down the front of my Websuit had chosen the same moment to give me a maximum kick. I was looking up at a wooden ceiling with old-fashioned electric lights hanging from it.

A man's face appeared above my head and frowned down at me.

'You're out of it, soldier,' he said, not unkindly. 'You're dead.'

I smiled bravely and tried to sit up. The man leaned forward and placed his hand on my chest. This was painful enough to make me lie back again.

'No need for you to see what you look like,' he said, 'nor what the other casualties look like, neither. Here, I'll give you a code.' He held his left wrist to mine. Cartoon lightning jumped the gap. 'Hit Enter and this'll take you straight to the lecture.'

'Lecture?'

He was smiling now. 'Look, kid, you just got yourself killed in a fight. Might be a good idea to find out why, yeah?'

'OK,' I said.

Without thinking, I tried to sit up. Again he pushed me down.

'You don't wanna look, kid. Just go.'

I hit Enter on my wristpad, and instantly found myself standing up at the back of a big shed built of rough timber and corrugated iron. At the front there was a table with a wallscreen behind it, faced by rows of chairs with scuffed plastic bucket seats and tubular legs. Through the large windows I could see trees beyond an area of packed and beaten earth. Dotted about were big chunks of machinery the size of tractors under tarps – armoured cars or big guns? I never found out.

Other people were spinning into the room, appearing out of nowhere with grey, shocked faces. Each new arrival would shake themselves or shudder, look down wonderingly at their bodies or raise a reluctant hand to their faces. Then, with their colour coming back and a look of relief, they'd shamble forward and sit on one of the chairs.

After a moment I did the same.

'Oh, there you are,' said Louise. The voice in my ear sounded shaky. I saw her single eye floating in front of me like an after-image. 'I lost you after the blast. I tracked your jump and tried to follow you, but the next place I found was like some kind of casualty unit.' She paused. 'People all burnt and mangled and bleeding. I looked for you, but—'

'I was there,' I said. 'Up to a minute ago.'

'Oh,' she said flatly.

I realized then what sights the kind man had been protecting me from. There might not have been much left of me to recognize, and the others in no better state. No wonder everybody looked so shocked.

'I'm sorry you had to see that,' I whispered.

'I've seen worse,' the tiny, tinny voice said. 'In Realworld. Mozambique. There's a rebel group there called Renamo that—' She took a deep breath. 'Ah, forget it. Just listen and find out what's going on.'

Good idea, I nodded. People around me were already giving me curious looks.

A man walked in at the back of the Shed and strode to the table and looked us over. I tried to shrink into my seat.

It was Bill MacCready.

CHAPTER NINE

DREAMLAND

MacCready recognized me all right. As he scanned the couple of dozen people who'd filled the rows of seats, his glance rested on me for a split-second smile. Then he took a step forward, leaned on the table and glared.

'You're all new here,' he said. 'That's not much of an excuse for youse all being *dead*, now is it?' His Belfast accent was harsher than ever, with an American undertone. He straightened and pointed at me, making me jump. 'You! There at the back! Links!'

'Yes?'

'What were you doing out there?'

'Trying to learn about real fighting,' I said.

'Good! Well you've learned something, haven't you? *Real fighting can get you killed*. But you're a smart lad. You knew that already, right?'

'Yes,' I said, rather sullenly.

'No you didn't,' MacCready said. 'And you still don't.' He switched his glare to the rest of the room, to my relief. 'However. That's not what your little lesson out there was mainly about. You all turned up and jumped straight into the exercise, like it was a combat-game. Well it ain't. It's a test we set up for fools like you. You want to know how to pass?' He looked down at something on the table as if he were checking a list. Perhaps he was. Then he looked us over again, pityingly. 'None of you lot did, by the way. What a sad shower. Most times at least *one* gets it right.'

'We didn't have a chance,' someone complained.

'"We didn't have a chance."' MacCready mimicked the guy's whinging tone exactly. 'What you mean is, you didn't have a chance to get past spysats and tanks and gunships and guards.' He snapped his fingers and the screen behind him lit up.

It displayed a perfect 3D image, like the view from a window, of the hillside where we'd all fallen to the bullets or the blast. One by one, we all appeared and all did the same thing, diving down the slope and taking cover and within minutes being wiped out.

The view pulled back a bit and the scene was replayed. This time I could see that, like everybody else, I'd arrived on the top of the ridge, with the opposite slope right behind me. It was almost comical to see everyone arriving and rushing into danger without so much as a backward glance.

And safety had been only that backward glance away.

'Right,' said MacCready. 'I can see the light dawning on some of you. The only way to survive that fight was not to get into it in the first place. The only way to pass that test was to look behind you and go back.'

Silence, then somebody a couple of rows in front of me spoke up.

'But that would be ... desertion, wouldn't it? Cowardice?'

MacCready gave the latest speaker an even less approving look than the previous one.

'Who told you to go down into the valley? You had no orders. You just assumed. You didn't ask questions, you just headed for the action, like you were in a combat-game. And you got gloriously killed. At least that's what we'd tell the folks back home.' He sighed. 'You know what the real armies have to spend most of their first weeks of training on these days? Knocking daft notions from Web shoot-em-ups out of lads' and lasses' daft wee heads!'

I shouldn't have been surprised by all this, but I was. I'd

expected MacCready to be a dangerous nutter. But he sounded sane and sensible. Maybe that made him all the more dangerous.

'OK, that's enough for today. Any of you want to come back, just remember what you learned. If I see you again I want it to be in basic training. Because you sure need it.'

Everybody shifted in their chairs, turned with wry smiles to their neighbours or said something or reached for their scuttle-buttons. I was just doing that when MacCready strode forward and laid a light hand on my shoulder.

'Not you, Links,' he said. 'I'd like to have a word with you.'

'Stick with it,' advised Louise, urgently whispering in my ear.

'OK,' I said, to her and to MacCready. All the other people in the room were disappearing from it, their images breaking up into swirls of pixels. In a few seconds I was alone with the former street-fighter. He spun a chair around and sat down.

'Relax, lad,' he said. 'I can't harm you here, can I? All I want you to do is listen for a minute.'

I nodded, still afraid of him.

'I can see you're not too happy about me,' he began, 'and I can guess why. You're from Belfast, your accent still gives you away, and you live in Scotland now. That's all I know about you. But I can tell a lot from that. For starters, that you had to leave because of the Troubles, right?'

'Yes,' I said, then added, feeling bolder, 'thanks to you!'

'I see I'm not the only one who knows more than they're saying,' he said. He frowned. 'You know who I am?'

'Sure I know,' I said. 'I remember you all right, Mr MacCready. You and your URF pals who messed things up for everybody, including us.'

'Aye, well.' He rubbed the back of his neck. 'You could say that, and I don't blame you for thinking it.'

'But you don't think so?'

'Not as such,' he said, with a dry chuckle. 'At least during the peace process – and even the war, come to that – your

family could still live in Ireland, and now they can't. Isn't
that true?'

'That's what I don't get about you, Mr MacCready—'

He raised a hand. 'Just call me Mac,' he said mildly.

'Mac – you used to be a Loyalist. Why were you talking like
some kind of extreme Scottish Nationalist? Scotland's going
to get independence anyway. Any talk about fighting for it
will only scare people off, and I think that's what you really
want. Because you're *still* a Unionist!'

There, I'd just blurted out my very own conspiracy theory
to the very man I thought was the chief conspirator. Not the
sort of move Tim would have recommended. I could hear
Louise's indrawn breath, see her floating, watchful eye
widen.

MacCready gave me a look of complete astonishment,
then tilted back his head and let out a roar of laughter.

'Links,' he said when he'd got his breath back, 'you've
been hanging out too long with those conspiracy nuts!' He
laughed again. '*Cydonia*! What a place!'

'That's where I met *you*,' I pointed out. 'Going on about a
Scottish Republic, and independence, and freedom.'

'Aye,' said MacCready, clasping his hands behind his head
and leaning back at a dangerous angle. 'But the independence your parliament is about to get is just that – independence for your parliament. Not for you. And it won't be much
of an independence, anyway. You'll still have the Luftwaffe
buzzing your glens, still have the Green settlers buying up
your land from the people who stole it from you in the first
place. Same goes for the freedom. Freedom for the politicians
in Edinburgh, not for you. And not much for them.'

'But bringing guns into it will just make people vote
against even *that* amount of independence,' I protested. 'Is
that what you want?'

He frowned at me, puzzled.

'Who's bringing guns into it?'

'You are,' I said.

'*Me*? How so?'

'You're asking me that?' I asked. 'You call yourself a Scottish Republican, and you're with the militias. Looks a bit obvious what you're up to.'

'There you go again,' said MacCready. 'Jumping to conclusions, like you did out on that hill.' He stood up and stalked to the front of the room and stood behind the table, as if he were about to give another lecture. This time, to a class of one. 'When did I ever call myself a Scottish Republican?'

'But—' I began, then realized that I'd never heard him say any such thing.

'I'm a Republican, all right,' he said. 'But not a Scottish Republican. What country do you think I live in?'

'Scotland,' I said.

He smiled thinly. 'Not likely. I live in the land of the free ... Canada.'

I felt like my brain was running at about one mip.

'So why are you—?'

'Mixed up with American patriot militias?' He grinned at my hopeless confusion. 'Because I like them. They're my kind of people.' He gave me an appraising look. 'Our kind. They just want to go on living their own lives in their own way and not be pushed around by a bunch of politicians. And they *are* getting pushed around. Even if they do have some wacky ideas about why it's happening, just like we used to believe in Papist plots.'

He looked at his watch. 'Speaking of conspiracies – I'm due to meet somebody in Cydonia in half an hour. What d'you say we take a stroll around there?'

'Interesting,' murmured Louise. 'Go along with it.'

'Fine by me,' I said, to her and to Mac. 'Which part?'

'Oh, somewhere we can walk around and chat. Not the Café.'

'Area 51?'

'What's that?'

'Part of the site based on a place in Nevada. Also called Groom Lake and Dreamland.'

MacCready nodded. 'Oh, aye, that. We'll go there.'

We linked hands and jumped. I snatched my hand away from MacCready's as soon as we arrived. He gave me an amused look and stepped a few paces away.

'Don't be so nervous,' he said. 'I don't bite.' He gazed around at the site. Although it's in Cydonia, once you're actually inside Dreamland you see a scene from Earth, not Mars. But it's in the Nevada desert, so, apart from the gravity, it's not like you'd notice.

Behind us, stretching off into the distance, was a chainlink fence topped with razor wire. Ahead of us, just visible over the rolling dunes and scrub, were some low buildings. Above, stealth fighters and flying saucers flitted through the cloudless blue sky. You could see how similar they were in their movements, their speed, and their silence. MacCready looked up at their aerial ballet with a wry smile.

'Very convincing resemblance,' he said. 'Question is, which came first … What's in yon sheds?'

I set off towards them. 'Hangar 18, links to the Roswell Room and so on. It's where they keep the crashed saucers and dead aliens, and test captured alien technology.'

'Like, Japanese?' MacCready grinned.

'I guess that's what is at the bottom of it,' I said.

'What do you think of the Roswell stories?' MacCready was keeping pace with me, striding along a metre or two away, still respecting my space, as they say.

'I don't know what to think,' I said. 'Have you heard the latest official USAF explanation of the Roswell Incident?'

'Can't say I have.'

'They say their Nazi rocket scientists were using orphan children in re-entry vehicle tests.'

MacCready grunted. 'That's shocking! And the poor kids were the wee dead aliens, eh?'

'That's what they're telling us *now*.'

'Oh, I see,' said MacCready. 'And you think, maybe if they'll admit to something as bad as that, they must be really covering up something worse?'

'Well, I don't think so. But I know people who do.'

'I'm sure you do,' he said. 'Forget it, Links. All that conspiracy nonsense is a waste of computer space and your time.' His final words were almost drowned out by a black helicopter that swept over us, low and fast, then took up position a hundred metres away and three metres off the ground. I wasn't bothered. It was just part of the scenery.

We stopped for a moment to brush virtual dust from our clothes. MacCready walked on, steadfastly ignoring the helicopter steadily following us.

'What about your militia pals?' I asked. 'They believe in conspiracies – in *The* Conspiracy.'

'Like I said. These guys have real problems, they just have unreal explanations for them.'

He jerked his thumb at the sky behind him. 'Take the black helicopters. They exist. They're not a strike-force for some New World Order – they're just the cops, or the army, or the Drug Enforcement Agency, snooping around looking for cannabis fields! And if they find so much as a leaf they can take your farm and house and money from under you, with no charge or trial and no chance of getting it back. Just try taking them to court when they can use *your* bank account to pay *their* fancy lawyers! No wonder the farmers get paranoid.'

'Aw come on,' I said. 'That can't be happening! We'd hear about it!'

MacCready just smiled, and went right on smiling at me until I had to admit he could be right. The story about Roswell, true or cover-up, was evidence enough that awful things could happen. And other stories I'd heard in Cydonia checked out – they were reported all right, in respectable newslines, and almost nobody paid them any attention. But—

I placed my right hand casually over my left wrist, ready to scuttle at any moment.

'There's two things I don't understand,' I said. 'One is that all your public records say nothing about how you were in the URF and all that.'

'Sure they don't,' said MacCready, frowning a little. 'It's the law. You can get certain criminal records purged after seven years.' He shrugged. 'And I really have changed, man! I make no secret of my past, but having it on public databases isn't exactly a credit reference. I've made a new life in Vancouver.'

So that was all there was to it, I thought. I felt quite embarrassed.

'Why hang out with the militia guys, then?'

'I told you why. As to what good I can do, I can use my experience to talk people out of romantic notions about armed resistance. Nothing wrong with knowing how to handle a gun, but knowing when to use it and when not is far more important.' He looked at me sharply. 'And teaching young fools that combat-games are not the same thing as combat, OK? It's practically social work. The government should be paying me for it. And what's your other question?'

'What about all the Scottish people on the training-range?'

'When did you see Scottish people there?' He sounded anxious.

'I didn't, but a couple of my friends did. This morning.'

'Ah,' he said. 'Morning to you, evening to me ... yes! Those were the friends of yours I met in the Café, Akay and ... Weaver, right?'

'Yes,' I admitted.

Mac laughed. 'Well, it's a rare Yank or Sassenach can tell the difference between a Scottish accent and an Ulster one! Some of my old comrades were on the range this evening. All Canadians now.' He looked at me sidelong. 'There goes your whole Scottish connection, man. So much for conspiracies, eh?'

That's when I told him about our encounter with the Realworld black helicopters. I didn't mention Louise by name, just described the incident.

For a moment he looked really alarmed, then forced a hearty smile.

'I don't know anything about that,' he said. 'I doubt it's

got anything to do with me, though. I think it's got something to do with *you*.'

'Me? But I haven't *done* anything!'

'That's what they all say,' he told me dryly.

By this time we'd reached the vast doorway of the famous Hangar 18. MacCready walked ahead of me and peered in, waiting for his eyes to adjust to the interior gloom. I took the chance to look around for Louise's triangular icon.

I couldn't see it. I couldn't think when I'd last seen it.

'Louise?' I said quietly.

No answer.

'Louise!'

Mac turned and gave me a puzzled look.

Then his eyes widened.

'Look out!' he said.

I suddenly noticed the rising sound of the black helicopter that had been pacing us. I whirled around. It was hovering right behind me.

'STAY WHERE YOU ARE!' a voice boomed from the helicopter. 'THIS IS A POLICE RAID. RAISE YOUR HANDS!'

'Scuttle!' yelled MacCready, vanishing.

I hit my scuttle-button just as the scene began to dissolve. As my room reappeared around me, I half-expected to see the Realworld black helicopter outside.

It wasn't. I sighed with relief and peeled off my hood. There was a ringing noise which after a moment I recognized as the doorbell.

Nobody seemed to be answering it, so I went downstairs. Yvonne's door was open, and she was cocooned in her little pink Websuit. My mum was in glove-and-glasses at her table, oblivious. Stitches chattered out of the Fiberfax as I padded past and opened the front door.

Two men in black suits and dark glasses stood on the doorstep.

CHAPTER TEN

MEN IN BLACK

One of the men was African, the other European. They both had white shirts and black ties. They looked exactly like the guys who're supposed to come round and silence people who *know too much*. The only thing missing was a big black car. The car parked on the road outside was a small blue Hyundai Solar.

'You're Dave Kennedy?' the white man said sternly.

'Yes,' I said. There didn't seem to be much point in denying it. I had that feeling you get in a fast lift, going down.

'Hello, Dave,' the man said. He took off his dark glasses and stuck out his hand. 'I'm very pleased to meet you.'

He didn't seem pleased at all.

His accent was unusual, but strangely familiar. After a moment I recognized it as the same as Louise's. 'I'm John MacPherson. Louise's father. This is Zebediah Matabele, one of my deacons.'

The black man took off his glasses and gave me a wide, white smile. He was much younger than the first man, about twenty, I guessed. I couldn't help noticing he had holes in his earlobes you could see the sunlight through.

'Hi, Dave,' he said. His smile was replaced by a worried frown as he shook hands. 'I'm the Reverend MacPherson's main man on the Web. He called me up because—'

'Louise seems to be in some kind of trouble,' said Rev. MacPherson. 'Trouble in the Web. We can't get her out of it.'

'*What*?'

I felt quite sick with dismay, much worse than when I'd thought they were from some sinister agency.

'Perhaps we'd better come inside,' said Zebediah Matabele.

'Oh, yes, sorry.' I stepped aside and backed off to let them in.

At this point my mother turned up and demanded to know what was going on. It's uncanny, this knack she has, like a heat-seeking missile. She ushered the two men into the front room and they sat down on the edges of seats.

'Louise mentioned you and your son at lunchtime,' the minister explained. He gave me a suspicious, checking-out stare. 'Then she disappeared off up to her room, saying she had some studying to do. When my wife took a cup of tea up to her, she was accessing the Web with her usual kit.' He glanced at my mother's gag set on the table. 'As you know, Mrs Kennedy, it should let her hear what's going on around her. She's used to her mother giving her a call. But she didn't respond, and nothing we can do will snap her out of it. I called Zebediah straightaway.'

'We could pull the plug, of course,' said Mr Matabele. 'But it can be a bit traumatic. I advised against it, short of a real emergency.'

'Do we have a real emergency? That's what we've come here to find out,' continued Mr MacPherson.

I became uncomfortably aware that everyone else in the room was giving me dirty looks.

'Where did you take her?' asked Anne-Marie.

'I didn't *take* her anywhere,' I said. 'We were checking out a training site and then we skipped over to, uh, Cydonia—'

'What's that?' Anne-Marie demanded sharply.

'I know what it is,' said Mr MacPherson. 'Unedifying, but fairly harmless.'

'Mostly harmless,' said Mr Matabele.

'And when did you last see her?'

'I'm not sure. I suddenly noticed she wasn't there. That's why—That's when I came out.'

'So,' said my mother shrewdly, 'that's not *why* you spun out?'

'No, not exactly.'

This wasn't a satisfactory answer, I could see that. I took a deep breath and was about to confess all when Zebediah Matabele raised his hand.

'Explanations later,' he said. 'For now, it would be a waste of time. David, can you go back in the Web and *find* Louise?'

I stared at him in surprise. 'Sure,' I said, with more confidence than I felt.

The deacon and the minister nodded. 'Go to it,' Matabele said. 'You can report back to your mother here, perhaps?'

'Of course,' said Anne-Marie, reaching for her glove-and-glasses. 'You can reach me at NeedleNet,' she told me. 'Same code.'

'Gotcha, Mum.'

I ran upstairs. As I passed the open door of Yvonne's room I heard a thin wail that almost stopped my heart. I halted and swung around the side of the door. She was lying propped on her pillow in her Websuit. But she was lying stiff and still, without the usual small twitches of someone in the Web, their movements just begun and then caught by the suit's transformers and turned into Web motion.

I leapt to the side of the bed and leaned over her. She was breathing normally, I saw with a rush of relief, but her mouth, visible below the mask of the hood, was a rectangular rictus of distress. Every other breath came out as another little wail.

'Yvonne!' I yelled.

I wanted to grab her, shake her, pull the plug, but I knew this might do more harm than good. At the very least it would give her nightmares for months. I thought of yelling at her again, or calling for help. Then it struck me that what was happening to Yvonne was what had happened to Louise.

The quickest way to get help for both of them was for me to get back into the Web. That was where the problem was, and there it would be solved.

But I felt very reluctant as I turned away and left her lying there, like one more doll among the dolls and stuffed toys on the bed.

'Good afternoon, Dave,' said Hal. 'What can I do for you?'

'Contact Mac, tell him we have an emergency. Also Akay. He's probably asleep, so wake him if you can. Otherwise leave a message on his terminal asking for help.' I paused, then decided I had nothing to lose, now, by appealing to Weaver – Webcop or not. 'To Weaver: Links calling Ariadne. We know who you are. You know who we are. Help us. Attach all of the following to all the messages: ID and current status of Yvonne, Louise, and me. Oh, and encrypt them all with PGP Plus.'

PGP+ (Pretty Good Privacy Plus) is a method of encrypting a message, turning it into unbreakable code that only the person it's intended for can read.

'I must remind you that PGP Plus is an illegal encryption method in the United States—'

'Do it.'

'Very well, Dave.' If Hal was bothered by being asked to do something that could have it decompiled, the faithful AI's voice didn't give it away. There wasn't much chance of being found out, anyway – even detecting that PGP+ is being used takes more mips than the universe has electrons. According to the US government, only terrorists, drug barons and other unsavoury characters could possibly have a use for it. Anyone with nothing to hide has nothing to fear, and should be quite happy to let government agents rummage through their mail. Naturally, every self-respecting Web phreak in America uses it to encrypt even their most trivial chat. In the Free World, as the patriots call the world beyond their government's reach, PGP+ is a standard feature on every software release.

'Get back to me as soon as you can, Hal.'

I leaned back on the futon and keyed in the NeedleNet code. The first thing I wanted to do was make sure I had a secure link with Anne-Marie. The next was to tell her about Yvonne. She might have a better idea about what to do than I had.

Again I found myself in the green, upward-curving land-scape. Anne-Marie was standing right in front of where I arrived. She was looking away and didn't notice me. Her big green dress was frozen in mid-swirl. I thought at first it was the same kind of cut-out image that Louise had presented when in gag.

'Mum—'

Her face was rigid, mouth half-open. She made some kind of grunt.

I looked around and saw that the whole site was frozen. The only moving figures were black-clad, visored Webcops, striding among the groups of women on the grass. In this imagined past, time had stopped – for everyone but the Webcops and, so far, me.

Anne-Marie's grunting became frantic, as she struggled to form words.

'Get ... out ... Dave!'

I didn't waste another second – I hit the scuttle-button. Whatever had entrapped Louise and Yvonne had now caught my mother. It looked like the Webcops were investigating – or perhaps responsible for it! I was thoroughly shaken as I lay there, staring up at the ceiling.

A red light blinked on, apparently in the middle of the air. Hal was back.

'Messages delivered,' it said. 'Mac is off-line, Weaver is reachable but not disclosing her location. Akay is awake and Webbing around. He says "Hang in there, Links." And Louise and Yvonne ...'

For the first time in my experience, Hal hesitated.

'Yes?'

'They are in the same place. Hangar 18.'

'See you there. Oh, and tell my father what's going on.'

'Dave, wait—'

I didn't. My next jump took me straight to Dreamland.

This time I'd made sure the coordinates were set to put me down inside the hangar. For a moment I stood blinking in the vast gloom. Pools of light here and there picked out phace technicians toiling over saucer wrecks. The usual parties of visitors were wandering through. No doubt there were many more visitors, present but invisible. No sign of Webcops, but that proved nothing. They could be as invisible to me as the majority of the other users were. I was well aware that I might be walking straight into a trap, baited by Yvonne's and Louise's location-codes.

'Dave, my analysis of similar situations suggests that this could be a trap,' Hal told me. 'The location-codes for Yvonne and Louise—'

'Where are they?' I whispered.

'Roswell Room. Autopsy theatre,' Hal said briskly, with just a hint of very human exasperation.

I jumped again.

The autopsy theatre has semicircular tiers of seats rising around the stage on which a scene is played out based on an ancient hoax video. Masked and gowned pathologists carving up deeply unconvincing Grey bodies. The aliens' innards look like moulded jellies, which they may well be.

'Where's Yvonne?' I asked Hal, as quietly as possible as I glanced around the fascinated, gullible audience.

'There,' said Hal, flashing a virtual pointer line.

I stared along the after-image track, feeling cold and sick. It was pointing at the alien on the operating-table.

For a moment, rage and pity almost sent me hurtling forward, along the pointer line. But I held back long enough to ask, 'And Louise?'

'Here, Dave.'

I looked around frantically. At last I saw her icon, a tiny triangle floating above the stage.

'I can't move,' she said. 'And I can't get out.'

'It's OK,' I said, desperately reassuring her with more confidence than I felt. 'We're working on it right now.'

I was still staring at the alien on the operating-table. Its chest was open and the site's phaces were lifting out mucky, dripping blobs. This was what poor little Yvonne was seeing! No wonder she was terrified! I was sure she wasn't *feeling* it, or she'd have been screaming herself hoarse, not wailing, in Realworld. And I knew she was smart enough to know at some level that it wasn't really happening.

But even so, my little sister was going through what must have seemed an eternity of sinister figures stooping over her with scalpels.

My rage got the better of me and I jumped. I hurled myself forward, barging through the watchers, and bounded on to the stage. The *surgeon* phaces, whose range of actions must've been pretty limited, got smartly out of my way and just stood there, green Grey blood still dripping from their latex gloves. Yells and other sounds of commotion came from the audience.

I looked down at the little Grey body. To my horror, it stirred. Creaking noises came from its opened chest. Its great black eyes rolled and looked at me.

'We need to talk,' it said, as if with an expiring gasp.

Then there was no sound from it, except Yvonne's reedy cry.

'We'll get you out, Yvonne,' I promised.

Something crashed behind me. I turned, fists balled, ready to lash out. Black-uniformed Webcops were appearing all through the theatre, one of them right beside me on the stage.

I stabbed a finger towards my scuttle-button – too late.

My Websuit froze up around me. I couldn't move.

Then the scene dissolved, and all of Dreamland vanished like a dream. It was replaced by a white floor. Out of the corner of my eye, I could see Yvonne, not in her Grey guise any more, but her usual Nintendo jumpsuit. My mother and

Louise were there, both of them in cardboard cut-outs of
their Web avatars. And Mac, standing like a statue on a war
memorial in his combat gear, an expression of foolish
astonishment on his face. He saw me, and with difficulty
closed one eye in a slow wink.

A Webcop strode into view. A black-gloved hand lifted a
black visor, to reveal a triumphantly grinning face.

It was Weaver.

'You're all under arrest,' she told us. 'For conspiracy.'

CHAPTER ELEVEN

THE CONSPIRACY THEORY

Weaver keyed some invisible pad. Whatever was holding me in place relaxed enough for me to move my head and speak. I ignored the now-exposed Webcop and her ridiculous accusation.

'Are you all right, Yvonne?' I asked. I wanted to ask her how she'd got mixed up in this, but decided to leave that for a later and gentler interrogation.

My little sister looked about, sniffled and blinked. 'Frightened,' she said tearfully. 'Can I go home?'

'Yes,' I said. 'Soon.'

I stopped ignoring Weaver. 'Let us go!' I snapped at her.

Weaver tapped out some more keystrokes and the others were also partly released. From the neck up, anyway. My mother turned from her anxious but reassuring gaze on Yvonne to give Weaver a glance of puzzled distaste. 'You can't keep us here!' she said.

Weaver looked back at us, still smiling. Louise and Mac were looking around, but they were saying nothing.

'I won't keep you long,' she said. 'Only until all your Realworld locations have been secured by the police in each place.' She smiled at me. 'And if you're hoping your friend Akay will come to the rescue, forget it. The FBI are kicking down his door and impounding his kit right now.'

'What on earth is this all about?' my mother asked indignantly. 'There must be some mistake.'

Weaver's smug smile turned contemptuous. 'Oh, don't waste your breath and my time, Mrs Kennedy. Save all that for the jury.'

'I'm relieved to hear we'll get one,' Mac said sarcastically. 'Would you mind telling us what we'll be charged with? Every second you keep us here is going to cost you or your force a year's pay in compensation to all of us, so take your time.'

Weaver laughed. 'You don't scare me. By the time we're finished with you, you'll be in jail or on the street, just another homeless beggar tugging at sleeves with a tale that only proves how crazy he is, if he can get anyone to listen.'

I felt a chill as I remembered what Mac had told me about asset forfeiture. Surely this couldn't happen *here*! Not to *people like us*! This was the Free World, not the United States!

'Make my day,' said Mac. 'Add slander to the charges clocking up against you. Tell us what this is all about.'

'Just to pass the time till the police arrive at your houses ...' Weaver shrugged. 'All right. You all know some of this already, but I'm sure none of you know how it fits together. That's just shows how clever your little conspiracy is.'

She started pacing about like a teacher in front of a wallscreen, lecturing us all.

'I'm not Ariadne,' she began, with a pitying glance at me. 'If such a person ever existed. My job is not to keep kids *out* of trouble. It's to find and deal with kids who *make* trouble. No matter what age they are, or pretend to be.' She smiled thinly at Yvonne, who looked back with blank innocence. 'Like you, young miss. We'll soon see if you're as young as you pretend. But even if you are, it's still my job to protect society from the likes of you.'

Yvonne looked quite alarmed until she warmed to the reassuring smiles being beamed at her by the rest of us. Our smiles were genuine. I think we were all relieved to hear Weaver saying something so absurd. It meant that whatever else she had to say was probably just as wrong. Weaver was still walking up and down, still talking. I noticed that whenever she had her back turned, Louise would contort her face into a strange grimace, her tongue flickering out like a snake's. It seemed a childish way to show her disrespect, but if it made Louise feel better I supposed it was all to the good.

'I've been assigned to keep an eye on any overlaps between Cydonia and combat-games,' Weaver was telling me. 'That's how I first caught on to you and Akay. When you met up with MacCready, everything became clear.' She shook her head, almost admiringly. 'You tried to warn me away from MacCready with your own nonsense conspiracy theory, but I could see it was a red herring because I found out at once that MacCready lives in Canada and isn't much interested in Britain any more.'

'So what,' MacCready asked heavily, 'are we supposed to have done?'

Weaver's triumphant grin came back. 'As far as we're concerned, Cydonia is a perfect honey-trap. It pulls all the dangerous paranoid nutcases into one place, where we can watch what they get up to. We have an expert system for sniffing out *real* conspiracies there, and when we turned its attention to you lot, all its lights went on! We can start with Links here – very apt name! He's the link between his father and the Web. Alan Kennedy sensibly keeps off it as much as he can, but he has his own worldwide connections. All those international trade unions, with communists and ex-communists in every position they can get! Then we had Akay, an American libertarian gun nut, already hanging out with the armed militias. We had MacCready, running a construction business in Vancouver, and keeping in touch with – in fact, employing – his former terrorist comrades. And there's Louise, who's a member of a Protestant fundamentalist cult which has had more experience of guerrilla war than the rest of you put together. Even some of its *elders* were once members of ZANU and Frelimo and the ANC! More ex-communist ex-terrorists! And finally, the spider at the centre of the web.'

Weaver spun around dramatically and pointed a finger at Anne-Marie.

I laughed out loud at this, but Weaver's pointed finger quivered as she spat out her accusations. '*You*, under the innocent cover of NeedleNet! A network, all right, its threads joining together people all around the world! And with your expert knowledge of how to turn designs in the Web into Realworld products, and ability to Web in to factories all over the place.' She frowned for a moment. 'I'm not quite sure yet what Yvonne's role was, but we think she was some kind of courier, a runner who would never normally be suspected. Anyway, when you put all these things together, the answer is obvious.'

'It certainly isn't obvious to me,' said my mother, in the weary tone she adopts when I come home with some wild tale from the Web.

'Like I said,' Weaver told her, in a similar tone, 'save that for the trial. *We* know what you're up to. Here's how it was going to work. The militias supply virtual images of weapons, every part accurate to the last detail. Akay provides propaganda, all that nonsense about inalienable rights that he's been well programmed to trot out. MacCready supplies military, *terrorist*, training. Anne-Marie Kennedy uses her knowledge of Fiberfax software to adapt machines in factories to start turning the virtual guns into real ones. The communist and trade union militants in the factories look after the process – and the products! – on site. No doubt they'll find uses for them in other countries. In Scotland, the Southern African Presbyterian Church, which has links with Ulster Protestants and experience of armed struggle in Africa, uses the guns to disrupt Scottish independence, because they fear Catholic influence in a free Scotland.'

'Rubbish!' shouted Louise. 'We live in peace with our neighbours! We have old people in Harare who knew the Pope when he was an altar-boy!'

'Besides that,' Weaver said, ignoring her, 'there are plenty of other tensions in Scotland to exploit: the Green settlers, the EU Air Force ... plenty of room for a few nasty provocations. The key is the new financial centre planned for Edinburgh. If independence doesn't pass, it never gets built. Investment is scared off, unemployment rises, the moderate leaders of Alan Kennedy's union are discredited, and his communist friends get control. And do you know where the new centre will be built, if the Edinburgh site falls through? *Vancouver* – where MacCready's firm has a good chance of winning juicy contracts on it! And what do the militias get out of all this? Lots of new friends, another defeat for gun control, and another inspiring struggle of good Christian people to support. And no doubt lots of other armed actions all over the world, even if these are carried out by communists. The militias will ally with anyone against the so-called New World Order.'

'Wow,' said Mac. 'You're really something. That is some story.'

Weaver shrugged. 'It was our expert system that worked it out,' she said modestly. 'It learns things.'

'It's learned paranoia from Cydonia,' Mac retorted. 'Now, let us go before we die laughing.'

Weaver cocked her head. 'I don't hear anyone laughing,' she remarked. She caught sight of Louise pulling faces, and frowned. 'You are in serious trouble, all of you, and—'

Then she screamed. Anne-Marie and Yvonne screamed too. I nearly screamed myself.

A three-metre-tall giant had just appeared right in front of Weaver.

The giant had long hair and a wild beard. He was dressed in mammoth skins, and his long, heavy spear was poised above Weaver's head. His free hand shot out and grabbed Weaver's right arm. She couldn't reach her scuttle-button. The giant's mighty paw slid down her arm and covered her hand like an enormous furry mitt. Then it forced her hand upward, and swatted it down, twice.

Suddenly, I could move again. So could we all. Yvonne

rushed over and grabbed Mum. As a flat shape, Anne-Marie couldn't give her much of a hug, but she tried.

'How did you do that?' I asked Louise.

'Glove-and-glasses,' Louise grinned. 'Called up some low-level software with my tongue. I nicked the giant and a few other things from Noah's Park. Weaver here has an invisible control-panel that responds to her fingers only. Looks like I guessed right for the keys to free us.' She laughed. 'Good old Esc Esc, actually. Bit obvious.'

'It won't do you any good,' yelled Weaver, still struggling in the Paluxy Man's grasp. 'This is a Webcop holding pen, closed off from any access but our own, and the rest of my team will be here any moment—'

There was a sound like shattering glass. The white floor and the featureless space around us vanished. I looked around frantically. We were in a huge, dark interior with pools of light all around and a big rectangle of sunlight in front of us. Hangar 18, Dreamland.

Shadowy figures stepped forward out of the darkness around us. All of them had guns levelled. Their faces came into view: my father, Mr Matabele, Akay, the militia woman who called herself Code, and Relay – the Korean girl I'd fought beside on the Moon that morning, which seemed so long ago.

Louise's flat image turned to face Weaver.

'You were saying?'

The giant phace shambled off into the darkness. Weaver had her hands on top of her head, and Akay was taking great pleasure in aiming his AK47 at her to make sure they stayed there. Virtual guns can't do real harm, of course, but because of the Web's underlying consistency rules they can do lots of *virtual* harm, even to a Webcop avatar.

'We're going to scuttle,' Anne-Marie said. 'Yvonne and I. She needs a hot drink, a hot bath and a real cuddle. I'll get the story later. Thanks, Louise, and all of you, whatever you did.'

She reached for her scuttle-button. It was a weird sight, because her image didn't bend like a cardboard cut-out at all, it flowed and changed like a flat picture – and hesitated.

'Will we find the house full of police?'

'Nah,' said Akay, still not taking his gaze or his gun-muzzle off Weaver. 'They were called off just after they got called out. Too late for our front door, mind you. My dad's lawyer is suing the FBI right now, and y'all should do the same to your local fuzz.'

'Oh, I don't know,' said Anne-Marie. 'They're good boys, really, our policemen.'

She and Yvonne vanished before Akay's cynical laugh reached their ears.

'Yeah, I suppose there are good cops,' he admitted. 'Even good Webcops.'

'Too right there are,' said Mr Matabele. 'Lucky for us all,' – he interrupted himself, with a smile at Louise, as if to say *don't repeat what I just said* – 'or, I should say, providential, that you found one by accident. Even your militia pals couldn't have broken in to that holding-site without her help.'

'I guess not,' said Code, with a shrug.

Other dark figures were stepping forward out of the gloom. They were Webcops, but they didn't seem interested in us. They were interested in carefully and rather gently arresting Weaver. Akay lowered his rifle to let them do it. Weaver gave us all a sour smile as they led her away.

'Can't win them all,' she said. 'And don't get too cocky, we're still watching you.' Her image dissolved as the Webcops scuttled with her, leaving her final words hanging on the air: 'I'll be back!'

'No doubt she will,' sighed Relay. 'Slap on the wrist, that's all she'll get. I really am sorry about all this. She's from London Metcops Limited, seconded to UN Special Forces, not a regular Webcop. Both these forces contain a whole barrel of bad apples. But it's not really her fault. She was misled by this expert system the UN Special Forces have set up to watch Cydonia. It's gone native – totally paranoid, turned into a sort of conspiracy buff itself, from watching the people it watches watching it right back, if you ask me.'

'How do you know all this?' I asked. I looked around at the folk who'd rescued us. They all looked like they knew something I didn't. 'What's going on?'

Akay gave me an aw-shucks-it-was-nothing sort of grin. 'I Webbed around, like I said. Roused the ARM and our pals from the game. Your AI gopher – hey, man, maybe you could slip me a copy of Hal, it's a venomous cool device – put me in touch with Mac and your old man and this church Webmaster.' He glanced at Mr Matabele. 'Another cool guy. Anyway, we've got the churches and the American Civil Liberties Union and the International Free Trade Unions screaming about this. We're Webwide famous!'

'Famous for fifteen minutes, I hope,' said Mac.

'Yeah, well. Anyway, like the deacon says, we'd never have broken through without a good Webcop on our side.'

'I don't see any—'

Relay clapped my shoulder. 'Yes you do,' she said. 'I'm a Webcop.' She drew herself up to her full height, which seemed taller than I remembered. 'I'm Ariadne.'

CHAPTER TWELVE

PROTOCOLS

With one sweep of its mighty tail, the plesiosaur turned at
the end of the huge aquarium along one wall of the Cydonia
Café. Spectators, splashed with virtual water, cheered as it
swam another length, turned again and swam back, turned
... you get the picture. Louise stepped around the side of the
aquarium, bowed and smiled to a storm of applause, and
formally fixed a polished brass nameplate to the side of the
aquarium.

I was standing at the bar, watching from nearly a hundred
metres away, but I knew what was written on the plate. I
knew because I'd written it myself, with the help of my old
Latin-spider phace.

Plesiosarus caledonis.

Scottish plesiosaur. Better known as Nessie, but there was
no need to put that on the brass plate. This was Cydonia,
after all.

Louise was making her way through the crowd, who'd
now gone back to their regular debates. The story of what
had happened to us had already spawned its own talk-
groups, spinning theories wilder than Weaver's. No doubt
they'll be arguing about it for years.

'It was a bit off,' said a voice beside me, 'nicking that
plesiosaur from Noah's Park. I have a soft spot for the
creationists.'

I turned to see a tall, dignified-looking elderly man, one of

the regulars. I couldn't remember his name, but I grinned at
him like an old friend.

'I hope you don't shop us to them,' I said.

'Oh, no,' he said. 'Never! Cydonia's the old homepage,
after all.'

'Good on you.' I turned, leaning back on the bar, looking
again at the huge display. 'Some cafés have tanks of tropical
fish. You have to admit, here at the Cydonia Café we have
people who think that little bit bigger.'

'I'll grant you that,' he said. He turned to the bartender.
'Another Coke Tingle, please.'

The drink was placed carefully on the counter by a big
hairy hand. Paluxy Man had found a job, and seemed in no
hurry to return to Noah's Park. I was idly wondering what
had happened to N'thota, the Martian phace, when Louise
shouldered her way through the last of the crush and stood
beside me.

'Well,' she said. 'That was fun! Where do we go now?'

Where indeed. About a month has passed since our adventure. Our fifteen minutes of Webwide fame have resulted in a
discreet flurry of Realworld activity. Rumour has it that
Weaver has been demoted and sent on a re-training course: a
slap on the wrist, just as Relay – Ariadne – had predicted. The
expert system that went mad listening to the Cydonia
debates is being re-trained too, so we're told, to give it more
rigorous protocols. We don't know who, or what, is watching Cydonia right now. But someone, or something, is. You
can count on it. Tim's father's lawyers are suing the FBI and
the UN Special Forces for millions of dollars. I wish them
luck.

The other Webcops – Relay's lot, not Weaver's – have
shown very little interest in our story. They're more concerned about investigating how all those alien phaces got
upgraded and started behaving oddly, like the one Yvonne
found herself trapped in when she innocently tried to follow
me to Dreamland. There are a whole lot of rumours about

the upgrades. Typical Cydonia babble, but you never know ...

MacCready and my father meet Friday nights in a virtual bar in Toronto and argue about politics. Well, about Ireland, actually. It's a start.

Or, perhaps, a continuation. MacCready and Alan must have known each other in Northern Ireland, even as enemies. In Ulster, everybody knows everybody else. I still don't know for sure if there wasn't *something* behind Weaver's conspiracy theory, some unlikely liason between the militias and the International.

Her idea about guns turning up in factories around the world may or may not be true. But according to Alan's me-paper, foremen in Korean shipyards and Party hacks in Cuban sweatshops and so on have started behaving with nervous politeness over the past few weeks.

In the run-up to the independence referendum the Scottish government has set up a Royal Commission to look into areas of tension in Scotland: Unionists, Green settlers, all that. It's headed up by a chap called Sir Brian Micklethwait. Tim was amazed that I'd never heard of him. Outside Britain, everybody's heard of him. Everybody Tim knows, anyway. Even Louise says he's a big name in what's called micro-diplomacy. Sorted out some brushfire banditry in Mozambique by winning over a few bandit leaders, she told me.

Just one more of those things I should have known about, but didn't. I have exams coming up, and I'm coming round to the idea that maybe I've spent too much time in Cydonia. The world is owned, all right, but its owners' names are no secret. Just look at the brand names around you, and you'll see them.

The old guy who'd spoken to me had found another listener. 'That's not my theory or version of it at all,' he was earnestly explaining. 'My version of it is that you had Mars sitting right over the Earth with an atmosphere shared between the planets and constrained by an electro-magnetic

bottle, and that human ancestors who looked very much like
the face on the pedestal base in Cydonia inhabited both
planets, getting from one to the other via aircraft, dirigible,
or possibly even by putting a saddle on one of the teratorns
or some such.'

I found myself smiling at Louise, and shaking my head.

'I know where to go!' she said. 'I've found a link in the
deep software. To another version of Mars – breathable
atmosphere, frozen canals. D'you fancy a bit of skating?'

Skating is a great excuse to hold hands, to bump into each
other, to fall and help each other up, to fall into each other's
arms. We'd done it in real and virtual places, but never, until
now, on Mars.

'Yes,' I said. 'Let's do that.'

Louise has learned a lot in all her years of working the Web
in gag: the deep codes, the consistency rules, the protocols.
She tapped at her wristpad, and suddenly a doorway opened
up in front of us.

A ribbon of ice stretched from in front of our feet to the
near horizon, between banks of red soil overgrown with
scrub and lichen. We held hands and stepped through,
morphing our footwear into skates.

As we passed through that gate she'd hacked in the deep
software of the site, I noticed a whirl of text in front of my
eyes. I can't swear to it, but I'm almost sure I saw a bright line
that read (before it faded):

> http:www/marsobserver/1993/june/nasa.gov

Then it was gone, and we were standing unsteadily on the
frozen canal. Louise gripped my hand firmly.

'Let's go,' she said.

I looked over my shoulder at Cydonia, and for another
fleeting, fading moment, I saw – or thought I saw – a
different Cydonia.

The Face was there, its chiselled features sharp and clear,
sharper even than they're shown on the Cydonia site. And
the City, and the Pyramids, were all there – all obviously,

blatantly, unarguably artificial, their dressed red rock gleaming under the small, pale sun of Mars. Machines, and people in spacesuits, were climbing all over them, USS and NASA Mars rovers were parked around them, tiny as toys beside that work of giants.

I blinked, and it was gone. Was it another of Cydonia's hoaxes, another deceit? Or was it—

'What is it?' asked Louise, looking up at me impatiently. She hadn't seen it.

I shook my head. 'Nothing,' I said. 'A glitch in telemetry. A trick of the light.'

I squeezed her hand and smiled and (with a few bumps and falls) we sped away, and turned our backs on Cydonia.

The truth is not there.

COMPUTOPIA
JAMES LOVEGROVE

CONTENTS

CHAPTER ONE

LORELAND

Jax wasn't all that fond of Loreland.

When it came to entertainment, he preferred Web game-zones that were action-packed – Dreamcastle, for instance, or Draculand.

On schooldays, and particularly on those two days a week when he attended Realworld school, Jax liked nothing better than to suit up afterwards and bat into a gamezone where you didn't have to think or, at any rate, didn't have to think very hard. You had to have quick reflexes to battle dragons or vanquish vampires, but that was all, whereas in Loreland you were required to concentrate all the time, and Jax's brain, weary after a day's learning, often found that a strain.

However, Loreland was Flygirl's favourite gamezone and Jax liked hanging out with Flygirl in the Web. That was why, this evening, he found himself once again in the company of his best and perhaps only friend, roaming among Loreland's cloud-capped castles and yellow-brick roads.

Unfortunately, on this occasion Flygirl had brought along Lioness, who lived next door to her. Lioness thought she was something rather special. She brimmed with pride.

Not only that, she was also one of life's great whingers.

'I *hate* this game,' Lioness said.

Lioness, Flygirl and Jax were passing through a dark, dense forest when she made this announcement. They were following a winding pathway and taking care not to step on

the cracks between the flagstones, since there were bears
lurking among the trees who took a particular dislike to
anyone who stepped on cracks. Flygirl – an ultravet at
Loreland – had advised Jax and Lioness not to stray from the
pathway either, no matter what might happen to catch their
eye. There were gingerbread cottages in the forest that
looked alluring (not to mention tasty) but were home to
witches who would attempt to make a pie out of you, and
there were picturesque little cottages where wolves dressed as
grandmothers waited in bed to mesmerize you with their big
eyes, and chomp on you with their big teeth if you failed to
answer their questions correctly. The knack to Loreland was
remembering all of its many rules and pitfalls. By learning
from your mistakes and not repeating them, you were able to
get further in the game and survive longer.

'Why do you hate it, Talisa?' Jax asked, using Lioness's
Realworld first name rather than her alias because he knew it
would annoy her.

'It's all European fairy-tale stuff,' Lioness replied, glaring at
Jax. She had altered her features (which, like Flygirl's, were
African) using top-grade cosmetic software. Her nose was
flattened, her eyes were amber with narrow pupil-slits, and
white whisker-like lines scored her cheeks. 'African folklore is
much more dangerous and exciting. *This*,' she said, dismiss-
ing the forest with an all-encompassing sweep of her hand,
'is for eggs.'

'Is that the real reason?' said Jax. 'Or is it because you're
completely six at playing Loreland and you're down to your
last life?'

He gestured at the amulet that hung on a chain around
Lioness's neck. At the start of a Loreland session, each player
was given one of these amulets on which there was a trio of
green gemstones representing the player's three lives. Every
time you lost a life, a gemstone was removed. Lioness had
one left.

'How was I to know that little man in the green jacket was

lying about the pot of gold worth 100 points?' Lioness retorted.

'All the phaces in this game are out to trick you, leprechauns included. That's the point. Anyway, you should have held on to his finger and not let go, like Flygirl told you to. Then you would have got the 100 points. And as for stepping on a crack . . .'

Lioness had accidentally done that moments after they had entered the forest. A vast, snarling grizzly bear had lunged out onto the pathway and removed the second gemstone from her amulet with one swipe of its sharp-clawed paw.

'Keep your mind on the game, Jax, or you'll be next,' Flygirl warned. 'You almost stepped on a crack yourself just then.'

Jax, with a surly grimace, returned his attention to where he placed his feet.

A moment later, Flygirl pointed ahead. There were hazy beams of sunlight slanting through the trees, brightening the pathway. 'Nearly there,' she said.

'We ain't outta the woods yet,' Jax said.

Behind the bulbous round lenses of the dark glasses she always wore in the Web, Flygirl rolled her eyes. 'We ain't outta the woods yet,' was the sort of clichéd line you might expect to hear spoken by a tough-guy character in an interactive movie in Hollywoodland. Coming from the lips of a thirteen-year-old boy, even one who hailed from California, it sounded totally gag.

The three of them emerged from the forest into the sunshine. The sun felt warm on their faces after the chilly darkness of the forest.

They found themselves at one end of a green valley. Sheer, craggy mountains rose on both sides. At the far end of the valley, about half a kilometre away, ran a river, spanned by a rickety wooden bridge. There appeared to be no other way out of the valley except by the bridge, so they set off towards it, their feet whisking through daisy-spangled grass.

They hadn't gone more than a hundred metres when
Lioness piped up again. 'This is cog. I've a good mind to go
bat.'

'Why don't you then?' said Jax irritably. He had had about
as much of Lioness's moaning as he could stomach. 'I'm fed
up with you egging along with us.'

'I asked Lioness to come with us,' Flygirl reminded him.
Her expression, however, suggested that she wished she
hadn't.

Flygirl's mother and father couldn't seem to get it into
their heads that she didn't like Lioness. Lioness's parents, Mr
and Mrs Makeba, and Flygirl's parents got along famously so
they naturally assumed that their daughters got along
famously, too. At her father's insistence, Flygirl had reluctantly agreed to invite Lioness along on one of her spins into
the Web.

'It doesn't matter, anyway,' said Lioness with a regal,
dismissive wave. 'We've just signed up with the Net at our
house, and there are much better gamezones there.'

'Izzit?' said Jax, using a piece of Zimbabwean slang he had
picked up from Flygirl.

Flygirl shot an interested glance at Jax – not because of the
slang, but for another reason.

'Yes,' said Lioness. 'I don't suppose either of you has
visited the Net brochure site yet, but it's absolutely awesome.
Our Net junction-box arrived this morning, as a matter of
fact. Unfortunately, we're off to Scotland tomorrow, on a
two-week safari, so I won't have a chance to use the box until
we get back. Everyone who's anyone is going over to the Net,
you know.'

Flygirl was still watching Jax closely. It seemed that Jax
wasn't going to let on that he had a certain connection with
the Net. A family connection.

'In fact,' said Lioness – now that she had started bragging,
it was hard for her to stop – 'I overheard the sales realoe at
the brochure site saying to my father that there are places in

the Net that are real *utopias*.' She had trouble correctly pronouncing that last, unfamiliar word.

'Utopias?' said Flygirl.

'Yes. I'm not sure what it means, but my father seemed pretty intrigued.'

Jax's face and tone of voice turned sly. 'The Net sounds great. I bet you wish you were there right now, huh, Lioness?'

The words were out of Lioness's mouth before she could stop herself. 'Oh, I wish I was, yes, definitely.'

A fairy with gossamer wings and an acorn-cup hat winked into existence in front of Lioness's nose. Hovering on a blur of gossamer wings, the tiny phace offered Lioness an impish smile and said, in a high-pitched, squeaky voice, 'You have expressed a wish in Loreland. You now have ten seconds to touch wood, or you forfeit a life. Ten. Nine. Eight . . .'

Lioness looked ahead of her, then behind her. They had walked nearly halfway along the valley. The forest was about 250 metres behind them, the wooden bridge a similar distance ahead. There was no other type of wood to be seen, and there was no way, even running, that Lioness would be able to reach either the forest or the bridge in time.

She fixed the fairy with a contemptuous stare and said, 'It's a useless, one-mip game, anyway.'

The fairy counted off the remaining seconds, then swooped towards Lioness's amulet. It snatched away her third and final gemstone and, with a light tinkling giggle, flew up into the sky.

Lioness dissolved into a spray of millions of fizzing pixels, vanishing.

'That wasn't very nice of you, Jax,' said Flygirl. But she was grinning.

'Serves her right,' Jax replied. 'She shouldn't have started boasting like that.'

'And why didn't you tell her your father owns the Net?'

Jax shrugged. 'Didn't seem important.'

Flygirl eyed Jax carefully. Jax saw his face reflected twice –

once in each lens of Flygirl's dark glasses, distorted. The glasses didn't, as dark glasses do in Realworld, shade Flygirl's eyes from bright light. They were a software add-on that enabled her to see visual code in enhanced detail. They were also capable of several other neat tricks.

Finally, Flygirl shook her head, making the beads rattle on her braided hair. 'You're strange, Jerry Hamlyn,' she said.

'You're strange, too, Anita N'Douba. That's why we're friends.'

They laughed.

'Well,' said Flygirl, 'shall we go and see what's waiting for us under that bridge?'

'Betcha it's a troll and it's got a riddle for us,' said Jax.

It *was* a troll and it *did* have a riddle for them. But no sooner had the hairy, malevolent creature crawled out and begun voicing its ritual challenge, than it froze, mid-sentence – and disappeared.

In its place, a d-box shimmered into view.

!!!WARNING!!!
Loreland will shut down in fifteen minutes
for systems analysis.
Please pause your game and exit.

Following the recent worldwide Webcrash, all sites in Webtown were undergoing regular checks to make sure their software was running smoothly and without hitch or glitch. The Webcops had promised that things would be back to normal within a couple of weeks. Until then, Web-users would have to put up with these occasional interruptions.

'Pick up where we left off tomorrow, then?' said Flygirl.

Jax nodded, and they scuttled.

Jax pulled off his gloves, headset and boots, and peeled himself out of his Websuit. The suit was top-of-the-range Gucci-wear, lightweight and comfortable, the best that money could buy.

He hung the suit on its hanger next to his spare Websuit, then exited his padded, windowless Webroom. The door slid shut behind him and the lights turned themselves off automatically. He strode along the corridor, gradually read-justing to the heavy sensation of walking in Realworld. After being in the Web, which gave the illusion of effortless movement, it sometimes took a conscious effort to remind himself how to put one foot in front of the other. Dyson-drones hummed along the floor, veering out of his way as they sucked up dust through their nozzle-snouts.

The corridor linked up with a glassed-in verandah that ran the entire length of one side of the house. Metallic cleaning-slugs clung to the windowpanes, sliding over them in regular patterns, leaving gleaming swathes of polished glass behind. Like the Dyson-drones, the cleaning-slugs were remote-con-trolled by the house's central processing unit. The CPU was almost solely responsible for domestic maintenance of the building. It also controlled the climate in each room and monitored security.

Of course, like every other computer in the world, the house's CPU had been affected by the Webcrash. Jax remembered that day clearly. The Dyson-drones had gone haywire, charging around the house trying to vacuum one another. The cleaning-slugs had started climbing the walls. Outside, the solar-powered lawn mower had switched itself on and gone careering around the back lawn, cutting crop-circle patterns in the grass. And all the doors and windows of the house had locked themselves. Jax and his father were trapped inside for several hours, prisoners in their own home, until eventually his father had managed to override the CPU and shut it down.

Looking back, Jax could see the funny side of what had happened. But at the time it had been quite alarming, and for days afterwards he had stepped warily around the domestic appliances, half-fearing that they were suddenly going to go mad again.

The house, a sprawling, one-storey building, stood on the

side of a hill overlooking Los Angeles. It was noon, and the sun hung high over the city's grid-pattern layout of palm-fringed streets. It was possible, on this bright April day, to see clear across the city to the Pacific Ocean, which glinted like a huge sapphire on the horizon. A couple of decades ago the sea would have been lost in the pall of pollution that used to hang permanently over LA, but now all that remained of the infamous thick blanket of smog was a faint haze.

Jax glanced out indifferently at the view which he had seen hundreds of times before, then headed along the verandah in the direction of his father's study.

Lioness's remark about *utopias* had got him thinking. He would ask his father what it meant.

But someone else was already in conversation with his father. As he reached the study door, Jax recognized the voice coming from the other side. The voice was an insinuating nasal drawl that set Jax's teeth on edge. It belonged to J Edgar Glote.

Most people thought Jax's father, multimillionaire Larry Hamlyn, was the man who had created the Net. In fact, Glote was the Net's true inventor. A computer-programming genius, Glote had dreamed up and developed a rival system to the Web that offered improved, more detailed graphics, faster and smoother movement, and a reduction in Websick-ness which allowed users to stay online up to 15 per cent longer. All Jax's father had done was invest a small fraction of his immense wealth in Glote's fledgling company, Mesh Incorporated.

Hamlyn hadn't been expecting Mesh Inc. to make him very much money. Indeed, quite the reverse. He had bought the company as a tax write-off, thinking it would not survive long. However, since coming onstream three months ago, the Net had surprised everyone – except, perhaps, Glote – by showing nothing but healthy and ever-increasing profits. Although time spent in the Net was more expensive than time spent in the Web, the Net was popular with certain people in the same way that the smarter, flashier makes of car – Ferrari, Rolls Royce, Skoda Excel – were popular with certain people, despite the fact that their batteries ate up electricity and their parts were expensive to replace. The Net cost more to use. It was superior. It had *snob-value*.

Jax halted outside his father's study. He knew it was wrong to eavesdrop but, nonetheless, he put his ear to the door and listened.

' . . . Webcrash was the best damn thing that could have happened to us,' he heard Glote saying to his father. 'A lot of people got a heck of a fright when Webtown went down back in January. They kinda had their confidence shaken, so we couldn't have chosen a better time to launch the Net than the following month. People saw us and thought, "Well, I don't know if I can trust the Web any more. Maybe I should try the Net. It seems safe. It's got a clean track record." And new subscribers have been signing up in their thousands.'

'But surely people realize that if the Net had been online during the Webcrash, it would have been affected, too,' said Hamlyn.

'Maybe so, Larry, but it's all about perception,' replied Glote. 'Doesn't matter what the truth is. The public still *perceives* the Net as being safer than the Web. And that's the angle our marketing people are going to use in our latest advertising campaign. They've come up with a slogan: *The Net – It Won't Let You Down.*'

'Catchy,' said Hamlyn, dryly.

'Isn't it, though?' said Glote. 'Which brings me to my next point. There's been a lot of interest in the Net among the Pacific Rim nations. Taiwan, Japan, Korea – they're all keen to get their hands on our junction-boxes. It's potentially a huge market, and we'd be foolish not to expand into it. It would enlarge our, if you'll excuse the pun, *net profits* considerably.'

'If you think we should, Edgar, then we should.' Hamlyn sounded tired and not at all interested in what his business associate had to say.

Jax became impatient. He couldn't be bothered to wait for Glote to finish. Raising his fist, he knocked on the study door.

'Come in,' said Hamlyn.

Command-recognition software triggered the door's opening mechanism. Jax entered the study.

Hamlyn was sitting in a leather-upholstered chair behind his imposing hardwood desk, on which sat a videophone and a computer terminal. He had his back to the study's windows, through which could be seen a large swimming pool and an expanse of well-tended lawn. Glote was sitting on the other side of the desk, facing Hamlyn. A stainless-steel briefcase rested on the floor at his feet. On the wall behind him hung two original and hugely valuable paintings by Van Gogh.

The bespectacled, ponytailed computer genius greeted Jax as though they were old buddies. 'Jerry! How ya doing, kiddo?'

'Not bad. Mr Glote, could I have a word with my dad, please? In private?'

'Sure, why not? We're about done here anyway. And Jerry, I keep telling you, you must remember to call me Edgar.'

'OK, Mr Glote.'

A hint of a frown flitted across Glote's face. It was like the brief disturbance caused by a breath of wind passing over the surface of an otherwise calm pond. It was short-lived, and Glote's smile quickly returned. But Jax had noticed the frown and was pleased to think that he had managed to annoy Glote, however mildly.

Glote gathered up his briefcase and left the room.

Hamlyn looked across the desk at his son. 'What do you want, Jerry? Is it about that fishing trip again?'

Actually, Jax had not been thinking about the often promised – and just as often postponed – fishing trip, but now that the subject had been raised, it seemed a good idea to try and get his father to fix a date. 'Well, when *are* we going, Dad?'

Hamlyn sighed. 'Soon, son. I've a lot on my plate at the moment.'

'*Dad*. You've been putting it off for months!'

'I know, I know.'

'And my schoolteachers keep going on about the importance of Realworld experiences over Web experiences.'

'Jerry . . .'

'*Your* dad used to take you fishing all the time.'

'He did, but things were different when I was a kid. There wasn't a Web, for one thing.'

'Or a Net,' said Jax, pointedly. 'Maybe I'd be better off going fishing in there.'

Hamlyn leaped to his feet. He strode around the desk until he was standing beside his son. He bent down until their faces were level. His expression, which was usually distracted and preoccupied, had become stern and serious.

'Jerry,' he said, 'listen to me, and listen to me good. Don't go batting into the Net. Don't even joke about it. Got that?'

Jax nodded, perplexed by the sudden change that had come over his father.

'The Net is not the sort of place a boy should visit,' his father continued. 'Do you understand me?' He placed a hand on Jax's shoulder, gripping him tightly enough to hurt. 'Do you understand me?'

Again Jax nodded, just a little scared now.

Hamlyn relaxed his grip. 'Good.'

The v-phone on the desk beeped demandingly. Hamlyn frowned at it. 'I'd better get that,' he said.

Jax nodded, turned, and left the study in a state of some confusion. Just a moment ago he had heard Glote say that the Net was safer than the Web. Yet here was his father suggesting something quite different.

Which of them was right?

CHAPTER TWO

NETSHARKS

Jax headed for the kitchen to fix himself a peanut-butter-and-jam sandwich and to have a good think.

Glote was in the kitchen, sitting on one of the stools at the breakfast bar and taunting Jax's PseudoPup. He had the little animatroid dog's favourite ball in his hand and was pretending to throw it. Each time he swung his arm, the PseudoPup shot off across the floor in the direction it thought the ball would be travelling. When it realized the ball had not been thrown and was still in Glote's hand, it would scrabble to a halt and come scampering back. Frustration was not in the PseudoPup's programming but Jax felt sorry for it all the same. Glote was exploiting its limitless enthusiasm for his own amusement.

Jax summoned the PseudoPup with a whistle. The PseudoPup ran over to him and jumped up against his legs, wagging its tail in demented delight. He stroked its nylon fur and petted it behind its ears.

'A boy and his dog – always a sight that warms my heart,' said Glote. 'Dogs are so adoring, aren't they? Even artificial ones. You can always rely on them for perfect, unconditional affection. Unlike people.'

'Yeah, some people you just can't rely on for anything.'

Jax meant this as a barbed comment on Glote's personality, but Glote chose to interpret it differently.

'Oh now,' he said, 'you and your dad didn't just have a fight, did you?'

'Kinda,' admitted Jax. 'You know that fishing trip he's forever been promising to take me on?'

'He postponed it again.'

Jax nodded.

'I'm sorry to hear it, Jerry. But don't forget, your father's a busy guy, and it's not easy for a man to bring up his son all by himself. And hey!' Glote gestured at the PseudoPup, and then at the kitchen in general, which was large and equipped with all the latest labour-saving gadgets, including a self-stacking dishwasher and an automatic cookie-maker that could produce a dozen different types of cookie at the drop of a hat, turning them out warm and oven-fresh every time. 'This is a heck of a lifestyle you've got going here. You have everything a kid your age could ever want – toys, a fabulous home, even your own Rhodium account at the Days home-shopping site in the Web. You've nothing to complain about. Me, I was brought up in a poor neighbourhood in San Bernardino, one of eight brothers and sisters. My pa was a waste-reclamation engineer, which is a fancy way of saying he worked on a dumpsite. We barely had two cents to rub together. I had to bootstrap myself to where I am today, through sheer hard work. You're a very lucky boy, Jerry.'

'I don't *feel* lucky,' said Jax. He sidled up to the breakfast bar and hoisted himself onto the stool next to Glote's. Much as he disliked Glote, the man was being sympathetic, and just then Jax was in need of a sympathetic ear. 'I mean, Dad has all this money he inherited from my grandparents, and it's a full-time job looking after it. You'd think he could employ someone else to do that for him, so he could spend more time with me, but no-o-o.'

'Your father's wise not to trust anyone else with his money. I think he hopes you'll be just as wise when your turn comes to inherit it.'

'I just wish Mom was still around.'

Jax had been three years old when his mother died, so he had only the vaguest memories of her. He knew what she looked like, because her father kept several framed photographs of her around the house and there was a holo-portrait of her, commissioned from one of America's foremost 3D artists, hanging in the entrance hall. She had been beautiful. What she had been like as a person, however, Jax could not remember.

One thing he did recall about her clearly was the smell of her favourite perfume, rose-water. The smell had lodged in his memory. Whenever he smelled the scent of roses, he immediately felt safe and secure and comforted.

'It'd be nice to have a mom,' he added wistfully.

'Your dad wishes she was still around, too, Jerry. He misses her terribly.'

Glote regarded Jax levelly through the flat lenses of his steel-rimmed spectacles. Nowadays, no one needed spectacles, not when laser surgery could correct any imperfections in vision. Glote, however, chose to wear a pair as a tribute to his personal hero, Bill Gates, the man who, over four decades ago, founded a company called Microsoft that revolutionized computing. By helping to make it easier for different types of computers to talk to one another, Microsoft was instrumental in paving the way for the creation of the Web. Microsoft also made Gates almost unimaginably wealthy.

Gates now lived the life of a recluse in a palatial home which he had built for himself inside a hollowed-out mesa in the Arizona desert. He never went outdoors, and it was rumoured that he had become quite eccentric in his old age. He would, it was said, do anything to avoid spending his fortune unnecessarily, for example walking around with shoeboxes on his feet (packed with tissue-paper for padding) so that he would not wear out the actual shoes that had come in the boxes.

'But you're right,' Glote said. 'Having everything you could want, every *material* thing, means nothing if you don't have a loving parent – someone you can trust, someone you can look up to. Life can seem pretty unfair when you look at it that way.'

'Unfair, yeah,' said Jax, nodding bitterly. Glote was making a lot of sense.

Glote's stainless-steel briefcase was lying flat on the breakfast bar. He reached for it and popped the catches. 'Y'know, there's somewhere you can go where you can even up the unfairness, Jax. Where you can work out all your frustrations.'

'Where?' Jax was so curious to see what was in the briefcase that he did not notice that Glote had addressed him by his nick.

Glote raised the briefcase lid.

Inside, nestling among squiggles of polystyrene-foam packing, was a Net junction-box.

It was a matt-black cube, its edges twenty centimetres long. All of its surfaces were plain and smooth except one, which featured a standard input socket and an output cable. On that same surface the Mesh Inc. corporate logo – the letters *MI* superimposed over a crosshatched square – was stencilled in blue.

'This is the latest version,' said Glote, removing the junction-box from the briefcase. 'The Mark III. The guys in Research and Development are pretty proud of it. It's the smallest model yet, and it's got an awful lot of processing power crammed inside. You can tell just by holding it. Here.' He proffered the box to Jax.

Jax took it from him. 'It's heavy,' he said, cupping the box in both hands.

'It's yours.'

Jax blinked at Glote. 'I'm sorry?'

'I said, it's yours. As in yours to keep. That is, if you want it.'

'You mean, it's mine, and I can use it to access the Net?'

Glote nodded. 'It's initialized for whoever first uses it.'

'But don't I have to subscribe? Sign up? Wait for credit approval?'

'Larry Hamlyn's kid wait for credit approval?' said Glote, chuckling. 'The son of the famous multimillionaire, having to have his finances checked out? I don't think so.'

'I don't know,' said Jax, uncertainly. A thought darted through the back of his mind – a memory of his father's warning: *Don't go batting into the Net.*

'Hey, fine, sure, whatever.' Glote leaned closer to Jax, and lowered his voice. 'But let me just say this. The Net's not policed by Webcops and it doesn't have the usual boring age-restriction protocols. There's some pretty neat stuff in there. *Venomous* stuff, as you kids would say. Games like you wouldn't believe. Zones like you couldn't imagine. Check 'em out for yourself. You'll see. All you have to do is bat in and ask for Davy Jones's Locker.'

Glote closed the briefcase and stood up.

'Anyway,' he said. 'Gotta go. I'm meeting with representatives of a Singapore tech-manufacture conglomerate in an hour. Nice talking with you, Jerry. I feel like you and I have really bonded.'

He tousled Jax's hair. Usually Jax would have hated this, but he was too busy staring at the junction-box to notice, or care.

'I'll see myself out,' said Glote. 'I know the way.' Glote, indeed, was such a frequent visitor to the Hamlyn household that he had his own code-number for the front door and the driveway gates.

Glote strolled out of the kitchen, briefcase under one arm.

Jax sat for several minutes, contemplating the junction-box. The PseudoPup was lying curled up in its basket. It had plugged itself into the mains and was quietly snoozing while its batteries recharged.

At last, Jax got slowly to his feet.

What the heck. It couldn't hurt just to have a peek into the Net.

Could it?

In his Webroom, Jax plugged his Websuit's output cable into

the input socket in the junction-box, and plugged the junction-box's cable into his Web-console. Then he suited up as normal. Took a deep breath. Put on his headset.

The world went blue.

Jax was floating. Way above him stretched a glowing field of azure light, patterned with bright ripples like the surface of the ocean viewed from beneath. Way below him lay a ribbed sandy seabed, dotted with wrecked galleons and coral reefs. In front of him, between the surface and the seabed, was a lattice of different-coloured Building Blocks, just like those in the Web, but stacked one on top of another, in tiers, as well as laid out in lines and rows.

The avatars of other Net-users were swimming through the spaces between the Building Blocks, browsing. If the contents of a block took a Net-user's fancy, he or she simply tapped its surface and vanished inside.

Jax was a little disappointed. To judge by first impressions, the only difference between the Net and the Web was the way the Building Blocks were arranged, in three dimensions instead of two, and the fact that you moved around by swimming rather than walking. The clarity of the graphics was perhaps marginally better, but nothing to write home about.

Then he noticed shapes roving around and among the blocks and the swimming avatars. They resembled torpedoes, thick and rounded at one end, tapering to a narrow, crescent-finned tail at the other.

He recognized them from the marine-biology classes he had attended at Webschool.

Sharks.

They moved lazily, propelling themselves with slow, easy lashes of their tails. They turned this way and that, apparently at random, as though casting about for a scent, or a purpose. And, watching them, Jax felt an unpleasant prickling in the pit of his stomach. Something about the shapes of the sharks stirred dread in him. This must have been some ancestral instinct that harked back to the time when mankind first ventured onto the ocean in cockleshell boats; a knowledge – passed down through the generations, imprinted in the genes – that these creatures were to be feared.

Then he recalled hearing somewhere that sharks were the Net's designated phaces. They patrolled the Net, and were on hand at all times to answer queries.

That made him feel a little better. But only a little. In the Web, after all, there were no phaces at the Building Block level. So why were they needed here?

Jax didn't know. But since they *were* here, it seemed like a good idea to take advantage of their presence. He decided to ask one of the NetSharks about Davy Jones's Locker. Spotting a tiger shark nearby, he aimed himself towards it.

He wasn't prepared for what happened next. He hadn't expected motion in the Net to be any different from in the Web, so he was startled by the speed with which he shot forwards. It was as though someone, without his knowledge, had strapped an outboard motor to his back. He found himself accelerating towards the tiger shark at an alarming rate.

He tried braking. Whereas in the Web he would have stopped straightaway, here he only slowed. His momentum carried him on. He was on a collision course with the NetShark and could not prevent himself crashing into its slash-striped flank.

The tiger shark rounded on him, yelling angrily, 'Hey, buddy!'

Jax's out-of-control progress had been halted by the impact. Turning himself around, he held up his hands, palms outwards. 'Sorry. I'm new here. Just getting my bearings.'

The NetShark scowled at him. Its eyes and mouth were disturbingly human-like. 'Yeah, well. In future, watch where you're going, OK?'

'I will. Excuse me, but can I ask you a question?'

The tiger shark grimaced. 'Guess so.'

'I'm looking for Davy Jones's Locker, and I was wondering—'

Before he could say any more, as if from nowhere another dozen NetSharks came streaking towards him. Within two heartbeats, Jax was surrounded by grey, torpedo-shaped bodies and mirthless, sickle-shaped grins.

The NetSharks circled around him, subjecting him to intimidating stares and hostile comments.

'Davy Jones's Locker? Ain't no such place.'

'Never heard of it.'

'Dumb kid! He should just curl up.'

'Stupid one-mip smallfry with a big mouth.'

'Get outta here, kid!'

'Yeah, go on. Scram!'

'Go back to the Web where you belong.'

Jax had a good mind to do exactly that. He knew the NetSharks were only computer constructs, merely software. He knew that they couldn't actually *harm* him. But, even knowing this, he was finding their sickle-grins just a little too sickly, a little too toothsome for comfort. Scuttling seemed a very appealing prospect. He was just reaching for the button on his wristpad when yet another NetShark, larger than any of the others, came finning towards him.

The other NetSharks respectfully cleared a path for the new arrival.

Jax identified it as a great white, a species now extinct in Realworld. Its face was oddly familiar, but it took Jax a couple of moments to work out who it looked like.

The great white's features bore a marked resemblance to those of J Edgar Glote.

CHAPTER THREE

UTOPIA

'It's Jax, isn't it?' said the great white. Its voice, too, was similar to Glote's. Jax assumed that Glote himself must have programmed this particular phace, furnishing it with his looks, voice-patterns and even a crude AI replica of his personality. 'Pleased to meetcha. Glad you could make it. Now, what can I do to help?'

'I was told to ask for Davy Jones's Locker,' said Jax, adding quickly, 'but it's not that important. Really. I don't *have* to go there.'

'Sure you do, Jax, sure you do,' said the great white reassuringly. 'That's where all the good stuff is. But you're gonna need the passcode.'

'Which is?'

The great white started to arch and spasm like a cat coughing up a hairball. It retched once, twice, then opened its mouth wide and spat out an octopus.

The octopus floated for a moment, furling and unfurling its tentacles as though to make sure they still worked. Its eyes, on their stubby stalks, looked bemused and bewildered.

Then the great white grabbed one of the octopus's tentacles between its two rows of evilly sharp teeth and bit it off.

The octopus did not seem distressed or alarmed to have been dismembered in this way. In fact, no sooner had the tentacle been bitten off than a new one budded from the stump and began to grow. Within seconds, the octopus had a full set of eight pulpy, sinuous limbs again.

A similar thing happened with the severed tentacle, although in reverse. The octopus had grown a new tentacle, and the tentacle grew a new octopus!

The body appeared first, swelling from the chewed-off end of the tentacle. Eye-stalks popped out on either side of the body, and seven more tentacles sprouted from beneath. In next to no time, there were two identical octopuses floating between Jax and the great white.

'There's your passcode,' said the great white.

The second octopus fondled its way elegantly over to Jax and attached itself to his arm, wrapping its tentacles tight around his wristpad.

'Davy Jones's Locker awaits,' said the great white, with a slow, sly wink.

Jax hesitated. Keen though he was to investigate Davy Jones's Locker, the NetSharks' behaviour had unsettled him. He didn't feel up to exploring the Net further on his own.

'You mind if I take a rain check?' he asked nervously.

'Of all the ungrateful—!' snarled a hammerhead, but it was interrupted by the Glote-like great white, who lashed out with a fin, whacking the hammerhead on its T-shaped nose to silence it.

'Of course we don't mind, Jax,' said the great white, with toothy politeness. 'You visit the Locker when you're good and ready. The octopus will still be on your arm when you next return to the Net.'

Without another word, Jax scuttled, returning himself to the padded confines of his Webroom where he tugged off his headset.

He had to Web round Flygirl.

The BiblioTech was vast. No one, not even the librarian-avatars who roamed its aisles, knew precisely how many books it contained. Millions, perhaps billions of them. One copy of every book ever published was filed away here in dusty silence, stacked on shelves that rose more than a hundred metres high, cliffs of words that reached all the way up to the lofty, vaulted ceiling.

The BiblioTech was a shrine to a habit that had nearly died out since the inception of the Web – book reading. Mainly it was visited by old people, who went there out of nostalgia to recapture one of the pleasures of their youth. Some college professors, too, liked to use the BiblioTech for research purposes. Sometimes it was easier to turn up a piece of information there than go trawling through a series of hyperlinked Webtown sites. After all, every scrap of knowledge that had ever been committed to print was available in the BiblioTech, ready to hand.

One of the youngest registered users of the BiblioTech was Anita N'Douba. Flygirl had an enquiring mind, a hunger to seek out facts and answers. If there was something she didn't fully understand, rather than forget about it or pretend it wasn't important, she preferred to go and find out everything she could about it. The BiblioTech was a wonderful place to do that.

She was in the BiblioTech now, looking up the word *utopia*. She had heard the term used before, but since Lioness had mentioned it she had been curious to learn what, precisely, it meant.

A quick check in one of the BiblioTech's dictionaries told her that a utopia was *an imaginary state of ideal perfection*, but Flygirl was not content to leave it at that. The dictionary listed a number of works of literature that dealt with the subject, including the book *Utopia*, written by an Englishman called Sir Thomas More back in 1516, in which the term had been coined. Flygirl made a note of the books' titles and reference numbers in a portable d-pad which she then handed to one of the librarians.

The librarian went away, and returned a few minutes later with an armful of leather-bound volumes.

Flygirl took the books, found herself a lectern and stacked the books on it in a pile. She adjusted a switch on the frame of her dark glasses, setting them to Digest Mode. This meant the glasses would highlight key sentences and passages, so that she could distil the essence of each book in a few minutes. Then she began flicking through the books one by one, rejoicing in the silken ease with which their pages turned.

While she read, every now and then a librarian came by to make sure she wasn't making too much noise and disturbing the other BiblioTech users. The librarians had uniformly stern, pinched faces and wore tweed jackets with leather patches on the elbows. They walked floating a few centimetres off the floor, so that their footsteps did not make a sound. Each kept an index finger permanently extended, ready to raise to his or her lips should a *ssh* be required.

The first book Flygirl went through was the aforementioned *Utopia*. It concerned an island where people lived happy, fulfilled lives, where laws were just, and where everyone behaved fairly towards each other. *Utopia*, in effect, was a blueprint for what the author, Thomas More, considered a perfect society, and it was clear that he had hoped that such a place could exist, and believed that such a place *would* exist if enough people followed the example of the Utopians in the book.

The next book she read was called *Erewhon* by Samuel Butler, and it used the concept of a perfect society to show what its author considered to be wrong with the Victorian society in which he lived. The Erewhonians led apparently idyllic lives, but they were hypocrites. How they acted and what they actually felt inside were two different things. In this way Butler, like More, seemed to be acknowledging that the perfection he was writing about was impossible (*Erewhon*, Flygirl realized, was an anagram of *nowhere*). Nonetheless, he seemed to be hoping to change things just a little with his book.

The third book in the pile was a novel called *Animal Farm* by George Orwell. Its simple story made the point rather well that a utopia was an unrealizable dream.

In the book, a collection of farm animals drove out the cruel, ruthless farmer who had been working them too hard and making their lives a misery. They then set about running the farm themselves, full of high hopes and with every intention of making their working conditions fairer. Eventually, however, the pigs took control of the farm and proved to be just as cruel and ruthless as the farmer had been.

The moral of the story was that the same happens in real life. However hard people try to get along and work together, however hard they try to treat one another as equals, inevitably somebody winds up with more money than the rest, or more power, or both. That was just the way things are – although Orwell evidently wished they weren't.

Flygirl thought *Animal Farm* was a very good novel, and resolved to save up enough pocket-credit to buy a copy from her local branch of Kingston's, the chain of shops in Zimbabwe where these brittle, antique, papery objects were sold, so that she could read the book more thoroughly, at her leisure.

One sentence in *Animal Farm* particularly amused her: "Four legs good, two legs bad." This was a sort of refrain that ran through the book, a chant the animals would repeat to stress how superior they were to humans. It amused her because a similar convention applied in the Web, where *eight* legs were good and *six* legs bad.

The next book in the pile was also by Orwell. It was called *Nineteen Eighty-four*, and the dictionary had described it as a *dys*topia, which was the opposite of a utopia, i.e. an imaginary place where everything was *far from* perfect. Flygirl didn't, however, get the chance to scan more than a few pages of it. A discreet cough caught her attention, and she looked round to find Samuel Jackson standing at her shoulder.

'Oh,' she said, and looked back down at the book, as if a visit from the President of the United States of America was an everyday occurrence.

'Excuse me, ma'am,' said the distinguished-looking president. In the subdued BiblioTech light, his brown, bald-shaven scalp gleamed like well-preserved leather.

A couple of nearby librarians turned in his direction and shushed him.

'Keep the volume down,' Flygirl ordered the president.

'Excuse me, ma'am,' said President Jackson, whispering this time. 'I've a message for you.'

This was not, of course, the avatar of the real President Jackson; it was a Web-crawler, sent by Jax to find Flygirl.

One of Jax's more peculiar peccadilloes was his staunch admiration for the President. Samuel Jackson, in Jax's opinion, was pretty venomous – for an old guy, that is. He had brains and attitude, and he didn't take all that presidential razzmatazz too seriously. Rather than a formal suit, shirtsleeves, slacks and a beret were his preferred attire for attending press conferences and White House briefings, and he had been known to take out foreign heads of state to fast-food restaurants and get down to intense political discussions over burgers and fries. But he could also be impressively statesmanlike when necessary. At last year's World Peace Day, the twentieth anniversary of the detonation of the nuclear bomb at Pusan, Jackson had delivered a speech that was a model of controlled, righteous indignation. He had echoed the sentiments of every civilized person on the face of the planet when he had said that if any country ever again deployed a nuclear weapon, the UN would 'strike down upon them with great vengeance and furious anger'. (This was a paraphrase of a line of dialogue famously spoken by the president in an old film he had starred in. It was a reference from the *Book of Ezekiel* in the Bible, slightly amended by the scriptwriter.)

Flygirl knew that Jax's relationship with his father was awkward and strained. She had a theory that Jax looked up to President Jackson as a kind of idealized father-figure, regarding him as the sort of man whose son he would like to be. But whether this was true or not, she had no idea.

Such was Jax's respect for the man, at any rate, that not only did he use his image as a Web-crawler, but he had taken the first syllable of his surname as an alias.

'So what does Jax want?' said Flygirl.

'He'd like you to meet him in Lonelycloud,' said the president. 'Now.'

Flygirl sighed. 'I don't suppose it'll wait.'

'Nuh-uh.' The president shook his head.

Flygirl stuck a *Reserved* tag on her lectern. She would come back and finish the remaining books later. Then she tapped out the code for Lonelycloud on her wristpad.

For the lover of space and solitude, there was only one place in the Web to go – Lonelycloud.

For those who wanted to discuss something in private, without any fear of interruption, there was a zone designed for just that purpose – Lonelycloud.

For anyone who lived in a built-up urban area without easy access to a park or common, there was a computer-generated land of rolling hills and beautiful vistas that could be visited at any time – Lonelycloud.

In Lonelycloud, you were guaranteed to have the entire zone to yourself, no matter how many other people might also be using it. Parallel-running subroutines meant that, as far as you were concerned, the Lonelycloud you entered was the only Lonelycloud in existence. If you wanted to share it with someone else, all you had to do was log his or her alias in a d-box. When that person arrived, he or she would immediately be transported to your side.

Thus Flygirl, after a split-second of singing blue blankness, found herself standing next to a babbling stream, halfway up a hillside. In front of her lay an expanse of English countryside – rolling fields spread out like a giant picnic-cloth beneath a gorgeous, cloud-puffed sky. The sun was shining, larks were trilling, sheep were grazing in a distant pasture . . . and Jax was sitting on a rock, looking glum and troubled.

'Hi,' he said. 'Thanks for coming.'

'*Ziko ndaba*,' said Flygirl. It meant *no problem*. 'Besides, it was an order from the president. I could hardly say *no*.' She sat down beside Jax. 'Well? What's up?'

Jax took a deep breath and told her everything that had happened since they had parted company in Loreland. He told her about the junction-box that Glote had given him, and about his trip into the Net, and about the NetSharks, and about a place called Davy Jones's Locker, wherever and whatever *that* was. The only thing he omitted to mention was his father's warning not to enter the Net. He didn't mention it because he didn't think it was important. Either his father was mistaken about the Net, or he had simply been trying to stop Jax having any fun. Both explanations seemed equally likely, to Jax.

'Davy Jones's Locker,' said Flygirl. 'In the olden days, sailors used to say that was the place where people who drowned at sea went. It's a sort of graveyard for dead seamen.'

'So who was Davy Jones?' Jax enquired.

'If I remember correctly, that's what sailors used to call the Devil,' said Flygirl. 'Much less of a mouthful than *Beelzebub*,' she added.

Jax laughed, but at the same time he couldn't suppress a small shiver. It seemed a bit creepy, to name a Net zone after a graveyard owned by the Devil.

'Anyway, don't you want to know what I've been up to?' Flygirl asked.

'Sure,' said Jax. 'What have you been up to?'

Flygirl told him what she had learned about utopias. 'Maybe,' she said, 'this Davy Jones's Locker is where we'll find them.'

'Maybe,' said Jax. 'It's worth a look, at any rate. I'd have gone there myself, of course, only I'm—'

'Too much of a coward?' Flygirl suggested, with a teasing smile.

'No,' said Jax emphatically, although there was a lot of

truth in what she had said. 'I just thought you'd like to come
with me. We do most things together, after all.'

'Well, Jax . . .' Flygirl drummed her fingers against her
chin. 'I suppose I could come with you into the Net. Hold
your hand so you won't get scared.'

Jax flashed her an annoyed look, which she ignored.

'There's just one small problem.'

'What?'

'I don't have a junction-box, you one-mip!'

Jax grinned. For once in his life, he was a step ahead of
Flygirl. 'Aha! You see, I've thought about that. Your friend
Lioness—'

Now it was Flygirl's turn to be annoyed. 'She's *not* my
friend.'

'OK, OK. But she *is* your next-door neighbour, and she
does have a junction-box.'

'And you want me to go round to her house and ask to
borrow it, is that what you're saying?'

'Yeah.'

Flygirl waved a hand. 'No way. Forget it. Curl up. Never in
a million years. I wouldn't ask Talisa Makeba to lend me a
toothpick.'

'Well, then,' said Jax, 'how about this? She's going away
on vacation tomorrow, right? Scotland, with her parents, to
see the wolves and the big cats and the genetically-engi-
neered loch monsters. There'll be no one in the house. You
could just—' He left the rest unsaid.

Flygirl thought hard. She had to admit she was extremely
curious to take a look in the Net. The utopias that Lioness
had referred to – what *were* they? What *were* these places of
perfection that the Net, allegedly, contained? Flygirl's
enquiring mind – that restless hunger of hers for facts, for
morsels of information, for *flies* – had not been wholly
satisfied by her trip to the BiblioTech. There was more to be
learned, and the answers, it seemed, might be found in the
Net.

Her parents and the Makebas had key-cards for each

other's houses so that while one family was away, the other could check up on their property, make sure everything was all right, turn on lights to deter burglars, and so on. She knew where the key-card was kept. She could nip in and out of the Makebas' house without any difficulty. She could use the junction-box, and no one would be any the wiser. Yes—

'Yes,' she said. 'Let's do it.'

'All right!' exclaimed Jax, and he punched the air.

They made a plan. Tomorrow evening, Flygirl would go round to the Makebas'. Then she and Jax would meet in the Net to find out what lay in the mysterious Davy Jones's Locker.

CHAPTER FOUR

GUARD HYENA

The following night, shortly after sunset, Flygirl removed the Makebas' key-card from its hiding-place inside the mouth of the Shona tribal mask that hung as decoration in her parents' hallway. She slipped the key-card into the pocket of her jeans and let herself out of the house, quietly easing the front door shut behind her with a soft click.

She stole across the garden to the front gate, avoiding the gravel driveway and keeping to the grass. She had told her parents that she was going to spin into the Web for the next couple of hours, which, while it wasn't exactly the truth, wasn't exactly a lie either. She just hadn't specified whose bedroom she was going to be in and whose Websuit she would be using.

The N'Doubas lived in Belgravia, a well-to-do suburb of Harare, the capital of Zimbabwe. Every home in the suburb was set in its own grounds, with security gates and high walls around the garden. While Harare was by no means as dangerous a place to live in as it had been at the end of the previous century when crime had been rife on its streets, it was still far from being the safest city on earth. The discovery, a decade ago, of several new and extensive gold fields in the country's eastern region had brought about an upturn in Zimbabwe's economic fortunes (gold-plated wiring, disks and circuitry being vital components of Web technology), and with this prosperity had come the peace and political stability which Zimbabweans had long craved. However, the new wealth had yet to filter all the way down to the lowest levels of Zimbabwean society, so there remained – especially in the cities – a restless, unhappy underclass who, lacking money and decent housing, looked with an envious eye on the better-off, on those who had what they did not have. Hence people with respectable incomes, such as Dr and Mrs N'Douba, still had to take care to protect their property and possessions.

Flygirl unlocked the front gate with her own key-card and stepped cautiously out onto the avenue which was lined with jacarandas and acacias. The avenue was deserted, and the blossom-heavy boughs of the trees swayed and sighed in a gentle, cool breeze. The clear night sky scintillated with stars, and crickets sang, their voices competing with the distant whirring hum of the condensation plants which were located over in the Highlands district of the city. From where she was standing, Flygirl could see the tops of the condensation plants' funnel-shaped towers, adorned with flashing red aircraft-warning lights. Like most of southern Africa, Zimbabwe had been suffering a continuous, relentless drought since the end of the previous century. The towers extracted moisture from the air, working through the cool of the night to supply the citizens of Harare with all the fresh water they needed for the following day.

It was just over a hundred metres from the N'Doubas' front gate to the Makebas'. Flygirl made her way along the pavement, keeping close to the wall and casting frequent glances over her shoulder. It was not wise to venture out after dark on foot, even if you had only a short distance to travel.

Reaching the Makebas' gate, she hurriedly inserted the key-card into the slot in the metal plate that was set into the gatepost.

Nothing happened. The lock on the gate did not open.

She muttered a curse under her breath and tried the key-card again.

Still the lock did not open.

She glanced at her wristwatch. Quarter to eight. Over in California Jax would be waiting, suited up, ready to bat in. They had agreed to rendezvous in the Net at eight p.m. her time (ten in the morning, Pacific Coast Time). Jax was counting on her to be there, and she had failed him at the first obstacle. She couldn't even get into the Makebas' house!

Then she realized why the key-card wasn't working. It was her own key-card, which only worked for her parents' house. The two key-cards looked exactly alike – plain grey wafers of plastic with a chip embedded in one side. They had both been in her jeans pocket, and she had got them mixed up.

Tutting at her carelessness, Flygirl swapped cards and inserted the right one.

The gate unlocked itself with a soft clank. She swung the gate open, stepped through, and closed it behind her.

All was shadowy and still in the Makebas' garden. The house loomed ahead, its whitewashed walls glowing palely in the moonlight, its windows empty black rectangles. A huge baobab tree stood in front, partly obscuring the house with its squat, knobbly trunk and thick branches.

The driveway that curved up to the front door was brick-paved, not gravelled. Flygirl began walking along it. She was wearing trainers, so her footsteps were all but silent. It occurred to her that she ought to avoid stepping on the cracks between the bricks, so that a bear would not leap out from one of the thickets of poinsettia or from behind one of the towering, cactus-like euphorbias that grew on either side of the driveway. Then she realized how absurd that was. She wasn't in Loreland now and, anyway, unless she went on tiptoes like a ballerina, there was no way she could avoid stepping on the cracks between the bricks. And – more to the point – there were no bears, or any other kinds of wild beasts, in the Makebas' garden!

A soft, wheezy chuckling from somewhere nearby brought Flygirl to a halt. She peered, big-eyed, in the direction from which the sound had come. All she could see was the leafy black silhouette of a poinsettia bush. She breathed shallowly, waiting for the sound to repeat itself, praying it would not. She hoped her ears had been playing tricks on her and that she had mistaken a perfectly innocent noise for something not so innocent. Perhaps it had just been some small nocturnal mammal snuffling around beneath the poinsettia. Yes. Perhaps.

Several further seconds passed before Flygirl was able to convince herself to start walking again. She told herself she had been fretting over nothing.

Then the noise came again.

There was a boy in Flygirl's class at Realworld school who suffered from asthma. Sometimes when he laughed, it sounded like he had thistles stuck in his throat.

This noise was similar, a whistling, wheezy *heh heh heh*.

Flygirl looked again at the poinsettia bush, and this time saw a pair of eyes staring at her. Glowing, yellowy eyes.

And then the creature that owned the eyes came slouching out from the shadow of the bush into the moonlight.

It looked a little like a dog, but its shoulders were higher and its haunches lower than those of an ordinary canine. It had rounded ears and a spotted pelt, and stood with its tail curled under its belly and its broad flat head hunched down, as though it was cowering. But it was not cowering. It was grinning at Flygirl, its tongue lolling floppily out between its wicked arrays of teeth, and as it regarded her with those large, bright, baleful eyes, it snickered again. Hungrily.

A hyena.

Flygirl didn't need to ask herself what a lone hyena was doing inside the Makebas' compound. All over Africa, hyenas were being bred and trained for use as guard dogs. They were cunning, which made them less predictable – and so more dangerous – than the traditional breeds of guard dog such as the Alsatian or the Doberman. They were also just as ferocious. If you were going to be away from home for a while, it didn't cost much to hire a guard hyena from a professional security firm to patrol your premises. This, evidently, was what the Makebas had done.

No doubt Flygirl's parents had known about the presence of the guard hyena in the Makebas' garden. If only she had told them where she was going.

But it was too late to think about that now.

The hyena took another couple of paces towards Flygirl. A glistening strand of drool leaked down from one corner of its jaws.

Flygirl glanced over to the door of the house. She could run to it, but even if she got there before the hyena did (which was unlikely), the hyena would catch up with her while she was trying to open the door with the key-card. The same thing would happen if she made for the front gate.

There was nowhere she could run to. No safe refuge.

Except . . .

Her legs started moving even before the idea had fully formed in her brain. It was as though her body knew before her mind did that she had only one chance to escape the hyena and if she didn't seize it now, it would be lost for ever.

She sprinted for the baobab tree. Out of the corner of one eye she saw the guard hyena take off after her, pursuing her with the loping, lolloping gait that was characteristic of its species. Flygirl ran faster, her feet thumping on the lawn, her heart thumping in her chest.

As she came closer to the baobab, she scanned its trunk for handholds. Its bark was smooth, but lumps protruded here and there.

She could hear the guard hyena behind – gaining on her rapidly.

A dozen paces to the baobab tree.

Half a dozen.

She thought she could feel the hyena's breath on the backs of her legs.

And then she was leaping.

And climbing, picking her way up the side of the baobab as surefootedly as though she were a real fly, not simply a

Flygirl. Panic lent her speed and agility. Within seconds she reached one of the baobab's lower branches, a feat which under any other circumstances would probably have been beyond her.

The guard hyena jumped up after her, snarling and snapping. Its gnashing teeth missed her heels by centimetres. The hyena went skidding back down the trunk and crashed to the ground, rolling onto its back. Immediately getting back on its feet, it launched itself at the tree again, leaving dozens of shallow gouges in the bark as it tried to claw its way up, but again, without success.

It tried once more, and failed, then settled down on its haunches and stared resentfully up at Flygirl, who was by now lying prone along the branch, hugging it tightly with her arms and legs. She could see the hyena thinking hard, trying to figure out how it might get to her. Hyenas, it appeared, could not climb trees, so as long as she remained where she was, she would be all right.

But she couldn't stay up there for ever. Sooner or later, for one reason or another, she would have to come down.

Damn Jax! This was all his fault.

There was nothing else for it, she was going to have to shout for help. Her parents would hear her cries. They would call the police who would come with animal-handlers to catch the hyena.

And then, of course, she would have to explain to her parents – *and* to the police – what she had been doing in the Makebas' garden, trespassing on their private property. The police would most likely let her off with a caution, but her parents . . . Her parents would be furious. She would be grounded for life, probably. Her father would get hold of a W-chip that would prevent her from visiting anything other than educational sites in Webtown. She would never see Jax again!

Actually, given how she was feeling about Jax just then, never seeing him again might not be a bad thing. For *his* sake.

She turned her head in the direction of her parents' house, ready to start shouting. It was then she noticed that one of the baobab's branches, slightly higher up than the one to which she was clinging, extended almost to the wall that divided the Makebas' garden from her own.

Flygirl could hardly believe her luck. The wall wasn't much more than three metres tall. She could reach the top of it from the branch, and then could lower herself over the other side and drop down into her own garden. If her memory served, there was a shrub bed at the foot of the wall on the other side – a nice, soft landing. She could get back home, and no one would ever have to know where she had been.

She got slowly to her feet, holding onto another branch for balance. The guard hyena got to its feet, too, cocking its head in curiosity. What was the human in the tree up to?

The baobab's branches spread out like the spokes of a wheel, at evenly-spaced intervals. Flygirl began climbing cautiously round from one to the next. The hyena followed her on the ground, tracking her progress. Much though she wanted to be out of the Makebas' garden as quickly as possible, Flygirl knew she must not hurry. One mistake – a misplaced foot, an insecure handhold – and she would fall, and that would be that.

At last she reached the branch she wanted to be on. It looked sturdy. She straddled it, legs dangling, and began shunt-shuffling herself along. The hyena prowled below her, slavering and licking its chops. No doubt it was praying to the god of hyenas, begging for some accident to befall the human.

The god of hyenas must have been listening.

Halfway along the branch, Flygirl heard a deep, low creak and felt the branch shudder between her thighs.

It's going to be all right, she told herself. The tree's old, but the branch is thick and strong, and I don't weigh much. Well, not *that* much.

She continued shunt-shuffling along. The branch continued to creak and shudder. Then it began to groan.

The guard hyena cackled eagerly.

Flygirl was within a metre of the wall and getting ready to leap for it when, with a loud, rending *creee-eeack*, the branch broke away from the baobab's trunk.

The next thing Flygirl knew, she and the branch were plummeting to earth.

CHAPTER FIVE

DAVY JONES'S LOCKER

Flygirl lay on her back on the ground, stunned. Now she understood what was meant when people who had received a knock on the head were said to *see stars*. For here, filling her vision, were stars. Hundreds of them.

It took her a few moments to realize that they were real stars, the ones you traditionally see at night.

Then she recalled where she was and what had just happened.

The hyena!

She struggled to sit up, but none of her limbs seemed to work properly. Her arms flailed uselessly around, her feet dug futile grooves in the grass.

At any moment, she expected to hear the hyena's asthmatic snickering right beside her ear, and to feel sharp teeth sinking into her throat, perhaps, or her stomach.

Still, she kept trying to sit up and, eventually, something came of her frantic efforts. She managed to push herself up into a kind of reclining position, then roll herself fully onto her side.

She was lying next to the branch. She looked around for the hyena. It was lying three metres away, sprawled beneath the branch. The branch had crushed it, flattening its torso in the middle. The hyena's forelegs were twitching, but it was quite dead.

Slowly, Flygirl got to her feet. She inspected herself all

over. Apart from a few bruises, she was unhurt. She had had a lucky escape.

She looked up at the baobab. There was a great pale scar on its trunk where the branch had torn away. With any luck the Makebas would think it had broken off of its own accord, and that the guard hyena had simply had the misfortune to be underneath at the time.

She consulted her watch. Ten to eight. Just five minutes had elapsed since she had entered the garden. She felt as if she had lived several lifetimes in those few minutes.

Jax would still be expecting to meet her in the Net. She was tempted not to keep their rendezvous. Jax, after all, was to blame for all of this. But she decided she couldn't let the stupid one-mip bat into the Net without her. Who knew what trouble he might get himself into!

She took one last glance at the hyena, which was now lying completely still. She felt rather sorry for the poor creature, now that it wasn't trying to bite her.

She set off towards the house.

At the front door she let herself in using the key-card. She didn't turn on any lights inside. There was a chance that her parents might see them and alert the police.

She had been in the Makebas' house a number of times before, most recently for Lioness's thirteenth birthday party. Most kids were content to hold their birthday parties in the Web, but not Lioness. Oh no. She had insisted on a full traditional Realworld celebration, complete with cake and games and a juggler and musicians and an inflatable bouncy castle on the lawn. And, Flygirl had to admit, as parties went it had been quite a success. Lioness had lorded it over everyone, of course, organizing the games and generally acting as though she were a queen and all the guests were her subjects. But apart from that the occasion, in its old-fashioned way, had been novel and interesting.

Flygirl groped her way through the darkened house, moonlight her only illumination. She found her way to Lioness's bedroom. Lioness did not have a Webroom – her parents weren't *that* rich – but she did have a top-of-the-line Websuit, a Calvin Klein, tailor-made for her in a spangly, shocking-pink material. Her Net junction-box was plugged in, ready for use.

Flygirl wriggled herself into Lioness's Websuit and zipped it up. It was roomier than her own Websuit, especially around the hips and backside, which pleased her immensely.

'OK, Jax,' she said, lowering the hood over her head. 'Here I come.'

They spun in almost simultaneously at a prearranged entry-point in the Net's Building Block level.

Immediately, Flygirl pointed at Jax's forearm and said, 'What's that?'

Jax glanced down at the octopus that was still attached to his left arm as the great white had said it would be.

'Passcode to Davy Jones's Locker,' he told her.

'You never said anything about needing a passcode.'

'Didn't I? Guess I forgot.'

'I don't believe it!' Flygirl was furious. 'Do you have any idea what I had to go through to get here, Jax? Do you? I was nearly killed. Twice! And now, after all that, you tell me I'm not going to be able to get into Davy Jones's Locker!'

'Killed?'

Flygirl, tight-lipped, explained about her encounter with the guard hyena.

'Well, I'm sorry,' said Jax, 'but I could hardly have known, could I? Anyway, the main thing is that you're OK. And as for getting you a passcode – *ziko ndaba*. Watch.'

He unpicked one of the octopus's tentacles from his arm. Taking a firm grip on the pulpy limb, he wrenched it off.

'Sus!' said Flygirl, wincing. (*Sus* was Zimbabwean slang for *gag*.)

'Don't worry. It's all right. See?'

As before, the octopus re-grew its missing tentacle, and the tentacle sprouted a brand new octopus.

'Self-replicating software,' said Flygirl, nodding in approval. 'Snice.' (*Snice* meant the opposite of *sus*.)

Jax held the new octopus out to Flygirl, and she let it wrap its tentacles around her arm.

'So now what do we do?' she said. For the first time since arriving in the Net, she took stock of her surroundings. Turning herself around in the water, she noticed that her movements seemed a little sluggish. She also became aware that she couldn't feel anything around her waist and hips. At first she thought there must be some funnel in Lioness's Net junction-box, but then she realized that in fact the problems were being caused by Lioness's Websuit. Because the Websuit didn't fit *her* perfectly, it wasn't giving her full interface with the Net. Websuits needed to be snug-fitting in order to work properly.

'Is Davy Jones's Locker in one of those, do you think?' she said to Jax, indicating the three-dimensional lattice of Building Blocks.

'Probably. Maybe we should ask one of the NetSharks.' Jax said this reluctantly.

'Maybe,' said Flygirl. 'Or maybe the octopuses know what to do. They look pretty intelligent.'

'That's a good idea,' said Jax, relieved. The prospect of talking to one of the Net's bad-tempered phaces again had not appealed to him. 'I hadn't thought of that.'

'You never do,' said Flygirl. 'That's why I'm the brains of this outfit.'

She brought the octopus up close to her face and looked it square in the eye. 'Would you show us the way to Davy Jones's Locker, please?'

The octopus flattened itself against her arm, tensed, then thrust away with all its might, but still keeping its grip on Flygirl so that she was yanked along behind it in a swirl of silvery bubbles. For something so small, the octopus was deceptively strong. With a single succulent throb of its body it was able to propel both itself and Flygirl a good ten metres.

Without having to be asked to, Jax's octopus did the same.

They both found themselves being tugged along by their left arms in a series of jerky ten-metre lunges.

The octopuses dragged them downwards. The galleons and reefs on the seabed loomed closer. Soon Jax and Flygirl were moving horizontally over the sand, with seaweed fronds slithering against their bodies and startled crabs scuttling out of their way.

They were drawn by the octopuses under the Building Blocks. The water was darker beneath the lattice of huge, coloured cubes, and there were strange sea creatures here that neither of the children recognized. Hideous skeletal things, like X-rays of fish. Blind white worms that writhed along the sand. Transparent jellyfish with arrays of glowing lights all over their bodies.

Then, ahead, Jax and Flygirl spotted a huge outgrowth of pink coral rising from the seabed. The outgrowth was roughly cube-shaped, and the coral's fronds were woven so densely together that they formed an apparently impenetrable surface.

The octopuses headed for the outgrowth and with one last powerful pulse of their bodies they brought Jax and Flygirl's left hands into contact with the coral's surface.

There was a moment of blue-and-tone, then Jax and Flygirl found themselves in a large undersea cavern the size of a ballroom. Illumination was provided by phosphorescent algae which coated the cavern's walls, floors and roof, giving off a glimmering blue glow. The octopuses remained attached to their arms.

The cavern was empty apart from a pirates' treasure chest which sat at its centre on a raised section of the floor. The wood of the chest was old and rotten, its brass fittings were tarnished, and it was fitted with a large padlock of a type neither Jax nor Flygirl had ever seen before. Rather than a single keyhole, the padlock had eight round openings arranged in a circle. Both Jax and Flygirl wondered what sort of key was required to open it.

The answer was, not a key at all, but an eight-limbed cephalopod.

Flygirl's octopus detached itself from her arm and swam over to the padlock. Inserting the tips of its tentacles into the eight holes, it performed a complicated twisting manoeuvre. The padlock came undone, and the octopus withdrew its tentacles and dextrously removed the padlock from the treasure chest's hasp.

Jax's octopus let go of his arm and joined the other one at the chest. First it lifted the hasp, then together the two octopuses raised the lid.

A bright blue light – far brighter than the glow of the phosphorescent algae – flooded out from the opened chest.

Jax and Flygirl shut their eyes against the light. Both heard the familiar brief tone that always accompanied a bat between sites in the Web.

Then they were somewhere warm and humid.

They opened their eyes.

They were in a tropical jungle. Overhead, palm-tree leaves were laced together tightly, forming a dense green canopy. Thick thickets of bamboo clustered all around them. Warbling birdsong filled the air. Insects chirruped and buzzed.

'Hmph,' said Jax, glancing around, unimpressed. 'I was expecting a bit more.'

'Me, too,' said Flygirl. 'Good sound quality, though.' She bent forward to inspect the bark of one of the palms, setting the mode-switch on her dark glasses to Magnification/Enhancement. 'And the graphics textures aren't bad, either. But if this is supposed to be a utopia—'

Jax finished the sentence for her. 'It's not very imaginative. Nothing you wouldn't find in a vacation zone in the Web.'

'Perhaps we ought to explore the place a bit before we write it off completely,' Flygirl suggested.

Before Jax could reply, they heard crashing and shouting coming from not far away.

'What on earth is *that*?' said Jax.

'See that kopje over there?' Flygirl pointed to a large
outcrop of rock the summit of which rose above the tops of
the trees. 'If we climb that, maybe we'll be able to get a better
view of what's going on.'

They scrambled up the side of the rock outcrop, Flygirl
lagging slightly behind Jax because of the looseness of
Lioness's Websuit. Shortly, they both emerged above the
trees into clear sunlight. The jungle spread as far as the eye
could see in all directions. The sun was an ordinary sun and
beat down with a fierce tropical heat, but the sky in which it
shone was weird. It was not a smooth, even blue, like the sky
in the Web or Realworld. Rather it was the rippled, flexing
blue of the sea-surface that stretched over the Net's Building
Blocks.

The shouting and crashing got louder. Between breaks in
the jungle canopy they caught glimpses of men and women
dressed in khaki safari suits and pith helmets. They were
running, apparently chasing something, but neither of the
children could see what it was.

Jax noticed that the men and women were carrying rifles.

'Hunters,' Flygirl said, her lip curling in sour disapproval.
'We're not supposed to be here, Jax. This is a grown-ups'
zone.'

Not far from the rock outcrop there was a large clearing.
From their vantage point, crouching on the outcrop's
summit, Jax and Flygirl were able to observe clearly – all too
clearly – what happened next.

A family of black-and-white bear-like creatures, two adults
and three cubs, came hurrying into the clearing. They were
obviously terrified. They were also, obviously, the prey that
the people with rifles were pursuing.

'What are those?' said Jax.

'Weren't you paying attention in your Historical Zoology
lessons?' replied Flygirl. 'They're pandas.'

Jax did pay attention in his Historical Zoology lessons, but
only when the animals he was learning about were predators
or creepy-crawlies. That was why he had been able to

identify Glote's NetShark phace as a great white, but had not recognized the pandas. 'Extinct?' he said.

Flygirl nodded solemnly. 'This is very bad. Hunting simulations are forbidden under UN Web regulations.'

'Maybe in the Web they are,' said Jax, 'but we're in the Net now.'

The panda cubs, squealing and trembling, huddled together in the middle of the clearing. Their parents prowled around them, urging them with prods and nudges to keep going. But it was no use. The cubs were exhausted and could not go another step.

The hunters closed in. Their shouts rose to a pitch of terrible, bloodthirsty intensity as they burst into the clearing. Halting, they raised their rifles and took aim at the defence-less pandas.

The adult pandas, hoping to protect their brood, placed themselves between the cubs and the hunters.

Flygirl averted her eyes. Jax would have looked away also, but he was both too appalled and too fascinated. He seemed incapable of moving his head.

The rifle shots were shockingly loud and seemed to go on forever. Mercifully, the din of the rifles drowned out the pandas' howls of pain.

When it was over, the clearing was filled with a drifting mist of gunsmoke. Jax was just about able to make out the bodies of the pandas lying in a heap on the ground. The adults had not been able to protect the cubs. All five of the pandas were dead.

Jax looked at the hunters' faces. Their eyes were huge and bright, and their grins were savagely wide. They whooped and yelped triumphantly, and high-fived one another.

Finally, Flygirl forced herself to look, too. What she saw filled her with disgust and outrage.

She had been responsible for the death of the guard hyena, a real animal in Realworld, and she felt bad about that but at least it had been an accident. She hadn't *intended* to kill the hyena, whereas these hunters had pursued the pandas for no other reason than to massacre them in cold blood. Admittedly, the pandas were only phaces but their wounds looked realistic – realistic enough to satisfy the hunters' horrible appetite for slaughter.

Incensed, Flygirl rose to her feet. 'Hey!' she shouted down to the hunters, and then, louder, 'HEY!'

The hunters turned and looked up at her, squinting and shading their eyes.

Flygirl was about to deliver an impassioned speech, telling the hunters that what they were doing was horrible and wrong and that they should be ashamed of themselves. But she never got the chance.

One of the hunters said, 'Look. Human prey!'

Instantly, all the hunters raised their rifles and took aim at Flygirl and Jax.

CHAPTER SIX

CARNIVAL

Flygirl stood there, dumbfounded. This couldn't be happening. These people couldn't, surely, be about to shoot at her and Jax. That sort of thing simply didn't happen in the Web.

Then she remembered. Like Jax had said, they weren't in the Web. They were in the Net which was not regulated the way the Web was. To be precise, they were in Davy Jones's Locker, where who-knows-what was permitted.

One of the hunters fired. The bullet ricocheted off the rock, mere millimetres from Flygirl's toes.

She flinched and instinctively ducked for cover. So did Jax. In the shock of being shot at, both momentarily forgot that nothing they experienced while wearing Websuits could actually hurt or harm them. They scrambled back from the summit of the rock outcrop, just as the rest of the hunters joined in the shooting. Bullets whizzed, whumped and whanged into the rock, sending up sprays of stone chips and splinters. Bullets also whizzed, whumped and whanged over the children's heads.

'Let's get out of here!' Flygirl shouted to Jax above the racket of gun-reports and ricochets.

They reached for the scuttle buttons on their wristpads. They pressed the buttons and, in a singing blue flash, found themselves . . . not, as expected, back in Realworld, but in a smoky bar filled with people dressed in denim and black motorbike leathers. The men were almost all burly and bearded, and each sported at least a couple of tattoos. Many of the women, too, were tattooed, and all of them wore their hair big and back-combed. Everyone was drinking and shouting raucously, and there were fights going on in various different corners of the bar. The fighters were hitting one another with pool cues, beer glasses, chairs, even tables. Onlookers cheered them on, encouraging them to greater heights of viciousness and passing them weapons if they were empty-handed. The air was filled with grunts and roars, the sound of things breaking and smashing, and the insistent grinding throb of very loud rock music.

Jax and Flygirl stared at the scene in disbelief.

'Must have been a malfunction with our scuttle buttons,' said Flygirl. 'A misaligned set of coordinates. Let's try again.'

Just as she said this, a pair of rotund, muscular bikers came swaggering up. One of the bikers had a pair of Hell's Angel wings tattooed on his neck, the other had a patch on the sleeve of his leather jacket that showed a skull in a helmet, with *Born To Be Wild* written below it in Gothic script.

'Well, lookee here,' said the Hell's Angel, pointing a stubby finger at Jax and Flygirl. There was a crust of black dirt under his ragged fingernail. 'Fresh meat.'

The other biker chuckled throatily and smacked his right fist into his left palm. 'OK, shrimps,' he said. 'Put 'em up.'

Jax and Flygirl, without needing to consult each other, scuttled . . .

They found themselves on the deck of a large, rusting ship that was heaving across the surface of a cold grey ocean. Hissing sprays of icy sea water splashed over the ship's gunwales, soaking Jax and Flygirl and making them shiver. A freezing wind whipped into their faces. The sky was a mass of dark, forbidding cloud, split here and there with flickering crackles of bright-blue lightning.

'What the heck's going on?' yelled Jax, grimacing with the cold. 'We're supposed to be home!'

'I don't know,' Flygirl yelled back. 'Something's wrong with our scuttle buttons, that's all I know.'

People in fluorescent-orange waterproofs and sou' wester hats were standing in a huddle at the ship's bows. They were looking out to sea, pointing and jabbering excitedly. The waterproofs were so big and heavy, it was hard to tell which of the people were men and which were women.

Jax and Flygirl craned their necks to see what the people were looking at.

Roughly half a kilometre ahead there was a pod of whales, swimming. There were at least a dozen of them, and they moved with a magnificent stately grace, their great barnacled grey backs arching slowly up from the water and then down again, their massive tails following, each one striking the waves with an almighty slap and splash. As each whale broke the surface, it shot a plume of white water from its blowhole fifteen metres into the air. It was an enthralling sight.

'This isn't so bad,' said Jax. 'Those people are just here to watch the whales.'

'I don't think so,' said Flygirl. 'Look.'

One of the people in waterproofs had stepped up onto a platform mounted on the ship's prow. Across his back, in large black letters, was the word 'SPECKTIONEER'.

On top of the platform sat a large object covered in a tarpaulin. The specktioneer pulled off the tarpaulin to reveal a harpoon gun.

The people at the bows looked on avidly as the specktioneer grasped the controls of the harpoon gun, took aim at the whales, and fired.

The harpoon shot from the gun with a loud percussive *whoosh!* and went hurtling towards the whales, trailing a line of cable behind it.

The harpoon struck one of the whales in the back, and its explosive tip detonated.

The whale went under and came up again, and this time the water that spurted from its blowholes was pink.

'That's it!' said Flygirl angrily. 'I've had enough of this. Our scuttle buttons may not work, but there's nothing to stop me pulling my Websuit hood off.'

'Let's give the buttons one more try,' said Jax.

'All right,' she said, reluctantly. 'One more.'

They scuttled . . . and found themselves in a carnival. All around them were brightly-coloured tents, sideshows, fairground rides and stalls. Calliope music parped and oom-pah-pahed merrily. The sky was rippling blue again, but other than that, everything about the scene seemed pleasant and normal.

'Well, no one seems to be killing anything here,' said Flygirl. 'That's *something* at least. So, before we bat out for good, let's decide what we're going to do.'

'What do you mean?' said Jax.

'Well, we have to tell the Webcops what we've seen here,' Flygirl said, spelling it out as if it was the most obvious thing in the world. 'About the hunting zones, and about that biker bar.'

'The biker bar? What was illegal about that? It was just a combat zone, wasn't it? Plenty of those in the Web.'

'Combat zones are meant to be fantasy-based,' Flygirl explained. 'You know, you fight aliens or dragons, that sort of thing. Hitting other human beings in a realistic setting isn't allowed.'

'Oh,' said Jax. 'I see. But will the Webcops be able to do anything? After all, they're *Web*cops, not *Net*cops. Technically, they don't have any say over how the Net is run.'

'Not right now they don't, no.' Flygirl knew that the UN was currently debating whether to extend the Webcops' powers to cover the Net as well as the Web. It was likely that the UN *would* pass a law giving the Webcops jurisdiction over the Net, but the decision would not be forthcoming for several months, and perhaps not even for a couple of years. Lawmaking was a slow, time-consuming process. 'But if someone told them what was going on here,' she continued, 'I think they'd find a way of shutting the Net down. Or, at any rate, shutting this part of it down.'

Jax nodded slowly. 'All right. I take your point. We'll go to the Webcops.'

Just then, to their left, a pair of women emerged ·from a tent, laughing. Usually laughter is a pleasant sound, but not in this instance. The laughter of these women had a hard, mocking edge to it.

'Did you get a load of *her*!' said one of them, shaking her head in disbelief.

'There was an awful lot to get a load of,' replied the other. 'Talk about a weight problem. She had a weight *crisis*!'

Flygirl glanced up at the sign above the tent entrance. It said:

Inside – Larger Than Life!
Three-Ton Tess!
The Fattest Lady in the World!
Ten Men to Her Hug Her –
A Freight Train to Lug Her!

'What a porker!' said the first woman. 'Oink oink!'

Her friend joined in. They strolled away, oinking merrily to each other.

The women's avatars were slim and well-proportioned, but Flygirl suspected that, in Realworld, both of them were somewhat on the portly side. Making fun of someone even larger than they were made them feel better about their own size.

She examined the signs on some of the other tents.

One said:

Bonzo, the Dog-faced Boy!
He Fetches! He Begs! He Rolls Over and Plays Dead!

Accompanying the words was a picture showing a boy with a face so hairy and ugly that it did, indeed, resemble a dog's.

Another sign showed a picture of a man with the worst case of acne Flygirl had ever seen. There wasn't a square centimetre of his body that didn't have at least one large, flaring, yellow-headed spot on it. Even his eyelids and the palms of his hands were affected.

The sign said:

> Zit-Man, The Living Pustule!
> Unbelievable!
> New Spots Will Appear Before Your Very Eyes!

Other tents showcased more people who, by virtue of some physical deformity or other, could be considered disgusting or freakish. There was a bearded lady, a man so thin he looked like a walking skeleton, a girl with scaly skin like an alligator's, and a host of midgets and pinheads and dwarves. All had been put on display so that Net users could come and have a shudder and a laugh at their expense.

The Webcops, thought Flygirl, are definitely going to hear about *this*.

She turned to say as much to Jax, only to discover that he was no longer by her side.

She looked around and caught sight of him entering a nearby tent, accompanied by a man who was dressed in a striped waistcoat and brown Derby hat.

Frowning, she set off after Jax.

While Flygirl had been busy gazing at the sideshow tents, Jax had heard someone calling out to him. 'Psst! Hey! Jax!'

Jax had turned around and pointed to himself quizzically, and a carnival barker had said, 'Yeah, you. I wanna word with you. C'mon over here.'

The barker, like the great white in the Building Blocks level bore a more-than-passing resemblance to a certain pony-tailed computer genius of Jax's acquaintance. Older, and puffier around the cheeks and chin, but still unmistakably J Edgar Glote.

Curious, Jax went over to him.

'You look like a young fella with a lotta stuff weighing on his mind,' the barker said. He gestured at the large tent behind him. 'And I know a place where you can unburden yourself. Step inside and I'll show ya how.'

The barker held aside one of the tent-flaps. From inside the tent Jax heard the sound of gunfire.

Tentatively, he ventured in.

It was a shooting gallery of some sort. There was a row of wooden booths, and in each one there was a person taking potshots at a target. From where he was standing Jax couldn't see what the targets were. The people were all wearing large plastic headphones, presumably to protect their ears from the sound of the gunshots.

The barker took Jax by the shoulder and led him along the row. 'This is where folks can get their own back on people they don't like,' he said. He pointed to one man as they passed him. 'This fella's boss didn't give him the pay rise he deserves.' He pointed to a woman. 'This lady's husband has been ignoring her for several months, treating her like she wasn't there.' He pointed to a teenage boy, perhaps five years older than Jax. 'This young fella's been getting hassle from his parents, wanting to know when he's going to get a job and start making something of his life.' He gestured along the entire row with a sweep of his arm. 'All of 'em have a grudge or a grievance against somebody. But instead of getting mad, they're getting even.'

The barker and Jax arrived at a vacant booth. The barker picked up the rifle that was lying on the shelf in the booth. It was similar to the rifles Jax had seen the panda-hunters carrying. It had a telescopic sight on top, and it looked powerful.

The barker handed the gun to Jax.

'Unlimited ammunition,' he said. 'Just aim and fire.'

Now, at last, Jax had a clear view of what everyone was shooting at. The targets were not concentric circles or tin ducks or little stars on pieces of paper. The targets were human figures, somewhat like mannequins, each suspended by chains from a scaffold frame. The figures were blank and featureless, except for their faces, which were fully detailed and realistic. Whenever a bullet found its mark, the figure that was hit would writhe as though in agony, its face contorting into a mask of pain and its mouth gaping in a soundless scream.

'The faces are 3D composites,' the barker informed him. 'We matte them in from identification photographs that are stored in various databases all over the world – banks, vehicle-licence offices, that kinda thing. Whoever's face you want, we can find it for you and put it on one of those figures. The screams are transmitted through the headphones. We thought it'd be better that way. Wouldn't want to alarm the folks outside, eh?'

Jax peered at the figure at the end of his aisle of the shooting gallery.

'There's already a face on my one,' he said.

'Sure there is,' said the barker. 'I kinda had a hunch you'd be coming, so I got one all ready just for you.'

'Who is it?' Jax asked, squinting.

'Take a look through the rifle sight.'

Jax held the rifle up to his eye, peered through its telescopic sight, and began adjusting the focus dial. Meanwhile the barker took a pair of headphones and slipped them on over Jax's head.

Muffled through the headphones, Jax heard the barker say, 'It's the guy who never has any time for you. The guy who's too wrapped up in himself to give you the attention you deserve. The guy who lets you have everything you want, except the one thing you really want – affection.'

Jax brought the figure's face into focus.

It was his father.

CHAPTER SEVEN

ROUSTABOUTS

'Go on,' said the barker to Jax. 'You know you want to. And it ain't really your father, only a digital representation of him. It'll scream like him and it'll kick and dance like it's in genuine pain – but it ain't really him. That's the wonder of it. You can get your own back without any comeback, because he'll never find out, never know. It's perfect, kid. Completely perfect.'

Jax stared through the telescopic sight at the image of his father's face. His father's face stared back, calm and impassive.

It wouldn't hurt, thought Jax. It might even feel quite good.

'Think about the fishing trip,' said the barker. 'Think about how many times he's said, "Maybe later, son." Too busy to bother, that's the truth of it. He made you a promise, you've tried to hold him to it, and he keeps wriggling out of it again and again. *Because he never meant to take you fishing at all, kid.* It was just something he said one day on the spur of the moment, hoping you'd forget about it. And to my mind, there ain't nothing worse than an idle promise.'

Jax's finger curled around the rifle trigger. He steadied the gun's butt against his shoulder, taking careful aim. The rifle felt right in his arms; felt natural.

'Nothing worse at all,' said the barker.

'Jax!'

Jax turned. Flygirl was standing just behind the barker. She had heard everything that had been said.

'Put the rifle down,' she said.

'Butt out, girlie,' growled the barker. 'This ain't got nothing to do with you.'

'This has everything to do with me,' replied Flygirl firmly. 'Jax is my friend, and you're trying to corrupt him. You're trying to make him like everyone else here in Davy Jones's Locker. You want him to be cruel, to do things without listening to his conscience.'

'Reckon you think you're pretty smart, dontcha, girlie?' sneered the barker. 'Smart and oh so worldly-wise. Well, for your information, what we do here isn't *corrupt* people. What we do is give them an outlet for their negative emotions. They can get things off their chests here, they can even up old scores, they can work out their problems and frustrations, and return to Realworld afterwards all the better for it. Calmer, more balanced, saner citizens. And that, if you ask me, ain't a bad thing at all.'

'No, it isn't a bad thing,' said Flygirl, 'it's a *terrible* thing. You're letting people do as they please without worrying about the consequences. That just encourages irresponsibility, both here and in Realworld.'

'If you say so, girlie,' said the barker with a patronizing smile. 'But you're wrong.'

'Don't call me *girlie*,' said Flygirl icily. She reached for Jax's hand. 'Come on, Jax. We're off.'

Jax glanced back at the figure with his father's face. Did he really want to see and hear his father scream?

No. No, he didn't.

He might resent his father sometimes, but he didn't *hate* him.

He lowered the rifle and removed the headphones. He set both items down on the shelf in front of him.

Flygirl, who was still holding on to his arm, gave him a reassuring squeeze. 'Well done,' she said.

'No, not well done,' said the barker. 'Big mistake.' He put

two fingers in his mouth and blew a shrill, piercing whistle. 'Hey, Rube!' he yelled.

Two men wearing checked shirts and flat caps entered through the tent-flap. They were broad-shouldered and barrel-chested, with faces like baked potatoes and fists like cooked hams.

In the days when real carnivals toured America, men like these were known as roustabouts. They were the ones who erected and dismantled the tents and sideshows, and carried out all the other manual tasks relating to the carnival. These two, however, looked as if their particular speciality was mangling, or perhaps crushing, or maybe pounding – one of those, certainly, and probably all three.

'These kids,' said the barker, indicating Jax and Flygirl, 'don't seem to appreciate the delights we got on offer.'

'Ain't *dat* a shame,' said one of the roustabouts.

'Real pity,' said the other.

They began moving menacingly towards Flygirl and Jax. 'Run!' said Flygirl.

Jax didn't need any further prompting. Together, they turned and ran. The roustabouts set off after them at a lumbering pace.

Jax and Flygirl sprinted along the row of booths. The roustabouts followed, two hulking great masses of meat and muscle. The people using the shooting gallery were so intent on inflicting pain on their enemies that they were oblivious to the drama behind them.

Jax reached the end of the shooting gallery first, several metres ahead of Flygirl, who was hampered by the unresponsiveness of Lioness's Websuit but was still, fortunately, quicker on her feet than the roustabouts.

Turning, Jax saw that there was nowhere to go. The only way in and out of the tent was by the flap through which he and Flygirl had entered. The pair of roustabouts were between them and it, and were gaining on them rapidly.

As Flygirl caught up with him, she reached down and pulled up the bottom edge of the tent, creating a gap between it and the ground. The gap was just large enough for them to squeeze through.

'Quickly!' she said.

Obediently, Jax got down on his hands and knees and wriggled through the gap. Standing up on the other side, he had a moment to register that he was in a narrow alley between two rows of tents before he grabbed the edge of the shooting-gallery tent from Flygirl and held it up for her.

The two roustabouts were almost upon her as she threw herself flat on the ground and thrust herself headfirst into the gap.

She was almost through when she felt a powerful hand grab her left ankle. She grunted and kicked at the hand with her right foot. Her heel connected with the roustabout's knuckles. He yelled and cursed but he did not let go.

'Jax!' said Flygirl as she felt herself being hauled back inside the tent. 'Grab my wrists!'

Jax pulled hard at Flygirl until her entire torso was dragged clear of the tent, but her legs remained inside.

The second roustabout seized Flygirl's other ankle, and together the two men tugged her back until only her head, shoulders and arms were outside the tent.

Jax dug his heels in and pulled with all his might. Flygirl slid forwards until she was half in, half out of the tent again.

It would have been comical if it hadn't been deadly serious – Flygirl being used as the rope in a desperate tug-of-war. She certainly failed to see the funny side of it.

'Come on, Jax, for heaven's sake!' she cried. 'Put your back into it! Pull!'

Jax bent over and braced himself for one last effort. At the same time, Flygirl started kicking her legs in the air like a swimmer, making it difficult for the roustabouts to maintain a proper grip on her. Jax's feet trowelled twin gouges in the grass as he heaved at his friend. Flygirl's waist emerged, then her bottom, her thighs, her calves, and finally her feet, still with the roustabouts' hands clasping her ankles.

Jax let go of her wrists and, before the roustabouts had a

chance to drag her back, he stamped on their hands one after another in quick succession.

The roustabouts yelped and snatched back their hands, uttering a stream of oaths.

Flygirl scrambled to her feet and dusted herself down. 'Thanks, Jax,' she said. 'I owe you one.'

'No, you don't,' said Jax. 'You stopped me doing something in there that I would probably have regretted forever. We're even.'

They smiled at each other.

'Hoods off, then?' said Flygirl, miming the action of removing a Websuit hood.

'Hey, Rube!'

The barker was standing at the end of the alley of tents. Three more of the roustabouts were with him. He pointed at Jax and Flygirl. 'Get 'em, boys!' he ordered.

The roustabouts lurched down the alley. Jax and Flygirl had no choice but to start running again.

The tents were lined up so closely together that their guy-ropes overlapped. Jax and Flygirl were forced to hurdle the guy-ropes one after another, which slowed them down. Luckily, the ropes slowed the roustabouts down even more. The roustabout who was leading the pack tripped on one of them and fell flat on his face, and the two following him, being phaces of limited mip-capacity, stumbled right over him.

Jax and Flygirl watched as one after another, like man-sized dominoes, the roustabouts went crashing to the ground. All three of them tried to get up at once with the result that none of them actually managed it. They all fell flailing to the ground again. One of them became so snarled up in the guy-ropes that when they all tried to rise a second time, the result was similarly disastrous. The three roustabouts writhed and cursed on the ground, calling one another rude names and struggling, without success, to pull themselves upright and resume the chase.

'Better keep going,' Flygirl prompted Jax.

They turned only to find their way was blocked by a peculiar-looking man.

He had coffee-coloured skin, a goatee beard, a long, aquiline nose, and limpid brown eyes, and he was dressed in white tie and tails. This might seem normal enough, but he also had a red silk turban on his head that was crowned with a long white feather. Not only that, but set into the middle of his forehead there was a large, sparkling ruby, and on his shoulder there perched a soot-black rook.

The man appeared to be Indian in origin, but his voice was like nothing Jax or Flygirl had heard before. It buzzed and flitted up and down through each word he spoke, like a bee uncertain where to alight.

'coMe wITh mE,' he said. 'i caN HeLP yOu.'

CHAPTER EIGHT

SWAMI

Both Jax and Flygirl took a wary step backwards.

'pLeaSe,' said the man. 'I CaN shOw You tHE wAy oUT of hErE.'

'How can we be sure you aren't with *them*?' Flygirl gestured over her shoulder at the tangle of roustabouts who were still struggling to get to their feet.

The strange man gave a sly smile. 'AlLOW me tO pRoVe It tO yOu. stEp AsIde.'

Jax and Flygirl cautiously did as he had asked.

The man raised his hand to his shoulder and let the rook step onto his index finger. As he brought his hand down, the rook flapped its wings to maintain its balance, cawing croakily.

Holding the rook in front of him, the man said the following words – an incantation, of sorts:

ROOK

ROCK

RACK

RANK

DANK

DARK

DARE

DIRE

DIVE

DOVE

Then he gave the bird a deft, double-handed twist, apparently turning it inside-out.

All of a sudden he was no longer holding a cawing black rook. He was holding a cooing white dove.

At the exact same instant that the rook changed into a dove, the three roustabouts disappeared in a big explosion and a puff of smoke.

When the smoke cleared, in their place were three white rabbits.

The rabbits looked perplexed for a moment, but then set about doing what rabbits do: hopping around, nibbling the grass and twitching their noses.

'Venomous,' said Jax. 'How did you do that?'

'THEre iS A sAyIng, iS thERe nOt? "a gOoD mAGicIaN NevEr REvEalS hIs seCreTS."'

'Is that what you are?' said Flygirl. 'A magician?'

'I pREfeR tO cAlL MyseLf A SwAMI,' said the man, placing the dove on his shoulder. 'iT Is a MOrE eXoTic aPpelLaTioN, aNd i Am, wIThoUt a doUBt, EXceEdIngLy exoTIc. nOw, COme. WE MuSt hIDE. OThErs wIlL bE lOokInG For YoU.'

The Swami led them along the alley, stepping over the guy-ropes. Soon they came to the back of a tent that was decked out in an Eastern style, with ornate trimming around its edges and hypnotically swirly patterns picked out in gold on its canvas.

The Swami traced a fingertip over some of the patterns, and an oval opening appeared in the tent canvas.

He stepped through the opening and invited Jax and Flygirl to follow him.

They exchanged glances.

'Well?' said Jax out of the side of his mouth.

'I think we can trust him,' said Flygirl, although she didn't sound entirely convinced. 'But if he tries anything funny, we do a bat, OK?'

Jax nodded, and they entered the tent.

The opening sealed itself silently behind them.

The tent was small and dimly lit by candles. It was filled

with a stage magician's props and paraphernalia: wands, top hats, boxes decorated with stars and crescent moons, sets of steel rings linked together, tall cabinets large enough to hold (and hide) a human being, dozens of packs of oversized playing cards, and lots of other items. Everything looked new and unused, as if it was all just there for show.

The Swami pulled out two chairs and invited the children to sit on them.

'YOu hAve hAD TroUbLe lEAvIng, hAVe yOU NoT?' he said.

'Our scuttle buttons are down the plug,' replied Flygirl. 'Instead of taking us back to Realworld, they've been transporting us from one zone of Davy Jones's Locker to another.'

'maY i INSpEct?'

Flygirl extended her left arm, and the Swami grasped her wristpad and peered hard at it for several seconds. At the same time, Flygirl surreptitiously touched the control knob on the frame of her dark glasses and peered hard at *him*.

'AH, yeS,' he said. 'It aPpEArS THaT SoMeoNE hAs BeEn tAMpErInG wITH yOur SOfTwAre. a virUs HaS beeN iNtrO-dUCed.'

'That's not possible,' said Jax. 'Our realoes get regular booster inoculations.'

'nONeTheLEsS,' said the Swami.

'The octopuses!' said Flygirl, with a snap of her fingers. 'It must have been them. They were wrapped around our wristpads for a while. They could easily have passed on a contact virus.'

'Can you get rid of the virus so we can get back home?' Jax asked the Swami.

'BuT Of cOURrSe,' said the Swami, with a small, polite bow. 'hOlD sTiLL,' he told Flygirl.

He leaned over her wristpad and began staring at it with a concentrated frown. A finger-thick beam of red light erupted from the ruby embedded in his forehead, bathing Flygirl's wristpad in a crimson glow.

Slowly, lugubriously, something gelatinous and green started oozing up from beneath her scuttle button. The gelatinous green thing wormed its way out as though the light from the Swami's ruby was making life so uncomfortable for it inside the wristpad that it was forced out into the open.

When the green thing had emerged completely, the beam of red light shut itself off.

'tHerE iS yOUr VIruS,' said the Swami, plucking the gelatinous green thing from Flygirl's wristpad. He held it up between thumb and forefinger. It squirmed and writhed stickily. It looked like a cross between a slug and a lump of phlegm.

The Swami frowned again, and another beam of light shot from his ruby, this one as narrow and focused as a laser beam. The virus, caught in the beam, began bubbling and sizzling like a sausage under a grill. In no time at all, it had shrivelled up to a charred lump of dead matter.

The Swami tossed it aside and repeated the whole process with Jax's wristpad.

'dONe,' he said, flinging aside a second cooked virus. 'NoW You mAy leAvE WhEn yOU sO DesIre.'

'Thank you,' said Flygirl.

'A plEaSurE,' said the Swami, bowing again. 'bUT fIrST, PLeAsE lIstEN tO ME. i HaVe BEen MonItorInG tHiS pLaCE foR SoME tiMe. IT iS nOT a GooD PLaCE to Be, EsPecIalLY fOr cHiLdRen.'

'We know,' said Flygirl, with feeling. 'And we intend to do something about it.'

'tHAt Is goOd.'

'Who *are* you?' said Jax. 'Are you a phace? An undercover Webcop?'

'i,' said the Swami, 'aM aN ObSeRVer. mY dUTiEs ArE TO rEconNOiTrE aND REPorT BAcK.'

'Like a scout,' said Flygirl.

'pREciSeLy.'

'But who for?'

'IT iS AgainSt My ORDeRs To tEll YOU. aLl wiLL bE REVeALeD in TimE. It Is ALSo AGAinSt mY ordErs tO INTeRFerE wiTH whATevEr i Am obsERvIng.'

'But you've done that already,' Jax pointed out. 'You saved us from those three men, and you got rid of the virus.'

The Swami acknowledged this with a resigned nod. 'I fElT oblIgeD tO hELp. i cOULld nOT MerELy stANd bY aND dO noThING. And SinCE I hAVe disOBeYed onE oRDer, I fEeL lESs rEluCTaNT abOut dISoBEyiNG ANOthER. i WISh tO hELp yOu FURthER.'

'That's very kind of you,' said Flygirl, 'but I'm not sure what you can do.'

'yOu sAW, wiTH thOse thREe mEn, hoW I ReNDeRED tHE harMfuL HaRMLesS.'

'With that dove,' said Jax.

The Swami nodded. He took the dove down and held it out to Jax.

'TaKE It,' he said. 'AnD RemeMBeR tHIS. eveRyTHInG conTainNS, inSiDE iT, elemENtS Of ITS oPPosIte. GoOD AnD bad, negATIvE anD POsItiVE, blaCk And WhitE – WHerEvEr yOU fiND tHE onE, yOU WiLL NEceSsArilY FinD ThE oTher. thUs iT Is eAsIEr thAn yoU Might tHinK tO trANsFORM ThE onE iNTo thE oThEr.'

Jax hesitated before accepting the dove from the Swami. He wasn't sure what possible use the bird could be to him.

It was almost as if the Swami had read his mind. 'wHEn tHE TimE COMeS,' he said, with a slow, enigmatic blink, 'yOU wiLl knOW whAT tO Do.'

From outside there came the sound of several men shouting at once. The children recognized, among the voices, the voice of the barker.

'gO,' said the Swami. 'IF TheY enTer hERe, I wIlL teLL ThEM i hAVE NoT seeN You.'

'Thank you,' Flygirl said to the Swami. To Jax she said, 'You and I had better talk again soon.'

They hit their scuttle buttons.

*

Jax yanked off the hood of his Websuit and took a long, deep breath of air. Familiar air. The air of his Webroom.

His father was standing in front of him, holding the Net junction-box, which was still plugged into his Websuit.

Larry Hamlyn did not look happy.

CHAPTER NINE
DEAL?

As he angrily unplugged the Net junction-box from Jax's Websuit, Larry Hamlyn said to his son, 'I don't make too many demands on you, Jerry. In fact, I let you do pretty much as you please. And yet, the one time I do instruct you specifically not to do something, what happens? You disobey me.'

Jax tried to protest, but his father would not listen.

'I don't want to hear it,' said Hamlyn, holding up his hand like a policeman stopping traffic. 'Whatever you've got to say, whatever excuse you have – I don't want to hear it. I don't even want to know where *this* came from.' He shook the junction-box. 'The Days home-shopping site, I'll bet. Well, I hope it's under guarantee, because I'm sending it back there first thing tomorrow.'

'But—'

'No, Jerry! This isn't something you can talk your way out of. I was serious when I told you I didn't want you batting into the Net, and I'm serious now when I say that you've let me down badly.'

'I know, Dad,' said Jax, and he tried to explain where the junction-box had really come from and then tell his father about Davy Jones's Locker and the things he and Flygirl had seen and experienced there. But again, Hamlyn cut him off.

'Not another word, Jerry. I'm taking this box and locking it away in my study where you won't be able to get to it – and *you* are going to your bedroom to sit and think about what you've done.'

That, for Jax, was the final straw. If his father didn't want to know what was going on inside the Net, then fine. He could learn about it from the Webcops.

Glaring at his father, Jax shrugged out of his Websuit, letting it fall in a crumpled heap around his ankles. Then he strode out of the Webroom without so much as a backward glance.

He had dinner that evening alone in his bedroom. A tray-drone brought him the meal on its back. After dinner, he played listlessly for a while with his PseudoPup, which got up to all sorts of mischievous pranks in a vain attempt to cheer him up. Then he turned on the TV and climbed into bed to watch. Normally television was a poor substitute for the intense virtual adventures he could have in his Websuit, but tonight, after his experiences in Davy Jones's Locker, it was a reassuringly two-dimensional and non-threatening source of entertainment. He channel-surfed until he grew too tired to operate the remote control. Soon he had fallen asleep, the TV set switching itself off automatically the moment his eyelids closed.

The following morning, Jax woke, got up, and went to the kitchen to make himself some breakfast. He was hoping his father would be there. In the light of a new day, his father's temper might have cooled. He might be in a calmer, more receptive frame of mind and might be willing to listen to what Jax had to tell him.

But his father was not there. Instead, sitting at the breakfast bar, sipping a cup of coffee and looking very much at home, thank you, was J Edgar Glote.

'Hiya, kiddo!' said Glote. 'How's it hanging?'

'Where's my dad?' Jax asked.

'Been and gone,' replied Glote. 'Meeting with his accountant, I think he said. Told me, if I saw you, to pass on a message. He's got a charity fund-raiser to attend this afternoon, so he won't be home for lunch, but this evening you and he are going to have a good long talk.'

'A charity fund-raiser? In the afternoon? That doesn't sound right.'

'Ah, you know these charity people – they'll ask for their handouts at any time of day,' said Glote with a sneer. 'Stop me if I'm being nosy here, Jerry, but from the way your father was talking, I got the distinct impression that you and he still haven't patched up your differences.'

Jax said nothing. He programmed the kitchen's pancake-maker to prepare him six wheat pancakes with maple syrup.

'You know what you guys' trouble is?' said Glote. Without waiting for a response from Jax, he went on. 'You're both as obstinate as each other. It must be a hereditary thing. Like father, like son. Neither of you's prepared to back down when you have an argument. Neither of you'll concede so much as a millimetre of ground. So you go around mad at each other all the time and nothing gets resolved.'

'Thank you for that penetrating insight,' said Jax sarcastically.

'Hey, you're welcome.'

The pancake-maker pinged, and Jax opened its hatch and took out a plate stacked with steaming, syrup-drenched pancakes. He carried the plate to the breakfast bar and set to work on its contents with a fork.

Glote watched him eat for a while, and then said, 'So how was it?'

'How was what?' said Jax through a mouthful of pancake.

'The Net.'

Jax phrased his answer carefully. 'It was . . . different.'

'Did you like Davy Jones's Locker?'

Jax laid down his fork. 'I had a few problems there.'

'Problems with your scuttle button?'

'Yeah.' Then Jax frowned. 'How did you know that?'

'Think about it, kid.'

Slowly it dawned on Jax. '*You* did it. *You* were responsible for the virus.'

'Give the boy a medal!' said Glote, chuckling.

'But why? Why did you want me not to bat out?'

'I didn't want you not to bat out, exactly. I wanted you to have the opportunity to experience all the different environments that Davy Jones's Locker has to offer, and I figured installing an anti-scuttle virus in the passcode was the best way to do that. As you no doubt discovered, there was a limit on the virus. Six presses on your scuttle button, and you were back in Realworld. I figured six zones would be enough to give you a good sample of the range of experiences available. So, what did you think? How was the whaling-ship scenario? And the seal-culling? And the Deep South plantation zone?'

Jax thought it best not to mention that, thanks to the Swami, he had not had to visit those last two zones.

'It was horrible,' he said. 'All the killing, the violence—'

'Yeah, but deep down, in your heart of hearts, didn't you find it just the teensiest bit thrilling, too?' said Glote. 'You see, Jerry, Davy Jones's Locker is a place where people can do as they please. That's the glory of it. It's a place where no one – not the Webcops, and especially not a father who ignores you most of the time – can tell you what to do. It's everyone's *dream*. A world without rules, restrictions, responsibilities.'

'Is that what the sales realoes at the brochure site mean when they talk about utopias?' Jax asked, remembering what Lioness had said in Loreland the other day.

'You could look at it that way, I guess. The word *utopia* is used as a kind of test for prospective subscribers. If a subscriber reacts in a certain way to it, gives certain specific reactions, that tells us that he or she may be the sort of person who would enjoy Davy Jones's Locker. Then one of the NetSharks will approach him or her in the Net and make an offer. There's a surcharge for using Davy Jones's Locker, but people don't mind paying it at all, once they've had a taste of the place.'

'And you've kept all this from my dad?'

'More easily than you'd think, Jerry. Your father's no fool, but he's only a money-man, an investor. He owns Mesh Inc., but I'm the one who actually runs the company. Besides, Davy Jones's Locker is kind of a shared secret. The only people who know about it are the Netware programmers who created it and the Net-subscribers who use it, and they all realize that in order for it to continue to exist, they mustn't tell anyone else about it.'

'So why are you telling *me*?' Jax asked.

'Isn't it obvious? Jerry, pal, I want to go into partnership with you.'

Jax paused a moment to let this sink in. 'What, like a business deal?'

'Not quite so formal. More a kind of *friends* thing. See, Jerry, your dad's investment is crucial to the Net and to Mesh Inc. I won't bore you with all the complicated financial stuff. Suffice to say that we're showing a profit, but if your dad were to pull out his money for whatever reason, the company'd go under. Glug glug glug. That would be bad at any time, but particularly now, because I'm right in the middle of delicate negotiations with several Pacific Rim nations to market and distribute Netware there. It's a multimillion-dollar deal, and if anything were to mess it up, I'd get pretty mad.'

Jax had the feeling that he didn't want to be around if Glote ever got mad. Glote acted all nice and friendly on the surface, but Jax sensed there was a simmering bad temper beneath, like the molten core of an apparently-dormant volcano, ready to boil over at the slightest provocation.

'And you want me on your side,' said Jax. 'That's what this is all about.'

'Exactamundo, Jerry, my boy! I want you on my side. I want you batting on my team, as it were.'

'In case my dad tries to pull his money out. You think I could talk him out of it, if necessary.'

'If you couldn't, who could?' said Glote, with a simple shrug.

'But why? Why would I want to help you?'

''Cause you liked it in Davy Jones's Locker, Jerry. I know what you said – how it was horrible and all that. That's what you said with your *lips*, but your *eyes* told me a whole different story.'

Jax could not deny that there was some truth in this. In the shooting gallery he had been sorely tempted to put bullets into the mannequin with his father's face.

'And I'm thinking about the future as well,' Glote went on. 'After all . . .' He scratched the top of his head. 'What's a tactful way of putting this? Your dad, Jerry, isn't going to be around for ever, if you know what I mean. And when he's gone, who's going to inherit his wealth? His one and only son, of course.'

Jax thought about Flygirl. Evidently Glote was unaware that he had not visited Davy Jones's Locker alone. 'What if,' he said, choosing his words carefully, 'someone was to report what they'd seen in Davy Jones's Locker to the Webcops?'

'Jerry,' said Glote, shaking his head. 'Use your brain. The public associate the name of one person, and one person alone, with the Net – Larry Hamlyn. Hardly anyone's heard of J Edgar Glote, and I'm happy for it to stay that way. I'm not a limelight kind of guy. I like to remain behind the scenes, in the shadows. Your dad's the one everybody immediately thinks of whenever the Net is mentioned. So if there were any kind of scandal involving the Net, the blame would *appear* to lie squarely with your dad, never mind who was really responsible. Eminent people live by their reputations, and Larry Hamlyn's reputation would be in ruins.' Glote's eyes turned as cold and steely as the spectacle-rims that framed them. 'You bear that in mind, Jerry,' he said, and finished his coffee and stood up. 'And also bear in mind the offer I've made.'

As he left the kitchen, Glote said, 'So long, *partner*.'

A couple of minutes later Jax heard the sound of Glote starting his car outside and driving away. Staring at the half-eaten pancakes in front of him, he pondered deeply over everything Glote had said.

Jax came to the conclusion that he didn't have any choice. For his father's sake, he would have to keep quiet about Davy Jones's Locker. He would have to do this even though it meant that he was going to be stuck, for the rest of his life, in an uneasy alliance with J Edgar Glote.

He felt as if he had made a pact with the Devil.

Then a thought occurred to him. What if Flygirl had already contacted the Webcops?

He leaped to his feet and headed for the nearest video-phone in the house.

The N'Doubas' v-phone number was stored in the house CPU's dial-memory. At the press of a single button, Jax was put through.

Mrs N'Douba answered. She was a handsome woman, with glossy, curly black hair held back by a gold headband, and fine smile-wrinkles around her eyes.

'Jerry,' she said. 'How nice to see you. How are you?'

'OK, thanks, Mrs N'Douba. Is Flygirl home?'

'Is *who* home? Oh, you mean Anita.'

'Yeah, sorry. Anita.'

'You children and your alter-egos,' said Mrs N'Douba, with a mildly despairing laugh. 'It's a whole different world. Yes, I believe she's in. I'll go and fetch her.'

A minute later, Flygirl's face appeared on the screen in front of Jax. On the rare occasions when Jax saw her without her dark glasses, such as now, it always took him a moment to adjust. She looked a completely different person. More approachable, less aloof and mysteriously wise.

'Flygirl,' he said, 'please tell me you haven't spoken to the Webcops yet.'

'Why?' she asked, with a hint of suspicion.

'Just tell me you haven't.'

'As a matter of fact I haven't.'

Relief surged through Jax.

'It was pretty late when I got back in last night,' Flygirl went on, 'and I thought that before we did anything we ought to agree on the best way of going about it. It's, what, just past eight a.m. where you are? I figured you'd only have just got up, so I was going to leave it till nine to call you. Give you a chance to suck some breakfast. So what's the problem, Jax? It sounds to me like you've changed your mind about telling the Webcops about Davy Jones's Locker.'

Jax explained to her why he didn't want the Webcops to know about Davy Jones's Locker. He also told her how Glote had sabotaged their scuttle buttons and then had offered him the prospect of a sort of partnership.

'You *have* to tell your father about Davy Jones's Locker,' said Flygirl, when Jax had finished. 'There's no alternative.'

'But then what? Dad would be forced to go to the Webcops, and then there'd be a huge scandal. Glote's right. Everyone would blame Larry Hamlyn, not him.'

'Why? Davy Jones's Locker wasn't your father's idea.'

'Yes, but that's not how it would look.'

'You've told me about this Glote person before. You've always said he gives you the creeps because he's so silky.'

'Well, he is.'

'So, why do you trust him now?'

'Because everything he's said sounds plausible.'

Flygirl sighed impatiently. 'Jax, haven't you learned any- thing from all those hours we've spent in Loreland? All the leprechauns and Rumplestiltskins and Snow Queens *sound* plausible, but you have to take everything they say with a pinch of salt.'

'That's the Web, Flygirl. This is Realworld. You know,' he added, viciously, 'sometimes you can be such a *phreak*.'

The comment clearly stung Flygirl, and he immediately regretted making it. He apologized. 'Sorry. That was a basement-level thing to say.'

'*Ziko ndaba*,' Flygirl replied, with a half-hearted smile.

There was an awkward silence. Then Jax said, 'If only there was some way we could stop everyone using Davy Jones's Locker and get the place shut down, but without involving the Webcops.'

'Well, there isn't, so we're just going to have to do as we

originally planned,' said Flygirl adamantly. 'Inform the Webcops. And while we're doing that, we ought to tell them about that Swami character as well. I had a squint at his code while he was looking at my wristpad. I've never seen code like it on any phace or realoe ever. It was weird, complex stuff. The algorithms were all back-to-front, and I'd swear it wasn't in binary. Jax, your eyes have gone all faraway. Are you listening to me?'

'Hmm? Oh, sorry, Flygirl. Something you said's just given me an idea.'

Flygirl's eyes narrowed. 'I'm not sure I like the sound of this.'

'No, seriously. I think I know what we can do. And if we do it right, the Webcops needn't ever be involved.'

He outlined his idea to Flygirl. She said it was a crazy plan and had the square-root-of-zero chance of succeeding. He said it might work, with her help. She said that even with her help, it wouldn't work. He begged her to give it a try, at least, and if the plan failed, *then* they would go to the Webcops.

Eventually, reluctantly, Flygirl gave in and agreed to help him.

'Thanks, Flygirl. You're widow.'

'Flatterer. All right, so when do you want to put this harebrained scheme of yours into effect?'

'My dad's not going to be back till this evening,' said Jax. 'Now seems as good a time as any.'

CHAPTER TEN

INSIDE-OUT

What Jax had asked of Flygirl wasn't, in theory, impossible. It was just that no one had ever tried it before.

Websuited-up, she batted into the Web, then punched buttons on her wristpad, entering a code Jax had given her.

The period of blue-and-tone went on for considerably longer than normal. Then, all of a sudden, Flygirl felt herself being wrenched and wrung and strangely *stretched*, as though her body was a lump of pâté that someone was forcing, millimetre by squidgy millimetre, down a drinking straw.

There were moments of claustrophobic panic, when she thought she was going to suffocate, thought she was never going to draw breath again . . .

And then, millimetre by squidgy millimetre, she found herself expanding again, opening out and able to inhale and exhale normally.

She was still herself, but she was also something else.

She had many eyes now, each electronically remote on the end of a long fibre-optic stalk, and each able to zoom and pan and memorize.

She had many ears, too, which waited, ever-ready, to hear certain preset verbal commands.

She had skin of brick and metal and glass, and dozens of delicate inner organs that were attuned to the tiniest movements and changes in temperature in all of the many compartments inside her.

She had several noses that were particularly sensitive to smoke, so that, if she smelled any, she could instantly raise the alarm and send down showers of water from a sprinkler system to extinguish a fire.

She could even, after a fashion, taste. Wherever there was dirt or dust, it was almost as though she could feel it on her tongue, and she could send cleaning-drones to rid the site in question of all offensive, unwanted matter.

She had accessed the central processing unit of the Hamlyn residence in Los Angeles. Jax had made this possible by setting up a channel between the CPU and the Web via his spare Websuit's interface. She and the CPU were now intimately linked. Its physical sensations were hers – a bizarre feeling, though not an entirely unpleasant one. The house had software routines that were like simple, homely emotions. Flygirl felt the pride it took in efficiently supplying shelter and comfort to its occupants. She felt its sense of vigilance as, twenty-four hours a day, it looked after and over the man and the boy who lived in it. In a way the house was a mother to both Larry and Jerry Hamlyn. It protected and provided.

Quickly adjusting to her new reality, Flygirl located Jax through one of the house's indoor surveillance cameras. He was where he had said he would be, waiting outside the door to his father's study. She looked down at him from the corner of the corridor ceiling. She couldn't talk to him – the CPU was not equipped with a voice synthesizer – but she showed him that she had arrived in the CPU by overriding the lock-command that Jax's father had put on the door.

The door slid open. Jax threw a thank-you wave to the surveillance camera's lens and entered the study.

He searched the room high and low for the Net junction-box, but it was in none of the drawers of his father's desk, nor was it on any of the shelves.

'Open safe,' he said.

The phrase 'Open safe' spoken by anyone but Larry Hamlyn automatically registered with the house CPU as *Voice-Pattern Mismatch*. The CPU was programmed not to respond unless Hamlyn himself uttered the command.

Flygirl overrode that programming.

In the study, one of the pair of Van Goghs swung away from the wall on hinges. Behind was the door to a reinforced ceramic safe.

Jax reached up and placed his right hand on the scanning plate on the safe door. The scanning plate read his palmprint and fingerprints and transmitted a second *Mismatch* signal to the CPU. The hand did not belong to Larry Hamlyn. Similar, but not quite.

Again, Flygirl arranged for the mismatch to be disregarded. The safe door unlocked and opened.

The Net junction-box was inside.

Jax took it and headed for his Webroom. Flygirl, meanwhile, closed and re-locked both the safe door and the study door.

For the time being, she couldn't do anything more for her friend, except wish him luck.

And remember the words, Jax, she thought. Remember the words.

Arriving at the Net's Building Blocks, Jax found the octopus passcode was, as before, still attached to his arm. That was good. If the octopus was there, it meant the anti-scuttle virus was being reinstalled in his wristpad. The virus was not crucial to his plan, but its presence would make things simpler.

The octopus, when asked, dragged him down under the Building Blocks to the coral outgrowth, and from there they passed through into the algae-illuminated cavern, where the octopus opened the treasure chest for him.

Then he was in the jungle again. The octopus was gone, but the dove that the Swami had given him was there, perched on his shoulder. Jax stroked the top of its white

head with one finger, and it closed its eyes and cooed
pleasurably.

'You and I,' he said to the dove, 'have work to do.'

It wasn't long before he heard the cry and crash of
hunters. He strode calmly in the direction of the sound, until
he was able to see a group of khaki-clad figures moving
between the trees. Ahead of them, a family of terrified
pandas were fleeing as fast as they could, which, for such
slow and docile animals, was not very fast.

Jax broke into a slow run, keeping pace with the pandas.
As he ran, he took the dove from his shoulder and clasped it
in both hands, the way the Swami had done.

Earlier, with Flygirl's help, he had pieced together the ten-
word incantation the Swami had used. Now he repeated it
aloud:

> ROOK
> ROCK
> RACK
> RANK
> DANK
> DARK
> DARE
> DIRE
> DIVE
> DOVE

At the same time, he copied the twisting action the Swami
had used, bending the dove with both hands as though
trying to push its belly up through its back.

The dove protested, flapping its wings and fluting shrilly.
Other than that, nothing happened. The hunters continued
their pursuit, closing in on the pandas.

Jax stopped in his tracks. Why wasn't it working? Why
hadn't the hunters been transformed into rabbits or chip-
munks or mice or something equally small and harmless?

Then he realized why. In the order he had spoken them,
the words changed 'ROOK' to 'DOVE'. But the rook was
already a dove. He had to change it back.

Grasping the dove again, he repeated the words, but in reverse order. With a certain amount of stumbling and hesitation he got from 'DOVE' to 'ROOK'.

And as he said, 'ROOK,' he gave the bird a twist, and felt it fold between his fingers as easily as a table napkin.

He looked down and saw that he had a croaking, coal-black rook in his hands.

Then he looked up and saw that the hunters were still hunters. As he watched, however, he saw their expressions shift from bloodthirsty determination to panic and fear. They turned on their heels and started running away from, instead of after, the pandas.

The pandas were now the ones doing the chasing. No longer were they rotund, cuddly, timid creatures. All of them, including the cubs, had grown to three metres tall, and long, sharp claws had sprung from their paws, and rows of fearsome fangs filled their mouths. They had morphed into monster-pandas, and they bellowed and snarled terrifyingly as they loped after the hunters, as intent on slaughtering the hunters as the hunters had been on slaughtering them.

One by one the scared hunters dropped their rifles and batted out. Their avatars became faint, blurry smears, as though a giant hand had rubbed them sideways. Swiftly the smears faded into invisibility.

Seeing this, Jax chuckled heartily to himself. The rook, apparently sharing his amusement, let out a hoarse cackle.

'Next zone,' Jax said, and pressed his scuttle button.

The anti-scuttle virus did its thing. He was transported to the biker bar, where, it transpired, there was a huge brawl going on. One of the two-person fights had got out of control, and now everyone in the room, men and women alike, had become involved. Fists were flying. Hair was being pulled. Punches and kicks were landing left, right and centre. Knocked-out teeth were hurtling through the air.

In the midst of this rowdy free-for-all, Jax cupped the rook protectively to his chest and again went through the incantation, ROOK to DOVE.

As he twisted the bird, a sudden calm fell. All fighting in the bar ceased, and everyone looked at everyone else, blinking, and perplexed.

Every person in the room except Jax had sprouted a pair of huge white wings and a halo. Their leather and denim outfits had been replaced by flowing white robes. Those who had been holding weapons now found themselves holding harps.

There were no Hell's Angels in the bar any more. Only angels.

Jax hadn't expected this. He had turned the rook back into a dove simply so that he would be able to turn it back into a rook again. However, in the event, he couldn't have hoped for a better outcome, for the bikers could not bring themselves to continue fighting. Angels, after all, did not hit one another. Angels were pure and serene and heavenly and holy.

Hopelessly confused, the biker-angels began batting out.

Jax scuttled again, and found himself on the deck of the whaling ship as it lurched ponderously across that turbulent, icy-grey ocean.

At the prow, whaling enthusiasts in their bright-orange waterproofs were taking it in turns to fire the harpoon gun. The specktioneer was giving each of them instructions on how to aim, how to keep the harpoon gun trained on the target while the ship rose and fell, and how and when to press the trigger. In between shots he would reload the gun with a fresh harpoon.

Again and again, a harpoon sprang from the gun-barrel and blasted into the back of one of the whales with a bloody red impact.

Teeth chattering with the cold, Jax ran through the reverse-incantation, DOVE to ROOK. This time he scarcely made a single mistake with the words. He flipped the bird inside-out, and as the rook reappeared in his hands, he heard the whaling enthusiasts' gleeful cries change to murmurs of consternation and then to yelps of alarm.

The whales that had not yet been harpooned were turning around and heading for the ship. The ones that had been harpooned and were still attached to the ship by cables began swimming, in a group, to starboard.

The unharpooned whales gathered by the ship's port side and began butting it with their massive heads.

With one set of whales pulling it and the other set pushing, slowly the whaling ship began to tip over.

The whaling enthusiasts shrieked and screamed as they slithered down the tilting deck. They clutched desperately at anything they thought they might be able to hold on to, but everything on the deck was slippery-slick with sea-water and their fingers could not get a grip. One after another they slid down, fetching up with a bump against the starboard railing.

The deck continued to tilt at an increasingly steep angle.

Jax, steadying himself against the starboard railing, grinned.

Then the whaling enthusiasts started falling overboard, plunging into the churning grey waves and surfacing moments later, bobbing up like bright-orange buoys.

As the whales continued to turn the whaling ship over, it began to sink sideways. Jax, no longer able to maintain his balance, decided that now was a sensible time to move on to the next zone. Glote had said that the anti-scuttle virus was good for six presses of the button. That meant Jax would pass through three more zones before he was returned to Real-world.

He and the Swami's rook/dove were causing some wonderful havoc in Davy Jones's Locker. With any luck, Net-users would think twice before visiting here again, and also warn their friends not to.

Next stop – the carnival.

J Edgar Glote was sitting in his solar-powered Volvo, which he had parked at the end of the winding road that led up to the Hamlyn residence. He was admiring the view of Los Angeles and dreaming of the day when he, too, would be able to afford to live in a *really* smart neighbourhood like this one, way above the throng and bustle of the city, in a big house crammed with all sorts of lavish furnishings and luxuries. It wouldn't be long. The Net was well on its way to becoming a viable rival to the Web. It already had the edge on the Web in terms of improved graphics and reduced Websickness, but these were minor advantages. Webware programmers would soon catch up. There was one thing, however, which the Net had and which the Web would never have – Davy Jones's Locker. *That* was the Net's ace-in-the-hole. A place where you could indulge in activities that most people frowned on. A land of do-as-you-please.

Yes, things were looking pretty good for the Net and for J Edgar Glote, especially now that he had the Hamlyn brat in his pocket. Jerry 'Jax' Hamlyn was a useful insurance policy, in case Larry Hamlyn ever found out what was going on inside – or, geographically speaking, *below* – the Net. Were Hamlyn ever to learn about Davy Jones's Locker, he would probably get all ethical and disapproving and threaten to pull the financial plug on Mesh Inc. But then all Glote would have to do was tell him that his own son had visited Davy Jones's Locker, and he had the subscription records to prove it. How would *that* look on the TV news? *Multimillionaire's Son Bats Into Illegal Zones*. CNN and Pravda International would have a field day. Hamlyn would have no choice but to let Davy Jones's Locker continue as it was.

Yes, no matter which way you looked at it, J Edgar Glote's future was looking very bright indeed. As bright as the sunny, cloudless sky that arched over Los Angeles in front of him.

Glote's musings were interrupted by a voice from the Volvo's dashboard.

'Edgar,' it said, in soft, seductive, feminine tones with a Swedish accent. 'I have an incoming emergency message for you. It's being patched through from your home.'

'Origin?'

'Davy Jones's Locker. There's been some kind of disturbance in Sectors 11 and 3. Users have been scuttling *en masse*.
Some undetermined factor is causing a software dysfunction.
Oh, apparently it's happening in a third sector now. Sector
18. The whaling-ship scenario.'

'Can it be contained?' Glote asked, keeping his voice
controlled and even. It was nothing to be worried about, he
told himself. A bug of some sort. Maybe a rogue cyberat that
had snuck across into the Net from the Web.

'It appears to be moving between zones in a pattern that
accords with the path of your anti-scuttle virus.'

'What?' exclaimed Glote. 'Give me the user-designation.'

There was a pause. Then the voice said, 'The user-designation is *Jax*.'

'No!' yelled Glote, pounding the steering wheel with the
heel of his hand. 'It can't be!'

'I'm afraid so, Edgar,' said the Volvo's in-car AI personality.
'And please calm down.'

'That ungrateful, little, no-good—!' growled Glote. 'Well,
I'll sort him out. Nobody interferes with J Edgar Glote's
plans! Nobody!'

'Start!' he instructed, and the ignition system, recognizing
his voice, started the engine.

'Apply containment procedures,' he said to the car
through clenched teeth.

'Understood.'

Glote executed a U-turn and drove back up the road
towards the Hamlyn residence.

On the way, he opened the dashboard glove compartment
and reached inside for something he kept concealed behind
a false panel.

Something he kept there in case of emergencies.

Jax had no idea how switching the rook back, yet again, to
the dove would affect the carnival zone. Nor did he have the
chance to find out.

He arrived at the carnival to find, standing in front of him, the barker who had lured him into the shooting gallery yesterday. The barker was flanked by two of the thuggish roustabouts.

Jax fumbled with the rook, and managed to blurt out, 'ROOK, ROCK, RACK—' but got no further than that. The roustabouts lunged at him and grabbed his arms. As they pinned his arms to his sides, the startled rook cawed and flew from his grasp. The barker caught the rook in mid-air, clutched its head in one hand and its body in the other, and, without a moment's hesitation, wrung the bird's neck with a hideous snap-crackle-and-pop of bones. He let the limp, dead rook drop to the ground.

Then he took a step towards Jax and bent down until his Glote-like face was directly in front of Jax's face.

'You ain't going nowhere, kid,' the barker said. 'You're staying right where you are until someone in Realworld reaches you and deals with you there.'

Flygirl detected movement out of the corner of one of her surveillance-camera eyes.

A car was pulling up at the front gates of the house. It came to a halt alongside a small brick pillar that stood beside the driveway, a couple of metres in front of the gates. Set on top of the pillar was a video-entryphone panel, with a bell-button and a number-pad.

The driver's-side window of the car slid down. A hand emerged and punched out a five-digit code on the number-pad. The gates swung inwards and the car drove through.

The house CPU registered the number as the personal access-code belonging to J Edgar Glote.

What was Glote doing there? Flygirl wondered. She continued to observe.

Glote's car travelled up the driveway and stopped outside the front door. Flygirl activated the surveillance camera mounted just above the door's fanlight.

Glote switched off the car's engine. She watched him

climb out of the car and ascend the short flight of steps that led up to the front door. He was hiding something inside the flap of his jacket, and looked agitated and furtive.

Flygirl made the camera zoom in on the object Glote was holding inside his jacket. She couldn't quite make out what it was.

With his free hand, Glote tapped his personal access-code into the number-pad set into the door frame.

As the door opened, Glote pulled out what he had been keeping inside his jacket.

It was a revolver.

Flygirl looked on in helpless disbelief as Glote, his face a mask of murderous intent, strode into the house.

CHAPTER ELEVEN

HOUSEKEEPING

Flygirl quickly assessed the situation. Jax was in his Web-room, suited up and totally unaware that Glote was in the building. Her friend was in mortal danger, and it was up to her to save him.

She would have to pull out of the house CPU, and somehow get a message through to the Los Angeles Police Department that a murder was about to be committed. But in the time it took her to bat out, take off her Websuit, get the relevant videophone number from International Directory Enquiries and call the LAPD, it would probably be too late. Jax would already be dead. And that was assuming the LAPD believed her and didn't think she was just some crank-caller playing a practical joke.

No, she would have to stop Glote herself. But how? As long as she was inside the house CPU, she was powerless.

Or was she?

Thinking fast, Flygirl located the burglar alarm in the CPU. The alarm was designed to come on automatically when the house was empty. It was connected to the nearest police precinct station, which was down on Sunset Boulevard, a couple of miles away.

She activated it. A signal sped along the wires to the police station, alerting the police computer to a possible break-in at the Hamlyn residence. Within the house itself, however, no bells rang and no lights flashed. This was so that any burglar who inadvertently tripped the alarm would not know he had done so until the police arrived to catch him red-handed.

Flygirl didn't know how long the police would take to get there. It all depended how close-by the nearest squad car was. According to the CPU, the response time could be as much as five minutes. Too long. Jax would be dead by then.

Via a camera in the hallway ceiling, she watched Glote cock the hammer on his revolver and start tiptoeing stealthily across the floor.

Then she noticed a Dyson-drone in one corner of the hallway. The drone was humming happily along, siphoning up dust through its nozzle-snout.

She recalled Jax telling her once about the day of the Webcrash, when the entire house and all its automated appliances had gone crazy.

And suddenly she had an idea.

Glote was halfway across the hallway when something collided with his left ankle. Hard.

Pain shot up from his tarsal bone. He yelped and hopped up and down on his right leg, massaging the spot where he had been hit.

Looking down, he saw the Dyson-drone bumbling away from him with its nozzle-snout waving in the air like a triumphant elephant's trunk.

'Damn hunk of junk!' he hissed. 'You're not supposed to bump into people. You're supposed to avoid us.'

He put his left foot gingerly back down on the floor and tested the ankle. It worked, but there would probably be a large bruise on it tomorrow morning.

Now to get on with what he had come here to do – sort out the Hamlyn brat.

He had already planned how he was going to get away with murdering the little troublemaker. He was going to shoot him, and then dispose of the revolver where no one could find it. He would smash a window from the outside, so that it would look like somebody had broken into the house.

Then he would summon the police and tell them that he had arrived at the house to find poor Jerry Hamlyn already dead. He would feign tearful distress. 'If only,' he would say, 'I had arrived a couple of minutes earlier . . .'

The security system was inactive. There would be no recorded evidence. No one would ever know it was he who had committed the deed.

Glote tightened his grip on the revolver and resumed his stealthy progress across the hallway, heading for the corridor that led to the Webroom.

The Dyson-drone came whirring at him again and struck him, this time on the shin.

'Ouch!' cried Glote. He spun round furiously and aimed a kick at the little robotic domestic appliance. The Dyson-drone darted backwards to avoid his foot.

Another drone came hurtling at Glote from the living-room doorway. It was a sweeper, with a brush attachment on the end of an articulated stalk. It rammed the brush-head into Glote's right buttock.

'Ouch!' cried Glote again. He grabbed for the brush attachment but the sweeper took evasive action and jabbed the brush-head into Glote's other buttock.

'OUCH!' cried Glote yet again.

Suddenly, it seemed as if he was being set upon by every cleaning-drone in the house. They came at him from all directions like a miniature tank battalion converging on a military target. Polishers and dusters and waxers and wipers surrounded and assaulted him with their various cloths, pads, brushes, and spinning scrubbers.

Glote reeled this way and that as the drones subjected him to a succession of blows to the legs and pelvis (none of them could reach any higher than Glote's waist). He lashed out with his feet in retaliation. Some of his kicks connected, sending drones skidding across the floor, but mostly the drones were too quick for him. Glote could scarcely believe what was happening. It was as if the entire house had gone mad!

Finally, he managed to battle his way through the encircling drones and stumble away. Flygirl sent the drones off after him in a pack.

He staggered into the kitchen, and ordered the door to close behind him.

Flygirl made the door refuse to obey, no matter how many times and how insistently Glote gave the *close* command.

The drones piled through the open doorway, brandishing their implements and attachments like an angry mob.

Glote scrambled up onto one of the kitchen counters, wincing at the pain this caused his bruised, battered legs. He levelled his gun at the drones and shouted, 'Back off! Back off or I'll shoot!'

Naturally, the threat did not perturb the drones in the slightest. They clustered at the foot of the counter in a whirring, whining, whirling throng.

Then the kitchen door slid shut.

Glote looked at the door in abject despair. Now he was trapped in a room with dozens of domestic appliances gone berserk. This was a nightmare!

And it wasn't just domestic appliances that had it in for him. Flygirl took command of Jax's PseudoPup, which, until Glote came charging into the kitchen, had been curled up asleep in its basket. The little artificial dog had a remote-control link to the house CPU, so that it could be shut down when the human occupants were out and thus would not drain its batteries needlessly by scampering about when there was no one around to be amused by its antics.

Flygirl had the PseudoPup leap from its basket and bound up onto the counter where Glote had taken refuge. The PseudoPup snarled and bared its teeth at the computer genius. Then it started snapping at Glote's legs with a ferocity that surprised Flygirl. She assumed that, at some point in the past, Glote had done something mean to the PseudoPup, and that as a result, somewhere in its tiny microchip brain the PseudoPup harboured a genuine resentment of Glote. Its programming forbade it to bite anything, but it was offering a very good impersonation of a dog that *could* and *would* bite, given half a chance.

By now Glote was thoroughly rattled. Sweating, eyes bulging, he aimed the revolver wildly around the room, threatening to shoot anything and everything.

Flygirl was glad to see how unnerved Glote had become, but she hadn't yet finished with him. She took control of the thermostat that regulated the ambient temperature in the kitchen and dropped it to well below freezing.

Soon Glote's panting breaths were emerging as chilly clouds. He started shivering. His teeth began to chatter. The sweat on his face turned to a crust of ice. A drip of clear mucus collected at the tip of his nose and froze to an icicle. His spectacles frosted over. Eventually, his fingers became too numb with cold to hold the revolver, and the gun dropped onto the countertop.

With the PseudoPup still yapping and snapping viciously at him and the cleaning-drones still besieging his perch, Glote sank down to the countertop and huddled himself into a shivering ball.

That was how the police found him a few minutes later.

All this time, Jax was still trapped at the carnival, completely oblivious of all that was going on in the house. The roustabouts had a good firm grip on his arms, so there was no way he could scuttle or bat out. The Glote-like barker was pacing to and fro in front of him, muttering vague threats.

'Maybe we could put you on show,' the barker said at one point. '*The Poor Little Rich Kid*. That'd give everyone a good laugh.'

Jax barely paid any attention. He was too busy worrying about what might be going to happen to his body in Realworld. Glote couldn't be planning to kill him, could he? Surely not. But what else could the barker have meant when he had said that someone was on his way in Realworld to deal with him?

A familiar and distinctive voice from behind him interrupted his thoughts.

'I sHalL WArN YoU genTLeMEn OncE, AnD ONCe onLy. STAnd AWaY fRom tHE BoY aND no HaRm WiLl CoME tO YoU.'

Jax turned his head round as far as it would go.

Sure enough, it was the Swami.

The Swami offered Jax a brief but reassuring smile, and then returned his attention to the roustabouts. 'WeLL?' he said.

'And just who in heck are *you*?' demanded the barker. 'You sure as hell don't sound like you come from round these parts.'

'WhERe i cOme fROm, YOu cANnoT poSsIBly IMagIne. ALl YOu NeeD knOW aBouT ME iS thAT i Am a FRieND oF thIS boY.'

'Well, lucky him,' the barker drawled sarcastically. 'Now buzz off back to India or wherever it is you turban-wearing types live. This here's got nothing to do with you. This is between me and the boy.'

The Swami sighed. 'DoN'T sAy i Didn'T WArN yoU.'

He raised his hands and made a series of quick, delicate gestures in the air as though he were manipulating a set of tiny invisible controls. Arcane energy crackled at his fingertips. Then a ball of light manifested around each of his hands.

He aimed a hand at each of the roustabouts and sent the two balls of light whizzing at them.

The startled roustabouts had no time to duck. The balls of light hit them simultaneously, and the result was impressive. The roustabouts shattered into millions of pieces like a pair of fragile china statuettes struck by bowling balls. Their powdered fragments sprayed over the grass in two long dusty streaks.

Jax's arms were free. He had never felt so relieved in all his life.

The barker, staring at the remains of the disintegrated

roustabouts, sputtered and stuttered. 'That ain't—! I mean, you can't—! I mean, that just ain't—!'

The Swami walked up to him. 'I KnoW YoU aRE jusT a VIRtuAL ConStruCT,' he said. 'i KNoW You HAvE No ConTroL OVEr whAt yoU DO; YOu sIMpLY oBEy YOuR proGRamMiNg. NonETHeLeSS, WHaT yOU dO Is WIckEd, aND tHat MAkEs yOU WIckEd.'

'No, no, you've – you've got me all wrong,' stammered the barker. 'I'm just a showman. I give folks what they want.'

'iF tHaT Is so,' said the Swami, 'THeN YoU wiLl HAVe nO oBJectIon TO WhAt i AM aBOuT to dO.'

So saying, the Swami brushed a hand over the barker's face.

Uttering a horrible groan, the barker fell to his knees. Where the Swami's hand had touched him, a lump like a wart appeared. It swelled rapidly until it was the size of a golf ball. Meanwhile, other similar lumps started sprouting around it.

Soon one half of the barker's face was covered in these tumorous growths, and they were spreading down his neck and beneath his shirt-collar to his chest. One of his eyes was puffed shut, and his Derby hat fell off, dislodged from his head by the lumps that had crept up beneath his hair. His groans were terrible to hear, and for all that he hated the barker, Jax couldn't help but feel a little sorry for him, too.

The barker's groaning attracted a small crowd of curious onlookers. It also drew some of the carnival's permanent residents out from their nearby tents.

Out they came, a bizarre selection of outcasts and medical oddities. Three-ton Tess, the Fattest Lady in the World. Bonzo the Dog-faced Boy. Zit-Man the Living Pustule. The Alligator Girl. And many of the other unfortunates who, for want of a better classification, could be called *freaks*. Out they came to join the crowd of onlookers. And the so-called normal people – many of whom had tailored their avatars to disguise certain minor deformities of their own, such as hair-loss and obesity – parted to give the freaks a space all to themselves. And together, the normal people and the freaks watched the barker's gradual transformation. Watched as his clothing tore at the seams and lumps pushed through. Watched as his hands became lost beneath a profusion of swellings. Watched as his entire body became one distended, warty mass, vaguely shaped like a man.

When it was over, the barker was left crouching on the ground, sobbing.

Then the freaks stepped forwards.

A dwarf took hold of the misshapen knot of flesh and skin that was the barker's right hand. Bonzo the Dog-faced Boy took hold of its counterpart on the other side. Together they helped the barker to his feet.

The other freaks surrounded them, and, with a gentle solemnity, the barker was escorted away.

He was one of them now. A freak himself. And that was how he would remain for as long as Davy Jones's Locker survived.

The crowd of onlookers dispersed and drifted away, having seen all there was to see. Jax and the Swami were left alone.

'YOu hAvE Done weLL,' the Swami told Jax. 'a GREaT disRuPtIon haS BeEn CAuSeD. THe rePuTatiOn oF daVY jONes'S LOcKer haS BeeN cAst inTo DOubT. I SUsPecT iT WiLL noT ConTInUE TO surVivE In ITs CUrreNT foRM muCh LOngEr.'

'Yeah, well, you had a lot to do with that,' said Jax. He pointed to the dead rook on the ground. 'And so did *it*,' he added regretfully.

The Swami bent down and picked up the bird. Cradling it in his arms, he stroked its body three times.

The rook stirred, opened an eye, and uttered a weak but encouraging caw.

'iT Will REcOVer,' the Swami said. 'IT MeREIY nEeDEd rEboOtinG.'

'Oh no!' Jax exclaimed abruptly, horrified. He had been so caught up in watching the grisly spectacle of the barker's transformation that, incredibly, he had clean forgotten about the danger he was in, in Realworld. 'I've got to leave here right now,' he said to the Swami.

'oNe moMEnT. I hAVe aN iMpoRTanT mESsaGE i MUst cONveY tO yoU. SOmEthINg iS sHortlY goInG tO hapPeN – aN EvEnt tHAT wILL CHangE yoUr eNtirE plANEt.'

'Please, can it wait?'

'wE ArE reVEaliNg ouR PreSEncE onLy To CHiLdreN. CHiLDReN HaVe MORe fLeXibLe MiNds. THEy aDApT anD ACcEpT moRe ReAdiLy tHan ADUltS.'

'I'm serious. I can't hang around.' Jax's finger was poised over his scuttle button.

'lIsTen To ME!' the Swami insisted. 'PLeasE! WE aRE hEre iN greAT nuMberS, anD soON tHeRe is GoinG To Be a TErRiBlE coNFusIon. SOoN WE arE GOinG tO lEAve thiS plACe anD TAkE FlESh. tHE sHocK wIll bE LesSEnEd iF somE haVe beEn WarNEd in ADVaNce. UNdERstAnd! I Am NoT HUmaN. i AM noT DIgiTal.'

'I'm really sorry. Thanks for everything.'

'I aM—'

Jax scuttled just as the Swami spoke two more words. The two words were almost drowned out by the sound of the batting-out tone. Almost.

Jax wrenched off his Websuit hood. He was alone in his Webroom. He commanded the door to lock itself and open for no one. He was safe!

He plumped himself down on the padded floor, feeling suddenly exhausted. It had been a close-run thing. If the Swami had gone on talking much longer—

A frown crossed Jax's face. The Swami's final two words. What *were* they? What had he been saying?

There was a loud pounding on the Webroom door.

Glote! thought Jax.

He scrambled to his feet and retreated swiftly to the corner of the room furthest away from the door.

The pounding went on.

Then a voice said, 'Jerry? Jerry, are you in there? Are you all right?'

It was his father.

'Yeah, Dad,' said Jax, his voice cracking with relief. 'Yeah. I'm fine.'

'Oh, thank God. Jerry, the police are here with me. We have Glote. They've taken him into custody and he's said he's willing to confess everything. Something kind of peculiar happened to him. The house— I don't know, as far as I can tell, the house *attacked* him. He's completely freaked out by it. I think he might even have gone a little insane. Jerry, can you hear me in there?'

'Yeah, Dad, I can hear you. Will you hold on a moment? I've just got to catch the fade on something.'

'All right. I'll be right here.'

The Swami's final two words . . .

Jax racked his brain. He had heard them, and he knew in the back of his mind that they were highly significant. He *had* to remember what they were.

At last they popped into his head.

And then he had to sit down on the floor again because the implication of those two small words made him dizzy and light-headed.

It couldn't be right. He must have misheard.

But the two words made sense of everything the Swami had said before. They made sense, too, of what Flygirl had observed about the Swami software – the algorithms all back-to-front, the code not being in binary.

Jax shook his head, and smiled, and then began to laugh.

It was crazy, but it could only be true.

The two words were: *aN aLieN*.

The Swami was from outer space. And he wasn't here alone.

CHAPTER TWELVE

GONE FISHING

Three days later, Flygirl was in the BiblioTech, completing her research into utopias (because she never liked to leave a job unfinished), when President Samuel Jackson appeared beside her again and politely begged a moment of her time.

Flygirl looked up from the book she was reading – *News From Nowhere* by William Morris – and sighed testily.

'It'll wait,' she said. 'Whatever it is, it'll wait.'

The President was taken aback. 'I appreciate you're busy,' he said, 'but this is kind of a special occasion.'

'So *you* say,' replied Flygirl, and she hunched over her book again, putting her elbows on the lectern and her face in her fists – the posture of someone very much determined not to be disturbed.

'Well, I guess I *could* come back at a more convenient time, Miss N'Douba,' said the President.

'You do that,' said Flygirl. Then her head snapped round. 'Wait a second. What did you just call me?'

'You *are* Anita N'Douba, right?' said the President. 'Or have I got the wrong person? I gotta admit, this technology stuff gets me pretty confused sometimes.'

Flygirl's jaw dropped. Her mouth gaped. This was one of those rare occasions in her life when she was lost for words.

'You didn't think it was me, did you?' said the avatar of the President of the United States. 'I get that a lot. Seems some folk've been taking my likeness in vain.'

'But— But—'

The president smiled. 'I heard 'bout what you did the other day, Anita. You and your pal Jerry, Larry Hamlyn's kid. You busted that whole Davy Jones's Locker thing wide open. Quite a feat.'

'But—'

'Saved your friend's life as well. Kept cool as ice in a tricky situation. Came up with a plan. You're a smart kid. I could use someone like you on my staff.'

'But—'

'In an advisory capacity,' the President went on. 'As a kinda Web liaison officer. I'm an old guy, after all, an' frankly I find mosta this Web stuff just a little bit baffling. Your job would be to keep me in touch with what's going on in here. You'd report, once a month, directly to me. Keep me up with the latest developments, the latest innovations. How's that sound?'

'But—'

'One thing, though,' said the President. 'You want the job, Anita, you're going to have to learn to say something else other than "But—"'

Flygirl closed her mouth, breathed in deep through her nose, composed herself, and said, 'I'm your Flygirl, Mr President.'

President Jackson grinned hugely. '*Flygirl*? That's your alias, right? Damn, that's funky! Y'know, I think you an' me, Flygirl, we're gonna make a great team.'

After the president had left, Flygirl was unable to concentrate on her reading any more. She was far too excited. In fact, she kept giggling to herself so much that eventually one of the librarians asked her to leave.

Web Liaison Officer to President Jackson! She couldn't wait to tell Jax about it. He'd burst with envy!

Then she remembered that Jax was incommunicado for the next few days. He was away in the mountains of Oregon . . .

*

Fishing.

The lake was placid and crystal-clear. Barely a breath of wind disturbed its surface. There were mountain ridges and pine forests all around. The great hiss of Nature's emptiness was all that could be heard.

The small fibreglass rowing-boat floated in the middle of the lake. Jax and his father sat aboard it, side by side. Each had a fishing rod in his hands, and each was gazing contentedly at the spot where his line entered the water, marked by a small, bobbing orange float, the bull's-eye at the centre of a set of concentric ripples. The silence between Jax and his father was companionable. It didn't matter that neither of them had had so much as a nibble on his line all morning. Being there, and the anticipation of a catch, were enough to keep them both happy.

Finally, Jax broke the silence. 'Dad,' he said, 'how long did you know about Davy Jones's Locker?'

'I thought we agreed when we set out on this trip that we weren't going to talk about any of that until we got back home,' said Hamlyn.

'I know, but it's been bugging me.'

'OK,' said Hamlyn, playing out a bit more line into the water. 'A couple of months ago the Webcops contacted me, saying they'd heard unconfirmed rumours of improper activities in the Net. They had a pretty good idea who was responsible, and so did I. Glote. Unfortunately, they couldn't prove anything at the time, so we decided to play a waiting game. We figured that Glote, left to his own devices, would eventually get over-ambitious. That's the kind of guy he is. Then he'd make a mistake, and we would ensnare him. So I kept stringing Glote along, pretending I knew nothing about Davy Jones's Locker so that his suspicions wouldn't be aroused. We needed absolutely watertight evidence if we were going to bring him down, and if he had gotten wind of what we were up to, he'd have shut Davy Jones's Locker down immediately and there'd be nothing to prove it had ever existed.'

'But weren't you worried what people would think? After all, this was going on inside a company *you* owned.'

'The Webcops made it clear that, as far as they were concerned, I was innocent of all involvement in Davy Jones's Locker, and that, if necessary, they would go on record, publicly exonerating me of all blame. And I believe people would think far worse of me if it turned out that I'd known about Davy Jones's Locker and *not* done anything about it.'

This had proved to be true. On the evening after his second bat into Davy Jones's Locker, Jax had watched his father on the TV news giving a statement to reporters, saying that he deplored everything that had gone on in Davy Jones's Locker and that, despite the financial loss he was going to incur, he was decommissioning the Net with immediate effect. From the presenter's comments afterwards, it was clear that opinion of Larry Hamlyn was entirely favourable. He had done the right thing, the decent thing.

Opinion of J Edgar Glote could not have been more different. Flygirl had used the surveillance cameras to record him going through the house with his revolver and being attacked by the cleaning-drones, and cornered in the kitchen. The footage was being shown repeatedly on TV. No one, it seemed, got tired of watching it, and late-night chatshow hosts couldn't stop making jokes about it and about Glote. Being attacked by a house was a fair and just retribution on the man who had attempted to kill Larry Hamlyn's son.

'And, of course,' said Jax, 'you didn't want me batting into the Net because—'

'Because I couldn't risk you winding up in Davy Jones's Locker.' Hamlyn rolled his eyes. 'I should have known that would be the *first* place you went.'

'Why didn't you say anything at the time, though?'

'I couldn't. To keep Glote completely in the dark, I had to pretend to everyone – you included – that I had no idea what was really going on.'

'Well, I wish you *had* told me.'

'Yes, and I wish I'd listened to you when you tried to tell me that you'd been to Davy Jones's Locker. But I was too preoccupied. Things had reached a crucial stage. Remember when I was supposed to be attending a charity fund-raiser? Actually I was in a meeting with the Webcops. I told them I couldn't hold out much longer. I couldn't keep lying to you, particularly since you'd gotten hold of that junction-box. I told them we had to spring the trap on Glote now, and we were trying to figure out how to do that when the call came through from the LAPD that there'd been a break-in at the house. And not long after that, word came that Glote had been caught on the premises with a gun—' Hamlyn's voice trailed off. The thought of how close Glote had come to killing his son, his only remaining family, was almost too much to bear. 'Well, hey, he's not our problem any more, is he?'

Jax nodded. 'I guess he was right about one thing, though. He said you and I haven't been communicating properly.'

'Maybe so. But I get the feeling that's going to change from now on. Don't you?'

Jax couldn't help but think then of the Swami. If what the Swami had said was true, then a lot more than a father/son relationship was about to change. The entire planet was in for a major shake-up. Mankind was about to have its first encounter with an extraterrestrial race!

Jax wanted to tell everyone, warn everyone what was about to happen, but he knew no one would believe him. It would have to remain his secret. For now.

Hamlyn inhaled a lungful of fresh mountain air and let it slowly out as a sigh.

'It doesn't get much better than this, does it?' he said, gazing around at the spectacular scenery. 'In fact, you and me in this boat, miles from anywhere, in the midst of all this beauty and tranquillity – I'd say this was pretty much perfection. Wouldn't you, Jerry?'

Jax sniffed the air. Suddenly, impossibly, inexplicably, he could smell roses.

'Yeah,' he said. 'Yeah, Dad, I'd say this was utopia.'

SPINDRIFT
MAGGIE FUREY

For the Bakiras family in Paleokastrista, whose kind hospitality over the years has provided so much joy and inspiration and especially for Eleni, who played a special part in the two Web novels

With love and thanks.

CONTENTS

CHAPTER ONE

THE WARNING

Globenet Times, August 23, 2028.
WEB INFESTED BY DEMONS?
A cult religious group calling themselves the Guardians of the Word have launched a campaign to have the Web dismantled and destroyed. They claim the network has become the home of demons, who take over the minds of Web-users and cause them to behave in a bizarre and dangerous manner. 'People must be warned,' a spokesman for the group said today. 'The Web is clearly an invention of the Evil One. It is being used to corrupt the world, and this must be stopped at any cost.'

Church leaders have dismissed these claims as hysterical nonsense.

'SUPERMAN' DEATH IN ITALY
In Milan, a man has been killed after jumping from a high roof in the city centre. Enrico Romero, an accountant, aged 43, was dressed as Superman. 'We are regarding this as an unfortunate accident,' said a spokesman for the police. 'It looks as though the man really believed he could fly.'

'Enrico has been behaving strangely,' Carlo Romero, the dead man's brother said. 'At first we thought it was a joke when he pretended to be various characters from fiction. One day he would be Sherlock Holmes, the next day, Darth Vader. We never thought he actually believed this stuff – until now.'

Police are investigating links with other reports of strange behaviour following time spent in the Web.

Cat was running, running through dark city streets. The
night around her was wet and raw cold, with a blustery wind
that cut through her clothing like a jagged knife. Pelting rain
battered her skin and plastered her hair to her face. Her feet
stung from pounding the hard pavement. How long had she
been running? She wasn't sure any longer. It felt like forever.
Her breath burned in her throat – she was panting, partly
through exhaustion, but also partly from pure terror. She
knew she was being chased, but had no idea who – or what –
was after her. It was far worse not knowing.

Suddenly, in front of her, loomed the cathedral, its
massive bulk rearing above her in the harsh white glare of
the floodlights like a cliff carved of crystal and ice. Cat was so
startled that she skidded to a stop on the slippery wet grass.
This had happened before! She discarded the thought almost
before it had formed. A swift glance over her shoulder
showed her that this time, there was no furious father in
pursuit. She could hear no sound of approaching feet.
Behind her, where the narrow lane opened onto the broad
lawns of Palace Green, she saw nothing but an old-fashioned
wrought-iron street lamp that cast a circle of pale light onto
the street.

Even as Cat watched, the light grew dimmer, as though
clouded by a smoky haze. A patch of formless darkness was
gathering in the mouth of the lane, coiling and writhing like
something alive. It looked like a cloud of thick, black smoke
– except that it stayed in place, instead of being blown away
by the gusting gale as any normal smoke would have done.
Tendrils of oily blackness crept across the open space,
reaching for her like the tentacles of some hideous sea-
monster.

Cat, frozen with horror, simply stood there as though her
feet had been glued to the ground . . . Suddenly, from
somewhere, she found her wits and fear once again lent
wings to her feet. Smothering a scream, she took off like a
scared rabbit towards the shelter of the cathedral.

In the olden days, the mighty building had been open

every hour, a sanctuary for those in trouble or danger, but that had ended long ago. In these harsher times the cathedral had to be protected from damage and theft, and was normally locked up through the night – yet Cat felt no surprise when she pushed at one great door and it shuddered open, just a chink – just enough to let her through. The cathedral had taken her in and sheltered her once before, a year ago, and the experience had changed her life.

As she slipped through the door, Cat risked another quick glance over her shoulder. The black ooze was still following her – closer now. It moved in eerie silence, the blunt tendrils, like curls of smoke, pushing out blindly ahead of the great shapeless mass, groping along the ground and probing the air as though it were sniffing out her trail. Somehow she knew – just *knew* – it had intelligence and purpose. Whatever it was, it was alive, and it was after *her* – Cat – not just any stray victim who had happened to come that way.

A shiver of terror ran down Cat's spine. She slammed the door shut and ran into the vast, echoing gloom of the cathedral. Already, she knew, the blackness would be beginning to seep into the cracks around the edges of the door and underneath it, too, where centuries' worth of pilgrim footsteps had worn hollows in the flagstones of the floor. There would be no sanctuary from the *thing* that pursued her, not even in this holy place.

At least Cat had won herself a few minutes – just enough time to realize that she'd made a serious mistake. Idiot! In her panic, she hadn't thought it through. She should have stayed in the open – tried to dodge and outrun the thing. But like a terrified animal, she'd headed instinctively for the nearest shelter – and had cornered herself. Unless there was another way out of here, she was down the plug, and no mistake.

At night, Durham cathedral was only dimly lit. The candles had all been put out, and only a few dim bulbs burned, high in the distant vaults of the ceiling. They cast a faint, half-hearted glimmer down into the bottom of that

great well of stone and air, as though the light was too lazy
to bother coming all the way to the ground. In the nave, all
along the central aisle to the delicately carved altar screen,
shadows stretched long limbs like wild beasts about to
pounce. Above the altar, the dark eye of the great round
window seemed to fade and grow dim as a vast black cloud
billowed up and began to ooze through the gaps in the lacy
stonework of the rood screen. Horror squeezed Cat's heart in
a fist of ice. *They* were already here! There was nowhere left
to run. She had been driven into a trap!

There was only one option left to Cat. Behind its curtain
the door to the ancient tower seemed to beckon her, as it
had done once before. It was hopeless – there was no way the
thing would fail to find her – but it was her only chance.
There was evil in the chill, mysterious blackness. Cat had
been close enough to feel it. Rather than be captured, she
could always jump off the top of the tower. But it was best
not to think of such things – at least, not yet. Instead, Cat
sped across the open space and dived behind the thick blue
drapes that hid the tower door.

The door still bolted from the inside and the candles were
there in their niche as they had been that other time, so long
ago. Cat shot the bolt into place, for all the good it would do,
and lit a candle. As she turned to go up the stairs, the
candlelight caught a row of pale spiky writing that scarred
the ancient stone. Some words had been gouged roughly
into the wall:

WHO IS THE HUNTER?

Cat, though faintly shocked by such vandalism, had too
many problems of her own to give much thought to the
writing. She had begun to feel that this whole business was
inevitable – that she had been herded here on purpose. But
why? If the thing had wanted to kill her, surely there were
simpler ways? Driven on by a growing feeling of fate at work,
she hurried up the tower stairs.

Higher and higher, Cat went, until eventually the sight of

a streak of dim light coming from underneath a door made her hesitate. 'Oh no,' she whispered. 'Oh, please, no.' But she couldn't stop herself. Like a sleepwalker, Cat stumbled forward, turned the handle of the old wooden door, and pushed.

Red light blossomed around her like an opening flower. 'Come in, my dear,' said an old voice like gravel and silk. Seated in her wheelchair like a queen upon a throne, with an array of bottles, tubes and wires in place of a sceptre and a crown, sat the gaunt, imperious figure of the Sorceress herself!

The old woman smiled at Cat. 'Close your mouth, my dear, before your brains fall out. You're safe here,' she went on. '*They* won't come into the Shadowzone. They're still afraid of me – they don't quite know what to make of me yet – so we'd better use that uncertainty while it lasts.'

Cat barely heard the last part. *You're safe here.* She had heard those words before, in this very room – but the first time Miss Aldanar had used that phrase, Cat had barely escaped with her life. Suddenly, the girl felt anger flare up inside her, a rage that had been buried for more than a year because she thought its target was dead and gone. 'You! Stay away from me!' she screamed at the old woman. I trusted you! I *loved* you, and you betrayed me!'

'You're right, I did.' Miss Aldanar's calm voice was like cool water poured on the flames of Cat's rage. 'At the time I felt I had no choice, but what I did was wrong. I see that now. I'm very sorry, Cat. I had no right to trap you as I did – to try to steal your young body to replace my failing old carcass!'

A grim smile flickered across her hawklike face. 'I failed, though. I was punished, and it served me right.' She sighed. 'Maybe some day, you'll be able to forgive me – I truly hope so – but I don't have time to wait. I must warn you now.' She leaned forward in her chair and fixed Cat with her dark glittering gaze. 'My dear, be careful. You are in grave danger. The whole world is in danger. *They are here.* The Web will not contain them any longer. They've found a way out, Cat.

They're loose in the world now, and no one knows! I don't understand what they are doing, or what they want – but people must be warned.'

Cat backed away from her. 'No!' she shouted. 'I don't believe you. You're lying! You never told me the truth! You want to trick me again, just as you did before! Stay away from me! *Leave me alone!*'

'Leave me alone! Leave me alone!'

'Cat? Cat! Wake up!'

Abruptly, Miss Aldanar and her tower vanished, to be replaced by Cat's dad, wearing his horrible striped bathrobe and a worried frown. He was leaning over the bed and shaking her. 'Kitten, are you all right?' he asked her. 'You were screaming loud enough to wake the whole street!' He sat down on the edge of the bed, looking sleepy-eyed but concerned. 'That nightmare again?' he asked her. 'I thought you'd managed to get rid of those – you haven't had one for ages.'

Cat was too old now to fling herself into his arms as she had done when she was little, but she took his hand and held it very tightly. 'Not the same one . . .' she shook her head. Ever since last year, when she had run away from home and met Miss Aldanar, she had been suffering terrible nightmares about being trapped forever in the Web, as the Sorceress had planned.

Still, Cat told herself, some good had come out of the terrifying experience. Dad was a friend to her now, instead of the bitter enemy who hated the Web and everything it stood for. He had been a teacher who ended up on the scrap-heap when education switched to the Web. As a result, he had forbidden his children to have anything to do with it. Cat had been forced to steal secret Web-time, sneaking off to the cybercafe whenever she had the chance – until she finally ran away from home and into the clutches of the evil Miss Aldanar, who was using children in experiments because she hoped the Web could give her some kind of everlasting life after her frail old body had failed her.

Following the defeat of the Sorceress, Cat's home life had come to the attention of the authorities. Her father had been taken away for counselling and treatment, and Cat had gone to stay in Ireland with Anna Lucas, the well-known game designer, who had played such an important part in the downfall of the Sorceress. Months later, a very changed, very shy dad had come to pick Cat up. To everyone's surprise, he and Anna were soon getting along as though they had been friends for years, and now they were working together in the Web, designing *interesting* ways of learning history that were partly games, and partly direct experience of what it was like to live in those times.

Seeing her father's worried expression, Cat pulled her thoughts back to the present. 'Miss Aldanar was in my dream,' she said, 'but this time, she saved me – from some horrible bad *thing*, like a cloud of darkness, but with *tentacles* . . .' She shuddered. 'She was trying to warn me about something. She said I was in danger – the whole human race was in danger. *They are here*,' she said.

'Who?' Dad asked. 'Who are here?'

Cat shrugged. 'Who knows? It was just another stupid dream, I expect. What time is it, anyway?'

'Just after three – there's plenty of night left. I'll get you some hot milk,' Dad suggested.

'Yuk.' Cat made a face. 'Hot milk is for babies. You know I loathe the stuff.'

He grinned. 'A cup of tea, then? If you're sure it won't keep you awake.'

'Mmm – yes please,' Cat said. 'I don't really feel like going back to sleep just yet.'

Nevertheless, she was asleep again before the tea came.

CHAPTER TWO

THE WRITING
ON THE WALL

Globenet Times, August 24, 2028.
WORLDWIDE CRIME WAVE CAUSES CONCERN
Law enforcement authorities across the globe joined together today to warn that there has been a dramatic rise in planet-wide crime over the past few months. Apparently the increase is mostly in crimes of theft such as burglary, shoplifting and mugging.

'It's the weirdest thing I've seen in almost forty years of police work,' said Commissioner Ben McLean of the NYPD. 'People just see a thing, decide they want it – and simply take it without a thought for the consequences.'

'It's as though these people have taken leave of their senses,' said Samotu Hanakiro, Head of the Tokyo Law Enforcement Network. 'Afterwards, many of them cannot even remember committing the crime.'

'Frankly, we don't understand this trend,' said Chief Inspector Anne Harrow of London's Scotland Yard. 'When the Web came into being, the numbers of street crimes dropped very sharply, and stayed low – until now. So far, we can find no real cause for the increase – most of the criminals themselves don't seem to understand why they did what they did.'

CONTROVERSY OVER NEW ALIEN MOVIE
The successful VRealie director Patrick Kickham, who began a distin- guished career thirty years ago in old-fashioned flatscreen films, has had a mixed response to his latest shock production, ALIEN HORDES, which is shot from the point of view of beings from another world. (Hotlink

Reviews, page 1906) The alien invaders here are actually the human race,
who are seen as brutal, barbaric and merciless destroyers.

Kickham, who was one of the pioneers of the Web-based VRealie,
where the watcher is inside the movie and takes part in the action, said
he was disappointed by the response. 'I'm not really surprised, though,' he
said. 'It takes a very open mind to see ourselves as the bad guys for a
change.'

When asked where the idea for the VRealie had come from, he said, 'I
don't know, to be honest. I hardly remember writing it at all. The idea
came from a weird dream I had, and after that, the whole thing just took
off on its own.'

'Eleni, this is magnificent! You've created a masterpiece!'

Eleni glowed with pride at Anna's praise. She had put in a
tremendous amount of hard work on this project, and it was
by far the most difficult and complicated thing she had ever
done. It felt great to have her work appreciated by a
professional like Anna Lucas.

Rom, who had paid Eleni the compliment of appearing in
human shape for once, seemed unable to stop looking
around. The view was well worth looking at. On one side of
the road, a steep slope dropped down to an ocean, the calm
waters of which were the vivid deep blue-green of a
peacock's tail. On the other side, steeply sloping terraces of
silver-green olive trees rose up, suddenly ending in spectacular 300-metre cliffs of grey-gold stone.

'I never imagined your home would look like this, Leni,'
Jack said. 'I never realized that Greece was so, well, green.'

'Most of it isn't,' said Anna, who had done a fair amount
of travelling when she was younger. 'It's because the winters
are so wet here in Corfu. Also, before you ask, the sea really *is*
that incredible colour.' She turned to Eleni. 'I'm glad I
advised you to stick to something you know for your first
solo design. My dear, this is a splendid effort.'

Eleni beamed with pleasure. She had decided long ago that
she wanted to make a living doing what Anna did and, to
her delight, the games designer had agreed to take her on as

a kind of unofficial apprentice. For the last few months, the Greek girl had spent most of her spare time working like a slave to learn the basic programming skills used by Anna and people like her to create the marvels of the Web.

'Wow,' the American boy said at last. 'Are those cliffs for *real*? Just look at those venomous caves. You could have dragons up there for sure.'

Eleni grinned. 'I plan to, Rom. I have some wildlife down in the garden to start with, just insects and stuff on a loop, but I had to start small.'

'I'll teach you to design proper phaces next,' Anna told her. 'It's a lot more difficult, but it's great fun.' She grinned. 'When I think of some of the weird and wonderful critters I used to come up with—'

'What do you mean, used to?' Jack teased her.

'Grrrr!' Anna's fingers danced over her wrist unit and, suddenly, in her place stood an enormous tiger that pounced on Jack, knocking him down into the dusty road.

'Peace, peace,' Jack yelled, laughing. 'I take it back!'

The tiger turned back into Anna again.

'All the same,' Jack added wickedly, 'that just proves my point.' Hooting with laughter, he scurried behind Eleni, putting himself well out of Anna's range.

'You horrible wretch!' Anna made a face at him.

'Do you think the Cat will get here?' Rom interrupted. 'It would be a real pity if she missed this.'

'I don't know, Rom. When D.L. called, he said she hadn't woken up just yet and he was letting her sleep. He sounded a bit worried.' Anna sighed. 'Poor old Cat. I thought those nightmares of hers had gone for good.'

Anna's friendship with Cat's father had come as a surprise to them all. Only last year, he had seemed the blackest of villains to Jack, Eleni and Rom, but in the end he had turned out all right 'after we trained him', as Jack always said. Sometimes he still tended to act a bit formally, like an old-fashioned professor, but Anna would never let him get away with *that* for very long. His name, David Lee, was a good example. When he had refused to let Anna call him *Dave*, she had come up with *D.L.* instead – and the nick had stuck for good. Now everyone called him that, and it suited him.

'Poor old Cat,' said Rom, but it was clear that his thoughts already were somewhere else. He always had a thousand things he wanted to do with his precious Web-time, and he was usually thinking about the next one. 'Never mind. She'll get here when she can, or you can bring her later, Leni. C'mon, show us your house. We're all dying of curiosity.'

Eleni led them off the edge of the road and downhill towards the sea, down a curving flight of rough steps that had been hacked out of the stony hillside. On the left was a chain-link fence, on the right another terraced olive grove. About halfway down the slope, the rough stairway and the olive trees came to an end. Beyond the grove was a square, two-storey white building with steps leading up to an iron-railed balcony that ran right around the upper floor. On the ground floor, a paved patio ran along the front of the house, shaded from the sun by an enormous grapevine that covered a wooden trellis overhead. Below the patio, the garden, a lush mixture of flowers, vegetables and herbs, stretched down to a wall that dropped directly into the sea some three metres below.

'Hey, you've been keeping this a secret! You never told us you lived in such a venomous place!' Jack said.

'I'm glad you like it.' Eleni glowed at the compliment. 'I haven't done the inside yet,' she added, as Rom headed towards the door, 'so there's no point in looking.'

'Give her a chance, Rom,' said Anna.

The garden went on sloping down to the sea. Near the house were terraces of brightly coloured flowers, and further down, where the land levelled out, was a vegetable patch. Jack was investigating. 'Wow,' he said, 'I see what you mean about the wildlife.'

From a crack between two stones, a small, chocolate-coloured lizard darted out. It sunned itself for a moment, then, as Jack moved, it darted away in a flicker of movement almost too fast to see. Almost hidden among the green leaves, a praying mantis turned her wicked, triangular head and watched them fearlessly with cold glittering eyes. Cicadas were zithering in the bushes, sounding, as Rom said, like grasshoppers on an amplifier. Big swallowtail butterflies, bright yellow or patterned black and white, whirled in a zigzag dance above the flowers and, surely, hovering beside a geranium—

'Hold on,' Rom said, 'that tiny thing *can't* be a humming-bird?'

Eleni laughed. 'No, it's a sort of moth. But doesn't it look *exactly* like a hummingbird?'

'It had me fooled,' said Jack from the far end of the patio. He vanished around the corner of the house — and everyone jumped as he let out a yell. 'Hey! You! Come back!'

They ran to see what was wrong. Jack had vanished – but after a moment he reappeared from around the back of the house. 'Someone was *here*,' he said indignantly. 'I saw him! Somebody dressed all in black. I chased him around the corner there – but he scuttled.'

'But that's impossible,' Eleni protested. 'This is part of Anna's design space. It's security coded!'

'Don't be daft, Jack,' Anna scoffed. 'You'll be seeing fairies next.'

Rom laughed. 'Come on – you'll never bite us with a basement-level stunt like that!'

'No?' Jack said grimly. 'Who did *that*, then?'

Eleni looked up at the side of the house. The spotless white wall was defaced by a series of huge, sprawling words, roughly scrawled in what looked like smears of blood.

WHO IS THE HUNTER?

The Cat finally caught up with the others in the Star Bar, which lately had become their favourite haunt. Cat loved the place. You entered through a window in E&R Webtown, and when the BAT had cleared, you found yourself hanging, suspended, in deep and endless infinity, with nothing around you but millions of blazing stars – and a scattering of brightly coloured tables floating in space, orbiting the Star Bar's central counter. Best of all, this was the Web and though there was the illusion of zero gravity there was nothing to fear in this place from the cold and vacuum between the stars, and no need to wear a clumsy, confining space suit.

The entrance point was beside the counter. Cat, well-practised by now with the Star Bar's zero gravity, made a grab for one of the handholds that stuck out from the fluorescent yellow structure where the robot bartenders worked, and pulled herself over to the serving area where she picked up a drinking bulb and a set of thrusters. These looked like chunky silver bracelets which she strapped around her wrists and ankles, triggering them in sequence with her own wristpad. Using the thrusters in small, skilful bursts, she drifted over to her friends.

Rom, who happened to be pointing in her direction, looked up and saw her. 'Yo, Sleeping Beauty!' he yelled. 'Where you been?'

'Hiding from you, Frog-Face,' Cat yelled back with a grin. Then she realized that Eleni was not with him. Rats, she thought. Is she mad at me because I didn't come to look at her site this morning?

'If I'm the Frog, does that make Eleni the Princess?' Rom asked as she drew near.

'Ha! You wish!' Cat snorted.

'It would take more than a kiss from Leni to turn Rom into a handsome prince,' Jack laughed.

Though a lot of people, particularly grown-ups, preferred to align themselves with the serving counter, there was no real *up* or *down* in this place. The circular tables were tilted every-which-way to each other, and quite a few were upside-down – or would have been, had there been a right way up. The benches were attached to the tables as part of the structure, so there was no danger of them floating away.

People who weren't used to the Star Bar always had a bit of

a struggle to get themselves into the space between the
bench and the table, but Cat was an old hand at this, and
slipped easily into position between Jack and Rom using the
table's handholds. Once she was seated she fastened a strap,
like the safety belt in a plane, across her lap to stop herself
drifting away again. The drinking bulb could be stuck into
position on the top of the table, using a simple velcro pad.

'Whoops! Watch out!' Jack laughed. Cat's arrival had set
the whole table tilting, so that the stars wheeled around
them in the mad display that everyone – except most adults
– enjoyed so much. This time, however, Cat noticed that
Rom and Jack, who normally enjoyed the cosmic carousel
effect, were no longer smiling.

'Look, I'm sorry I didn't make it this morning,' Cat said
quickly, worried that their black mood must be her fault. 'I
had no idea my daft dad would let me oversleep like that!'

'Never mind,' Jack told her grimly. 'You only missed all
the trouble.'

'Trouble? What trouble?' Cat asked him sharply. 'Is Eleni
all right?'

'She's upset, is all,' Rom said. 'I've never seen her so angry.
We've no idea how they could have gotten in, but some one-
mip, basement-level gag had been messing with her site.'

Prompted here and there by Jack, he quickly told her what
had happened. 'Not even Anna could put it right,' he went
on in an awed voice. 'She said she doesn't know how he did
it, but there seems to be no way of changing the programming to wipe it out.' Rom's eyes were like saucers. 'Poor old
Leni,' he went on. 'Her site was awesome, too! And then,
after all the hard work she put in, someone comes along and
writes WHO IS THE HUNTER? all over the place—'

'He wrote *what*?' Suddenly, the image of those very words
carved into the stone of an ancient staircase flashed into
Cat's mind – and all the details of her nightmare, forgotten
in the scramble of being late, came flooding back to her. In
that moment, an icy cold feeling struck through her like a

knife. It was the same fear she had felt a year ago and had expected never to feel again.

Cat leaned towards the boys. 'Listen,' she said urgently, fighting an irrational urge to whisper. 'Something is very wrong here.' Then she told them about her dream – about being hunted by the formless black evil, and about the writing on the wall of the cathedral bell tower.

'Are you sure it was the same words?' Rom asked her. '*Who is the Hunter*?'

'That's exactly what it said,' Cat replied. 'But that wasn't all.' Finally, she told them about the Sorceress – and the old woman's warning. 'I know this sounds crazy,' she said, 'but it wasn't like the other dreams at all. It was so *real*.' She shuddered. 'Miss Aldanar told me the world is in danger. *They are here*, she said, whatever *they* are. She said they had found some way to get out of the Web. They're loose in the world now, she said, and no one knows! She wanted people to be warned.'

'But Cat,' Jack protested, 'it was only a dream.'

'Was it?' Rom looked from one to the other, his eyes sparkling as he savoured the drama. 'If it was only a dream, Jack, how do you account for the writing in the tower? I'm telling you guys, there's something extremely weird going on here.'

'But it had to be a dream,' Jack insisted. 'The Sorceress is dead!'

'Is she?' Rom said. 'Her body died, but what about her mind? What if she fooled us all? What if there's a hidden place, somewhere deep in the Web, where she lives on?'

CHAPTER THREE

THE GREY MAN

Globenet Times, August 25, 2028.
SCANDAL OF BANQUET BATTLE
Embarrassed world leaders have been forced to make a public apology
today, after the United Nations conference on the future of space
exploration broke up in chaos. Disgraceful scenes broke out at last night's
formal banquet. Police had to be called to break up a food fight between
formerly respectable prime ministers and presidents that caused thou-
sands of euros worth of damage to the Great Hall of Dublin Castle, where
the conference was being held.

'I can't understand what came over everyone,' a delegate said today.
'The conference had gone very well, with an unusual amount of
agreement on all sides. We had spent a useful afternoon in the Web,
attending a demonstration of the latest advances in space probes, and
everyone was looking forward to the banquet. That was when everything
went wrong.'

'Certain personal comments were passed by one or two of the
delegates,' another delegate admitted. 'Then people started taking sides,
and before we knew it, the whole thing had got completely out of hand.'

A third delegate was quoted as saying, 'Afterwards, we were all deeply
ashamed of ourselves – but it was great fun while it lasted.'

Next morning, Cat was squabbling with her oldest brother
over the last piece of toast when the buzzer sounded.

'But you can make some more,' Mark was protesting.

'*You* make some more, you lazy one-mip! It's your turn!'

''S'not – it's yours—'

'Will somebody get that blasted *door*!' Dad, halfway out of his websuit, yelled down from the upstairs landing. In the abrupt silence that followed, the blaring of the door buzzer was very loud. Mark went across and switched on the video display. He groaned, and twisted his face as though he smelled something bad. 'It's the Grey Man,' he whined. 'Cat, you go. He scares me.'

'Then you're a silly little egg,' Cat snapped. Then she took pity on him. He was only eleven, after all. 'Why don't you take Brian and Susie out for a while?'

Glad of the chance to escape, Mark hurried off to get his little brother and sister into their jackets while Cat went to answer the door. Cold and unsmiling, the Grey Man towered over her on the doorstep, looking down at her as though she were some kind of insect. 'About time,' he said. 'What kept you?'

A spark of annoyance began to burn inside Cat. 'I didn't expect you today.'

He raised an eyebrow. 'Really? I'm sure I sent word. Perhaps the message went astray.' His tone hinted that it was her fault.

Cat sighed. 'Will this take long?' She saw her plans for the rest of the day going down the plug there and then.

The Grey Man shook his head. 'Not this time, Catherine. I have a few documents for you to sign, that's all.'

Well, there was no escaping it. Cat stood back from the door and invited him to come inside.

These sessions with the Grey Man were an unexpected result of Cat's meeting with the Sorceress. Not long after Miss Aldanar's death, it had come as a tremendous shock when the girl found out that the old lady had made a new will before she died, and had left everything to her. It had been a bigger shock to discover just how much *everything* amounted to. Miss Aldanar's business empire was huge, and her wealth beyond imagining.

Luckily, Cat had been staying with Anna while this was

happening, and the designer had at once grasped the true
purpose of the will. 'You know what the cunning old witch
has done, don't you?' she'd said to Cat. 'She left everything
to you because she planned to steal your body. It was all
meant to come back to *her*! She wouldn't lose a thing,
wouldn't need to start over. As soon as she came of age, she
would get it all back. Why, the devious old besom.' Anna
laughed. 'And in the end, she outsmarted herself. She
planned to make you her victim, but it all backfired on her,
and you've wound up with the lot!'

After the first shock had died away, Cat was left with
mixed feelings about such wealth. First had been disbelief,
then delight, followed by confusion. On the one hand, of
course, it was a dream come true. Why, with all that money,
she could do anything – when she was older, at any rate. At
this point, though, it all seemed so unreal. Everything was
held in trust for her and would stay that way until she
turned eighteen.

On the other hand, the idea of such a huge responsibility
weighed her down. Should she keep Miss Aldanar's empire
and learn to run it as the old lady had? Was she even capable
of such a thing? Or should she just sell the lot and live out
the rest of her life in idleness and comfort? Give it all away to
good causes? Sell part of it, and just hold on to the
companies that interested her?

Again, wise Anna had come to the rescue. 'The best thing
you can do right now is to forget about the whole thing,'
she'd said firmly. 'You're in your growing-up years, Cat, and
you're changing every day. You'll be an entirely different
person by the time you reach eighteen, so any decision you
make now won't count for much then. Put it out of your
mind, love, as much as you can. Why worry about something that won't happen for another few years? Enjoy your
monthly allowance and let those lawyers and executives take
care of the rest. Goodness knows, they get paid enough to do
it. If you're worried, I can help you hire some lawyers and

accountants of your own, to make sure that Miss Aldanar's Grey Men aren't cheating you.'

So that was exactly what Cat had done, although Anna's nick of *Grey Men* had stuck to the executives of Miss Aldanar's Black Widow Corporation. When Cat's father had come home, and the family could get back together again, Anna had helped Cat persuade the trustees to part with enough money to buy them a roomy house in an old street that ran steeply uphill from the marketplace in Durham. Though it wasn't the expensive area of the city, it was much nicer than the crowded estate where they had lived before, and Cat knew they would be happy there. It was a new start for all of them.

Unfortunately, Cat couldn't get rid of the Black Widow Corporation entirely. To her dismay, there had been a special clause in Miss Aldanar's will stating that Cat must look over every decision made by the directors and approve them. Every month, Mr Craven, the greyest of all the Grey Men and the bane of her life, would arrive with his exec-screen and his unsmiling face, and she would have to waste the best part of a day going over stuff that, to her, was tedious and dull.

Cat knew why the Sorceress had done it, of course. If everything had gone according to plan, then Miss Aldanar would have been there in Cat's body, supervising her empire. *She*, of course, would have enjoyed it, and would have understood what was going on. Sometimes, as she sat fidgeting under the eye of the unsmiling Craven, who clearly thought the whole affair was a waste of *his* valuable time, Cat found herself wishing that the old woman was still alive, so that she could strangle her.

Cat's father didn't care for Mr Craven either. Lately, he had taken to sitting in on their sessions, and though he never really said much, Cat found it a great help just to have him there. Sure enough, as soon as Cat had settled her unwelcome visitor in the living room and was making him some coffee, D.L. came galloping downstairs, his face like thunder. Cat knew he would be in a warlike mood after staying up all night to work with Anna in the Web. They were producing Vikings at present, and it always took Dad an hour or so to shake off the ghosts of those ancient Norse warriors.

Cat took one look at her dad's expression, and sighed. She hoped his next project would involve a more peaceable civilization. In case of accidents, she quickly hid the bread-knife in the drawer. D.L. picked up a table knife instead, and started brandishing it like a broadsword. 'What's *he* want?' he hissed. 'This isn't his week to come here.'

Cat shrugged. 'The sooner we find out, the sooner we can get rid of him.'

It turned out, however, that Mr Craven wasn't to be got rid of so easily. After a time, Cat found herself wondering what was so urgent that the Grey Man couldn't have waited for the proper day. This was all so trivial! As Craven droned on about streamlining and efficiency, she found her mind wandering. I wonder who, or what, this Hunter really is? she thought. What could be the key to the mystery?

'The Shadowzone, of course—'

Cat jumped. It was almost as though the Grey Man had answered the question in her mind – and surely she had heard that phrase somewhere before? 'Sorry, what did you say?' she asked him.

Craven grimaced with irritation. 'I *said*, we have certain sites and domains within the Web that have fallen into disuse. Our plan is to reclaim and cleanse them – wipe out anything left cluttering them, so that they can be re-used.'

Cat frowned. 'I don't understand what you mean by reclaim and cleanse. Why can't you just reprogram them?'

For an instant the Grey Man scowled at her, then quickly hid his anger under a plastic smile. 'Don't worry about it, Catherine, it's a technical term. It's nothing that need concern a little girl.' He pushed the light-pen into her hand. 'Just sign the authorization, and we can get on.'

At her side, Cat could feel Dad start to bristle. 'I might

remind you, Craven, that this little girl happens to be your boss. Your job is to explain anything that Catherine doesn't understand – so I suggest you get on with it.'

'I'm not signing anything,' Cat added, 'until I understand what's going on.' From the way he was trying to rush her, she was sure he was hiding something.

The Grey Man turned white with anger. 'She'll be my boss when she comes of age,' he snarled, 'and not a minute before. In the meantime, I answer to the Board, not some snotty-nosed kid.' He banged the exec-screen shut without even bothering to log off.

Cat jumped when D.L. shot out of his seat as though on springs. 'Poltroon!' he roared. 'Split-tongued traitor! Spineless whelp of a mangy hound!'

'What? Now look here . . . How dare you?' Craven scrambled up from the sofa and started backing towards the door. His wary expression turned to stark fear as Dad grabbed the poker from its strictly ornamental position beside the fireplace and charged at him with a wild and awful yell. 'Odin! Odiiiiin!'

The Grey Man took to his heels and fled for the safety of his car, and the last Cat saw of him, he was driving away down the street as though he was being chased by all the fiends from Hell. She went back inside, collapsed on the sofa and laughed until she was breathless.

After a few moments Dad came back, shaking his head and frowning in puzzlement. He was holding the poker at arm's length as though it were a live snake. 'Good heavens,' he muttered. 'I'm sorry, Kitten. I don't know what came over me.'

'It served him right,' Cat said. 'That horrible *creep*!'

'I only hope the trustees see it that way.' It had been a long time since Cat had seen her father look so grim. 'I'm going to call them now, and get our side of the story in first,' he said. 'Just let Craven try to complain! I'll tell them if he ever shows his face around here again, I'll personally *kick* him all the way back to head office. Next time, they can send somebody with some manners. Don't worry, Kitten. He won't be back – not after the shock I gave him.' He shook his head again. 'Mind you, he wasn't the only one who got a shock. I think I might need a day or two off work.'

Cat leaped up to hug him. 'Don't worry, Dad, I thought you were a real hero.'

When he had left the room, however, she sat there for a long time wondering just what was going on. Who was the Hunter? What was the Shadowzone, and why were the Grey Men so desperate to wipe it out?

Then all at once, Cat remembered. Miss Aldanar had used those very words in that dream the other night! '*They* won't come into the Shadowzone,' the old woman had said. So the dream *had* been some kind of warning! But surely, that could only mean—

'No,' Cat said aloud. 'No, no! NO! I saw her body. She couldn't have survived! The Sorceress is *dead*!' But, suddenly, she wasn't so sure.

CHAPTER FOUR

DOWN INTO DARKNESS

Globenet Times, August 26, 2028.
PRESIDENTIAL PLANE IN NEAR DISASTER
Air Force One, the presidential stratoplane, has been forced to make an emergency landing in the Nevada desert. According to Ground Control at the Clinton Air Base, the plane had taken off normally, en route to Washington to pick up the president and his family, when the pilot appeared to go mad at the controls. According to one eyewitness, the plane was looping, diving, and trying to buzz the control tower before the co-pilot succeeded in overpowering his partner and made an emergency landing.

Three people of the crew, security and cabin staff, sustained minor injuries during the incident.

Neither the pilot nor the co-pilot will be named until there has been a full inquiry into the incident.

MIRACULOUS SURVIVAL OF LION MAN
Keepers at San Diego Zoo were forced to use nets and tranquillizer guns to remove a man from the lion enclosure last night. The man, Milton Barnes from Boise, Idaho, had removed his clothing and broken into the enclosure after the zoo had closed for the night. 'I wanted to communicate with a predator,' he told the keepers at the time of his rescue.

'Later, when we interviewed him, he seemed frightened and confused,' said Sergeant Alan Janisch of the San Diego Police. 'He had no explanation for what he had done.'

Amazingly, not one of the five lions had made a move to harm him. 'This idiot must be the luckiest guy alive,' Sergeant Janisch said.

'It was an appallingly stupid thing to do,' said Dr Susan Brown, the zoo's curator. 'These big cats may look cute from a distance, but we're dealing with extremely dangerous predators. Even the keepers don't enter those enclosures without taking precautions.'

To prevent any further incidents, the zoo have increased security around the lion enclosure.

Usually, there was nothing Rom liked better than a good puzzle, but he was beginning to wonder if this one might be beyond even him. He had spent a sleepless night, racking his brains in search of a way to solve the mysteries of Cat's nightmare, Eleni's intruder, and the weird graffiti. So far, he hadn't come up with a single answer. It was frustrating but, worse, it could be dangerous. If this business was connected in some way with the Sorceress – if it turned out that the old woman was still alive in the Web – then she was bound to be involved in something far more serious and far reaching than simply messing up the site of an unimportant student. But was Leni really so unimportant? In the end, it had been she who defeated the Sorceress. Was the message only a warning? Had the old hag come back to seek her revenge? Somebody ought to be finding out – and who better than Rom?

Over the last couple of years, Rom had become much closer friends with Cat, Jack and Eleni. Before that, he had spent most of his time playing Dreamcastle with Surfer and Kilroy, two game vets who also lived in Oakhills, his home town in New England. Though they were great fun to be around, they had both been older than Rom, and about the time Dreamcastle had closed, they had developed an interest in each other which kept them out of the Web a good deal, and made Rom feel he was in the way whenever he saw them. Though he was glad that things had worked out for them, he'd been pretty lonely for a while. Then he had found himself mixed up with Jack and the two girls, and their battle against the Sorceress had cemented a lasting friendship – especially with Eleni.

Of all the friends, Rom probably best understood the Greek girl's anger when her work had been tampered with. He and Leni were spun from the same silk. In a way, Jack and the Cat were tourists. They looked on the Web as a vast, ever-changing playground that they could visit whenever they wanted. Rom and Eleni, on the other hand, saw its complex structure as a kind of second home that could be rebuilt, refurbished and changed to suit their own wants and needs. He had shared her triumph in creating an actual part of the Web – in adding to its wonders – and now he shared her dismay that someone could break into a secured site and spoil the results of her hard work.

How the mip had they done that, anyway? The site had been part of Anna's design space and, because of commercial competition, game design security was tighter than an outgrown Websuit. Besides, after Anna's Dragonville proto-type had been hijacked by the Sorceress, the designer had added modifications that made her sites impenetrable – or so they had thought. Had he not been one of the privileged few who had a limited visitor's password, Rom doubted whether he could break in himself – and that was saying a lot.

Outside his window, there was a faint glimmer of daylight beyond the thin summer curtains. Somewhere in the distance, a single bird broke into a sleepy whistle. Rom still hadn't been to sleep. This was crazy! Though his folks were pretty strict about him getting his rest, he figured that today at least, he'd be better off in the Web, trying to solve the problem of Leni's trespasser. He slid out of bed quietly, anxious not to wake his parents. He was the youngest of his family – the others were grown and had all left home now – and his mother seemed determined to keep him a baby forever.

Naturally, Rom had had a lot of practice at sneaking into his Websuit in the middle of the night. Was it his fault if his friends lived in different time zones? After the trouble with

Dreamcastle, his parents had decided that hanging out with the vets and phreaks in the VR Bar was bad for him, and had bought him a suit of his own so he could surf from home.

Like many parents who didn't use the Web much, it never seemed to cross their minds that he'd be meeting exactly the same people as soon as he'd spun in. Things were a lot handier this way, too. There was no way Rom could be sneaking unofficial Web time if he had to get out of the house and go to the VR Bar – and he had discovered long ago how to hack into the Central User Records and wipe the evidence of his night-time adventures from his folks' monthly account, hiding the extra cost here and there between his Education Modules, Dad's ball games and Mom's romantic VRealies.

It didn't take long to spin into Leni's site – he was one of the few people she trusted with the access code. The entry point was at the top of the steps. Once again he glanced behind him at the incredible cliffs with their high cave mouths that could so easily hide a dragon, or lead to a zillion other adventures. Rom allowed himself a small, envious sigh. Wow, he thought. What a venomous place to live!

Wasting no more time, Rom scrambled down the rough rock steps until he reached the house. Feeling a bit like a burglar, he crept across the vine-shaped patio and rounded the far corner. Again he felt a twinge of anger as he looked at the spiky letters that scarred the white wall. 'Just who the *mip* is this stupid Hunter?' he wondered out loud. 'I wish I could get my hands on him.' He was far too preoccupied to spot the many eyes that watched him from among the branches of a nearby olive tree.

Rom spent ages on the graffiti, trying one code after another in the hope of finding a combination that would restore the wall to its former perfect state. Eventually, he was interrupted by a bleeping alarm on his unit, and realized he had run out of time – at least for now. Back in Realworld, his parents would be waking up any minute – and he had better be innocently back in bed before they did, or he'd be down the plug with vengeance.

Even as he lifted his hand to hit his scuttle button, he heard the voice.

'You are leaving already? I think not.'

All thoughts of his parents were wiped from Rom's mind as the dark, gangling form dropped down from the olive tree. Looming over him was a creature of terror – a gigantic silver-black praying mantis that seemed to grow once it had hit the ground, until it towered some four or five metres over his head.

Held by the hypnotic glitter of the monster's dark eyes, Rom found he could no longer move. His hand remained frozen in mid-air above the scuttle button.

'Fool,' the creature said with mocking contempt. *'All humans are fools. You and your friends are fools – but at least you may be of some use.'* It stretched out its long, barbed forelimbs and grabbed the helpless Rom, pulling him towards its armoured body in a deadly embrace. Thick black mist like oily smoke came spiralling out of its glittering eyes, pulling his mind down into darkness.

Eleni was swimming in the bay below the house with her younger sister Toula, when she heard her mother calling from the top of the garden. Before the echoes of the second call had died away, she had grabbed her towel, scrambled across the narrow strip of shingle beach and was running up through the garden, taking the steps two at a time. Eleni hurried. She had never heard her mother sound so scared and angry.

Mama's face was very white, but her dark eyes were flashing as she grabbed her daughter by the arm. 'What have you been doing – you and that Lucas woman?' she demanded. 'I just had a call from Mrs Williams in New England. The poor woman is out of her mind with worry.'

It took Leni a moment to realize that her mother was

talking about Rom's mother. 'What's wrong?' she pleaded. 'Has something happened to Rom, Mama?'

Her mother, in a sudden switch of mood, let go of Eleni's arm and hugged her hard. 'God forgive me, but I'm glad it wasn't you,' she said softly. 'Rom's mother found him this morning, unconscious in his Websuit. They took him to hospital, but he's in a coma – he won't wake.'

Again, her mother's voice became stern. 'Eleni, this is a serious matter. When they found the boy, he was logged into your site in Anna Lucas's design space. Just what have you been doing in there?'

CHAPTER FIVE

ALPHA RUN

The wolves were running very fast across the tundra. The pack leader could feel the icy Arctic wind flowing through his thick grey fur, and silvery clouds of hot breath streamed out behind him as he raced swiftly onwards. Thick moss, brittle and chilled from the frost, crunched beneath his paws with every bounding stride. His muscles moved with efficient ease in a springy loping gait that devoured the ground. The rest of the pack, half a dozen in all, ran close behind him. He could hear their breathing, and the soft, rapid drum of their speeding feet.

From the corner of his eye the leader could see another wolf running beside him. Her coat was almost silver – much lighter than his own shadowy grey, and her silhouette was a little more slender than his own, a little less heavy about the neck and shoulders. His wolf senses told him that she was his mate and fellow pack-leader – the alpha female as he was the alpha male. A faint memory in the back of his mind also reminded him that she was truly human, as was he. This was the Web, and he was Jack, and this was his friend Cat. In Realworld, they were studying – Ecology and Wildlife Module 3051W, to be precise.

For a moment the wolf's swift run faltered as a feeling of dizzy confusion swept over Jack. As a wolf he felt the fresh, cold wind in his face and the crisp mossy hummocks of the endless tundra beneath his feet, yet at the same time he could feel the soft pressure of the couch at his back, the slight constriction of his helmet and visor, and the touch of the websuit that clung tightly to his human body.

'Idiot!' Jack told himself. 'Stop acting like an egg! Carry on like this and you'll give yourself the voms.' With the ease of experience, he relaxed and let the human thoughts drain out of his mind. Wolf, wolf, he thought. Keen eyes, sharp, pricked ears, thick grey coat. Brave heart, keen brain, wiry strength. A lonely voice to span great distances, a tireless, sinewy body designed to hunt and run. The comradeship of the pack, the call of the ceaseless wind, the lure of the far horizon . . . The tundra came back into focus and the wolf ran on. For the present, Jack had vanished.

The pack were hunting. Surprisingly, the greatest part of their diet was mice, for larger creatures were more difficult to catch. The prey could either burrow like the marmot, fly like the ptarmigan, or, like the Arctic hare, run swifter than a hungry wolf. Life was hard on the bleak tundra. The pack worked hard to survive.

After a time, the grey hunters reached the southern boundaries of their territory, and passed like ghosts into the shadows of the forest. As they prowled through the pine-scented gloom beneath the trees, the pack-leader was startled by the sound of human voices. The alpha male stopped, and sniffed the air suspiciously. He had not expected to find humans in his territory. The other wolves froze obediently and waited to see what their leader would do. From their hiding place in the low, scrubby undergrowth, the pack watched as a number of large, heavy deer came into sight, plodding patiently through the woods, their pale cream and brown coats gleaming faintly in the shadows beneath the trees.

The caribou herders walked along beside their animals, the sound of their cheerful voices carrying clearly to the wolf pack. The part of the wolf that was Jack watched with interest. The part of Jack that was the wolf shrank away from the feared and hated humans. He knew about poison, traps and guns. There was nothing for the pack here. Wolves might run down a caribou that was old or injured, and they might take a newborn calf if its mother had ventured too far from the safety of the herd, but adult reindeer in their prime, with sharp hooves and fearsome antlers, were more than a match for the grey raiders.

With the added danger of the humans, the caribou presented more of a threat to the wolf pack than an opportunity. A wolf, of course, couldn't reason this out as a human could, but the leader's experience and instincts were telling him to get away. He glanced across at the alpha female, whose flattened ears and tucked-in tail showed similar fear and reluctance. Though human speech was not included in this study module – the students were supposed to *be* wolves, after all – she was clearly saying it was time to take the pack to safety before the herders spotted them. She was right. The leader tried to turn and slink off through the bushes but, suddenly, to his horror, he found himself running the other way, heading *towards* the men!

This was all wrong! Infected by the alpha male's fear, Jack tried to stop or turn, but the wolf's body would not obey him. It was as though something else had overridden the study programme and taken control. Alarmed by this new feeling of helplessness, Jack tried to scuttle – but nothing happened. He was trapped in the Web and out of control!

The caribou herders were closer now. Soon the pack would be on them. At his side, Jack saw the female that was Cat. From the jerkiness of her movement and the terrified rolling of her eyes, she was clearly having a similar struggle. The two of them were the alpha wolves – where they went, the pack must follow. Jack could hear the others behind him, racing towards destruction.

The caribou were scattering in panic, stampeding through the trees. By this time the herders had spotted the attacking wolves. Jack saw the steely glint of guns in their hands. Shots ripped through the once-silent forest. One of the wolves screamed and fell. Another followed. Gathering his muscles in a mighty leap, the alpha male left the ground, launching himself at the nearest herder. From the corner of his eye, Jack saw the Cat-female doing the same, when, suddenly, her image flickered and disappeared. The herder fired – and missed. He screamed the words, *'WHO IS THE HUNTER?'*

The voice was cut off abruptly as the wolf's teeth met in the herder's throat, tearing into gristle and flesh.

Sheer horror gave Jack the strength to break free at last. Suddenly, the forest vanished and became Jack's own untidy room, with the holographic posters and the giant flatscreen dominating one wall. In his panic, he must have torn off his helmet and visor instinctively, for he found them clutched in his trembling hands. At that point, he was forced to run for the bathroom before the voms caught up with him.

Cat looked in horror at her precious helmet which she was holding as though it were an unexploded bomb. She let it drop to the floor, where it rolled unnoticed into a corner. Lying back on her couch she took deep breaths, and forced herself to become calm. It had been a long, hard struggle to get her dad to accept the Web. The last thing Cat needed at this point was for him to start panicking.

Cat stayed on her couch until she had managed to shake off the wolf. It always took a fair amount of adjustment time to come back from an animal avatar, especially the vividly accurate forms used in the Education programs. The first time she'd tried out the cat shape she so often used in the Web, she had spun out and promptly fallen flat on her face because she'd tried to land on all four feet when she jumped off the couch.

She used the few minutes while her brain caught up with her human body to do some hard thinking. What the mip had happened back there? The Education Modules were supposed to be completely true to life, but *real* wolves would never attack a large group of humans like that! Something had taken over the wolf forms that she and Jack had been using, and used them to attack the program's human phaces.

But why, for goodness' sake? And why am I thinking it's some*thing*, instead of some*one*? Cat wondered. Maybe *they*, whoever they were, had been using the wolf program for their own ends, and didn't even know, or care, that she and Jack were there at all.

She shivered. It had been a scary feeling to be trapped as a helpless passenger in a body that was committing an act too horrible even to think about, but there was another mystery that disturbed her even more. Before the wolf attacked the caribou herder, someone had rescued her. She remembered it clearly. As the animal, under the control of the interloper, had gathered itself to spring, Cat had felt *another* presence enter the wolf's mind. It felt as though the first invader had been shoved roughly aside, and Cat had regained control for long enough to hit the scuttle button.

I must tell Jack, she thought. Normally, they had a standing arrangement to meet in the Star Bar, and chase the fade. Today, however, Cat was sure her friend would be as reluctant as she to go back into the Web. She dialled his flatscreen code instead. Although she tried and tried, there was no answer.

Cat was disappointed that she couldn't reach Jack, but she was also worried. What had happened in the Education Module after she had spun out? She had assumed that Jack would follow her – but had he? What if the program was down the plug and he had somehow been trapped?

She decided she was probably getting into a panic for nothing. Perhaps she had overreacted about the business with the wolves. Maybe all that scary stuff was supposed to happen – though she doubted it. The Education Modules were supposed to be true to life, but that was taking things a bit too far. Anyway, it was more than likely that Jack had gone to meet her in the Star Bar as planned, and she was keeping him waiting. Without giving herself time to get nervous about going back into the Web, Cat crammed her helmet back onto her head and punched the Star Bar code into her wrist unit.

To Cat's disappointment, there was no sign of Jack in the bar. There was only one other customer around her own age, a boy who sat alone at a nearby table. Cat frowned. Do I know him? she thought. Sometimes, in the Web, it was hard to tell. You might meet the same person every day of the week and he or she might be in an entirely different form each time. That was why Cat always tried to recognize the little tricks that gave away a person's identity – a figure of speech, a shrug, a trait of posture or expression.

There was something familiar about this boy – his upright posture on the bench, a tilt of his head that was almost arrogant – but no, she couldn't place him. Besides, she thought, if I had seen him before, I'm sure I wouldn't have forgotten. There was a very dramatic look about him. His long, straight hair was very fair, his eyes were a silvery grey, and his skin was very pale. He was dressed in black from head to foot.

Then, to Cat's complete embarrassment, he suddenly turned his head and saw her staring at him. Oh no, he was beckoning her over! For an instant, Cat's finger hovered over her scuttle button, but then she told herself not to be such a gag. It was better to brazen things out. She took her time choosing a drink from the counter, then jetted over to the boy's table. 'Sorry I was staring,' she said brightly. 'I thought I knew you from somewhere.'

The boy grinned at her. 'If we had met before, I would have remembered *you*.'

Cat knew perfectly well that this was rubbish. If they had met before, she might have been in any shape from a dinosaur to a dragonfly. 'Silky,' she accused him, but she couldn't help feeling just a bit flattered.

The boy laughed. 'I've been called worse than that.'

'And what do they call you when they aren't calling you names?' Cat asked him.

'I'm called the Hunter,' said the boy.

For an instant, Cat's world stood still.

CHAPTER SIX

GUARDIANS OF THE WORD

Normally, Jack would never have dreamed of running to his parents because he was scared. He had grown out of that years ago. This time, though, it was different. Something had gone wrong with the Web. Should he report the fault to the Education authorities, or did the problem lie with his own equipment? At any rate, something must be done. The experience of attacking a man with claws and fangs was something Jack never wanted to repeat.

Jack's parents shared a workroom, though often they were busy with separate projects in different parts of the Web. His father was a musician, his mother a visual effects wizard whose work was in great demand. At this time of the afternoon, the curtains would be drawn to block out the sunlight and the two couches, side by side in the gloom, would be almost lost in shadow. Not wanting to interrupt his folks if they were in the middle of something, he keyed their access code into his flatscreen. A BUSY message flashed up.

Jack sighed, but he could use a break anyway. He fetched himself a cola from the fridge, then settled back on his couch to see what they were working on today.

The drink, forgotten, grew warm in Jack's hand as he stared at the screen. This stuff was *strange*! The music, a mixture of old-fashioned Stratocaster and ultra-slick Megasynth, seemed to swirl and pulse in harmony with patterns of shimmering light, and weird half-glimpsed images flashed into being and were gone before Jack could understand them. He had never seen anything like it. The effect was so creepy, so alien – and yet it seemed to be trying to tell him something. Jack was sure there was a message there, yet it remained tantalizingly just beyond the reach of his understanding.

With a shudder, he turned off the screen. What the mip were his parents playing at? The stuff they normally came up was, to be truthful, a bit old-fashioned these days. It was *never* so unearthly and unsettling as this. Jack wondered what had come over them.

At least he could count on Anna to be her sensible self. The Webware designer should be up and about by now. Like programmers the world over, she would usually work all night on her latest project, and sleep through the morning. He checked his watch, just to make sure. Yes, she would even have had time for that first cup of coffee, so he could count on getting a sensible conversation out of her. He left a note telling his folks where he had gone, and went out.

The August heat hit Jack like a hammer as he stepped out of the house. Around him, the parched countryside seemed to shimmer in the brassy glare. He hurried down the lane, trying to stay as much as possible in the shade of the tall hedge. It seemed incredible, he thought, that he had crept down here in pitch darkness that night last year, with a desperate plan to break into Anna's house and outwit the police who were guarding the property.

The authorities had arrested the designer after her new game had been hijacked and misused by the Sorceress, the evil old woman who had planned to live on forever in one new body after another, leaving their original inhabitants trapped and formless in the Web. In the end, Jack and his friends Rom, Eleni and Cat, had been responsible for putting an end to her plans. Ever since then, life had been peaceful. Almost too peaceful, Jack thought. Maybe that's why I'm reacting to the Wolf Module going wrong. Am I just looking for some mystery and excitement again? A shiver ran through him at the memory of his attack on the caribou herder. If that's excitement, he thought, I can do without it!

When he reached Anna's house, Jack noticed a small, flat package in a plain brown wrapper lying on the front doorstep. Strange, he thought. Couriers don't usually leave stuff behind if no one answers the door. It has to be signed for. He picked it up and turned it over in his hands, looking for the label of the delivery firm, but there was nothing, only Anna's name, hand-printed across the front in blocky black letters. Weird. What could it be? Itching with curiosity, he took the package round to the back door.

The smell of coffee met Jack as he walked into Anna's bright, airy kitchen. A deafening chorus of meows filled the air, followed by an abrupt silence as the cats' owner put three bowls of food down on the floor. Anna straightened up and grinned at her visitor. 'That's better. Now we can hear ourselves think. Want some coffee?'

Jack shook his head. 'No thanks. I don't know how you can drink that stuff in this heat. I nearly melted just coming down the lane.'

'Cold drinks in the fridge. Help yourself.' Anna sat down at the kitchen table and took the day's first sip of coffee. She closed her eyes in bliss. Had she been one of her cats, Jack thought, she would have been purring.

Jack handed her the parcel. 'Here, I found this on your doorstep.' Then he noticed that the kitchen table was covered by a snowdrift of sketches, diagrams and notes. Excitement leaped inside him. 'Hey, are you starting a new game?'

'Didn't take you long to notice.' Anna made a face at him. 'The working title will be Star Pirates. Basically, you'll start off in some exotic spaceport with about 50 credits and a treasure map for some mysterious place far away across the galaxy. You'll join a trading vessel or a pirate craft – your choice – as part of the crew and work up to being a captain yourself with your own ship. Then you'll be able to take on newcomers to the game, as well as more experienced players,

as your own crew. Wealth can be earned, or found – or stolen
from the other people in the game, so there'll be plenty of
scope for both puzzles and battles. It's just the germ of an
idea so far, but it has possibilities. Besides, it's about time,
don't you think?'

'I think it's eight!' Jack told her with delight. 'I'm really
glad you're going back to designing games, Anna, instead of
all that dull coggy educational stuff.'

Anna laughed. 'I hope it's not *that* dull, or I'd be out of a
job.'

'Well, you know what I mean. It's just not the same.' Jack
couldn't wait to tell the others this news. They had all been
worried about Anna, since the affair of the Sorceress. That
horrible old woman had a lot to answer for, Jack thought.
Ever since the designer had been in trouble with the
Webcops over her Dragonville game, she had seemed to lose
confidence. Even though it had not been her fault, it had
shaken her badly when her own creations had escaped and
started running loose all over the Web, stealing irreplaceable
information from other sites. Though the authorities had
cleared her of any blame, she had never designed another
game.

Anna had torn the package open. 'What on earth—' It
contained a single sheet of thin paper, something unheard
of these days when all mail went through the Web. As she
read, Jack saw her turn pale. 'Summoner of Demons,' she
read aloud. 'Destroyer of innocents. Cut down the Tree of
Evil by its roots.' Her fist hit the table with a thump,
overturning her coffee bulb. 'Just who *are* these idiots?' Then
she remembered that Jack was there. 'Still, I wouldn't worry
about it, it's probably just somebody's idea of a stupid joke.'
She didn't sound very convinced.

'It's more than any joke.' Jack's mother Sheila stood in the
doorway. 'I just read on Globenet that a group of anti-Web
fanatics called Guardians of the Word, or some such
nonsense, have burned down the home of Glen DelRoy, the
designer of the Dreamcastle game. He wasn't hurt, but . . .'

She came across to Anna and read the piece of paper over her shoulder. 'If I were you, love, I'd call the police.'

At that moment, they heard the buzzer for an incoming flatscreen call. Anna leaped to her feet and ran into her combined workroom and office to answer it.

'Phew, it's hot out there!' Jack's mum sat down at the table and helped herself to a long swing of his cola. 'I got your note, so I thought I'd come down,' she told him. 'I needed a breath of fresh air after being cooped up in a websuit all morning.'

'Mum, do you think Anna is really in danger?' Jack blurted out.

'I don't know, love.' His mother never lied to him. 'Let's hope not, but who knows what a bunch of crazy fanatics will do next? Let's just hope the police can round them up before they do any further damage.'

Really, there was nothing more to be said. Jack tried to think of a less worrying subject. 'I looked in on the stuff you and Dad were doing this afternoon,' he said. 'Mum, it was really weird. Was it some kind of new experiment?'

Mum looked embarrassed. 'Oh, that piece. You would discover *that*. It wasn't so much an experiment as a big mistake, I think. When we looked at it afterwards, we couldn't believe it. We just wiped the whole thing.' She looked at him and chuckled. 'I can see by your face that you're relieved, and I quite agree. To be honest, I don't know what came over us.'

It seemed to Jack that he had heard that phrase a lot lately – in the news and, more worryingly, among the people he knew. What is going on? he thought. Is the whole world going mad?

When Anna came back, her face was grim. 'That was Rom's mother,' she told them. 'He's in hospital. The little idiot got into Eleni's site this morning and started messing about, I suppose. His mother found him in a coma.' She slumped down at the table and put her head in her hands. 'Oh, *why* didn't I think to change those access codes!'

'Anna,' Jack's mother protested. 'It wasn't your fault!'

'Wasn't it?' Anna said wildly. 'This is the second time something has gone wrong with one of my sites. Those kids got into enough danger in Dragonville, and this time I've put one of them in hospital!'

With a sweep of her arm, she gathered up the scattered papers, the precious plans for her new game. Ignoring Jack's cry of protest, she crumpled them up viciously and stuffed them into the recycler. 'Enough,' she said abruptly. 'It's time I found some other way to make a living. And now, if you'll excuse me, I'm going to change those access codes.' She ran off into her workroom, slamming the door behind her.

Jack's mother put an arm around his shoulders. 'Don't worry,' she said softly. 'Anna's upset and, what with this news coming on top of those horrible threats, I don't blame her. Let's give her some time to calm down. I'll come back and talk to her later.'

She got up to leave, and Jack was about to follow her when he noticed something. There was no red light on the recycler. Anna had forgotten to switch it on! He darted across the room and pushed his arm as far as it would go down the chute.

'You idiot! That's dangerous,' his mother yelled. 'Come out of there!'

'It's switched off.' Jack groped around until he found the crumpled wad of plans and pulled them out. They were a bit damp and stained but, hopefully, they would still be legible. 'Sorry, Mum,' he said, 'but these are tremendously important. Anna will be wanting them later. At least, I hope so.'

CHAPTER SEVEN

THE PERFECT STRANGER

Suddenly, the incident with the Wolf Module didn't seem so important any more. Jack was glad he'd not had a chance to mention it to his mother or Anna. After what had happened to Rom, they might decide to keep him out of the Web for a while, too. In the meantime, he must get the news to Cat. He remembered, with a guilty pang, that he'd been supposed to meet her in the Star Bar, ages ago. He only hoped she would still be there.

Jack had the codes for the Star Bar stored in his wrist unit, and spun directly into their meeting place. To his relief, Cat was still there – but who was that with her? Whoever it was, he looked like a real one-mip wearing all that stupid black! Who have I seen recently, dressed like that? Jack wondered. Cat and the stranger were sitting with their heads close together. Then, as the boy looked up, Jack suddenly remembered where he had seen him before, and his brows drew together in a scowl. Picking up a set of thrusters from the serving counter, he jetted over to Cat and her new companion.

Cat's face lit up when she saw him. 'Jack, thank goodness you've come! This is the Hunter. He's been trying to find out about these mysterious things that have been happening in the Web. He says—'

'I bet he says a lot of things,' Jack said coldly. 'Perhaps he would like to start by explaining why he put that brainless graffiti in our friend Eleni's site.'

'*What*?' Cat gasped.

'It's true. Remember, I saw someone running away that day? Well, guess what they were wearing? Besides, what other mipless wonder would write WHO IS THE HUNTER? all over the place?'

'But he said that had nothing to do with him,' Cat protested. 'I already asked him.'

'And you *believed* that?'

'You listen to me.' The unexpected note of command in the boy's voice made the others shut up abruptly. 'It happens to be true,' the Hunter went on in a quieter tone. 'I was there that day, but I was watching the ones who were watching *you*. All over the world, people who have been using the Web have started to act in strange, irrational ways. Where I come from, we know the reason. Only we can expose the invaders. Of all of us, I'm the only one right now who can be active in the Web. So far, they're not sure of my identity, but they want to know. Of course they want to know who, and what, is the Hunter.'

Suddenly, he looked around wildly. 'They're here. I can feel their presence. Talking about them draws them to us. I'll come back when I can. Trust in your dreams. Cat. And, remember, beware the Outsiders. They are everywhere. Only the Shadowzone is safe from them.'

'Hunter, wait!' Cat cried. 'I just remembered—' She was talking to thin air. Hunter had hit his scuttle button and was gone.

'Beware of them,' Jack mimicked. 'They are everywhere—' He made a rude sound of disgust. 'Oh, right. Of course they are. He doesn't know *who* they are, mind you, or what or where or even how – and he certainly can't explain why he's the only one who seems to know about them.' He rolled his eyes and made a face. 'Honestly, Cat, you do find them! How did you end up talking to that total gag?'

Suddenly, he noticed that Cat's eyes were boring into him,

as cold and hard as jade. 'When you've finished mocking,' she said acidly, '*you* try explaining what's going on in the Web, if you're so clever.'

Almost too late, Jack noticed the danger signs. 'All right, all right.' He held up his hands in surrender. 'You liked him, I didn't. One of us will turn out to be right in the end – if he ever turns up again.'

But Cat was still bristling. 'You idiot! Why did you have to come barging in just then? He was just starting to tell me a whole lot of stuff!'

I bet he was, Jack thought grimly, but he knew better than to say it. Besides, he had more important things to talk about.

'Cat, never mind the Hunter. I've got some bad news.' He told her about Rom.

'But that's awful,' Cat cried. 'Poor Rom! What can have happened to him?'

'I wish I knew,' Jack said. 'Maybe your friend the Hunter can tell you – if you plan on seeing him again.' It came out sounding a lot nastier than he had intended.

'You mind your own business.' There was a flash of hot anger in Cat's eyes that Jack had never seen before. 'I have other things to worry about. The Hunter was right about people acting weirdly. My dad was acting like an ancient Norse berserker yesterday— Don't grin like that, it wasn't funny. It frightened us both. If he gets to hear about this business with Rom, he'll probably keep me out of the Web too. I won't be seeing anybody in a hurry.'

'Trust you to be thinking about yourself, instead of poor Rom. Well, I don't see how you can stop your dad finding out,' Jack said grimly. 'He and Anna are working together just now, and as soon as they meet, she'll tell him. And, considering the sort of lunatics you've started keeping company with, that might be no bad thing.'

'Oh, curl up, Jack!' Cat blazed. 'You give me the voms! Of course I care about poor Rom! It's typical of you not to understand. You've never had to do without anything in

your life. You don't know what it's like to be deprived of
something that everyone else takes for granted. You've
always had Anna, and your rich successful parents, and the
best equipment and all the Web time you ever wanted!'

'That's not fair!' Jack protested, but it was too late. Cat was
gone before he'd even had a chance to tell her about Anna.

Though Cat had spun out of the Star Bar, she didn't scuttle
from the Web. Even though she was seething with anger, she
had more sense than that. If her father wanted to be difficult,
who knew when she'd get back again? But she did need a
place to be alone, to think.

Cat had punched a code blindly, almost at random, into
her wrist unit. When the BAT cleared, she was astonished at
where she'd ended up. 'Goodness!' she gasped. 'I had
forgotten all about this!'

The half-finished castle still sat square on its golden plain,
just as it had a year ago, when she had seen it last. Cat and
her friends had outgrown the place. After the excitement
and danger of their battle with the Sorceress, building their
own childish idea of a castle had seemed too tame. Looking
back on those days, Cat suddenly felt far older than she had
ever felt before. This place was full of memories.

Then Cat realized that she was not alone. A solitary figure
stood high up on the battlements, looking away across the
golden plain. Somehow, it came as no surprise to see Eleni
here. The castle had originally been her idea, and it was
always her pet project more than anyone else's. It had never
occurred to Cat before, but even back in those days, Leni
knew what she wanted to do with her life. Even before the
Greek girl got her own suit, and could only access the Web
with gloves and glasses, she had wanted to program and
design Webspace. We were wrong in thinking the copy of
Eleni's home was her first design, Cat realized. In reality, it
was this old place.

'Cat!' Eleni was waving, and beckoning to her to come up.

'Coming!' Cat hurried across the drawbridge, and through the great arched doors into the shadowy hallway.

Inside, the castle was very different from the bare, echoing space that Cat remembered. Stained-glass pictures filled the once blank windows. The rooms held heavy old furniture of dark, carved wood. There were wax-dripping candles, tapestries on the walls stitched in jewelled colours and silver and gold thread, and roaring log fires in the massive fireplaces. Eleni, it seemed, had never abandoned this site. She must have been working on it all along, just for fun, in whatever spare Webtime she could scrounge.

Cat climbed the broad curved staircase, then the smaller spiral of steps that led up to the battlements. Leni was waiting for her at the top, an unhappy expression on her face.

'Is there still no news of Rom?' Cat asked her as they strolled out onto the flat roof.

'No, the fool!' Eleni growled. Cat had never heard her sound so angry. Leni was striding up and down, too agitated to stay still. 'Who asked him to go meddling with my site?' she demanded. 'Cat, if I wasn't so desperately worried about him, I could kill him! He couldn't resist interfering where he wasn't needed. Isn't that just *like* a boy!'

For a moment, her words tailed off, as she and Cat shared a wry, empathetic grin. Then Eleni's face darkened again, and she sighed. 'And now he's got both of us into trouble. Something bad has happened to him, and we don't know how to help. Anna has locked me out of my site, but that's not all—' She was fighting to keep her voice steady. 'My mother doesn't want me to learn programming any more – especially not with Anna – and Anna doesn't want to teach me. I talked to her on flatscreen just before I spun in, Cat. She's giving up Web design completely. She says too many young people have been endangered by her work.'

Cat was stunned by this latest piece of bad news. 'Anna giving up the Web? Why, she might as well give up breathing! Surely Jack must have known about this, and he hadn't even bothered to tell her. Though that might explain why he'd been in such a foul temper—'

'What's the matter with Jack?' Eleni asked.

Only then did Cat realize that she must have been thinking out loud. She shrugged. 'Oh, I don't know. We just had the most colossal fight. That's why I came here. I wanted somewhere quiet to think things out.'

Eleni's eyebrows went up. 'You and Jack fighting! But why?'

Cat shrugged. 'I met a boy in the Star Bar and Jack didn't like him. That's the short answer.' She was reluctant to say any more, but honesty drove her to it. 'Leni, I suppose you should know. He's calling himself the Hunter, this boy, and Jack is convinced he was the one who meddled with your site.'

'But, plainly, you don't think so.'

It wasn't the first time that Cat had felt grateful for her friend's quiet understanding. 'How can I explain?' she said. 'He said it wasn't him, and I believed him. He seemed more hunted than hunter. He said something bad had invaded the Web. He said he knew what was going on and, because of that, he was in danger. He was a bit weird, it's true, but I liked him. More than that, I *trusted* him, even though he was saying all this crazy stuff that I normally would just have laughed at, and told him to take a bat. You know, after the business with Miss Aldanar, I've never trusted a single stranger. After the way she deceived me, I thought I had learned my lesson, but—'

In spite of her dark mood, Eleni burst out laughing. 'Oh my, Cat, he *must* have been something special, this boy! If only I had been there! I wish I could have seen him!'

'As you wish.'

Both girls spun around at the sound of the voice. There, sitting in one of the square dips of the battlements, was the black-clad boy from the Star Bar.

'How did you get here?' Cat gasped.

'I followed you.'

'But that's impossible! And anyway, *you* spun out first.'

He grinned. 'Why do you think they call me the Hunter? I have my ways.' He nodded to the Greek girl. 'Ah. Eleni the Webmistress.'

'How do you know my name?' Leni demanded.

'I know you all,' the Hunter replied. 'I'm very sorry about your site. I didn't do the damage, I promise you – but it probably came about because of me.' He held out his hands to the two girls. 'Look, I know this is all very mysterious, but I'm begging you to trust me. You need to come with me to the Shadowzone.'

'But wait,' Cat interrupted. 'That's what I was trying to tell you when you spun out of the Star Bar. Hunter, I don't understand what you mean about the Shadowzone being safe, but it isn't. The place is in deadly danger. The Black Widow Corporation are planning to have it wiped. *Reclaim and cleanse* were the words that Craven used.'

'*What?*' The Hunter looked stunned. 'But you can't let them do that!'

Cat stared at him. 'Just who the mip *are* you, anyway? Why all this mystery?'

The Hunter shook his head. 'I'm sorry, Cat. I can't tell you yet, not without permission. But please don't let them wipe the Shadowzone. You *must* find a way to save it! I've managed to get your friend Rom out of trouble. That's what I really came to tell you. When you spin out, you'll find that he's fine.'

'What?'

'But how?'

Cat and Eleni were bursting with questions, but the Hunter gave them no chance. 'Listen,' he said firmly. 'If you trust me enough to come with me, meet me here tomorrow at the same time. Bring Rom with you if you can.' He made a wry face. 'And the suspicious Jack if you must.' He leaped down from the wall, held out his hand, and a single red rose appeared in his fingers. With a smile, he handed it to Cat, and vanished.

Cat looked at the rose. 'Ugh! How silky can you get?' she demanded, but she couldn't prevent a broad silly grin from spreading across her face.

Eleni was watching her with sparkling eyes. 'Come on,' she said. 'There are a lot of questions to be asked, but first I want to know if Rom is really all right. That's the most important thing. Let's spin out, and see if your new boyfriend was telling the truth.'

CHAPTER EIGHT

SPINDRIFT

Rom was drifting . . . bodiless, he drifted in darkness . . . like *them*, he thought. They came so far, just to drift. They haunt the Web, and drift into our minds like hitchhikers. When we spin out, they are there with us. Passengers in our bodies. Wondering what it's like to be human, to be us and live in our world. They tried to talk at first but were unsure about the best way to communicate. No one believed in them. The Web has clouded our view of what is real and what is not. They were jokes, they were phaces, they were part of the Web. So now they observe, and experiment . . . trying to understand . . . making people do weird things . . . things we always wanted, in our most secret hearts to do. They want to learn what it is to smell, to feel, to live on our planet . . . . what it is to be human . . . maybe then, they can reach an understanding with us . . .

But why tell me? I'm only a kid, for goodness' sake. Sure, I'm smart, I know the Web inside out, but why not a grown-up? A congresswoman, a general, a scientist? Someone in authority? Even as he asked, he knew the answer. They had already tried that. Some people have been treated as mad – all those reports of irrational behaviour. Others are hiding the knowledge, in fear of being thought insane. And maybe some poor grown-ups really believe they're crazy. So, the Outsiders are turning to us, the kids, as a last desperate resort. But who'll believe *us*? I'm sure not going to tell anyone, but there must be some way . . .

'Doctor? I think he's waking.' It was his mother's voice – anxious, tired, tearful, but with one bright thread of hope. Rom took hold of the thread, and let it pull him to the surface.

He opened his eyes to a white ceiling, and a collection of wires, tubes and machinery that reminded him, for one awful moment, of the Sorceress. Then he saw the faces of his folks – worried, weary and scared, but alight, too, with happiness and relief. Rom had never been so glad to see them in his life.

'Honey!' His mother's voice broke on a sob. 'Honey, are you all right?'

'What happened, son?' his father was asking. 'How do you feel?'

In the few minutes of commotion while the doctors took over, Rom tried to think of some answers. He failed. He remembered the brilliant peacock blue of Eleni's ocean, something dark and threatening, and strange, silvery fluid shapes thronging around him. Curiosity battering at him, and a feeling of *wanting* so intense that it hurt. He couldn't escape. They had fenced him in with their need, and they wouldn't let him go. Then, after what had seemed a long, long time, there was a human form, bursting in among the alien shapes of the Outsiders. Black clothing, a flash of pale, bright hair, a voice:

'*Let him go. He's not the one you want.*'

As the aliens turned on the invader in a fury, the voice came again. '*Get out, while they're distracted. NOW!*'

This time, Rom's scuttle button had worked, and he was free. It couldn't have been the button really, of course. How could he still have been inside the Web? They had taken his suit off him at the hospital. But somewhere, he had been trapped, maybe in his own mind, by the aliens, and somehow, he had been rescued. By someone. *Who?*

'How do you feel, son? Can you tell us what happened?' They were all asking him the same questions, over and over.

If I told you, what would you think? What would you do to me? Rom thought. He closed his eyes. 'I'm OK,' he said. 'I guess I must have stayed in the Web too long. I don't remember.'

It was very late when Cat finally got the call she had been waiting for. In the end, she had agreed to go to bed, though she and her father both knew she wouldn't sleep. She had been surprised, when she had spun back out of the Web, to find that Anna had not yet been in contact with D.L. to tell him what had happened, so she had decided it would be best to tell him herself – especially now she was secretly confident that Rom would be all right.

Her father had taken the news surprisingly well, all things considered. He had heard a lot from Anna about Rom's habit of getting into places where he had no business to be. Sadly, Anna was not answering his calls that evening, so there were no answers there. 'We'll sleep on it, Kitten,' he had said at last. 'Maybe there'll be some better news in the morning. But until we have some answers, one way or another, I want you to be specially careful in the Web. Don't spin in again tonight, and maybe none of us should stay in there as long as we've been doing. These days, I understand how easy it is to get carried away.'

Cat knew he was remembering the incident with Craven. Weak with relief to find him so understanding, she hugged him hard. 'Thanks, Dad,' she said. 'Thanks.'

It was almost midnight when Cat's flatscreen chimed softly. The caller was Eleni, her face alight with relief. 'Cat, Rom's all right. His mother just called mine. She said he can't remember what happened, but the doctors say there's nothing wrong with him, and he's going home tomorrow.' For the flicker of a second, she hesitated. 'Cat, do you really think the Hunter rescued him?'

'Yes,' Cat said firmly, 'I do. I can't wait to talk to Rom. I bet it's rubbish about him not remembering. I don't suppose his parents will let him back into the Web for a while – they'll be watching him like hawks after this – but maybe he'll be able to call us tomorrow.'

'I hope so,' Eleni said. 'After this news, I don't have to ask you if you're going to see the Hunter tomorrow. I'll meet you in the Star Bar first, and we can make some plans – unless you want him all to yourself!' She grinned. 'Goodnight, Cat. Sweet dreams.'

As she turned the flatscreen off, Cat could feel her face growing hot with blushes. 'I don't know what she seems to find so amusing,' she muttered. After a couple of minutes, she went off to tell her dad that Rom was OK.

Cat woke to find herself standing in a dark place, all alone. She stretched out a hand and touched the cold, rough surface of stone. A few minutes frantic groping told her that she seemed to be surrounded by rock, trapped in some kind of air pocket in a pile of huge, fallen boulders. Only the floor felt fairly smooth beneath her feet.

Oh, gag, Cat thought. I didn't wake up at all. This is another one of those wretched dreams, isn't it? She felt surprise on two counts. Firstly, she didn't usually realize she was dreaming until after she'd woken in a panic; and, secondly, if this was a dream, why couldn't she just wake up? After trying very hard to open her eyes and get back to her own bed, she found it to be impossible. She just stayed where she was in the cold, dark place.

Well, all right, Cat thought at last. It's obviously not going to set me free until I find out what happens. For once, the dream seemed to be waiting for her to take some kind of action to start things. off. But how could she go anywhere? As far as Cat could feel, she was completely enclosed by the great boulders. Well, if this is my dream, I should be able to change things, she thought. Light. Some light is what I need.

Even as she wished for it, the light began to grow, glimmering faintly on the rough outlines of the surrounding rocks. It wasn't really much help, though. Cat's eyes could tell her little more than her groping hands. She seemed to be trapped underground and, at first sight, there was no way out. No problem, Cat thought. Surely, if I could wish for some light, I can wish for a doorway, or an opening in these rocks. She concentrated until she almost burst, but nothing happened. She was still trapped.

Just typical of a stupid nightmare, Cat thought angrily, but she was beginning to panic. Desperate to escape, she wedged her fingers into a space between two big stones and tugged with all her might. At first, nothing happened – the rock seemed to be wedged in place – but as her pulling and pushing grew more frantic, she felt the boulder shift. To her horror, that set everything moving. Above her, the ceiling gave an ominous creak and a thread of dust came pattering down. She had upset the balance of the rock pile and, suddenly, everything was shifting around her with a low, grinding noise like the crunch of gigantic jaws.

Cat's blood froze in horror. In her panic, she was forgetting that it was only a dream. The light went out abruptly and everything was dark again. She flung herself to the ground, curled up like a small terrified animal, and waited for the end.

It never came. After a moment, the rocks settled into a new balance, and her air pocket had been saved.

As the hammering of her heart slowed down, Cat noticed that there were small, sharp-edged, gritty fragments rolling on the floor beneath her hands. One piece pierced the tip of her finger, making her cry out in pain. What on earth? Cat stuck her stinging finger into her mouth, and tasted blood. This seemed awfully real for a dream, and yet, what else could it be?

By concentrating hard, she managed to make it lighter again. Very carefully she sat up, hardly daring to breathe and keeping one eye on the ceiling in case there should be any more movement. Nothing shifted, however. The rocks seemed to have settled into their new position. Cat looked down at the gritty stuff beneath her, and saw coarse grains of some sparkling, blue-white stuff lying in drifts across the stony floor. She frowned, wondering. It looked like broken glass— Then everything seemed to snap into focus. She recognized the stuff, and knew where she was. The glittering white fragments were bits of broken data crystal. Cat was trapped beneath the ruins of the old Dragonville game.

This has got to be a dream. It *must* be, Cat thought desperately. But still she couldn't wake. How will I ever get out of here? She racked her brains for an answer and, after a time, an idea came. She had not used her cat shape for some time but, perhaps, since the dream seemed to be taking place in the Web, she could use it now. Cat felt for her wrist unit, and was not surprised to find it there. She was also not surprised to find that the scuttle button didn't work. Naturally, she thought with some irritation. Some day, something in one of these dreams will work as it's supposed to and I'll probably die of shock! Still, if only the rest of the wrist unit is OK. Quickly, her fingers went to the buttons and, muttering a swift prayer to whatever gods of luck might be listening, she punched in the code.

It worked! Cat let out an enormous sigh of relief. As soon as she had shrunk down to cat size, the space beneath the rockfall seemed far less cramped. Suddenly, it seemed a lot easier to breathe and, just as Cat had hoped, it was now possible to slip her small, lithe, feline body through the spaces between the boulders. She didn't know which direction was out, but anything was better than being stuck here forever. Hoping for the best, the small grey tabby cat wormed its way into the dark heart of the mound of rubble.

The going was very difficult. The spaces between the stones were narrow and awkward. Cat was terrified that she might accidentally shift one of the boulders again and bring the whole pile grinding down to crush her. If this was really a nightmare, it was one of the worst she'd ever had. She was bruised and scraped by the rough, angular surfaces of the rocks and felt utterly exhausted but didn't dare rest. She was sure that if she stopped, she'd have neither the strength nor the courage to go on again. Suddenly, Cat twisted her body round a sharp angle between two great stones, and felt herself slipping. There was no surface beneath her feet. She was falling!

With a cat's sure instincts, she wrenched round in mid-air and came down on her feet. Miraculously, light and space were around her again. Cat took wonderful gulps of fresh, free air and blinked her eyes against the sudden dazzle.

'That was very well done, my dear. Against all the odds, you have reached me where no one else could.' At the sound of the voice, Cat jerked her eyes open. Towering above her, up and up, was the menacing form of a gigantic, golden dragon.

This time, Cat was beyond being shocked or fearful. Too many weird things had been happening lately, both in her dreams and out. She sighed. 'Miss Aldanar. I might have guessed it would be you again. If we must do this, let's meet face to face in our proper shapes, shall we?'

'Very well,' said the dragon.

Even as Cat changed back, growing into her proper shape, the gigantic creature shrunk. A woman clad all in silver stood there – not old, feeble and withered, but young and standing tall. Even though so many years had fallen away, Cat recognized the proud, hawk-like features and dark, penetrating eyes of Miss Aldanar. She swallowed hard. 'So,' she said softly, 'you did get your wish. I'm glad.'

Miss Aldanar smiled. 'Thank you for that, my dear. Yes, in a way I got my wish. I miss having a true body, and I even miss the human world, flawed as it is – but really I have done better than I expected, and better, probably, than I deserved.'

Cat nodded. 'It took me a long time to forgive you, but—'

'And can you forgive me, too?' From the shadows behind Miss Aldanar stepped the slight, black-clad figure of the Hunter.

This time, Cat was shocked, and furious. Miss Aldanar had sent the Hunter to her to soften her up, to win her trust. The

Sorceress had deceived her once again! She looked helplessly from one of them to the other, utterly lost for words to express her hurt and anger.

'My dear, I'm sorry,' Miss Aldanar said. 'You've no need to be unhappy. Don't blame the Hunter – the fault is mine. I can't leave the Shadowzone, so I asked him to watch over you in my place. I've been worried about you ever since the aliens arrived.'

'Aliens?' Cat said numbly. There were so many questions bubbling up in her mind that she didn't know where to start. 'As in aliens from space? From another planet?'

'Ridiculous, isn't it?' Miss Aldanar said. 'We expected that one day a spaceship would land, and there would be a momentous meeting between races that spanned the Galaxy . . .' She grimaced. 'Instead, the Outsiders downloaded their consciousness into digitized form, and crossed space as a series of energy pulses. They got into the Web with the SETI data, but they soon learned the limits of what they had done. They've skulked around ever since, afraid to make official contact because they're vulnerable in the Web, and they're afraid that humans would take steps to control them – or even do to them what my enemies plan to do to me, if what you told the Hunter about Black Widow is true.'

Cat swallowed hard. 'Somebody could just wipe the aliens? They could wipe *you*?' What am I saying? she thought. I'm talking calmly about aliens as if this sort of thing happens every day. Aliens! *Actual, genuine aliens!*

'Cat!' Miss Aldanar said sharply.

Cat shook her head. 'I'm sorry. I just can't take it in.'

'Well, never mind the aliens for now. That problem we can deal with later,' the Hunter said impatiently. 'First, we have to worry about saving the Shadowzone.' Hunter's grey eyes were fixed on Cat's face. 'Cat, will you come with me?' he pleaded. 'I know we deceived you, and you have every right to be angry, but we really need your help.'

CHAPTER NINE

BLACK WIDOW

Globenet Times, August 27, 2028.

NEW FORM OF WEBSICKNESS FEARED

A report has been leaked today from the Swiss Psycho-Cybernetics Institute in Berne, warning of a new danger from too much exposure to the Web. The physical symptoms of Websickness have long been known, but in the last year, according to the report, there has been an increasing number of hospital cases dealing with mental disturbance. People spending too much time in the Web are suffering from blackouts, memory loss and irrational behaviour. Patients tend to recover within a few hours, but the spread of this sickness, called spindrift syndrome by researchers, is giving cause for concern.

A spokesman from the Institute has advised the public not to panic. 'This investigation is still in its early stages,' he said. 'As yet, we don't even know if there's a genuine problem.'

WEB RESTRICTIONS URGED

The Executive Governing Council of the Soviet Confederation has urged that public use of the Web be restricted to essential applications such as business and education. Giorgi Kamaverov, Secretary for Domestic Affairs, said that the current trends of usage were a matter of some concern:

'We are becoming completely dependent on this artificial environment, and many people now are living in a fantasy world, as reports on recent mental disturbances would seem to demonstrate. The Web is like a parasite, sapping our resources, destroying our capacity for original thought, and taking over our lives. Already our society can barely

function without it – and for that reason among others, its growth should be halted now, before it can expand any further.'

Mr Kamaverov said that he expected a great public outcry at his suggestion. 'And does that not prove people are already addicted to this thing?' he said. 'It simply serves to demonstrate that our worst nightmares have already come true.'

Next morning, Cat spun into the castle site to find Jack and Eleni both waiting for her, and looking very puzzled. 'Good,' she said. 'You got my message, then.'

'What's going on?' Jack demanded, and Cat suddenly realized that they had not made up after yesterday's quarrel. She had forgotten all about it but, clearly, Jack had not.

'Cat, is something wrong?' Eleni looked worried. 'Has something happened to the Hunter? I thought we were supposed to meet him this afternoon.'

'The plans got changed. I—' Before she could get any further, Jack had broken in with a groan. 'Oh, no. This isn't some basement-level scheme of that one-mip you were talking to yesterday? Because if it is, you can count me out.'

'Take a bat, then. We could have used Rom's help, but we don't need *you*.'

They all spun round at the sound of that cool voice. The Hunter was standing in the doorway of the castle.

Jack glowered at him. 'That's fine by me,' he said, making no attempt to move. After a moment, he spoke again. 'Look, I don't know what you're up to, but it's plain that no good is going to come of it. You've absolutely no right to get these girls involved.'

'What?' Cat spluttered.

'How dare you talk about us as if we had no minds of our own?' Eleni shouted.

The Hunter only laughed. 'And have *you* a right to spout such drivel when you don't understand the situation?' he said. 'You've known Cat and Eleni for years. If you don't realize by now how intelligent and capable they are, then there's no hope for you.'

Inwardly, Cat smiled. Though she'd had no chance yet to explain anything to Eleni, Jack had just put the Greek girl squarely on the side of herself and the Hunter. Serves him right, she thought. Why couldn't he just listen, for a change?

Jack must have been reading her mind. 'All right,' he said. 'Why doesn't somebody explain it to me, then?'

Cat and the Hunter exchanged a long look. 'All right,' Cat said. 'This morning we're going to break into the most secret, confidential files of the Black Widow Corporation.'

Then she stood back and waited for them both to stop spluttering.

In the end, of course, it took a lot of explaining, especially about the dreams. Cat wasn't sure she understood that part herself, completely. In the end, the Hunter helped her out. 'They only seemed like dreams to Cat,' he explained. 'When she was scuttling, we diverted her and arranged those meetings. Afterwards, we made her forget them, until after she was out of the Web and asleep.' He glanced apologetically at Cat. 'We never would have hurt you. It was just a simple hypnotic technique.'

'But why?' Eleni asked. 'I don't understand why you'd do it in such a roundabout way.'

'Because it took me such a long time to forgive Miss Aldanar,' Cat replied. 'If the authorities knew she wasn't really dead, they would still see her as a criminal. She couldn't reveal that she was still alive until she was sure she could trust me. Until then, she was forced to keep making me believe that she was only a figment of my imagination.'

Jack was scowling. 'She still *is* a criminal,' he said. 'It's all right for you, Cat, you escaped her. But what about the other poor kids who didn't? What about those children in India that Rom told us about? Don't you think she should be punished for that?'

'I think she already has been,' the Hunter put in quietly. 'In a way, she lost her struggle against death. Her personality only lives on as data in the Web, and it's very vulnerable. She's imprisoned forever in the Shadowzone. If she comes out, sooner or later either the authorities or Black Widow will get her. She has been punished, Jack, and since she came to the Shadowzone she has done everything in her power to help those condemned to exist in that lost place.'

Slowly, Jack nodded in acceptance. 'OK,' he said. 'I suppose I can live with that.'

Cat breathed a sign of relief. She knew it wasn't easy. She had already gone through the same struggle with her own conscience.

'But what is this Shadowzone place?' Jack went on. 'Is it dangerous? I don't understand—'

'I can't explain, but you'll understand when you get there,' the Hunter said.

'And we can't do that until after we've dealt with this Black Widow business,' Cat put in. 'Are you both with us?'

Eleni nodded . . . and then Jack. Cat smiled at him. 'Thank you,' she said, and their quarrel was well on the way to being healed.

Suddenly, Eleni was all business. 'Well, with Rom the ultravet hacker out of the picture, I suppose it's my job to get us into the place.'

Cat nodded. 'If you can get us into the Commercial block, the access to Black Widow itself shouldn't be too hard. As owner of the company, they had to give me top level security clearance, though I've never actually used it before. The problem is, to get in without being spotted and caught.'

Within moments, the air was thick with plans.

Eleni had never been in the Finance & Commerce Webtown before. Though she and Rom had worked out how to break into it ages ago, just for the challenge, she had never been interested enough to actually go there. She had always imagined it as a dull, grey place, full of harsh angles and ugly, plain-looking blocks, so the reality came as a great surprise. The blocks looked as though they were carved from gleaming white marble, and were arranged in pleasing, gracious squares that contained greenery and sparkling fountains, with tables and seating laid out for people to meet.

The strands were wide and brightly-lit, and laid out with a fast-moving strip in the centre for people going places in a hurry, and plain paved walkways on either side for people wanting to look into the blocks. Unlike the E&R Webtown, where the destination sites were scrolled across the outsides of the blocks for people to pick and choose, jump-sites in Finance & Commerce were inside the blocks which were entered from the strand. Privacy and even secrecy were important in this competitive world, and no company wanted to give too much away.

Cat's elbow poked sharply into Leni's ribs. 'Disguise!' she hissed. 'Stop dreaming!' The others had already changed shape. Guiltily, Eleni punched a pre-set code into her wrist unit and triggered her disguise. She tried not to think about what her mother and father would say if she was caught. Impersonating a spider was not looked upon kindly by the Web's controlling authorities, but these low-level spiders were definitely the best disguise. They swarmed all over the Commercial Zone, some busy with cleaning and maintenance, others acting as gofers or messengers with company logos etched on their sides.

'Come on!' the Hunter hissed. 'Spiders never stand about! We can be spotted as fakes a mile off!'

Eleni checked that her Black Widow logo was in place, and hurried after the others. At first it was very difficult to control eight legs after being used to only two, but by concentrating hard, she soon managed to get the hang of it.

The bigger corporations were not located in the general blocks, but stood alone in vast beautifully landscaped parks. 'What a waste of Web resources,' Leni whispered disapprovingly to Cat.

'It's a status thing, so they tell me,' replied the reluctant owner of one of the world's most powerful corporations. 'It's to prove they can afford it.'

The Black Widow block nearly took Eleni's breath away. It

stood on a large island in the midst of an artificial lake, with woods and gentle rolling hills all around. It suddenly hit home to her that all of this actually belonged to her friend. She looked at Cat and gulped.

Even as a spider, Cat was looking far from impressed. 'That lying Craven,' she growled. 'This wasn't the site they brought *me* to visit. That one was much smaller. I wonder what else they've been up to behind my back?'

'I wouldn't worry about it now,' Jack said. He was looking at the businesslike security post at the end of the only bridge. 'The problem is, how will we get in?'

'Leave that to me,' said Cat. She marched, eight-legged, to the window beside the barrier, where a gigantic spider coloured metallic grey towered over her. Unconcerned, Cat reeled off a long series of numbers and letters, and Eleni let out her breath in a long sigh of relief as the security spider raised the barrier to let them pass.

'Was that your own code?' she whispered when they were safely away.

'You must be joking,' Cat chuckled. 'I want to leave it as late as I can before I risk tipping them off that I'm here. That was Craven's code. He uses it to access his exec-screen, and I memorized it ages ago. I never did trust that lying, slippery slime-ball.'

Craven's code was enough to get them into the block. The inside was a vast, echoing white space, with a massive hologram of the company logo floating in the centre, a black spider within a gigantic red jewel. The white walls stretched away on every side, covered in a series of differently-shaped portals that looked like open doorways. Groups of people were entering and leaving the portals, flashing in and out, all looking serious and busy.

'Keep moving,' the Hunter muttered. 'Try to look as if we know where we're going.'

There was a soft little laugh from Cat that sent a shiver down Eleni's spine. A sudden memory of the Sorceress flashed across her mind. Cat laughed again. 'I do know where I'm going. The one place that those cheating snakes who are running Black Widow don't even know exists.' She hurried away down the line of doorways with the Hunter at her heels, not seeing the looks of worry and doubt exchanged by Eleni and Jack.

'Look at that,' Jack whispered to Eleni as they scurried along. A group of nearby portals flashed images of corporate offices in exotic places all around the world. Information in a d-box above each entrance flashed information about the departments that could be reached. Other portals had more ordinary looking destinations, with such titles as MARKET-ING, ADMINISTRATION, and RESEARCH & DEVELOP-MENT. Leni hesitated by a magnificent portal marked EXECUTIVE LEVELS, but Cat marched straight on past, confidence and determination in every line of her small, spidery body.

To take her mind off her nervousness, Eleni began to pick out and recognize people from the various departments by the way they were dressed. Some were grey-garbed and sombre. Administration, she guessed, or maybe Finance. Those from Research & Development were dressed in crisp white overalls, but the ones going in and out of Programming were determinedly casual. A group from Marketing were as brightly-clad as a flock of tropical birds, and were probably making about as much noise with their chatter.

At the far end of the hall was a small, insignificant-looking entrance marked MAINTENANCE. Cat stopped here, and tapped what seemed to be a long code into her wristpad. Then she held her wrist unit up to the doorway and spoke softly but clearly. 'Security Override. Code Triple Platinum.' The portal, which had been scrolling through the various Maintenance departments, suddenly turned black.

'Follow me. Hurry up,' said Cat. Stepping forward, she vanished. Eleni felt suddenly afraid, but told herself not to be stupid. With a fast-beating heart, she followed Cat.

CHAPTER TEN

ELIMINATOR

The darkness vanished as the BAT flared around Eleni. When it cleared she found herself standing in a room that was a complete opposite to the vast white chamber she had left. It was very cosy, with laden bookshelves and panelling of glowing wood on the walls. The floor had a deep carpet with an intricate pattern of red, blue, and green, and a fire blazed in the big fireplace. An old-fashioned desk and a green leather chair stood in the deep alcove of the bay window, and there was a comfortable old sofa in front of the hearth.

'Where are we?' Eleni gasped.

Cat blurred into her human shape. 'You can change back now. We're quite safe in here.' She gestured around her. 'Welcome to Miss Aldanar's private office. Apart from herself, and me, you folk are the only ones who even know of its existence.' She grinned. 'What that creep Craven and his friends wouldn't give to know about this! This place is the true heart of Black Widow, and a lot more besides. She told me that from here, she can even access files that the other Board members think are protected by their private security codes.'

'Wow,' Jack said. 'No wonder they're trying to get rid of her. If she held that kind of power, they must be absolutely terrified she'll try to come back.'

Eleni looked around at the bare desk and the walls that

were covered in old-fashioned books. No screen, no keyboard was in sight. 'Do you know where she keeps her system files?'

'I'll show you,' Cat said. She crossed to the desk and sat down. There was nothing on the surface other than what looked like a beautiful paperweight of glittering crystal, in the shape of a spider. As Cat picked it up it began to glow, the light pulsing gently with the regular rhythm of a heartbeat. Holding it close to her face, she spoke to it so softly that even Eleni, who was standing nearest, didn't hear what she said.

The spider glowed more brightly, and pulsed a little faster. Eleni jumped as it began to speak. *'Rebirth codes accepted,'* said a clear, melodious voice. *'Merlin system activated. System allegiance transferring.'*

Jack poked Leni. *'Allegiance?'* he whispered.

Eleni nodded. 'It's a dedicated, one-person system,' she told him softly. 'They were supposed to be the closest thing to true artificial intelligence, but they were always said to be impossible! Identification works on brain-wave patterns. Only the Sorceress could use this Merlin system, but now, she's passed it on.' Eleni let out her breath in a low whistle. 'She really *has* passed her whole empire on to Cat!'

'Yes,' Cat's grim little voice interrupted. 'She has. And when I'm old enough to take it over, Craven and his pals are going to be sorry.'

'Allegiance transfer complete,' came the voice of Merlin.

'Good,' Cat said. 'Access: Black Widow Executive Files, hyper-level secrecy. Override code: Sorceress. Search: Shadowzone.'

There was a brief pause, then the spider pulsed once more. *'Executive hyper-encrypted system. Shadowzone: four files found.'* Above the surface of the desk, glowing letters appeared in the air:

BRATFIX
CRONETRACK
ELIMINATOR

HUNTER

'Crone,' Cat said bitterly. 'They mean Miss Aldanar. The pigs!'

'Access Hunter,' Jack said to the crystal spider.

'No!' the Hunter cried.

'*Unauthorized command: access denied,*' said Merlin firmly.

Cat glared across at Jack, but spoke to Merlin. 'Access Bratfix,' she said, in a voice that shook a little. 'I have a horrible feeling.'

The area above the desk seemed to shimmer. Words scrolled across.

File 1: Nightmare.

Suddenly, Eleni saw an image of Cat, running through dark streets, pursued by a sinister black shadow. She ran into an open space, and Eleni saw a huge old floodlit building with a square grey tower. She recognized it at once from holos that Cat had sent her. As Cat vanished through the doors, the scene changed to show her running through the vast, echoing interior of the cathedral, with the black shadows closing in on all sides. Then she darted through a doorway that was concealed by a blue velvet curtain, and the shadows stopped, blocked and balked by some invisible barrier. Some words scrolled across the bottom of the image:

Mission incomplete. Nightmare implant blocked. Possible Crone interference?

'It was Black Widow!' Cat gasped. 'My nightmare – it was them all along! And Miss Aldanar protected me!'

The image vanished, then more words scrolled across:

File 2: Bratsnatch.

This time everyone gasped as the screen showed an image

of Rom in Eleni's site. They saw him confronted by a gigantic insectlike creature. He was trying to back away in terror – then just as the creature made a grab for him, something appeared from the side of the image, a silvery shape moving so fast that it was just an indistinct flicker. It snatched Rom up and whirled him away.

Once more, words scrolled across the screen:

Mission failure. Mistaken identity of victim. Intervention by forces unknown. Investigation pending.

Jack's mouth was hanging open. '*Black Widow* tried to kidnap Rom?'

'Only because they expected him to be me.' Cat was scowling.

'But what was that other thing?' Eleni said. 'What did grab him?'

'The Aliens.'

Everyone looked at the Hunter as he spoke.

'Why didn't you tell us this before?' Jack demanded.

'Why Rom?' Cat asked at the same time.

The Hunter answered her first. 'They've spent more than enough time in the Web to come across Rom, hacking his way in and out of everything. I think they wanted to pick his brains – quite literally. It's probably a good thing I got him out of there before they had a chance to try it.'

Then he looked at Jack. 'Until now, it's been difficult to distinguish between the actions of Black Widow and those of the aliens. Too much was happening at once. Without the evidence of your own eyes, would you have believed me?'

To that, Jack had nothing to say.

An impatient bleep from Merlin brought their attention back to the display.

File 3: Wolfscare.

Cat muttered a word she definitely wasn't supposed to

know. 'So they hijacked the Education Module, too.' She was speaking through clenched teeth. 'Craven and his cronies are trying to get rid of me, aren't they? Trying to scare me out of the Web so I'll sell the company, and they can keep control.'

On the screen, they saw the image of the Hunter appear beside the female wolf. He touched her, and they both vanished. 'It was *you*!' Cat cried. She looked at him with shining eyes. 'Thank you.'

More writing was scrolling through the air above the desk:

Mission failure. Intervention by Hunter. Extermination proce-dures progressing. See exec-encrypt file Eliminator.

'Extermination procedures?' Cat said in a very small voice that didn't sound like her own. Hunter reached out and took her hand. It suddenly seemed to Eleni that she and Jack might as well not have been there. For the other two, they had ceased to exist.

'I didn't want to tell you like this,' the Hunter said. 'I wish I didn't have to tell you at all. When a game or a site is wiped, there's some sort of rift created in that space – like a whirlpool, or a black hole. It's a kind of a tear in the fabric of the Web, if you like. If any parts of the program accidentally get sucked into this rift, then they find themselves in the Shadowzone – an unknown alternate dimension of the Web, if you like. There are all sorts of weird things living in the Shadowzone, right from way back when people used to play games on the old-style Internet. No one knows they exist – except those who have also been deleted, one way or another.'

'*Deleted*?' Cat whispered, her eyes wide.

The Hunter nodded. 'Cat, I may look like one of you, an ordinary boy surfing the Web, but it's not true. I'm part of an old Websearch engine that Miss Aldanar created long ago when the Web was in its formative stage.' He bit his lip. 'The engine was thrown out as a failure while it was still in the research stage. It was just too far ahead of its time. When it was wiped, I somehow fell into the Shadowzone, and I've been living there ever since. When Miss Aldanar came across, I started to help her.' His mouth took on an ironic twist. 'In a way, she was the only mother I ever had. Cat, I'm sorry I deceived you. I'm not human, but I wanted . . . I wish . . .' He let go of her hand and turned away. 'I think Miss Aldanar made too good a job of me. I don't have a body outside the Web, but in here I have a mind, and a history, and I have feelings.'

For a long moment, Cat stood there, stunned, as though she had been turned to stone. Then she took a long, shuddering breath. 'I don't care,' she said firmly. Reaching out, she took hold of the Hunter's hand again. 'Here in the Web, bodies are only a detail. For all I know, Rom and Eleni might only be programs. I've never met them in the flesh, and probably I never will. That doesn't stop us from having fun, and being friends – and caring for each other. As far as I'm concerned, this makes no difference, and if those rats on the Board think they can wipe you, they'll have to get through me to do it!' Her eyes sparkled fiercely and, once again, Eleni was reminded of Miss Aldanar.

Jack spoke abruptly, making everyone jump. 'That's all very well, but hadn't we better look at the Eliminator file? It would help to know what we're up against.'

'You're right.' Cat rubbed her eyes, as though waking from a dream. 'Access exec-encrypt file Eliminator,' she said crisply, and gasped with horror as a long, slender, wicked-looking artefact appeared, turning gently as it floated in mid-air above the desk. It was a polished, smoky grey in colour. Its streamlined shape looked alive, like a shark, but the great jaws, like a collection of rotating scythes, were clearly part of a machine. The blades were set within a mouth that was designed to suck up whatever was left of its prey when the blades had finished with it.

Underneath the image of the Eliminator was a list of

specifications, including dimensions. Jack's jaw dropped open. 'Have you seen the *power* of that thing?'

The Hunter's face had turned a ghastly shade of white. 'If they set that monster on the Shadowzone,' he said, 'there'll be nothing left.'

'Well, they plan to.' Jack jabbed with a finger at more information that was scrolling past. 'Tomorrow!' He exchanged a horrified look with the others. 'If we're going to save the Shadowzone, we don't have much time.'

CHAPTER ELEVEN

PASSWORD: REDROSE

As the castle site shimmered into being through a blue haze of clearing BAT, Cat let herself relax. Safe at last! It had been a nightmare getting out of Black Widow. She'd insisted on bringing them back the way they had come. 'If we scuttle from this office we can be backtracked here,' she had said. 'It's *got* to remain hidden. We daren't risk leaving a trail.' No one had thanked her for putting them through the extra danger.

Tired and frustrated, they had come back briefly to the castle site to think about the next step. Eleni was cast down by her failure to infiltrate the Eliminator file. 'I'm sorry,' she told the others. 'There just seemed no way to get at that thing to disable it. It's so well protected, I couldn't have reached it without letting Black Widow know we were there.'

'No, you were right to leave it,' Cat told her. 'They mustn't discover Merlin. That would be a disaster. Somehow, we've got to find another way.'

Everyone was beginning to run out of Web-time, and the alarm in Leni's wrist unit went off.

'Look,' Jack said, 'we've all been in here far too long. We'd better scuttle. After what happened to Rom, I can't see a real bad dose of the voms going down too well with our folks. We can come back later and talk again.'

'*Endaxi*,' Eleni said. 'OK. In the meantime, I'll talk to Rom as soon as I get back. If the two of us put our heads together, maybe we can find a way to destroy that horrible thing.'

'And if you can't?' the Hunter asked quietly.

'Then I'm sorry,' Eleni said, 'but the only way we can save the Shadowzone is to hide it somehow – and that will mean sealing it off completely from the rest of the Web.'

'But the Hunter would be imprisoned in there for good!' Cat protested.

'Would you rather he was wiped?' Leni said wearily. 'I'm sorry, Cat. It may be the only thing we can do.'

There was nothing more to be said. No one had enough energy left to come up with any bright ideas. After arranging to meet again in six hours, Jack and Eleni spun out, but Cat lingered with the Hunter, her eyes full of questions. With a flourish, he created another red rose and pressed it into her hand. 'Go on,' he said softly. 'Don't make yourself ill.'

'Wait,' Cat said. 'I have something for you, in exchange.' From her pocket, she took something that glittered brightly. 'Here.' Cupped in her open palm was the crystal spider, the access point to Merlin.

The Hunter's eyes widened. 'You brought it *out* with you?'

Cat nodded. 'I took an awful risk, removing it from the security of the private office. If the Black Widow Execs get their hands on this much power, the consequences don't bear thinking about. But to save you and Miss Aldanar, and the Shadowzone, we may need Merlin. I had to take the chance.'

Holding up the spider, she spoke to it softly. 'Password: Daughter.'

'*Cleared and Activating.*' The crystal access link began to glow and pulse in her hand. Cat looked at Hunter. 'Security Override. Code Triple Platinum,' she said clearly. 'Modify Allegiance Files. Add temporary subfile: Grey Wolf.'

'*Invalid Command. Unlimited access, single subject only.*'

'Rats!' Cat's brow creased in a frown. She racked her brains for a solution, trying to remember Miss Aldanar's instructions. 'Emergency override. Code Maxus. Modify Allegiance

Files. Add temporary subfile: Grey Wolf. Unlimited Access, 24 hours only, to AI master-program The Hunter.'

Merlin gave a harsh squawk of protest. *'Warning. Irregular command. May result in danger to system. Do you wish to continue?'*

'Continue.'

There was a long moment of silence before Merlin spoke again. *'Accepted.'*

With a smile, Cat held the spider up to the Hunter's face. 'Commence subject scan.'

'Scanning . . .'

'Cat, you can't!' the Hunter protested. 'This was never meant for me! It's too great a trust!'

Cat shook her head. 'Too great a trust for *you*? Never,' she said softly. 'I trust you more than any Realworld person I know. When the scan's complete, you'll give it your own password at the prompt.'

'Scan completed.'

The Hunter took a deep breath. 'Password: Redrose.'

'Accepted.'

'Good.' Not without a pang of reluctance, Cat placed the precious spider into the Hunter's hands. 'Here. Take Merlin into the Shadowzone with you. It's the only place where Black Widow can't get at it. I don't know if Miss Aldanar will still be able to access it after the Allegiance Transfer, but if she can, she may be able to use it to help us in ways I don't know. I need some time out now, but I'll meet you here in six hours, and you can take us all into the Shadowzone. In the meantime, take Merlin back and make sure he's safe.'

'All right.' Hunter was still looking absolutely stunned. Cat kissed the velvety petals of the rose, and handed it back to him. Then she was gone. When she was safely away, the Hunter buried his face in his hands. 'Why?' he whispered. 'Why couldn't I be human?'

When Cat spun out of the Web she took off her helmet and sat for a moment, gazing blindly at the wall. 'It won't make any difference,' she whispered fiercely. Then the room

shimmered around her like a BAT as her eyes filled with
tears.

Rom was glad to be home again, but furious because his
parents wouldn't let him back into the Web – yet. He
supposed it was only to be expected, but *that* wasn't much
help. He was taking out his frustration on the flatscreen,
scrolling his way through a screed of recent news reports.
With every one he read, another piece of the jigsaw was
falling into place, and the picture was looking blacker and
blacker.

Could it really be true that the aliens were everywhere,
tinkering with people's minds and making them behave in
strange, and sometimes lethal ways? How many of these
cases had been alien interference, and how many just plain
human idiocy? Curiosity drove them, that much he understood – a deep need to understand, to experience, to *know*.
Rom wondered what would happen if one of their victims
actually died, like the man in Italy who had tried to fly. No,
surely that couldn't have been the Outsiders. How could
they get safely back into the Web? Surely they would die too.
No, the man must just have been plain crazy. As crazy as *he*
was, to be thinking of these things.

'This is nuts,' Rom said to himself. The authorities should
be told – the Government, the Webcops – somebody. If it
was all true, there might even be ways of helping the
sensation-hungry aliens. I would volunteer to take an alien
around in my mind and show it how to be human, he
thought. So long as I knew it was there, and if it left when it
was told, then playing host to a being from another planet
might be fun. *But what if I'm doing that right now? What if
they did get into my mind. What if they've been there all along?*
Rom felt sick. It was the not knowing that was horrible.

An urgent buzz from his flatscreen interrupted his
thoughts and, for once, Rom wasn't sorry. A *call waiting*
signal flashed up, so he closed down his file of news reports
and opened up the line, using his own private scrambler in

case his folks decided to listen in. Normally, they wouldn't have dreamed of eavesdropping but, lately, since he'd been in hospital, they had been acting a little weird.

Rom's fingers froze on the flatscreen keys as the chilling thought flashed into his mind. Oh no . . . No, no, no! Surely the aliens couldn't be using his own mom and dad to spy on him? I won't think about it, he decided. I'll just be a bit more careful. There's no way of knowing, after all. Putting the matter firmly out of his mind, he accessed the call, and was delighted to find Eleni on the other end of the line.

She looked absolutely exhausted, but her face lit up at the sight of him. '*Yiasou*, frog-face. It's good to see you back in one piece! *Ti kanis*?'

Rom rummaged through his mind for some Greek words to answer her, then gave it up. 'I'm fine, Princess.'

Eleni smiled. Though she hadn't been there, she knew all about the conversation between Rom, Jack, and Cat that had taken place in the Star Bar a few days ago. The new nicks were already beginning to stick. That had been the very day, Rom thought suddenly, when the strange writing had appeared in Leni's site, and all this trouble had started.

'Rom, I have such a lot to tell you. We know now who the Hunter is.' It was as though Eleni had been reading his mind. Before he had a chance to bring up the subject of the aliens she had launched into the whole story, and by the time she'd finished telling him everything that had been happening, the thoughts of his own experience had been pushed to the back of his mind.

'It's only been a couple of days,' he protested indignantly. 'How can so much have happened?' There was a tremendous amount to take in – Miss Aldanar, the Hunter, the Shadow-zone, Black Widow, Merlin, and this dreadful device called the Eliminator.

'Hold on. Did I miss something here?' he demanded. 'Are you telling me we're trying to *save* the Sorceress now? What changed, all of a sudden?'

'*She* did, according to Cat and the Hunter,' Eleni tried to explain. 'And Cat says that the Black Widow executives are trying to grab control of the company for themselves, and they've been trying to frighten her out of the Web. The Hunter says the inhabitants of the Shadowzone have as much right to survive as anything else in the Web, and we can't let Black Widow wipe them out.' She paused for an instant. 'Rom, I know about the aliens. Are you really all right? They didn't hurt you?'

Eleni was just as shocked by Rom's encounter with the aliens as he had been by her news of the Sorceress. By the time he had reassured her, and told her as much as he could understand about what had happened, their call had already lasted ages.

Suddenly, Rom glanced at the charges readout on the screen and let out a yelp. 'Leni, your folks will go ballistic when they see how much this is costing! Listen, you've given me what codes you could scrounge for this Eliminator thing. I'll sneak in tonight and try to take a look when my mom and dad have gone to bed. They told me I couldn't go back into the Web until the doc had cleared it, but this is an emergency.'

'It's no good,' Eleni said. 'You can't get anywhere near the thing without Cat's access to Merlin. Not only is Eliminator hyper-encrypted, it's surrounded by all kinds of alarms and watchdogs, too. The Black Widow execs aren't messing about.'

'Maybe, but they haven't tangled with *me*, yet.' Rom gave her a confident grin.

Leni sighed. 'Look at this. I copied the data from Merlin into my wrist unit.'

There was a brief pause as she sent the file across. Rom said a word that would have shocked his mother to the core.

'See?' Eleni said. 'We can't take that thing on until Black Widow unleash it tomorrow – and then we'll have to be extremely fast. It's a tall order, Rom.'

'I hear you! Listen, Leni. I'll try to meet you at the time you said, but if I should run into a delay, or any other kind of trouble, you're going to have to seal off the Shadowzone. Wait ten minutes for me, and if I'm not there by then, don't hang around. And don't try to get in touch, just in case Black Widow are on to me. Just get inside, and do your stuff. It would be awful to lose Cat's friend – but that Eliminator is too much for one person to handle.'

'OK.' Eleni swallowed hard. 'Look, Rom, I've really got to go. I can hear Mama coming. See you soon. And take care.'

When she had gone, Rom scanned the data for the Eliminator again, and did some hard thinking. In the face of such power, his usual brash self-confidence was beginning to crumble. He had never seen anything like it. I'm going to need some help, he thought, but who has ever seen anything like this? It's like nothing on earth. Nothing on earth—

Suddenly, Rom had an idea, but the risk involved turned him cold right to the bone. It's a terrible risk, he thought, and would it work anyway?

Well, there was only one way to find out. In half a minute he had shed his clothes, pulled his Websuit out of the closet and put it on.

Rom spun into Eleni's site, left the road, and hurried down the uneven steps into the garden. Once there, he paused and looked around him. Though he could see nothing unusual, he was convinced that he could feel eyes on him, or was that just his imagination?

He took a deep breath. 'Hey, you aliens, anybody home?' Was that a movement in the shadowy olive grove? A flash of quicksilver in the corner of his eye? Rom swallowed hard, his mouth gone dry with fear. Clearing his throat, he tried again.

'Hey, you aliens, listen to me! You've got to trust me. I came back, didn't I? I can't help you, but I sure know someone who can! She's called the Sorceress, and she's done more work on getting into other people's bodies than anyone I know. Right now, though, she's in deadly danger, and before she can help you, you'll have to help her. Is it a deal?'

Suddenly, the shadows beneath the olive trees were thronged with a host of silvery shapes.

CHAPTER TWELVE

SHADOWZONE

Globenet Times, August 28, 2028.
TWO KILLED IN WEBSTORE BLAZE
Two people have lost their lives as a fire swept through a Dublin store
selling Web systems and accessories. Before emergency services could
reach the scene the Weborium in St Stephen's Green was devastated by
the blaze in which the manager and one of the sales staff lost their lives.
Police suspect the fire was started deliberately.

When Cat spun into the castle site, she saw that both Eleni
and the Hunter had arrived before her. They were seated up
on the battlements, their heads close together, deep in talk.
Cat felt a swift pang of jealousy, then told herself firmly not
to be so stupid. To the best of her knowledge, the Hunter had
never given red roses to Leni. She called to them from the
ground, and had the immense satisfaction of seeing the
Hunter's face light up at the sight of her. 'Wait there,' he
called. 'We're coming down.'

They emerged from the shadows of the castle doorway
looking very pleased with themselves, but before Cat had
time to feel jealous again, the Hunter had come across and
taken both of her hands. 'Merlin is safe,' he told her. 'And
Miss Aldanar is very proud of you. She told me to tell you
that she chose well in her heir.'

Cat felt a glow of happy pride, but reminded herself
sharply that this affair was a long way from being over yet.

'No sign of the others?' she asked. The words were barely out of her mouth before there was a shimmer in the air as Jack spun in.

Though she tried to hide it, Eleni's face fell at the sight of him. 'I wish Rom would come,' she said anxiously. 'I can't take on the Eliminator without him. He promised to be here if there was any way he could manage it, but there might be some problem if his parents are around. He said if he wasn't here in ten minutes, not to wait.'

Cat felt a chill deep inside her as the implications of Eleni's words sunk in. 'And if he doesn't come?'

There was a long pause. 'Cat, I'm sorry,' she said at last. 'If he doesn't come, the only way to save the Hunter and Miss Aldanar will be to seal off the Shadowzone.'

When Jack joined them, Eleni told them of her conversation with Rom. Jack checked the time on his wrist unit. 'Time's nearly up,' he said, with a sidelong glance at Cat, who barely noticed. She just stood there, still and silent, holding tightly to the Hunter's hand.

It was the Hunter who finally broke the grim spell that held them all in thrall. 'Well,' he said briskly, 'I don't think he's coming now, so let's get on with it, shall we? Eleni and I have worked out a way to get you humans into the Shadowzone, we think. We believe that when a site is wiped and the rift appears, it flicks in and out of existence so fast that very few things slip through – and *they* do it by accident.'

'We had to find a way to slow down our relative time,' Eleni said. 'Normally, when a site is wiped, everything takes place in nanoseconds. The Hunter and I worked out that if something *does* happen then, it happens too fast for anyone to notice, so we decided that if we could kind of stretch the process out, we'd have enough time to see just what was going on, and follow the lost data to wherever it goes.'

Cat looked at Eleni in amazement, and wondered how she had failed to notice this change in her friend long before now. While she and Jack were just generally messing about and playing games, Leni had been very busy turning herself into a formidable Web-wizard!

'Anyway, it turned out that we couldn't slow things down,' Eleni was saying. 'Not without reprogramming the entire Web!' Her dark eyes sparkled with mischief. 'We were really tempted to try, but we decided we should maybe do it in a less noticeable way, in case we attracted the attention of Black Widow. We realized we couldn't slow down the Web, but we *could* speed up ourselves!'

'So that's exactly what we did.' The Hunter looked at the stunned faces of the others. 'And now, when we wipe this site—'

'*What?*' Jack was looking at the Hunter as though he had sprouted another head. 'You want to wipe the site with us inside it? Have you lost your *mind?*'

Eleni shrugged. 'Don't be such a gag, Jack.'

Cat looked at her in astonishment. This wasn't like Eleni at all!

'What can happen?' the Greek girl went on. 'Either we make it to the Shadowzone, or the site disappears and we find ourselves back in Webtown. What can possibly go wrong?'

A shiver ran down Cat's spine. *Don't say that!* she thought, but of course it was too late. Eleni had already tempted fate. With a sinking heart, she looked across at Jack. There was a reflection of her own dismay on his face, and she knew he was thinking exactly the same thing. Cat, prideful as always, would rather die than say anything, though. She didn't want Leni, of all people, calling *her* a gag, too.

The Hunter spoke at last. 'I trust Eleni. She knows her stuff.' There was a challenge in his voice as he looked at Jack.

Cat was looking at her friend. 'Leni, are you absolutely certain that everything will be all right?' she asked.

'No,' Eleni said cheerfully. Then she hit a code in her wristpad, and the world collapsed around them.

To Cat, everything seemed to happen in slow motion. The castle and its surrounding plain began to smudge and streak like wet paint, as the colours swirled and ran into one another. A pinpoint of black nothingness appeared in the ground, right in front of Cat's feet. She jumped back, but didn't move as far as she had expected. Already, the forces gathering around the tiny opening were vast, and becoming greater all the time.

There was no way out now. As Cat watched in fascinated horror, the hole began to grow as the details of the castle spun faster and faster around it, blurring into a whirlpool of colour and light. Everything was vanishing, being pulled into the opening like water swirling down the drain. Down the plug, Cat thought wildly. We're going down the plug!

'No! This is insane!' Jack shook his head, backing away from the hole. Then with a wild yell he was gone, down into nothingness.

'Go on, quick!' Leni urged Cat. 'I'll follow!'

Without giving herself time to think about it, Cat held tightly to the Hunter's hand and dived down into the hole.

Cat felt that there should have been a sensation of falling, but there was nothing – no sound, no sensation. They had jumped from light into absolute blackness. Then she realized that she could feel one thing. She still held the Hunter's hand, and his grip was firm and strong. That helped Cat find her own courage.

'It's all right.' His voice, still calm and cheerful, came out of the darkness. 'It's just the Shadowzone playing tricks. It does that, sometimes. Just use your wrist unit and turn up the light gain as far as it'll go.'

That meant letting go of the Hunter's hand, and being all alone in the darkness. There was a short pause while Cat screwed up her courage. Then she let go and fumbled at her wristpad. After a moment, the black blanket that covered her eyes became grey, then was pulled back to reveal a dusky, gloomy landscape like a barren plain, littered with rocks of various shapes and sizes.

'The Shadowzone,' Eleni breathed.

'Look at those rocks,' Jack said. 'They must all be data – just chunks of ancient data that can't be recognized now, by our modern programming.'

'Just like me, eh?' the Hunter said with grim humour. He met Jack's eyes and, suddenly, the tension that had always existed between them seemed to relax a little.

'Is it all like this?' Cat was anxious to change the subject.

The Hunter shook his head. 'No. Just around the rift. As it opens and closes, anything in the locality can be torn apart by the forces involved.'

Eleni looked around uneasily. 'Don't you think we should be moving, then?'

'Don't worry,' the Hunter told her. 'We'll be leaving in a minute.'

At that moment, a distant buzzing could be heard – the first sound, save for their voices, to break through the sullen silence of the arid plain. Squinting into the distance, Cat saw a cluster of far-off specks above the wasteland, travelling high and fast. As they came nearer they grew and took on a definite and distinctive shape – four delicate, double-winged dragonflies with a dragon's roar.

Jack let out a low whistle. 'Oh, wow! Camels!'

Eleni looked around wildly, puzzled to find no hump-backed creatures in sight. Cat burst out laughing. She knew what Jack meant. She was not an historian's daughter for nothing, and she too had recognized the distinctive shape of the fierce yet fragile-seeming aircraft. 'Sopwith Camels, Leni. Fighter planes from the 1914-1918 War,' she explained.

'Aren't they beautiful?' Jack was lost in adoration. Cat had to admit he was right. Somehow they gave a lift to her heart, these elegant, brave little craft. There was a kind of romance about them. The biplanes looked as flimsy as paper kites, yet their appearance was deceptive, she knew. They were beautiful but deadly – tricky and fractious in the air, a difficult and dangerous plane to fly, and their guns were dealers of powerful death.

'You like them?' The Hunter's voice tore Cat's eyes away

from the sky. 'They're relics from an old Fighter Ace game.'
He grinned at Cat. 'Watch out for their tempers.'

Cat had no time to ask him what he meant, for the Camels
were landing. One after the other they set down as lightly as
birds, the throbbing roar of their engines drowning out all
hope of speech. Now that they were down, Cat was shocked
to see they had no pilots.

The little biplanes lined up, their engines idling. The
Hunter led Cat and her friends down the row and made the
introductions. 'Eleni, Jack and Cat, this is Gold Leader, and
these are Gold One, Gold Two and Gold Three.'

'Glad to make your acquaintance.'

'Delighted to meet you.'

'It's a pleasure.'

'Charmed.'

Cat was stunned when the planes replied in clipped
accents, their voices a throaty growl.

'What did you expect?' the Hunter said softly. 'They're as
alive and intelligent as I am. In the Shadowzone, we're all
the same, no matter what we look like. Anyway, come on.
Let's all get aboard. We don't have a lot of time to spare.'

Already Jack was nattering away to Gold One, asking
questions, examining the bracing wires, and running his
hands lovingly along the plane's sleek, tilted wings. The two
of them were clearly getting on like old friends. Sadly, the
same could not be said for Cat and Gold Two. Though the
planes had no eyes or faces, they had very forceful personal-
ities and, somehow, Cat could feel Gold Two looking down
on her with haughty distain.

'A girl?' the biplane growled at Hunter. 'I'm a Sopwith
Camel, the most dangerous aircraft in the skies. I don't suffer
fools at all. I kill a third of my pilots on their first flight, and
now you want me to fly a *girl*?'

Hunter sighed. 'Look,' he said, 'we don't have time for
tantrums. You volunteered to take a passenger and here she
is. You behave yourself, or Miss Aldanar will hear of it.'

The mention of Miss Aldanar was enough to stop Gold

Two's complaints, but Cat could still hear it muttering peevishly under its breath as its engine idled. She felt an ominous chill. I have a feeling this is going to be one memorable ride, she thought.

The Hunter showed her which part of the lower wing to stand on, and she climbed into the cockpit. 'I'm sorry,' he said to Cat, as he helped her to strap in. 'That's the trouble with some of these antique constructs. He'll behave. He'd better . . .' He scowled at the biplane. 'All the same,' he added as an afterthought. 'Better keep those straps tight, just in case.'

With a last, reassuring squeeze of her hand the Hunter was off, scrambling up into Gold Leader's high cockpit. The sound of Gold Leader's engine changed from a muffled throb to a throaty roar. The plane began to roll along the ground, moving faster and faster, until with a wild whoop of joy it was airborne, sweeping up into the skies and climbing fast. Gold One, with Jack in the cockpit, followed on its tail, and then it was Cat's turn.

Every jolt from the bumpy ground jarred up through Cat's spine and into her skull, grinding her teeth together. She couldn't see a thing in front of her, her view obscured by the high, humped engine cowling that gave the Camel its name. As the plane gathered speed, the ground on either side blurred past. Cat clung tightly to the sides of the cockpit. Just when she thought they could go no faster without the biplane jarring itself to pieces, Gold Two finally hurled itself up into the air with a howl of exhilaration.

'Hold tight, little girl,' the aircraft snickered. Without warning, Cat found herself hanging upside-down in her straps as Gold Two flipped over. She closed her eyes in terror as the ground streaked past beneath her. She was completely at the biplane's mercy. She didn't dare touch anything in the cockpit. She was just about to shriek for help when she realized that was exactly what Gold Two wanted. Cat shut her teeth with a snap and clenched them tight. She'd rather die than let this arrogant brute see that she was scared!

When it got no reaction, Gold Two tried another tack, flipping over on to its left wingtips then upright again. Before Cat could snatch a gasp of relief, it was screaming up into the sky, standing on its tail, then toppling backwards into a spectacular loop. For an instant Cat's stomach heaved but, suddenly, as they swooped like a hawk through the skies, she found herself caught up in the plane's exultation. She joined Gold Two's roar of joy with a wild yell of her own. 'Again,' she urged, as it levelled out. 'Do it again!'

She felt the shock of surprise shudder through the bracing wires on the biplane's wings. 'Well,' it admitted reluctantly, 'perhaps I was wrong, after all. You do have courage enough to fly with me, girl.'

'Gold Two, Gold Two, this is Gold Leader. What the blazes do you think you're playing at? Get back into formation AT ONCE!'

Gold Two and Cat shared a guilty chuckle, and slipped meekly back into line.

No longer afraid, Cat peered over the side of the cockpit as they flew onward, looking down through a framework of struts and wires at the changing landscape below. The barren grey stretches of desert had long since vanished, to be replaced by forests, hills and rivers, all in clear crystalline colours as though the Shadowzone had been constructed from pieces of stained glass, laid on top of each other in overlapping layers of colour and richness. In the far distance, islands floated like emeralds in a sparkling sapphire ocean.

Though the sky was unclouded blue on the horizon, higher up it grew gradually darker, until above Cat's head it was the starry black of space. Spacecraft, silvery and stream-lined, could be seen zooming across the starscape, firing long tracers of red or green light. All sorts of weird creatures inhabited the green landscape – people and animals, mon-sters and machines. Entrances to dark and sinister tunnels pierced some of the hillsides, and sleek cars hurtled endlessly round looped tangles of road, going nowhere at a tremen-dous speed.

Cat wished she could appreciate this incredible flight as it deserved, but all the time her worried thoughts tugged at her attention, taking it away from the landscape below. Would they be on time? Would they find a way to defeat the monster that Black Widow had created? What if they had to seal off the Shadowzone, and she lost the Hunter for ever?

It seemed an eternity before the biplanes circled down to land in a green meadow beside a shimmering blue lake. On the lake shore, a high slender tower, made all of faceted glass, glittered with the blinding brilliance of a diamond. In the doorway of the tower, at the top of a long flight of steps, Cat could see Miss Aldanar waiting. She was young and straight and beautiful, just as in Cat's dream, but this time, she was looking deeply worried and – if such a thing could be possible – almost afraid.

'Hurry!' she shouted. 'Into the tower! The Eliminator has already been unleashed!'

CHAPTER THIRTEEN

AVENGING ANGELS

Eleni clambered out of Gold Three, belatedly remembering to thank the aircraft. She hurried across the grass and saw Cat ahead of her, exchanging brief words with Miss Aldanar on the tower steps. A shiver of nervousness went through her. It was all very well for Cat – she was the chosen heir of the Sorceress – but how would this fearsome and powerful woman react to the girl who had been responsible for her defeat and destruction? Despite the urgency of their situation, her feet dragged with reluctance as she followed Jack towards the tower.

With one arm around Cat's shoulders, and beckoning to the others to follow, Miss Aldanar hurried back into the slender spire of crystal, and led the way up the spiral of stairs inside. As she entered, Eleni gasped in awe. The place was stunningly beautiful. The sunlight struck through the facets of the crystal and filled the stairwell with a host of dazzling rainbows. As she climbed the seemingly endless stairs, she noticed that there were no rooms on the way up the glass tower – it was merely a stem to support whatever lay at the top. If the Sorceress is so powerful and clever, why didn't she put a lift in here? Eleni thought as she toiled her way up the stairs. Somehow, it made her feel better to be able to find fault with one of Miss Aldanar's constructs.

At last, the staircase reached the very top of the tower, and opened into a great circular chamber with a domed roof of transparent glass. Save that the walls were crystal instead of panelling, and the furnishings were made to fit into a differently-shaped area, the room was a copy of Miss Aldanar's cosy secret office in the Black Widow headquarters. The Sorceress led Eleni to one side, a little apart from the others. The girl trembled as she confronted the woman whose doom she had brought about. Miss Aldanar looked at Eleni with a curious glitter in her fathomless dark eyes. 'So,' she said, 'we meet again. I congratulate you, my dear. I completely underestimated you when you destroyed me.'

She continued before Eleni could protest. 'It's all right, child, you beat me fair and square, and it would be a waste of time to bear you a grudge. Use that cleverness of yours to save the Shadowzone, and we'll call it quits, shall we?'

Eleni nodded, feeling very much relieved by the woman's attitude. She took a deep breath. 'I'm glad I didn't really destroy you.'

Miss Aldanar grimaced. 'It wasn't for the want of trying,' she said feelingly, 'but let's get to the problem in hand.'

She gestured towards her heavy, antique wooden desk. There sat the crystal spider that was the access to Merlin. In the air above it was an image that chilled Eleni's blood. She had no doubts about what she was seeing. Clearly, this was a view from the outside of the Shadowzone. The interface between the secret domain and the rest of the Web was shown as a fragile-looking curved surface sleeked with swirling, iridescent patterns of energy like the colours on a soap bubble. Unfortunately, the barrier also looked as fragile as a soap bubble in comparison with the vast, black, sharklike shape that loomed over it – a menacing shadow that crept slowly but relentlessly towards its prey.

A shiver of fear went through Eleni. 'Is it true that you can't leave the Shadowzone?' she asked Miss Aldanar. To the last, she had held out the hope that she wouldn't have to tackle the Eliminator alone.

'I can leave, but I have little power outside any more. Certainly not enough to tackle *that*. It was created by

Realworld people, and must also be destroyed by one of them.'

Cat was looking on anxiously, barely aware of Jack and the Hunter by her side. Would Eleni succeed? Everything depended on her now.

'Cat, come here!' Eleni called. 'I need your help. I want to access data on both the Eliminator and the Shadowzone, so you'll have to talk to Merlin for me.'

It was better to have something to do. For the next few frantic minutes, Cat found herself acting as the interface between her friend and Merlin as Eleni fired a long and complex list of questions and instructions at the computer, storing the data in her own wrist unit. Between them they managed to create a double display above the desk, where Eleni's information was scrolling across one side, and, on the other, they could see the image of the Eliminator with its multiple scythelike jaws, descending on the helpless Shadowzone.

For a time, as Eleni worked, Cat began to hope that the Greek girl would find a way, against all the odds, to deal with the threat. But as the minutes ticked by and the Eliminator drew nearer and nearer, her confidence began to falter. The air in the circular room almost sang with the suspense, and the eyes of everyone were fixed, as though fastened with tightly-stretched threads, to Eleni and to the computer display that showed an ever-shrinking distance between the lethal-looking monster and their unprotected haven.

The black hulk of Eliminator drew closer, closer and, suddenly, there was no need to look at the display. There was a tearing crash like a thousand thunderclaps, and they staggered, clutching each other as the floor heaved and shook under their feet. Cat picked herself up, rubbing a bruised elbow, and stopped, transfixed, her eyes on the glass dome above her head. The interface had been breached. There was a jagged tear across the sky, through which they could see bright nothingness, and part of the looming bulk of the Eliminator, its fearsome mandibles gnawing at the edges of the hole.

Miss Aldanar broke the horrified silence. 'Eleni, thank you for trying, but our options have run out. You've got to seal off the Shadowzone before even that last chance is lost.'

Eleni's shoulders slumped. 'I'm sorry,' she murmured.

'Not your fault,' Miss Aldanar said firmly. '*I* couldn't have stopped it. No one could. Those vermin at Black Widow have made the cursed thing well-nigh invincible.'

'At least I can seal off the Shadowzone,' Eleni said. 'I'll take a few seconds of stored memory from when the interface was unbroken, and put them into a permanent loop. That way, it doesn't matter how many times the barrier is breached, it'll instantly seal back up again. The only thing is, I'll have to do it from outside. How can we get out?'

'Don't worry.' The Hunter's voice was quiet and strained. 'We anticipated this. Gold Squadron will take you. They know you're sealing off the Shadowzone. They know it's a one-way mission, but they're following in the tradition of the hundreds of their Realworld brethren who went out to confront the enemy and never came back.'

'Go now, all of you.' Miss Aldanar ordered. 'Don't get trapped here.'

'Wait!' Leni turned back. 'Cat, tell Merlin to send these files to the destination I give you! Quick, it's important!'

She clung to Cat's sleeve, not letting her move away from the computer until she had delivered the instructions. Cat repeated the words like a robot and hardly knew what she was saying. Her eyes were on the Hunter, storing up memories.

It was done. Caught up in the action of the moment, Jack and Eleni raced downstairs, heading for the planes. Cat lingered, dragged back by the ties of love.

'Go, please,' Hunter whispered. 'Don't drag it out. Cat . . . I'll never forget you.'

'And I won't forget you.' Cat's throat was too tight with

tears to say any more. It just couldn't happen like this. It was all too fast! There was no time to say goodbye.

'Go,' Miss Aldanar said roughly. 'Be well, child. You are the daughter I never had.' She crammed the crystal spider into Cat's hands. 'Don't forget Merlin. Avenge us one day.'

At that moment, Jack burst back into the room. 'Cat, come *on!*'

'Goodbye.' Cat found her voice, and ran, not daring to look back. If she looked back once, she would never leave. Jack almost hurled her into the cockpit of Gold Two and ran for his own plane. Cat fumbled for her straps, barely able to see for the sheen of tears in her eyes. Angrily, she blinked her vision clear. 'Not now,' she muttered savagely. 'There'll be plenty of time for that later.'

With a scream of engines Gold Two shot forward, following its companions and picking up speed every second. Cat was pressed into her seat as they surged into the air. Then she noticed that there were four planes in the sky, not the three she had expected. Their leader had followed them. 'Gold Leader's coming!' she shouted above the engine roar.

'Naturally. He wouldn't desert his squadron in times of need.' The tone of Gold Two warned Cat not to discuss the matter any further, but she understood and sympathized. Gold Leader would rather perish with his companions than stay behind, all alone. Suddenly, she realized that she had stopped thinking of the fierce little craft as *it*. These brave, hot-tempered warriors were no mere machines!

The dauntless biplanes climbed higher and higher, towards the jagged rift in the sky that was enlarging every second as the Eliminator's fearsome multiple jaws ripped into the fabric of the Shadowzone. Already, Eleni was keying frantically at her wristpad, trying to start the healing process even before she reached the gap. If she couldn't stop the destruction soon, the rip would have grown too big to be patched, and the Shadowzone could never be sealed off.

'We've got to delay it – give Leni a chance to work,' Cat shouted.

'I know! Don't tell me my job!' snarled the biplane. 'Hold on tight, girl!' Gold Two swooped in a high, banking turn towards the monster, but was too late. Gold Leader was suddenly ahead, diving into danger to protect its comrade.

Gold Leader swooped closer and closer, a darting dragon, firing his guns right into the jaws of the behemoth, until one of the gigantic mandibles caught the gallant little plane. Struts snapped with the dry sound of breaking bones as his wings crumpled like paper. There was a muffled boom and a flash as his fuel tank exploded, then he was spiralling down and down with a whistling screech, trailing a long plume of black oily smoke behind. Then, in a split second flash, Cat glimpsed the tiny figure in the cockpit, beating helplessly at the flames. Her heart froze. Gold Leader had not come without a pilot after all. The Hunter, too, could not bear to be left behind alone.

The horror was almost too great to comprehend. 'No!' Cat wailed in anguish, and realized too late that she was next. Already she had been noticed. Already those long, hinged jaws were springing out towards Gold Two. With a howl of engines the plane flipped on its right wingtip and turned in its own length, dodging the deadly predator. Again the jaws snaked out. Again Gold Two dodged, dropping out of the sky in a screaming dive. Cat heard a sharp crack as a strut snapped, and Two pulled itself out of the plunge with a curse. 'If we try *that* again,' it muttered, 'I'll tear my wings off.'

With a chill, Cat realized that they were running out of options. What would happen if she went down in flames like the Hunter? Would her body survive the shock? Would terror destroy her mind? Black Widow have been trying to get rid of me, she thought. Maybe they've succeeded after all.

She glanced down at the ruined interface. Eleni was having problems because Gold Three couldn't hover, but could only fly back and forth along the interface. She didn't look anywhere near finished, and the rip was getting bigger all the time as Eliminator tore at the fabric of the Shadow-zone.

It was all going wrong. Suddenly, there were two sets of jaws reaching out towards her, one on either side. This was the end. Gold Two was trapped. Cat closed her eyes, waiting for the crushing mandibles to close – and opened them again as Gold Two let out a howl of triumph.

Out of nowhere, a swarm of great winged silver creatures were plunging down like avenging angels towards the Eliminator. They reminded Cat of the gigantic manta rays of Earth's oceans, but these were strange and alien in form. As they swept down on the Black Widow death-machine, they spat crimson bolts of energy that cut through the Elimina-tor's armour like lasers, chewing great chunks from its body.

Eliminator screamed like a wounded animal. Its many jaws clashed again and again on empty air, and its long, sharklike body twisted and squirmed, trying to escape its attackers, but to no avail. There were just too many of them. Cat watched with triumph singing in her heart as, bit by bit, the monstrous machine was being torn to pieces.

The great, silver ray-like creatures curved round and swept towards Cat, where she circled in Gold Two with Jack and Gold One close by. From below, Eleni was climbing to meet them. There was no need to seal off the Shadowzone now, everything was all right. Then Cat remembered with a sick surge of misery that everything was *not* all right. It didn't matter if the Shadowzone was safe – the Hunter was gone. She would never see him again.

But what was this? Cat squinted her eyes against the dazzle of the silvery forms. There, riding the foremost creature was a small familiar figure. Cat gasped in astonishment. Despite her sorrow, she suddenly burst out laughing.

'Hey, guys!' Rom yelled. 'Are you all right? I brought the cavalry! How do you like these for aliens?'

CHAPTER FOURTEEN

KNIGHT
IN SHINING ARMOUR

All at once, everything was too much for Cat. So what if there were aliens? The loss of the Hunter was too raw and too recent to let her share in any triumphant celebrations. Without even a word to Gold Two, she hit her scuttle button, only wanting to get out of the Web and go home. She spun out, only saving herself in time from hurling her helmet savagely across the room. Instead, she stuffed it under the bed where she wouldn't have to look at the wretched thing. Flinging herself face-down on her bed, she cried until at last, worn out, she fell asleep.

When Cat woke she saw the late summer twilight outside her window, and a note from her dad on her pillow.

Taking the youngsters out for a burger. Thought I'd let you sleep, you look absolutely shattered. Too much Web-time! It's got to stop! Love, Dad.
p.s. Answer your calls!

He needn't worry about the Web-time, Cat thought drearily. Right now, I don't care if I never spin into the Web again! She bit her lip, determined not to start herself off crying again. Answer your calls, the note had said. Well, she supposed it would be a distraction.

Cat keyed up the data on her flatscreen. There were messages stacked up and waiting from Eleni, Rom and Jack –

and someone else, who had left no identification. Curious, Cat called it up, and nearly fell off her bed. There, on the screen, was the proud and lovely face of Miss Aldanar. The Sorceress had risked leaving the Shadowzone to contact her!

On the recording, Miss Aldanar shook her head in mock dismay, but her smile was kind. 'Cat, you little idiot. You forgot, didn't you, that in the Shadowzone everything is only data? What I programmed once, I can fix again. I've worked out some new access codes that will get you back.' By that time, she was speaking to empty air. With a wild yell, Cat was down on her hands and knees, scrabbling under the bed for her helmet.

Eleni's site had never seen so many visitors. Cat was there with her dad and her brothers and sister, Jack stood nearby with his parents and an amused-looking Anna, not to mention Rom and his parents who were managing to look both bemused and resigned. Eleni was there with her parents and Toula, her younger sister, whose eyes were shining with delight. Ariadne, the Webcop who had first met the friends during their battle with the Sorceress the year before, was also there, standing at the edge of the wall where the garden dropped down to the sea.

'I don't believe it.' The Webcop sounded stunned. 'Why *me*?' she added plaintively. 'First you wretched youngsters end up getting the entire Board of Directors of the world's biggest Web corporation arrested – and now this! Couldn't you have lumbered someone else with the job of convincing my superiors that the Web is full of aliens? They'll never believe me!'

'That's why we had to drag the folks along,' Rom said cheekily. 'If it had just been us, you'd have put it down to one of my practical jokes.'

Ariadne looked out across the peacock-blue ocean where dozens of silvery shapes hovered patiently above the calm ripples like sleek manta rays who had strayed, and were somehow swimming above the water rather than in it. 'I should be so lucky,' the Webcop said faintly.

Eleni, relieved that her plans had worked out, smiled to herself, and caught Cat's eye. Cat grinned, and made a thumbs-up sign. 'You ought to get a medal,' she whispered. In those last frantic minutes when the Shadowzone had been attacked, Leni had realized she could get data out, because the barrier had been breached. She had taken her chance, and dumped copies of all the Black Widow Eliminator files into the Webcop database. The authorities, discovering that Black Widow had developed a machine powerful enough to hold the entire Web to ransom, had just about fallen over themselves in their hurry to act. And while the Webcops swooped on Black Widow, Eleni and Miss Aldanar has used the brief breathing space to make a hasty repair of the interface, so that the Shadowzone and its rare and precious refugees could live as they had always done, in safety and in secret.

Ariadne was still peering, all amazement, at the aliens. At last, the reality seemed to be sinking in. 'This is incredible,' she murmured. 'Will they talk to me?'

'Talk?' said the irrepressible Rom. 'Ma'am, once you get them started, the problem is how to stop them!' He beckoned to the aliens, and one silvery, streamlined creature came towards them, swooping low over the incredible blue-green ocean. The alien hovered above the edge of the wall, shimmered, blurred, and changed its shape.

When the patch of glitter disappeared, there stood an odd-looking man in an antiquated white tail coat and a red turban with a long white feather. On his shoulder perched a gleaming, jet-black rook. The alien looked down and blinked. 'ExCUSe me – wrong SHape! I mean, wrong shape!' The second time, his voice sounded quite normal. If our sort of normal is normal for an alien, Eleni thought in a bemused sort of way. The strange form shimmered again. The white coat turned into silvery armour, and the turban became a silver helmet with a long red plume. The black rook

vanished, expanded, and became a white, winged horse so
utterly gorgeous that both the girls gave a kind of gulping
sigh.

The knight turned to Ariadne. 'I greet you,' he said
formally. 'My last form was known as the Swami, but in my
current appearance I am Galahad, a name suggested by our
friend Rom when he proposed this shape for me.'

Ariadne swallowed hard. 'I'm Ariadne.' The Webcop led
the alien a little distance away from the others so that they
could not be heard while they got acquainted. Eleni, Jack,
Cat and Rom reluctantly took the hint.

'Spoilsports!' Jack muttered. 'I want to know what they're
saying to each other.'

Rom laughed. 'I betcha Ariadne couldn't think of anything grand and quotable enough for the history sites!'

'Yeah, and she's embarrassed to let us hear her saying the
same old boring stuff that adults are always twittering on
about,' Cat added, her eyes sparkling with glee.

'We'll find out later,' Eleni reassured them. 'This is *my* site,
remember, and some of those insects in that flower bed are
bugs in more ways than one!'

Jack turned to Anna, who was aglow with delight as she
watched the scene. 'Once the news of the aliens gets out,
those Guardians of the Word won't have a leg to stand on,'
he said. 'Wait till they find out that their demons are really
beings from another world!'

The Game Designer nodded. 'I must admit, it's a relief.
Ariadne thinks the news will probably smoke the last of the
cult out of hiding, then maybe the designers can live in
peace again, with no more threats.'

'And now you can go back to work,' Jack prompted,
'because it was the aliens who were making people act
strangely, and not your programming at all.'

Anna's mouth fell open. 'I never said it was!'

'I know,' Jack said, 'but it was pretty clear that you thought
so.'

Anna laughed. 'All right, I give in! It'll be a relief to get back to work.' She sighed. 'If only I hadn't destroyed those notes for the Star Pirate game.'

Turning his face away from her, Jack allowed himself a secret, triumphant grin. When Anna got home, did he have a surprise for her!

Ariadne and Galahad were walking back towards the others, deep in conversation. 'Of course I will investigate,' the alien was saying. 'We would certainly have the *ability* to hide in people's minds and alter their actions, but my own lawmakers would disapprove most deeply of such a thing. Nevertheless, as *you* know all too well, there are always some who will bend the law, if not break it outright.'

'Well, it may not be your fault at all.' At Ariadne's words, the ears of the four friends pricked up. 'Black Widow, the ones who built that dreadful Eliminator you so kindly destroyed for us, have been experimenting along those lines. The previous owner practised all sorts of horrific experiments in mind control and we think her successors may have been continuing her work in secret.'

Cat could stand it no longer. 'Ariadne, you're right! Think of those nightmares they gave me, not to mention the way they mucked about with the wolf-program.' Suddenly realizing that she might give away too much of the secret knowledge she had discovered in the Merlin files, she shut her mouth quickly.

Ariadne lifted her eyes in a give-me-patience kind of look. 'Yes, all right, you meddlesome wretch. But that's Webcop business. It will all be investigated in good time.'

'Well, just remember to let me know what you find.' Cat refused to be squashed. 'As the owner of Black Widow, it's my business too!'

'Oh, help!' Ariadne muttered. 'Well, hopefully, by the time you're old enough to step into Miss Aldanar's shoes, I'll be ready to retire from police work!'

'Rom,' Anna intervened quickly, to keep the peace. 'Just out of interest, why did you suggest that Galahad appear in the form of a knight?'

Though it was impossible to blush in the Web, it was clear that Rom found the question very inconvenient. 'Er . . . I . . . it was a thought, you know. It kinda popped into my mind.'

'Perhaps I can help.' Galahad was smiling. 'I recall the conversation exactly. You described this shape, then you laughed, and you said it ought to please your friend as she seemed to have a thing for knights in shining armour right now.'

The rest of his words were drowned out in a furious shriek. 'Rom! You *pig!*' Even as Cat launched herself at him, Rom hit his scuttle button, but the sound of his laughter seemed to echo through the garden even after he had disappeared.

Two days later, there was no sign inside the Shadowzone that the place had almost been destroyed. The gaping rent in the sky had been sealed, and everything was peaceful. In Realworld, it was very early in the morning. Cat had been unable to sleep all night. In the end she had given up and spun in using Miss Aldanar's new secret access codes. She'd been driven out of her bed by a sudden urgent feeling that the Shadowzone was where she must be as soon as possible.

The green meadow, sparkling as always in the sunlight was deserted and peaceful. Nothing moved, and there was no sound, but Cat was confident that she had been drawn here for a purpose. She stood very still and waited. After a time, the door at the bottom of the tower swung open. There, on the steps, stood a slight, black-clad figure with sunlight glinting gold on his pale hair.

Cat let out a cry of joy, and ran – and the Hunter ran to meet her. He swung her around, hugging her tightly, both of them laughing and weeping with sheer happiness all at the same time. From the top of the tower, they heard a voice, and looked up to see Miss Aldanar, standing on the high balcony that ran around the edge of the glass dome. 'I told you I'd fix him, didn't I?' she called. 'Be well, my children!'

Jack spun into the Shadowzone, to emerge in the green

meadow by the glass tower, where Rom and the sleek, silver forms of half a dozen aliens clustered on the grass beside three twin-winged shapes from Gold Squadron. Jack was glad to see Gold Leader restored to its former splendour, and looking as though it had never gone down in that dreadful, screaming fireball. He was also amused by the fascination that the biplanes held for the alien contingent. The wanderers from another world had clearly spent the entire morning getting acquainted with the cranky little aircraft.

'They're getting on like long-lost cousins.' The voice at Jack's shoulder made him jump. He spun to see that while he had been watching the biplanes, the Sorceress and Eleni had come quietly out of the tower and were standing behind him. 'You wouldn't believe it, would you?' Miss Aldanar went on. 'The aliens find it quite difficult to make any distinction between real and artificial intelligence.'

Jack thought about it for a moment, struggling with the difficult idea.

'I suspect it's an effect of the Shadowzone,' Miss Aldanar went on. 'This place is different from the rest of the Web. Some of the constructs here have been able to go their own way without any outside interference for a very long time now. I think they've actually been evolving.'

'They're turning into real native inhabitants of the Web,' Eleni said in an awed voice.

Miss Aldanar laughed. 'Not until they actually start to breed, but you never know.' Her eyes twinkled. 'I wouldn't put it past them. The aliens have been giving them a lot of information.' She pointed to where two young armour-clad warriors, a broad-shouldered knight and a flame-haired woman archer, clearly refugees from another old game, were wandering across the grass hand in hand.

'Where's Gold One?' Jack asked, missing his special friend.

Miss Aldanar shrugged. 'One of them has been away, off and on, these last couple of days. The others just say it has urgent matters to attend to. You know how independent

they are.' She sighed. 'I'm going to miss Gold Squadron.
You'll have to send me news of them when I'm gone.'

'You really decided to go, then,' Eleni said. 'When are you
leaving?'

'In a day or two.'

'I think you're very brave.'

Miss Aldanar smiled at Eleni. 'Well, to tell you the honest
truth, I was getting a bit bored with being stuck here in the
Shadowzone all the time. Even with the Black Widow Board
gone, your friend Ariadne would take a dim view if she knew
I still existed. This is a much safer option for me and, you
must admit, it will be very exciting.'

Her eyes shone. 'Just imagine being the first one to
actually visit the alien world, even if it is only the inside of
their equivalent of the Web. They say my insights will be
invaluable, and that I can be a kind of unofficial ambassador
for the human race.'

'I'm glad,' Eleni said. 'And who knows? Maybe if you do a
good job, the authorities here will pardon you. After all,
having the aliens on your side will have to help a lot.'

'That's just what I told Cat,' Miss Aldanar replied. 'Poor
child, she was a bit upset when I said I was going. Still, if
everything works out, I hope you'll all be able to come and
visit me soon. In the meantime, she won't be alone.' She
gestured across to the green hillside beyond the tower, where
Cat and the Hunter sat, their heads close together, deep in
talk.

Jack hesitated for a moment, then took the plunge. 'If you
don't mind me saying so, do you really think it's a good idea,
Cat getting so, well, *close* to someone who doesn't even
exist? It's just not natural! As far as I can see, she's letting
herself in for a lot of heartache sooner or later.' He couldn't
keep the accusing edge out of his voice.

Miss Aldanar laid a hand on his shoulder. 'So is the
Hunter,' she replied, to his surprise. 'Jack, how can you
define *real*? He exists, he lives, and he certainly feels as much

as you do. In the battle he was willing to sacrifice himself in order to protect Cat. Is that not a very human reaction?'

The Sorceress met his eyes with a steady gaze. 'Jack, nothing in this world lasts for ever. Cat and the Hunter are making the most of their happiness while they can. Sooner or later, there'll be someone for her in Realworld, but she will always keep a place in her heart for her Shadowzone companion. Why should she not? And, remember, whatever may happen to her in Realworld, she will always have one faithful friend on whom she can depend inside the Web. She'll need that support, you know. She told me she's determined to take her place at the head of Black Widow as soon as she's old enough, *and* she's going to learn to run it as well as I ever did.'

Miss Aldanar smiled fondly. 'She'll do it, too. Of that I've no doubt. She's one determined young woman. But I know how demanding and difficult and lonely such a life can be. I'm glad the Hunter, at least, will be there for her.'

Suddenly suspicious, Jack eyed her narrowly. 'You programmed the Hunter in the first place. You planned this deliberately, didn't you?'

Miss Aldanar looked him in the eye, her face absolutely expressionless. 'I wouldn't waste time worrying about that if I were you, young man, because it's something you'll never know.'

Gold One circled above the glass tower and recognized her friend Jack talking to the Sorceress. She rocked her wings at him, and was happy to see him wave back in return. She wished she had time to skim down and take him flying, but she knew she was going to be pretty busy for the foreseeable future. With one last look down, she sped off towards the distant hills where a high grassy plateau rose up out of the surrounding meadowland. It was a perfect spot. She and Gold Leader had chosen it carefully – with a nice, flat, even surface for take-offs and landings, and that sheltering, grassy hollow nearby.

Landing smoothly, she trundled over to the sheltered dip,
her engines idling. As she approached, a high-pitched whir
of tiny motors rose expectantly. At the edge of the hollow,
Gold One looked down proudly at the four tiny Sopwith
Camels, each one of them a perfect replica of its parents.

AVATAR
PAT CADIGAN

This is for my son,
Bob Fenner
Gamesmaster, Bobmeister,
And most definitely,
The Man

CONTENTS

CHAPTER ONE

THE ACCIDENT

This will probably sound strange. I'm trying to do it fast. *Gotta*. I'm not in a hurry, I'm just lots slower than anybody else, even in this shorthand. Next time you're frustrated by something, try spelling out everything you want to say with the tip of your tongue on a surface you can't see. Sometimes letter by letter, sometimes word by word. You got to learn symbols – like code – for all the common words, and even some phrases. You have to trace the symbols with your tongue, just right. Then a voice a lot like yours used to be says them out loud. Takes some getting used to. I miss talking, almost as much as moving around. The next time you moan and groan about having to make an extra trip up and down the stairs or—

No. Sarah Jane says not to do that. She says it's unfair to use ordinary things as clubs on people. She—

She's special.

In the end, I have to say that even if what she did wasn't right, it was best for Sarah Jane.

Before I tell about how Sarah Jane fixed up my rig, I guess I have to tell about the accident. I'm going to make that short, if you don't mind, 'cause I don't like to talk about it. Maybe someday it won't bother me so much, but don't ask me when I think that'll be.

It was a stupid accident. Meaning, I was being stupid.

Showing off, being the big man because I'd learned to dive.
And that's as much of it as I remember firsthand. I was
standing at the end of the raft in the middle of the lake, my
arms straight out in front of me, preparing to dive. I was
looking at everyone on the shore, my parents, my little
brother Gary, lots of other people from our community,
families, kids, lots of my friends. I remember thinking how I
was going to show off my form and I remember (or I *think* I
remember) Sarah Jane standing near the edge of the water,
about to call out to me. It was nearly lunchtime; my parents
had waved at me to come eat something. I was going to dive
off the raft, swim to shore, and have some fried chicken.

The next thing I knew, I was looking up at a really white
ceiling and I couldn't feel *anything*. After a while, I started
hearing this gentle *beep-boop* noise, a lot like my mother's
extremely polite alarm clock (that's what we all call it,
because it wakes you so gently). Then a woman's face hove
into sight above me and I knew right away she was a nurse. I
was in the hospital, hurt worse than I'd ever been in my life.

When I understood exactly how I was hurt, I figured that
was probably the last time I'd ever feel any pain. But the Imp
in charge of Life's Practical Jokes, as my cousin Dee would
say, wasn't done with me yet.

Luckily, the Council of Elders decided in favour of high-tech
prosthetics before I had much opportunity to stare at the
ceiling, or the TV, and think about what being paralyzed in a
community like ours was going to mean. Plenty of people
couldn't have lived in Bonner Springs, Kansas, with all their
physical abilities intact – it just isn't the most exciting place
in the world. I knew kids who'd been born here, same as I
was, who took off for bigger and better places as soon as they
were of legal age. I'd thought about it once in a while myself.
I think everybody did.

It's not like you can't be comfortable here. Contrary to
what a lot of people Out There believe, we're not Luddites or
religious fanatics, and we do have indoor flush toilets and

electricity and television. Even cable TV, with remote controls for those who want them. The local paper has a hook-up to some news-gathering places on the Web, so we're all up-to-date on what's happening in the world, same as any other place. Maybe even more up-to-date, because current events don't have to fight their way through all that other stuff the rest of the world is draped in, all that Web stuff and artificial this and that.

Maybe that sounds like sour grapes, and maybe if I hadn't got a chance to try it all out, it would be. Sarah Jane always used to say, 'Don't knock it if you haven't tried it.' Well, I *have* tried that Web stuff, so I guess I can knock it if I want to.

Anyway, we're a community that simply believes in appropriate technology, and no more than necessary. It's true that a lot of us in Bonner Springs use horse- or mule-drawn carriages, or bicycles to get around, and there are very few motorized vehicles. That's simple enough – Bonner Springs is a small place, you don't really need a motor to get around. Hospital's got ambulances with regular old electric generators for emergencies. I was unconscious when I had my one and only ride in one, but my mother told me about it. She rode with me. It must have been pretty exciting, in a scary way.

We have school classroom-style, but we have computers and videos. For entertainment, we have theatre and cinema and old-style television. In fact, we have our own television station, where specially trained technicians re-format stuff from the Web for flat, non-interactive broadcast. One time, we even had the cast of *Julius Caesar – The Early Years* come out and visit in person. They were all curious as to how they'd look, and how the episodes would run. The guy who played Julius said he thought it was kind of nice just watching and not having to be in it, but most of the Roman senators said they couldn't get used to just seeing little images in a frame, and they missed having all the detailed textures and things to go with the story. And that set off Ms Evans, who teaches drama and literature. It didn't set her off right away. She waited until the next day and then let loose in class when we were going to rehearse a scene from the original *Julius Caesar*. True to Ms Evans' form, she had us doing it in a barn, because she said that would be more like the conditions the Shakespearean actors worked under, but she also had Gladys Brown playing Caesar and Sarah Jane playing Brutus, because she said it would help us understand Shakespeare's universality. I was a senator.

So, we were all waiting for one of Ms Evans' big lectures on Shakespeare's timelessness and all that and she suddenly started in on how there were plenty of textures and details in the real world if you kept your senses open, and anyone so jaded that they had to go in the Web— (*'Spin in,'* I heard Sarah Jane whisper behind me. *'You spin into the Web and spin out again.'*). 'Well, anyone that jaded might as well be paralyzed from the eyelids down, they could so little appreciate the world as it was.'

So weird that she said that, months and months before I hit that rock diving off the raft. Ms Evans came to see me in the hospital, and I'd wanted to tell her she sure was right, but I didn't have the speech rig then. After I got it, I was ready not only to set her off but join in some as well, only she never found time to come back after that. Funny how that works.

CHAPTER TWO

BACK TO LIFE

So that's how I ended up needing a whole artificial what'sit rig. I didn't hear till later how the Bonner Springs elders voted on it. They convened a special meeting at the Agricultural Hall of Fame (which is more interesting than most people think), and then they faxed the Department of Health, Education, and Welfare, and the Food, Drug, and Software Administration. In a month or so, they brought in all this stuff and wired me up. A therapist came in and helped me work on the communications part. By then, we knew everything I could and couldn't move, and she showed me how to use the tip of my tongue on a touch-pad, and drilled me on the shorthand symbols.

It was like learning a new language. Ms Mankiller – that was her real name – was a Native American, Cherokee and Kickapoo mix, from the reservation which is not too far from here. She taught all kinds of sign language, from traditional Native American to the American Sign Language, as well as a lot of the native languages. She was part of a general cultural project partly funded by the government to keep the old native languages from dying out. She told me that they weren't doing as well with that as they'd hoped, and I told her I wished I could help.

Made her laugh, but not in a mean way. Done wiping her eyes, she said she just thought it was pretty wild, me wishing *I* could help *her*. Couldn't think why, right away. When I did, I couldn't even show I was embarrassed. But maybe Ms Mankiller knew, because right away she changed the subject back to tongue-signing on the touch-pad.

We drilled letters and symbols, phrases, whole sentences, over and over again. After a few weeks, she started training some of the nurses and aides on how to drill me, to help me transfer my talking impulse from my vocal chords to my tongue-tip. That's what she said we were doing, anyway. Then one day, Sarah Jane came in to visit and I told her about it (using my cheat-sheet, which Ms Mankiller left clipped up in front of me on the display board). Sarah Jane thought it was pretty cool, said she wanted to help me, too. So that's how we started getting to be even better friends than we'd been already.

My other friends visited, too, don't want to make out like they didn't. Knew it was pretty dull stuff for them, though, and I couldn't blame them for not coming back. *I* thought it was dull, compared to my old life. If I could just go back and keep myself from diving off the raft and hitting that rock. Found out later it was one of the rocks the raft had been moored to. Mooring broke, raft drifted into a slightly different position. We'd all noticed it had, but hadn't thought anything. Somehow, though, the rock got moved, too. Currents, maybe. Funny things happen underwater.

Wish I could go back and warn myself. Wished it a lot more at first – all I could think about, sometimes.

Ms Mankiller and Sarah Jane thought up the remote together. Back-to-school season, I got all sad. Two favourite things: New Year's Eve, and the way we get real violent weather when we go back to school in the fall.

Didn't know how exactly I'd be able to keep up school – tutor, maybe. Figured they'd send someone with some videotapes and workbook software I could use with my tongue-pad. Day before school starts, Sarah Jane and Ms Mankiller came into my room at the hospital *giggling*. They got to be pretty close friends over the summer, helping me.

Figured they'd been shopping, but then Sarah Jane said, 'Hey, Max, how'd you like to go to school?'

Was pretty good by then with my new talking, and I tongued out how? You carry me piggyback? I didn't have a vocalizer then. The words appeared on a monitor screen next to my bed.

They looked at each other surprised, then looked at me. 'Well ... yeah,' Sarah Jane said. 'I mean, *kinda*.'

More equipment got brought in, and the next thing I knew, I was wearing those goggle-things and I was looking all around. Only *I* wasn't. Sarah Jane was. Had this little camera strapped to her forehead, and I could see and hear everything she could.

'But here's the *big* surprise, Max,' she said. 'Say something.'

Like what? I tongued – and was startled to hear my own voice saying, 'Like what?' just as plain as, well, my old, real voice.

Ms Mankiller looked into my eyes, except she was actually looking into the camera on Sarah Jane's forehead. 'You're going to school,' she said. 'And other places. Sarah Jane will take you to school. Your family will take you home, to the movies, to plays, picnics, church, wherever. And your other friends will take you different places. If you're real good,' she said, '*I'll* take you to the reservation and introduce you around.'

So *weird*; how she could look so deep at me, like she was looking into me, and she wasn't even looking in my direction. It made me dizzy.

Found out later it was Websickness. I was having it right away, because I wasn't controlling the movements. We started out with just Sarah Jane taking me to school. Those first few days, I could hardly stand it sometimes. Everything'd be fine if Sarah Jane was just sitting in the classroom looking at the teacher, or a video or something. But then she'd forget and turn to look at something real quick – to the side, or worse, up or down – and it would be like I'd gone from just sitting to being on some wild amusement park ride, a crack-the-whip or a roller coaster (if anyone outside of Bonner Springs still knows what those are). One time, I actually fainted, and they thought I'd had a seizure.

For a while, it looked like we'd maybe have to give up. Then Sarah Jane came up with the idea of her wearing goggles too, and adding a glove, so when she handled something, I would feel more like I was handling it, kinda.

That was *really* weird. Sarah Jane wearing a camera on her head that would feed her the same image of the outside world as I got, but that she could have seen *without* the camera or goggles. I thought it was too weird to work, but it wasn't.

We *both* got Websick. Then Sarah Jane figured out how to move more carefully, and we started getting *attuned*. It was real spooky, that part.

Not at the time, but later, when I thought about it. At the time, it was just a relief. I guess it happened because she was the body for both of us, but I sort of took over the seeing and balance, in a way. Don't know exactly how to put it.

The trouble started when Sarah Jane tried to help our other friends – well, *my* other friends – learn to use the cam/goggle/glove rig. Some of the kids got Websick right off, which upset the elders. But the kids who really liked it and wanted to use it a lot upset the elders even more. The Web and its technology had no place in our lives, the elders said, and we had no place in the Web. That was inappropriate technology, it was crippling to the spiritual nature of human beings, it was one of the things that caused us to get so far away from real things that we messed up the earth's ecology and places like Bonner Springs were all but blowing away in the wind, and what didn't blow away was roasting to death in the summers.

And for a couple of days, I stared at the ceiling and thought about messed-up ecology and wondered how the elders would like to trade places with me. I *could* have stared at the television, but it was my way of protesting.

By then, Ms Mankiller had gone back to the reservation, but they sent for her and asked her if she could come up with any ideas. I'm not sure why they sent for her, or even who did, exactly – that was never clear. Some people said her turning up was a complete surprise. Anyway, she helped figure out a list of rules and stuff so that I could use my rig and not contaminate the Bonner Springs community ideals. And the first rule was that, except in an emergency, only Sarah Jane or my parents could use the remote rig. Ms Mankiller insisted that Sarah Jane stay with the rig because she was a close friend, and it would be better for me to go to school with my friend rather than my mom or dad. And she was already trained.

Sarah Jane had to promise in a court of law, under oath, that she wouldn't let another person use the rig unless it was some kind of horrible emergency. So did my parents.

It turned out that my parents were mostly glad to have Sarah Jane wearing it, because it made them both real uncomfortable – not so much Websick as just, well, unhappy. It was something they didn't believe in, and it was almost too hard for them to get around that even for my sake.

You're probably wondering about Sarah Jane's parents. Well, we all wondered about them. Bonner Springs never claimed to be like the Garden of Eden, with a lot of perfect people. Sarah Jane's parents were both, well, drunks. Most of the time, they didn't know where *they* were, let alone where she was. I'm not sure they even noticed when she went to stay at my house, with my family.

It was only supposed to be temporary, of course, though my mom was thrilled as anything. None of us knew how much she'd wanted a daughter. Maybe even she didn't know till Sarah Jane moved into the guest bedroom.

Ms Mankiller went back to the reservation, kinda.

CHAPTER THREE

ME AND SARAH JANE

Attuned. Attuned to Sarah Jane.

Never gotten so close to anyone in my whole life. OK, maybe thirteen isn't a very long life, but it's *my* life. Spend it trapped in your body instead of just living, and you'll see how time has a way of stretching endlessly, even when someone else is carrying you around with them.

Other people's waiting is hard. I mean, when Sarah Jane and I used to wait for something together, it was bad enough. But, now, if Sarah Jane is waiting for something just for her, like sitting in a movie theatre waiting for the movie to start – wow. It's almost as bad as just staring at the ceiling in my hospital room.

Then one day I thought: when am I going home? Why are they keeping me in the hospital?

That was a bad time. Because I tried to get Sarah Jane to find out and tell me, and she *wouldn't*. Thought she was just being mean till she told me it was one of the things she wasn't supposed to get involved with.

We were having this conversation at lunchtime, outside. It was early November and the weather was really mild. They told us in school that early November in Bonner Springs used to be real cold, and it would even snow, or there would be ice storms that would bring down power lines, make pipes freeze and even burst. Hard to picture now.

Anyway, we were talking about her finding out why they

wouldn't send me home, or why my mom and dad wouldn't just come and get me.

'I'm not supposed to get *involved* in that, Max,' she said, in that stubborn Sarah Jane way she had. She could make her voice sound real old when she did that, too. Old at *seventeen*, for crying out loud. And thinking of Sarah Jane four years on at seventeen made me feel funny deep inside, so I tried not to think about it. Now, it's even harder.

So, I said to her, just as a joke, that she could come up and break me out herself.

'But don't you *feel* like you're out, Max?' she said.

'Not the same. I know the difference,' I told her.

It had been a long time since Sarah Jane had come to see me, in person.

Weeks.

No, *months*. Since just after Ms Mankiller had got us the rigs.

Realizing that, I got awful sad. Sarah Jane felt it, too, right through the rig, even though stuff like that isn't supposed to be possible. I think maybe at that point, some things had already started to happen, and neither of us knew about it – the beginning of what happened later, but I don't want to get too ahead of myself, even if I do have to tell this quick.

Right after I realized how long it had been since Sarah Jane had seen me in person, it occurred to me I hadn't seen *myself* for even longer.

Seeing yourself is something you take for granted. Look in a mirror, see yourself. Do it whenever you want ... unless you're like me.

When Sarah Jane took up wearing the rig, she looked in mirrors sometimes, and I started taking her reflection for granted – Sarah Jane in goggles and glove, with the cam on her head. Almost as if it were me. I didn't really think about *me*, my own reflection. I figured I must look the same as I always had.

The nurses and aides took care of my body, I knew. They told me I was fed in a special way, which I thought was like intravenous, liquid food through a needle in my arm. Glad I couldn't feel that – hate needles! They'd work my arms and legs and turn me so I wouldn't get bedsores. But there was a lot I didn't understand when I started having this conversation with Sarah Jane about wanting her to come to the hospital and *look* at me, so I could see myself.

She kept changing the subject and changing the subject and then we started arguing. I got scared, because I understood that Sarah Jane didn't want to look at me. Not because of what she'd see, but because of what *I'd* see.

Don't ask how I knew that. Part I mighta figured out because I knew she'd already seen me. And when she came up to visit on her birthday, nobody took a picture of us together.

I thought: *Uh-oh – what if I got my legs cut off or my arms?*

Or was it even worse than that? But … like *what?*

Like maybe my face got torn off—

Thought of this real old book Mr Feder talked about in the World Conflicts section of history class: *Johnny Got His Gun.* Guy in a twentieth century war got hit by a bomb. Blew off his arms, legs, his face, made him deaf and blind. It was fiction, but things like that had happened to people, Mr Feder told us.

What if that happened to me, I thought.

Wouldn't let Sarah Jane rest then. In the book, after he figures out what happened, the guy taps out a message in code with his head on the pillow, over and over, till the doctors figure it out. I didn't have to do that – and couldn't have anyway – but I just kept sending Sarah Jane the same message over and over with my repeat button: *Johnny Got His Gun. Johnny Got His Gun. Johnny Got His Gun. Johnny Got His Gun.* Knew she'd understand, too – she had that history class with me.

She knew I wouldn't give up then. She could have gone to somebody, but it wouldn't have done any good. I'd just keep pushing the repeat button – *Johnny Got His Gun, Johnny Got His Gun* – till they either had to take the rig away from me or give in. If they took it away and then gave it back after a while, they'd just get the same thing again – *Johnny Got His Gun, Johnny Got His Gun.*

Sarah Jane knew that because we were *attuned*. We were so

attuned that I could feel when she gave in, before she even asked me when the best time was to come up to the hospital so we wouldn't get caught.

'Because they told me not to,' she said. 'Everybody told me never to let you see.'

'Even Ms Mankiller?'

'Ms Mankiller said to help you even when the doctors said not to help you. I didn't know what she meant, but maybe this is what she was talking about, kinda.'

'Maybe it kinda is,' I said, and told her that the dead spot on Sunday afternoon just before dinnertime was good. The staff was changing shifts and everyone who'd been working all Sunday would be draggy and bored, and the ones coming on to work Sunday night would be thinking about other things and not paying close attention.

Lie in a hospital bed without moving twenty-four hours a day, you get to know the routine without having to study.

She told me that the best thing to do would be for her to come up bareheaded – goggles and cam off, stashed in a bag just in case anyone did notice her. That's smart, I told her, so that's what she did.

But it was so *hard*, cut off! Solitary confinement boosted a hundred times. I tuned the audio on my goggles to music with my tongue control but it was like I couldn't really hear it over the roaring silence.

Not like *complete* silence, of course. I could hear the background noise everybody hears. But after having the company of Sarah Jane's talking, it was just too quiet. I'll remember this for the rest of my life, I thought: silence is the loudest noise of all.

Sarah Jane tried to prepare me. Told me that it wasn't like in the movies, where you just see someone lying still in bed. I could feel how she wanted to say more, even ask me not to make her do it, but I wasn't letting her get out of it. She put on the goggles, the cam, powered up, and looked straight at me.

I didn't realize she was looking at *me* right away. I thought it was somebody else, someone sharing the room that I didn't know about. But then I knew from the way Sarah Jane was breathing – it was almost as loud as the silence had been – that it *was* me.

Looked myself over real good but in the end, I couldn't see much of myself in the half-contorted body. Or that face. That really awful face. One eye was closed for good, some kind of muscle thing. When you're paralyzed, you don't just go limp – some muscles contract. Others stretch. It's not handsome. You wouldn't want a picture.

If they brought me home, I thought, Gary'd have to look at that every day. *He* might get used to it, but Mom never would. Then I saw the tube running from the equipment next to the bed, under the sheet and becoming some weird shape I knew was plugged into my stomach. How they fed me.

Another tube, plugged into my throat. How I kept breathing. At least the machine's quiet, I thought. If it had wheezed or something, the sound woulda driven me crazy.

'Happy?' Sarah Jane said after a bit.

'I didn't do this to be happy,' I said. 'I did it to *know*. Now I do. You don't have to look any more, Sarah Jane.'

Hesitated before looking away from me. 'Do you want me to look at you again?' she asked. 'I could sneak up and look at you again, if you wanted.'

'You'd do that?'

'Sure. If it was important to you.'

''K.'

'You want me to?'

'Yeah.'

'Oh.' She took a breath. 'Um, when?'

Took a breath myself. 'I'll, uh, I'll let you know.'

We never talked about it again.

CHAPTER FOUR

SARAH JANE
CROSSES THE LINE

Don't know why I felt better after that. Like, *really* better, about as cheerful as I ever remembered being just day-to-day before the accident. Wait, maybe I *do* know. Seeing myself showed me that if I had to be like that, I was lucky to have the remote, and Sarah Jane to be my remote body. It meant that every day, my hearing, my vision would be filled with things outside myself. I would be able to think about anything and everything except the way I really was.

And that made me laugh deep inside, because it meant that I was actually using the rig exactly the way the Elders said was wrong – to escape reality so completely that it was a denial. Except I was escaping from reality *into* reality.

Of course, Sarah Jane picked up on the fact that I was laughing inside. There was something about that rig, like I said. Made us closer than if we'd been handcuffed together for real.

That worried me, too. I kept waiting for the Elders or somebody to start talking about how improper it was, a boy and a girl together so much. Communities like ours, there's no shortage of prudes and dirty-minded, self-appointed guardians of the public morals. Weird, though – nobody said boo. Couldn't for the *life* of me figure out why, either.

Anyway, I was laughing inside sometimes and worrying inside other times, as the mood took me. And I knew that Sarah Jane was picking up on the differences – I was sensing her sensing me. And when I sensed her, she sensed that, too. It felt kind of like being two tennis players who once they started hitting a ball back and forth to each other they never missed and never stopped, because they couldn't. They were locked into the game, until, well, who knew? Until there was no more ball, maybe?

Pretty soon, I could feel all this was building up between us – this no-words communication we were getting from each other and not doing anything about. The feelings were piling up and something needed to be done. Except, I couldn't even figure out how to describe what was going on and even if I could have, it was supposed to be impossible. There's no room in the Bonner Springs community for things like telepathy or clairvoyance. That stuff was classified as occult, and our law said anything occult ran the risk of exposing people to the demonic.

Now, this is the part of life here where most outsiders hearing about it get this fixed, overly polite smile while they're wondering when we had our last witch-burning and do we speak in tongues when we cast out devils and so forth. I admit, it's a pretty old-fashioned sort of belief. Maybe it *is* too extreme to say that mental telepathy is a tool of the devil, which is pretty much what the law says in a more dignified kind of way. Most people don't even believe in the devil any more, and I mean, a lot of people here in the community don't. I don't believe in the devil, when the sun's out and all the lights are on.

But the sun's not always out, and all the lights aren't always on ... even when they are, if you get my drift. It's not like I'm thinking the devil is something like the bogeyman in the closet or anything. That would be so easy. Too easy. The devil doesn't live anywhere but inside every human mind. It has to be that way, because then we always have free will to choose what's good over what's bad.

You get into the supernatural – the occult, things like telepathy or seeing the future – well, that's a violation of all the natural laws anyway, without bringing anything like the devil into it. Cheating's what it is.

Well, that's the way I was thinking then, and I won't deny it or apologize for it. Those were my values. Can't really say I've changed a whole lot. Not really.

At the end of February, the Arctic Express paid us a visit and dumped about a foot of snow in the space of a day. It was great, like something out of real old movie or news footage. I kept begging Sarah Jane to keep watching it come down and she was laughing and saying I didn't have to ask because she just wanted to look at it forever.

We went to every window in the house, upstairs, downstairs, back, front. Then Sarah Jane got real daring and went outside with me. Of course, you're not supposed to get the rig wet, so she covered everything over as much as she could with scarves and her coat and all. We stood out under the cotton-white sky for a few minutes and I saw snowflakes coming down onto my face – our faces – our face. Blurred the lenses, of course, but Sarah Jane wiped them clean with the edge of a tartan scarf and took me back under the shelter of the porch.

The wind had blown a lot of snow up the steps and across the old warped wooden planks so that the stuff looked like miniature sand dunes done in white. Sarah Jane dug into one with her mittens on.

'You're ruining it,' I said, before I could stop myself. Sarah Jane and I had resolved to always try to be extra-*extra* polite with each other because of how close we had to be. (Although, now that I think of it, we'd somehow decided this without actually talking about it.)

'Sorry, didn't mean to,' Sarah Jane said. 'I'm trying to make a snowball.'

She patted the stuff into something that was shaped more like a cross between a lemon and a giant stuffed ravioli.

'Try circling your hands around it,' I said. 'Like, I don't know, like petting a cat into a round ball.' I stared hard at her hands, trying to imagine that they were my hands, trying to feel the cold wet mittens around them, trying to feel the ball of snow to make it rounder.

'Keep doing that,' Sarah Jane said as her hands worked the snow.

'Keep doing what?' I asked her.

'What you were doing. Concentrating, I guess. I don't know. Thinking? Keep *thinking*.'

'Why?'

'Because if you keep thinking, in another moment, I'll—'

I don't know what she was going to say, what words she could have possibly found, because in that following moment, it happened, whatever it was. Only for a moment, barely a moment, that fast. But so *vividly* that I never doubted, *never* doubted, that it had really occurred.

I was wearing her hands the way she was wearing her mittens. I could feel them covering my own, moving for me, feeling the texture of the snow and the cold of it, the wet, the way it crumbled some places and packed down on others on that snowball. For a moment, about as long as it might take you to breathe in without thinking about it, I was moving again.

Sarah Jane had been crouched down on the porch. Now she stood up and stared at the sky.

'Sarah Jane?' I asked, a little bit scared. I was afraid that maybe I'd done something wrong.

'Did you feel that?'

She didn't have to ask, I thought, so why was she?

'I just want to make sure,' she went on, as if I'd actually said it, 'that I really didn't imagine it.'

'If you did, then I must be imagining you,' I told her.

'OK,' she said. I heard/felt her take in this shuddery deep breath, but when she let it out, she gave a little laugh. 'OK.'

'I guess we're gonna have to talk about this, ain't we?'

'This?' she asked.

'Don't make believe you don't know what I mean.'

'I wasn't going to,' she said. 'I just—'

'What?' I asked after a real long minute or so. 'Are you thinking it's bad or something? Do you want to quit, train somebody else?'

'No,' she laughed. 'No. What it is, is, I know you think it's the rig somehow, all by itself. But it isn't. It's something—' she stopped and took a slow breath. I waited. 'It's something I did to the rig.'

'That *you* did?' Now she was surprising me. 'When did you have time to do anything?'

'When you were asleep.' She looked down at the bad snowball sitting in the middle of her wet mitten and let it drop onto the toe of her boot, where it fell apart. 'I did this thing to it – I did something wrong.'

She was waiting for my reaction, I realized. Waiting for me to get it, first, of course, and then waiting for my reaction to it. And suddenly, I was going slow, my mind was like doing underwater ballet or something. Maybe it was just wanting to take the time to think it through without missing a step. Anyway, I took my big slow mental steps towards what she wanted me to know. Something wrong she'd done, while I'd been asleep. Must have taken her a while, she could only work maybe an hour or so after I went to sleep, in order to get enough sleep herself.

Something *wrong*. She'd done something wrong, with the rig. That was important, it wasn't something wrong that she could have done without the rig. And the only thing I could think of was—

'The Web?' I said finally. 'You been on the Web?'

'I spun in,' she corrected me. 'Spun in, and spun out again.'

Well, now we had to talk out loud, because it was like I had to pull away from her to think this thing through.

'You spun in and out using the rig?' I said slowly.

'Yeah. Using the rig.'

It seemed like I couldn't get my slow-motion mind any further than that. Finally, she burst out, 'Are you mad at me? Do you think I'm bad?'

'Well … no. No, I'm not mad at you, Sarah Jane, and I know you're not bad,' I said, feeling very uncomfortable. Not because I was lying to her – I really *wasn't* mad at her, and I *didn't* think she was bad, but I was scared of what was going to come next. Because I just knew that whatever it was, nothing was ever going to be the same again.

'I had to,' she said, and I knew that she was going to confess everything to me just like Catholic kids confess to priests, only with a lot more gusto, if you see what I mean. 'I just *had* to. Ms Mankiller gave me the idea. She even told me how.'

'Why'd she do *that?*'

'Because I begged her to.'

'Oh.'

'Max, I'm— It's like I'm dying here. This place is killing me. I can't stand it. I don't belong here. I feel trapped. I feel just the way you must feel. Locked in. Paralyzed.'

'Well,' I said. 'I used to feel that way. I don't any more. Since we got the rig, and you agreed to—'

'Yes, I know. Don't you see? I'm helping you be free, or at least free-*er*. And so, for me—' she stopped.

'The Web?' I said after a bit. 'That's for you what you are for me?'

'You're so smart, Max,' she said and laughed a little. 'I always said you weren't like any other dumb old boy.'

'Well, that's a relief,' I said. 'I always thought it took brains to be me.'

She was supposed to laugh, but she didn't. 'I want to show it to you,' she said. 'I want to show you the Web.'

'I figured you did.'

'It's *important*, Max. It really is. I have to make you understand. I have to make *everyone* understand.'

The snow was coming down harder now and the sky was getting darker.

'Everyone?' I said. A snowflake landed on one of the cam lenses and melted, blurring our vision; I waited for her to wipe it clear.

'Everyone here, in the community. In Bonner Springs.' Any minute, my mother or father was gonna come out and tell her to get inside before she froze her giblets. 'They all have to realize, we're being cheated, deprived, short-changed.' She paused, and I guess she was waiting for me to say something, but I didn't know what to say. 'It isn't fair!' she burst out.

The front door opened and my dad peered at her through the screen. 'Sarah Jane, honey, I think you'd best come in now. Wind's picking up.'

'Switch on my external speaker so I can tell him it's my fault,' I said, but she wouldn't do it. Just went inside and watched a movie on the TV.

CHAPTER FIVE

I CROSS THE LINE
WITH SARAH JANE

I fell asleep in the middle of *Gone With the Wind*. I always do. Those big old movies douse me like a candle. Sarah Jane was always teasing me saying that I snored, but I don't think I did. I don't think I could, being on a respirator.

Anyway, I had this real vivid dream that I was in *Gone With the Wind*, in the movie. Even though I corked off in the middle, I dreamed I was walking around the big plantation, at the picnic with a plate of food in my hand. Like always when I dream I'm walking on my own, I could feel my leg muscles working. That is, I was real conscious of how they would stretch and contract. I could feel the terrain under my boots, big old riding boots like I've never worn in my life.

I'd wandered pretty far from the house so I turned around and headed back toward it, and I knew I was gonna miss my cue. I was supposed to be up there for the big scene when war's announced and all the men ride off to enlist in the Confederate Army. I started to run but, this being a dream, I couldn't get any closer to the house. I kept running, thinking any minute the director was gonna pop out of the bushes and holler about me not being where I was supposed to be.

Even though it was a film set, I couldn't see any cameras. It was as if I really was down South back in the 1800s. *Gone with the Wind* was made long after the Civil War had ended. Movie-making was still new and was a clumsy old business with lots of unwieldy equipment, cameras, lights and reflectors, microphones and camera booms, and loads of assistants running around fetching and carrying. But there was nothing like that, just women in big hoop-skirts floating back and forth across the grass, accompanied by a lot of Clark Gable clones.

One of the women in a pretty pastel blue skirt turned toward me. It was Sarah Jane, smiling at me. I found if I focused on her, I could actually make some forward progress. So I just kept looking at her while I trudged up the broad expanse of back yard.

'You did that real well,' she said when I reached her. 'You got the hang of it right away.'

'Well,' I said. 'I wanted to be in the movie. Couldn't pass *that* up.'

She laughed. 'Is that what it feels like to you?'

'Is that what *what* feels like to me?' I asked her, not understanding. I looked around, trying to see where the director and all the cameras and everything were. If I hadn't missed my cue after all, and it looked like I hadn't, then I didn't want to make the director mad by talking on the set when I wasn't supposed to.

Something was all screwy with the set – well, either the set or my eyes. I couldn't see it properly any more, it was like anything I wanted to look at would slide away from my eyes like oil skating on water. It *was* my eyes, I thought after a moment; they felt so heavy, I was having trouble opening them. If I kept them closed, I could see better—

'Max,' said Sarah Jane from somewhere close by, 'where do you think you are?'

'*Gone With the Wind*,' I said.

She laughed, and it sounded like drops of water hitting bells or crystals. 'You're gone,' she said, 'but not with the wind.'

'Sarah Jane—' I stopped. the antebellum (period before a war) South was disintegrating around me. I was standing in front of some kind of big ... *thing* ... and Sarah Jane was standing right next to me, watching me wake up. 'I was asleep,' I said.

'I know. *Now.*' I saw her move in my peripheral vision but I couldn't yet get my eyes to focus. 'I didn't realize you'd conked out. You were talking and answering me just like you *were* awake.'

'I do that sometimes,' I said, still trying to make my eyes work. 'I mean, I used to do that. I'd make my mother so mad. She'd come into my room in the morning and tell me a whole list of chores and errands I had to do. I'd say yes to everything and promise to get it all done. I'd wake up after she'd gone downstairs and not remember any of it. Guess things aren't any different now, in that area.'

I'd been about to say something else when my eyes finally focused on my feet. I registered that I was awake ... and I was *standing*.

Instant vertigo! I was flat on my back staring up at a blue featureless nothing that might have been a sky. Sarah Jane hove into view like the nurse had all that time ago when I first woke up in hospital. Except this Sarah Jane looked more like a paper doll replica of her.

'Well, you can sleepwalk,' she said cheerfully. 'That's a start.'

I used to sleepwalk – back when I *could* walk. Well, a long, long time before the accident, when I was little, I did it more often. I hadn't done it much in the year before the accident, though. The doctor always said it was something kids grew out of mostly, but trauma of some kind can jolt people back into it. Maybe that's what I'd been doing, sleepwalking the only way I could.

Bad luck – soon as I knew what I was doing, couldn't do it any more. Sarah Jane hovered over me and I saw her tap her wrist with her fingers, like she was typing.

'OK,' she said, 'a guide frame is going to come up in the lower part of your vision.'

There was a click I felt more than heard and, sure enough,

there was a transparent line drawing taking up the lower third of my field of vision. There was a little arrow cursor in the middle of it, just like on my old computer, and all these commands, like: forward, back, stand, sit, raise right/left arm, jump, duck, turn right/left, fast, slow, and a bunch of others. The frame scrolled as well, another thing that was like my old computer. At least I was working with something familiar here.

'Your tongue tip is the cursor,' she said. 'All you have to do is put it to the touch pad and you activate the guide frame. Put the cursor on raise right arm and see what happens.'

I saw this flat, paper-doll arm rise just as a real arm would have, if it had been me lying on the ground lifting my arm. I didn't feel anything. Even though I'd known I wouldn't, I was disappointed anyway.

Sarah Jane's flat hand took my flat hand. 'Stand up,' she said. 'Look for the command.'

I touched it with my tongue and up I went, smooth as chocolate sauce.

'Wow, that was graceful,' Sarah Jane said.

'Yeah, maybe I'll become a dancer in here.' I looked at the big something in front of us. It looked like a pile of blocks abandoned by a giant baby. 'This is it, isn't it? The Web, I mean.'

'That's right, Max. It's the Web.'

'How'd you do it?'

Sarah Jane laughed, and I heard music in it. Nice effect. 'It's actually more of a problem *not* to do it. Ms Mankiller showed me. Everything is hooked up to the Web, one way and another, including us. Bonner Springs has the feed; it comes with the cable and the telephone. We just don't use our codes to access it. Ms Mankiller showed me how to find out what the codes are just by using the telephone. You dial a number, and you get these tones. I recorded the tones and entered them into the rig software.

'You and I were already transmitting back and forth to

each other. It wasn't that hard to add another point to communicate with. We've got wireless access.'

'Wow,' I said. 'That's like – you're a genius, I guess.'

The paper doll shrugged. Sarah Jane was actually a very modest person but I could tell how pleased she was with herself. Not from the way she looked, but from the way things felt between us on the rig.

'It wasn't that hard. Anyone could figure it out. Probably people have before now. For all we know, there could be a whole secret society of Web junkies in Bonner Springs. Maybe we'll even run into them.'

'I guess anything's possible. But I'm wondering, um ...' I hesitated. 'I don't want to seem stupid or anything, but what are we supposed to do now? This isn't all, is it?'

'You know it isn't, Max.'

'Well, yeah, but we don't have all the fancy equipment, those suits and helmets and things.'

'We don't really need them for access,' Sarah Jane said. 'Though it would be nice to have the whole experience. But to get in, all you need are the right codes. And a little courage.'

Of course, she could feel my hesitation. Part of it was wondering if I could manage a virtual body with just the tip of my tongue. The rest was wondering what would happen if someone caught us. The Elders had made such a big deal out of it, what with making Sarah Jane take an oath in a court of law and all. On the other hand, they'd left us pretty much to ourselves. No one came around checking on us or anything like that. Bonner Springs isn't that kind of place, and I guess they figured my parents would keep us in line anyway.

The whole thing about the community in Bonner Springs was that it was all voluntary. We were all here because we wanted to live this way, not because we were ordered to, or felt we had to because of some religious kind of thing. So if my parents, say, had caught me and Sarah Jane on the Web, I guess we'd get talked to about what we wanted. Not that we could just leave Bonner Springs and go off somewhere – we were just kids, after all. But if we could have gone to a boarding school Outside, or lived with relatives or friends, I think my parents would have considered it. Well, for me. I kept forgetting that they couldn't really make any decisions like that for Sarah Jane, because she still had parents legally, even if they hadn't seemed to have noticed that she wasn't living with them any more.

'Are you afraid of getting caught?' Sarah Jane asked me finally.

'Not really,' I said. 'Well, maybe a little. I mean, I don't think we'd get arrested or anything, but my parents might feel hurt, or guilty. And I was raised – I don't know how to put it. I was raised not to want it. I don't see what good it can do. The world out here has so many problems, it feels like a sin to turn your back on it and go play in something that's just a hyped-up theme park.'

'The Web connects the world,' Sarah Jane said. 'We can go around the world in an instant if we want to. We can talk to other people anywhere on earth, trade ideas, learn new things. The way we are right now, we're cut off. *We're* the ones turning our backs on the world and pretending that we live in a simpler time. Bonner Springs is the theme park, not the Web.'

'I don't know about that,' I said, feeling shaky under the force of how she felt. 'I'd have to think about that. I mean, if you want to talk about being cut off, I'm an expert.'

'I know. That's why I wanted to bring you here. Just give it a chance. Let me show you what you're missing.' Her paper-doll face smiled at me; it looked just like her school photo. 'And then if you don't want it, that's your choice. You don't get to knock it if you haven't tried it, OK?'

'OK,' I said, understanding at last that this was the same thing as my transmitting *Johnny Got His Gun, Johnny Got His Gun* at her until she gave in and did what I wanted. I owed her one.

'Thanks, Max,' she said. 'Now are you ready to go bat?'
Go bat?

CHAPTER SIX
BIZARRE BAZAAR

To tell you the truth, I was a little bit scared, just because it was the Big Bad Web. My parents used to whisper to each other, when they thought I couldn't hear, about strange, dangerous people who used to troll the Web looking for people to hurt. I didn't actually think anyone could hurt Sarah Jane or me while we were in the Web, but I did wonder if a strange, dangerous person could find out where we lived and come after us for real.

Of course, Bonner Springs is a long way from anywhere, so it would have to be someone really nuts, and that's not the kind of stranger who would pass unnoticed around here. Few strangers of any kind do. So I suppose I didn't have a whole lot of real stuff to be afraid of – just the unknown. And it wasn't the unknown any more for Sarah Jane, so I'd just have to trust her.

We 'did a bat'. Everything turned blue and there was a musical tone sound (more like a chime I thought) and we were in.

All I had to do to move forward was keep the cursor on the word *forward*, which changed to an arrow icon. It was like floating in a dream. It felt sort of weird – as if I should have felt like I was walking. I could feel something in myself – in my mind – kind of trying to reach out and get hold of the feeling. But that was too much to concentrate on.

Sarah Jane's paper-doll self had changed slightly. Her dark

brown hair was a little longer and shinier, and she looked a bit older. Well, not older, exactly, just more ... more finished. Less like she was growing into an adult and more like this was how she would always look. I wondered how I looked, but there didn't seem to be any mirrors here.

Here: the place Sarah Jane had taken me to was a great big space like a cross between a cathedral and a palace, in which a circus had merged with a gypsy camp and an Egyptian bazaar on New Year's Eve.

'Good Lord!' I said, staring up at the vaulted ceiling. It seemed to be about a mile up, and there was silver mist floating around everywhere. From time to time, little pin-points of light flashed out. Shadows moved behind it, like maybe there were moving pictures on the ceiling.

Abruptly, something enormous ran out of the mist up there, moving up and down along the vaults. No mistaking that movement – it was a spider, a tarantula the size of a sports car. I looked at Sarah Jane, too frightened to speak.

But she was smiling up at the thing like it was a cute furry animal. Then she put two fingers to her mouth and whistled.

'Wow,' I said, 'where'd you learn to do that?'

'Ms Mankiller,' she said, in a real casual way, as if she saw Ms Mankiller every Thursday and Saturday or something.

I was gonna say something else to her, but all of a sudden, the sports-car-sized tarantula was dangling in front of us on a silver thread. That made me suspicious.

'Tarantulas don't spin web,' I said.

'What can I say? I'm a lousy tarantula, but I'm a pretty good spider.'

'I don't know about that, either,' I said after a moment, feeling a little queasy looking at those hairy legs. 'Spiders don't talk.'

'I only said, *pretty good*. I didn't say *the best*.'

Sarah Jane giggled. 'This is my friend, Max, that I was telling you about.'

'Pleased ta meetcha, Max,' the spider said, and offered me one of those legs, like a dog offering a paw. 'How ya doin'?'

I couldn't help it. I drew back. The spider laughed.

'Just kidding, Maxie. You can't actually touch me, I'm information and miscellaneous. Anything you wanna know, you ask me, or any of the other eight-legged beasties you see running around.'

I looked up at the ceiling again. Now it was *swarming* with them up there. I wanted to put my hands over my head and run, except I was too scared to tongue the cursor through the positions quickly enough. 'Uh ... where is this?' I asked finally.

The spider laughed. 'Well, you're not in Kansas any more, Toto.'

'How original,' Sarah Jane said. 'I'd never have thought of *that* one.' She winked at me.

'Hey, I'm *informational*,' the spider said. 'All I know is what I've been told. Not an original thought in my head, such as it is. Everyone here has heard all my jokes, what can I do?'

'Well, you still haven't told me where I am,' I said. 'Only where I'm not.'

'Good point, kid. I can see you're going to do well in here. You know that place Oz, over the rainbow?'

'Yeah?' I said cautiously, thinking, *Oh, God*, not that. It's not like I have anything against *The Wizard of Oz*, it's just that I've seen it about a billion times.

'This ain't it. Welcome to Bizarre Bazaar.' The words *Bizarre Bazaar* appeared briefly in the air in front of me, the letters bright blue flames. The spider laughed again. 'I had you going there for a moment, didn't I?'

'Oh, I don't know,' I said, looking over at Sarah Jane.' I didn't think she'd take me to any place so corny.'

For the next hour, Sarah Jane and I moved through Bizarre Bazaar, taking in the sights, occasionally accompanied by the tarantula, who would pop up – or down from the ceiling – to offer little bits of information. For example, the Romany people were the shifting cast of an historical recreation run and paid for by a university somewhere on the east coast.

The people playing the gypsies came here to blow off steam, or gear up for a session in the recreation, or gear down after doing one. They had staked out an area that wasn't quite a camp and wasn't quite a bar-room, but was some weird combination of the two. That was Bizarre Bazaar itself, in a nutshell – some weird combination. Sometimes, I could have sworn we were outdoors; other times, I knew for certain we were in the biggest one-room structure ever built. Sometimes, I thought maybe it was more of a canopy than a complete building. The surface we walked on – well, the surface below me, that I could see Sarah Jane's paper doll walking on – was sometimes earth, and sometimes cement, and then when I'd look again, it was marble or tile. For a while, it was thick glass over the clearest, cleanest water I'd ever seen. It was filled with giant mantas and big sharks of every variety, including the extinct ones like the great white and the hammerhead.

That really got me. I had to stop and take a closer look. Using the cursor, I managed to get right down on the glass, as if I was lying on my stomach with my nose pressed up against it, trying to see as much as possible. I couldn't take my eyes off the mantas. A lot of them were even bigger than the tarantula, and I'd never seen anything move so gracefully.

'That's actually a transmission from a place in New Zealand,' Sarah Jane said. 'A really amazing aquarium where they keep all of these different species.'

An octopus crawled through the water, its tentacles furling and unfurling as if it were dancing. 'They've got great whites in New Zealand?'

'Well, no. Not yet, anyway. They're working on a way of cloning them, but they don't have it yet. The great whites are images inserted into the transmission. The images are programmed to avoid the real creatures, so they don't have eels and blow-fish swimming through them and ruining the effect.'

'Pretty neat,' I said, and then felt like a real weenie. *Neat*, for heaven's sake; how about a real strong term, like *nifty?*

Sarah Jane sensed my wincing. Of course. 'In here, when they want to say that something's really, um, great, they say it's *eight*. As in the number eight, not like *ate dinner*.'

'Well, no,' I said. 'Because then they'd have to say *eaten*, wouldn't they?'

I was surprised when Sarah Jane burst out laughing about as hard as I'd ever seen her. 'What?' I said. 'It wasn't that funny, was it?'

It took about half a minute before she could wind down enough to speak. 'It is if you realize that it's the first time you've made a joke since ... since a very long time.'

'You sounded like the old Max,' she said after a bit, 'always cracking jokes.'

I wanted to tell her that it also could have been that this was the first time since the accident that she'd dared to laugh at any jokes I made. But all I said was, 'Maybe.'

Sarah Jane was real patient about letting me watch the fish and all. Of course, she got her own back.

Man, it must have been the biggest flea market in the whole world. Some of the voices I overheard called it a *swap meet*, and others a *car-boot sale*, which was really puzzling. What kind of special boots did you have to wear in a car nowadays? Sarah Jane said it was every market and mall that had ever been, multiplied and divided and added to again and again, past and present and, who knew, maybe even future, too.

'No one's ever found where it ends,' she said dreamily as we stood at the entrance to it.

'Now how can that be?' I asked. 'Nothing can go on forever. Not even in here.'

'No?' she said. 'OK, maybe not. The grains of sand on every beach in the world, there's a finite number of them, too. But no one's ever counted them all.'

'All right, I see what you mean,' I said. 'But I gotta tell you right now, I sure didn't think you were bringing me into the Web to go *shopping*.'

Sarah Jane laughed again. 'Did you realize, you're talking much easier in here?'

'Fastest tongue in the midwest,' I said.

'It's the vocalizer,' she said. 'It's started to anticipate you and learn your speech patterns. And it can do that more easily in here, because there's more power for it to draw on, more memory.'

'That's good,' I said.

'Yes, it *is* good. So it can't be wrong to be in here, can it? And it's wrong of anyone to keep us from it?' She hesitated at the entrance to the market, and then moved on toward the circus.

'I didn't grow up with this, so I don't know,' I said, following after her. 'Life seems normal to me without it. Well, when I had a normal life, anyway.'

'That's my point,' she said as we passed a fire-eater. He obligingly huffed out a stream of fire at least five metres long. I tongued my cursor to applause. 'You can no longer have anything *like* a normal life in Bonner Springs, or out of it. It's not fair to keep you from accessing the Web. It's like forcing you to be locked in.'

'It's not that anyone's keeping me from doing anything,' I said as she stopped in front of the freak show. I felt a shiver – a real shiver – go down my spine. Freak shows are not the most comfortable places for me. I guess they're not supposed to be comfortable for anyone except the freaks, but still. 'My parents chose their way of life. I had no choice, but it's the life I know, and I'm willing to give it a chance.'

'It's not giving *you* a chance any more,' she said hotly. 'You've got *no* chance if you stick with what they want.'

'I don't see it that way,' I told her, wondering what she was getting so upset about. We'd already talked about how she felt like Bonner Springs was killing her. It wasn't like she had to convert *me* just because she'd told me how *she* felt.

Or did she? I zoomed in on her paper-doll face, as if that

was going to tell me anything. But then something really weird happened. Instead of just stopping at her face, I kept on zooming, right into her left eye, right into the pupil until all I could see was black.

It was dizzying. I made myself look down – or where I thought was down – and tried to get my bearings so I could reverse out of there and back to a reasonable distance from her. This was so weird, I thought. Then I wondered, was it something that was even supposed to happen?

Suddenly, there was a big, bright light, like someone had just turned on the sun, and I felt something that was definitely not me, and not Sarah Jane.

'Get out,' it said. 'I was here first.'

CHAPTER SEVEN

BAD CONNECTION

For the second time, I was suddenly flat on my back, staring up. The ceiling seemed further away than ever, and was getting even more distant as I lay there. The paper-doll figure of Sarah Jane appeared over me. This was getting to be a habit, I thought.

'Oh, dear, you're Websick,' she said. 'I should have known better than to keep you in here so long on your first time.'

'I'll be all right,' I said. 'Help me up—'

'No need,' she said. 'We can scuttle.'

'What?'

'Get out. Exit.'

'But—'

I'd wanted to tell her we didn't have to leave yet, but we were already out.

'Sarah Jane, what happened to me back there?'

I was speaking into darkness and silence. It must have been real late at night. Maybe Sarah Jane was changing into her pyjamas and getting ready for bed, so she had the visual turned off.

'Sarah Jane?' I beeped for her attention. 'Are you there, or are you still in the Web?'

Still no answer.

'Come on, Sarah Jane,' I said, getting nervous. 'Gimme a holler. Even just a shut-up-I'm-busy.' I waited some more. 'At least turn on the lights?' The silence stretched and the darkness seemed to get deeper and deeper, as if I were slowly sinking into some kind of nothing. 'Sarah Jane, you're kinda scaring me, which as you might guess is not something I care to admit to.' I tried a laugh but it sounded even more fake than my vocalizer laugh usually did. 'Come on, now. I'm not kidding around any more. This is awful, Sarah Jane, to be in the dark like this, can't move, can't call out—' I shut up for a moment. 'Are you hurt, is that it? Are you – did you fall, or – or faint?'

Something was in the dark with me.

Except ... where *was* I, exactly? Was I still in the Web, somehow still connected to it? Was I in some weird, shorted-out place halfway online and halfway off?

Power failure? Maybe all of Bonner Springs was blacked out?

That had happened from time to time, especially during the thunderstorm season, but even when Bonner Springs was flat-line, so to speak, the hospital never was. It had emergency generators that kicked in almost before you even noticed there was something wrong.

I searched around for my usual control screen overlay, thinking it should come up any second, but there was nothing. Just me and the darkness.

And something else. Unless I was imagining it. Or dreaming it. Except I knew for sure I wasn't dreaming.

'Sarah Jane,' I tried again. 'Please? I don't want to stay like this. It's *Johnny Got His Gun* land.'

The vocalizer wasn't great on expressiveness. It wasn't a dull, monotone robot voice. Like I said, it was pretty much like my voice, and could do a lot of things a human voice could. The tone would rise on questions, and fall for answers, but strong feelings just didn't come across. I might have been talking about the weather. That made it sound really horrible, now that Sarah Jane wasn't answering.

I don't know how much longer I waited. When you hang in the dark like that, seeing nothing, hearing nothing, thirty seconds could be an hour or a day, or a week. And I didn't know why I couldn't hear anything, except maybe the hospital was real quiet and I was too upset.

Suddenly there was a bright light. It was like fear punched a hole in the chest I wasn't supposed to feel any more. I was scared it was whatever that thing was in Sarah Jane's eye—

Get out. I was here first.

The light dimmed and I was looking into Sarah Jane's face from below. She had put the cam on the bedside table in her room.

'Well,' she said. 'How did you like it?'

'Like *what?*' I said. 'Being alone in the dark?'

'No.' She looked mildly surprised. 'You mean, when we came out?'

'I could do without the period in limbo,' I told her, wishing like anything that my vocalizer had a setting for angry. Didn't she have *any* idea? We were supposed to be so attuned—

Get out. I was here first.

'Oh, that. You were just Websick.' She smiled down at the cam. It was like looking up at Mount Rushmore. Sarah Jane usually kept the cam at eye-level if she talked to me when she wasn't wearing it. 'You probably still are, a little. So everything's going to seem a little strange for a while. Don't worry, it will go away.'

'Sarah Jane, come down here closer to the camera,' I said.

She obliged without hesitation, kneeling down in front of the bedside table. 'Like this?'

'Closer,' I said, focusing on her left eye.

'OK. How's that?'

'Can you get any closer?'

'I don't think the cam will focus any closer than that,' she said. 'Why? What's up?'

I hesitated. 'I thought ... I thought you had something in your eye.'

She stood up again and turned away, waving a hand dismissively. 'Oh, you're just Websick. It'll pass.'

But I knew it wouldn't. Sarah Jane and I were no longer attuned.

It felt awful.

Sarah Jane wore the camera and goggles just like she had before, just as much, but I felt cut off, almost as bad as I'd felt right after the accident. I wasn't seeing things the same way with her. It was practically no different to watching TV. The All Boredom Channel – all boredom, all day, all night.

The worst part, though, was that Sarah Jane didn't seem to notice.

No ... no ... that's not quite right, either. Sarah Jane had changed and didn't know it.

Was that possible? I kept asking myself. When you ask yourself a question over and over, eventually, you're bound to get an answer: *Not for a human!*

Get out. I was here first. Remembering it was like hearing it again.

What *was* that? An hallucination from being Websick, like Sarah Jane kept insisting? Was Sarah Jane the one who was Websick? Or was this something else entirely?

I was asking myself all the questions because I wasn't talking much to Sarah Jane, or anyone else. Watching the world go by on the goggles, I began thinking that I understood how a bank security camera felt.

Then I began thinking that maybe Sarah Jane understood that, too. Sarah Jane as she was now, anyway. Because, as far as I could tell, that was all she was doing – watching. Like, surveillance.

March came and good weather hit as suddenly as the blizzard had in February. Sarah Jane just couldn't seem to hold still. It wasn't that she was fidgety or nervous, just on the move constantly. It was like watching out of the window of a train that never stops, goes too fast when you want to be slow, and too slow when you want to be fast.

It was even more like a carnival ride that I couldn't get off.

Or rather, I could, and sometimes I did, to watch TV, or read a book. The Bonner Springs library donated a subscription to their DiscoText collection so I had free access to everything from Shakespeare to DC Comics. That was pretty cool, actually, and I wasn't the only one who thought so. I overheard my father say that lying on his back with an unlimited, free library was his idea of a great vacation. I had to agree, with one condition – I'd get to say when the vacation ends.

Anyway, disconnecting from Sarah Jane was OK for a while, but I'd gotten used to being 'out'. I didn't want to go back to staying in all the time.

My father's remark rubbed me up the wrong way, even though I knew he wasn't being deliberately insensitive. It really grated because I wanted to say to him it might make a great vacation but not a great life – except I couldn't. It was something I shouldn't have heard. Sarah Jane had been spying on him and my mother, kind of. She'd started doing that a lot.

What I mean is, she did a lot of listening and watching when they didn't know she was there. They'd think they were alone in the living room and be talking about me, or Gary, or even Sarah Jane. They wanted to start adoption proceedings, and it was going to be expensive. Or my mother would be depressed about what had happened to me and feel guilty because she didn't like seeing me the way I was in the hospital, but she still wanted to hug me. My dad would talk about how much he missed doing simple stuff with me, like tossing a football around, or us watering the yard and the trees together, and how I wouldn't ever know what it was like to go to my first school dance with a girl.

See, it wasn't usually anything bad that I'd hear – we'd hear – but it wasn't meant for anyone else but the two of them. Our hearing it was wrong, and I knew it. But I kept connected to the cam because I wanted to find out what she could possibly be up to. This wasn't anything like Sarah Jane as I knew her. I had a feeling that pretty soon, somebody, probably Sarah Jane herself, was going to need me to be like a witness.

Or something.

CHAPTER EIGHT

SARAH JANE
V. THE WORLD

Now, I know what you're thinking, even if we're not *attuned*, ha ha. I mean, it's probably so obvious now. But you have to remember where I lived and how I grew up and all – what kind of community I lived in. I mean, the world was full of fantastic things for us in Bonner Springs, but not the same kind of fantastic that you'd find in the Web.

And that was another reason why we chose to refrain, or abstain, or whatever you want to call it, from the Web. I have to keep saying 'we chose' about all of it because, later on, there was a lot of stuff in the news about how the Bonner Springs elders wouldn't allow people to access the Web or to play computer games or drive cars. That was all a bunch of hooey. It's like no one can understand that there could be a community of people who'd agreed on a code they wanted to live by, but didn't force anybody to stay who *didn't want* to live the same way. We didn't force anyone to attend religious services or donate all their belongings to some guru, and we didn't go door-to-door Out There, trying to persuade people to burn their goggles or suits or repent or whatever.

But Sarah Jane was a minor, and while my parents were responsible for her in a way, they weren't her legal guardians. And her parents were really hopeless. Her father had disappeared again, and her mother had been sent to a special clinic in one of our sister-towns in Arizona to dry out – or rather, to see if she *could* dry out. So it was up to the elders in Bonner Springs to take charge of Sarah Jane's welfare.

But that was later when the elders got involved. Right then, it was just me and Sarah Jane.

Anyway, whatever was going on, I really didn't tip to it right away. I really couldn't have even *imagined* the truth. I realised later that if I'd been Gary's age, seven going on eight, I probably would have gotten it sooner, maybe even right away, because little kids aren't as convinced about what's impossible and what isn't.

I thought people like Ms Evans were not only right about the Web being a corrupting influence, but that they didn't go far enough. It wasn't necessarily an evil place, but it sure had a way of bringing out the worst of human nature. Sarah Jane had never been one for sneaking around listening in on private conversations. And the way she was treating me—

It wasn't like it was mean, but, like I said, we weren't attuned any more and she didn't seem to care. It was like we'd never been attuned, like she'd forgotten. For maybe thirty seconds, I wondered if Sarah Jane might have gotten embarrassed and uncomfortable about being that close to someone, especially a boy. Then, when I remembered how she was spying on my parents, I decided that she probably wasn't all that torn up about personal privacy.

When she wasn't doing that, she was on the move. Walking everywhere, looking at everything. Spring break came and she walked from one end of Bonner Springs to the other, north to south, east to west and then on the diagonals. Like someone had sent her out to map the place. She only stopped to look at stuff in people's yards, their gardens or birdbaths, kids' toys left out, stuff like that.

One time, Sarah Jane saw the mail carrier delivering letters and she followed her, watching how she'd open each mailbox, slip the letters in, then raise the rod with the little red flag on the side of every box to signal there'd been a delivery. That wouldn't have been so bad, but after about a block, she started opening the mailboxes and taking out whatever was inside. She'd shuffle through each bundle of mail and then put it back before going on to the next box.

'Sarah Jane!' I said. 'What do you think you're doing?'

She didn't answer me, just kept shuffling through envelopes. I amped up the volume.

'*SARAH JANE!*' I blared, and didn't care when she flinched.

'*What?* I heard you the first time, you don't have to blast me.' She put envelopes back into the mailbox and went on to the next.

'What are you doing?' I asked her.

'What does it look like?' That was when I noticed the way her hands were moving. So efficiently, like she'd been sorting mail at the post office for twenty years. It wasn't like watching a kid's hand do something.

'Don't play games now,' I said, really irritated. 'You're looking at everybody's mail. Why?'

'Why?'

She moved to the next mailbox.

'Yes, why? You know it's wrong.'

'I do? It is?'

'*Yes,*' I hollered. 'You know you can't take mail out of someone else's box, that's a federal offence! You can go to prison, or have to pay a big fine. Or rather, my parents might, because you're living with them. And because I'm kind of with you, they could nail me as your accomplice and I'd be in trouble, too.'

'That doesn't sound right,' she said, pausing at an envelope with lots of flowers all over it. 'Why would any of that happen? It's not like I'm opening it or destroying it. I'm putting it back.'

'But what are you *doing?*' I had to force myself to lower my voice, or every nurse on the floor would be running in to see what was up. 'What do you *think* you're doing?'

Her laugh grated. It was like she'd forgotten how and was trying to make a laughing kind of noise to make up for it. 'I'm *looking* at this stuff.'

'But *why?* What's with you, all of a sudden, that you're doing stuff like this?'

She stopped again to look at a postcard from Texas. 'What are you talking about? I've never done *this* before.'

'Yes, you have. You've gotten real nosy all of a sudden,' I said. 'You listen in on my parents when they don't know you're there, you've been poking through everyone's yards and looking at stuff. Any minute, I keep expecting you to start looking in people's windows, for crying out loud—'

Immediately, her head turned toward the house she – we – were standing in front of. She put the mail back in the box and went into the front yard.

'Stop it!' I hollered.

She flinched again. 'If you keep hurting my ears like that, I'm going to kill your sound.'

'Sarah Jane, you get out of this yard and go home right now!' I said, and this time, *I* flinched, because I sounded just like a stereotypical schoolteacher in an old movie.

'Why should I?' she said, sounding not so much offended as genuinely curious, like she couldn't imagine what my problem was.

'Because you're really being, um, *foolish.* People don't do this, Sarah Jane. It's against the law to go through people's mail and peek into their windows.'

' "Against the law." ' She said it like she was tasting the idea. '*The* law?'

'Sarah Jane—'

'Which law would that be, *the* law? Is that the law of gravity? Second law of thermodynamics?' That laugh noise again. '*Ohm's* Law? Murphy's Law?'

'Stop,' I said. 'Just please stop. I don't know what's up with you right now, but I think we should go home and talk. A *lot.*'

She sniffed. 'You want to stop, then *you* can stop. Go do something else.' She moved toward the front window of the house.

'*Now* what are you talking about? How am I supposed to do that?'

'Like this.'

She cut the connection. I couldn't believe it. Sarah Jane had never done that to me. Except for the way she'd left me in the dark and the quiet after we'd come out of the Web, she had never shut me off. And she knew how upset I'd been. Didn't she?

I waited for the goggles to clear so I could tune in the TV or call up something from the library. Not for entertainment, but so I could throw myself into something else for a while to take away the bad taste of the whole rotten experience. Get my mind clear so I could try to figure out what to do. Or if there *was* anything I could do about Sarah Jane being so weird. Sometimes when you throw yourself completely into some activity, it lets your thoughts settle and ideas come easier.

It took a long time for the goggles to clear. When they finally did, I realized I wasn't going to be throwing myself into a TV show or a book or anything like that. Sarah Jane had already done that for me; when she had cut the connection, she'd thrown me into something else.

She'd thrown me into the Web. Alone.

CHAPTER NINE

FLYING SOLO

'Yo, Maxie!'

The tarantula dangled in front of me on a silvery thread, revolving slowly.

'Glad to see you decided to come back.'

There was that click, and the guide came up in the lower half of my vision. That was a relief. But then I looked closer and saw that it had changed some. The symbols all looked a little different. There was nothing that said *exit* or *quit* or *goodbye*.

'Are you the same one?' I asked.

'Well, *actually*, much as I would hate to admit this if I were capable of emotion which I'm not, spiders are not what you'd call the last of the red-hot rugged individualists. What one of us knows, the rest of us know. It just isn't always dialed up to the fore.'

Whatever *that* meant. I let it go and tried to think. But Bizarre Bazaar wasn't exactly the sort of place that encouraged concentration. Not that kind, anyway.

Bizarre Bazaar had changed, too. Oh, the vaulted ceilings almost lost in the mist were still there, and the place was still the biggest room full of marvels in the history of, well, anything, I guess. But there was lots of new stuff, and the stuff I'd already seen was all re-arranged.

'If you're looking for something in particular,' the spider said, 'I've got to warn you, Bizarre Bazaar just doesn't come with a map. You come here to get lost, if you see what I mean. So if there's something you want, you should just ask me, and I'll see if I can hunt it up for you. But also – and I hope, Maxie, that you're not averse to a little constructive criticism here – you need an extra eyepiece on that thing.'

I'd been scanning the place looking for something I couldn't put into words. Now I turned back to the spider. 'A what?'

'Extra eyepiece,' said the tarantula. 'You got no binocular vision there.'

'Huh?'

I wouldn't have thought of a tarantula as patient, even a fake that was actually an infomercial, or whatever it had told me it was last time. 'For some reason, you are not using two eyes. I can help you with that.'

'You can?'

'Want me to show you?'

'OK.'

It was like the goggles blinked, or maybe more like a shutter in a camera taking a picture. And then everything looked *better*. A lot more like it was really there, and not like something I was watching on a monitor.

'What did you do?' I asked.

'Put a correcting input on your visuals, so that you get binocular vision. Now you got depth perception like most people. What do you think?'

'It's great,' I said, feeling ridiculously happy in spite of everything. I wondered if it was a software thing I could keep after I logged out – spun out – so I could use it on the rig with Sarah Jane. And then everything came back to me and I felt like an idiot for messing around with Web toys when something really serious was going on in the real world.

'Something else?' asked the spider.

'Yeah. Only – I don't know what it is or how to ask for it.'

'I can't help you there,' the spider told me, still cheerful. 'Maybe you can find a sage in here.'

'A what?'

'We got mystics, we got philosophers, we got fortune-tellers, Gypsy and non-gypsy, we got mad alchemists, magicians, oracles, astrologers, tarot readers, servants of the *I Ching*, and I think there's even a substitute maths teacher somewhere giving a short course in how to use statistics for games of chance. That's gambling to you, which is something you should not even attempt to do around here, I am required by law to mention. And there's a medium who claims to be able to send messages to the spirit world—'

'Send a message,' I said. 'That's what I want to do. I want to send a message. But not to the spirit world. More like e-mail to the real world.'

'The *real* world? Which world is that?' The tarantula stared at me for a moment. 'You mean your Realworld. Whatever world I'm in is the real world.'

'Have you been in other worlds?' I asked, not even sure that I knew what we were talking about.

'Don't know. Real is real is real. Don't worry about it. You want to send e-mail?'

'Yeah. I think – yeah. That'll work. I hope.'

The spider raised two legs and did a tarantula-style impression of whistling between two fingers. I was afraid to ask it if it had learned this from Ms Mankiller.

'You whistled?'

A guy about eighteen years old had popped into existence on my left. He was wearing a marathoner's tank top and shorts. The number on his shirt was 1. His curly yellow hair was covered by something that looked a lot like an upside-down metal soup-bowl. His running shoes looked like someone had put every hot athletic look for the last fifty years in a barrel and stirred it all up with an eggbeater, and then added weird little wings to the heels. While I watched, the wings flexed themselves and stretched, like they were getting ready.

'Hermes?' I said.

'Got it in one, Maxie,' said the tarantula.

'A scholar,' said the guy and bowed. 'Hermes I am, ready to take your message.'

That was so weird. I didn't remember seeing Mount Olympus when I'd been here before. Of course, that didn't mean anything. It wasn't like I'd been here long enough to see everything. 'How do I give it to you?' I asked him.

'Just tell me. I'll remember.' Hermes smiled and twirled his caduceus like a baton. The snakes hissed, but didn't seem to be upset for real.

'OK. I guess. Anyway. Dear Ms Mankiller, Hi, this is Max in the hospital, I really need to talk to you about something that's happ—'

'Hold it, Maxie,' said the spider. 'You don't need to do that.'

'What are you talking about?'

Hermes vanished, and a bolt of fear went through me like lightning.

'You don't have to e-mail Ms Mankiller,' the spider said. 'She's here.'

CHAPTER TEN

WE ARE NOT ALONE

'I hope you do not feel betrayed by me,' said the crow. It was the biggest crow I'd ever seen, about the size of an eagle, and its voice was a bit scratchy and out-of-tune, but not unpleasantly so. This was Ms Mankiller in the form of her totem animal. I didn't believe this bird was her right away, but after we talked about the time she had spent training me to talk in the hospital, I had to admit it really was her.

'Why would I feel betrayed?' I asked. We were sitting in one of the break areas on the fringe of Bizarre Bazaar. This was where you went if you got to feeling overloaded with all the colours and sounds and fireworks and acrobats and whatever else was in here. With my new binocular vision patch, I couldn't stop looking round. I could hardly manage to get a complete sentence out on the first try. So Ms Mankiller gave me a code to take me instantly to what she descrbed as a chill-out room. I didn't notice any change in temperature (but then, I wouldn't). It didn't seem to be anything more than a lounge with big, comfortable-looking chairs and sofas, nice pictures on the walls, subdued lighting and soft background music. There wasn't any ice or snow, which was too bad. I'd been hoping for a blizzard replay. I could probably find that someplace else in the Web, though, I thought. There was probably a virtual Antarctica, come to that, with icebergs and penguins and snowmen that never melted.

I realized my mind was wandering again. 'I'm sorry,' I said to Ms Mankiller. 'I guess I'm not too good at this.'

'Well, this is no place for a beginner,' she said. 'Sarah Jane should have been more patient. She should have walked you through an orientation session.'

'I thought this place was so regulated,' I said. 'I thought it was really strict about where kids could go and how long you stay and all that.'

'It is.' A crow doesn't really have a very expressive face, but Ms Mankiller's avatar managed to look amused. 'It's just that you seem to be invisible to the hierarchy.'

'How's that again?'

The crow stretched its wings and tucked them in again. 'You're in here not-quite-legally. But it's not-quite-illegal, either, so for the moment, the system is ignoring you ... however, that's not the only reason you can go wherever you please.'

Go wherever I please? Oh, if only!

'Certain areas and levels of the Web have become ... less clear than they used to be. Out of focus, but not so much to raise an alarm or trigger a diagnostic routine.'

'I'm sorry, Ms Mankiller,' I said, watching a mandala on the wall opposite go through a slow and pretty gorgeous shift in its colours. 'I just don't understand, I guess.'

'The Web has been ... there is ... oh, boy.' The big wings unfolded again and beat the air briefly. 'Did you ever hear the expression, "We are not alone"?'

' "We are not alone," ' I repeated, mystified. 'You mean, like, arguments for the existence of angels or Gods, or other supernatural beings? Or aliens in UFOs?'

'Aliens in UFOs,' Ms Mankiller said, and I had this crazy idea that we were teaching each other phrases in English. Repeat after me: *We are not alone. Aliens in UFOs.* 'Did you ever think that maybe when aliens – extraterrestrial life, that is, just to make sure you know exactly what I mean – that when these beings came, that they might not come in spacecraft or flying saucers or, indeed, even in bodies?'

I began to feel dizzy. Then I replayed what Ms Mankiller had said in my mind – I think – and I realized she had said *when* and not *if* about aliens coming to earth.

'I'm glad you're not afraid of heights,' Ms Mankiller said. We were both crows now, and we were perched on what she said was a handsome simulation of the Triboro Bridge in New York City, circa 1982, watching, alternately, the sun going down in the west and the night coming up in the east. I wasn't sure that it had ever really looked this good in real life, with the sky so clear and the stars coming out to twinkle like diamonds, but I wasn't about to criticize. 'Maybe there's some of my people's blood in you.'

'Why?' I asked. My wings unfolded and folded again, adjusting for something. Balance maybe. I wished I could have told Ms Mankiller that it felt different being a crow but the truth was, it didn't. Not for me. I couldn't feel anything any better as a crow than I could as a paper doll, or whatever I'd been in Bizarre Bazaar. But that was just physically. Mentally, I sure did like it better. What a way to travel! And boy, it sure beat all that bat stuff and steering myself around with the guide panel. Of course, I wasn't doing a whole lot of flying on my own, exactly. What I had was an automatic virtual crow body, where Ms Mankiller had set the destination for me and kicked the autopilot into go.

I couldn't *feel* the lift under my wings when we first took off, but at the same time, I got that thrill, the kind you get on a roller coaster, or a really fast elevator. I felt like yelling for joy, like *yeehaw!* And suddenly, I heard this great big *Caw! Caw!* come from my direction – something had registered my feelings in that virtual bird body, and expressed it for me. That idea would have scared me if I hadn't been in the Web. Don't ask me why. Maybe it's the idea of a virtual bird body being attuned to me like that.

Ms Mankiller had taken me for a long, head-clearing flight over a landscape that looked pretty much like real land, except for the fact that all of the colours were wrong – too many, too bright, and not the ones you'd see for real. But it was beautiful, and so was the sky. My bird body worked just fine – I had a sense of the way it moved. But as for feeling, I might as well have been a balloon on a string attached to Ms Mankiller's beak.

She said the Triboro Bridge was one of her places to go and think things out.

'I know some people from certain tribes – Algonquin, Mohawk, mostly – who are descended from men who built and maintained this bridge and others, as well as many of the skyscrapers,' Ms Mankiller said. 'They had no fear of heights, and they were as surefooted on the high steel as they were on the solid earth.'

'I don't know,' I said. 'But I like it fine.'

'Are you comfortable?'

'I guess.'

Ms Mankiller's crow head tipped to one side in a way that was so human I almost laughed. 'You guess? You don't know?'

'I don't feel anything,' I told her. 'I mean, I wish I did, because this is so cool, and I'd like to tell you it felt good. But I can't lie about that, and I won't try. I like it, but I don't feel it.'

'I didn't mean physically. I mean, emotionally, are you relaxed? Are you comfortable, or uneasy?'

'Both.'

Ms Mankiller's head tipped the other way, and I started thinking that maybe a bird face was more expressive than I'd given it credit for being.

'Well, it *is* both. I'm worried about Sarah Jane. But at the same time, it's great being a crow for a while. It helps.'

'That about sums it all up,' Ms Mankiller said. 'The human condition. We find things that help, though we don't let go of our worries.'

'Well, I just can't stop worrying about Sarah Jane. I told you, back in Bizarre Bazaar, what she was doing, how she was spying and snooping and she couldn't see anything wrong with it. And then cutting me off like that. Not just cutting me off but sending me in here without even asking if I wanted to go. What happens if someone in the hospital finds out what I'm doing right now, that I'm in the Web? What if they catch Sarah Jane looking in someone's windows, or looking through their mail like it was addressed to her? What else is she going to take it into her head to do?'

'This is, indeed, a worry,' Ms Mankiller said. 'If I were you, I would be almost out of my mind, I think. But the biggest part of your worry is what you do *not* know.'

'Well, yeah. Like, I don't know what's gotten into her—' I stopped.

Get out—

'What's gotten into her,' I repeated.

I was here first.

'What's—' I couldn't say anything else. The Web, I thought. Was that it, the Web had gotten into her?

'It must be very confusing for you,' said Ms Mankiller. I saw the wind playing with her feathers, couldn't feel it playing with mine but I knew it must have been. 'But I do want you to know that in fact, you actually can stop worrying about Sarah Jane.'

'If that's what you think,' I said, feeling really irritated now, 'then you don't know me as well as I thought you did.'

'I mean, I know more about this than you do,' Ms Mankiller replied. 'And I know that Sarah Jane is all right. She's in no danger at all.'

'Well, just how do you know *that*?' I demanded.

'Because I have seen her several times a day, every day, since she took you on your first foray into the virtual.'

'What? How? *Where?*'

'Here,' said Ms Mankiller. 'Sarah Jane is safe and well and right here. In the Web.'

The last sliver of setting sun disappeared and left us in a twilight that was too dark.

CHAPTER ELEVEN

SARAH JANE?

As far as I know, crows do not fly at night. I'm sure no expert on birds, but when you live in Kansas all your life, some things just sink in, and knowing that crows aren't nocturnal is one of them. So I was not crazy about being perched on this bridge under the stars. I still wasn't afraid of heights, but I was developing a serious dislike for the dark.

Also, I thought Ms Mankiller was lying to me. Anyone would have thought the same, the whole thing was preposterous. That was the only word for it, preposterous. I'd always thought that was a clumsy word that only pompous windbags would use to exaggerate about stuff they didn't understand and jokes they didn't get. But man, there it was, I thought; if you looked that word up in the dictionary, Ms Mankiller's whole story about Sarah Jane would be right there so you'd understand the meaning exactly.

I wanted to lift up and just fly away, leave Ms Mankiller on top of her precious bridge and send myself back to the real world. But I just couldn't bring myself even to try flying alone in the dark.

'You've been silent a long time, Max,' Ms Mankiller said suddenly, and I realized that was probably true.

'I think I'm Websick,' I said. 'I want to go home.'

'I was afraid you'd say that.'

Another bolt of fear, like an electric shock that was

powerful enough to hurt but so fast it was gone before you could yell in pain.

'Why are you afraid?' I asked her.

'I'm not afraid, not for me.'

'For *me?*' Another scare. One more and I was pretty sure my heart would go wonky and set off the cardio alarm.

'You're in no danger in here,' Ms Mankiller said, but she sounded so serious I decided she had to be lying again. 'It's just that there are some technical problems.'

'What kind of technical problems?'

I have to give her credit, she didn't hesitate. 'Well, you may have noticed you're shy an exit command. I'm afraid I have to tell you that means you won't be able to spin out for a while, until we can make you a new one.'

'OK,' I said. 'So how hard is that? Just programming, right? I mean, even with the graphics and the virtual reality and all, how hard is it to code an exit command?'

Now she did hesitate and I didn't like that a bit. 'There are complications.'

'There are?'

She didn't answer.

'So, what is it? Do you just want to keep me in suspense, or haven't you had enough time to think up what they are?'

'So you don't believe me.'

'Did you really expect me to?'

'No.'

That startled me. 'Is that so? The way you told it to me, it sounded like you expected me to swallow it all in one gulp, no questions asked.'

'Hardly. I've been waiting for you to accuse me of lying or of being crazy or sick or evil. When you didn't, I began to wonder what you *would* do. Try to ring your call-button, summon a nurse, confess to being in the forbidden Web, maybe? I didn't know.'

'Is that why you deleted my exit icon?'

'I didn't delete it.'

'So who did? Was it Sarah Jane? Or this life-form from out

of town that's taken up residence in her body?' My crow
voice was a lot better at conveying sarcasm. But then, crows
would sound sarcastic, I guess, whether or not they really
were.

'I think it's just a glitch,' she said. 'Caused by the presence
of things in the Web that were never meant to be there.'

'Like a human being's brain? Excuse me, *not* her brain, just
her mind. Like that?'

'Or the living consciousness of other kinds of beings, who
have discovered how to survive without bodies. Which is, in
a way, how you live.'

'Oh, right. What's that lump of flesh in that hospital bed,
then?'

'A very flawed vessel, unfortunately beyond repair at this
time. But perhaps—'

'No,' I interrupted. 'Don't do that. Don't say that maybe
sometime in the not-too-distant future, they'll be able to fix
neck and spinal injuries, promising research, blah, blah,
blah. Because that's too mean, and no matter how evil you
really are, I don't want to believe you're that evil.'

There was a long silence. I could just see one crow eye
reflecting some distant light from the city. Otherwise, I'd
have thought she'd flown away and left me to endure the
dark until day cycled around again. If it did.

'Shall I say instead that I can take you to Sarah Jane?' Ms
Mankiller said at last. 'Or is that also too mean?'

'Take me anywhere,' I said, 'as long as it's out of this
darkness.'

'I didn't want you to know until I could work my avatar with
perfect control and coordination,' Sarah Jane said. 'I didn't
want you to see me all messed up and unable to do
anything.'

'You call that fair?' I said.

She took me off her shoulder and held me up on her wrist
at eye level. 'What do you mean?'

'I mean, *I'm* all messed up and unable to do anything, and you can see me any time you want to.'

'I was afraid that you'd think I was mocking you.'

'Well, thanks for the act of faith, pal,' I said and cawed. We both laughed, me mostly from relief. As soon as Ms Mankiller had brought me to the encampment in the forest clearing, I knew Sarah Jane was there – *really* there, the *real* Sarah Jane. In spite of the fact that she was now a cartoon – literally – of the way she had looked in real life, and someone – something – else was walking her body around Bonner Springs and getting it into who knows what kind of trouble, we were still *attuned*. It was still there.

No doubt about it, this was the real Sarah Jane – and boy, how weird was *that?* The real one being the cartoon in the Web and the fake being the flesh-and-blood avatar in the real world.

The encampment belonged to a group that Sarah Jane said were called The Newest Age Travellers, a loosely organized group of Web nomads. They had a circle of really odd-looking vehicles, converted buses and mobile homes and trailers that looked like they'd been made up of parts scavenged from Cinderella's pumpkin coach. There had once been a real group of people who called themselves new age travellers, Sarah Jane told me, but she didn't know too much about them, other than that they had also been nomads in the Realworld.

These Newest Age Travellers should have called themselves Mutant Travellers, I thought. They were all roaming around the encampment picking up odd bits of stuff I couldn't quite see, and every single one of them was what Sarah Jane called *enhanced*. Some had extra limbs, and others had extra ... *somethings*. I didn't know what they were, except that they were supposed to be body parts, I think. I didn't see anyone take any of them off the way you would a hat or a pair of glasses. A few of them had multi-faceted eyes like insects, and a few were real close to being insects.

That sounds real weird and scary but it wasn't. I didn't

even think till much later that maybe it should have been weird and scary, seeing people who'd been altered to the point of deformity, even if they were avatars. But I just felt very peaceful, perched on Sarah Jane. It was a lot like the old arrangement with my rig. She sat on this great big old boulder and didn't move around a whole lot. I think she was still not as sure with her avatar as she'd have liked.

Ms Mankiller had given me a short, fast version of what had happened. When I had arrived – in full daylight, thank you – and known for sure that I was with Sarah Jane again, I thought maybe *she'd* tell me everything in detail. But while she did tell me more than Ms Mankiller had, it wasn't a whole lot more. There were some differences, too.

When Sarah Jane had first realized some form of life was moving around in the Web, she hadn't been as quick as a lot of others, including Ms Mankiller, to believe it was an alien presence. She'd thought that maybe parts of the Web were just waking up, kinda. Evolving faster than any organic life on earth ever could.

But then she'd made direct contact with it. Or them. Or one of them – she wasn't sure exactly which described the life form properly. Maybe even none of those. 'The old rules don't work,' she said, 'so you end up entertaining ideas that you'd have called absurd in the past, if you could even have thought them up.'

Anyway, as soon as she and the whatever-it-was met, Sarah Jane said, she knew it wasn't anything that could have originated on earth. 'Not because it told me in so many words,' she said. 'In fact, even though you can say we're in contact, we aren't really communicating. Not like humans know communicating, that is. Sometimes, I can make sense of *it* making sense of *me* – if that makes sense?' We giggled together, and if you want something strange in your day, listen to a crow giggle sometime. 'But it doesn't happen too often. That I can sense that happening, I mean. And I don't have a clue what makes sense to it and what doesn't, or why,

or whether what makes sense to it would make sense to
me—'

'Sarah Jane,' I said, 'in the words of the prophet, *stop
making sense.*' We giggled some more.

'Anyway,' she said after a bit, 'I didn't understand about
the body swap. Even after it happened, I had trouble.'

'Well, I'm not surprised,' I said. 'For one thing, you can't
say it's a real swap. It's not like he – it – they – oh, jeez, I'm
gonna be crazy in an hour, if it takes that long – well, it's not
like the other one traded you a body for a body.'

'Actually …' Sarah Jane leaned forward and looked down
at the grass. I followed her gaze and found myself looking at
something that seemed to be a cross between a spider-web
and Stonehenge after it had been moved to Egypt to be with
the pyramids. (I know, but that's the best description I've
come up with yet.)

'Don't tell me that's supposed to be the body you swapped
for,' I said.

'OK. I won't tell you.' She giggled. I didn't.

'If you want to be a warped version of some other
country's national monuments,' I said, 'I bet you can find
some in the flea market in Bizarre Bazaar.'

'It's not so much a body as a concept.'

'Of what? Chaos? Non-organization?'

'Of location, sort of,' she said, ignoring how I was baiting
her. 'It's— Location is a lot of things. You're located in time,
in space, in ecologies, as seen by others, in—'

'Wait a minute. I'm still stuck back at "ecologies". What's
that supposed to mean?'

'Ecology means ecology,' she said, shrugging. I was back
on her shoulder and I almost fell off. 'Every group, every
system, every organization has an ecology to it.'

I thought I might understand now, but I didn't want to
risk asking and find out I wasn't even close. 'OK. So what's
this "seen by others" stuff?'

'As near as I can tell, anyway, it's like everyone around you
has to vote yes on you before you can actually exist.'

I almost fell off her shoulder again. 'Like, voting for or against you being alive?' I said.

'No,' said Sarah Jane, and she suddenly sounded strange and old and far away. 'No. More like they all have to agree that they believe in you. That you exist.'

'Wow,' I said. 'So how can you tell if they do?'

'I don't know.' Sarah Jane's wistfulness came to me as clear as a radio signal on a cloudless starry night. I felt like she'd run me through with it and didn't realize how intense it was. 'I don't have the faintest idea, so it's going to be extra hard for me. Wish me luck?'

CHAPTER TWELVE

BACK AGAIN

My first thought was that I'd misunderstood her. No, that's not quite right. My first thought was to tell myself that I had misunderstood her, even though I knew right off I hadn't.

My next thought was, *I gotta talk her out of this!* Then, of course, *how?*

I couldn't do it alone, certainly, and Ms Mankiller hadn't come back from wherever she'd flown off to so Sarah Jane and I could talk privately. But when she did come back, would she help me try to change Sarah Jane's mind, or try to get me to accept her decision?

A lot of time must have passed while I agonized over it, because suddenly Sarah Jane made a throat-clearing noise and said, 'That bad, huh?'

'I ... I don't know,' I told her. 'I don't know exactly what you're doing, and I have a feeling that you don't either.'

'I don't,' she admitted. 'Isn't it wonderful?'

'Oh, Sarah Jane,' I said, and I could feel myself starting to cry. I can't actually produce tears, but that doesn't mean I can't or don't cry.

'What is it?' she said, alarmed now.

'You don't understand,' I said. 'I'm stuck with that ... imposter ... out there, and it, she, the thing – well, I can't talk to it. It doesn't hear me. And it's so stupid, I tried to tell it what not to do so you – *it* wouldn't get you into trouble, but it just locked me out and tossed me in here. Without even asking.'

'It doesn't know where you really are,' she said. 'Or what you are. It's never been a physical being, at least not in its memory. Which may be corrupted or even erased altogether. Or maybe it doesn't even have a memory and never did, not the way we think of memory. I don't know. I don't even know if they're all the same kind, from the same place, or if they're all as different from each other as they are from us. Some of them I know just can't see me – sense me in any way. And I get the feeling that there are others that *I* can't find, no matter how hard I concentrate or try to open my mind to ideas. The only thing I do know for sure is that they aren't native to our planet.'

'How?' I asked.

'Feeling. You can feel what's alien.'

'Then I guess there's something wrong with me, because I didn't feel anything alien about the one in your body.'

'Well, that's probably because it's not really *in* my body. The way you're not really *in* the body of a crow.'

It took me a little bit to get my mind around that one, and when I did, I was afraid I might throw up.

'Eventually, that might change,' she went on. 'At least, for some of them. The contact with us has already changed them greatly. And the change is still happening. If it keeps up, by this time next month, they won't be anything like the way they are now.'

'And what's that supposed to mean?' I said, exasperated.

'It could mean any number of things but, mostly, to me, it means that I'd better hurry and do what it is I want to do before I have to learn a whole new set of ... of ... protocols, I guess you'd call it.'

I felt like flying up to a branch and sulking, except I was afraid that if I left her shoulder, she might get up and walk away and I'd never see her again. 'So that's it, then. The clock is ticking and you gotta go?'

She didn't say anything.

'And what am *I* supposed to do, try and train your avatar to fetch and shake hands?'

Sarah Jane wet her lips and swallowed, which I thought was showing off, kinda. 'Actually, I thought I'd talk to you about doing something entirely different.'

'It's something to consider,' said Ms Mankiller.

The Newest Age Travellers were packing up in earnest now. They were all human avatars, Sarah Jane had told me, so I couldn't test out her premise about being able to feel alien-ness, or whatever it was. She was off helping them with some kind of task I probably wouldn't have understood, even if I'd known what it was. If she's asked me, I'd have told her that everyone felt alien to me now, and maybe that was because I was the one who was completely different from everybody else. Which would actually make me the alien, even if I hadn't started out that way.

In the words of the prophet, I thought, some are born alien, some acquire alien-ness, and some have alien-ness thrust upon them.

'Pretty good, Max,' said Ms Mankiller. 'You must be an incredible student.'

'Huh?' I said, and then, 'Oh.' I hadn't realized that I had assembled my thought and not muted the vocalizer.

'The way of speaking I helped you learn, it seems to have become second nature to you.'

'Yeah, well. I had a lot of spare time to practise. Next year I'm taking up the violin.'

To my surprise, Ms Mankiller burst out with hearty laughter, which I swore I could hear quite well beneath the caws.

'You think that's funny?' I said. 'You must be a secret sicko.'

'Perhaps. And then again, perhaps it's just something I read today in the news. About the development of a prosthetic body for survivors of certain kinds of accidents. It'll take a lot of delicate operations, but they re-channel the nerves to transmit to the prosthesis. Then there's a lot of physical therapy to make the brain learn new routines.'

I knew she was waiting for my reaction. 'Didn't anybody ever tell you there's no Santa Claus?' I said after a bit.

'Actually, nobody ever told me there *was*. But I did grow up believing in Coyote Trickster, and it was quite amazing to meet him in here,' said Ms Mankiller, sounding confident. 'It would be like a physical avatar, you know. The prosthesis, I mean, not—'

'I know what you meant, not Coyote Trickster.' I thought about flapping my wings, or rather, how nice it would be to be able to flap my wings whenever the whim hit me. Suddenly, I was flapping my wings – so vigorously I almost lifted off from the boulder without meaning to.

'They say not every paralyzed person could manage to cope with a prosthetic body, and that certain kinds of patients are better candidates than others. I think you might get the idea already which group you belong to.'

'Sarah Jane,' I said automatically.

'Pardon?'

'It's because of Sarah Jane,' I said. 'When we became attuned. With her helping—' I stopped.

'Well, actually,' said Ms Mankiller, 'you could do it alone now.'

'I could,' I said.

When I wouldn't go on, Ms Mankiller went on for me.

'But,' she prompted.

'Yeah,' I said. 'But.' I paused. 'I'd like to get out of here now. I'm Websick.' Among other things.

'OK,' said Ms Mankiller.

'OK?' I said. 'There's still the little matter of my not having an exit command.'

'Funny you should mention it,' she said, 'but I managed to dig up a patch for you. However, we'll have to remove your binocular vision plug-in first.'

Ms Mankiller did it for me. By the time she got the exit

icon to show up on my guide, I really was feeling kind of Websick. Getting out just in time, I thought.

'Tell Sarah Jane—' I broke off. Tell Sarah Jane *what?*

But Ms Mankiller just nodded her crow head in a very human-looking motion. 'I will.'

My goggles had just cleared when I heard a nurse say, 'He's out of it now.'

They were pulled off me a lot less gently than I was used to, and I found myself looking up at a circle of faces that included the nurse who had spoken, both my parents, and the chief of the Bonner Springs Police. For the first time, I was glad my face was frozen into an unreadable mask.

'Max,' said my mother looking worried. 'Are you ... are you all right?'

'Yes,' said my vocalizer.

'Not Websick?' asked my father. Strangely enough, he didn't look angry or offended or anything. Just concerned.

'Maybe a little.'

My parents were about to say something else when the police chief spoke up. 'Then you must be up to answering a few questions about your little gal pal Sarah Jane. We just picked her up about an hour ago. She broke into a house over on the west side.' He waited, letting me absorb this. 'Didn't steal anything, but probably only because she didn't get a chance to get away. The owners came home and found her in the kitchen, asleep on the floor, empty vodka bottle in her hand. They said there'd been half of it left when they'd gone out.' He waited again and I saw my parents look at each other.

'When we finally brought her to, she said it had all been your idea,' he said finally. 'You care to comment on that?'

'Not without a lawyer,' I said automatically. I don't know why I blurted that out. Too much TV, maybe. Anyway, it was my right, but my mother burst into tears.

CHAPTER THIRTEEN

BUSTED

Of course, they wouldn't let me see or talk to 'Sarah Jane'. Not that I could have without the rig, or a whole lot of help, and they weren't about to give me either. The police confiscated the rig, leaving me the TV and my library subscription, to keep me from dying of boredom.

Oh, brother – talk about being cut off! I hadn't known what *cut off* really was until I lost the use of the rig. I cried a lot. Inside, of course, where no one could see. It was so awful, like prison – a one-hundred per cent escape-proof prison, with a population of one. I hadn't realized just how much I'd gotten used to being 'out' via the rig and Sarah Jane. I'd even started taking it for granted in some ways.

For a while, right after the police left with my rig, I was actually hysterical. My head was full of silent screaming and I found myself instinctively … trying to move? Getting ready to move? Making as if to move? Whatever you call it, the reflex to move was still there in my mind. I could feel how I wanted to move. I wanted to roar and beat my fists on the walls and curse everyone and everything. But when I'd go to do it, I'd find that I hadn't actually gone anywhere, hadn't budged.

Then I started to feel really warm, like I was all wrapped up in blankets in the middle of July. My heart beat real hard and fast and I thought, well, I'd make history for being the first-ever locked-in person to explode, literally. Then a nurse must have come in with a syringe, because that was all I knew for about twelve hours.

The dreams were pretty wild. All about Bizarre Bazaar and talking spiders, long lines of mobile homes and trailers rumbling through the flea market, shopping. I mean, the vehicles themselves were shopping, while the people inside them slept or ate or watched TV. I ran into my father, who said that he was on his way to take a vacation, so he was going to have his spine unplugged from his head for two weeks. I asked him if he'd seen Sarah Jane, but he didn't hear anything I said to him because of the crows, which were very loud. But whenever I looked around for them, of course, I couldn't see any. I couldn't see much of anything because the light was really bad, more towards the blue-purple end of the spectrum. It made my eyes tend to roll up in my head for some reason.

After a while I realized my eyes were rolling up because I was trying to open them while I was still pretty drugged. The cawing crows were real enough, though. There seemed to be an awful lot of them outside my windows. It sounded like a whole convention of crows.

That would be a *murder*, I remember; a *murder* of crows. I shivered inside.

Ms Evans' face appeared above me. 'Hello, Max,' she said. I watched the underside of her chin wobble a little as she spoke. 'You're probably surprised to see me, so I'll get right to the point: I'm Head Elder, as of the last election. I'm pretty sure you didn't know that, as I don't think you've been following much of what's been going on in Bonner Springs lately. I imagine the Web eats up a lot of your time.'

Another face appeared opposite hers, a young guy, or at least he was younger than Ms Evans. He looked familiar, but I couldn't quite place him. 'I'm pretty sure you remember me, Max, although you may not recognize me. I taught you to swim at day-camp when you were maybe six or seven.'

Billy Fiore. The last time I had seen him close up, he'd

been wearing swimming trunks, standing in water up to his knees and showing me and about seven first-graders how to breathe in and blow out bubbles underwater. Later on, he got to be County Champ three years in a row on the swim team. Sometimes Mom and Dad would take me and Gary to the meets. Sarah Jane used go too. She used to have a crush on him, I remembered. Now Billy was wearing a suit, and his dark, curly hair wasn't cut as close to his scalp as it used to be. I thought he looked like a history teacher. I thought wrong.

'Your parents hired me to be your lawyer,' Billy went on, with a glance at Ms Evans. 'I'm here to help you with the problem of Sarah Jane and if you want, I can also advise you on community matters. Of course—' He glanced at Ms Evans again. 'That means we'll need privacy and enough undisturbed time so I can get the full story from you.'

They locked gazes, Ms Evans and Billy, but she finally had to give in and leave. Bonner Springs is a special community with its own standards, but it's still in the state of Kansas, which is in the U.S., where anyone accused of a crime has a right to an attorney, and you're innocent until proven guilty. What a relief.

Billy didn't waste any time. As soon as the door closed behind Ms Evans, he took off his suitcoat, whipped out a palmtop, and cranked up my bedside tray so it was high enough for him to lean on. He was sitting on a high stool, probably borrowed from the nurses' station, so I could look at him while we talked. If I could have, I'd have hugged him with gratitude for that little bit of consideration. Nobody else except Sarah Jane, the real one, ever thought of doing that.

'Is Sarah Jane doing drugs?' he asked me, right out of the blue, as he made sure I could work my vocalizer.

'Don't know. Don't think so. Why?' I asked. I could tell I'd been spoiled in the Web. The rig anticipated a lot. Out here in *Johnny Got His Gun* land, my conversation went a lot slower.

'Well, for one thing, she was found passed out after drinking about a third of a litre of vodka. She hadn't thrown up, and the examining doctor said there were no signs of alcohol poisoning, which I would have thought would happen with a thirteen-year-old girl. But even more important—' Billy looked partly worried and partly sheepish 'I dropped by the jail where they're holding her, and I swear she didn't know me. Didn't know me, didn't remember me, nothing. And not to sound real stuck on myself or anything, but I know she used to have a crush on me when she was little.' He rolled his eyes. 'It was cute, guys on the swimming team used to tease me about her coming to the meets and leaving little presents wrapped in my towel for me to find later. But that doesn't necessarily mean anything. She may very well have forgotten everything about me.

'But your folks said you and she were always pretty good pals, and after your accident – rotten luck, my man, I wish I'd known back when it happened – after your accident, she volunteered to be your sort of remote body. And you two worked together so well it was really spooky. Did you ever notice anything weird about her then?'

This was going to be it, I thought. We were approaching a moment of truth here, when I would either have to tell the truth as I knew it, or the truth that people in Bonner Springs could believe.

And maybe not just Bonner Springs, but anywhere. Because this wasn't just a matter of deciding what level of technology was appropriate technology, or a disagreement over the cultural value of the Web. This was— Well, it was Sarah Jane to start with, and everyone else after.

So weird! People would get together and agree to pretend a place like Bizarre Bazaar was real, but when something real happened they'd suddenly go all sceptical. There's one of Bonner Springs' sister cities in Idaho where most of the people are convinced that we aren't actually on Mars and we never landed on the moon, either. And just outside Kansas City, there's this fundamentalist religious group who believe

the teachings of some old preacher from hundreds of years
ago, who was convinced he had figured out how old the
universe really was by adding up all the ages of everyone in
the Old Testament. Or something like that.

But they're harmless – not like that bunch in the Ozarks
who don't even believe the Holocaust happened. I suppose
they'd be harmless, although awfully repellent, except that
they're fanatics. Every so often, their fanaticism boils over
and they feel an irresistible urge to come out from under
their rock and supply the immediate world with tracts and
videos and holographic stickers and buttons and all kinds of
other tacky doodads to spread their irrational hatreds.

I guess it's stupid to expect a group like that, say, who
think historical facts are matters of opinion, to believe a
story like mine. On the other hand, the Winter Olympics
could be held in an open-air tent in Death Valley in July
before I'd look for help from people like that.

Maybe, considering that's in the Web, I should specify that
I mean the Realworld Winter Olympics and not anything
virtual.

'Max?' said Billy, and I jumped, but inside where he
couldn't see it. 'Did you fall asleep, or are you having trouble
with the question?'

'No,' I said. 'I'm awake. No trouble. Just ... before
answering ... question for you.' I had to wince at the way my
speech was deteriorating into something near pidgin.

'Go ahead,' Billy said, genially. 'However, if you're asking
about client-lawyer confidentiality, the answer is, you have
nothing to worry about. Even though your parents are
paying the bills, I still won't tell them anything unless you
allow me to.'

'Good, but not that. You remember the old saying by
Holmes?'

'Who?' said Billy.

'Sherlock.'

'Oh. That. Sorry, Max. You must think I'm stupid.'

'No.' Not yet, anyway. 'Holmes said: "eliminate the

impossible and then whatever is left, no matter how improbable, is truth." '

Billy tilted his head and gazed at me thoughtfully. He would make a good crow, I thought. 'Yeah, I'm familiar with that one. Does this mean you're about to tell me a story I'm going to have a hard time believing? Or more than one?'

'One more question,' I said.

'Go ahead.'

'Live here?'

'All my life,' Billy said. 'However – and I'm pretty sure this is why your parents chose me – I'm about to leave. At the end of May I'm planning to move to Detroit.' He waited for me to react. When I didn't, he went on. 'It's not that I'm opposed to the Bonner Springs way of life. When I wanted to go to law school, the University of Kansas accepted me as a special restrictions student and still gave me a good education. The elders paid part of my tuition as well and didn't attach any strings about what I could and couldn't do. Even if I'd been caught playing in the Web, I wouldn't have lost the financial support. I had to respect that.'

Then he laughed a little. 'Of course, that might have been different if Ms Evans had been Head Elder back then. But she wasn't, and I didn't ever do anything more than take a quick peek into somebody's helmet. Was sorry I did that, too, but that's another story. Anyway, I've been feeling a bit … restricted, I guess, is the word. I'm going to give it a try with a practice in Detroit. I'm allowing myself a year to decide if I want more than appropriate technology in my life, or whether I want to come back here and shut all that out again. Which is more than you really wanted to know, right, Max?'

'Wrong,' I said. 'Needed to know.'

'I figured. Just from what they told me about how they caught you in full access. However, does this have anything to do with Sarah Jane possibly being on drugs?'

'Long story,' I said.

'Take your time,' he said, shifting position slightly on the stool. 'Would you really be heartbroken if Ms Evans got tired of waiting to see you and went out for a pig-foot and a bottle of beer? So to speak.'

'Pig-foot? Ms Evans?'

Billy smiled broadly. 'Sorry to break it to you like that, but you'd have heard eventually. No, I don't know. Anyway, let's talk about Sarah Jane and only Sarah Jane right now. Is she on drugs?'

'More improbable.'

'You mean, something more improbable than that?' he asked.

'More improbable than anything.'

CHAPTER FOURTEEN

HELP?

There was bad news, good news, and weird news.

Right – Billy didn't believe me. That was the bad news.

The weird news was that, in cooperation with Sarah Jane's court-appointed lawyer, Billy started building a case for diminished capacity, which he figured would take care both of my legal problems and my violation of community standards. Even Ms Evans wouldn't be able to argue with that. Well, actually, she probably would, but only to her mirror. Diminished capacity got both me and my family off the hook, as long as I took the required counselling. I just hoped that wouldn't turn out to be Ms Evans coming in three afternoons a week and reading old archives to me about oil shortages and Ebola viruses and how many species became extinct in the last century alone.

The good news travelled a lot slower.

Actually, there was some other good news, and I thought that would be all of it. My parents decided to make arrangements for me to live at home.

Oh, man, when my mother came to tell me that, thought I would explode, this time from sheer happiness. And I hadn't even been thinking about it. Not consciously, anyway. I'd just accepted that, what with the respirator and the feeding tube and all the rest of it, I was now permanently in the room at the end of the corridor on the second floor, east wing of the hospital. Things weren't the way they were in the last century, when hospitals were so expensive and overcrowded even in Kansas that surgery was done on practically a drive-through basis. So it wasn't like my living in the hospital was a problem. And yeah, I did have a problem with it, but I had a problem with being paralyzed.

When my mother said I'd be moving back home, it hit me all at once just how homesick I was, how much I needed to see that old room of mine. No, not just see it, through the lens of a camera but to be in it. To smell it. To hear the sounds I'd always heard in it.

I know my face never moves, never changes, but my mother saw something, or maybe just sensed it because she's a mother. She put her cheek down on my forehead and talked to me for a long time, all about how she and Dad had let me down by not trying to argue the hospital into letting them bring me home sooner.

'That was bad enough,' she said, 'but we've compounded the problem by relating to you through a third party instead of directly. Oh, I know Sarah Jane did you a lot of good. But she was only meant to help you with school and some socializing, things like that. She wasn't meant to stand in for you with us, or to stand in for us with you. But that's what she ended up doing and while I wish we could lay all the blame on the technology – inappropriate technology – well, I just don't think we can.'

I had my vocalizer ready, but I couldn't bring myself to use it. I didn't want the emotionless, mechanical voice ruining what I wanted to say.

'We were so concerned with using only appropriate technology, only proper things, that we forgot something important,' my mother went on after a moment. 'We forgot that the whole idea of our community was to take the focus off technology and put it back on people. Their real needs, their ideas, their values. And their emotions. I can't tell you how very sorry your Dad and I are – that we neglected you. And we didn't do Sarah Jane any big favours, either, other

than giving her a clean place to sleep without drunks
coming and going at all hours of the day and night. But in
our own way, we were even harder on her. It's no wonder
both of you broke down the way you did and turned to
breaking into people's homes.'

I tried to will my mother to feel me bristling, to feel me
yelling *Wrong! Wrong! You're wrong!* in my mind. But of
course, she didn't feel anything of the sort. She just stayed
like that with her cheek on my forehead, talking softly,
apologizing and talking about how she and Dad were going
to try their best to make it up to me.

No mention any more of Sarah Jane, I realized with a chill,
and that was probably because she'd been found passed out
with a vodka bottle in her hand. Well, she hadn't. Mom and
Dad probably figured that Sarah Jane had chosen the way
she wanted to follow, and it was a case of like father and
mother, like daughter, and who needs that kind of problem
around the house? Especially when you're not the legal
guardian and you already have a paralyzed son to take care
of. So, now things would be a lot better. We would all live
happily ever after. Then she started to talk about a new
development she'd seen on the news, a prosthetic body for
paraplegics.

Jeez. That was all I could think, over and over. My mind
was full of that word and its echoes and nothing else. *Jeez.
Jeez. Jeez.*

But, finally, the really good news showed itself, right at the
point where Billy Fiore was going to file a motion for
dismissal of the case for reasons of diminished capacity.
Good news, also known as Ms Mankiller (what was her first
name, I wondered) walked into my hospital room and sat
down on the edge of my bed.

'I just got a subpoena from someone who says he's your
lawyer, defending you against some kind of weird breaking-
and-entering charge, along with Sarah Jane. So what's going
on, and why did it take so long for me to hear?'

'Long story,' I said. 'Glad you're here. If I had a tail, I'd wag it.'

'I'd get pneumonia. The gusts from your sighs of relief are bad enough. What do you need me to do?'

'Bring Sarah Jane back.'

Ms Mankiller frowned. 'How about peace in the Middle East? Since we're making requests.'

Of course, bringing Sarah Jane back, and putting her back were two different matters. Neither was quite possible, but fortunately, Sarah Jane was willing to help me any way she could, Ms Mankiller told me the following day.

'Swell,' I said in my dead-calm voice. 'I'm so happy I could jump for joy. Or I will be just as soon as you tell me how you think she can help me from her spot among the Newest Age Travellers.'

'It would take too long to tell,' Ms Mankiller said. 'Just leave it all to me.'

I figure that Ms Mankiller was absolutely the only person in the world who could have persuaded everyone, from the elders to my own parents, that allowing me to make one last visit to the Web was a good idea. Was, as a matter of fact, the only thing to do that would help both me and Sarah Jane, as well as my mother and father, Gary, Billy Fiore, Ms Evans, and maybe even the entire world. That was thinking big on a scale that I could barely get my mind around. But I didn't have to. All I had to do was get Sarah Jane to show herself and convince everybody that she was, without a doubt, the real thing.

Waiting for Ms Mankiller to show up with my rig, I thought a lot about that – how to do it, but mostly how I could go about doing it. I mean, it's not like there are a whole lot of instructions out there on how to get people to believe in something. Or someone.

And then, just as clear as anything, I heard Sarah Jane's voice in my head. *First, start with yourself, and work outward.*

*

My sense of time was screwed up by being sedated for that
super-stress/hysteria spell I'd had, so I wasn't sure how many
days it had been since I had talked to Sarah Jane and then
come out to find the police chief waiting for me. It couldn't
have been more than three or four days. But when Ms
Mankiller slipped the goggles and rig back onto my face and
batted me into Bizarre Bazaar, I felt homesick all over again,
this time for the Web.

For the Web?

That didn't sound right to me. Oh, it wasn't anywhere
near as intense as how I'd felt when my mother had told me
I was going home, but I knew what I was feeling and it took
me by surprise.

My next surprise was Ms Mankiller. She'd told me that she
was going to join me in the Web, but I'd thought she was
going to use a regular Web version of her appearance out
here. Instead, she appeared the way she always had, as a
crow. How many crows did you have to have, I wondered,
before you could say you had a full murder of crows? I tried
to squelch the thought, but it just kept sneaking up on me.

CHAPTER FIFTEEN

THE REAL SARAH JANE

My third and final visit to the Web was being televised, but to a very select audience consisting of Billy Fiore, an older woman named Vera Penn that the county seat had sent to be Sarah Jane's public defender, my parents, Ms Evans, the police chief, and a couple of nurses. They all assembled in front of a closed-circuit monitor in my hospital room (which I only had a week more to endure, hurray, hurray), which put them in the same room with me even though I was also about as far away from them all as I could get. I'd have felt weird about that, except that by the time I got to that point, I was too weirded-out to feel any more weird than I already did.

Anyway, as soon as I was in Bizarre Bazaar, I pretty much forgot anyone was watching from outside the Web. There was no sign of open surveillance, but Ms Mankiller had said that they'd be able to see us, or at least me, all the time. Maybe it was something like the way the aliens had used Sarah Jane to keep us under surveillance. I didn't ask; I had enough to think about.

According to Ms Mankiller, Sarah Jane would be waiting for us where the flea market began. She had already been on her way to somewhere else with the Newest Age Travellers when Ms Mankiller had contacted her and called her back to help.

That part I wasn't too sure I understood. I mean, the Web was virtual, so all Ms Mankiller had to do was hit the right codes and she should have spun in right where Sarah Jane was. It wasn't like a real city, say, where you had to travel real distance over a period of time to get from point A to point B.

Was it?

Jeez. I tried not to think about that, too, but that and the question of how many crows in a murder kept chasing each other around my mind like hyperactive house-cats so that I might as well have been sleepwalking for all the impression Bizarre Bazaar was making on me today. And for my last visit, too. Considering that I'd felt homesick, there should have been something sad about that for me, maybe.

I had to walk through the freak show to get to where the flea market began – no great pleasure for me. There was a two-headed strong-man juggling cannonballs and doing this really corny comedy routine about what it was like being a two-headed husband married to a two-headed wife, while a woman with holographic tattoos all over her body proved she was a contortionist, too. For a moment, I could almost smell the sawdust and feel the heat. Knowing I couldn't and never would made me feel a little less homesick for this place.

Don't know how she did it, but Sarah Jane had duplicated her Realworld appearance perfectly. The likeness was so true to the person currently sitting in the Bonner Springs' makeshift juvenile cell that everyone in the room gasped. I know, because I heard them all quite clearly.

Now, that gave me a turn – being in the Web, and hearing things out there. I'd never noticed before. Why not? Don't ask me, I just lurk here.

As soon as I reached Sarah Jane, the crow that was Ms Mankiller appeared on my shoulder, and then fluttered to Sarah Jane's. Sarah Jane smiled at me, a little sadly, and said, 'Should I face any particular direction?'

'Only if you want to,' said Ms Mankiller.

Sarah Jane decided to look right at me.

'Ms Mankiller's told me that I was arrested for breaking and entering and drinking vodka,' she began, without preamble. 'Or rather, my body, which everyone thinks is me, was.

'But it isn't me. There is a … a passenger, a strange life-form, using my body to move around in our world. If one of you had come in here with Ms Mankiller and Max, you'd know right away I was telling the truth. Because I no longer have a flesh container around who I am, it's real easy to, uh—' She looked slightly embarrassed for a moment. 'Smell isn't really the word I'm looking for, but it has more of the sense of what I mean. So let's just say, for a minute, that there's such a thing as a virtual smell and a virtual nose to detect it.'

'Ask her who's supposed to be in her body now if she isn't,' said the police chief. I heard him and relayed the question to her.

'For lack of a better word, Chief,' and I wondered if he flinched at her talking to him directly from the TV monitor, 'I have to call it an alien. And to answer your next questions, no, I don't know why it's here or what it wants, I don't know if it's friendly or not, I don't even know if it understands anything about the Web or Bonner Springs, or anything else. Nor do I know if it's the only one, or if there's actually more than one.

'I also don't know how it managed to steal my body to go walking in,' she went on, and I knew she was talking only to me in reality. 'Sometimes, I think it was actually a gradual kind of thing, like that old question about remodelling the boat while it's at sea. You know which one I mean – about how if you took a boat across the ocean, and replaced every board and nail and what-have-you so that you arrived at the other harbour having replaced every single component, could you say you were arriving in the same boat, or in a different one? I think that's what happened to me. I think I was the boat, and the alien replaced me little by little, until I was all gone over here, and he, or she, or it – or they – was firmly rooted out there.' She paused.

'Or maybe that's the only way I can understand what happened, but not the way that it really happened. The only thing I know for sure, though, is that it did really happen. And now you have this Sarah Jane person who's acting nothing like the one you know. But I guess that doesn't prove it for you, does it?'

'Ha,' said the police chief flatly. I could picture him sitting in front of the TV with his skinny arms folded over his chest.

'Police chief says, "Ha," ' I told her.

'I'd have been surprised if he didn't,' Sarah Jane replied. She seemed very calm, very relaxed and sure of herself, in a way that I hadn't ever seen her be until now. Was that the Web's effect? Or was it just Sarah Jane being herself without the constraints she felt Bonner Springs put on her? 'However, I have a *Ha* of my own for him.

'I've been in here for quite a while without anything to get between me and the Web,' she said. 'And that means I've been changing some more, on my own. Time in here runs a bit faster because it *is* the Web, so while a few days have passed for you Outside, it's been a lot longer for me.'

So that was it, I thought, and I swear my heart was literally sinking. Sarah Jane wasn't really my age any more.

'But it's more than that,' she went on. 'I'm ... enhanced. The Web has added some things to me, and changed other things around. So there are certain things I can do now that I couldn't do before. And one of those things is to prove to you – I mean you all, watching Max and Ms Mankiller and me in the Web – that I really am Sarah Jane, and there really is an alien sitting in the jail in the town centre.'

There was murmuring, but I couldn't make out what anyone was saying.

'Hang on, Max,' she said to me, smiling. 'This is going to feel a little funny.'

A moment later she had put her hand over my face, as if it were something she meant to pick up and hold, or carry around. That wouldn't have been so remarkable, except I *felt* it.

Everybody who was in the room pretty much agrees on what happened next.

In my hospital bed, my body was suddenly enveloped in flames. My mother started to get up and go to me, so she was first to be speared by the bright white light-beam that shot out from my head.

But that only took about a quarter of a second. Everybody there was hit with a light beam, some in the chest, some in the head, others in their mid-section. It didn't hurt, exactly, but everybody agreed they wouldn't care to have it happen again.

The light was the essence of Sarah Jane, the essence that she had built up within herself so she could convince anyone – or anything – that she did, indeed, exist, and was therefore a being to believe in. The way it came through for everyone in the room, however, was as memories of her life in Bonner Springs. My mother remembered when she had come to live with us, my father remembered her out on the porch in the snow in February, the nurses remembered the way she had trained and trained to use the rig with me. The chief of police saw mental pictures of her and the alien in her body side by side and was able to see otherwise invisible differences in their appearance. Billy Fiore saw every single little piece of candy or gumball machine trinket she'd sneaked into his towel where he'd left it on a bench by the pool – love tokens from a six-year-old. Ms Evans took a concentrated dose of Sarah Jane's presence from first grade through to the present, and never doubted again.

The public defender had never seen Sarah Jane before, but she wasn't left out. Sarah Jane let her feel how being in the presence of an alien really differed from being in the presence of another human. I think that must have been the scariest of all, myself.

I don't know how long it lasted, exactly. Not in Web time, anyway. In Bonner Springs time, it was over in thirty seconds, but in Web time it might still be going on, for all I know.

CHAPTER SIXTEEN

AS I AM

After that, there's not much to tell. The police chief was left with the problem of dealing with a minor who wasn't actually a minor, or even human, except to the untrained and inexperienced eye. Ms Evans wouldn't talk to anyone; she just packed up and took off for the Caribbean. Maybe she won't come back. I don't know what her problem is. All I know is that she was always the person in Bonner Springs who was most opposed to the Web, and maybe what Sarah Jane did to her made her feel unclean or something.

Billy Fiore and the public defender got together with the police chief to try and figure out who they should approach with the story and how to do it. The nurses gave each of my parents a stiff drink out of somebody's secret whisky supply and Ms Mankiller made sure that everyone was too distracted to question me about anything immediately.

Except, of course, about my face. That was natural enough, and it was only natural for me to say I didn't know a thing about it. One of the doctors who examined me later said it could have been the shock to the nerves that did it, and that sounds as good to me as anything else. I can't say I really give it a lot of thought, except to be happy about it. I mean, if there could have been one thing I'd have wished for, other than for the damage to be reversed, it would have been for my face to unfreeze from the way it had been, so that when my parents and my brother Gary looked at me, they'd see me as normal as possible under the circumstances.

But, yeah, I lied when I said I couldn't remember and I didn't know. I can, and I do.

Web time is a slippery matter. I think it's one of the biggest reasons people get Websick, but don't quote me, I've only made three trips in, and I don't plan to spin in again in this lifetime.

In the moment between the last second the beams of light were on everyone and the first second they shut off – in that moment, there's a whole universe of other moments. Most of the time, the presence we fill is too large to slip between moments. But if you know how to draw your presence in, you can manage it. And if you know how to keep drawing your presence in, you can keep slipping between moments over and over, and enter a zone of timelessness. Hours can pass for you between one watch-tick and the next. But it *is* cheating, and if you do it too often, Sarah Jane told me, you run the risk of dying of old age in the space of ten seconds. Wild.

In fact, I thought that part of living in the Web was even more wild than what she wanted me to do, which was to go with her. Or stay with her, I'm not sure how to put it. And so now you know that I lied about that, too, when I said that Sarah Jane never offered to help me out of my own body and into the Web.

'You can be free,' she said as we moved through timelessness, simultaneously going away from and toward regular time (don't ask). 'You don't have to be locked inside your own body, it doesn't have to be a prison. Not only that, you can be freer than people who aren't paralyzed. They can only move around in the world. You can have the universe.'

What was bothering me, was that Sarah Jane had been wrong about something. Which was to say, yes, it was her, but at the same time, it wasn't. She was all enhanced now. But that wasn't the Sarah Jane in my ... ecology.

Beng Web-enhanced, she picked all that up from me almost as soon as it occurred to me. I got irritated for a moment, because un-enhanced types like me, and you, and every other regular human on the face of the earth, we all need to express ourselves, not have it slipped out of us by intuition. For humans, that's too much like having your pocket picked. But I'll say this for Sarah Jane, when she picked up on my irritation, she backed off right away and let me do my own communicating.

'It's not just that,' I told her. 'I want to feel the sun on my face. I want to smell the wind. I want to be too warm sometimes and too cold other times. I want to go outside. It looks good for the prosthetic body being available for general use soon. And if that's the case, then I should be taking walks by myself before the next school year starts.'

'It couldn't do everything, though,' Sarah Jane said.

'I know,' I told her. 'It would probably short out if I tried to go swimming in it, but I have to tell you that I'm not that keen on water sports any more.'

We laughed together, and for a moment, everything was the way it used to be. But that's not one of those moments you can keep in a timeless zone.

'You know, then,' she said, 'that I'm not coming back.'

'Yeah. I think maybe I knew somehow the first time we went in the Web together.'

'It was a real turning point, wasn't it?' She finally took her hand from my face. 'I'm not going to say I understand why you want to be anchored to an earth that's practically one-dimensional compared to what's possible here.'

'I know,' I said. 'Same way I can't understand why you'd choose an unreal universe over things you can touch.'

'What do you suppose will happen to the alien in my body?'

'Don't know. Maybe it'll have to go to reform school.'

'Why do you say that?' Sarah Jane asked me, horrified.

'How many people you think are going to believe the real story? How long do you think the chief of police in Bonner Springs is going to hold out against the ridicule he's going to get? This time next month, I bet people will be calling him Elvis.'

Regret was an aura around her. 'It's never going to be a perfect world, is it, Max?'

'Not here, not anywhere, I imagine. But I think people should live in the worlds they know they belong in.' She started to say something in protest. 'It's OK, Sarah Jane, I wasn't saying that you had to belong in that one just because I know that I do.' And we both knew I meant Outside.

So Sarah Jane's gone to, well, just gone. Alive, but gone. I miss that being attuned stuff, but the more I think about it, the surer I am that it wasn't going to last. We got attuned while she was changing from Sarah Jane to alien, and maybe it was the alien replacing her in this world that allowed it to happen. You know, breaking down her barriers, that kind of thing. I do know that if I had stayed in the Web, we wouldn't have had it any more. I don't know for sure, but I think that's a pretty good guess on my part.

See, it's that slippery Web time again. I grew some, too. I know I'm not thirteen any more. But I'm not going to try and figure out how much. I'm just going to take it easy, actually. Try not to upset anyone, or myself. I have to rest up, after all. My parents are taking me to the Mayo Clinic for the first in the series of operations to connect me to a prosthetic body. I'm going to like that a lot. It's probably going to be the hardest thing I've ever done in my life, getting that thing under control and learning to manoeuvre it like a real body but I do have an advantage. I've been an extra in *Gone With the Wind*, a paper doll, and a crow. The doctor at the clinic says the fact that I was a sleepwalker will probably work in my favour, too. That's so cool.

So that's all I know. It's sure all I can tell, anyway, and that's all I want to say right now. What it all comes down to is, there's something in the Web, and it's not from around here.

But even if there wasn't something in the Web, I'd still go with my decision. I don't have anything really against it. But when my parents offered to move just outside the city limits so I could have a Web feed if I wanted it, I wasn't even tempted to say yes. Because this is me, me *here*. I know I wasn't any less me in the Web, but it's just not my ecology. This is where people believe in me, no matter where they are themselves. Like Sarah Jane. I'm real sure that she believes in me here from wherever she is in the Web, just the same way I believe in her in the Web from where I am here.

Can't ask for more than that, can you?

WALKABOUT
ERIC BROWN

For
Josh Lacey and Andrea Doder
(and for Pushkin, of course)

CONTENTS

CHAPTER ONE

DARJEELING

Suzie decided to be herself today.

She strode down the strand between the building blocks, each one pulsing with a dozen different scenes like a Rubik's cube gone mad. This was only her third time in the Web. The first time, she had commanded her wristpad to give her the avatar of a tall white boy, just to see what it was like. The second time she had appeared as a woman in her twenties, as pretty as a vid-star. Each time, she had found that people in the Web had treated her differently, just because she *looked* different. Soon she had found herself acting strangely – acting how people might expect a young boy or vid-star to act. She had been in danger of forgetting who she really was, and that had frightened her.

So today she was herself. She was tall for her age, and her hair was a mass of jet black curls, her skin as dark as that of any other Aboriginal she had ever met. She wore shorts and a T-shirt and went barefoot. At first she was self-conscious about showing her true self in the Web. Then she told herself not to worry; no one gave her a second glance. She was part of a crowd of a thousand different avatars and phaces. She passed brightly coloured animals, real and mythical, a host of cartoon characters, scurrying spiders the size of dingoes and boys and girls like herself.

The reason Suzie was here today was that she was doing badly at school. Ms Walker, her History teacher, had told

her, 'You'll have to buck your ideas up, Miss Wollagong. This
essay is way below standard. You're letting your fame go to
your head!'

Well, for a few days she had been famous – the first
Aboriginal girl to be selected for the Australian under-sixteen
mixed soccer team. But she didn't think that her selection
had changed her.

She had always found her lessons difficult. 'Face it, Suzie,'
Uncle Tom had said, 'Some people have it up here.' He had
tapped his head. 'And some down here.' He pointed to his
feet. 'Me and you, we play soccer. So we're not brain-boxes.
We sure can kick that ball, but—'

Then a sadness had crept into his eyes, because Tom
hadn't kicked a ball in almost ten years, since his injury.

Yesterday, Ms Walker had set an essay: 'A day in the British
Raj.'

'I want you to imagine what it might have been like to
have been an Indian under British rule in the 19th century.
One thousand words by Friday.'

Now Suzie paused on the strand, a thousand brightly
coloured avatars flowing around her, and looked for a spider.

'Excuse me!' She stepped in front of a hairy purple spider,
halting its scurrying progress. 'I'm looking for the Indian Raj-
zone. Can you give me the code?'

'Sure thing, Miss! Whadya think I'm here for?' The spider
lifted a thick leg and pretended to scratch its head, as if deep
in thought. 'Hokay, found it! You ready?'

Suzie waited, finger poised over her wristpad. 'Ready.'

'So here it is, Miss.' And the spider reeled off the code
number.

Suzie tapped it into her wristpad, and before she could
thank the spider she saw a blue flash and heard a high
pinging chime, and she was no longer in Webtown.

She looked about her. Even though this was her third time
in the Web, she was still amazed by the instant scene-
changes.

She was standing on a street that climbed up a hillside,

with shops on either side. Men and women passed by, many
of the men in the khaki uniform of a British Army officer,
the women in long dresses and big hats. They were talking in
posh, pommy accents.

There were a few Indians in suits, but mainly they wore
traditional dress: the women in saris, and the men in dhotis,
white ankle-length garments like tight skirts.

Everyone seemed to be strolling up the hill, so Suzie joined
them. She saw a sign above a doorway: Darjeeling Post
Office. So she was in the Hill Station of Darjeeling, in West
Bengal, where the British had come in summer to get away
from the heat of Calcutta. As she looked about her, it was as
if she had been magically carried back in time.

Donkeys laden with wooden crates and wicker baskets
trotted past her, driven by thin boys and girls with sticks.
Strange Indian cries filled the air. 'Chai!' a man called, and
beckoned her over to where he squatted next to a big kettle.
'You like spiced chai, girl?'

'Mooli!' a thin young man cried. 'Mooli, Mooli, Mooli!'

Mooli, it seemed, was a long white vegetable shaped like a
carrot. The man was selling them peeled and sprinkled with
red powder.

Suzie stared about her in wonder. She would have more
than enough material to put in her essay!

She reached the top of the hill and came to a broad
promenade filled with strolling couples. Indians with old-
fashioned box cameras took pictures of proud officers in
uniforms, and others sold donkey rides.

'Hi, there! This your first time in Darjeeling?'

Suzie turned, realizing that someone was talking to her.

A thin Indian girl, perhaps her age but shorter, was smiling
up at Suzie. She was dressed in a white T-shirt and baggy
shorts. Her face was round and friendly, with a small, red
velvet circle on her forehead.

'Don't tell me,' the girl went on. 'You're here to research a
project, ah-cha?'

Suzie laughed. 'How do you know?'

The girl beamed. 'Every day, schoolkids from all around the world spin into the Raj-zone to see what it was like.'

'Is that why you're here?'

'No. I *work* here.'

Suzie was confused. 'But you're not a phace, are you? You're real, in Realworld? How can you work here?'

'Simple. I work as a guide. I show schoolkids around Darjeeling – show them what it was like to be Indian, all those years ago.'

'Neat-o,' Suzie said. She frowned. 'But why? I mean, who pays you? The Web authorities?'

The girl pulled a scowling face. 'They don't know what I do! I work for myself!' She puffed out her chest, proudly. 'You see, I show you around here, and you transfer VR credits into my wristpad. That way I can spend more time in the Web, here and in the gamezones.'

'Hey, that's a great idea!' Suzie said. 'How much do you charge?'

'Ah-cha. I show you around the town for thirty minutes, and you give me one hour of credit. Deal?'

Suzie thought about it. Time in the Web was expensive, and she didn't have a lot of credit, but seeing as this was going to get her a good grade for her essay . . .

'OK. Sounds fair enough.' Suzie shook hands with the girl. 'What's your name?'

'Ana Devi,' the girl said. 'Yours?'

Suzie told her. 'From Australia. A town called Stewart's Creek, fifty kilometres west of Sydney. You from India?'

Ana nodded. 'I live in New Delhi—'

'New Delhi? Hey, I might be going to Delhi next month.' She told Ana about the soccer competition. Australia were in the final of the qualifying games. If they beat New Zealand in Sydney on Monday night, they would play in a competition at the Olympic Games in India – an exhibition tournament of mixed-sex teams. Depending on the success of the tournament, mixed soccer might be allowed into the Olympic Games as an official sport.

Ana stared. 'You play soccer for Australia?'

'The Australian under-sixteen mixed team,' she said. 'You see, Uncle Tom was a pro-soccer player in Sydney, ten years ago. He's coached me since I was four years old.'

'Your parents must be proud.'

Suzie shrugged. 'Never knew my father. And my mother died three years ago, when I was ten.'

'My parents died when I was young.' Ana looked up. 'So we're both orphans.'

Suzie smiled. 'I live with my Uncle. Well, really I have my own tree house—'

Ana stared at her with goggle eyes. 'You live in a tree trunk?'

Suzie laughed. 'No! Uncle Tom built me a house in a tree in the back paddock for my tenth birthday. It's like a shed high up in the branches. That's where I am now, in Realworld. I have my Websuit and junction box in the tree house, connected to the power supply in Uncle Tom's bungalow.' She paused. 'Where do you live?'

'Oh . . . ' Ana seemed reluctant to talk about it. 'Here and there. I live with my brother, Ajay. He goes to school now.' She said this with pride, as if it were a great achievement.

Suzie said, 'And you didn't?'

Ana shook her head. 'I had to beg for a living. At least Ajay will have an education, the chance of a good job.'

They moved down the hill, and Ana gave Suzie a brief history of the town. This was certainly better than reading about the subject on boring computer screens!

She told Suzie about a caste of Indians called Untouchables, the things they were not allowed to do, jobs they could not take, places they could not visit.

'You know a lot about them,' Suzie said.

Ana nodded. 'It's always been difficult for my people,' she said. 'Perhaps you could write an essay about a day in the life of an Untouchable?'

Suzie looked at Ana. 'But can people tell, just by looking at you?'

The small Indian girl nodded. 'Everyone knows who everyone else is, in India. It's – what do you call it? – instinct. We just know. I might be able to beg outside cafés and restaurants, but they wouldn't let me come inside and spend my rupees.'

'How can people do that to other people?'

'It's always been that way. Those in power will always find ways to control others.' She looked at Suzie. 'Haven't you found it difficult in Australia, because of your colour?'

Suzie thought about it. 'Sometimes people have said . . . *things*,' she said. 'My uncle tells me to ignore them, and to prove myself by doing well, by trying harder. But – I don't know – why *should* we always have to try harder than anyone else?'

'It's the same in India,' Ana said. 'It always has been, for an Untouchable. Come on, I'll show you.'

She took Suzie's hand in hers and pulled her through the crowds to a long, low building at the side of the sloping street. A sign above the door read: Glengary Tea Rooms.

'This is where the mem-sahibs and officers go for afternoon tea,' Ana said.

'The mem-what?'

Ana smiled. 'Mem-sahibs. English ladies,' she said. 'Would you like to be one?'

Suzie stared at her. 'What do you mean?'

'Just tap this code into your wristpad.' Ana gave her the code, tapped it into her own wristpad, and began to change in front of Suzie's eyes.

She grew, soon becoming taller than Suzie. Her skin changed colour, from a dark brown to pale pink. Also, her clothing changed. Now she was wearing a beautiful long dress of the period.

Suzie entered the code into her own wristpad and changed her appearance too, becoming white and fashionably dressed. Now they were like all the other – what had Ana called them – mem-sahibs, who were strolling up and down the hill.

They climbed the steps of the Glengary and entered a big room full of small round tables, each set with a fine lace tablecloth and shining cutlery. The hum of polite conversation filled the air, along with the tinkle of a piano. Old-fashioned ladies and gentlemen enjoyed afternoon tea and pastries. Even though Suzie was dressed for the period, she still felt out of place among them.

A waiter with a big moustache hurried across to them. 'Ladies, a table for two? Please, if you would care to follow me . . . We have a window table free with a spectacular view of the hills.'

Ana winked at Suzie as they were led across the room towards the window overlooking the steep, wooded hillside and the distant mountain peaks.

The Indian girl put on a posh voice, in keeping with her appearance. 'I will have a pot of Lapsang Souchong and a salmon sandwich,' she said. 'The same for my friend.'

The waiter bowed. 'Thank you, madame. One minute . . . ' He hurried towards the kitchen.

Ana was grinning mischievously. 'Now just watch this! When he comes back, enter your old code—'

'But—'

The waiter returned, wheeling a trolley carrying two plates of sandwiches and a silver teapot. As he turned to the trolley, Ana quickly entered a code on her wristpad. Suzie did the same.

Ana changed. No longer was she the posh British lady. In a second she was the Ana of old, the thin, dark Indian girl in baggy shorts and a T-shirt.

Suzie felt herself changing. She looked down. She was her old self again, dark-skinned and casually dressed.

The waiter turned to the table, carrying the plates of sandwiches. 'What!' he cried, and in his shock dropped the plates. Small triangular sandwiches spilled across the floor.

'How did you get in here?' I'll fetch the police! It'll be jail for you, you no-good gutter rats!'

To think that all they had to do to become accepted was to change the colour of their skin . . .   ·

'Go fetch the police, then!' Ana shouted.

Before Suzie could stop her, Ana stood and pushed over the table, sending flowers and ash trays bouncing across the carpet.

By now, all the diners in the restaurant had stopped eating and were staring at the two girls who were causing the commotion. Suzie felt herself blushing, even though she knew that the diners were nothing more than computer-generated phaces.

'You can keep your awful tea rooms!' Ana was shouting. 'We wouldn't eat here if we were starving hungry! Come on, Suzie.'

The head-waiter approached, shaking his fist. 'I'll have the police on you!' he yelled.

Suzie and Ana stepped over the spilled sandwiches and flowers and ran from the tea rooms. Suzie said, 'Won't we be in trouble if the police catch us? They might tell the Web authorities and we'll be fined!'

They hurried down the sunlit hillside. 'Don't worry, Suzie,' Ana said. 'The authorities have got other things to worry about, these days.'

'They have?'

Ana stopped and hiked herself onto a wall at the side of the road. 'How long have you been spinning onto the Web, Suzie?'

'This is only my third time,' Suzie admitted. 'I've never had the money before now. Then a newspaper paid me five hundred dollars for my story – first Aboriginal girl to play for a mixed soccer team, and all that. I'd always wanted a Websuit, so I went out and bought a secondhand suit and a junction box.'

'I've been spinning in for a year now,' Ana told her. 'Lately things have been getting – I don't know – *strange*. Loads of Websites and zones have been closed down. More spiders have been patrolling certain zones, and I've noticed more

Webcops, men in black uniforms. Then, sometimes there are
– well, Rom calls them leaks.'

'Rom?'

'A friend of mine. He's a real Web-wizard. He's trying to
investigate what's going on, but he keeps getting arrested
and fined. He's seen the leaks. You're in a site or zone – say
Dreamcastle or Bellatrix – and suddenly strange things begin
to happen, like the sky changes colour, or bits of other zones
creep into yours. Once we were playing a really venomous
game in the Camelot gamezone when a spaceship crash-
landed on the castle.'

'Hairy.'

'The authorities claim it's just routine malfunction, but
Rom thinks something big is happening.'

A golden butterfly dancing through the air came to rest on
the wall beside Suzie. She watched it flex its wings open and
shut – for all the world like a Realworld butterfly.

Ana asked, 'Do you have many friends in the Web?'

Suzie shook her head. 'I don't really know anyone. It's
hard to make friends after just three visits. Everyone seems to
have their own groups.'

'It takes time, Suzie.'

'Do you know a lot of people?'

Ana shrugged. 'A few. There's Sanjay and Rom, they're my
best friends. And then I know Flygirl and Jax and Metaphor.
Every week we spin into the eightest game going.'

It sounded fantastic, to be part of a group of friends
exploring the many worlds of the Web.

In Realworld Suzie lived so far from town that it was
difficult to get out and meet people. Her best friend was
Wilkie, an Aboriginal who played for the same local soccer
team. And then of course there was Uncle Tom, who she
loved like nobody else.

'Who's the egg, Ana?' a voice from nowhere asked.

Suzie looked around, but they were quite alone on the
wall.

The voice called again. 'I said, who's the one-mip egg?'

Ana said, 'Is that you, Rom?' She was staring all around her, on the floor, on the wall – as if she might find Rom hiding there!

'Can't you find me?' he laughed. 'You're both basement-level cogs and that's a fact!'

Ana looked cross. 'He sometimes does this, Suzie. You'll have to excuse him. Rom! Show yourself at once!'

'My word, we are getting angry! Look closely, Ana. I'll give you a clue. The first part of my name is spread on bread, and the second is what birds do!'

Suzie worked it out. 'Butterfly!' she cried.

She stared in wonder at the big, golden butterfly sunning itself on the wall beside her.

'OK, Rom,' Ana said. 'Enough's enough. Why don't you introduce yourself to Suzie?'

As Suzie watched, the butterfly underwent a miraculous transformation. Its body grew, swelled, became a grinning head with a mop of ginger hair and a million freckles. The butterfly's wings became pink ears. Then Rom grew a thin body in a one-piece blue body suit.

'But how did he do that!' Suzie said. She had no idea you could make yourself *that* small.

Ana sighed. 'Like I said,' she whispered. 'Rom's a wizard – but don't tell him I said that.'

Rom perched on the wall and wiped a cocky wave at the girls. 'Hi, there, Ana,' he said in an American accent. 'Just battled in from Webtown. Thought you might be here, somehow. Who's the egg?' he asked, staring at Suzie.

'Curl up, Rom! She's no egg. Meet Suzie, a good friend of mine.'

Rom laughed. 'Hey, I've been listening to you for ten minutes. You've only just met.'

Ana sighed. 'We might have only just met, but sometimes you meet people and you just know they're going to be good friends. Unlike you, Rom. When I met Rom,' she explained to Suzie, 'all he could do was insult me. It's how he works. So don't be upset by his bad manners.'

Suzie smiled. She wasn't sure about Rom, though. He seemed extra big-headed to her.

'Anyway,' Ana said, 'what are you doing here?'

'Thought you might want to spin into a gamezone.'

'Are Flygirl and Jax coming?'

'They said they'd be along soon, and Sanjay's coming too.'

'Venomous!' Ana jumped from the wall and reached for her wristpad. She stopped and looked up at Suzie. 'Why not come along, Suzie? I'll introduce you to the others.'

Suzie wondered if she could afford an extra hour or so in the Web. It would be expensive, but how could she miss this opportunity to meet Ana's friends?

'Are you sure they won't mind?' she asked.

Rom laughed. 'They're not all as rude as me. Of course they won't mind.'

Perhaps Rom wasn't so bad, after all.

Ana touched her hand. 'I'll give you the code, Suzie. See you there!'

Suzie tapped the code into her wristpad. She experienced a sudden flash of blue and a ringing chime in her ears. Then she opened her eyes. She was no longer in Darjeeling.

CHAPTER TWO

TRIASSIC PARK

Suzie was standing on the wooden observation platform of an hexagonal safari hut, overlooking an incredible landscape. Not for the first time she marvelled at the reality of the Web. She gripped the rail in front of her and stared down the hillside. At the foot of the hill was a swamp, coated with a scum of bright green algae, and beyond was a steaming jungle. In the distance, on the horizon, a row of volcanoes smoked as if ready to erupt at any second.

Ana and Rom were standing beside her. 'Welcome to Triassic Park, Suzie,' Rom said. 'My all-time favourite game-zone.'

'This is amazing,' she said. 'I never imagined—'

Rom laughed. 'What Websites have you visited, Suzie?'

She shrugged, 'I've been to Gulliverzone – because I've always loved the book – and last week I visited Lunazone and watched the first moon landing. And then Darjeeling.'

'I've been spinning in for five years now,' Rom boasted, 'and there's still a million worlds I haven't explored.'

Suzie looked at him. 'And you keep coming back to this one?'

He nodded. 'It's *truly* venomous,' he said.

'Look!' Ana cried, pointing.

Suzie swung round and stared down the hillside. At first she didn't see what had attracted Ana's attention – then she heard the roar.

A great, grey dinosaur was moving with colossal grace from the jungle and into the swamp. It had a body the size of a school bus, a long tail and an even longer neck. It swung its head from side to side, scanning the swamp, and then waded into the thick mud. Like a wallowing hippo, it collapsed slowly onto its side and rolled.

'A brachiosaurus,' Rom said.

'And it's taking a morning mud bath,' Ana finished.

Further along the wooden verandah, the air began to shimmer. As Suzie turned, a million pixels fizzed like a shaken soft drink – and one by one three figures appeared.

'Flygirl!' Rom said. Flygirl was a tall teenager in a bright yellow one-piece. Her skin was as brown as mahogany and she wore her hair in dreadlocks.

Behind her was a handsome white boy, and beside him a short Indian boy.

Ana made the introductions. 'This is Suzie, from Australia,' she said. 'Suzie, meet Flygirl, Jax and Sanjay.'

Suzie nodded at each of them and they smiled and waved in return.

'So,' Flygirl said, 'is it find the egg?'

'Why not?' Jax said. 'Two teams of three? We take on you, OK?'

'Great!' Ana turned to Suzie. 'You're with Rom and me.'

'Hey,' Rom said. 'Why do we get the new girl?'

'Because I say so!' Ana said, staring at him. Suzie felt like hugging the small Indian girl. She glared at Rom.

'OK,' Jax said, 'get your weapons!'

While the others stepped inside the hexagonal hut, Ana explained. 'Are you feeling brave, Suzie? You see, we're going in search of a brontosaur's egg. They live on the far side of the swamp, through the jungle. We find their lair, take an egg, and bring it back here. First team back is the winner.'

Suzie gulped. 'We're stealing the egg of a dinosaur?'

'Like Rom said, it's a venomous game. The very best. I make it sound easy, but there's a hundred dangers on the way!'

'I can imagine,' she said. But, the more she thought about it, the more excited she became.

The others emerged from the hut carrying long poles. Rom passed one each to English and Suzie. He indicated a red ferrule at the end of his pole.

'They might not look much,' he explained to Suzie, 'but if anything attacks us just swipe it with the red end and it'll drop dead, OK?'

'Even a brontosaur?'

'Even old bronto. But they aren't the most dangerous predators out there. We've got to watch out for the smaller, faster things.'

'Like scelidosaurs and phytosaurs,' Ana said.

Rom was nodding, his face pulled into a grimace. 'Last week a phytosaur – that's a prehistoric alligator – got Flygirl. Bit off her leg!'

Flygirl laughed. 'It didn't hurt, of course. But it was a strange feeling to see my left leg carried off by the little monster!'

'OK,' Jax said. 'If we're all ready, let's set off. We'll go left around the swamp. You go right.'

Jax, Flygirl and Sanjay jumped from the verandah and ran off down the hillside. Rom led Suzie and Ana from the observation hut and towards the swamp, skirting the right-hand shore.

Suzie gripped her pole and looked around for any sign of danger.

'I'll scan ahead,' Rom said. 'Do whatever I say, OK? Suzie, you follow me and keep your eyes left. If you see anything move – anything at all! – shout. Ana, you bring up the rear and scan right.'

They were creeping around the swamp. One hundred metres away, the brachiosaurus slapped its great tail in the mud and snorted. Suzie felt her feet sink centimetres into the soft ground with every step. She was sweating in the hot and humid air.

Across the swamp she saw the three small figures of Flygirl,

Jax and Sanjay moving quickly towards the jungle. As she watched, she saw something dart from the green mud and launch itself at Jax – a fearsome creature like a crocodile with spines. Jax, Flygirl and Sanjay beat at it with the poles, but the creature dodged and dived and evaded their swipes.

Rom laughed aloud. 'That'll slow them down. Hey!' he called across the swamp. 'Give it a whack from me!'

He shouldn't have been so cocky, Suzie thought. What happened next served him right. A green, long-legged beast as tall as Rom himself strutted out from behind a stand of pineapple-top ferns and lunged, trying to bite him with snapping jaws.

Suzie cried out in fright and tried to whack the animal. That was a mistake. The creature transferred its attention to her. It darted forward, sickle teeth slashing the air before Suzie. She lashed out with her pole and missed.

Ana crept behind the animal and jabbed it with her pole. Instantly, it collapsed in a heap at Suzie's feet. She stared at it, aware of her heart thumping.

'That was your fault!' Ana hissed at Rom. 'If you hadn't shouted, it wouldn't have heard you and attacked. We'd be in the jungle by now. Look, the others are well ahead.'

Sure enough, there was no sign of the other team across the swamp.

Rom nodded, looking sheepish. 'OK, it was a one-mip thing to do. Sorry, and all that.' He flashed them a grin. 'Forgiven?'

Ana swiped at him playfully with her pole. 'We're wasting time standing around like this. Let's get going!'

This time the small Indian girl led the way. Minutes later they left the swamp behind and entered the jungle. Suzie felt even more vulnerable now. Strange plants and trees pressed in from every side, providing abundant hiding places for hostile predators.

She held her pole at the ready. They were creeping swiftly down a path worn through the undergrowth, brushing past spiny ferns and cacti-like growths. The sun pierced the

canopy overhead like dazzling spears, illuminating the
flitting shapes of massive insects and colourful birds. Weird
calls and whoops echoed through the jungle.

Something touched Suzie's shoulder. She jumped and
screamed. 'What was that?'

A black shape was moving on the edge of her vision. She
turned her head and saw a tarantula – like a Brillo pad with
legs – crawling down her arm. She screamed again. Ana
turned and brushed the spider away with the back of her
hand.

'Don't worry,' the Indian girl said. 'It can't do you any
harm.' She smiled reassuringly.

Suzie nodded, aware of her rapidly beating heart.

They continued their march.

She was concentrating on the undergrowth to her left
when she saw him. At first she thought she was seeing
things, an odd pattern of leaves that looked like . . . She
blinked, but he was still there: an Indian, with a hooked nose
and a sparkling ruby set into the middle of his forehead,
wearing a red turban. The man wore a white suit and was
sitting cross-legged, levitating a metre from the ground and
staring at Suzie with big brown eyes.

He smiled and moved his lips, but no sound reached her.
She was about to tap Rom on the shoulder when the man
vanished. She shook her head. Had she really seen him, or
imagined it?

She recalled Ana telling her about the leaks. Was that what
the Indian had been, a stray image leaking from another
Website?

She pushed the thought to the back of her mind. There
were more important things to be thinking about – like
making sure they remained safe and won the game.

They pressed on, and five minutes later came to a silver
stream gurgling through the jungle. Ana paused on the bank.
'We're nearly there,' she told Suzie. 'Two hundred metres
beyond the stream is where the brontos have their lair.'

'One of us should go for the egg,' Rom said, 'while the other two act as decoys. I volunteer for egg duty!'

'You always want all the glory!' Ana complained. 'Why don't we let Suzie try for the egg while we distract the brontos?'

'Because,' Rom said, wearily, 'I don't want an egg going for the egg. I'll go.'

Ana looked at Suzie and gave a despairing shrug.

They located a series of stepping stones and crossed the stream, Ana leading the way, Suzie in the middle and Rom bringing up the rear. Suzie was stepping onto the far bank when she heard a cry from behind her.

She turned in time to see something long, thin and red – an eel with legs? – wrap itself around Rom's right leg and begin to climb, like the helix on a barber's pole. He was standing transfixed, staring down at the creature in horror.

'Where's your pole?' Suzie cried.

'I . . . I dropped it in the river when . . . when *it* attacked me.'

The creature reached the top of Rom's leg, opened its jaws and sank its needle-sharp teeth into his thigh.

Suzie jabbed out with her pole and the creature slithered back down Rom's leg and flopped into the river.

Rom was staring down at where the thing had bitten him, a look of horror on his face. The legging of his one-piece was ripped. 'It doesn't hurt,' he was saying to himself. 'Nothing can hurt you in the Web. But—' He stepped from the last stone and joined Ana and Suzie on the bank, limping. 'But I can't walk properly. We've been handicapped for not being vigilant.'

'You mean,' Ana pointed out, 'that we've been handicapped because *you* weren't vigilant. Well, you can't go for the egg now. How about it, Suzie?'

Rom interrupted, 'But she's not experienced! We can't risk it. You go, Ana.'

'Hey,' Suzie said, 'what makes you think I'm no good? I

might not have played this game before, but I bet I can outrun you any day.' She looked at Ana. 'I'll go for the egg.'

Ana smiled. 'Just remember that even if a bronto does try to stomp on you, you can't be hurt in the Web.'

Rom had stormed off and was peering into the stream. 'I can't find my pole.'

'You one-mip no-brain!' Ana cried. 'Come on, we're wasting time. The others will get there before us! You'll just have to hope you don't get attacked again.'

Ana led the way through the dense undergrowth, Rom dragging his leg slowly. Suzie came last, looking around her for the next sign of trouble.

Two minutes later they came to a vast clearing in the jungle. Ana ducked behind a low bush. Suzie and Rom joined her, crouching low and peering through the leaves. A great outcropping of rock reared into the sky, perhaps one hundred metres away. In the sandy area before the rock, half a dozen massive brontosaurs moved slowly, snacking on leaves and guzzling water from a stream.

Suzie gulped at the sight of them. She knew they couldn't hurt her, so why did she feel an instinctive pang of fear at the thought of what she had to do next?

Ana pointed with her pole. 'There, on the far side of the clearing at the foot of the first rock, can you see a hollow in the sand?'

Suzie nodded. 'Next to that ugly looking brute?'

'All you have to do,' Ana went on, 'is run across the clearing, dive into the hollow and dig until you come across an egg. Then grab it and run. Don't worry, we'll distract the brontos first. Meet you back here in two minutes.'

'And if you don't get an egg,' Rom said, staring at her, 'you'll never spin in with us again!'

Ana turned to Rom. 'Look who's talking! As if you've been very helpful today! Thanks to you we've got less chance of succeeding.' She smiled at Suzie. 'Don't listen to him, ah-cha? You can spin in with me any time.'

Suzie glared at Rom. 'Let me show you how it's done,' she said.

First, Ana and Rom left the cover of the bush and ran into the clearing, shouting to attract the attention of the grazing beasts. Suzie crouched like a sprinter in the blocks, ready to run at the first opportunity.

Three of the dinosaurs heard the commotion created by the tiny humans and ponderously swung their heads around. They moved off to get a closer look at Ana and Rom, the ground shaking beneath their feet. A gap opened in their ranks. There were still two monsters nearby, but they were facing the other way. The mother brontosaur seemed to be napping beside the hollow where the eggs were buried, sprawled out on its belly with its long neck protectively encircling the sand pit.

Suzie ran. She felt her heart pumping as she sprinted across the clearing. She thought she had never run as fast in all her life, even when going for goal with the ball at her feet. She passed the massive grey bulk of the first dinosaur, which was pulling leaves off a nearby tree, quite oblivious to her.

She was halfway across the clearing when the second brontosaur turned, blocking her way to the sand pit. For a second she was convinced that it had seen her, would lift its great, tree-trunk leg and attempt to squash her flat, but it seemed unaware of her. The problem was how to get past. Its long tail was curled against the rock, blocking the rear route, and she couldn't go around the front for fear of it seeing her.

So . . . there was only one way to go. *Underneath* the animal.

She ducked and sprinted between its four stocky legs, her head brushing against its belly. If it decides to sit down now, she told herself, I'm mincemeat. Or rather, she would be ejected from the gamezone and would find herself back in Webtown. A failure.

She emerged from beneath the dinosaur's belly. She was nearly there. She felt a sudden thrill bubbling within her chest, just like receiving the ball in front of an open goal.

She ran past the bulk of the dozing mother and leaped over its neck into the sand pit. She dropped her pole and, on her knees, dug frantically through the sand.

But what if there were no eggs at this time of year? she asked herself. What if the other team had got there before her?

She dug a hole as deep as her arm, and then gave up. She tried again two metres away, scooping up the warm sand and breathing hard. Just as she was beginning to give up hope, her fingers hit something hard and smooth.

A dinosaur's egg!

She dug the sand from around the big, creamy dome and lifted it free. She was surprised by how heavy it was as she hugged it to her chest and rose to her feet, elation flowing through her. All they had to do now was to get back safely to the observation hut, and the game was theirs.

But first, of course, there was the small matter of evading the dinosaurs.

She crept from the pit and past the creature's head, clutching the egg like a trophy. Then she took off and ran like the wind. Across the clearing, she saw Ana. The small Indian girl was waving madly at her and shouting.

'. . . behind you!' Suzie heard.

She turned in panic. The sleeping brontosaur was asleep no longer. It raised its head and peered at her, then looked at the disturbed sand pit. Its small brain made the connection. It gave a high screech and lumbered awkwardly to its feet.

Suzie felt a surge of high voltage fear pass through her. She had left her pole back at the sand pit! Should she run back into the jungle, hoping she could outpace the brontosaur, or return for the pole and hope she got there before the monster reached her?

She knew what she must do. Her heart in her mouth, she sprinted for the pit. The dinosaur stomped towards her, screeching in anger. Suzie skidded into the sand, looked about for her pole. It wasn't there.

The brontosaur approached, bellowing. It was perhaps five

metres away, seconds from lifting its front leg and mashing her to a pulp, when Suzie saw the red tip of the pole protruding from the sand. She had accidentally buried it while digging up the egg. She dived and grabbed the weapon with one hand, swinging it around in a wild arc as the brontosaur lifted a leg above her.

She missed and fell onto her back. She screamed as the massive foot fell towards her. In desperation she lashed out again with the pole, and then rolled away.

More through good luck than skill, the pole struck the underside of the monster's foot. It gave a grunt and, as if in slow motion, toppled towards her. Suzie yelped and scram- bled across the sand. Seconds later the brontosaur hit the ground where she had been with the impact of an earth- quake.

She picked herself up and ran . . . then tripped over a rock. She sprawled head first, and the egg flew from her arms and rolled across the ground like a rugby ball.

She saw a pair of legs run to the egg and felt thankful that Ana had joined her. She would feel more confident crossing the clearing with her Indian friend.

Only then did she notice that the girl was not Ana, but Flygirl.

'Hey!' she cried out. 'You can't do that?'

'Who says I can't?' Flygirl laughed. 'I just have!' She snatched up the egg and ran. Jax and Sanjay began cheering from where they were watching in the jungle.

Enraged, Suzie surged to her feet. She sprinted across the clearing and shoulder-charged Flygirl. The girl screamed and went sprawling across the ground, the egg tumbling from her grasp. Suzie picked it up and ran into the jungle.

'Hey!' Flygirl called out. 'You can't—'

Suzie laughed. 'Who says I can't?' she shouted back. 'I just have!'

Ana was jumping up and down, clapping her hands in delight. 'Well done!' she cried.

Suzie stopped in front of Rom. She presented him with the egg. 'So, I couldn't get the egg, wise guy?'

Rom smiled, and Suzie saw acceptance in his eyes. 'So I was wrong,' he said. 'Hey, even *I* can be wrong, sometimes. Welcome to the gang.'

Ana took the egg from Rom. 'Let's get back to the observation hut!'

They ran off through the jungle, Rom limping behind them. Seconds later the world went mad.

The first indication that something was wrong came when Suzie saw the white-suited Indian, and then another, then dozens of them hanging on a nearby tree like so many Christmas baubles. She was about to shout to Ana when she saw something else.

A brontosaur was lumbering through the jungle towards them, and as Suzie stared at the animal it suddenly changed into . . .

Suzie closed her eyes and opened them again, hardly believing what she was seeing. The dinosaur was no longer a dinosaur but a steam engine, punching fists of white steam into the air. It even whistled as it careered towards them.

'Ana!' Suzie cried. 'Watch out!' She flung herself at her friend and pulled her from the path of the oncoming train. They rolled through the undergrowth and seconds later the engine hurtled by, roaring and snorting like a mechanical dragon. They crouched behind a stand of ferns and watched it pass.

'What's happening?' Suzie shouted. 'Look. Over there!'

She pointed to a tree which had suddenly turned into a skyscraper, its silver windows reflecting the sun. They heard a cry from behind them, and seconds later Rom appeared limping through the jungle. He was rapidly followed by a line of cartoon characters. Suzie recognized some of them. Old Disney favourites from the last century: Mickey Mouse, Donald Duck and Goofy. They ran after Rom, calling and waving as if they wanted him to stop. Suzie reached out from behind the ferns and grabbed Rom as he passed. Mickey

Mouse, Donald and Goofy cavorted merrily by, still waving and shouting at some invisible quarry.

'It's a mega-leak!' Rom told them. 'The Web's going mad!'

Something was happening to the quality of the light. Suzie looked into the sky. It was a sky no longer, but a canopy of red and white stripes, as if Triassic Park was enclosed within a vast marquee. As they stared, holes appeared in the canopy and things dropped through, floating gently to earth – cars and trees, umbrellas and whales, sailing ships and giant bananas.

Suzie heard a sound behind her. She turned and screamed. Something . . . something green and scaly, like the ugliest lizard in the world, was walking upright towards her.

She ran, grabbing Ana's hand and pulling the little Indian girl after her. 'Wait for me!' Rom wailed, limping as fast as he was able.

Suzie looked over her shoulder. The lizard was still following, reaching out as if imploring her to stop. She cried out and sprinted even faster. Then she heard something that made her blood run cold.

'Suzie,' said the lizard in a dull monotone. 'Suzie, we need to speak with you.'

How did it know her name, and what did it want with her?

She had no desire to find out. She increased her pace, pulling Ana along behind her. She looked over her shoulder to see the lizard falling behind. As if in desperation, it called out to her. 'Suzie, you met the prime minister . . . we need . . . '

Ana stared at her. 'What does it mean?'

Suzie shook her head, too confused and shocked to speak. She looked behind her. The lizard was halted, waving at her like a stranded castaway.

Before she could feel relieved, the ground began to move beneath her feet. Nearby trees and bushes were moving slowly away from her. It was as if the jungle were floating on a river, and separate chunks of it were drifting apart. The scene was like an optical illusion. Suzie felt dizzy and sick.

She gripped Ana's hand as the patch of jungle on which they stood began to rock unsteadily. All around them the land was breaking up, crumbling into individual fragments and floating away like small islands.

'Ana!' Rom cried. He was kneeling on a nearby island as it bobbed past. 'I'm scuttling out of here! Catch you later!'

He hit his scuttle button and his image dissolved in a whirlwind of multi-coloured pixels.

Ana and Suzie held hands as all the islands moved away from each other, separated by gulfs as black as deep space.

'I think it would be a good idea to scuttle,' Suzie said.

Ana looked at her. 'What did that lizard-thing mean?' she asked. 'Why did it say you've met the prime minster? What does it want with you?'

Suzie shook her head. Its words had scared her more than the visual chaos. 'I don't know,' she said. 'But it's right, I have met the prime minister of Australia. When I became the first native Australian to be picked for my country. And I'm due to meet him again when we play in the qualifying final.' She shook her head, exasperated. 'But what could the lizard want with me?'

Ana never replied. The small island on which they were riding suddenly tipped, pitching them into the darkness. Suzie screamed and fell head over heels. She lost her grip on Ana's hand and watched her friend cartwheel away.

Then, in the darkness before her, the lizard-thing appeared. 'Suzie,' it began.

She screamed, reached out and hit her scuttle button.

Instantly, she was no longer in the Web. She pulled off her hood and goggles and stared up at the timber ceiling of her tree-house. She was breathing hard, her heart banging in her chest. She felt a sudden loneliness at being parted from Ana.

She thought about the Indian girl and the fact that they were now in their separate countries, thousands of miles apart.

Then Suzie considered the lizard and its words, and shivered.

CHAPTER THREE

ZOMBIE

Suzie peeled off her Websuit and folded it away under the bed. The tree-house consisted of one small room, with her bed in one corner and a big padded armchair by the open window. A warm breeze blew in from the paddock, carrying with it the cough-sweet scent of eucalyptus leaves.

She glanced at the alarm clock. It was noon, a hot Saturday in May. In Realworld she had been gone for three hours, but it had passed like a flash in the Web.

Three hours. She stood up, and immediately felt dizzy. If she'd stayed in the Web any longer, she realized, the Websickness would have been even worse.

She felt a pang of guilt. She had promised Uncle Tom that she would be gone just one hour. When she bought the suit a month ago, Tom had told her that she could spin into the Web for an hour every day. Her junction box was connected to the metered power supply in the house, and Tom would be able to tell if she disobeyed him. He didn't have much money these days, and electricity to power the junction box was expensive.

He would mention it, over the next day or so. He was never angry; that wasn't his style. Suzie had never heard him raise his voice. He told her off with a glance, a shake of his greying head.

She pulled her hold-all from under the bed and threw her soccer kit into it: a blue and white striped shirt, blue shorts and socks, and brand new Adidas boots which Uncle Tom had bought her when she was picked to represent Australia.

She had a league game at three o'clock. Wilkie was picking her up in his old Holden truck at one-thirty on the main road. It took an hour to get into Stewart's Creek. She often wished that Tom had bought a small-holding a bit closer to civilization.

'Suzie, you up there?'

'Here, Tom,' she called down.

She heard his slow progress up the ladder, rung by creaking rung, pausing a couple of times to rest his knee.

His head appeared in the trap-door, a mop of unruly grey curls surrounding his dark, round face. He was dressed in his customary denim shorts and Foster's Lager T-shirt. He was a small man with a little pot belly and a right knee scarred like a hot-cross bun.

He'd been a good footballer in his day. He had played professionally for a few Sydney clubs before the knee injury forced him to quit at the age of thirty. Since then he'd raised chickens and goats on his small-holding, coached Suzie at soccer and watched her get better season by season.

He limped over to the armchair and sat down with a sigh. 'Hot today, girl. Who you playing?'

'Ballaran, at home.'

'I'll be along to watch. Take it easy, but. Don't want you picking up an injury before the big game.'

'No worries. I'll take care.'

Tom sighed, looking around the tree-house approvingly. 'I did a beaut job here, ay? Solid as a rock.'

She could tell that he had something on his mind. She wondered if he'd read the meter, worked out that she'd been in the Web all this time.

'Suzie . . . ' he said at last. 'In a couple of months I'll be leaving this place for a while, going away.'

He looked through the window at the sun-browned hills of central New South Wales, rolling off into the distance like the humps of so many camels. His expression was far away, as if in his mind he was already out there.

'You know how I got to get away once in a while,' he said.

Suzie nodded. Every year, when his knee felt up to it, Tom set off. He would say goodbye the night before, and in the morning he would be gone. Suzie had woken early one time, and watched him go. He had been wearing only his shorts, and carried a spear, a boomerang and a goatskin full of water.

He never called it walkabout, but Suzie knew that's what it was.

A couple of months later, Tom would suddenly be back. The pot belly would be gone. He'd be leaner, fitter, and happier.

She shifted uncomfortably. She knew what was coming. A month ago he'd mentioned, casually, that perhaps she would like to come with him, the next time he left.

Now he said, 'Maybe in July, after the Indian tournament.'

'We haven't got through, yet!' she said.

'You'll get through, no worries, Suzie. When you get back, during the school holidays . . . Wilkie'll look after the chooks an' goats.' He paused, looked down at his scarred knee and began massaging it absently.

'You know something? I was fourteen when I first went. Your grandfather, Bill, he took me.' He smiled at the memory. 'Followed the river into the hills, then cut west and walked into the desert. Gone nearly four months, and jeez, what a time . . .'

Suzie swallowed, unable to meet his big brown eyes. She didn't want to hurt his feelings, after everything he had done for her, but how could she tell him that she wasn't interested?

'Things are different, out there,' he went on. 'You come to understand what really matters. You come to know yourself, and your connection to your ancestors. Living like they did, learning the old ways, you become one with the land and the spirits.'

'Tom,' she said softly. It was the only way she could

protest. She wondered why she was so against accompanying her uncle into the interior. It was something more than the hardship they would endure, the food they would have to eat, witchetty grubs and ants and dingo meat. It was more than the heat and the lack of water.

He laughed. 'I know, Suzie. You're a modern girl. You're not interested in the old ways.'

She shrugged. She *was* interested in the old ways – in reading about them, studying Aborigine history and lore. But she was living in the twenty-first century. How could she go back to something that her ancestors did, hundreds of years ago?

'I know how you feel,' Tom said. 'I didn't really want to go, when I was your age. But remember,' he went on, 'remember, Suzie, you won't be giving anything up. You'll be gaining something.'

'It's just that—' she began. 'You see, I like how I live now. I have my own interests. The Web—'

'Hey, girl,' Tom said gently. 'I like the Web, you know.' Tom used the VR-bar in Stewart's Creek from time to time. 'We can do both, but. We can live in the modern world, and in the old world, too.' He sighed. 'Keep it in mind, Suzie. If not this year, maybe next, OK?'

She nodded, aware that she had been let off, at least for a year.

He changed the subject. 'Hey, you enjoying the Web?'

'Reckon. Today was . . . it was just great! I met some people, kids who've been spinning in for ages. They know all the best zones. We played a game called snatch the dinosaur's egg!' She thought about telling Tom of the strange leaks, and the lizard which had chased her, but decided not to. She didn't want him pulling the plug on her fun.

Tom smiled. 'That's another thing I wanted to see you about, Suzie. I don't mind you spinning in, but the Web just sucks up the old power.'

'I know I was in for a long time today,' she said. 'But in future I'll try to stick to one hour.'

Tom winked at her.

A horn sounded, muffled by the distance. 'That'll be Wilkie,' Tom said. 'Time you weren't here, girl!'

She grabbed her bag, bent to hug her uncle, and climbed down the ladder to the paddock. She ran past Tom's tumbledown weatherboard bungalow to the access road and sprinted the half-kilometre to the main road.

Wilkie was furiously pounding the horn and leaning through the window of the truck. 'Run, Suzie! Faster, faster! You'll never skin the defender running like a possum!'

She dived into the passenger seat and Wilkie accelerated off down the road. 'Can run faster than you any day, Wilkie.'

'Reckon?' he laughed.

She had known Wilkie all her life. They'd grown up on neighbouring farms, gone to school together, began kicking a soccer ball around with Uncle Tom almost before they could walk.

Wilkie was sixteen, three years older than Suzie. He was a good player, but Suzie was better. When she'd been picked for Australia, she'd noticed something change in his attitude towards her. It was almost as if he resented her success. For a few weeks, they'd hardly talked. Then, when he saw that she was just the same old Suzie he had always known, that success hadn't changed her, he became friendly again.

Now he was proud that he knew a real Socceroo.

Suzie wound the window down and stuck her head out into the hot wind. 'Hey,' she called, 'your dad ever gone walkabout, Wilkie?'

He stared at her. 'What? You kidding? No way. Dad couldn't walk to the dunny without stopping halfway.'

She looked at him as he sat hunched over the steering wheel, almost hugging it.

'You never wanted to go?' she asked.

'What, walk into the desert with no food and no bed to kip in? Nah, not me. Where'd I get me pie an' sauce?' He glanced across at her. 'You?'

She shook her head. 'Nah.'

She remembered what Tom had said. *'You won't be giving anything up. You'll be gaining something.'*

She considered telling Wilkie about her adventure in the Web, but she knew he wouldn't be interested. Wilkie had never used the Web. 'Give me soccer any day!' he'd told her.

Stewart's Creek was a small town of just two thousand people, a pub, a post office, a VR-bar, half a dozen shops and no creek. That had dried up years ago.

The soccer field was next to the school. Cars and trucks were parked beside the red-brick changing rooms. Wilkie skidded his truck to a noisy halt and Suzie felt a surge of excitement at the thought of the game.

Thirty minutes later she was changed and out on the pitch, stretching her leg muscles and kicking the ball with Jenny, the only other girl on the team. One by one the others emerged from the dressing room, followed by the Ballaran team all in red. Around fifty people stood on the touchline, a good turn-out for an end of season under-sixteen game. Perhaps some of them had come to watch her, after all the TV and newspaper coverage. There was not much else to do in Stewart's Creek on a Saturday afternoon.

The coach gave a team talk before the match began, reminding them that Ballaran was a good team. If Stewart's Creek won their last two matches, they were in with a chance of finishing second in the league.

Just as they were about to kick off, Uncle Tom turned up on his old Suzuki motorbike. He took his usual place by the halfway line and waved to Suzie. She returned his greeting, and then forgot about everything else as the game kicked off. She was deaf to the cries of the crowd and heard only the shouts of her team-mates and the ref's whistle.

She played wide on the left wing and had a couple of good touches in the first five minutes. She received the ball in the opponent's half and ran at the defender. He dived in at her, trying to intimidate with his first crunching tackle, but Suzie just shrugged him aside and crossed the ball high to the far post. From then on she gained confidence. Her marker was smaller than her, and slower, and every time Suzie picked up the ball she beat him for pace, reached the by-line and crossed. Her breathing came easily, despite the heat, and she felt as if she could go on running for ever.

The first goal came a minute before half-time – for Stewart's Creek. Suzie picked up a loose ball on the edge of the penalty area and dribbled past the right back. She reached the goal line and tried to cross the ball, but the defender kicked her legs from under her. She fell heavily and rolled, but the sound of the referee's whistle awarding the penalty compensated for the pain shooting through her shoulder.

Jenny placed the ball on the spot and took five steps back. Suzie watched, aware of her beating heart, as Jenny stepped up and blasted an unstoppable shot past the diving keeper.

Seconds later the whistle went for half-time. They gathered by the touchline for a team talk.

'We're doing beaut!' Suzie said, biting into her half an orange.

'Just keep on pressing,' the coach said, 'and you've got the game won. Keep it tight at the back, remember. Suzie, you've got that full-back on toast! OK, get back out there and finish it off.'

Five minutes into the second half, Suzie threaded a pass through to Wilkie who rounded the keeper and side-footed the ball into the gaping net. From then on the result was never in doubt. Suzie enjoyed her game, receiving the ball deep and running at the defence. Only bad luck robbed her of making a goal herself.

She intercepted a loose ball in the centre circle, played a one-two with Jenny, and carried the ball forward. The line of defenders seemed to melt away before her. In a split second she decided to shoot. She whacked the ball with her left foot. It cannoned towards goal, always rising, cracked against the crossbar and rebounded. Wilkie dived, meeting the ball with his head and driving it into the back of the net.

Three-nil, and the game was won.

At full-time, her marker reluctantly shook her hand. 'Not bad,' he said, 'for an Abo.'

Suzie could only laugh. She remembered playing her first organized game at the age of nine. 'Not bad,' an opponent had told her, 'for a girl.'

Now Suzie laughed. 'Better luck next time, mate. You'll need it.'

Uncle Tom met her with a hug on the touchline. 'Well played, Suzie. I'm going into town for a while, OK? See you back home.'

Suzie waved. 'I won't be late.'

She showered and changed in the girls' dressing room and met Wilkie and the rest of the team outside fifteen minutes later. Everyone piled onto the flat-bed of the truck and Wilkie drove into town. It was customary after the game to celebrate victory, or mourn defeat, at Jack's Milk Bar and Café.

Suzie sat with Wilkie and Jenny on high stools at the counter, swivelling her seat to shout at her team-mates around the tables. She sucked on a malted chocolate milkshake while Wilkie ate his way through three Four 'n' Twenty pies smothered in tomato sauce.

'Two-goal hero, Wilkie!' She slapped him on the back.

'Reckon!' he said, dribbling sauce.

'And both made by me, don't forget.'

'You're a star, Suzie. Hope you play as well Monday night, but.'

Jenny glanced up from her bottle of Royal Crown Cola. 'Looking forward to the big game?'

Suzie frowned. 'Not been thinking about it that much.'

When she did think about it – her first game for the national under-sixteens, in front of a crowd of thirty thousand in the Olympic stadium, with a trip to India awaiting the winners – she felt weak at the knees. It was just too much to contemplate.

Wilkie jabbed her shoulder. 'Y' never know; might be the first girl to play for the full national side.'

Suzie grunted. 'If they ever allow women to play at senior level.' She had often wondered what she would do when she reached seventeen, and was not allowed under FIFA laws to play in a mixed team. Join a women's team, she supposed. But it would be up to her, and players like her, to prove they could compete with the best of the men.

For the next few hours they ran down the stock of pies and milkshakes and talked about the game, soccer in general, school . . .

Wilkie looked at his watch. 'Jeez, it's eight, Suzie. Time I was getting back.'

She said bye to Jenny and the others, then wandered out into the heat of the summer's evening.

'Just got to fill her up. Won't be a sec.' Wilkie drove his truck into the petrol station. Suzie stood on the empty street, staring across at the lighted sign of the VR-bar, a big neon symbol shaped like a spider's web.

It was a small place, as VR-bars went – just six single couches with three worn Websuits and three sets of glasses and goggles. Suzie had used the bar once, which was all it had taken to persuade her that she wanted her own suit.

Someone emerged from the lighted foyer of the VR-bar and turned left along the main street, heading out of town. In the gathering twilight, Suzie didn't recognize her uncle at first. She peered, saw his familiar squat figure and beer belly.

'Tom!' she called, waving and crossing the street towards him.

She called again, but he didn't slow down. And why was he heading out of town, when he always parked his motorbike outside the pub?

As she caught up with him, something else struck her as odd. Tom was moving like a zombie, walking as if wading through treacle, and looking around him in a daze. She was glad that no one else was around to witness his strange behaviour.

She tugged at his T-shirt, worried. 'Tom? Tom, what's wrong?'

He didn't so much as glance at her, just went on walking slowly, staring all around as if in amazement.

'Tom! Please, what's wrong? Talk to me!'

He stepped from the sidewalk and entered a paddock, knelt slowly and brushed his hands through the tall grass.

Suzie felt tears stinging her eyes. There was something strangely childlike in his behaviour, innocent and full of wonder.

He had just come from the VR-bar, but what could have occurred in there to make him act like this?

Now he was on his hands and knees, crawling like a child, his rapt gaze inches from the grass and wild flowers.

She heard the sound of a car horn. Wilkie was driving along the street towards her. She ran out into the road and waved.

Wilkie hung from the window. 'Suzie? What's wrong?'

'It's Tom, he's— I don't know. I think he's sick.'

Wilkie jumped from the cab and joined her. They hurried back to where Tom was still on all fours in the grass. To her surprise, Wilkie began laughing. 'He's had a few tinnies too many, Suzie. He'll be right!'

'No. He isn't drunk. He never has more than one or two. It isn't alcohol, Wilkie. There's something wrong. Help me get him into the truck.'

Wilkie nodded, suddenly serious. 'No worries.'

Between them they managed to lift Tom by his shoulders and steer him towards the truck. Trying to squeeze him into the cab was a little more difficult. Suzie forced his head down, but when she had done this his legs refused to bend. It seemed that he'd lost all comprehension of how to climb into an automobile. Wilkie lifted one leg, then the other, and pushed Tom into the passenger seat. Suzie squeezed herself in after him while Wilkie climbed in behind the wheel and gunned the engine.

'We'd better pick up his bike!' Suzie remembered. 'It'll be outside the pub.'

Wilkie reversed at speed, climbed out and manhandled the

Suzuki into the flat-bed. Then they set off, accelerating away from Stewart's Creek and into the gathering darkness.

For the next hour, Suzie gripped her Uncle's hand and whispered to him, asking him where he'd been and what had happened. Tom said not one word, just stared ahead at the probing beams of the headlights and the dancing mosquitoes, as if all the world was new and wonderful to him.

Back at the bungalow, Wilkie lifted the motorbike from the truck. He helped Suzie pull Tom from the cab and walk him inside. 'We'll put him to bed, Suzie. If he's still like this in the morning, reckon we'll call in the doctor. OK?'

Suzie nodded. They guided Tom through the old house to his bedroom and laid him on the bed. He lay still, not protesting, staring at the pattern of cracks in the plaster of the ceiling. Suzie paused at the door, watching him.

'He'll be right in the morning,' Wilkie said. 'Had a couple of beers, went into the Web, it's knocked him out.'

Suzie nodded, but she knew that Wilkie's explanation was way off the mark.

They moved through the house and paused on the verandah. 'You OK, Suzie?'

'I'll be fine, Wilkie. Thanks.'

'Call you in the morning. OK?' He touched her hand on the way out.

Suzie listened to the truck growling down the drive, the noise dying into silence. Soon there was only the intermittent creaking of the bungalow, as the timber cooled after the long, hot day.

She decided to sleep in the spare room and look in on Tom from time to time. Before she went to bed, she paused by his door. He was still lying flat on his back, gazing in rapture at the ceiling. Suzie shivered. She wanted to go to him, hug him, but at the same time she could not bring herself to approach her uncle. It was as if he was no longer himself, and Suzie was frightened.

She was awoken in the early hours by the banging of the

flyscreen door. She got up, pulled on her dressing gown, and hurried out onto the verandah. Tom was standing in the middle of the fruit garden, staring up at the dazzling globe of the full moon as if he had never seen it before.

As she watched, he walked into the back paddock and climbed the ladder to her tree-house. The window became a yellow square in the darkness of the night as he switched on her bedside lamp. Suzie watched him sit on the bed and pull on her VR-hood and goggles. He lay down, disappeared from sight, and switched off the light.

She returned to bed and tried to sleep. She lay awake for what seemed like hours, staring at the pattern the moonlight flung against the far wall. She must have dropped off at some time, because she awoke with a start to find bright sunlight filling the room.

The smell of frying bacon wafted through the bungalow.

Suzie jumped out of bed, dressed and hurried to the kitchen.

Tom stood by the stove in his shorts and T-shirt, cooking bacon and eggs in a frying pan. He turned and smiled at her. 'Morning, girl. You hungry?'

Suzie could only stare. 'Are you all right?' she asked.

He frowned. 'Never better, girl. Hey, why the concern?'

She shook her head. 'No reason. I just . . .' She paused. 'Can you remember yesterday?'

'Too right. Great game. You played like a star.'

'And after?'

'Had a couple of schooners down the pub with Jim.' He shrugged, frowned. 'Then I spun into the Web, looked up a couple of soccer mates.'

'How did you get home?' she asked.

Tom laughed. 'Flew, Suzie. You know.' He pumped his elbows in a flapping gesture. 'How'd you think I got home? Motorbike's in the drive, isn't it?'

Suzie persisted. 'But do you *remember* getting home?'

He sighed. 'OK, so I had a couple too many and I don't

remember getting in. I'm sorry. Won't happen again, I promise. Now, you want some breakfast?'

'No, I'm not hungry.'

The phone rang in the lounge. Suzie answered. It was Wilkie, asking after Tom.

'Oh, he's fine now. I think you were right. He had a bit too much to drink.'

Wilkie laughed and hung up, and Suzie slowly replaced the receiver and left the house. She crossed the garden and entered the back paddock. She climbed up the ladder to her tree-house and sprawled on the bed.

Tom might be fine now, but something had been very wrong last night, and Suzie was sure that drink was not responsible.

She looked at the alarm clock. It was nine-thirty. At nine yesterday, she had met Ana Devi in the Darjeeling Website.

Suzie hoped the little Indian would be there again today. She had a lot to tell her new friend.

Quickly she pulled on her suit and entered the Web.

CHAPTER FOUR

LADY-BUGS

The strand between the building blocks was not so busy today. There were fewer avatars moving from block to block, but there seemed to be more spiders patrolling the long avenues. For the first time, Suzie noticed the Webcops.

They were big, grossly muscled men in black uniforms. She thought she recognized their faces. They all had the appearance of a film star from the last century. What was his name? Arnie something-or-other. At any rate, they looked frightening.

She wondered why they were suddenly here in force, if it had anything to do with the recent leaks, or the lizard that had chased her yesterday, or whatever had happened to Tom last night.

She was about to tap the Darjeeling code into her wristpad when a big silver spider pranced up to her. 'Suzie?' it asked.

She backed off, afraid. 'What do you want?'

'Hey, lighten up, girl. We don't bite, you know. Well, not often. Got a message for you.'

Suzie wondered if it was the lizard again, trying to contact her. 'Who from?'

'You know Ana?'

Suzie smiled to herself at the thought that Ana had contacted her. 'A friend,' she said.

'She says to meet her at this code.' The spider rattled off a short string of digits. 'She'll be there at nine, your time. Be seeing you.'

Suzie watched the spider scurry away. Nine, her time . . . which meant that Ana would have been there for half an hour already.

She lost no time in entering the code. She experienced a flash of blue and a quick ringing in her ears, and she was no longer on the strand.

She seemed to be— She blinked. She was in a lush green landscape of rolling hills, forests of oaks, and . . . were those fairytale castles in the distance?

'Suzie!' called a voice from behind her. 'Thought you'd never get here!'

Ana Devi was sitting on a fallen log, smiling at her. She wore her usual baggy shorts and white T-shirt. She indicated the idyllic landscape with a small hand. 'What do you think?'

'It's . . . beaut. Where are we?'

'Camelot gamezone. You ever jousted, Suzie?'

'Never even ridden a horse!'

'Well, we could stay here, or we could bat into some other zone. Rom is joining us soon.'

Suzie thought of something. 'Hey, if it's nine-thirty my time, what time is it in India?'

'Around six in the morning.'

'You start early!'

Ana shrugged. 'It's cheap rates between midnight and seven.'

That reminded Suzie. 'Hey, I owe you VR-credits from yesterday, remember? You showed me around Darjeeling.'

'Forget it. I don't take creds from friends.'

Suzie sat beside Ana on the log. 'Did you notice all the spiders on the strand? And the Webcops?'

'Strange things are happening in the Web,' Ana told her. 'A lot of zones are closed down. I tried to bat into Bellatrix before I came here. It was being repaired, according to a spider I asked. I've never known that before.'

'Last night, Ana,' Suzie began, 'something odd happened in Realworld. I wondered if it was connected to the leaks.' She told Ana about her Uncle Tom, his strange behaviour after leaving the VR-bar.

'He's OK this morning, but he has no memory of what happened last night.' She shivered. 'It's creepy.'

'I've never known that before, and I've been spinning in for a year. But then a lot's happening that I've never seen before.'

'Ana, why do you think that lizard-thing wanted me yesterday?'

'Spiders usually bring messages – and the lizard was struggling . . . as if it didn't really know how to use the Web. I don't know.'

Something moved before them. Suzie watched as a small tornado of pixels appeared in mid-air. The pixels formed into the smiling, ginger-haired image of Rom. 'Got your message, Ana.' He looked around. 'Camelot gamezone? Bor-ing!'

'Can you suggest anywhere better?' Ana asked.

'Matter of fact I can do just that,' Rom said. 'I've been batting around for the last fifteen minutes, investigating certain things, talking to people.'

Ana rolled her eyes at Suzie, 'And?'

'Well, first of all, I found out that the Web-authorities have flooded the Web with cops and spiders. They're crawling all over the place.'

'Very observant,' Ana commented. 'Have you noticed anything else so obvious?'

'I do know that the authorities are stopping certain people entering the Web.'

'Are you sure?' Ana asked. 'I mean, what for?'

'All around the world, spiders are ejecting law-abiding, fully paid-up citizens. If they do get through, cops are sent to scuttle them.'

'Hairy!'

'There's more. The cops have closed down almost a hundred sites, but there's massive security around one site in particular. It's called Cydonia, a zone for conspiracy theorists. You know, people who have crazy ideas, like the Titanic was sunk by a UFO. The Webcops have thrown up a cordon around the site like you wouldn't believe. And it has something to do with the citizens who've been denied entry. You see, they were all batting into Cydonia.'

Suzie shook her head. 'I wonder what's going on in there?'

Rom grinned from Ana to Suzie. His expression was insufferably smug.

'What?' Ana asked at last. 'Tell us.'

'Well,' he said, 'I did say that I knew somewhere more interesting to bat to.'

'But you said it was closed down.' Ana began.

'No, I said it was surrounded by security like you wouldn't believe. The strange thing is that they've kept it operating. Word is that they're investigating something in there.'

Ana stared at him. 'And you think you can get into Cydonia?'

'I don't *think*, girl. I know I can. I've been working on an over-ride code.'

'But we'll be seen!' Suzie objected. 'We'll be arrested!'

'We'll be seen if we bat in looking like we do now. Of course we will. But remember yesterday when I batted into Darjeeling and you didn't even see me?'

'You were a butterfly!' Suzie said.

'And I know the codes for even smaller things,' Rom said. 'How do you feel about being a lady-bug?'

Ana was frowning. 'But . . . surely the cops will be able to detect us. They'll pick up our signal.'

'I don't think so, or at least it'll take them a while. We'll bat in and have a poke around. If there's any sign of them detecting us, we'll scuttle. What do you think?'

Ana looked uncertain. Suzie thought about all the strange things that had happened lately. Perhaps what was going on in Cydonia might answer a few questions.

Hesitantly, she nodded. 'OK. Yes. I want to go. But at the first sign of danger, I'm scuttling.'

At last Ana nodded. 'Ah-cha. I'll come too.'

'All right!' Rom whooped. 'Now, this is the code to change us to lady-bugs.'

He gave the code, and Suzie entered it into her wristpad. 'But!' she cried, just as she felt her perspective shift.

She was no longer sitting on a log on the grass, but hovering in the air. She bobbed up and down, hardly aware that she was using her wings. Everything seemed much bigger. The nearby daffodils were the size of trees, and the trees were as vast as clouds. Oh, to experience the world through the eyes of a lady-bug!

She had been about to ask Rom how they would bat from this site, but it was a silly question. Fixed to her left leg – a thin black leg covered with tiny hairs – was her wristpad. She practised moving her other front leg towards her wristpad, marvelling at the authenticity of the experience.

She saw two other lady-bugs hovering beside her, their tiny wings in arc-shaped blurs of motion.

'Hi there, Suzie,' the first insect said, in Ana's voice.

'You two ready?' said the larger lady-bug in an American accent.

Suzie tried to nod her head, then realized that the gesture was impossible. 'Ready,' she said, instead.

'Ready,' Ana called.

They formed a tight circle in the air like free-fall parachutists. 'OK,' Rom said. 'Let's stick together once in Cydonia and remember, we scuttle at the first sign of danger.' He gave the code.

Suzie moved her stick-leg and tapped the code into her wristpad. Camelot disappeared with a flash of blue and a high pinging chime.

CHAPTER FIVE

CYDONIA

They were hovering high above a vast plain of red sand. Suzie recognized the flat landscape. She had seen pictures and film of the place in geography lessons at school. She was on Mars, or rather a clever Web-simulation of the Red Planet.

The horizon fell away to the left and right in a perceptible curve, and overhead the two moons tumbled like giant potatoes.

Suzie and her friends formed a line in the air, holding onto each other with their front legs.

Suzie scanned the alien landscape. Beneath them was a vast dome, covering what looked like a small town. Beside it was a big stone carving – the Face discovered by the Viking lander last century.

'Look!' Rom called.

There was activity on the red sand beside the dome. Suzie saw a whirlwind of pixels form as a Web-user batted into the site – then another and another. In fact, hundreds of citizens were appearing all around the bubble-shape of the dome.

Or rather they were trying to.

No sooner had their images solidified than they were set upon by the imposing Arnie-phaces in black uniforms. There were thousands of the cops patrolling the perimeter of the dome, zapping citizens with machine guns, punches or karate chops. The avatars under attack disappeared in a quick fizz of pixels. Others tried to change appearance, becoming smaller to evade detection – birds, butterflies and bats swarmed around the dome. Spiders joined the Arnie-phaces in repelling the invaders.

'Look!' Ana called, pointing to the hatch of the dome.

The Arnie-phaces were facing retaliation. A hundred avatars of all shapes and sizes swarmed through the hatch from inside the dome and set about the cops and spiders. Suzie watched in disbelief as grizzly bears and lions, tigers and kangaroos attacked the Webcops. She even saw sharks swimming through the air and bearing down on the Arnie-phaces with open jaws. The cops and spiders detonated on impact with their attackers, disappearing in an explosion of pixels.

As she watched, more avatars batted into Cydonia. Pixels appeared like colourful tornadoes from every direction. All across the vast sea of sand avatars gained form, then quickly miniaturized themselves before the Arnies could pounce.

In the air around them, images gained solidity. Small birds, flying squirrels and locusts formed squadrons and homed in on the dome, entering through the main hatch.

'That's obviously where the action is,' Rom said. 'How about we go take a look?'

'Why not!' Ana said.

'OK by me,' Suzie agreed.

She tipped herself forward, angled her wings and set off in pursuit of Rom and Ana. She seemed to have perfect control of her new body, even though she had no idea quite how she was achieving that control. She had no sensation of her old self in the Websuit. All she could feel was her small domed body, tiny legs and powerful wings.

The sensation of flight filled her with exhilaration. They swooped through the cold Martian air towards the dome, which expanded before them like a blown soap bubble.

'Hey!' Rom called. 'We have company!'

Suzie angled her body and peered to their right. The Webcops had become wise to the miniaturization process of the avatars and were taking action. As she watched, a

hundred Arnie-faced bald eagles dived from the pink sky
high above, picking off insect and bird avatars one by one.

'This way!' Rom called, tilting and diving to their left. The
dome rushed to meet them. Below, the entrance hatch was a
chaotic melee as the Arnies and spiders fought a pitched
battle with Web-users of a thousand shapes and sizes.

Among the colourful riot, Suzie saw something which set
the alarm bells of her memory ringing. She saw the figure of
the white-suited, turbaned Indian doing battle with the
hulking Arnie-phace. Then she saw a green, upright lizard
attacking a spider. Soon she realized that there were more
than just one Indian and lizard fighting down below. She
counted perhaps a dozen in all. But, she asked herself,
were they the avatars of Web-users, or phaces? She decided
that they had to be avatars because why would computer-
generated phaces attack their own Webcops?

But if the lizards and Indians *were* the avatars of real
people, then who had tried to contact her yesterday in
Triassic Park?

Her confused thoughts were interrupted by Rom's shout.
'It's too dangerous down there!' he called. 'We'll try to enter
the dome some other way!'

He veered away from the entrance, and Suzie and Ana
followed. The silver skin of the dome expanded to fill Suzie's
entire field of vision, then she was stretching out her legs
and slowing her wing-beats in an attempt to effect a soft
landing.

She hit the dome with a bump, Ana and Rom banging
down beside her. Now, for the first time, she used her tiny
legs to walk. After a few seconds, she gained co-ordination of
her scurrying limbs and turned to face her friends. They
were, she realized, quite beautiful, now that their wing-cases
had closed to show their crimson carapaces spotted with
black dots.

She peered about her. It was as if she were walking on a
big, transparent planet, with the pink sky above the curved
horizon. She glanced down. Beneath her, through the skin

of the dome, Suzie made out a collection of buildings, parks and gardens. There were no Arnie-phaces or spiders within the dome. Far below, she saw the forms of the avatars which had made it through the entrance, and others which had batted straight into the protection of the dome itself.

She stared. The bird and bug avatars were changing into the images of normal, everyday humans, then approaching other figures and reaching out to hold them in odd embraces.

Rom was calling instructions. 'This way, troops! There's some kind of maintenance hatch on the horizon!'

He turned and scuttled off towards an irregularity above them. Suzie and Ana gave chase, scurrying with their tiny legs to keep up. They reached Rom, who had halted and was lowering his head over the lips of a vent.

'I think we can get in through here,' he called back to them. Without waiting, he moved forward, rolling over the edge and disappearing from sight. Suzie went next, scurrying around the lip of the vent and finding herself hanging upside-down.

Far below she could see the buildings and gardens of Cydonia, with the materializing avatars and the figures who were receiving them.

What on Earth – or rather on Mars – was going on down there?

'So what now?' Rom asked. 'Do we stay here and watch what's happening, or do we fly down and take a closer look?'

Suzie said, 'I say we take a closer look. We can always scuttle in an emergency.'

Ana was unsure. 'I don't know . . . I mean, will we be able to see much more?'

The decision, in the event, was made for them.

Suzie heard a sound coming from outside the dome. She turned, peered through the translucent membrane, and screamed.

An eel-like thing was slithering through the vent, and where its head should have been was the face of an Arnie-phace. It reared above her, ready to snap her up with its massive, grinning mouth.

'Get out!' said the Arnie-phace.

'Fly!' yelled Rom.

Suzie flew. She dropped from the underside of the dome, tumbling before righting herself and diving towards the ground. She was aware of the tiny figures of Rom and Ana beside her, their wings a blur of motion.

She made a broad swoop towards a garden, where she hoped she would be able to lose herself. She looked up and saw the Arnie-eel drop from the vent towards them. It tumbled over and over before morphing in mid-air, expanding into the shape of a diving eagle still with the hostile face of Arnie.

Its beady eye caught sight of the fleeing lady-bugs, its wings adjusted and the Arnie-phace knifed down towards them.

Ana screamed. 'We've had it! I'm scuttling. Catch you later!'

'Wait!' Rom cried. 'I have an idea. Enter this code!'

He called out a string of digits, and Suzie tapped them into her wristpad. Instantly, she was no longer a lady-bug, but something much sleeker and faster. She was aware of the ground passing by in a blur beneath her. Ahead, she saw the darting shapes of Ana and Rom. They were swifts, with sickle wings and forked tails. She twisted and turned, feeling the air streaming through her feathers. When she looked back, she could see the Arnie-eagle falling behind. In an instant, though, it had morphed into a smaller, faster bird, and was gaining.

'Down here!' Rom commanded.

The leading swift alighted on a patch of grass. Ana and Suzie landed beside him. 'What now?'

'Now we change again. I think I know the code . . .' But he hesitated, as if unsure.

'OK,' he said at last. 'Are you ready?'

Suzie looked up. The Arnie-phace in the shape of a smaller bird was fast approaching.

Rom reeled off the code.

Suzie entered the figures – tapping at the wristpad awkwardly with her thin, bird's claws – and then felt herself shrink. Now she was tiny, even smaller than a lady-bug. Blades of bright green grass rose around her like a forest of massive swords. She glanced down at herself. She was a small green insect with tiny fore-legs and pincer mandibles.

She looked around for the others. 'Where are you?' she called out.

She glanced up. The Arnie-bird, monstrously huge, landed nearby with a rush of air like the downdraught of a helicopter. She saw its great predatory shape strutting around above her, occasionally dipping to jab at something with a rapier beak protruding from Arnie's face where the human nose should have been.

'Over here!' Ana yelled. Suzie scurried through the thick grass, heading in the direction of the call. She butted her way past fallen leaves and cigarette ends the size of cars, desperate to find her friends.

'Suzie!' Rom called. 'Here!'

Rom and Ana were hiding beneath a fallen leaf, huddling close to each other. Suzie stared at the ugly emerald insects, with squat bodies, short legs and heads like gargoyles.

'We certainly won't win any beauty contest,' she said.

The insect that was Rom clacked his mandibles, and his unsynchronized voice said, 'We might not be pretty, but we're well camouflaged.'

A sound approached, the twitchy ferreting of the bird's beak in the grass. Its long stick legs came into sight as it hop-hopped a matter of inches away.

'I told you we should have scuttled!' Ana wailed.

'I don't know,' Rom said. 'I think this is dead venomous! Beats all the gamezones I've tried!'

Suzie huddled close to her friends and shut her eyes, aware

of her heart thudding in her human chest. In time the sound of the bird grew distant, replaced by the silence of the lawn.

Rom said, 'I think it's gone. Let's make a move. There's a path this way. Follow me.'

They set off, marching in single file, three small insects like bright green army tanks trundling over the uneven terrain of the lawn. Wait until she was back in Realworld, telling Wilkie of all her adventures! He wouldn't believe a word.

It was a long trek to the path. What would have taken a human less than a single stride was a gruelling marathon for the three little insects. 'Don't you know the code for – I don't know – a millipede?' Ana asked. 'Then we could move a bit faster.'

'Sorry,' Rom called back. 'This is the best I can do.'

Perhaps twenty minutes later they came to the sheer wall of the concrete path. Suzie followed Rom up the vertical face, suckers at the end of her legs making easy work of the climb.

They emerged on top of the path and paused side by side, scanning the way ahead for danger. In the distance they saw activity, far away blurs of arriving Web-users and one or two Arnie-phaces.

'How about we go back to being lady-bugs?' Rom suggested. 'We'll take off and see what gives.'

He gave the code. Suzie felt the familiar shape of the lady-bug's body enclosing her. She took off, following Rom and Ana as they launched themselves from the path and climbed slowly into the air.

They flew over a grassy knoll towards a building bearing the sign: Cydonia Café. There seemed to be activity going on beyond the café. 'We'll land on the roof and try to find out what's happening,' Rom began.

They didn't see the diving bird until it was too late.

Suzie heard a rush of wings, saw a quick shadow pass across Rom and Ana, and then the Arnie-phace, disguised as the eagle with an emotionless human face, was upon them.

Ana didn't stand a chance. The Arnie-phace opened its

beak and scissored the tiny lady-bug. Ana screamed, mashed in half by the great beak. Suzie saw Ana's frantic legs reach for her scuttle button, and she popped out of existence in an effervescence of pixels.

'I'm outta here!' Rom cried. 'See you around!'

He hit his scuttle button and vanished.

The eagle swooped towards Suzie. Fright kicked at her heart. She tried to reach her wristpad, but she could not co-ordinate her limbs. She closed her eyes and waited for the inevitable. She knew the eagle could not hurt her. She would simply be ejected and returned to Webtown. But even so she was seized with irrational fear.

She waited . . . but the expected attack never came.

She opened her eyes and could not believe what she was watching. The eagle was no longer intent on chasing her, but on saving itself. It was under attack from the most unlikely foe.

The white-suited Indian sat cross-legged and levitated through the air, chasing the Arnie-eagle. As Suzie watched, the Indian raised both arms. Crackling blue light streaked from his finger-tips and hit the eagle. The Arnie-phace squawked and vanished in an instant.

Still sitting cross-legged in the air, the Indian soared towards Suzie, 'mY FrieNd,' he said with a strange up and down tone, like a verbal roller-coaster. 'I aM a SwaMi. CoME, yOU deSErve AN eXPlaNatioN. FoLLow Me.'

He floated off through the air above the Cydonia Café. Suzie felt her pulse quicken. She had the almost irresistible urge to hit her scuttle button and get out of here, but at the same time she wanted to know what was going on.

She flew after the strange Indian.

'We NeED yOUr helP,' the Swami was saying, 'aND iN reTuRN wE WiLL reWArd yOU.'

'How?' she managed at last.

'FirST,' said the Swami, 'LoOK dOwn thERe.'

The Swami's brown eyes indicated the plaza in front of the café. A typhoon of pixels denoted the arrival of another avatar. Suzie watched, staring in disbelief, as a human figure materialized on the plaza.

'Tom!' she cried. 'Uncle Tom!'

He did not look up, but strode forward, towards . . .

Suzie stared, wanting to shout to her uncle not to do it. She had seen this before, this strange sacrifice of the avatars to the lizards. She had watched them approach each other earlier, embrace and join as one, before dissolving in a whirlwind of ejected pixels.

Now, Uncle Tom was doing the same. He stepped forward, arms outstretched, and reached for the upright lizard. Suzie could not tell who consumed whom: they seemed to merge, become one, before vanishing.

She cried out in fear and anguish.

'SUzIE,' the Swami said. 'Do NOt bE aFRaiD. I wiLL eXPlaiN.'

'No!' Suzie cried. Her mind was a whirl. How could she trust the Swami, no matter what he said, after watching the lizard do *that* to her uncle; whatever *that* was.

She was overcome with fright, and could do only one thing.

'NO!' the swami wailed.

She reached out and hit the scuttle button.

And Cydonia vanished.

CHAPTER SIX

THE GATHERING

Suzie yanked off the hood and goggles and struggled from her Websuit.

Her heart was still hammering from her experience in Cydonia. She glanced at the alarm clock. It was almost eleven. She had been in the Web for almost two hours, despite her promise to Tom.

Not that she was much bothered right at this moment about the cost of electricity!

The thought of what she had seen in the Web brought stinging tears to her eyes.

She pushed herself from the bed, and experienced the slows for the very first time. She was desperate to get to the bungalow, to see if Tom was at home or if he really *had* spun into the Web. But her movements seemed retarded, as if she were wading through golden syrup. She knew that she was really moving at the normal speed, but in relation to the accelerated pace of things in the Web, Realworld *seemed* like a slow motion action replay.

It took Suzie an age to get to the trapdoor, lower herself down the ladder, then run across the back paddock to the bungalow.

She pushed through the fly-screen door and ran through the house to Uncle Tom's bedroom. Her heart seemed to pound slowly in her chest as she made her way down the passage and flung open the door.

She stared into the room, hardly believing her eyes.

The bed was empty.

She retraced her steps, moved into the kitchen and out through the back door. She made her way around the house, to the drive where Tom usually left his Suzuki.

It was no longer there, of course.

So what she had seen in the Web was no hallucination. It had really happened – Tom had spun into the Web. She considered what to do next. Even her thoughts seemed slowed down, moving through her head like honey from a pot. She had to get to Stewart's Creek, get Tom from the VR-bar.

She ran back through the paddock, past the tree-house, and across the fields to Wilkie's place half a kilometre away. As she ran, the effects of the slows lifted from her. Soon she was flying, her heart beating rapidly and her arms and legs pumping. She seemed to eat up the metres between her place and Wilkie's. She sprinted into the back paddock and approached the house.

Nan Wilkinson sat in a big armchair on the back porch, chuckling to herself.

'G'day, Nan!' Suzie called. 'Wilkie home?'

Nan Wilkinson peered at her. 'The Wollagong girl? How's young Tom these days?'

Young Tom? Well, Nan did look about a hundred years old.

'He's fine, Nan. Is Wilkie in?'

She chuckled and pointed a big thumb over her shoulder. 'Reckon the bludger's still asleep, knowing him. Go on through.'

Suzie ran into the house. Wilkie's mum was baking in the kitchen. 'Hi, Suzie,' she smiled. 'Come for Wilkie?' Go wake him up, will you?'

She hurried down the passage and banged on his bedroom door. 'Wilkie, you decent? I'm coming in!'

She pushed open the door. The room smelled of sweat and old socks. 'Wilkie! You've got to help me!'

His tousled head appeared from a mound of bed linen. He dragged his watch from a bedside table, peered at it and groaned. 'Eleven-thirty on a Sunday morning! Can't a bloke get some kip around here?'

'Wilkie!' She almost hauled him from the bed. 'You got to help me. I need to get to Stewart's Creek! It's Tom!'

Wilkie shook his head. 'What's happened?'

'I was in the Web. Something attacked him. I think he's in trouble. I think maybe— The way he was last night, well, what happened in the Web might be responsible!'

'Suzie! Slow down. You aren't making sense.' Wilkie found his jeans and tugged them on. He struggled into his T-shirt. His head popped through the neck hole and he stared at Suzie.

'What attacked Tom?' he asked.

'I don't know . . . a lizard-thing.'

'It was in the *Web*, but,' Wilkie said. 'You always told me you can't get hurt in the Web.'

'You can't. He wasn't hurt none, I don't think. He was just . . . *attacked* by the lizard. I think that's what happened to him last night, before he left the VR-bar. You saw him then. He wasn't himself.'

Wilkie stumbled from his room, muttering.

Suzie gave chase. 'Will you *please* take me to Stewart's Creek.'

'If you wanna go to the Creek, I'll take you, Suzie. Just give my ears a rest. OK?'

He grabbed a handful of freshly-baked lamingtons from the table-top on the way out, passed one to Suzie and made his way around the house to his truck.

He climbed into the cab. Suzie hauled open the rusty door and joined him. Still half asleep and his cheeks full of sponge cake, Wilkie gunned the engine and they bucked from the drive and out onto the main road.

Suzie returned the lamington. She had no appetite, despite not having eaten today. Wilkie grunted, stuffed the cake into his mouth and hunched over the wheel as if wanting to go back to sleep.

He drove in silence, peering ahead at the road. Suzie stared through the side window at the passing bush, the hills dry and lifeless under the searing sun. She went over what had happened in Cydonia, trying to make sense of the series of events.

Wilkie turned to her. 'Was I hearing right, Suzie? You said a *lizard* attacked Tom in the Web?'

So she went through it all again. She told him about the leaks, the Swami and the lizard that had chased her, and the Arnie-phaces. Explaining all this to someone who had never used the Web was like trying to describe colour to a blind person.

When she fell silent, Wilkie just shook his head. 'Tell you something, girl. Glad I don't bother with the thing. Sounds like hell to me.'

'It's great, usually. But something strange is happening now.'

'Tell me about it! Fighting lizards and flying Arnies.'

Thirty minutes later they roared down the main street of Stewart's Creek. Wilkie braked with a screech outside the VR-bar and Suzie leaped out.

She pushed through the swing doors of the bar. The proprietor was sweeping the floor around the vacant Web-couches. 'Oh,' Suzie said, staring at the empty room. 'I thought Tom might still be here.'

'Left about half an hour ago.'

'Was he . . . I mean, did he seem OK?'

The man stared at her. 'OK?' He shrugged. 'Can't say I took much notice.' He looked at her oddly.

Suzie returned to the truck.

'Well?' Wilkie asked.

'He left thirty minutes ago.'

'OK, we'll try the pub.'

Wilkie drove along the street, braking before the big stone-built building. 'His motorbike isn't there,' Suzie said, climbing out.

She ran into the bar and looked around. A lonely drinker sat in the corner, staring at a bottle of Toohey's beer.

The barman said, 'How can I help you, Suzie?'

'Hi, Jim. You seen Tom today?'

'Sure. Drove by on his bike about . . .' He looked at his watch, 'about half an hour gone, I reckon.'

'Back home?' But why hadn't they passed him on the way?

'Nah. Other way, into the hills.'

'Thanks!' She waved and ran out into the heat and dazzling sunlight.

She climbed up next to Wilkie. 'He headed into the hills half an hour ago.'

Wilkie pulled a face. 'Wonder where he's going.'

He started the engine and they motored out of town, past the school and the soccer field. Within a minute they were out in the bush, following the long, straight road that climbed into the hills about ten kilometres away.

Wilkie braked about every five hundred metres, climbed from the cab and walked out in front of the truck. There he knelt and examined the dusty road.

He returned to Suzie. 'Tyre tracks still there,' he reported each time. 'So he hasn't turned off yet.'

Whenever Tom had his goats go missing, he called Wilkie to help track them down. Suzie kidded him that he had the ability handed down in his genes, but Wilkie just shook his head and claimed that any fool could do it.

Suzie knew how he felt. The old way of life was long gone now, and alien. They were creatures of modern Australia, and playing at the old way of life was just that, a game they didn't really understand.

As they drove, Suzie stared ahead for any sign of her uncle.

Perhaps ten kays out of town, as the road climbed into the hills, Wilkie got out and examined the ground. Something in his attitude alerted Suzie. He looked into the bush to the south.

He hurried back to the truck. 'He turned off here,' he said, 'heading along the track there.' He pointed to a rough track leading from the road at right angles.

He started the engine and turned left, bouncing along the pot-holed road between stands of gum and acacia. From time to time he braked and climbed out to look for tyre tracks, then set off again.

The odd thing was, Tom never usually came out this way. So why had he done so now?

Suzie held onto the dashboard as the truck bucked over the uneven surface. Once or twice she hit her head on the padded roof as the suspension creaked in protest.

Wilkie stopped again and examined the sandy track. He waved back at Suzie and pointed into the bush, then beckoned her to join him.

She climbed down and hurried to where he was kneeling. 'Over there,' he said.

Tom's old Suzuki was leaning against the trunk of a nearby eucalyptus. 'So wherever he went from here,' Wilkie said, 'he went on foot. Come on.'

They passed the motorbike and walked up the rise of the hill through the trees, Wilkie staring at the ground and stopping from time to time for a closer look.

They came to the crest of the hill and halted.

Far below on the plain was the town of Ballaran, laid out in a neat grid pattern. A rough track snaked up the hillside. Perhaps two hundred metres down the hill, on a straight stretch of track, a dozen cars and trucks were parked.

Wilkie gripped her arm. 'Look!'

Men and women were climbing from the vehicles and moving up the hill through the trees. They were walking like— Suzie stared. They moved in a familiar way, as if distracted by the wonder of the world around them. They were walking just as Uncle Tom had, the night before.

Then Suzie saw Tom.

He was making his way slowly down the hillside, as if to meet the others climbing the hill. He moved slowly, staring

about him, from time to time reaching out to caress the tall
grass. The others were doing the same, pulling leaves from
branches and inhaling their scent, or kneeling and running
the red soil through their fingers.

'What's wrong with them?' Suzie said to herself. 'It's as if
they've never seen the world before!'

Tom met the others in a clearing. Suzie watched in
disbelief as he greeted these strangers. He reached out to a
woman with both arms and touched his fists to her
shoulders, and then stood still as the woman did the same to
him. He moved to the next person and repeated the strange
movement. All around the clearing, people were greeting
each other with identical gestures.

Then they formed a circle and raised their arms to the sun.

Suzie set off slowly down the hillside.

Wilkie caught her up and tried to pull her back. 'Where're
you going?' he hissed.

'I want a closer look. I want to know what's going on!'

'I— Don't, Suzie. They might not want you watching.'

Suzie looked at her friend. 'I'm not sure they'll even notice
me,' she said. 'Remember how Tom was last night? He was
out of it.'

'OK, but I'm coming with you.'

She smiled to herself. Typical boy! As if she needed his
protection.

Still, she was glad of his company as they made their way
carefully down the hillside, keeping the gum trees between
themselves and the gathering.

They came to the edge of the clearing where Tom and the
others were standing with their arms in the air. Suzie
crouched behind a fallen eucalyptus, Wilkie beside her.

The people were standing very still. Slowly, they lowered
their arms and linked hands with each other. Suzie could see
that the men and women facing her had their eyes closed.
Their expressions were calm and content.

She wondered if they were high on some kind of drug.

Still holding hands, one of them spoke. The man was

standing perhaps three metres from where Suzie crouched, and she could hear every word he said. Unfortunately, she could understand nothing.

Wilkie stared at her. 'What language is *that*?' he said.

Suzie shook her head, a sick feeling in her stomach. She had never heard anything like it in her life.

The man fell silent, and the woman next to him began to speak in the same low, slow tone.

'Gahran . . . Mahruh lang dahbar. Pahray nahn lahti ro . . .'

It went on, low and sonorous – and utterly incomprehensible.

The men and women on the far side of the circle had opened their eyes now, and were staring at the speaker. The woman stopped, and the man next to her spoke. They were taking it in turns, obviously.

Suzie saw that Tom was standing next to the man speaking now. Wilkie reached out and gripped her hand.

To see her uncle acting like this was bad enough, but to hear him speak this strange language would be worse – confirmation that something was seriously wrong.

The man came to the end of his speech. The eyes of the others turned to her uncle.

'Dahbar lahti ro,' Tom said. 'Mahru tayah nau. Kiree . . .'

Suzie felt some strange emotion block her throat. She told herself not to be so irrational. She knew before he spoke that something terrible had changed him, so why did she feel like screaming at the thought, now?

Tom fell silent and the next man spoke, and so it went all around the circle. Perhaps thirty minutes later, the group lapsed into silence. Then they knelt, picked up handfuls of grass, stones, twigs, and passed them around the circle, examining their finds with eyes full of wonder.

Wilkie stared, open-mouthed.

Minutes later, the meeting broke up. The men and women dropped the twigs and stones to the ground, turned and walked back slowly down the hillside.

Tom made his way up the hill, passing just metres from where Suzie and Wilkie were crouching. Suzie had the urge to run after him, but something stopped her.

Fear, she knew. Fear of what her uncle had become.

They waited until Tom was almost out of sight, then followed. He moved like a zombie up the incline, trailing his hands through the long grass, staring about him in childlike wonder.

He came to where he had left his motorbike and pushed it onto the track. He seemed not to notice Wilkie's truck standing there. He straddled his bike, pressed the starter and rode off carefully down the track.

They waited until he had reached the main road, then returned to the truck and set off after him. The Suzuki raised a pall of sandy dust on the main road, marking Tom's position. They kept a couple of hundred metres between themselves and Tom all the way back to Stewart's Creek. Wilkie drove without comment, keeping his thoughts to himself, and Suzie said nothing to break the silence.

She was surprised when Tom pulled up outside the VR-bar, propped up his bike and went inside. Wilkie braked the truck fifty metres away and raised his eyebrows at Suzie.

'What now?'

She told him what had happened before, when Tom had got up in the middle of the night and used the Web-facility in her tree-house. 'You see, in the morning he seemed . . .' she shrugged, 'back to normal.'

He stared at her. 'So you reckon when he comes out of the VR-bar, he'll be himself again?'

Suzie frowned. 'Reckon . . . I don't know.' She stared glumly at the unlighted neon web above the bar. 'I honestly haven't got a clue what's going on, Wilkie.'

Ten minutes later Tom stepped from the bar, walking quickly. He waved to someone across the street, shouted a greeting and laughed. He was, Suzie could see, back to his old self.

Wilkie shook his head. 'You were right.'

Tom climbed onto his bike and roared off out of town, towards home. Wilkie gave him a minute, then started the engine.

Suzie clutched his wrist. 'Not yet,' she said. 'Look.'

She pointed through the windscreen.

As they watched, a big black saloon car pulled up outside the VR-bar. Two men climbed out as if they meant business and strode into the bar. They wore dark glasses and suits as black as the coachwork of their vehicle.

'Who the hell are *they*?' Wilkie asked.

Suzie shook her head. 'Search me. But I don't like the look of them.'

Five minutes later the men emerged, carrying what looked like Web junction boxes, Websuits and leads. They moved back and forth between the bar and the car, loading the boot, until they had confiscated all the Web-equipment.

Next, they came out with the bar's proprietor and hurried him into the back seat, handcuffed. One of the men shackled the door of the bar with a chain and padlock, then climbed into the driving seat. The car started up and accelerated out of town on the Sydney road.

A minute later only the silver chain on the VR-bar's double doors indicated that the men in black had ever visited Stewart's Creek.

Wilkie puffed out his cheeks. 'Heavy!' he said. He started the truck and headed home.

They were silent for a long time. At last Wilkie said, 'What do you think we should do, about what we saw back there – the gathering?'

Suzie thought about it. 'If we go to the police . . . I mean, will they believe us?' She shook her head. 'I don't know . . . I'll talk to Tom, see if he remembers anything. The good thing is, now the VR-bar is closed he won't be able to spin in again.' She thought of her own Websuit. He could always use that, of course. She wondered whether to hide the junction box somewhere.

Wilkie pulled the truck into the drive next to Tom's bungalow. The Suzuki was propped against the wall.

'You sure you're OK?' he asked. 'I could come in with you, if you want?'

Suzie smiled. 'I'll be fine. See you later, Wilkie. Thanks.' She climbed from the truck and made her way around the bungalow. She paused on the verandah, took a deep breath and pushed open the fly-screen door.

Tom was in the kitchen. He turned from the electricity meter as she entered.

'Hi, Tom.'

He nodded. 'Suzie.'

She noticed an unusual coolness in his manner. 'Where've you been?' she asked.

He shrugged. 'Stewart's Creek.'

'The VR-bar?'

'Thought I'd spin in, look up a few mates. Talking about the Web . . .' He tapped the glass face of the meter. 'Told you one hour a day, Suzie.'

She pulled an apologetic face. 'I know. Sorry. You know what it's like. You get in a venomous gamezone . . .'

He stared at her. 'I don't want you spinning in every day from now on, you got that?'

His words hurt. She felt a tightness in her throat. She wanted to hold her uncle, ask him what was going on.

Things had changed. He had never been this angry with her before.

Now a shadow crossed his face, as if he were trying to recall something. 'I said, did you hear me? I don't want you spinning in every day!'

She nodded, turned to hide her tears, and left the bungalow.

She ran across the back paddock to the tree-house and climbed the ladder. She sat on the bed and stared at her Websuit. More than anything she wanted to spin in, find Ana and Rom and tell them what had happened. But what good would that do, anyway? There was nothing they could do to find out what was going on.

Then she thought about her uncle. If he wanted to spin in again, and discovered the VR-bar in town closed down . . .

She picked up the junction box, disconnected it from the lead and crossed to the window. She climbed up so that she was standing on the narrow sill, then reached up and lodged the box on the flat roof of the tree-house, where it couldn't be seen from below.

She returned to the bed and lay down.

She stared at the timber ceiling and tried to occupy her mind by thinking about the big match tomorrow night, but it was useless.

Her thoughts turned to what she had seen in Cydonia earlier, and then to what was happening to Uncle Tom.

CHAPTER SEVEN

MEN IN BLACK

She was startled from sleep by the sound of an engine.

She sat up and rubbed her eyes. Through the window she could see the sun rising over the distant horizon. She must have dozed off in the heat of the afternoon and slept all night.

It was Monday morning, and the sudden thought of school made her groan. She glanced at her alarm clock. It was only six. Why had Wilkie come for her so early? They didn't normally leave for school until eight.

She moved to the window and peered out.

It was not Wilkie.

She stared at the two tall men in black as they climbed from the big car and stepped onto the verandah. They didn't bother knocking, just opened the back door, pulled open the fly-screen and slipped into the bungalow. Suzie felt panic grip her chest. For a second she was paralysed, hardly able to think what to do next.

Then she acted. Yesterday, the men in black had confiscated the VR-bar's Web equipment. What if they planned to do the same today? They would see the VR-lead snaking from the bungalow to her tree-house, and come looking for her junction box and suit.

She jumped up, gathered the suit, hood and goggles, and climbed through the window. She pushed them onto the roof next to the junction box, then slipped through the trap-door and scrambled down the ladder. She jumped the last few rungs, landed like a parachutist and rolled.

As she was righting herself, she saw the fly-screen door open. She dived behind a row of raspberry canes and peered out at the men in black.

One of them was taking Tom from the bungalow in handcuffs, leading him down the drive to the car. The other was kneeling to inspect the VR-lead that snaked from the kitchen. He yanked it, and the lead came slithering from the trap-door of the tree house. He pulled it towards him, coiling the cable as if it were a hose pipe.

Suzie looked around. She could move from the back paddock and down the side of the house without being seen. She took off, keeping Tom's fruit bushes between herself and the men in black. She ducked behind the fence that bordered the drive and crept towards the car. She peered through the loose boards. One of the men pushed Tom into the back seat, while the other tossed the rolled VR-lead into the boot.

'You check the bungalow for any more equipment,' she heard one say. 'I'll take a look in the tree-house.'

They moved around the side of the bungalow, and Suzie took her chance. She jumped over the fence and ran to the car. Tom looked up, opened his mouth as if to say something. Suzie tried the door handle. Of course it was locked. She moved around the car in desperation, trying each door in turn. All locked.

So what next?

She was considering physical violence – maybe she could attack the men with a spade when they returned – when she noticed the boot of the car.

When one of the men in black had stowed the VR-lead in the boot and closed it, the latch had not caught. The boot was open half an inch.

Even as she acted, she knew she was being foolhardy. At the same time, she saw no other course of action. She ran to the boot, opened it and slipped inside. She pulled the catch down and held it shut with her forefinger.

If they found nothing else to put in the boot, then she might go undiscovered. At their destination, wherever they were taking Tom, she would climb out and try to rescue him.

She knew she was dreaming. The chances were that she would be discovered and arrested, too. But what else could she do? She could hardly return to the bungalow and do nothing while they took her uncle away.

She waited. It seemed an age before the men in black returned. She held her breath as she heard their voices.

'Nothing,' one of them said.

'Just the lead,' the other replied. 'OK, so we'll take him in for questioning.'

She heard their footsteps beside the car, and screwed her eyes tight shut. If they had anything else to store in the boot, or decided to lock it, imprisoning her—

The car rocked on its suspension as they climbed in, and Suzie began breathing again.

The engine started up and the car rolled from the driveway and turned left along the main road towards Sydney.

After only five minutes, her finger holding the boot shut began to ache painfully. She switched fingers and considered what was going on.

Who were the men in black? Did they work for the government? But why didn't the government use the regular police to arrest the Web-users and confiscate Web equipment?

Perhaps the men in black worked independently of the government. Perhaps they worked for the Web itself? After all, the men who had arrested Uncle Tom were dressed like Webcops.

Her head was beginning to pound as she considered all the possibilities. She lay in the darkness and wondered when they might reach wherever they were going. A part of her wanted the journey to last forever, dreading what might

•

happen when they stopped. Another part wanted an end to the agonizing period of not knowing what was happening.

She told herself that the worst that could happen was that she might be arrested. Even if that happened, she had nothing to worry about. She had done nothing wrong, really. But would the men in black agree with her?

The journey seemed to be taking hours. They left the unmetalled road and hit the smooth highway, so the chances were that they *were* heading to Sydney. Suzie guessed that they were travelling at speed. She heard the quickening purr of the tyres on tarmac.

What seemed like ages later, the car slowed and veered left as it moved from the highway. They braked, turned right and left. They were moving more slowly now, turning down the streets of the city, perhaps?

At last the car slowed to a crawl, the engine idling. Suzie held her breath, her heart hammering. The car came to a sedate halt. This is it, she thought. This is where they open the boot and find me, caught like a pig in a trap.

She readied herself to leap out and run if they opened the boot.

She heard the car doors open and the men climb out. The back door opened. 'OK,' she heard a muffled voice say. 'Get out. Hurry up!' The car rocked as her uncle climbed out. She heard footsteps moving away.

OK, so what now? Do I get out, she asked herself, or wait? But wait for how long? She decided that she might be waiting for ever. She had to act *now*.

She opened the boot a fraction and peered out. She was in some kind of underground garage, full of similar big, black cars. There seemed to be no one about.

Swiftly, she pushed open the boot and slipped out. She ducked behind the car and looked around the garage. She was quite alone. At the far end of the chamber, she made out a door, and through the glass panel a flight of stairs.

She left the cover of the car and sprinted towards the door, pulling it open and slipping into the stairwell. She climbed the steps, trying to appear confident. She knew that at any second she might be discovered – but would they automatically arrest her? She would say that she was looking for her father who worked here. As if they would believe *that* story!

She came to a swing door and peered through the glass panel. She saw a long corridor lined with barred cells, like some kind of jail.

She continued up the stairs until she came to the next floor. She peered through the glass panel, then ducked away. Men in black, dozens of them, moving up and down a long corridor.

She turned and ran back down the steps. Now that she knew where they were keeping her uncle, she would try to get out and raise the alarm. Quite who she might ask for help, she didn't know. The government? She was, after all, supposed to be meeting the prime minister tonight with the rest of the team, before the game.

She turned, intending to run back down into the garage, and found herself staring into the faces of two tall men in black.

They seemed as surprised to see her as she was to see them. She tried to take off, back up the stairs, but she stood no chance. They gave chase, one of them grabbing her and pinning her arms painfully to her sides. She tried to struggle, kick out, but her captor squeezed all the harder.

'OK! You win. I won't struggle.'

'Now, just what are you doing here?' the other man laughed.

'I . . . I'm looking for my father. He works here.'

'Oh, of course. I should have realized. Forgive me for not recognizing you. Now, who's your father?'

Suzie opened her mouth, but no words came.

'What are you doing here?'

She could only shake her head in fear.

The men looked at each other, and nodded.

They carried her up the steps and through the door on the second floor. Here they allowed her to walk along the corridor to a windowless, barred cell. They pushed her inside and locked the bars behind her.

So much for helping her uncle to get out of here.

Suzie sat on the bunk and stared at the floor. Only now, when the fact of her captivity was slowly sinking in, did she begin to shake with fear.

She looked up. Across the corridor she saw a door open and a man enter a room equipped with Web-couches. When the door swung shut, she saw the spider-web logo of the Web organization affixed to the woodwork.

So the men in black *did* work for the Web!

Five minutes later two men strode along the corridor, a different pair from those who had captured her. One stationed himself outside the cell while the other joined her inside.

He knelt before her, reached out and gripped her jaw with fingers like steel. 'I want to know who you are and how you came to be here, do you understand?'

Suzie nodded, her movement restricted by his grip.

He released her. She felt the blood pounding back into the flesh of her chin. 'Suzie Wollagong,' she heard herself saying.

'Hey,' the man said. 'What do you know? The socceroo!'

Suzie tried to ignore him. She stared down at her fingers.

'So, soccer star, how did you get here?'

'Two men took my uncle. I climbed in the boot of the car and . . .' Tears began leaking from her eyes, tracking down her cheeks. She felt ashamed to be showing her weakness before this bully.

The man turned to his colleague outside the cell. 'Hear that? Get onto records. I want the file on—' He turned to Suzie. 'Your uncle's name?'

Suzie hesitated.

The man's hand reached out, grabbed her jaw, and squeezed.

'*Shokay!*' Suzie managed. The fingers relaxed. 'Tom,' she said. 'Tom Wollagong.'

The man nodded, stood and strode from the cell. He locked the bars and disappeared along the corridor.

Suzie lay on the bunk, shaking uncontrollably. Now she knew that all those vid-programmes about kids who hold out against interrogation, defy their captors and make amazing escapes, were just so much fantasy. Reality was different. Reality was terrifying. She hadn't meant to give in, tell them what they wanted. But they were bigger than her, and stronger, and she knew that they would have had no qualms about hurting her, badly.

Every time she heard a door open along the corridor, she braced herself. Men in black passed back and forth outside her cell, and each time Suzie felt sick. Long minutes elapsed, then hours. The terrible thing was not knowing what they might do to her, how long they might keep her imprisoned.

Tonight, she was due to play the most important game of soccer in her life, but would the men in black be bothered about that?

She smiled to herself. She thought not. They would probably take great delight in making her miss the match.

She wished she had never made the stupid decision to jump into the boot of the car.

But she had been acting unselfishly, hadn't she? She had not thought of herself – only of her uncle. She could hardly criticize herself for that.

She seemed to have been imprisoned for an age when she heard a door open. She looked up. A tall, blond man stepped from the Webroom. Her stomach knotted and she felt sick. He paused before her cell, looked in at her through the bars, and she knew that her destiny began here.

She told herself to be strong.

There was something at once strange, and familiar, in his expression as he stared through the bars at her. She had seen this look before, somewhere.

On the Arnie-phace in the Web? On the other men in black?

She felt herself trembling.

'What do you want with me?' She had meant it to sound strong, confident, but the question came out in a feeble whisper.

The man swung open the cell door. Instead of entering, he looked up and down the corridor. There was something curiously slow about his movements.

'Suzie Wollagong?'

'You know I am!' she wailed. 'What do you want?'

'Come with me, Suzie,' said the man in black.

She remained seated on the bunk. 'Where are we going?'

The man ignored her question. He stared at her. 'Come, quickly!'

Later, she would wonder why she had been so slow to realize, but at the time she was too frightened to understand anything.

He moved into the cell, reached out for her. His movements were slow, deliberate.

'You're—' she began, backing away.

The man looked at her with bright blue eyes, their expression distant. He gave a slow nod. 'This body has been . . . donated . . . for two, three hours. Come with me!'

Her heart began hammering in panic. 'Who . . . what are you?'

'That doesn't matter!' He looked desperate. He glanced down the corridor. 'Please, Suzie! They'll hold you here for weeks, maybe even months.' He paused. 'They might even keep you in here for ever. I can get you out!'

Who to trust? Where did he want to take her?

She found her voice. 'What do you want with me?'

The man in black looked at his watch. 'It is six o'clock,' he said. 'At eight you play for your country. I will take you to the stadium.'

He was offering her freedom, the chance of making it in time to play for Australia. So why was she hesitating?

She realized that she had to trust him.

'Quickly!' he said.

She stepped from the cell and his grip tightened on her shoulder. 'Come with me,' said the man in black.

CHAPTER EIGHT

ESCAPE

He steered her down the corridor, towards the swing door giving onto the stairwell. Suzie felt that at every step they might be challenged, that the man would be found out and she would be returned to the cell.

They pushed through the door and walked down the steps. 'Why are you doing this?'

'Quiet!' the man hissed. His grip tightened painfully on her shoulder.

He was taking her to the stadium, to play soccer for her country. It didn't make sense. Her thoughts were a jumbled confusion.

As they passed the door to the first floor, it opened and a man stepped out. He stopped when he saw them. 'Where you taking her, Roberts?'

'Interrogation,' the man said.

'Connery authorized the move?'

The man beside her nodded. 'He gave me the order.'

'Very well.' the other man moved off up the stairs.

The man in black eased her forward, his hand suddenly gentle on the back of her neck.

They hurried into the underground garage and across to a long black car. He took keys from his pocket and opened the door. 'Inside, quickly!'

Suzie slipped into the padded front seat, feeling herself sink into the soft leather. She was almost free. In seconds she would be out of here. She expected a shout to apprehend them, men in black armed with guns to come swarming into the garage.

The man, Roberts – or whoever or whatever was controlling his body – hurried around the car and climbed into the driving seat. He started the engine, moved the car slowly forward. Ahead, the garage door lifted. The man glanced into the rearview mirror, gripping the steering wheel anxiously.

They swept from the garage and turned right. Suzie felt an enormous weight lift from her, then realized that they were not quite free yet.

They were in a compound, surrounded by high concrete walls. They approached a checkpoint beside the gate. The man slowed the car and reached into the inside pocket of his jacket, pulling out a pass card. He lowered the window and reached out.

The guard on duty hardly gave the card a glance, nodded and swung open the gates. The car accelerated out onto the road.

As the gates were closing, Suzie heard a shout from within the compound. She turned in her seat. Two men were running from the garage, gesturing towards the gates. She had a glimpse of one of the men drawing a pistol, kneeling to take aim as the gates closed.

'They know we've got away!' she cried.

The man nodded. 'They will come after us, Suzie. But we have a start.' He accelerated along the road, turned down a side street. The sun was going down over the city, casting long shadows. Suzie looked behind them. There was no sign of pursuit.

She glanced at the man. 'You're not like the others I've seen. My uncle, the other people he met on the hillside. You have more . . .' She searched for the word. 'More co-ordination.'

He glanced into the rearview mirror, then at her. 'It takes time to learn how to control a body,' he said. 'We become more practised with each period of usage.'

His words sent icicles down her spine. 'Just . . . *who* are you?' she whispered.

'That is not important,' he said. 'You will find out in time. What matters is that we get you away from them.'

'But what about my uncle?' she said. 'He's still in there.'

'Don't worry. One of my colleagues will free him, and the other prisoners.'

He looked again into the mirror. Alarm crossed his face.

Suzie turned in her seat. A motorbike was threading its way towards them through the traffic.

The car gained speed, not too much, which would have attracted attention, but enough to pull away from the motorbike. They screeched round a corner, and another, attempting to shake off their pursuer. Suzie looked through the rear window. The bike appeared, gaining on them. Behind it, another bike came into view.

The first bullet hit the rear window, creating a perfectly circular hole. It zipped past Suzie's head, exiting through the windscreen. She screamed in fright and scrunched herself down in the seat. She realized she was crying.

These people, the men in black, were actually *shooting* at her. They meant to do her harm – even kill her. Her heart banged in her chest with terror. This wasn't some venomous gamezone in the Web. This was Realworld. The bullets aimed at her were real. If they hit her, if just one bullet found its target, then she would be *really* dead.

She thought of Uncle Tom, and Wilkie. The possibility that she might never see them again made her sob.

She heard bullets crunch into the car's coachwork, a quick rainstorm of metal. She closed her eyes, expecting to feel hot lead ripping into her back at any second.

The car swerved and skidded as the driver tried to lose the following motorbikes.

'Soon I will stop the car,' the man told her. 'When I do, quickly climb out and follow me.'

She nodded, a sick feeling in her stomach.

'OK!' the man shouted. 'Now!'

The car screeched to a halt and Suzie dived out.

'This way!' the man cried.

She sprinted after him. They were running down a narrow alley between tall buildings. She glanced back. Their abandoned car filled the end of the alley. A motorbike pulled up, tried to force its way past the car. Its driver gave up, jumped off and gave chase on foot. Suzie felt confidence surge through her. If it was to be a contest of speed, then she knew she would win.

She took deep breaths, felt her muscles respond. She lengthened her stride. Even the friendly man in black had difficulty matching her pace. They turned down a narrow back street, sprinting past some surprised delivery men. When Suzie looked back, there was no sign of their pursuers.

'Suzie!' he called. 'This way.'

She stopped, turned and followed him down another narrow alley strewn with rubbish from toppled trash cans. They sprinted to the end of the alley, and the man in black took her arm and pulled her into the recessed doorway of an underground night club.

He leaned back against the wall, panting. Suzie regained her breath. The man smiled. 'I think . . . I think we've lost them – for the time being. But we must be careful when we approach the stadium. They might have agents waiting.'

Suzie shook her head. 'For me?' The idea seemed absurd.

'Tonight, Suzie, you meet the prime minister.'

She recalled that the lizard had mentioned the meeting, back in Triassic Park.

'I don't understand.'

'This is important, Suzie. We made contact with your prime minister last week. We told him that we were going to give him the code for a secure Website. Until now we have been unable to establish a secure site in the Web. Today we accomplished this – but the Webcops stopped us from communicating with him again.' The man paused, staring at her. 'When you meet the prime minister, give him this simple message, and the code.'

He told her the code and the message she was to relay to the prime minister of Australia. 'Can you remember that?'

Suzie repeated the message and the code. 'But what's happening?'

'Later,' the man said. He took her arm, and they stepped from the alley and rounded the corner. Ahead, the Olympic stadium filled the sky, its floodlights dazzling in the twilight.

They hurried through the milling crowd and passed into the shadow of the vast arena. The man touched her shoulder. 'Over there, the players' entrance.'

Ahead, Suzie was greeted with a familiar sight. She stopped, staring in disbelief.

A beat-up Holden truck stood outside the players' entrance.

Wilkie jumped down from the cab and held out her sports bag.

She surprised her friend by greeting him with a tight hug.

'Saw the men in black take Tom away this morning,' Wilkie explained. 'I looked for you everywhere. Thought you must've followed. So I picked your boots up and drove here.' He glanced suspiciously at the man in black beside Suzie.

'Don't worry, Wilkie,' she said. 'He's with me. It's a long story.'

They made their way down the players' entrance. An official barred their way, until Suzie convinced him that she was playing tonight and had brought friends along. While Wilkie and the man in black made their way to the stand, Suzie hurried to the changing rooms.

The girls looked up when she pushed through the door. Most had changed and were lacing their boots. 'Suzie!' a girl called Shelly cried with relief. 'Thought you'd never make it.'

Suzie smiled. 'Had a bit of a hold up,' she said.

She looked at her kit hanging on the peg, the gold shirt and green shorts and socks. She took down the shirt and stared at the name above the number 11: Wollagong, it read. She sat down and closed her eyes, feeling tears streaming down her cheeks. She sat for a minute and controlled her breathing, trying to forget the drama of the past few hours.

Then she stood, undressed, changed into her kit, and joined the boys and the coach in the neighbouring dressing room.

'Quiet while I speak!' the coach yelled. 'OK, I know you all want to go to India next month,' he began, 'and here's how we're going to do it.'

For the next ten minutes he gave a team-talk, going over New Zealand's strengths and weaknesses. He told his team how he wanted them to play, giving each player detailed instructions and encouragement.

'That's it. The rest is up to you. Remember, you're playing for your country. Thousands of people'll be watching tonight, so go out there with conviction and courage. Good luck!'

Suzie stood and stretched her leg muscles. She felt a mounting sense of anticipation, not only because she was about to play the most important game of soccer in her life.

In two minutes they were due to meet the PM.

Suzie repeated the code to herself, and the message from the man in black, or rather from whoever was controlling him.

There was a knock at the door. The players glanced at each other in excitement. Suzie felt her stomach churning.

An official poked his head into the dressing room and spoke briefly with the coach.

'OK, everyone,' the coach said. 'I'm afraid the prime minister has been delayed by some unforeseen business, so he won't be able to make it before the game. But I've been assured that he'll meet us after the match. So . . .' he looked around the players, 'let's make sure he's congratulating us come the full-time whistle! Out you go.'

As they left the dressing room and filed down the tunnel, Suzie tried to control her disappointment. She had to concentrate on the game, now. She would give the message to the PM later.

They emerged to the roar of the crowd and the diamond bright dazzle of the floodlights.

Some soccer matches, Suzie knew from experience, passed in a blur of action and excitement. She hardly recalled the best games she had played in. She concentrated, and played as well as she could, and later remembered very little of the game itself.

This was such a game.

The first half seemed to be over almost before it had begun. Australia were the better team, pinning the opposition back in their own half and almost scoring twice, the first time with a close-range header, then with a long, curving shot. Suzie played well on the wing, time after time beating the girl who was marking her.

There was no score at half-time.

After the interval, Australia mounted wave after wave of attack. Suzie screamed for the ball, and when it came to her she ran at the defender. She recalled what Tom had told her, over and over. 'Run at the opposition at every opportunity, girl. Frighten them into making mistakes!'

The first goal came from a mistake, sure enough, but it was Australia that made the telling error. They were attacking yet again. A mid-fielder was carrying the ball into the New Zealand half. She tried to play a one-two with a forward, but the pass was intercepted by an opposition player who slotted the ball through to an attacker running unopposed towards the Aussie goal.

Suzie could only watch in despair as the forward chipped the keeper, and New Zealand were one-nil up with just ten minutes to play.

'We've got to dig deep and fight for this one, Australia!' the captain yelled at the restart. 'One hundred per cent from everyone! Let's go for it.'

They did. They attacked again and again. Suzie was only half-aware of the roar of the crowd, urging them on. With five minutes to go, she picked up the ball on the edge of the penalty zone. She feinted to shoot, then pushed the ball past the defender and sprinted to the by-line. She almost ran the ball out of play, then lunged and sent a looping cross to the far post. Suzie went skidding into the advertising boards, and could only watch as a forward headed the ball back across goal – to be met by the towering Australian centre-half who steamed in and blasted a header into the back of the net.

The crowd went mad. Suzie felt as if she were bursting with joy and pride. She picked herself up and embraced the scorer, then ran back into her own half as the game resumed. 'Two minutes, Australia!' the captain said. 'Let's give it everything!'

They attacked relentlessly down the wing, crossing high balls into the goal mouth. The opposition defended desperately, wildly kicking the ball anywhere in an attempt to force extra-time.

With a minute to go, Suzie was brought down on the edge of the penalty zone. She shaped to take the free kick herself, but touched it to the boy beside her.

What happened next seemed to take place in slow motion. The forward drew back his foot and kicked, connected with the ball and sending it curving around the wall. The players in the wall turned slowly, watching the trajectory of the goal-bound shot. Suzie felt emotion swell in her throat. The ball was heading into the corner of the net – until the keeper somehow flung herself across the face of the goal and managed to get a finger to the ball. Suzie watched it hit the post, rebound back into play. It seemed to bounce and hang in the air for ages as a melee of players struggled to be the first to make contact.

An Aussie forward stuck out a boot. The ball dribbled over the line and Suzie leaped into the air. The roar of the crowd reached her as if from a great distance. Somewhere amid the celebrations, the referee blew the final whistle and Suzie threw her arms around her nearest team-mate and felt tears trickle down her cheeks.

The next few minutes were a blur. She recalled shaking hands with the New Zealanders, hugging her own players.

She punched the air and stared around the packed stadium through a mist of tears.

'Ana Devi,' she said to herself, 'I'm on my way.'

They moved to the touchline, hugging officials and fans. Suzie saw someone through the press of the crowd, trying to get to her. He was stopped by a steward.

'No!' Suzie cried. 'Let him through!'

She opened her arms and Uncle Tom hugged her tight, as if never wanting to let her go. Wilkie joined them, his face alight with jubilation. 'You little beaut!' he said, lifting her into the air.

Seconds later they were filing down the tunnel, the confined space echoing with their cries.

'Suzie!' The coach caught up with her. 'There's someone here to see you.'

Suzie turned. A tall, silver-haired man made his way down the tunnel and held out his hand. 'Suzie Wollagong,' said the prime minister. 'It's great to meet you again. Many congratulations!'

She seemed to exist in a bubble of reality removed from the outside world. She was aware only of herself and the PM.

At last she found her voice.

'I have a message from the Pharanians,' she said. 'They come in peace, and give you this Web-code.'

CHAPTER NINE

PHARAN

Suzie decided to slip away early from the party in the stadium function room. She turned to Wilkie and said, 'I want to show you something.'

'Where're we going, Suzie?'

'Can't tell you yet. It's a surprise. Wait here.'

Across the room, Uncle Tom was talking about old times with an Australian soccer official, a team-mate from his playing days.

She joined them. 'And here's the girl herself!' Tom cried. 'Didn't she play like a star?'

Suzie squirmed with embarrassment. 'Tom, can I ask you a favour?'

'Sure. Anything.'

'Can I borrow your Web-card for an hour?'

Tom laughed. 'Kids these days! Spend all their time spinning in!' He slipped the card from the back pocket of his shorts. 'No worries, Suzie. Don't be long. OK?'

'Great! We won't be.' She found Wilkie and they hurried from the room.

The man in black was stationed in the corridor. He smiled at Suzie's look of surprise. 'I thought I'd stay,' he said. 'Just in case.'

Suzie held up the Web-card. 'We're spinning in,' she said. 'Thought we'd bat into the code you gave me.'

The man in black nodded. 'Very well. I'll be your guide.'

Wilkie stared at her. 'We're going into the Web?' he said.

Suzie laughed at his goggle-eyed expression. 'Why not? This is as good a time as any for your first Web experience!'

They left the stadium and the man in black guided them through the streets of the city centre to the nearest VR-bar. They took a three-couch booth and suited up.

Wilkie looked unsure. 'This is weird,' he said, pulling on his hood.

'Ready?' Suzie said. 'OK, let's go!'

Seconds later they were standing on a strand in Webtown. Wilkie stared around him in amazement. 'I . . . This is amazing, Suzie. Where are we?'

She told him. 'If you think this is venomous, just wait till you see some of the really eight sites!'

She hailed a passing spider and asked it to summon Ana Devi and Rom. It paused, closed its sieve-like eyes while it transmitted the information, then scurried away.

A minute later Rom appeared before them. 'Suzie!' he said. 'What a surprise.' He looked at the man in black. 'Who's your friend?'

'Long story,' Suzie said. She introduced Rom to Wilkie. 'We're batting somewhere special, Rom. Do you know where Ana is?'

'In Realworld,' he said. 'But we could get a spider to contact her local VR-bar. They'll send out a runner to find her.' He found a spider and spoke to it briefly.

They sat down while they waited for Ana to appear. 'So,' Rom said. 'Where are we going? And what's with the bodyguard?'

The man in black smiled. 'I'll guide you around a new Website. There is much to explain. The leaks, the actions of the Web-authorities.'

Rom stared at him. 'But don't you work for the Web?' he asked. 'I mean, you're dressed like a Webcop.'

The man shook his head. 'As Suzie said, it's a long story. All will be explained when we reach the site. But, no, I'm not a Webcop, or anything else to do with the authorities.'

Ana appeared before them in a swirl of coloured pixels. 'Suzie!' the small Indian girl said. 'Great to see you.'

Suzie introduced Ana to Wilkie and the man in black. 'A lot's been happening in Realworld since I saw you last,' she said. She told Ana and Rom about the odd behaviour of her uncle and the others, her arrest by the men in black and her escape. 'I know, Ana. I'm confused too.'

The man in black interrupted. 'I don't want to alarm you, but I think we're being watched.'

They looked up. Beside the nearest building block, a group of spiders and Webcops were glancing their way.

'They'll probably try to follow us to the site,' said the man in black. 'Don't worry. Keep together when we get there. Do you all know the code?'

Suzie gave the code to Ana, Rom and Wilkie. They stood and entered it into their wristpads. Blue light flashed in Suzie's eyes, a ringing tone sounded in her ears, and she was no longer in Webtown.

Quite where she was, however, she had no idea.

She took Ana and Wilkie's hands in hers.

Rom whispered, 'Ultra-venomous!'

Truly, it was the most amazing experience she had ever had in the Web. The colours were brighter than anything she had ever seen in virtual reality, the definition of images far sharper. Even the sounds – the soughing of the wind and the call of birds – came to her with a greater fidelity. It was as if Web technology had progressed a hundred years since the last time she had spun in.

'This is truly awesome!' Rom breathed beside her.

Quite apart from the greater reality of the site, it was spectacular to look at, too.

They were standing on a floating oval platform high above a plain of bright blue grass. Here and there on the plain were what looked like tall, leafless trees. Other platforms were moored to these, some of the craft occupied by small figures. In the distance was what looked like a dense jungle, but the vegetation was red and arranged in stands of tall fronds.

Beyond the jungle, on the horizon, was a range of silver mountains.

As if to emphasise the fact that this Website was alien, the sky was a light shade of green, with two huge white moons riding low above the mountain-tops.

She heard the voice of the man in black behind her. 'Welcome to Pharan,' he said.

Suzie, Ana, Wilkie and Rom turned together.

She expected to see the man in black, but standing where he should have been was . . .

She stared and backed away.

An upright lizard gestured towards her. 'Please, don't be alarmed,' he said in a familiar voice. 'This is the form I adopt when in the site of Pharan.'

Seconds later the invasion began.

All around them, big silver spiders materialized in the air. They swooped towards the platform, legs waving in an attempt to reach Suzie and the others. Behind the spiders, Webcops batted in and hovered over the blue plain. They were soon joined by Arnie-phaces in the form of vultures.

The lizard took evasive action. He reached out and pulled a lever on the platform. 'Hold on!' it cried, as the platform surged forward at high speed.

Suzie and the others fell to their knees, scrabbling for handholds. They found short straps fixed to the deck and held on as the platform weaved left and right, fleeing the pursuing Webcops and spiders. The lizard turned from time to time, lashing out with a silver swordstick to dash away an advancing spider.

Before the platform, a dozen floating Webcops materialized, lined up in the air like a sinister male voice choir. The lizard halted the platform, attempted to make a tight left turn. The vehicle tipped, and Suzie found herself tumbling head over heels through the air.

She screamed, then realized that she was not falling as she would in Realworld. This was a Website where the gravity was much lighter than that of Earth. She fell as slowly as a floating leaf and landed softly in the tall blue grass. Around her, Wilkie, Ana and Rom also came to rest. They picked themselves up and stared into the air. The battle continued in the pale green sky, silver spiders, Webcops and Arnie-vultures attacking the floating platforms bearing the small shapes of other upright lizards.

Suzie heard a rustling in the grass behind her. She screamed as a pig emerged through the fronds, a fat pig with the face of Arnie.

'Get out!' it grunted.

The others scattered, ran in fright through the long grass. Suzie tried to follow. She took off, tripped and sprawled headfirst. She heard the pig, grunting a laugh behind her, and felt it touch her back.

And she was ejected back into Webtown.

Instantly, a Webcop dived at her, trying to scuttle her into Realworld. Suzie dodged him, took off down the wide strand between the pulsing, multi-scened building blocks.

'Security alert!' She heard a cry behind her. 'Security alert!'

She barged past a hundred startled avatars, turned a corner and ran down another strand. She paused for breath beside a building block. Across the strand, a spider scurried towards her. She felt her heart beating like a woodpecker. She turned. She was facing a building block showing a forest scene.

Well, why not?

She leaped through and found herself in a dense, humid rainforest. She ran and dodged behind a tree, regaining her breath. She heard a spider crash through behind her.

Frantically, she tried to recall the code for the Pharan Website. Panic had erased it from her memory. She concentrated, stared at the array on her wristpad. OK.

5723/7 . . . now was it A or E?

She stabbed E, and batted from the forest.

She was standing on a floating platform high above the blue plain. All around her, lizards were doing battle with Webcops and spiders. Far below, she saw the tiny shapes of

Ana, Wilkie and Rom running through the grass, the obscene Arnie-pig snorting along behind them.

She recalled how the lizard had controlled the platform. She reached out for the lever and pushed it forward. The platform responded, diving towards the grass. Suzie steered over to where her friends were fleeing from the pig. She swooped over their heads and brought the platform down in the grass before them. Seconds later they reached her and scrambled aboard. She lifted the platform and they swooped away, gaining height.

'I thought it'd got you!' Wilkie cried.

'It did! But I batted back in. Six!' she cried out in alarm.

The pig had morphed. Now it was a flying pig, with silly stubby wings flapping ludicrously on either side of its fat body.

'Why don't we morph too!' Rom yelled at them. 'Reduce ourselves.'

'Great!' Suzie said. 'What's the code?'

Silence. She looked at Rom.

He made a comical face. 'I can't remember!' he wailed. He held his head and tried to concentrate.

Suzie steered the platform towards the red jungle, hoping to lose the Arnie-phace among the trees.

'It's gaining!' Ana cried. 'Can't we go any faster?'

Wilkie gripped onto the handholds, looking petrified.

Other Webcops were in pursuit, too. Spiders floated after them, along with a squadron of Arnie-vultures. Just when Suzie thought that they would be caught for sure, help arrived.

'Look!' Wilkie cried, pointing into the jungle.

Suzie stared, hardly able to believe her eyes.

Thousand upon thousand of platforms, each holding a dozen lizards armed with swordsticks and lasers, emerged from the tall, frond-like trees and advanced towards the Webcops and spiders. There were so many that, as Suzie stared open-mouthed, the entire range of distant mountains was lost to sight.

But the Arnie-pig was still in pursuit. Their only hope was to lose the thing in the jungle. Suzie pushed the lever forward.

At that second, a lizard materialized on the platform beside them. It ran to the back of the craft, knelt and aimed a laser. Blue light lanced out. The pursuing pig exploded in a million coloured fragments.

Rom and Wilkie cheered like soccer fans.

'Good to see you're still here,' the lizard said. 'I think we're winning the battle.' It took control of the platform and steered it at speed through the jungle. 'And now for the explanation I promised earlier.'

They emerged from the jungle and flew towards the distant mountains. Down below, a magnificent city came into view. Silver canals criss-crossed blue fields and gardens. Strange buildings, like bulbous dwellings blown from glass, lined the waterways. Suzie saw a thousand lizards going about their everyday lives on barges and ferries.

'Magical,' Ana breathed.

They came to rest on the roof of one of the bloated, glass-like buildings. They stepped from the platform and the lizard led them across the roof to a balcony area overlooking the city. Suzie gripped the rail and stared out. She felt a small hand find hers and hold on. It was Ana.

They were joined by two other lizards, these dressed in flowing red robes. The first lizard greeted the newcomers with a familiar gesture. It raised its fists and touched the shoulders of its friends.

'Permit me to introduce myself,' said the first lizard. 'I am Aphar, and my friends here are Marhu and Rahan, the avatars of the Pharanians who first discovered your planet.'

Suzie stared at the lizard, Aphar. She shook her head in disbelief. 'What?' was all she could manage.

The lizard smiled. 'Please, take a seat. I will explain.'

They sat on strangely-shaped, but comfortable, glass chairs. Aphar gestured with both arms indicating the city of Pharan and the world beyond.

'We Pharanians are an ancient race,' he began. 'We evolved on a planet far away from your sun, on the very rim of the galaxy. We passed through periods of hostility, where we fought each other in futile wars which almost brought about the end of our race. Somehow, with luck, we survived. Over the millennia we became a peaceable people, leaving behind the ways of conflict and hostility. In time, over the period of millions of years, we evolved yet again, from beings of flesh and blood to entities of pure energy.'

Suzie stared at her friends. 'Pure energy?' she repeated, shaking her head.

'I don't understand,' Ana said.

'It is a difficult idea for you to comprehend, I know,' said Aphar. 'Perhaps I can explain by saying that you humans are really so many units of energy, of electrical and chemical information, stored in flesh and blood bodies. Imagine if you were just brains, without your bodies, but able to move around merely by thinking about it. We achieved this many thousands of years ago. We Pharanians are small packets of electrical information, capable of beaming ourselves light years through space.'

'But,' Rom said, 'once in your history you used to look like . . . like lizards, right?'

Aphar smiled. 'That is correct. Many millions of years ago, we looked like this.' He indicated his avatar. 'Like the creatures you call lizards.'

Suzie stared in wonder at the alien before her, at the strange city laid out beneath the glass tower.

'For hundreds of your years,' Aphar went on, 'we have been exploring space, beaming ourselves across the galaxy to a hundred different stars and their planets, in search of intelligent life. Here and there, on planets few and far between, we have come across life, but not intelligent life, merely plants and organisms in the early stages of their evolution. We have despaired again and again of ever finding intelligent life. We thought that we were alone in the universe, destined to wander through space forever, finding no other race with which to communicate. Imagine our joy when we – when Marhu and Rahan – came upon planet Earth and found human beings.'

'When was this?' Suzie asked.

'Only a matter of three years ago,' Aphar said. 'Had we discovered you in the last century, say, before you had developed virtual reality, then we might never have been able to communicate with you. However, to our great delight, we found that you possessed the Web.'

For the first time, Marhu spoke. 'I recall when I beamed myself to Earth and discovered the virtual reality network covering the entire planet.'

'It was like,' said Rahan, 'oh, it was like stumbling upon paradise in a desert.'

Aphar continued, 'Marhu and Rahan communicated their find to the rest of our people, and for two years we debated how we should go about contacting you. We decided to infiltrate the Web, to learn as much about *Homo sapiens* as we could, your languages and cultural and political history, your technology and science. We decided to keep our presence a secret, until we could determine whether or not you were a hostile race. We set up a receiving station in the Website you call Cydonia.'

'For a while,' Marhu said, 'we were against making ourselves known to you, because some of us thought you might react aggressively.'

'However,' Aphar said, 'while we were debating this point, our presence in Cydonia was discovered. The Web authorities tried to exterminate us. In a bid to save ourselves, we moved to other sites in the Web, places where we thought we might go undetected. The activity of our movement, and the Web-authorities trying to banish us, caused the Web-crash of several months ago, and the leaks and other disturbances more recently.'

'All the time,' Marhu said, 'we were learning more about the Web, teaching ourselves how to use it. We bent our efforts towards constructing a site that the Web-authorities could not invade or destroy.'

'Then,' Rahan said, 'we made an accidental discovery that amazed us.'

Aphar nodded. 'When attempting to contact the individual avatars you humans use while in the Web, we found ourselves channelled down the Web-leads and inhabiting human minds. Imagine our reaction at being granted this amazing opportunity! For millions of years we have not known what it was to experience the physical, flesh and blood reality of planet-dwellers, and then suddenly we found ourselves able to control the bodies of Web-users all over the world!'

'Of course,' Marhu said, 'we debated for a long time on whether this control was right or wrong. We decided that if we inhabited human bodies only for a few hours at a time, and left the individuals with no memories of what they were doing during those periods, then we would not be committing a crime.'

'Oh, the wonder we experienced in your physical world!' Rahan said. 'The sights, the sounds, the smells. Truly it was a wonderland, for which we can only thank you.'

Suzie recalled watching her uncle – or rather her uncle's body, possessed by a Pharanian – as he moved about the world in amazement. She remembered the gathering of the Pharanian-controlled human bodies on the hillside above Ballaran, and how they had marvelled at their surroundings.

'However,' Aphar said, 'when the Web-authorities found out what we were doing, they redoubled their efforts to evict us from the Web. We tried to communicate to them that we were a peaceful people. We came to Earth to experience your way of life, to share knowledge with you, not to invade your planet. But they would not listen. We tried to contact your leaders, politicians and statesmen and women, but they were all warned off using the Web by the Web-authorities. They told your world leaders that we were hostile extraterrestrials, bent on invading and taking over your planet. We almost despaired of ever communicating the truth to you. Then we decided to contact the children of your world. We discovered that human children do not have the hostility and suspicion of their elders. Because they have no real power in their world, they are more likely to listen than to fight. We did all we could to communicate with children all around the world. Fortunately, we succeeded in perhaps a hundred cases. You, Suzie, were one of them, and the fact that you were due to meet your prime minister helped our cause. A week ago we managed to contact him with a long document describing our history, our arrival on Earth, and our plans while we are here. We told him that we were planning to construct a secure Website, where he and other curious humans could visit us, find out for themselves that we are a peaceable people. However, before we could reach him with the new code, the Web-authorities curtailed our activities, closed the channel we used to communicate with your leaders . . . Now, however, thanks to you, he knows the new code. We can only hope that in time he will visit us.'

'This,' Marhu said, gesturing at the city, 'is the Website we have created as a stronghold against the attack from the Web-authorities. So far they have been unable to destroy it. Only when they discovered the code were they able to follow you in. But the attack is under control, now. We have superior numbers and technology. Here we are safe.'

Aphar said, 'Over the next few days, we will communicate with all the world leaders, through the children of Earth, telling them about the Pharan-site and how we can help you.'

Rom leaned forward. 'Help us?'

Aphar inclined his head in assent. 'We have at our disposal limitless energy from the stars. We can help humanity make the Web even more realistic, as authentic as the site you experience here. We will construct sites based on the many amazing worlds we have discovered on our travels between the stars. All we ask in return is to be allowed to use human bodies from time to time. We will request human volunteers, *donors*, people who are willing to give up a few hours every week, so that we can experience their physical reality. In return, we will give these donors free access to the Web.'

Suzie said, 'I only hope they'll listen to you.'

'I think they will. And I think, also, that we will be able to persuade the Web-authorities that they have nothing to fear from us. In fact, they can only gain from our presence here. Once all the world learns of us, more people will want to use the Web, and so the authorities running the Web can only profit.'

'Perhaps,' said Marhu, 'our guests have heard enough of all our talk and lofty aspirations. Perhaps you would like a guided tour of the city?'

'May I suggest a canal trip, to begin with?' Aphar said.

'That'd be eight!' Rom cried.

Marhu rose and bowed. 'It will be a minute or two before I can arrange transport,' he said. He hurried across the rooftop and disappeared down a flight of stairs.

Suzie stared out over the glittering canals of the fabulous city, trying to take in everything the Pharanians had said.

Ana was leaning over the balcony rail, gazing up at the double moons. Suzie joined her. 'Three days ago I didn't know you,' Suzie said. 'And now here we are—' She hesitated. 'Next month I'll be in Delhi, Ana. Perhaps we could meet, in Realworld?'

Ana looked unsure. She shrugged. 'Why would you want to do that, when we can meet in the Web?'

Suzie smiled. 'Oh, I don't know. Curiosity, I suppose.'

'You'd be disappointed, Suzie. I'm poor. I live on the streets.'

Suzie took Ana's hand and squeezed. 'I'm not exactly rich,' she said. 'You should see Uncle Tom's tumbledown bunga-low! Look, the Web has proved that no matter what our backgrounds, no matter what our differences, we can be friends. I want to meet you in New Delhi. OK?'

Ana smiled, almost shyly. 'Ah-cha,' she said.

Suzie felt a touch on her shoulder. It was Aphar. 'Perhaps I can have a private word, Suzie?'

She followed the Pharanian across the rooftop.

'If all goes well,' Aphar said, 'and we can persuade the Web-authorities to accept us, I would be honoured if you would be my donor. I would like to see planet Earth through your eyes.'

Suzie smiled at the thought of having an alien riding in her head.

'If I can visit you here,' she said, 'then you've got yourself a deal.'

The alien smiled. 'The pleasure will be mine.'

Suzie looked out across the canal-laced city. She frowned. 'I was wondering,' she said. 'Why this place, this city? You could have created any place from the history of your people. Why this city, from millions of years ago?'

Aphar smiled. 'It is important to keep in contact with the past, with your heritage,' he said. 'We Pharanians, even though we are creatures of pure energy, have memories, like dreams, of this period of our history. It was the time when we were no longer an aggressive race, when we were taking the first steps on the road of peace. Now that we have the city of Pharan, we will all revisit it from time to time.'

Marhu returned. 'The boat awaits us,' he said.

Suzie joined Ana, Wilkie and Rom, and together with the Pharanians they climbed down the stairs to the waterway and the waiting boat.

CHAPTER TEN

WALKABOUT

Suzie lay on the cooling sand of the desert and stared up at the massed stars overhead.

It had been an interesting year, she told herself. Her many adventures in the Web; her visit to India, and second place in the four team soccer tournament; her meeting with Ana Devi at a chai stall on Connaught Place . . .

The night had gone well. They had met dozens of times in the Web, knew each other as well as it was possible for two people to know each other. What did it matter that in Realworld Ana was a beggar girl with only one leg?

Suzie met Ana's brother, Ajay, who was no longer blind, and Ana explained how one year ago she had bought him brand new eyes.*

They drank sweet chai and talked like sisters long into the night, and finally said a tearful goodbye and arranged to meet next time in the Web.

And then there had been the times when Suzie had visited the new zones in the Web. She had marvelled at the Websites created by the aliens using their advanced technology, enjoyed the incredible experience of the improved gamezones and strange new planet-sites.

The Web-authorities had seen sense at last and come to realize that the Pharanians were a peaceful race. They did not

*Read UNTOUCHABLES in THE WEB series.

want to invade Earth, or the Web. They were happy merely to give the human race the benefit of their knowledge in return for using human donors to experience planet Earth.

Suzie had spent many free hours in the new sites with Ana, Rom and the others. Even Wilkie had enjoyed himself in the gamezones and alien Websites.

She had often visited Aphar in Pharan, and they had sat and talked while gazing out over the magnificent alien city. On one occasion Suzie told him all about her people and had mentioned that her uncle wanted her to go walkabout.

Aphar gestured. 'Walkabout? What is walkabout?'

Suzie explained. 'It's when you leave the city or the town, or wherever you live, and walk for a long time in the bush and the desert. But it's more than just a long walk. It's a religious thing with my people, somehow spiritual. It's a time when you become one with the land, and live as your ancestors lived.'

'Ah,' Aphar said. 'I begin to understand. It is something like what we Pharanians do when we come here, to Pharan.'

Suzie smiled and shrugged. 'Well, I suppose it is, really.'

Aphar was watching her. 'I would like to experience this walkabout,' he said at last.

Shortly after that meeting with Aphar, Suzie asked Tom if he was going walkabout this year. He told her that he was due to set off in two weeks. 'Why, don't tell me you want to come with me, Suzie?'

She smiled at him. 'You know something? I think I would.'

Tom just stared at her. Then his face broke into a big grin. 'Beaut, girl! You don't know how pleased that makes an old man feel!'

Two weeks later they set off and walked into the desert, and at first it was hard for Suzie. The ways of her people were not her ways, but she had learned. She put up with the hardships, and listened to her uncle when he told her what to do.

It had been strange, sharing her body with Aphar.

The Pharanians had perfected a way of inhabiting a

human donor for just two hours a day, and then retreating into the subconscious until the following day. For these two hours, Suzie was not aware of what her body was doing. It was like being asleep. At first she would feel a tickling sensation in her head, then she would lose consciousness. Two hours later she would wake up, in a different place in the desert.

She would hear Aphar's voice in her head, asking questions, and she would *think* her replies.

'Today,' Aphar whispered in her mind, 'I ate a witchetty grub for the first time. A truly marvellous experience!'

'A witchetty grub?' Suzie thought, disgusted. 'You mean to say that you ate a witchetty grub with my mouth? Augh! That's just *gross!*'

'Do you mean,' Aphar spoke in her head, 'that you have never eaten a witchetty grub before?'

'Never! Give me a Mars bar any day!'

'Also, I watched kangaroos cross the desert, hundreds of them, and I watched the sunrise, all orange and blood red. You cannot imagine how wonderful it is to inhabit a human body and experience the miracle of the five senses, after being without a body for so long.'

'I'm glad you're having such a good time.'

'Please, tell me again the stories of your ancestors.'

Suzie smiled and thought of the stories Uncle Tom had told her. The tale of how Yhi, the sun goddess, brought life to the world; how Baiame, the Great Spirit, became the first man on Earth. She told Aphar the stories of Tiddalick the frog, and of the many other animals.

Later, the voice in her head quiet now, she lay with Tom beneath the stars. 'What made you change your mind, Suzie?' he asked.

She smiled. In her mind's eye she saw the beautiful city of Pharan, the city that no longer existed in reality. It was a million years gone, now, even though its likeness lived on in the Web. She thought of her conversation with Aphar as they sat above the city, and how the alien had wanted to experience walkabout.

She considered what Aphar had told her. *'It is important to keep in contact with the past.'*

She was a modern Australian, she lived in the twenty-first century, but she was also Aboriginal, and in her blood ran the memory of another time, far away and almost lost.

'It's a long story, Tom,' Suzie said at last. She smiled, and began at the beginning – her meeting with Ana and Rom three months ago in the wonderful world of the Web.

WEBSPEAK – A GLOSSARY

AI Artificial intelligence. Computer programs that appear to show intelligent behaviour when you interact with them.

avatar or realoe Personas in the Web that are the representations of real people.

basement-level Of the lowest level possible. Often used as an insult, as in 'You've got a basement-level grasp of the situation.'

bat The moment of transition into the Web or between sites. You can 'do a bat' or 'go bat'. Its slang use has extended to the everyday world. 'bat' is used instead of 'come in', 'take a bat' is a dismissal. (From *Blue And Tone*.)

bite To play a trick, or to get something over on someone.

bootstrap Verb, to improve your situation by your own efforts.

bot Programs with AI.

chasing the fade Analysing what has happened in the Web after you have left it.

cocoon A secret refuge. Also your bed or own room.

cog Incredibly boring or dull. Initially

	specific to the UK and America this slang is now in use worldwide. (From *Common Or Garden* spider.)
curl up	'Go away, I don't like you!' (From *Curl Up and Die*.)
cyberat	A Web construct, a descendant of computer viruses, that infests the Web programs.
cybercafe	A place where you can get drinks and snacks as well as renting time in the Web.
cyberspace	The visual representation of the communication system which links computers.
d-box	A data-box; an area of information which appears when people are in Virtual Reality (VR).
download	To enter the Web without leaving a Realworld copy.
down the plug	A disaster, as in 'We were down the plug'.
egg	A younger sibling or annoying hanger-on. Even in the first sense this is always meant nastily.
eight	Good (a spider has eight legs).
flame	An insult or nasty remark.
fly	A choice morsel of information, a clue, a hint.
funnel	An unexpected problem or obstacle.
gag	Someone, or something, you don't like very much, who you consider to be stupid. (From *Glove And Glasses*.)
glove and glasses	Cheap but outdated system for experiencing Virtual Reality. The glasses allow you to see VR, the gloves allow you to pick things up.
Id	Interactive display nodule.

mage	A magician.
mip	Measure of computer power.
nick or alias	A nickname. For example, 'Links' is the nickname of Dave Kennedy.
one-mip	Of limited worth or intelligence, as in 'a one-mip mind'.
phace	A person you meet in the Web who is not real; someone created by the software of a particular site or game.
phreak	Someone who is fanatical about virtual reality experiences in the Web.
protocol	The language one computer uses to talk to another.
raid	Any unscheduled intrusion into the Web; anything that forces someone to leave; a program crash.
realoe	See *avatar*
Realworld	What it says; the world outside the Web. Sometimes used in a derogatory way.
scuttle	Leave the Web and return to the Realworld.
SETI	Search for Extra-Terrestrial Intelligence.
SFX	Special effects.
silky	Smarmy, over-enthusiastic, untrustworthy.
six	Bad (an insect has six legs).
slows, the	The feeling that time has slowed down after experiencing the faster time of the Web.
spider	A web construct. Appearing in varying sizes and guises, these are used to pass on warnings or information in the Web. The word is also commonly applied to teachers or parents.
spidered-off	Warned away by a spider.
spin in	To enter the Web or a Website.

spin out   To leave the Web or a Website.

strand   A gap between rows of site skyscrapers in Webtown. Used to describe any street or road or journey.

suck   To eat or drink.

supertime   Parts of the Web that run even faster than normal.

TFO   Tennessee Fried Ostrich.

venomous   Adjective; excellent; could be used in reference to piece of equipment (usually a Websuit) or piece of programming.

vets   Veterans of any game or site. Ultra-vets are the *crème de la crème* of these.

VR   Virtual Reality. The illusion of a three dimensional reality created by computer software.

warlock   A sorcerer; magician.

Web   The worldwide network of communication links, entertainment, educational and administrative sites that exists in cyberspace and is represented in Virtual Reality.

Web heads   People who are fanatical about surfing the Web. (See also phreaks.)

Web round   Verb; to contact other Web users via the Web.

Websuit   The all over body suit lined with receptors which when worn by Web users allows them to experience the full physical illusion of virtual reality.

Webware   Computer software used to create and/or maintain the Web.

widow   Adjective; excellent; the term comes from the Black Widow, a particularly poisonous spider.

wipeout   To be comprehensively beaten in a Web game or to come out worse in any Web situation.